D0294431

BRISINGR

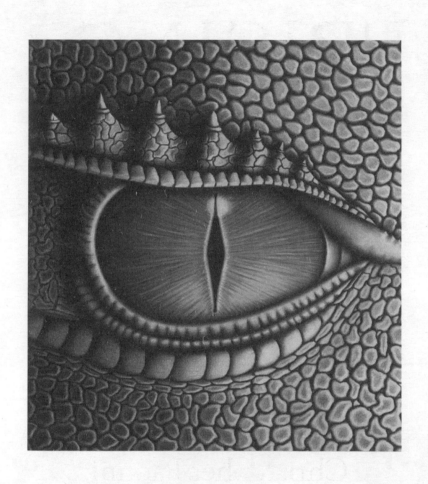

BRISINGR

or

THE SEVEN PROMISES OF ERAGON SHADESLAYER
AND SAPHIRA BJARTSKULAR

INHERITANCE

BOOK THREE

Christopher Paolini

DOUBLEDAY

BRISINGR
A DOUBLEDAY BOOK 978 0 385 60791 9 (cased)
978 0 385 61385 9 (trade paperback)

Published in Great Britain by Doubleday,
an imprint of Random House Children's Books
A Random House Group Company

This edition published 2008

11

Copyright © Christopher Paolini, 2008
Jacket art copyright © John Jude Palencar, 2005
Illustrations on endpapers, pages ii-iii, iv copyright © Christopher Paolini, 2002

The right of Christopher Paolini to be identified as the author of this work has been asserted in
accordance with the Copyright, Designs and Patents Act 1988.

All rights reserved. No part of this publication may be reproduced, stored in a retrieval system, or
transmitted in any form or by any means, electronic, mechanical, photocopying, recording or
otherwise, without the prior permission of the publishers.

The Random House Group Limited supports the Forest Stewardship Council (FSC), the leading
international forest certification organization. All our titles that are printed on Greenpeace-
approved FSC-certified paper carry the FSC logo. Our paper procurement policy can be found at
www.rbooks.co.uk/environment.

Mixed Sources
Product group from well-managed
forests and other controlled sources
www.fsc.org Cert no. TT-COC-2139
FSC   © 1996 Forest Stewardship Council

Set in 12-point Goudy

RANDOM HOUSE CHILDREN'S BOOKS
61–63 Uxbridge Road, London W5 5SA

www.kidsatrandomhouse.co.uk
www.rbooks.co.uk

Addresses for companies within The Random House Group Limited can be found at:
www.randomhouse.co.uk/offices.htm

THE RANDOM HOUSE GROUP Limited Reg. No. 954009

A CIP catalogue record for this book is available from the British Library.

Printed and bound in Great Britain by
Clays Ltd, St Ives plc

As always, this book is for my family.
And also for Jordan, Nina, and Sylvie,
the bright lights of a new generation.
Atra esterní ono thelduin.

CONTENTS

Synopsis of *Eragon* and *Eldest*

Eragon—a fifteen-year-old farm boy—is shocked when a polished blue stone appears before him in the range of mountains known as the Spine. Eragon takes the stone to the farm where he lives with his uncle, Garrow, and his cousin, Roran, outside the small village of Carvahall. Garrow and his late wife, Marian, have raised Eragon. Nothing is known of Eragon's father; his mother, Selena, was Garrow's sister and has not been seen since Eragon's birth.

Later, the stone cracks open and a baby dragon emerges. When Eragon touches her, a silvery mark appears on his palm, and an irrevocable bond is forged between their minds, making Eragon one of the legendary Dragon Riders. He names the dragon Saphira, after a dragon mentioned by the village storyteller, Brom.

The Dragon Riders were created thousands of years earlier in the aftermath of the devastating war between the elves and the dragons, in order to prevent their two races from ever again fighting each other. The Riders became peacekeepers, educators, healers, natural philosophers, and the greatest of all magicians—since being joined with a dragon makes one a spellcaster. Under their guidance and protection, the land enjoyed a golden age.

When humans arrived in Alagaësia, they too were added to this elite order. After many years of peace, the warlike Urgals killed the dragon of a young human Rider named Galbatorix. The loss drove him mad, and when his elders refused to provide him with another dragon, Galbatorix set out to topple the Riders.

He stole another dragon—whom he named Shruikan and forced to serve him through certain black spells—and gathered around himself a group of thirteen traitors: the Forsworn. With the help of those cruel disciples, Galbatorix threw down the Riders; killed their leader, Vrael; and declared himself king over Alagaësia. His actions forced the elves to retreat deep within their pinewood forest and the dwarves to hide in their tunnels and caves, and neither race now ventures forth from its secret places. The stalemate between Galbatorix and the other races has endured for over a hundred years, during which all of the Forsworn have died from various causes. It is into this tense political situation that Eragon finds himself thrust.

Several months after Saphira hatches, two menacing, beetle-like strangers called the Ra'zac arrive in Carvahall, searching for the stone that was Saphira's egg. Eragon and Saphira manage to evade them, but they destroy Eragon's home and murder Garrow.

Eragon vows to track down and kill the Ra'zac. As he leaves Carvahall, the storyteller Brom, who knows of Saphira's existence, accosts Eragon and asks to accompany him. Brom gives Eragon a red Dragon Rider's sword, Zar'roc, though he refuses to say how he acquired it.

Eragon learns much from Brom during their travels, including how to fight with swords and use magic. When they lose the Ra'zac's trail, they go to the port town of Teirm and visit Brom's old friend Jeod, who Brom thinks may be able to help them locate the Ra'zac's lair. In Teirm, they learn that the Ra'zac live somewhere close to the city of Dras-Leona. Eragon also has his fortune told by the herbalist Angela and receives two strange pieces of advice from her companion, the werecat Solembum.

On the way to Dras-Leona, Brom reveals that he is an agent of the Varden—a rebel group dedicated to overthrowing Galbatorix—and that he had been hiding in Carvahall, waiting for a new Dragon Rider to appear. Twenty years ago, Brom was involved in stealing Saphira's egg from Galbatorix and, in the process, killed Morzan, first and last of the Forsworn. Only two other dragon eggs still exist, both of which remain in Galbatorix's possession.

In and near Dras-Leona, they encounter the Ra'zac, who mortally wound Brom while he is protecting Eragon. A mysterious young man named Murtagh drives the Ra'zac away. With his dying breath, Brom confesses that he too was once a Rider and that his slain dragon was also named Saphira.

Eragon and Saphira then decide to join the Varden, but Eragon is captured at the city of Gil'ead and brought before Durza, an evil and powerful Shade who serves Galbatorix. With Murtagh's help, Eragon escapes from prison, bringing along with him the elf Arya, another captive of Durza's and an ambassador to the Varden. Arya has been poisoned and requires the Varden's medical help.

Pursued by a contingent of Urgals, the four of them flee across the land to the Varden's headquarters in the giant Beor Mountains, which stand over ten miles high. Circumstances force Murtagh — who does not want to go to the Varden—to reveal that he is the son of Morzan. Murtagh, however, has denounced his dead father's villainy and fled Galbatorix's court to seek his own destiny. And he tells Eragon that the sword Zar'roc once belonged to Murtagh's father.

Just before they are overwhelmed by the Urgals, Eragon and his friends are rescued by the Varden, who live in Farthen Dûr, a hollow mountain that is also home to the dwarves' capital, Tronjheim. Once inside, Eragon is taken to Ajihad, leader of the Varden, while Murtagh is imprisoned because of his relation to Morzan.

Eragon meets with the dwarf king, Hrothgar, and Ajihad's daughter, Nasuada, and is tested by the Twins, two rather nasty magicians who serve Ajihad. Eragon and Saphira also bless one of the Varden's orphan babies while the Varden heal Arya of her poisoning.

Eragon's stay is disrupted by news of an Urgal army approaching underground, through the dwarves' tunnels. In the battle that follows, Eragon is separated from Saphira and forced to fight Durza alone. Far stronger than any human, Durza easily defeats Eragon, slashing open his back from shoulder to hip. At that moment,

Saphira and Arya break the roof of a chamber—a sixty-foot-wide star sapphire—distracting Durza long enough for Eragon to stab him through the heart. Freed from Durza's spells, which were controlling them, the Urgals are driven back.

While Eragon lies unconscious after the battle, he is telepathically contacted by a being who identifies himself as Togira Ikonoka—the Cripple Who Is Whole. He urges Eragon to seek him for instruction in Ellesméra, the elves' capital.

When Eragon wakes, he has a huge scar across his back. Dismayed, he also realizes he only slew Durza through sheer luck and that he desperately needs more training. And at the end of Book One, he decides that, yes, he will find this Togira Ikonoka and learn from him.

Eldest begins three days after Eragon slays Durza. The Varden are recovering from the Battle of Farthen Dûr, and Ajihad, Murtagh, and the Twins have been hunting down the Urgals who escaped into the tunnels underneath Farthen Dûr after the battle. When a group of Urgals takes them by surprise, Ajihad is killed and Murtagh and the Twins disappear in the fray. The Varden's Council of Elders appoints Nasuada to succeed her father as new leader of the Varden, and Eragon swears fealty to her as her vassal.

Eragon and Saphira decide they must leave for Ellesméra to begin their training with the Cripple Who Is Whole. Before they go, the dwarf king, Hrothgar, offers to adopt Eragon into his clan, the Dûrgrimst Ingeitum, and Eragon accepts, which gives him full legal rights as a dwarf and entitles him to participate in dwarvish councils.

Both Arya and Orik, Hrothgar's foster son, accompany Eragon and Saphira on their journey to the land of the elves. En route, they stop in Tarnag, a dwarf city. Some of the dwarves are friendly, but Eragon learns that one clan in particular does not welcome him and Saphira—the Az Sweldn rak Anhûin, who hate Riders and dragons because the Forsworn slaughtered so many of their clan.

The party finally arrives in Du Weldenvarden, the forest of the elves. At Ellesméra, Eragon and Saphira meet Islanzadí, queen of the elves, who, they learn, is Arya's mother. They also meet with the Cripple Who Is Whole: an ancient elf named Oromis. He too is a Rider. Oromis and his dragon, Glaedr, have kept their existence hidden from Galbatorix for the past hundred years while they searched for a way to overthrow the king.

Both Oromis and Glaedr are afflicted with old wounds that prevent them from fighting—Glaedr is missing a leg and Oromis, who was captured and broken by the Forsworn, is unable to control large amounts of magic and is prone to debilitating seizures.

Eragon and Saphira begin their training, both together and separately. Eragon learns more about the history of Alagaësia's races, swordsmanship, and the ancient language, which all magicians use. In his studies of the ancient language, he discovers he made a terrible mistake when he and Saphira blessed the orphaned baby in Farthen Dûr: he intended to say "May you be shielded from misfortune," but what he actually said was "May you be *a shield* from misfortune." He has cursed the baby to shield others from any and all pain and misfortune.

Saphira makes quick progress learning from Glaedr, but the scar Eragon bears as a result of his battle with Durza slows his training. Not only is the mark on his back disfiguring, but at unexpected times it incapacitates him with painful spasms. He does not know how he will improve as a magician and swordsman if his convulsions continue.

Eragon begins to realize he has feelings for Arya. He confesses them to her, but she rebuffs him and soon leaves to return to the Varden.

Then the elves hold a ritual known as the Agaetí Blödhren, or the Blood-oath Celebration, during which Eragon goes through a magical transformation: he is turned into an elf-human hybrid—not quite one, not quite the other. As a result, his scar is healed and he now has the same superhuman strength the elves have. His features are also altered, so he appears slightly elvish.

At this point, Eragon learns that the Varden are on the brink of battle with the Empire and are in dire need of him and Saphira. While Eragon has been away, Nasuada has moved the Varden from Farthen Dûr to Surda, a country south of the Empire that still maintains its independence from Galbatorix.

Eragon and Saphira leave Ellesméra, along with Orik, after promising Oromis and Glaedr that they will return to complete their training as soon as they can.

Meanwhile, Eragon's cousin, Roran, has been having his own adventures. Galbatorix has sent the Ra'zac and a legion of imperial soldiers to Carvahall, looking to capture Roran, so as to use him against Eragon. Roran manages to escape into the nearby mountains. He and the other villagers attempt to drive the soldiers away. Numerous villagers die in the process. When Sloan, the village butcher—who hates Roran and opposes Roran's engagement to his daughter, Katrina—betrays Roran to the Ra'zac, the beetle-like creatures find and attack Roran in the middle of the night in his bedroom. Roran fights his way free, but the Ra'zac capture Katrina.

Roran convinces the people of Carvahall to leave their village and seek refuge with the Varden in Surda. They set out westward for the coast, in the hope that they can sail from there to Surda. Roran proves himself as a leader, bringing them safely through the Spine to the coast. In the port town of Teirm, they meet Jeod, who tells Roran that Eragon is a Rider and explains what the Ra'zac were looking for in Carvahall in the first place—Saphira. Jeod offers to help Roran and the villagers reach Surda, pointing out that once Roran and the villagers are safely with the Varden, Roran can enlist Eragon's help in rescuing Katrina. Jeod and the villagers pirate a ship and sail toward Surda.

Eragon and Saphira reach the Varden, who are readying for battle. Eragon learns what has become of the baby upon whom he bestowed the ill-phrased blessing: her name is Elva, and though, chronologically, she is still a baby, she has the appearance of a four-year-old child and the voice and demeanor of a world-weary adult.

Eragon's spell forces her to sense the pain of all the people she sees, and compels her to protect them; if she resists this urge, she herself suffers.

Eragon, Saphira, and the Varden ride out to meet the Empire's troops on the Burning Plains, a large swath of land that smokes and smolders from underground peat fires. They are astonished when another Rider appears astride a red dragon. The new Rider slays Hrothgar, the dwarf king, and then begins to fight with Eragon and Saphira. When Eragon manages to wrench the Rider's helm off, he is shocked to see Murtagh.

Murtagh did not die in the Urgal ambush under Farthen Dûr. The Twins arranged it all; they are traitors who planned the ambush so Ajihad would be killed and they could capture Murtagh and take him to Galbatorix. The king forced Murtagh to swear loyalty to him in the ancient language. Now Murtagh and his newly hatched dragon, Thorn, are Galbatorix's slaves, and Murtagh asserts that his oaths will never allow him to disobey the king, though Eragon pleads with him to abandon Galbatorix and join the Varden.

Murtagh is able to overwhelm Eragon and Saphira with an inexplicable display of strength. However, he decides to free them because of their previous friendship. Before Murtagh leaves, he takes Zar'roc from Eragon, claiming it is his inheritance as Morzan's elder son. Then he reveals that he is not Morzan's only son—Eragon and Murtagh are brothers, both sons of Selena, Morzan's consort. The Twins discovered the truth when they examined Eragon's memories the day he arrived at Farthen Dûr.

Still reeling from Murtagh's revelation about their parentage, Eragon retreats with Saphira, and he is finally reunited with Roran and the villagers of Carvahall, who have arrived at the Burning Plains just in time to aid the Varden in the battle. Roran fought heroically and succeeded in killing the Twins.

Eragon and Roran make peace over Eragon's role in Garrow's death, and Eragon vows to help Roran rescue Katrina from the Ra'zac.

THE GATES OF DEATH

Eragon stared at the dark tower of stone wherein hid the monsters who had murdered his uncle, Garrow.

He was lying on his belly behind the edge of a sandy hill dotted with sparse blades of grass, thornbushes, and small, rosebud-like cactuses. The brittle stems of last year's foliage pricked his palms as he inched forward to gain a better view of Helgrind, which loomed over the surrounding land like a black dagger thrust out from the bowels of the earth.

The evening sun streaked the low hills with shadows long and narrow and—far in the west—illuminated the surface of Leona Lake so that the horizon became a rippling bar of gold.

To his left, Eragon heard the steady breathing of his cousin, Roran, who was stretched out beside him. The normally inaudible flow of air seemed preternaturally loud to Eragon with his heightened sense of hearing, one of many such changes wrought by his experience during the Agaetí Blödhren, the elves' Blood-oath Celebration.

He paid little attention to that now as he watched a column of people inch toward the base of Helgrind, apparently having walked from the city of Dras-Leona, some miles away. A contingent of twenty-four men and women, garbed in thick leather robes, occupied the head of the column. This group moved with many strange and varied gaits—they limped and shuffled and humped and wriggled; they swung on crutches or used arms to propel themselves forward on curiously short legs— contortions that were necessary because, as Eragon realized, every one of the twenty-four lacked an arm or a leg or some combination thereof. Their leader sat upright upon a litter borne by six oiled slaves, a pose Eragon regarded as a rather amazing accomplishment, considering that the man or woman—he could not tell which—consisted of nothing more than a torso and head, upon whose brow balanced an ornate leather crest three feet high.

"The priests of Helgrind," he murmured to Roran.

"Can they use magic?"

"Possibly. I dare not explore Helgrind with my mind until they leave, for if any *are* magicians, they will sense my touch, however light, and our presence will be revealed."

Behind the priests trudged a double line of young men swathed in gold cloth. Each carried a rectangular metal frame subdivided by twelve horizontal crossbars from which hung iron bells the size of winter rutabagas. Half of the young men gave their frames a vigorous shake when they stepped forward with their right foot, producing a dolorous cacophony of notes, while the other half shook their frames when they advanced upon the left foot, causing iron tongues to crash against iron throats and emit a mournful clamor that echoed over the hills. The acolytes accompanied the throbbing of the bells with their own cries, groaning and shouting in an ecstasy of passion.

At the rear of the grotesque procession trudged a comet's tail of inhabitants from Dras-Leona: nobles, merchants, tradesmen, several high-ranking military commanders, and a motley collection of those less fortunate, such as laborers, beggars, and common foot soldiers.

Eragon wondered if Dras-Leona's governor, Marcus Tábor, was somewhere in their midst.

Drawing to a stop at the edge of the precipitous mound of scree that ringed Helgrind, the priests gathered on either side of a rust-colored boulder with a polished top. When the entire column stood motionless before the crude altar, the creature upon the litter stirred and began to chant in a voice as discordant as the moaning of the bells. The shaman's declamations were repeatedly truncated by gusts of wind, but Eragon caught snatches of the ancient language— strangely twisted and mispronounced—interspersed with dwarf and Urgal words, all of which were united by an archaic dialect of

Eragon's own tongue. What he understood caused him to shudder, for the sermon spoke of things best left unknown, of a malevolent hate that had festered for centuries in the dark caverns of people's hearts before being allowed to flourish in the Riders' absence, of blood and madness, and of foul rituals performed underneath a black moon.

At the end of that depraved oration, two of the lesser priests rushed forward and lifted their master—or mistress, as the case might be—off the litter and onto the face of the altar. Then the High Priest issued a brief order. Twin blades of steel winked like stars as they rose and fell. A rivulet of blood sprang from each of the High Priest's shoulders, flowed down the leather-encased torso, and then pooled across the boulder until it overflowed onto the gravel below.

Two more priests jumped forward to catch the crimson flow in goblets that, when filled to the rim, were distributed among the members of the congregation, who eagerly drank.

"Gar!" said Roran in an undertone. "You failed to mention that those errant flesh-mongers, those gore-bellied, boggle-minded idiot-worshipers were *cannibals*."

"Not quite. They do not partake of the meat."

When all the attendees had wet their throats, the servile novitiates returned the High Priest to the litter and bound the creature's shoulders with strips of white linen. Wet blotches quickly sullied the virgin cloth.

The wounds seemed to have no effect upon the High Priest, for the limbless figure rotated back toward the devotees with their lips of cranberry red and pronounced, "Now are you truly my Brothers and Sisters, having tasted the sap of my veins here in the shadow of almighty Helgrind. Blood calls to blood, and if ever your Family should need help, do then what you can for the Church and for others who acknowledge the power of our Dread Lord. . . . To affirm and reaffirm our fealty to the Triumvirate, recite with me the Nine Oaths. . . . By Gorm, Ilda, and Fell Angvara, we vow to perform homage at least thrice a month, in the hour before dusk, and then to make an offering of ourselves to appease the eternal hunger of our Great and Terrible Lord. . . . We vow to observe the strictures as they are presented in the book of Tosk. . . . We vow to always carry our Bregnir on our bodies and to forever abstain from the twelve of twelves and the touch of a many-knotted rope, lest it corrupt . . ."

A sudden rise in the wind obscured the rest of the High Priest's list. Then Eragon saw those who listened take out a small, curved knife and, one by one, cut themselves in the crook of their elbows and anoint the altar with a stream of their blood.

Some minutes later, the angry breeze subsided and Eragon again heard the priest: ". . . and such things as you long and lust for will be granted to you as a reward for your obedience. . . . Our worship is complete. However, if any now stand among you who are brave enough to demonstrate the true depth of their faith, let them show themselves!"

The audience stiffened and leaned forward, their faces rapt; this, apparently, was what they had been waiting for.

For a long, silent pause, it seemed as if they would be disappointed, but then one of the acolytes broke ranks and shouted, "I will!" With a roar of delight, his brethren began to brandish their bells in a quick and savage beat, whipping the congregation into such a frenzy, they jumped and yelled as if they had taken leave of their senses. The rough music kindled a spark of excitement in Eragon's heart—despite his revulsion at the proceedings—waking some primal and brutish part of him.

Shedding his gold robes so that he wore nothing but a leather breechcloth, the dark-haired youth sprang on top of the altar. Gouts of ruby spray erupted on either side of his feet. He faced Helgrind and began to shiver and quake as if stricken with palsy, keeping time with the tolling of the cruel iron bells. His head rolled loosely upon his neck, foam gathered at the corners of his mouth, his arms thrashed like snakes. Sweat oiled his muscles until he gleamed like a bronze statue in the dying light.

The bells soon reached a manic tempo where one note clashed

against another, at which point the young man thrust a hand out behind himself. Into it, a priest deposited the hilt of a bizarre implement: a single-edged weapon, two and a half feet long, with a full tang, scale grips, a vestigial crossguard, and a broad, flat blade that widened and was scalloped near the end, a shape reminiscent of a dragon wing. It was a tool designed for but one purpose: to hack through armor and bones and sinew as easily as through a bulging waterskin.

The young man lifted the weapon so that it slanted toward the highest peak of Helgrind. Then he dropped to one knee and, with an incoherent cry, brought the blade down across his right wrist.

Blood sprayed the rocks behind the altar.

Eragon winced and averted his eyes, although he could not escape the youth's piercing screams. It was nothing Eragon had not seen in battle, but it seemed wrong to deliberately mutilate yourself when it was so easy to become disfigured in everyday life.

Blades of grass rasped against one another as Roran shifted his weight. He muttered some curse, which was lost in his beard, and then fell silent again.

While a priest tended to the young man's wound—stanching the bleeding with a spell—an acolyte let loose two slaves from the High Priest's litter, only to chain them by the ankles to an iron loop embedded in the altar. Then the acolytes divested themselves of numerous packages from underneath their robes and piled them on the ground, out of reach of the slaves.

Their ceremonies at an end, the priests and their retinue departed Helgrind for Dras-Leona, wailing and ringing the entire way. The now one-handed zealot stumbled along just behind the High Priest.

A beatific smile graced his face.

"Well," said Eragon, and released his pent-up breath as the column vanished behind a distant hill.

"Well what?"

"I've traveled among both dwarves and elves, and nothing they did was ever as strange as what those people, those *humans*, do."

"They're as monstrous as the Ra'zac." Roran jerked his chin toward Helgrind. "Can you find out now if Katrina is in there?"

"I'll try. But be ready to run."

Closing his eyes, Eragon slowly extended his consciousness outward, moving from the mind of one living thing to another, like tendrils of water seeping through sand. He touched teeming cities of insects frantically scurrying about their business, lizards and snakes hidden among warm rocks, diverse species of songbirds, and numerous small mammals. Insects and animals alike bustled with activity as they prepared for the fast-approaching night, whether by retreating to their various dens or, in the case of those of a nocturnal bent, by yawning, stretching, and otherwise readying themselves to hunt and forage.

Just as with his other senses, Eragon's ability to touch another being's thoughts diminished with distance. By the time his psychic probe arrived at the base of Helgrind, he could perceive only the largest of animals, and even those but faintly.

He proceeded with caution, ready to withdraw at a second's notice if he happened to brush against the minds of their prey: the Ra'zac and the Ra'zac's parents and steeds, the gigantic Lethrblaka. Eragon was willing to expose himself in this manner only because none of the Ra'zac's breed could use magic, and he did not believe that they were mindbreakers—nonmagicians trained to fight with telepathy. The Ra'zac and Lethrblaka had no need for such tricks when their breath alone could induce a stupor in the largest of men.

And though Eragon risked discovery by his ghostly investigation, he, Roran, and Saphira *had* to know if the Ra'zac had imprisoned Katrina—Roran's betrothed—in Helgrind, for the answer would determine whether their mission was one of rescue or one of capture and interrogation.

Eragon searched long and hard. When he returned to himself,

Roran was watching him with the expression of a starving wolf. His gray eyes burned with a mixture of anger, hope, and despair that was so great, it seemed as if his emotions might burst forth and incinerate everything in sight in a blaze of unimaginable intensity, melting the very rocks themselves.

This Eragon understood.

Katrina's father, the butcher Sloan, had betrayed Roran to the Ra'zac. When they failed to capture him, the Ra'zac had instead seized Katrina from Roran's bedroom and spirited her away from Palancar Valley, leaving the inhabitants of Carvahall to be killed and enslaved by King Galbatorix's soldiers. Unable to pursue Katrina, Roran had—just in time—convinced the villagers to abandon their homes and to follow him across the Spine and then south along the coast of Alagaësia, where they joined forces with the rebel Varden. The hardships they endured as a result had been many and terrible. But circuitous as it was, that course had reunited Roran with Eragon, who knew the location of the Ra'zac's den and had promised to help save Katrina.

Roran had only succeeded, as he later explained, because the strength of his passion drove him to extremes that others feared and avoided, and thus allowed him to confound his enemies.

A similar fervor now gripped Eragon.

He would leap into harm's way without the slightest regard for his own safety if someone he cared for was in danger. He loved Roran as a brother, and since Roran was to marry Katrina, Eragon had extended his definition of family to include her as well. This concept seemed even more important because Eragon and Roran were the last heirs of their line. Eragon had renounced all affiliation with his birth brother, Murtagh, and the only relatives he and Roran had left were each other, and now Katrina.

Noble sentiments of kinship were not the only force that drove the pair. Another goal obsessed them as well: *revenge!* Even as they plotted to snatch Katrina from the grasp of the Ra'zac, so the two warriors—mortal man and Dragon Rider alike—sought to slay King Galbatorix's unnatural servants for torturing and murdering Garrow, who was Roran's father and had been as a father to Eragon.

The intelligence, then, that Eragon had gleaned was as important to him as to Roran.

"I think I felt her," he said. "It's hard to be certain, because we're so far from Helgrind and I've never touched her mind before, but I *think* she's in that forsaken peak, concealed somewhere near the very top."

"Is she sick? Is she injured? Blast it, Eragon, don't hide it from me: have they hurt her?"

"She's in no pain at the moment. More than that, I cannot say, for it required all my strength just to make out the glow of her consciousness; I could not communicate with her." Eragon refrained from mentioning, however, that he had detected a second person as well, one whose identity he suspected and the presence of whom, if confirmed, troubled him greatly. "What I *didn't* find were the Ra'zac or the Lethrblaka. Even if I somehow overlooked the Ra'zac, their parents are so large, their life force should blaze like a thousand lanterns, even as Saphira's does. Aside from Katrina and a few other dim specks of light, Helgrind is black, black, black."

Roran scowled, clenched his left fist, and glared at the mountain of rock, which was fading into the dusk as purple shadows enveloped it. In a low, flat voice, as if talking with himself, he said, "It doesn't matter whether you are right or wrong."

"How so?"

"We dare not attack tonight; night is when the Ra'zac are strongest, and if they *are* nearby, it would be stupid to fight them when we're at a disadvantage. Agreed?"

"Yes."

"So, we wait for the dawn." Roran gestured toward the slaves chained to the gory altar. "If those poor wretches are gone by then, we know the Ra'zac are here, and we proceed as planned. If not, we curse our bad luck that they escaped us, free the slaves, rescue

Katrina, and fly back to the Varden with her before Murtagh hunts us down. Either way, I doubt the Ra'zac will leave Katrina unattended for long, not if Galbatorix wants her to survive so he can use her as a tool against me."

Eragon nodded. He wanted to release the slaves now, but doing so could warn their foes that something was amiss. Nor, if the Ra'zac came to collect their dinner, could he and Saphira intercede before the slaves were ferried away. A battle in the open between a dragon and creatures such as the Lethrblaka would attract the attention of every man, woman, and child for leagues around. And Eragon did not think he, Saphira, or Roran could survive if Galbatorix learned they were alone in his empire.

He looked away from the shackled men. *For their sake, I hope the Ra'zac are on the other side of Alagaësia or, at least, that the Ra'zac aren't hungry tonight.*

By unspoken consent, Eragon and Roran crawled backward down from the crest of the low hill they were hiding behind. At the bottom, they rose into a half crouch, then turned and, still doubled over, ran between two rows of hills. The shallow depression gradually deepened into a narrow, flood-carved gully lined with crumbling slabs of shale.

Dodging the gnarled juniper trees that dotted the gully, Eragon glanced up and, through clumps of needles, saw the first constellations to adorn the velvet sky. They seemed cold and sharp, like bright shards of ice. Then he concentrated on maintaining his footing as he and Roran trotted south toward their camp.

AROUND THE CAMPFIRE

The low mound of coals throbbed like the heart of some giant beast. Occasionally, a patch of gold sparks flared into existence and raced across the surface of the wood before vanishing into a white-hot crevice.

The dying remnants of the fire Eragon and Roran had built cast a dim red light over the surrounding area, revealing a patch of rocky soil, a few pewter-gray bushes, the indistinct mass of a juniper tree farther off, then nothing.

Eragon sat with his bare feet extended toward the nest of ruby embers—enjoying the warmth—and with his back propped against the knobby scales of Saphira's thick right foreleg. Opposite him, Roran was perched on the iron-hard, sun-bleached, wind-worn shell of an ancient tree trunk. Every time he moved, the trunk produced a bitter shriek that made Eragon want to claw at his ears.

For the moment, quiet reigned within the hollow. Even the coals smoldered in silence; Roran had collected only long-dead branches devoid of moisture to eliminate any smoke that unfriendly eyes might spot.

Eragon had just finished recounting the day's activities to Saphira. Normally, he never had to tell her what he had been doing, as thoughts, feelings, and other sensations flowed between them as easily as water from one side of a lake to another. But in this instance it was necessary because Eragon had kept his mind carefully shielded during the scouting expedition, aside from his disembodied foray into the Ra'zac's lair.

After a considerable gap in the conversation, Saphira yawned, exposing her rows of many fearsome teeth. *Cruel and evil they may*

be, but I am impressed that the Ra'zac can bewitch their prey into want-
ing to be eaten. They are great hunters to do that. . . . Perhaps I shall
attempt it someday.

But not, Eragon felt compelled to add, *with people. Try it with sheep*
instead.

People, sheep: what difference is there to a dragon? Then she laughed
deep in her long throat—a rolling rumble that reminded him of
thunder.

Leaning forward to take his weight off Saphira's sharp-edged
scales, Eragon picked up the hawthorn staff that lay by his side. He
rolled it between his palms, admiring the play of light over the polished tangle of roots at the top and the much-scratched metal fer-
rule and spike at the base.

Roran had thrust the staff into his arms before they left the Varden on the Burning Plains, saying, "Here. Fisk made this for me after the Ra'zac bit my shoulder. I know you lost your sword, and I
thought you might have need of it. . . . If you want to get another
blade, that's fine too, but I've found there are very few fights you
can't win with a few whacks from a good, strong stick." Remembering the staff Brom had always carried, Eragon had decided to forgo a
new sword in favor of the length of knotted hawthorn. After losing
Zar'roc, he felt no desire to take up another, lesser sword. That
night, he had fortified both the knotted hawthorn and the handle to
Roran's hammer with several spells that would prevent either piece
from breaking, except under the most extreme stress.

Unbidden, a series of memories overwhelmed Eragon: *A sullen or-*
ange and crimson sky swirled around him as Saphira dove in pursuit of
the red dragon and his Rider. Wind howled past his ears. . . . His fingers
went numb from the jolt of sword striking sword as he dueled that same
Rider on the ground. . . . Tearing off his foe's helm in the midst of com-
bat to reveal his once friend and traveling companion, Murtagh, whom he
had thought dead. . . . The sneer upon Murtagh's face as he took
Zar'roc from Eragon, claiming the red sword by right of inheritance as
Eragon's elder brother. . . .

Eragon blinked, disoriented as the noise and fury of battle faded and the pleasant aroma of juniper wood replaced the stench of blood. He ran his tongue over his upper teeth, trying to eradicate the taste of bile that filled his mouth.

Murtagh.

The name alone generated a welter of confused emotions in Eragon. On one hand, he *liked* Murtagh. Murtagh had saved Eragon and Saphira from the Ra'zac after their first, ill-fated visit to Dras-Leona; risked his life to help extricate Eragon from Gil'ead; acquitted himself honorably in the Battle of Farthen Dûr; and, despite the torments he no doubt endured as a result, had chosen to interpret his orders from Galbatorix in a way that allowed him to release Eragon and Saphira after the Battle of the Burning Plains instead of taking them captive. It was not Murtagh's fault that the Twins had abducted him; that the red dragon, Thorn, had hatched for him; or that Galbatorix had discovered their true names, with which he extracted oaths of fealty in the ancient language from both Murtagh and Thorn.

None of that could be blamed on Murtagh. He was a victim of fate, and had been since the day he was born.

And yet . . . Murtagh might serve Galbatorix against his will, and he might abhor the atrocities the king forced him to commit, but some part of him seemed to revel in wielding his newfound power. During the recent engagement between the Varden and the Empire on the Burning Plains, Murtagh had singled out the dwarf king, Hrothgar, and slain him, although Galbatorix had not ordered Murtagh to do so. He had let Eragon and Saphira go, yes, but only after defeating them in a brutal contest of strength and then listening to Eragon plead for their freedom.

And Murtagh had derived entirely too much pleasure from the anguish he inflicted upon Eragon by revealing they were both sons of Morzan—first and last of the thirteen Dragon Riders, the Forsworn, who had betrayed their compatriots to Galbatorix.

Now, four days after the battle, another explanation presented itself to Eragon: *Perhaps what Murtagh enjoyed was watching another person shoulder the same terrible burden he had carried his whole life.*

Whether or not that was true, Eragon suspected Murtagh had embraced his new role for the same reason that a dog who has been whipped without cause will someday turn and attack his master. Murtagh had been whipped and whipped, and now he had his chance to strike back at a world that had shown him little enough kindness.

Yet no matter what good might still flicker in Murtagh's breast, he and Eragon were doomed to be mortal enemies, for Murtagh's promises in the ancient language bound him to Galbatorix with unbreakable fetters and would forevermore.

If only he hadn't gone with Ajihad to hunt Urgals underneath Farthen Dûr. Or if I had just been a little faster, the Twins—

Eragon, said Saphira.

He caught himself and nodded, grateful for her intervention. Eragon did his best to avoid brooding upon Murtagh or their shared parents, but such thoughts often waylaid him when he least expected it.

Drawing and releasing a slow breath to clear his head, Eragon tried to force his mind back to the present but could not.

The morning after the massive battle on the Burning Plains—when the Varden were busy regrouping and preparing to march after the Empire's army, which had retreated several leagues up the Jiet River—Eragon had gone to Nasuada and Arya, explained Roran's predicament, and sought their permission to help his cousin. He did not succeed. Both women vehemently opposed what Nasuada described as "a harebrained scheme that will have catastrophic consequences for everyone in Alagaësia if it goes awry!"

The debate raged on for so long, at last Saphira had interrupted with a roar that shook the walls of the command tent. Then she said, *I am sore and tired, and Eragon is doing a poor job of explaining himself. We have better things to do than stand around yammering like jackdaws, no? . . . Good, now listen to me.*

It was, reflected Eragon, difficult to argue with a dragon.

13

The details of Saphira's remarks were complex, but the underlying structure of her presentation was straightforward. Saphira supported Eragon because she understood how much the proposed mission meant to him, while Eragon supported Roran because of love and family, and because he knew Roran would pursue Katrina with or without him, and his cousin would never be able to defeat the Ra'zac by himself. Also, so long as the Empire held Katrina captive, Roran—and through him, Eragon—was vulnerable to manipulation by Galbatorix. If the usurper threatened to kill Katrina, Roran would have no choice but to submit to his demands.

It would be best, then, to patch this breach in their defenses before their enemies took advantage of it.

As for the timing, it was perfect. Neither Galbatorix nor the Ra'zac would expect a raid in the center of the Empire when the Varden were busy fighting Galbatorix's troops near the border of Surda. Murtagh and Thorn had been seen flying toward Urû'baen— no doubt to be chastised in person—and Nasuada and Arya agreed with Eragon that those two would probably then continue northward to confront Queen Islanzadí and the army under her command once the elves made their first strike and revealed their presence. And if possible, it would be good to eliminate the Ra'zac before they started to terrorize and demoralize the Varden's warriors.

Saphira had then pointed out, in the most diplomatic of terms, that if Nasuada asserted her authority as Eragon's liegelord and forbade him from participating in the sortie, it would poison their relationship with the sort of rancor and dissent that could undermine the Varden's cause. *But,* said Saphira, *the choice is yours. Keep Eragon here if you want. However, his commitments are not mine, and I, for one, have decided to accompany Roran. It seems like a fine adventure.*

A faint smile touched Eragon's lips as he recalled the scene.

The combined weight of Saphira's declaration and her impregnable logic had convinced Nasuada and Arya to grant their approval, albeit grudgingly.

14

Afterward, Nasuada had said, "We are trusting your judgment in this, Eragon, Saphira. For your sake and ours, I hope this expedition goes well." Her tone left Eragon uncertain whether her words represented a heartfelt wish or a subtle threat.

Eragon had spent the rest of that day gathering supplies, studying maps of the Empire with Saphira, and casting what spells he felt were necessary, such as one to thwart attempts by Galbatorix or his minions to scry Roran.

The following morning, Eragon and Roran had climbed onto Saphira's back, and she had taken flight, rising above the orange clouds that stifled the Burning Plains and angling northeast. She flew nonstop until the sun had traversed the dome of the sky and extinguished itself behind the horizon and then burst forth again with a glorious conflagration of reds and yellows.

The first leg of their journey carried them toward the edge of the Empire, which few people inhabited. There they turned west toward Dras-Leona and Helgrind. From then on, they traveled at night to avoid notice by anyone in the many small villages scattered across the grasslands that lay between them and their destination.

Eragon and Roran had to swathe themselves in cloaks and furs and wool mittens and felted hats, for Saphira chose to fly higher than the icebound peaks of most mountains—where the air was thin and dry and stabbed at their lungs—so that if a farmer tending a sick calf in the field or a sharp-eyed watchman making his rounds should happen to look up as she passed overhead, Saphira would appear no larger than an eagle.

Everywhere they went, Eragon saw evidence of the war that was now afoot: camps of soldiers, wagons full of supplies gathered into a bunch for the night, and lines of men with iron collars being led from their homes to fight on Galbatorix's behalf. The amount of resources deployed against them was daunting indeed.

Near the end of the second night, Helgrind had appeared in the distance: a mass of splintered columns, vague and ominous in the ashen light that precedes dawn. Saphira had landed in the hollow where they were now, and they had slept through most of the past day before beginning their reconnaissance.

A fountain of amber motes billowed and swirled as Roran tossed a branch onto the disintegrating coals. He caught Eragon's look and shrugged. "Cold," he said.

Before Eragon could respond, he heard a slithering scraping sound akin to someone drawing a sword.

He did not think; he flung himself in the opposite direction, rolled once, and came up into a crouch, lifting the hawthorn staff to deflect an oncoming blow. Roran was nearly as fast. He grabbed his shield from the ground, scrambled back from the log he had been sitting on, and drew his hammer from his belt, all in the span of a few seconds.

They froze, waiting for the attack.

Eragon's heart pounded and his muscles trembled as he searched the darkness for the slightest hint of motion.

I smell nothing, said Saphira.

When several minutes elapsed without incident, Eragon pushed his mind out over the surrounding landscape. "No one," he said. Reaching deep within himself to the place where he could touch the flow of magic, he uttered the words "Brisingr raudhr!" A pale red werelight popped into existence several feet in front of him and remained there, floating at eye level and painting the hollow with a watery radiance. He moved slightly, and the werelight mimicked his motion, as if connected to him by an invisible pole.

Together, he and Roran advanced toward where they'd heard the sound, down the gulch that wound eastward. They held their weapons high and paused between each step, ready to defend themselves at any moment. About ten yards from their camp, Roran held up a hand, stopping Eragon, then pointed at a plate of shale that lay on top of the grass. It appeared conspicuously out of place. Kneeling, Roran rubbed a smaller fragment of shale across the plate and created the same steely scrape they had heard before.

"It must have fallen," said Eragon, examining the sides of the gulch. He allowed the werelight to fade into oblivion.

Roran nodded and stood, brushing dirt from his pants.

As he walked back to Saphira, Eragon considered the speed with which they had reacted. His heart still contracted into a hard, painful knot with each beat, his hands shook, and he felt like dashing into the wilderness and running several miles without stopping. *We wouldn't have jumped like that before*, he thought. The reason for their vigilance was no mystery: every one of their fights had chipped away at their complacency, leaving behind nothing but raw nerves that twitched at the slightest touch.

Roran must have been entertaining similar thoughts, for he said, "Do you see them?"

"Who?"

"The men you've killed. Do you see them in your dreams?"

"Sometimes."

The pulsing glow from the coals lit Roran's face from below, forming thick shadows above his mouth and across his forehead and giving his heavy, half-lidded eyes a baleful aspect. He spoke slowly, as if he found the words difficult. "I never wanted to be a warrior. I dreamed of blood and glory when I was younger, as every boy does, but the land was what was important to me. That and our family. . . . And now I have killed. . . . I have killed and killed, and you have killed even more." His gaze focused on some distant place only he could see. "There were these two men in Narda. . . . Did I tell you this before?"

He had, but Eragon shook his head and remained silent.

"They were guards at the main gate. . . . Two of them, you know, and the man on the right, he had pure white hair. I remember because he couldn't have been more than twenty-four, twenty-five. They wore Galbatorix's sigil but spoke as if they were from Narda. They weren't professional soldiers. They were probably just men who had decided to help protect their homes from Urgals, pirates, brigands. . . . We weren't going to lift a finger against them. I swear to you, Eragon, that was never part of our plan. I had no choice, though. They recognized me. I stabbed the white-haired man underneath his chin. . . . It was like when Father cut the throat of a pig. And then the other, I smashed open his skull. I can still feel his bones giving way. . . . I remember every blow I've landed, from the soldiers in Carvahall to the ones on the Burning Plains. . . . You know, when I close my eyes, sometimes I can't sleep because the light from the fire we set in the docks of Teirm is so bright in my mind. I think I'm going mad then."

Eragon found his hands gripping the staff with such force, his knuckles were white and tendons ridged the insides of his wrists. "Aye," he said. "At first it was just Urgals, then it was men and Urgals, and now this last battle. . . . I know what we do is right, but *right* doesn't mean *easy*. Because of who we are, the Varden expect Saphira and me to stand at the front of their army and to slaughter entire battalions of soldiers. We do. We have." His voice caught, and he fell silent.

Turmoil accompanies every great change, said Saphira to both of them. *And we have experienced more than our share, for we are agents of that very change. I am a dragon, and I do not regret the deaths of those who endanger us. Killing the guards in Narda may not be a deed worthy of celebration, but neither is it one to feel guilty about. You had to do it. When you must fight, Roran, does not the fierce joy of combat lend wings to your feet? Do you not know the pleasure of pitting yourself against a worthy opponent and the satisfaction of seeing the bodies of your enemies piled before you? Eragon, you have experienced this. Help me explain it to your cousin.*

Eragon stared at the coals. She had stated a truth that he was reluctant to acknowledge, lest by agreeing that one could enjoy violence, he would become a man he would despise. So he was mute. Across from him, Roran appeared similarly affected.

In a softer voice, Saphira said, *Do not be angry. I did not intend to upset you. . . . I forget sometimes that you are still unaccustomed to these emotions, while I have fought tooth and nail for survival since the day I hatched.*

Rising to his feet, Eragon walked to their saddlebags and retrieved the small earthenware jar Orik had given him before they parted, then poured two large mouthfuls of raspberry mead down his gullet. Warmth bloomed in his stomach. Grimacing, Eragon passed the jar to Roran, who also partook of the concoction.

Several drinks later, when the mead had succeeded in tempering his black mood, Eragon said, "We may have a problem tomorrow."

"What do you mean?"

Eragon directed his words toward Saphira as well. "Remember how I said that we—Saphira and I—could easily handle the Ra'zac?"

"Aye."

And so we can, said Saphira.

"Well, I was thinking about it while we spied on Helgrind, and I'm not so sure anymore. There are almost an infinite number of ways to do something with magic. For example, if I want to light a fire, I could light it with heat gathered from the air or the ground; I could create a flame out of pure energy; I could summon a bolt of lightning; I could concentrate a raft of sunbeams into a single point; I could use friction; and so forth."

"So?"

"The problem is, even though I can devise numerous spells to perform this one action, *blocking* those spells might require but a single counterspell. If you prevent the action itself from taking place, then you don't have to tailor your counterspell to address the unique properties of each individual spell."

"I still don't understand what this has to do with tomorrow."

I do, said Saphira to both of them. She had immediately grasped the implications. *It means that, over the past century, Galbatorix—*

"—may have placed wards around the Ra'zac—"

—that will protect them against—

"—a whole range of spells. I probably won't—"

—be able to kill them with any—

"—of the words of death I was taught, nor any—"

—attacks that we can invent now or then. We may—

"—have to rely—"

"Stop!" exclaimed Roran. He gave a pained smile. "Stop, please. My head hurts when you do that."

Eragon paused with his mouth open; until that moment, he had been unaware that he and Saphira were speaking in turn. The knowledge pleased him: it signified that they had achieved new heights of cooperation and were acting together as a single entity—which made them far more powerful than either would be on their own. It also troubled him when he contemplated how such a partnership must, by its very nature, reduce the individuality of those involved.

He closed his mouth and chuckled. "Sorry. What I'm worried about is this: if Galbatorix has had the foresight to take certain precautions, then force of arms may be the only means by which we can slay the Ra'zac. If that's true—"

"I'll just be in your way tomorrow."

"Nonsense. You may be slower than the Ra'zac, but I have no doubt you'll give them cause to fear your weapon, Roran Stronghammer." The compliment seemed to please Roran. "The greatest danger for you is that the Ra'zac or the Lethrblaka will manage to separate you from Saphira and me. The closer we stay together, the safer we'll all be. Saphira and I will try to keep the Ra'zac and Lethrblaka occupied, but some of them may slip past us. Four against two are only good odds if you're among the four."

To Saphira, Eragon said, *If I had a sword, I'm sure I could slay the Ra'zac by myself, but I don't know if I can beat two creatures who are quick as elves, using nothing but this staff.*

You were the one who insisted on carrying that dry twig instead of a proper weapon, she said. *Remember, I told you it might not suffice against enemies as dangerous as the Ra'zac.*

Eragon reluctantly conceded the point. *If my spells fail us, we will be far more vulnerable than I expected. . . . Tomorrow could end very badly indeed.*

Continuing the strand of conversation he had been privy to, Roran said, "This magic is a tricky business." The log he sat on gave a drawn-out groan as he rested his elbows on his knees.

"It is," Eragon agreed. "The hardest part is trying to anticipate every possible spell; I spend most of my time asking how can I protect myself if I'm attacked like *this* and would another magician expect me to do *that*."

"Could you make me as strong and fast as you are?"

Eragon considered the suggestion for several minutes before saying, "I don't see how. The energy needed to do that would have to come from somewhere. Saphira and I could give it to you, but then we would lose as much speed or strength as you gained." What he did not mention was that one could also extract energy from nearby plants and animals, albeit at a terrible price: namely, the deaths of the smaller beings whose life force you drew upon. The technique was a great secret, and Eragon felt that he should not reveal it lightly, if at all. Moreover, it would be of no use to Roran, as too little grew or lived on Helgrind to fuel a man's body.

"Then can you teach me to use magic?" When Eragon hesitated, Roran added, "Not now, of course. We don't have the time, and I don't expect one can become a magician overnight anyway. But in general, why not? You and I are cousins. We share much the same blood. And it would be a valuable skill to have."

"I don't know how someone who's not a Rider learns to use magic," confessed Eragon. "It's not something I studied." Glancing around, he plucked a flat, round stone from the ground and tossed it to Roran, who caught it backhand. "Here, try this: concentrate on lifting the rock a foot or so into the air and say, 'Stenr rïsa.' "

"Stenr rïsa?"

"Exactly."

Roran frowned at the stone resting on his palm in a pose so reminiscent of Eragon's own training that Eragon could not help feeling a flash of nostalgia for the days he spent being drilled by Brom. Roran's eyebrows met, his lips tightened into a snarl, and he growled, "Stenr rïsa!" with enough intensity, Eragon half expected the stone to fly out of sight.

Nothing happened.

Scowling even harder, Roran repeated his command: "Stenr rïsa!"

The stone exhibited a profound lack of movement.

"Well," said Eragon, "keep trying. That's the only advice I can give you. But"—and here he raised a finger—"if you *should* happen to succeed, make sure you immediately come to me or, if I'm not around, another magician. You could kill yourself and others if you start experimenting with magic without understanding the rules. If nothing else, remember this: if you cast a spell that requires too much energy, you *will* die. Don't take on projects that are beyond your abilities, don't try to bring back the dead, and don't try to un-make anything."

Roran nodded, still looking at the stone.

"Magic aside, I just realized there's something far more important that you need to learn."

"Oh?"

"Yes, you need to be able to hide your thoughts from the Black Hand, Du Vrangr Gata, and others like them. You know a lot of things now that could harm the Varden. It's crucial, then, that you master this skill as soon as we return. Until you can defend yourself from spies, neither Nasuada nor I nor anyone else can trust you with information that might help our enemies."

"I understand. But why did you include Du Vrangr Gata in that list? They serve you and Nasuada."

"They do, but even among our allies there are more than a few people who would give their right arm"—he grimaced at the appropriateness of the phrase—"to ferret out our plans and secrets. And yours too, no less. You have become a *somebody*, Roran. Partly because of your deeds, and partly because we are related."

"I know. It is strange to be recognized by those you have not met."

"That it is." Several other, related observations leaped to the tip of Eragon's tongue, but he resisted the urge to pursue the topic; it was a subject to explore another time. "Now that you know what it feels like when one mind touches another, you might be able to learn to reach out and touch other minds in turn."

"I'm not sure that is an ability I want to have."

"No matter; you also might *not* be able to do it. Either way, before you spend time finding out, you should first devote yourself to the art of defense."

His cousin cocked an eyebrow. "How?"

"Choose something—a sound, an image, an emotion, anything—and let it swell within your mind until it blots out any other thoughts."

"That's all?"

"It's not as easy as you think. Go on; take a stab at it. When you're ready, let me know, and I'll see how well you've done."

Several moments passed. Then, at a flick of Roran's fingers, Eragon launched his consciousness toward his cousin, eager to discover what he had accomplished.

The full strength of Eragon's mental ray rammed into a wall composed of Roran's memories of Katrina and was stopped. He could take no ground, find no entrance or purchase, nor undermine the impenetrable barrier that stood before him. At that instant, Roran's entire identity was based upon his feelings for Katrina; his defenses exceeded any Eragon had previously encountered, for Roran's mind was devoid of anything else Eragon could grasp hold of and use to gain control over his cousin.

Then Roran shifted his left leg and the wood underneath released a harsh squeal.

With that, the wall Eragon had hurled himself against fractured into dozens of pieces as a host of competing thoughts distracted Roran: *What was . . . Blast! Don't pay attention to it; he'll break through. Katrina, remember Katrina. Ignore Eragon. The night she agreed to marry me, the smell of the grass and her hair . . . Is that him? No! Focus! Don't—*

Taking advantage of Roran's confusion, Eragon rushed forward and, by the force of his will, immobilized Roran before he could shield himself again.

You understand the basic concept, said Eragon, then withdrew from Roran's mind and said out loud, "but you have to learn to maintain your concentration even when you're in the middle of a battle. You must learn to think without thinking . . . to empty yourself of all hopes and worries, save that one idea that is your armor. Something the elves taught me, which I have found helpful, is to recite a riddle or a piece of a poem or song. Having an action that you can repeat over and over again makes it much easier to keep your mind from straying."

"I'll work on it," promised Roran.

In a quiet voice, Eragon said, "You really love her, don't you?" It was more a statement of truth and wonder than a question—the answer being self-evident—and one he felt uncertain making. Romance was not a topic Eragon had broached with his cousin before, notwithstanding the many hours they had devoted in years past to debating the relative merits of the young women in and around Carvahall. "How did it happen?"

"I liked her. She liked me. What importance are the details?"

"Come now," said Eragon. "I was too angry to ask before you left for Therinsford, and we have not seen each other again until just four days ago. I'm curious."

The skin around Roran's eyes pulled and wrinkled as he rubbed his temples. "There's not much to tell. I've always been partial to her. It meant little before I was a man, but after my rites of passage, I began to wonder whom I would marry and whom I wanted to become the mother of my children. During one of our visits to Carvahall, I saw Katrina stop by the side of Loring's house to pick a moss rose growing in the shade of the eaves. She smiled as she looked at the flower. . . . It was such a tender smile, and so happy, I decided right then that I wanted to make her smile like that again and again and that I wanted to look at that smile until the day I died." Tears gleamed in Roran's eyes, but they did not fall, and a second later, he blinked and they vanished. "I fear I have failed in that regard."

After a respectful pause, Eragon said, "You courted her, then? Aside from using me to ferry compliments to Katrina, how else did you proceed?"

"You ask like one who seeks instruction."

"I did not. You're imagining—"

"Come now, yourself," said Roran. "I know when you're lying. You get that big foolish grin, and your ears turn red. The elves may have given you a new face, but that part of you hasn't changed. What is it that exists between you and Arya?"

The strength of Roran's perception disturbed Eragon. "Nothing! The moon has addled your brain."

"Be honest. You dote upon her words as if each one were a diamond, and your gaze lingers upon her as if you were starving and she a grand feast arrayed an inch beyond your reach."

A plume of dark gray smoke erupted from Saphira's nostrils as she made a choking-like noise.

Eragon ignored her suppressed merriment and said, "Arya is an elf."

"And very beautiful. Pointed ears and slanted eyes are small flaws when compared with her charms. You look like a cat yourself now."

"Arya is over a hundred years old."

That particular piece of information caught Roran by surprise; his eyebrows went up, and he said, "I find that hard to believe! She's in the prime of her youth."

"It's true."

"Well, be that as it may, these are reasons you give me, Eragon, and the heart rarely listens to reason. Do you fancy her or not?"

If he fancied her any more, Saphira said to both Eragon and Roran, *I'd be trying to kiss Arya myself.*

Saphira! Mortified, Eragon swatted her on the leg.

Roran was prudent enough not to rib Eragon further. "Then answer my original question and tell me how things stand between you and Arya. Have you spoken to her or her family about this? I have found it's unwise to let such matters fester."

"Aye," said Eragon, and stared at the length of polished hawthorn. "I spoke with her."

"To what end?" When Eragon did not immediately reply, Roran uttered a frustrated exclamation. "Getting answers out of you is harder than dragging Birka through the mud." Eragon chuckled at the mention of Birka, one of their draft horses. "Saphira, will you solve this puzzle for me? Otherwise, I fear I'll never get a full explanation."

"To no end. No end at all. She'll not have me." Eragon spoke dispassionately, as if commenting on a stranger's misfortune, but within him raged a torrent of hurt so deep and wild, he felt Saphira withdraw somewhat from him.

"I'm sorry," said Roran.

Eragon forced a swallow past the lump in his throat, past the bruise that was his heart, and down to the knotted skein of his stomach. "It happens."

"I know it may seem unlikely at the moment," said Roran, "but I'm sure you will meet another woman who will make you forget this Arya. There are countless maids—and more than a few married women, I'd wager—who would be delighted to catch the eye of a Rider. You'll have no trouble finding a wife among all the lovelies in Alagaësia."

"And what would you have done if Katrina rejected your suit?"

The question struck Roran dumb; it was obvious he could not imagine how he might have reacted.

Eragon continued. "Contrary to what you, Arya, and everyone else seem to believe, I *am* aware that other eligible women exist in Alagaësia and that people have been known to fall in love more than once. No doubt, if I spent my days in the company of ladies from King Orrin's court, I might indeed decide that I fancy one.

However, my path is not so easy as that. Regardless of whether I can shift my affections to another—and the heart, as you observed, is a notoriously fickle beast—the question remains: should I?"

"Your tongue has grown as twisted as the roots of a fir tree," said Roran. "Speak not in riddles."

"Very well: what human woman can begin to understand who and what I am, or the extent of my powers? Who could share in my life? Few enough, and all of them magicians. And of that select group, or even of women in general, how many are immortal?"

Roran laughed, a rough, hearty bellow that rang loud in the gulch. "You might as well ask for the sun in your pocket or—" He stopped and tensed as if he were about to spring forward and then became unnaturally still. "You cannot be."

"I am."

Roran struggled to find words. "Is it a result of your change in Ellesméra, or is it part of being a Rider?"

"Part of being a Rider."

"That explains why Galbatorix hasn't died."

"Aye."

The branch Roran had added to the fire burst asunder with a muted *pop* as the coals underneath heated the gnarled length of wood to the point where a small cache of water or sap that had somehow evaded the rays of the sun for untold decades exploded into steam.

"The idea is so . . . *vast*, it's almost inconceivable," said Roran. "Death is part of who we are. It guides us. It shapes us. It drives us to madness. Can you still be human if you have no mortal end?"

"I'm not invincible," Eragon pointed out. "I can still be killed with a sword or an arrow. And I can still catch some incurable disease."

"But if you avoid those dangers, you will live forever."

"If I do, then yes. Saphira and I will *endure*."

"It seems both a blessing and a curse."

"Aye. I cannot in good conscience marry a woman who will age and die while I remain untouched by time; such an experience would be equally cruel for both of us. On top of that, I find the thought of taking one wife after another throughout the long centuries rather depressing."

"Can you make someone immortal with magic?" asked Roran.

"You can darken white hair, you can smooth wrinkles and remove cataracts, and if you are willing to go to extraordinary lengths, you can give a sixty-year-old man the body he had at nineteen. However, the elves have never discovered a way to restore a person's mind without destroying his or her memories. And who wants to erase their identity every so many decades in exchange for immortality? It would be a stranger, then, who lived on. An old brain in a young body isn't the answer either, for even with the best of health, that which we humans are made of can only last for a century, perhaps a bit more. Nor can you just stop someone from aging. That causes a whole host of other problems. . . . Oh, elves and men have tried a thousand and one different ways to foil death, but none have proved successful."

"In other words," said Roran, "it's safer for you to love Arya than to leave your heart free for the taking by a human woman."

"Who else *can* I marry but an elf? Especially considering how I look now." Eragon quelled the desire to reach up and finger the curved tips of his ears, a habit he had fallen into. "When I lived in Ellesméra, it was easy for me to accept how the dragons had changed my appearance. After all, they gave me many gifts besides. Also, the elves were friendlier toward me after the Agaetí Blödhren. It was only when I rejoined the Varden that I realized how *different* I've become. . . . It bothers me too. I'm no longer just human, and I'm not quite an elf. I'm something else in between: a mix, a halfbreed."

"Cheer up!" said Roran. "You may not have to worry about living forever. Galbatorix, Murtagh, the Ra'zac, or even one of the Empire's soldiers could put steel through us at any moment. A wise man would ignore the future and drink and carouse while he still has an opportunity to enjoy this world."

"I know what Father would say to that."

"And he'd give us a good hiding to boot."

They shared a laugh, and then the silence that so often intruded on their discussion asserted itself once again, a gap born of equal parts weariness, familiarity, and—conversely—the many differences that fate had created between those who had once gone about lives that were but variations on a single melody.

You should sleep, said Saphira to Eragon and Roran. *It's late, and we must rise early tomorrow.*

Eragon looked at the black vault of the sky, judging the hour by how far the stars had rotated. The night was older than he expected. "Sound advice," he said. "I just wish we had a few more days to rest before we storm Helgrind. The battle on the Burning Plains drained all of Saphira's strength and my own, and we have not fully recovered, what with flying here and the energy I transferred into the belt of Beloth the Wise these past two evenings. My limbs still ache, and I have more bruises than I can count. Look. . . ." Loosening the ties on the cuff of his left shirtsleeve, he pushed back the soft lámarae— a fabric the elves made by cross-weaving wool and nettle threads— revealing a rancid yellow streak where his shield had mashed against his forearm.

"Ha!" said Roran. "You call that tiny little mark a bruise? I hurt myself worse when I bumped my toe this morning. Here, I'll show you a bruise a man can be proud of." He unlaced his left boot, pulled it off, and rolled up the leg of his trousers to expose a black stripe as wide as Eragon's thumb that slanted across his quadriceps. "I caught the haft of a spear as a soldier was turning about."

"Impressive, but I have even better." Ducking out of his tunic, Eragon yanked his shirt free of his trousers and twisted to the side so that Roran could see the large blotch on his ribs and the similar discoloration on his belly. "Arrows," he explained. Then he uncovered his right forearm, revealing a bruise that matched the one on his other arm, given when he had deflected a sword with his bracer.

Now Roran bared a collection of irregular blue-green spots, each the size of a gold coin, that marched from his left armpit down to the base of his spine, the result of having fallen upon a jumble of rocks and embossed armor.

Eragon inspected the lesions, then chuckled and said, "Pshaw, those are pinpricks! Did you get lost and run into a rosebush? I have one that puts those to shame." He removed both his boots, then stood and dropped his trousers, so that his only garb was his shirt and woolen underpants. "Top that if you can," he said, and pointed to the inside of his thighs. A riotous combination of colors mottled his skin, as if Eragon were an exotic fruit that was ripening in uneven patches from crabapple green to putrefied purple.

"Ouch," said Roran. "What happened?"

"I jumped off Saphira when we were fighting Murtagh and Thorn in the air. That's how I wounded Thorn. Saphira managed to dive under me and catch me before I hit the ground, but I landed on her back a bit harder than I wanted to."

Roran winced and shivered at the same time. "Does it go all the way . . ." He trailed off, and made a vague gesture upward.

"Unfortunately."

"I have to admit, that's a remarkable bruise. You should be proud; it's quite a feat to get injured in the manner you did and in that . . . *particular* . . . place."

"I'm glad you appreciate it."

"Well," said Roran, "you may have the biggest bruise, but the Ra'zac dealt me a wound the likes of which you cannot match, since the dragons, as I understand, removed the scar from your back." While he spoke, he divested himself of his shirt and moved farther into the pulsing light of the coals.

Eragon's eyes widened before he caught himself and concealed his shock behind a more neutral expression. He berated himself for overreacting, thinking, *It can't be that bad*, but the longer he studied Roran, the more dismayed he became.

A long, puckered scar, red and glossy, wrapped around Roran's right shoulder, starting at his collarbone and ending just past the middle of his arm. It was obvious that the Ra'zac had severed part of the muscle and that the two ends had failed to heal back together, for an unsightly bulge deformed the skin below the scar, where the underlying fibers had recoiled upon themselves. Farther up, the skin had sunk inward, forming a depression half an inch deep.

"Roran! You should have shown this to me days ago. I had no idea the Ra'zac hurt you so badly. . . . Do you have any difficulty moving your arm?"

"Not to the side or back," said Roran. He demonstrated. "But in the front, I can only lift my hand about as high as . . . midchest." Grimacing, he lowered his arm. "Even that's a struggle; I have to keep my thumb level, or else my arm goes dead. The best way I've found is to swing my arm around from behind and let it land on whatever I'm trying to grasp. I skinned my knuckles a few times before I mastered the trick."

Eragon twisted the staff between his hands. *Should I?* he asked Saphira.

I think you must.

We may regret it tomorrow.

You will have more cause for regret if Roran dies because he could not wield his hammer when the occasion demanded. If you draw upon the resources around us, you can avoid tiring yourself further.

You know I hate doing that. Even talking about it sickens me.

Our lives are more important than an ant's, Saphira countered.

Not to an ant.

And are you an ant? Don't be glib, Eragon; it ill becomes you.

With a sigh, Eragon put down the staff and beckoned to Roran. "Here, I'll heal that for you."

"You can do that?"

"Obviously."

A momentary surge of excitement brightened Roran's face, but then he hesitated and looked troubled. "Now? Is that wise?"

"As Saphira said, better I tend to you while I have the chance, lest your injury cost you your life or endanger the rest of us." Roran drew near, and Eragon placed his right hand over the red scar while, at the same time, expanding his consciousness to encompass the trees and the plants and the animals that populated the gulch, save those he feared were too weak to survive his spell.

Then Eragon began to chant in the ancient language. The incantation he recited was long and complex. Repairing such a wound went far beyond growing new skin and was a difficult matter at best. In this, Eragon relied upon the curative formulas that he had studied in Ellesméra and had devoted so many weeks to memorizing.

The silvery mark on Eragon's palm, the gedwëy ignasia, glowed white-hot as he released the magic. A second later, he uttered an involuntary groan as he died three times, once each with two small birds roosting in a nearby juniper and also with a snake hidden among the rocks. Across from him, Roran threw back his head and bared his teeth in a soundless howl as his shoulder muscle jumped and writhed beneath the surface of his shifting skin.

Then it was over.

Eragon inhaled a shuddering breath and rested his head in his hands, taking advantage of the concealment they provided to wipe away his tears before he examined the results of his labor. He saw Roran shrug several times and then stretch and windmill his arms. Roran's shoulder was large and round, the result of years spent digging holes for fence posts, hauling rocks, and pitching hay. Despite himself, a needle of envy pricked Eragon. He might be stronger, but he had never been as muscular as his cousin.

Roran grinned. "It's as good as ever! Better, maybe. Thank you."

"You're welcome."

"It was the strangest thing. I actually felt as if I was going to crawl out of my hide. And it itched something terrible; I could barely keep from ripping—"

"Get me some bread from your saddlebag, would you? I'm hungry."

"We just had dinner."

"I need a bite to eat after using magic like that." Eragon sniffed and then pulled out his kerchief and wiped his nose. He sniffed again.

What he had said was not quite true. It was the toll his spell had exacted on the wildlife that disturbed him, not the magic itself, and he feared he might throw up unless he had something to settle his stomach.

"You're not ill, are you?" asked Roran.

"No." With the memory of the deaths he had caused still heavy in his mind, Eragon reached for the jar of mead by his side, hoping to fend off a tide of morbid thoughts.

Something very large, heavy, and sharp struck his hand and pinned it against the ground. He winced and looked over to see the tip of one of Saphira's ivory claws digging into his flesh. Her thick eyelid went *snick* as it flashed across the great big glittering iris she fixed upon him. After a long moment, she lifted the claw, as a person would a finger, and Eragon withdrew his hand. He gulped and gripped the hawthorn staff once more, striving to ignore the mead and to concentrate upon what was immediate and tangible, instead of wallowing in dismal introspection.

Roran removed a ragged half of sourdough bread from his bags, then paused and, with a hint of a smile, said, "Wouldn't you rather have some venison? I didn't finish all of mine." He held out the makeshift spit of seared juniper wood, on which were impaled three clumps of golden brown meat. To Eragon's sensitive nose, the odor that wafted toward him was thick and pungent and reminded him of nights he had spent in the Spine and of long winter dinners where he, Roran, and Garrow had gathered around their stove and enjoyed each other's company while a blizzard howled outside. His mouth watered. "It's still warm," said Roran, and waved the venison in front of Eragon.

With an effort of will, Eragon shook his head. "Just give me the bread."

"Are you sure? It's perfect: not too tough, not too tender, and cooked with the perfect amount of seasoning. It's so juicy, when you take a bite, it's as if you swallowed a mouthful of Elain's best stew."

"No, I can't."

"You know you'll like it."

"Roran, stop teasing me and hand over that bread!"

"Ah, now see, you look better already. Maybe what you need isn't bread but someone to get your hackles up, eh?"

Eragon glowered at him, then, faster than the eye could see, snatched the bread away from Roran.

That seemed to amuse Roran even more. As Eragon tore at the loaf, he said, "I don't know how you can survive on nothing but fruit, bread, and vegetables. A man has to eat meat if he wants to keep his strength up. Don't you miss it?"

"More than you can imagine."

"Then why do you insist on torturing yourself like this? Every creature in this world has to eat other living beings—even if they are only plants—in order to survive. That is how we are made. Why attempt to defy the natural order of things?"

I said much the same in Ellesméra, observed Saphira, *but he did not listen to me.*

Eragon shrugged. "We already had this discussion. You do what you want. I won't tell you or anyone else how to live. However, I cannot in good conscience eat a beast whose thoughts and feelings I've shared."

The tip of Saphira's tail twitched, and her scales clinked against a worn dome of rock that protruded from the ground. *Oh, he's hopeless.* Lifting and extending her neck, Saphira nipped the venison, spit and all, from Roran's other hand. The wood cracked between her serrated teeth as she bit down, and then it and the meat vanished into the fiery depths of her belly. *Mmm. You did not exaggerate,* she said to Roran. *What a sweet and succulent morsel: so soft, so salty, so deliciously delectable, it makes me want to wiggle with delight. You should cook for me more often, Roran Stronghammer. Only next time, I think you should prepare several deer at once. Otherwise, I won't get a proper meal.*

Roran hesitated, as if unable to decide whether her request was serious and, if so, how he could politely extricate himself from such an unlooked-for and rather onerous obligation. He cast a pleading glance at Eragon, who burst out laughing, both at Roran's expression and at his predicament.

The rise and fall of Saphira's sonorous laugh joined with Eragon's and reverberated throughout the hollow. Her teeth gleamed madder red in the light from the embers.

An hour after the three of them had retired, Eragon was lying on his back alongside Saphira, muffled in layers of blankets against the night cold. All was still and quiet. It seemed as if a magician had placed an enchantment upon the earth and that everything in the world was bound in an eternal sleep and would remain frozen and unchanging forevermore underneath the watchful gaze of the twinkling stars.

Without moving, Eragon whispered in his mind: *Saphira?*

Yes, little one?

What if I'm right and he's in Helgrind? I don't know what I should do then. . . . Tell me what I should do.

I cannot, little one. This is a decision you have to make by yourself. The ways of men are not the ways of dragons. I would tear off his head and feast on his body, but that would be wrong for you, I think.

Will you stand by me, whatever I decide?

Always, little one. Now rest. All will be well.

Comforted, Eragon gazed into the void between the stars and slowed his breathing as he drifted into the trance that had replaced sleep for him. He remained conscious of his surroundings, but against the backdrop of the white constellations, the figures of his waking dreams strode forth and performed confused and shadowy plays, as was their wont.

ASSAULT ON HELGRIND

Daybreak was fifteen minutes away when Eragon rolled upright. He snapped his fingers twice to wake Roran and then scooped up his blankets and knotted them into a tight bundle.

Pushing himself off the ground, Roran did likewise with his own bedding.

They looked at each other and shivered with excitement.

"If I die," said Roran, "you will see to Katrina?"

"I shall."

"Tell her then that I went into battle with joy in my heart and her name upon my lips."

"I shall."

Eragon muttered a quick line in the ancient language. The drop in his strength that followed was almost imperceptible. "There. That will filter the air in front of us and protect us from the paralyzing effects of the Ra'zac's breath."

From his bags, Eragon removed his shirt of mail and unwrapped the length of sackcloth he had stored it in. Blood from the fight on the Burning Plains still encrusted the once-shining corselet, and the combination of dried gore, sweat, and neglect had allowed blotches of rust to creep across the rings. The mail was, however, free of tears, as Eragon had repaired them before they had departed for the Empire.

Eragon donned the leather-backed shirt, wrinkling his nose at the stench of death and desperation that clung to it, then attached chased bracers to his forearms and greaves to his shins. Upon his head he placed a padded arming cap, a mail coif, and a plain steel helm. He had lost his own helm—the one he had worn in Farthen

Dûr and that the dwarves had engraved with the crest of Dûrgrimst Ingeitum—along with his shield during the aerial duel between Saphira and Thorn. On his hands went mailed gauntlets.

Roran outfitted himself in a similar manner, although he augmented his armor with a wooden shield. A band of soft iron wrapped around the lip of the shield, the better to catch and hold an enemy's sword. No shield encumbered Eragon's left arm; the hawthorn staff required two hands to wield properly.

Across his back, Eragon slung the quiver given to him by Queen Islanzadí. In addition to twenty heavy oak arrows fletched with gray goose feathers, the quiver contained the bow with silver fittings that the queen had sung out of a yew tree for him. The bow was already strung and ready for use.

Saphira kneaded the soil beneath her feet. *Let us be off!*

Leaving their bags and supplies hanging from the branch of a juniper tree, Eragon and Roran clambered onto Saphira's back. They wasted no time saddling her; she had worn her tack through the night. The molded leather was warm, almost hot, underneath Eragon. He clutched the neck spike in front of him—to steady himself during sudden changes in direction—while Roran hooked one thick arm around Eragon's waist and brandished his hammer with the other.

A piece of shale cracked under Saphira's weight as she settled into a low crouch and, in a single giddy bound, leaped up to the rim of the gulch, where she balanced for a moment before unfolding her massive wings. The thin membranes thrummed as Saphira raised them toward the sky. Vertical, they looked like two translucent blue sails.

"Not so tight," grunted Eragon.

"Sorry," said Roran. He loosened his embrace.

Further speech became impossible as Saphira jumped again. When she reached the pinnacle, she brought her wings down with a mighty *whoosh*, driving the three of them even higher. With each subsequent flap, they climbed closer to the flat, narrow clouds.

As Saphira angled toward Helgrind, Eragon glanced to his left and discovered that he could see a broad swath of Leona Lake some miles distant. A thick layer of mist, gray and ghostly in the predawn glow, emanated from the water, as if witchfire burned upon the surface of the liquid. Eragon tried, but even with his hawklike vision, he could not make out the far shore, nor the southern reaches of the Spine beyond, which he regretted. It had been too long since he had laid eyes upon the mountain range of his childhood.

To the north stood Dras-Leona, a huge, rambling mass that appeared as a blocky silhouette against the wall of mist that edged its western flank. The one building Eragon could identify was the cathedral where the Ra'zac had attacked him; its flanged spire loomed above the rest of the city, like a barbed spearhead.

And somewhere in the landscape that rushed past below, Eragon knew, were the remnants of the campsite where the Ra'zac had mortally wounded Brom. He allowed all of his anger and grief over the events of that day—as well as Garrow's murder and the destruction of their farm—to surge forth and give him the courage, nay, the *desire*, to face the Ra'zac in combat.

Eragon, said Saphira. *Today we need not guard our minds and keep our thoughts secret from one another, do we?*

Not unless another magician should appear.

A fan of golden light flared into existence as the top of the sun crested the horizon. In an instant, the full spectrum of colors enlivened the previously drab world: the mist glowed white, the water became a rich blue, the daubed-mud wall that encircled the center of Dras-Leona revealed its dingy yellow sides, the trees cloaked themselves in every shade of green, and the soil blushed red and orange. Helgrind, however, remained as it always was—black.

The mountain of stone rapidly grew larger as they approached. Even from the air, it was intimidating.

Diving toward the base of Helgrind, Saphira tilted so far to her left, Eragon and Roran would have fallen if they had not already strapped their legs to the saddle. Then she whipped around the apron of scree and over the altar where the priests of Helgrind observed their ceremonies. The lip of Eragon's helm caught the wind from her passage and produced a howl that almost deafened him.

"Well?" shouted Roran. He could not see in front of them.

"The slaves are gone!"

A great weight seemed to press Eragon into his seat as Saphira pulled out of her dive and spiraled up around Helgrind, searching for an entrance to the Ra'zac's hideout.

Not even a hole big enough for a woodrat, she declared. She slowed and hung in place before a ridge that connected the third lowest of the four peaks to the prominence above. The jagged buttress magnified the boom produced by each stroke of her wings until it was as loud as a thunderclap. Eragon's eyes watered as the air pulsed against his skin.

A web of white veins adorned the backside of the crags and pillars, where hoarfrost had collected in the cracks that furrowed the rock. Nothing else disturbed the gloom of Helgrind's inky, windswept ramparts. No trees grew among the slanting stones, nor shrubs, grass, or lichen, nor did eagles dare nest upon the tower's broken ledges. True to its name, Helgrind was a place of death, and stood cloaked in the razor-sharp, sawtooth folds of its scarps and clefts like a bony specter risen to haunt the earth.

Casting his mind outward, Eragon confirmed the presence of the two people whom he had discovered imprisoned within Helgrind the previous day, but he felt nothing of the slaves, and to his concern, he still could not locate the Ra'zac or the Lethrblaka. *If they aren't here, then where?* he wondered. Searching again, he noticed something that had eluded him before: a single flower, a gentian, blooming not fifty feet in front of them, where, by all rights, there ought to be solid rock. *How does it get enough light to live?*

Saphira answered his question by perching on a crumbling spur several feet to the right. As she did, she lost her balance for a moment and flared her wings to steady herself. Instead of brushing against the bulk of Helgrind, the tip of her right wing dipped into the rock and then back out again.

Saphira, did you see that!

I did.

Leaning forward, Saphira pushed the tip of her snout toward the sheer rock, paused an inch or two away—as if waiting for a trap to spring—then continued her advance. Scale by scale, Saphira's head slid into Helgrind, until all that was visible of her to Eragon was a neck, torso, and wings.

It's an illusion! exclaimed Saphira.

With a surge of her mighty thews, she abandoned the spur and flung the rest of her body after her head. It required every bit of Eragon's self-control not to cover his face in a desperate bid to protect himself as the crag rushed toward him.

An instant later, he found himself looking at a broad, vaulted cave suffused with the warm glow of morning. Saphira's scales refracted the light, casting thousands of shifting blue flecks across the rock. Twisting around, Eragon saw no wall behind them, only the mouth of the cave and a sweeping view of the landscape beyond.

Eragon grimaced. It had never occurred to him that Galbatorix might have hidden the Ra'zac's lair with magic. *Idiot! I have to do better,* he thought. Underestimating the king was a sure way to get them all killed.

Roran swore and said, "Warn me before you do something like that again."

Hunching forward, Eragon began to unbuckle his legs from the saddle as he studied their surroundings, alert for danger.

The opening to the cave was an irregular oval, perhaps fifty feet high and sixty feet wide. From there the chamber expanded to twice that size before ending a good bowshot away in a pile of thick stone slabs that leaned against each other in a confusion of uncertain angles. A mat of scratches defaced the floor, evidence of the many times the Lethrblaka had taken off from, landed on, and walked about its surface. Like mysterious keyholes, five low tunnels pierced the sides of the cave, as did a lancet passageway large enough to accommodate Saphira. Eragon examined the tunnels carefully, but they were pitch-black and appeared vacant, a fact he confirmed with quick thrusts of his mind. Strange, disjointed murmurs echoed from within Helgrind's innards, suggesting unknown *things* scurrying about in the dark, and endlessly dripping water. Adding to the chorus of whispers was the steady rise and fall of Saphira's breathing, which was over-loud in the confines of the bare chamber.

The most distinctive feature of the cavern, however, was the mixture of odors that pervaded it. The smell of cold stone domi-nated, but underneath Eragon discerned whiffs of damp and mold and something far worse: the sickly sweet fetor of rotting meat.

Undoing the last few straps, Eragon swung his right leg over Saphira's spine, so he was sitting sidesaddle, and prepared to jump off her back. Roran did the same on the opposite side.

Before he released his hold, Eragon heard, amid the many rustlings that teased his ear, a score of simultaneous clicks, as if someone had struck the rock with a collection of hammers. The sound repeated itself a half second later.

He looked in the direction of the noise, as did Saphira.

A huge, twisted shape hurtled out of the lancet passageway. Eyes black, bulging, rimless. A beak seven feet long. Batlike wings. The torso naked, hairless, rippling with muscle. Claws like iron spikes.

Saphira lurched as she tried to evade the Lethrblaka, but to no avail. The creature crashed into her right side with what felt to Eragon like the strength and fury of an avalanche.

What exactly happened next, he knew not, for the impact sent him tumbling through space without so much as a half-formed thought in his jumbled brain. His blind flight ended as abruptly as it began when something hard and flat rammed against the back of him, and he dropped to the floor, banging his head a second time.

That last collision drove the remaining air clean out of Eragon's lungs. Stunned, he lay curled on his side, gasping and struggling to regain a semblance of control over his unresponsive limbs.

Eragon! cried Saphira.

The concern in her voice fueled Eragon's efforts as nothing else could. As life returned to his arms and legs, he reached out and grasped his staff from where it had fallen beside him. He planted the spike mounted on the staff's lower end into a nearby crack and pulled himself up the hawthorn rod and onto his feet. He swayed. A swarm of crimson sparks danced before him.

The situation was so confusing, he hardly knew where to look first.

Saphira and the Lethrblaka rolled across the cave, kicking and clawing and snapping at each other with enough force to gouge the rock beneath them. The clamor of their fight must have been unimaginably loud, but to Eragon they grappled in silence; his ears did not work. Still, he felt the vibrations through the soles of his feet as the colossal beasts thrashed from side to side, threatening to crush anyone who came near them.

A torrent of blue fire erupted from between Saphira's jaws and bathed the left side of the Lethrblaka's head in a ravening inferno hot enough to melt steel. The flames curved around the Lethrblaka without harming it. Undeterred, the monster pecked at Saphira's neck, forcing her to stop and defend herself.

Fast as an arrow loosed from a bow, the second Lethrblaka darted out of the lancet passageway, pounced upon Saphira's flank, and, opening its narrow beak, uttered a horrible, withering shriek that made Eragon's scalp prickle and a cold lump of dread form in his gut. He snarled in discomfort; *that* he could hear.

The smell now, with both Lethrblaka present, resembled the sort of overpowering stench one would get from tossing a half-dozen pounds of rancid meat into a barrel of sewage and allowing the mixture to ferment for a week in summer.

Eragon clamped his mouth shut as his gorge rose and turned his attention elsewhere to keep from retching.

A few paces away, Roran lay crumpled against the side of the cave, where he too had landed. Even as Eragon watched, his cousin lifted an arm and pushed himself onto all fours and then to his feet. His eyes were glazed, and he tottered as if drunk.

Behind Roran, the two Ra'zac emerged from a nearby tunnel. They wielded long, pale blades of an ancient design in their malformed hands. Unlike their parents, the Ra'zac were roughly the same size and shape as humans. An ebony exoskeleton encased them from top to bottom, although little of it showed, for even in Helgrind, the Ra'zac wore dark robes and cloaks.

They advanced with startling swiftness, their movements sharp and jerky like those of an insect.

And yet, Eragon still could not sense them or the Lethrblaka. *Are they an illusion too?* he wondered. But no, that was nonsense; the flesh Saphira tore at with her talons was real enough. Another explanation occurred to him: perhaps it was *impossible* to detect their presence. Perhaps the Ra'zac could conceal themselves from the minds of humans, their prey, just as spiders conceal themselves from flies. If so, then Eragon finally understood why the Ra'zac had been so successful hunting magicians and Riders for Galbatorix when they themselves could not use magic.

Blast! Eragon would have indulged in more colorful oaths, but it was time for action, not cursing their bad luck. Brom had claimed the Ra'zac were no match for him in broad daylight, and while that might have been true—given that Brom had had decades to invent spells to use against the Ra'zac—Eragon knew that, without the advantage of surprise, he, Saphira, and Roran would be hard-pressed to escape with their lives, much less rescue Katrina.

Raising his right hand above his head, Eragon cried, *"Brisingr!"* and threw a roaring fireball toward the Ra'zac. They dodged, and the fireball splashed against the rock floor, guttered for a moment, and then winked out of existence. The spell was silly and childish and could cause no conceivable damage if Galbatorix had protected the Ra'zac like the Lethrblaka. Still, Eragon found the attack immensely satisfying. It also distracted the Ra'zac long enough for Eragon to dash over to Roran and press his back against his cousin's.

"Hold them off for a minute," he shouted, hoping Roran would hear. Whether he did or not, Roran grasped Eragon's meaning, for he covered himself with his shield and lifted his hammer in preparation to fight.

The amount of force contained within each of the Lethrblaka's terrible blows had already depleted the wards against physical danger that Eragon had placed around Saphira. Without them, the Lethrblaka had inflicted several rows of scratches—long but shallow—along her thighs and had managed to stab her three times with their beaks; those wounds were short but deep and caused her a great deal of pain.

In return, Saphira had laid open the ribs of one Lethrblaka and had bitten off the last three feet of the other's tail. The Lethrblaka's blood, to Eragon's astonishment, was a metallic blue-green, not unlike the verdigris that forms on aged copper.

At the moment, the Lethrblaka had withdrawn from Saphira and were circling her, lunging now and then in order to keep her at bay while they waited for her to tire or until they could kill her with a stab from one of their beaks.

Saphira was better suited than the Lethrblaka to open combat by virtue of her scales—which were harder and tougher than the Lethrblaka's gray hide—and her teeth—which were far more lethal in close quarters than the Lethrblaka's beaks—but despite all that, she had difficulty fending off both creatures at once, especially since the ceiling prevented her from leaping and flying about and otherwise outmaneuvering her foes. Eragon feared that even if she prevailed, the Lethrblaka would maim her before she slew them.

Taking a quick breath, Eragon cast a single spell that contained every one of the twelve techniques of killing that Oromis had taught him. He was careful to phrase the incantation as a series of processes, so that if Galbatorix's wards foiled him, he could sever the flow of magic. Otherwise, the spell might consume his strength until he died.

It was well he took the precaution. Upon release of the spell, Eragon quickly became aware that the magic was having no effect upon the Lethrblaka, and he abandoned the assault. He had not expected to succeed with the traditional death-words, but he had to try, on the slight chance Galbatorix might have been careless or ignorant when he had placed wards upon the Lethrblaka and their spawn.

Behind him, Roran shouted, "Yah!" An instant later, a sword thudded against his shield, followed by the tinkle of rippling mail and the bell-like peal of a second sword bouncing off Roran's helm.

Eragon realized that his hearing must be improving.

The Ra'zac struck again and again, but each time their weapons glanced off Roran's armor or missed his face and limbs by a hairsbreadth, no matter how fast they swung their blades. Roran was too slow to retaliate, but neither could the Ra'zac harm him. They hissed with frustration and spewed a continuous stream of invectives, which seemed all the more foul because of how the creatures' hard, clacking jaws mangled the language.

Eragon smiled. The cocoon of charms he had spun around Roran had done its job. He hoped the invisible net of energy would hold until he could find a way to halt the Lethrblaka.

Everything shivered and went gray around Eragon as the two Lethrblaka shrieked in unison. For a moment, his resolve deserted him, leaving him unable to move, then he rallied and shook himself as a dog might, casting off their fell influence. The sound reminded him of nothing so much as a pair of children screaming in pain.

Then Eragon began to chant as fast as he could without mispronouncing the ancient language. Each sentence he uttered, and they were legion, contained the potential to deliver instant death, and each death was unique among its fellows. As he recited his improvised soliloquy, Saphira received another cut upon her left flank. In return, she broke the wing of her assailant, slashing the thin flight membrane into ribbons with her claws. A number of heavy impacts transmitted themselves from Roran's back to Eragon's as the Ra'zac hacked and stabbed in a lightning-quick frenzy. The largest of the two Ra'zac began to edge around Roran, in order to attack Eragon directly.

And then, amid the din of steel against steel, and steel against wood, and claws against stone, there came the scrape of a sword sliding through mail, followed by a wet crunch. Roran yelled, and Eragon felt blood splash across the calf of his right leg.

Out of the corner of one eye, Eragon watched as a humpbacked figure leaped toward him, extending its leaf-bladed sword so as to impale him. The world seemed to contract around the thin, narrow point; the tip glittered like a shard of crystal, each scratch a thread of quicksilver in the bright light of dawn.

He only had time for one more spell before he would have to devote himself to stopping the Ra'zac from inserting the sword between his liver and kidneys. In desperation, he gave up trying to directly harm the Lethrblaka and instead cried, "Garjzla, letta!"

It was a crude spell, constructed in haste and poorly worded, yet it worked. The bulbous eyes of the Lethrblaka with the broken wing became a matched set of mirrors, each a perfect hemisphere, as Eragon's magic reflected the light that otherwise would have entered the Lethrblaka's pupils. Blind, the creature stumbled and flailed at the air in a vain attempt to hit Saphira.

Eragon spun the hawthorn staff in his hands and knocked aside the Ra'zac's sword when it was less than an inch from his ribs. The Ra'zac landed in front of him and jutted out its neck. Eragon recoiled as a short, thick beak appeared from within the depths of its hood. The chitinous appendage snapped shut just short of his right eye. In a rather detached way, Eragon noticed that the Ra'zac's tongue was barbed and purple and writhed like a headless snake.

Bringing his hands together at the center of the staff, Eragon drove his arms forward, striking the Ra'zac across its hollow chest and throwing the monster back several yards. It fell upon its hands and knees. Eragon pivoted around Roran, whose left side was slick with blood, and parried the sword of the other Ra'zac. He feinted, beat the Ra'zac's blade, and, when the Ra'zac stabbed at his throat, whirled the other half of the staff across his body and deflected the thrust. Without pausing, Eragon lunged forward and planted the wooden end of the staff in the Ra'zac's abdomen.

If Eragon had been wielding Zar'roc, he would have killed the Ra'zac then and there. As it was, something cracked inside the Ra'zac, and the creature went rolling across the cave for a dozen or more paces. It immediately popped up again, leaving a smear of blue gore on the uneven rock.

I need a sword, thought Eragon.

He widened his stance as the two Ra'zac converged upon him; he had no choice but to hold his ground and face their combined onslaught, for he was all that stood between those hook-clawed carrion crows and Roran. He began to mouth the same spell that had proved itself against the Lethrblaka, but the Ra'zac executed high and low slashes before he could utter a syllable.

The swords rebounded off the hawthorn with a dull *bonk*. They did not dent or otherwise mar the enchanted wood.

Left, right, up, down. Eragon did not think; he acted and reacted as he exchanged a flurry of blows with the Ra'zac. The staff was ideal for fighting multiple opponents, as he could strike and block with both ends, and often simultaneously. That ability served him well now. He panted, each breath short and quick. Sweat dripped from his brow and gathered at the corners of his eyes, and a layer greased his back and the undersides of his arms. The red haze of battle dimmed his vision and throbbed in response to the convulsions of his heart.

He never felt so alive, or afraid, as he did when fighting.

Eragon's own wards were scant. Since he had lavished the bulk of his attention on Saphira and Roran, Eragon's magical defenses soon failed, and the smaller Ra'zac wounded him on the outside of his left knee. The injury was not life-threatening, but it was still serious, for his left leg would no longer support his full weight.

Gripping the spike at the bottom, Eragon swung the staff like a club and bashed one Ra'zac upside the head. The Ra'zac collapsed, but whether it was dead or only unconscious, Eragon could not tell. Advancing upon the remaining Ra'zac, he battered the creature's arms and shoulders and, with a sudden twist, knocked the sword out of its hand.

Before Eragon could finish off the Ra'zac, the blinded, broken-winged Lethrblaka flew the width of the cave and slammed against the far wall, knocking loose a shower of stone flakes from the ceiling. The sight and sound were so colossal, they caused Eragon, Roran, and the Ra'zac to flinch and turn, simply out of instinct.

Jumping after the crippled Lethrblaka, which she had just kicked, Saphira sank her teeth into the back of the creature's sinewy neck. The Lethrblaka thrashed in one final effort to free itself, and then Saphira whipped her head from side to side and broke its spine. Rising from her bloody kill, Saphira filled the cave with a savage roar of victory.

The remaining Lethrblaka did not hesitate. Tackling Saphira, it dug its claws underneath the edges of her scales and pulled her into an uncontrolled tumble. Together they rolled to the lip of the cave, teetered for a half second, and then dropped out of sight, battling the whole way. It was a clever tactic, for it carried the Lethrblaka out of the range of Eragon's senses, and that which he could not sense, he had difficulty casting a spell against.

Saphira! cried Eragon.

Tend to yourself. This one won't escape me.

With a start, Eragon whirled around just in time to see the two Ra'zac vanish into the depths of the nearest tunnel, the smaller supporting the larger. Closing his eyes, Eragon located the minds of the prisoners in Helgrind, muttered a burst of the ancient language, then said to Roran, "I sealed off Katrina's cell so the Ra'zac can't use her as a hostage. Only you and I can open the door now."

"Good," said Roran through clenched teeth. "Can you do something about this?" He jerked his chin toward the spot he had clamped his right hand over. Blood welled between his fingers. Eragon probed the wound. As soon as he touched it, Roran flinched and recoiled.

"You're lucky," said Eragon. "The sword hit a rib." Placing one hand on the injury and the other on the twelve diamonds concealed inside the belt of Beloth the Wise strapped around his waist, Eragon drew upon the power he had stored within the gems. "Waíse heill!" A ripple traversed Roran's side as the magic knit his skin and muscle back together again.

Then Eragon healed his own wound: the gash on his left knee.

Finished, he straightened and glanced in the direction that Saphira had gone. His connection with her was fading as she chased the Lethrblaka toward Leona Lake. He yearned to help her but knew that, for the time being, she would have to fend for herself.

"Hurry," said Roran. "They're getting away!"

"Right."

Hefting his staff, Eragon approached the unlit tunnel and flicked his gaze from one stone protrusion to another, expecting the Ra'zac to spring out from behind one of them. He moved slowly in order that his footsteps would not echo in the winding shaft. When he happened to touch a rock to steady himself, he found it coated in slime.

After a score of yards, several folds and twists in the passageway hid the main cavern and plunged them into a gloom so profound, even Eragon found it impossible to see.

"Maybe you're different, but I can't fight in the dark," whispered Roran.

"If I make a light, the Ra'zac won't come near us, not when I now know a spell that works on them. They'll just hide until we leave. We have to kill them while we have the chance."

"What am I supposed to do? I'm more likely to run into a wall and break my nose than I am to find those two beetles. . . . They could sneak around behind us and stab us in the back."

"Shh. . . . Hold on to my belt, follow me, and be ready to duck."

Eragon could not see, but he could still hear, smell, touch, and taste, and those faculties were sensitive enough that he had a fair idea of what lay nearby. The greatest danger was that the Ra'zac would attack from a distance, perhaps with a bow, but he trusted that his reflexes were sharp enough to save Roran and himself from an oncoming missile.

A current of air tickled Eragon's skin, then paused and reversed itself as pressure from the outside waxed and waned. The cycle repeated itself at inconsistent intervals, creating invisible eddies that brushed against him like fountains of roiling water.

His breathing, and Roran's, was loud and ragged compared with the odd assortment of sounds that propagated through the tunnel. Above the gusts of their respiration, Eragon caught the *tink, clink, clatter* of a stone falling somewhere in the tangle of branching tubes and the steady *doink . . . doink . . . doink* of condensed droplets striking the drumlike surface of a subterranean pool. He also heard the grind of pea-sized gravel crushed underneath the soles of his boots. A long, eerie moan wavered somewhere far ahead of them.

Of smells, none were new: sweat, blood, damp, and mold.

Step by step, Eragon led the way as they burrowed farther into the bowels of Helgrind. The tunnel slanted downward and often split or turned, so that Eragon would have soon been lost if he had not been able to use Katrina's mind as a reference point. The various knobby holes were low and cramped. Once, when Eragon bumped his head against the ceiling, a sudden flare of claustrophobia unnerved him.

I'm back, Saphira announced just as Eragon put his foot on a rugged step hewn out of the rock below him. He paused. She had escaped additional injury, which relieved him.

And the Lethrblaka?

Floating belly-up in Leona Lake. I'm afraid that some fishermen saw our battle. They were rowing toward Dras-Leona when I last saw them.

Well, it can't be helped. See what you can find in the tunnel the Lethrblaka came out of. And keep an eye out for the Ra'zac. They may try to slip past us and escape Helgrind through the entrance we used.

They probably have a bolt-hole at ground level.

Probably, but I don't think they'll run quite yet.

After what seemed like an hour trapped in the darkness—though Eragon knew it could not have been more than ten or fifteen minutes—and after descending more than a hundred feet through Helgrind, Eragon stopped on a level patch of stone. Transmitting his thoughts to Roran, he said, *Katrina's cell is about fifty feet in front of us, on the right.*

We can't risk letting her out until the Ra'zac are dead or gone.

What if they won't reveal themselves until we do let her out? For some reason, I can't sense them. They could hide from me until doomsday in here. So do we wait for who knows how long, or do we free Katrina while we still have the chance? I can place some wards around her that should protect her from most attacks.

Roran was quiet for a second. *Let's free her, then.*

They began to move forward again, feeling their way along the squat corridor with its rough, unfinished floor. Eragon had to devote most of his attention to his footing in order to maintain his balance.

As a result, he almost missed the swish of cloth sliding over cloth and then the faint *twang* that emanated from off to his right.

He recoiled against the wall, shoving Roran back. At the same time, something augered past his face, carving a groove of flesh from his right cheek. The thin trench burned as if cauterized.

"Kveykva!" shouted Eragon.

Red light, bright as the midday sun, flared into existence. It had no source, and thus it illuminated every surface evenly and without shadows, giving things a curious flat appearance. The sudden blaze dazzled Eragon, but it did more than that to the lone Ra'zac in front of him; the creature dropped its bow, covered its hooded face, and screamed high and shrill. A similar screech told Eragon that the second Ra'zac was behind them.

Roran!

Eragon pivoted just in time to see Roran charge the other Ra'zac, hammer held high. The disoriented monster stumbled backward but was too slow. The hammer fell. "For my father!" shouted Roran. He struck again. "For our home!" The Ra'zac was already dead, but Roran lifted the hammer once more. "For Carvahall!" His final blow shattered the Ra'zac's carapace like the rind of a dry gourd. In the merciless ruby glare, the spreading pool of blood appeared purple.

Spinning his staff in a circle to knock aside the arrow or sword that he was convinced was driving toward him, Eragon turned to confront the remaining Ra'zac. The tunnel before them was empty. He swore.

Eragon strode over to the twisted figure on the floor. He swung the staff over his head and brought it down across the chest of the dead Ra'zac with a resounding thud.

"I've waited a long time to do that," said Eragon.

"As have I."

He and Roran looked at each other.

"Ahh!" cried Eragon, and clutched his cheek as the pain intensified.

"It's bubbling!" exclaimed Roran. "Do something!"

The Ra'zac must have coated the arrowhead with Seithr oil, thought Eragon. Remembering his training, he cleansed the wound and surrounding tissue with an incantation and then repaired the damage to his face. He opened and closed his mouth several times to make sure the muscles were working properly. With a grim smile, he said, "Imagine the state we'd be in without magic."

"Without magic, we wouldn't have Galbatorix to worry about."

Talk later, said Saphira. *As soon as those fishermen reach Dras-Leona, the king may hear of our doings from one of his pet spellcasters in the city, and we do not want Galbatorix scrying Helgrind while we are still here.*

Yes, yes, said Eragon. Extinguishing the omnipresent red glow, he said, "Brisingr raudhr," and created a red werelight like that from the previous night, except that this one remained anchored six inches from the ceiling instead of accompanying Eragon wherever he went.

Now that he had an opportunity to examine the tunnel in some detail, Eragon saw that the stone hallway was dotted with twenty or so ironbound doors, some on either side. He pointed and said, "Ninth down, on the right. You go get her. I'll check the other cells. The Ra'zac might have left something interesting in them."

Roran nodded. Crouching, he searched the corpse at their feet but found no keys. He shrugged. "I'll do it the hard way, then." He sprinted to the proper door, abandoned his shield, and set to work on the hinges with his hammer. Each blow created a frightful crash.

Eragon did not offer to help. His cousin would not want or appreciate assistance now, and besides, there was something else Eragon had to do. He went to the first cell, whispered three words, then, after the lock snapped open, pushed aside the door. All that the small room contained was a black chain and a pile of rotting bones. Those sad remains were no more than he had expected; he already knew where the object of his search lay, but he maintained the charade of ignorance to avoid kindling Roran's suspicion.

Two more doors opened and closed beneath the touch of Eragon's fingers. Then, at the fourth cell, the door swung back to admit the shifting radiance of the werelight and reveal the very man Eragon had hoped he would not find: Sloan.

DIVERGENCE

The butcher sat slumped against the left-hand wall, both arms chained to an iron ring above his head.

His ragged clothes barely covered his pale, emaciated body; the corners of his bones stood out in sharp relief underneath his translucent skin. His blue veins were also prominent. Sores had formed on his wrists where the manacles chafed. The ulcers oozed a mixture of clear fluid and blood. What remained of his hair had turned gray or white and hung in lank, greasy ropes over his pock-marked face.

Roused by the clang of Roran's hammer, Sloan lifted his chin toward the light and, in a quavering voice, asked, "Who is it? Who's there?" His hair parted and slid back, exposing his eye sockets, which had sunk deep into his skull. Where his eyelids should have been, there were now only a few scraps of tattered skin draped over the raw cavities underneath. The area around them was bruised and scabbed.

With a shock, Eragon realized that the Ra'zac had pecked out Sloan's eyes.

What he then should do, Eragon could not decide. The butcher had told the Ra'zac that Eragon had found Saphira's egg. Further-more, Sloan had murdered the watchman, Byrd, and had betrayed Carvahall to the Empire. If he were brought before his fellow vil-lagers, they would undoubtedly find Sloan guilty and condemn him to death by hanging.

It seemed only right, to Eragon, that the butcher should die for his crimes. That was not the source of his uncertainty. Rather, it arose from the fact that Roran loved Katrina, and Katrina, whatever

Sloan had done, must still harbor a certain degree of affection for her father. Watching an arbitrator publicly denounce Sloan's offenses and then hang him would be no easy thing for her or, by extension, Roran. Such hardship might even create enough ill will between them to end their engagement. Either way, Eragon was convinced that taking Sloan back with them would sow discord between him, Roran, Katrina, and the other villagers, and might engender enough anger to distract them from their struggle against the Empire.

The easiest solution, thought Eragon, *would be to kill him and say that I found him dead in the cell*. . . . His lips trembled, one of the death-words heavy upon his tongue.

"What do you want?" asked Sloan. He turned his head from side to side in an attempt to hear better. "I already told you everything I know!"

Eragon cursed himself for hesitating. Sloan's guilt was not in dispute; he was a murderer and a traitor. Any lawgiver would sentence him to execution.

Notwithstanding the merit of those arguments, it was Sloan who was curled in front of him, a man Eragon had known his entire life. The butcher might be a despicable person, but the wealth of memories and experiences Eragon shared with him bred a sense of intimacy that troubled Eragon's conscience. To strike down Sloan would be like raising his hand against Horst or Loring or any of the elders of Carvahall.

Again Eragon prepared to utter the fatal word.

An image appeared in his mind's eye: *Torkenbrand, the slaver he and Murtagh had encountered during their flight to the Varden, kneeling on the dusty ground and Murtagh striding up to him and beheading him.* Eragon remembered how he had objected to Murtagh's deed and how it had troubled him for days afterward.

Have I changed so much, he asked himself, *that I can do the same thing now? As Roran said, I have killed, but only in the heat of battle . . . never like this.*

He glanced over his shoulder as Roran broke the last hinge to Katrina's cell door. Dropping his hammer, Roran prepared to charge the door and knock it inward but then appeared to think better of it and tried to lift it free of its frame. The door rose a fraction of an inch, then halted and wobbled in his grip. "Give me a hand here!" he shouted. "I don't want it to fall on her."

Eragon looked back at the wretched butcher. He had no more time for mindless wanderings. He had to choose. One way or another, he had to choose. . . .

"Eragon!"

I don't know what's right, realized Eragon. His own uncertainty told him that it would be wrong to kill Sloan or return him to the Varden. He had no idea what he should do instead, except to find a third path, one that was less obvious and less violent.

Lifting his hand, as if in benediction, Eragon whispered, "Slytha." Sloan's manacles rattled as he went limp, falling into a profound sleep. As soon as he was sure the spell had taken hold, Eragon closed and locked the cell door again and replaced his wards around it.

What are you up to, Eragon? asked Saphira.

Wait until we're together again. I'll explain then.

Explain what? You don't have a plan.

Give me a minute and I will.

"What was in there?" asked Roran as Eragon took his place opposite him.

"Sloan." Eragon adjusted his grip on the door between them. "He's dead."

Roran's eyes widened. "How?"

"Looks like they broke his neck."

For an instant, Eragon feared that Roran might not believe him. Then his cousin grunted and said, "It's better that way, I suppose. Ready? One, two, three—"

Together, they heaved the massive door out of its casing and threw it across the hallway. The stone passageway returned the resulting boom to them again and again. Without pause, Roran rushed into the cell, which was lit by a single wax taper. Eragon followed a step behind.

Katrina cowered at the far end of an iron cot. "Let me alone, you toothless bastards! I—" She stopped, struck dumb as Roran stepped forward. Her face was white from lack of sun and streaked with filth, yet at that moment, a look of such wonder and tender love blossomed upon her features, Eragon thought he had rarely seen anyone so beautiful.

Never taking her eyes off Roran, Katrina stood and, with a shaking hand, touched his cheek.

"You came."

"I came."

A laughing sob broke out of Roran, and he folded her in his arms, pulling her against his chest. They remained lost in their embrace for a long moment.

Drawing back, Roran kissed her three times on the lips. Katrina wrinkled her nose and exclaimed, "You grew a beard!" Of all the things she could have said, that was so unexpected—and she sounded so shocked and surprised—that Eragon chuckled in response.

For the first time, Katrina seemed to notice him. She glanced him over, then settled on his face, which she studied with evident puzzlement. "Eragon? Is that you?"

"Aye."

"He's a Dragon Rider now," said Roran.

"A Rider? You mean . . ." She faltered; the revelation seemed to overwhelm her. Glancing at Roran, as if for protection, she held him even closer and sidled around him, away from Eragon. To Roran, she said, "How . . . how did you find us? Who else is with you?"

"All that later. We have to get out of Helgrind before the rest of the Empire comes running after us."

"Wait! What about my father? Did you find him?"

Roran looked at Eragon, then returned his gaze to Katrina and gently said, "We were too late."

A shiver ran through Katrina. She closed her eyes, and a solitary tear leaked down the side of her face. "So be it."

While they spoke, Eragon frantically tried to figure out how to dispose of Sloan, although he concealed his deliberations from Saphira; he knew that she would disapprove of the direction his thoughts were taking. A scheme began to form in his mind. It was an outlandish concept, fraught with danger and uncertainty, but it was the only viable path, given the circumstances.

Abandoning further reflection, Eragon sprang into action. He had much to do in little time. "Jierda!" he cried, pointing. With a burst of blue sparks and flying fragments, the metal bands riveted around Katrina's ankles broke apart. Katrina jumped in surprise.

"Magic . . . ," she whispered.

"A simple spell." She shrank from his touch as he reached toward her. "Katrina, I have to make sure that Galbatorix or one of his magicians hasn't enchanted you with any traps or forced you to swear things in the ancient language."

"The ancient—"

Roran interrupted her: "Eragon! Do this when we make camp. We can't stay here."

"No." Eragon slashed his arm through the air. "We do it now." Scowling, Roran moved aside and allowed Eragon to put his hands on Katrina's shoulders. "Just look into my eyes," he told her. She nodded and obeyed.

That was the first time Eragon had a reason to use the spells Oromis had taught him for detecting the work of another spellcaster, and he had difficulty remembering every word from the scrolls in Ellesméra. The gaps in his memory were so serious that on three different instances he had to rely upon a synonym to complete an incantation.

For a long while, Eragon stared into Katrina's glistening eyes and mouthed phrases in the ancient language, occasionally—and with her permission—examining one of her memories for evidence that someone had tampered with it. He was as gentle as possible, unlike the Twins, who had ravaged his own mind in a similar procedure the day he arrived at Farthen Dûr.

Roran stood guard, pacing back and forth in front of the open doorway. Every second that went by increased his agitation; he twirled his hammer and tapped the head of it against his upper thigh, as if keeping time with a piece of music.

At last Eragon released Katrina. "I'm done."

"What did you find?" she whispered. She hugged herself, her forehead creased with worry lines as she waited for his verdict. Silence filled the cell as Roran came to a standstill.

"Nothing but your own thoughts. You are free of any spells."

"Of course she is," growled Roran, and again wrapped her in his arms.

Together, the three of them exited the cell. "Brisingr, iet tauthr," said Eragon, gesturing at the werelight that still floated near the ceiling of the hallway. At his command, the glowing orb darted to a spot directly over his head and remained there, bobbing like a piece of driftwood in the surf.

Eragon took the lead as they hurried back through the jumble of tunnels toward the cavern where they had landed. As he trotted across the slick rock, he watched for the remaining Ra'zac while, at the same time, erecting wards to safeguard Katrina. Behind him, he heard her and Roran exchange a series of brief phrases and lone words: "I love you . . . Horst and others safe . . . Always . . . For you . . . Yes . . . Yes . . . Yes . . . Yes." The trust and affection they shared were so obvious, it roused a dull ache of longing inside Eragon.

When they were about ten yards from the main cavern and could just begin to see by the faint glow ahead of them, Eragon extinguished the werelight. A few feet later, Katrina slowed, then pressed herself against the side of the tunnel and covered her face. "I can't. It's too bright; my eyes hurt."

Roran quickly moved in front of her, casting her in his shadow. "When was the last time you were outside?"

"I don't know. . . ." A hint of panic crept into her voice. "I don't know! Not since they brought me here. Roran, am I going blind?" She sniffed and began to cry.

Her tears surprised Eragon. He remembered her as someone of great strength and fortitude. But then, she had spent many weeks locked in the dark, fearing for her life. *I might not be myself either, if I were in her place.*

"No, you're fine. You just need to get used to the sun again." Roran stroked her hair. "Come on, don't let this upset you. Everything is going to be all right. . . . You're safe now. *Safe*, Katrina. You hear me?"

"I hear you."

Although he hated to ruin one of the tunics the elves had given him, Eragon tore off a strip of cloth from the bottom edge of his garment. He handed it to Katrina and said, "Tie this over your eyes. You should be able to see through it well enough to keep from falling or running into anything."

She thanked him and then blindfolded herself.

Once again advancing, the trio emerged into the sunny, blood-splattered main cavern—which stank worse than before, owing to the noxious fumes that drifted from the body of the Lethrblaka— even as Saphira appeared from within the depths of the lancet opening opposite them. Seeing her, Katrina gasped and clung to Roran, digging her fingers into his arms.

Eragon said, "Katrina, allow me to introduce you to Saphira. I am her Rider. She can understand if you speak to her."

"It is an honor, O dragon," Katrina managed to say. She dipped her knees in a weak imitation of a curtsy.

Saphira inclined her head in return. Then she faced Eragon. *I searched the Lethrblaka's nest, but all I found was bones, bones, and more bones, including several that smelled of fresh meat. The Ra'zac must have eaten the slaves last night.*

I wish we could have rescued them.

I know, but we cannot protect everyone in this war.

Gesturing at Saphira, Eragon said, "Go on; climb onto her. I'll join you in a moment."

Katrina hesitated, then glanced at Roran, who nodded and murmured, "It's all right. Saphira brought us here." Together, the couple skirted the corpse of the Lethrblaka as they went over to Saphira, who crouched flat upon her belly so that they could mount her. Cupping his hands to form a step, Roran lifted Katrina high enough to pull herself over the upper part of Saphira's left foreleg. From there Katrina clambered the looped leg straps of the saddle, as if a ladder, until she sat perched upon the crest of Saphira's shoulders. Like a mountain goat leaping from one ledge to another, Roran duplicated her ascent.

Crossing the cave after them, Eragon examined Saphira, assessing the severity of her various scrapes, gashes, tears, bruises, and stab wounds. To do so, he relied upon what she herself felt, in addition to what he could see.

For goodness' sake, said Saphira, *save your attentions until we are well out of danger. I'm not going to bleed to death.*

That's not quite true, and you know it. You're bleeding inside. Unless I stop it now, you may suffer complications I can't heal, and then we'll never get back to the Varden. Don't argue; you can't change my mind, and I won't take a minute.

As it turned out, Eragon required several minutes to restore Saphira to her former health. Her injuries were severe enough that in order to complete his spells, he had to empty the belt of Beloth the Wise of energy and, after that, draw upon Saphira's own vast reserves of strength. Whenever he shifted from a larger wound to a smaller one, she protested that he was being foolish and would he please leave off, but he ignored her complaints, much to her growing displeasure.

Afterward, Eragon slumped, tired from the magic and the fighting. Flicking a finger toward the places where the Lethrblaka had skewered her with their beaks, he said, *You should have Arya or another elf inspect my handiwork on those. I did my best, but I may have missed something.*

I appreciate your concern for my welfare, she replied, *but this is hardly the place for softhearted demonstrations. Once and for all, let us be gone!*

Aye. Time to leave. Stepping back, Eragon edged away from Saphira, in the direction of the tunnel behind him.

"Come on!" called Roran. "Hurry up!"

Eragon! exclaimed Saphira.

Eragon shook his head. "No. I'm staying here."

"You—" Roran started to say, but a ferocious growl from Saphira interrupted him. She lashed her tail against the side of the cave and raked the floor with her talons, so that bone and stone squealed in what sounded like mortal agony.

"Listen!" shouted Eragon. "One of the Ra'zac is still on the loose. And think what else might be in Helgrind: scrolls, potions, information about the Empire's activities—things that can help us! The Ra'zac may even have eggs of theirs stored here. If they do, I have to destroy them before Galbatorix can claim them for his own."

To Saphira, Eragon also said, *I can't kill Sloan, I can't let Roran or Katrina see him, and I can't allow him to starve to death in his cell or Galbatorix's men to recapture him. I'm sorry, but I have to deal with Sloan on my own.*

"How will you get out of the Empire?" demanded Roran.

"I'll run. I'm as fast as an elf now, you know."

The tip of Saphira's tail twitched. That was the only warning Eragon had before she leaped toward him, extending one of her glittering paws. He fled, dashing into the tunnel a fraction of a second before Saphira's foot passed through the space where he had been.

Saphira skidded to a stop in front of the tunnel and roared with frustration that she was unable to follow him into the narrow enclosure. Her bulk blocked most of the light. The stone shook around Eragon as she tore at the entrance with her claws and teeth, breaking off thick chunks. Her feral snarls and the sight of her lunging muzzle, filled with teeth as long as his forearm, sent a jolt of fear through Eragon. He understood then how a rabbit must feel when it cowers in its den while a wolf digs after it.

"Gánga!" he shouted.

No! Saphira placed her head on the ground and uttered a mournful keen, her eyes large and pitiful.

"Gánga! I love you, Saphira, but you have to go."

She retreated several yards from the tunnel and snuffled at him, mewling like a cat. *Little one . . .*

Eragon hated to make her unhappy, and he hated to send her away; it felt as if he were tearing himself apart. Saphira's misery flowed across their mental link and, coupled with his own anguish, almost paralyzed him. Somehow he mustered the nerve to say, "Gánga! And don't come back for me or send anyone else for me, I'll be fine. Gánga! Gánga!"

Saphira howled with frustration and then reluctantly walked to the mouth of the cave. From his place on her saddle, Roran said, "Eragon, come on! Don't be daft. You're too important to risk—"

A combination of noise and motion obscured the rest of his sentence as Saphira launched herself out of the cave. In the clear sky beyond, her scales sparkled like a multitude of brilliant blue diamonds. She was, Eragon thought, magnificent: proud, noble, and more beautiful than any other living creature. No stag or lion could compete with the majesty of a dragon in flight. She said, *A week: that is how long I shall wait. Then I shall return for you, Eragon, even if I must fight my way past Thorn, Shruikan, and a thousand magicians.*

Eragon stood there until she dwindled from sight and he could no longer touch her mind. Then, his heart heavy as lead, he squared his shoulders and turned away from the sun and all things bright and living and once more descended into the tunnels of shadow.

RIDER AND RA'ZAC

Eragon sat bathed in the heatless radiance from his crimson werelight in the hall lined with cells near the center of Helgrind. His staff lay across his lap.

The rock reflected his voice as he repeated a phrase in the ancient language over and over again. It was not magic, but rather a message to the remaining Ra'zac. What he said meant this: "Come, O thou eater of men's flesh, let us end this fight of ours. You are hurt, and I am weary. Your companions are dead, and I am alone. We are a fit match. I promise that I shall not use gramarye against you, nor hurt or trap you with spells I have already cast. Come, O thou eater of men's flesh, let us end this fight of ours. . . ."

The time during which he spoke seemed endless: a neverwhen in a ghastly tinted chamber that remained unchanged through an eternity of cycling words whose order and significance ceased to matter to him. After a time, his clamoring thoughts fell silent, and a strange calm crept over him.

He paused with his mouth open, then closed it, watchful.

Thirty feet in front of him stood the Ra'zac. Blood dripped from the hem of the creature's ragged robes. "My massster does not want me to kill you," it hissed.

"But that does not matter to you now."

"No. If I fall to your staff, let Galbatorix deal with you as he will. He has more heartsss than you do."

Eragon laughed. "Hearts? I am the champion of the people, not him."

"Foolish boy." The Ra'zac cocked its head slightly, looking past him at the corpse of the other Ra'zac farther up the tunnel. "She was my hatchmate. You have become ssstrong since we firssst met, Shadeslayer."

"It was that or die."

"Will you make a pact with me, Shadeslayer?"

"What kind of a pact?"

"I am the lassst of my race, Shadeslayer. We are ancient, and I would not have us forgotten. Would you, in your songsss and in your hissstories, remind your fellow humans of the terror we inssspired in your kind? . . . Remember us as *fear*!"

"Why should I do that for you?"

Tucking its beak against its narrow chest, the Ra'zac clucked and chittered to itself for several moments. "Because," it said, "I will tell you sssomething secret, yesss I will."

"Then tell me."

"Give me your word firssst, lest you trick me."

"No. Tell me, and then I will decide whether or not to agree."

Over a minute passed, and neither of them moved, although Eragon kept his muscles taut and ready in expectation of a surprise attack. After another squall of sharp clicks, the Ra'zac said, "He has almossst found the *name*."

"Who has?"

"Galbatorix."

"The name of what?"

The Ra'zac hissed with frustration. "I cannot tell you! The *name*! The true *name*!"

"You have to give me more information than that."

"I cannot!"

"Then we have no pact."

"Curssse you, Rider! I curssse you! May you find no roossst nor den nor peace of mind in thisss land of yours. May you leave Alagaësia and never return!"

The nape of Eragon's neck prickled with the cold touch of dread.

65

In his mind, he again heard the words of Angela the herbalist when she had cast her dragon bones for him and told his fortune and predicted that selfsame fate.

A mare's tail of blood separated Eragon from his enemy as the Ra'zac swept back its sodden cloak, revealing a bow that it held with an arrow already fit to the string. Lifting and drawing the weapon, the Ra'zac loosed the bolt in the direction of Eragon's chest.

Eragon batted the shaft aside with his staff.

As if this attempt were nothing more than a preliminary gesture that custom dictated they observe before proceeding with their actual confrontation, the Ra'zac stooped, placed the bow on the floor, then straightened its cowl and slowly and deliberately pulled its leaf-bladed sword from underneath its robes. While it did, Eragon rose to his feet and took a shoulder-wide stance, his hands tight on the staff.

They lunged toward each other. The Ra'zac attempted to cleave Eragon from collarbone to hip, but Eragon twisted and stepped past the blow. Jamming the end of the staff upward, he drove its metal spike underneath the Ra'zac's beak and through the plates that protected the creature's throat.

The Ra'zac shuddered once and then collapsed.

Eragon stared at his most hated foe, stared at its lidless black eyes, and suddenly he went weak at the knees and retched against the wall of the corridor. Wiping his mouth, he yanked the staff free and whispered, "For our father. For our home. For Carvahall. For Brom. . . . I have had my fill of vengeance. May you rot here forever, Ra'zac."

Going to the appropriate cell, Eragon retrieved Sloan—who was still deep in his enchanted sleep—slung the butcher over his shoulder, and then began to retrace his steps back to the main cave of Helgrind. Along the way, he often lowered Sloan to the floor and left him to explore a chamber or byway that he had not visited before. In them he discovered many evil instruments, including four metal flasks of Seithr oil, which he promptly destroyed so that no one else could use the flesh-eating acid to further their malicious plans.

Hot sunlight stung Eragon's cheeks when he stumbled out of the network of tunnels. Holding his breath, he hurried past the dead Lethrblaka and went to the edge of the vast cave, where he gazed down the precipitous side of Helgrind at the hills far below. To the west, he saw a pillar of orange dust billowing above the lane that connected Helgrind to Dras-Leona, marking the approach of a group of horsemen.

His right side was burning from supporting Sloan's weight, so Eragon shifted the butcher onto his other shoulder. He blinked away the beads of sweat that clung to his eyelashes as he struggled to solve the problem of how he was supposed to transport Sloan and himself five thousand–some feet to the ground.

"It's almost a mile down," he murmured. "If there were a path, I could easily walk that distance, even with Sloan. So I must have the strength to lower us with magic. . . . Yes, but what you can do over a length of time may be too taxing to accomplish all at once without killing yourself. As Oromis said, the body cannot convert its stock-pile of fuel into energy fast enough to sustain most spells for more than a few seconds. I only have a certain amount of power avail-able at any given moment, and once it's gone, I have to wait until I recover. . . . And talking to myself isn't getting me anywhere."

Securing his hold on Sloan, Eragon fixed his eyes on a narrow ledge about a hundred feet below. *This is going to hurt,* he thought, preparing himself for the attempt. Then he barked, "Audr!"

Eragon felt himself rise several inches above the floor of the cave. "Fram," he said, and the spell propelled him away from Helgrind and into open space, where he hung unsupported, like a cloud drift-ing in the sky. Accustomed as he was to flying with Saphira, the sight of nothing but thin air underneath his feet still caused him unease.

By manipulating the flow of magic, Eragon quickly descended

from the Ra'zac's lair—which the insubstantial wall of stone once again hid—to the ledge. His boot slipped on a loose piece of rock as he alighted. For a handful of breathless seconds, he flailed, searching for solid footing but unable to look down, as tilting his head could send him toppling forward. He yelped as his left leg went off the ledge and he began to fall. Before he could resort to magic to save himself, he came to an abrupt halt as his left foot wedged itself in a crevice. The edges of the rift dug into his calf behind his greave, but he did not mind, for it held him in place.

Eragon leaned his back against Helgrind, using it to help him prop up Sloan's limp body. "That wasn't too bad," he observed. The effort had cost him, but not so much that he was unable to continue. "I can do this," he said. He gulped fresh air into his lungs, waiting for his racing heart to slow; he felt as if he had sprinted a score of yards while carrying Sloan. "I can do this. . . ."

The approaching riders caught his eye again. They were noticeably closer than before and galloping across the dry land at a pace that worried him. *It's a race between them and me,* he realized. *I have to escape before they reach Helgrind. There are sure to be magicians among them, and I'm in no fit condition to duel Galbatorix's spellcasters.* Glancing over at Sloan's face, he said, "Perhaps you can help me a bit, eh? It's the least you can do, considering I'm risking death and worse for you." The sleeping butcher rolled his head, lost in the world of dreams.

With a grunt, Eragon pushed himself off Helgrind. Again he said, "Audr," and again he became airborne. This time he relied upon Sloan's strength—meager as it was—as well as his own. Together they sank like two strange birds along Helgrind's rugged flank toward another ledge whose width promised safe haven.

In such a manner Eragon orchestrated their downward climb. He did not proceed in a straight line, but rather angled off to his right, so that they curved around Helgrind and the mass of blocky stone hid him and Sloan from the horsemen.

The closer they got to the ground, the slower they went. A

crushing fatigue overcame Eragon, reducing the distance he was able to traverse in a single stretch and making it increasingly difficult for him to recuperate during the pauses between his bursts of exertion. Even lifting a finger became a task that he found irritating in the extreme, as well as one that was almost unbearably laborious. Drowsiness muffled him in its warm folds and dulled his thoughts and feelings until the hardest of rocks seemed as soft as pillows to his aching muscles.

When he finally dropped onto the sun-baked soil—too weak to keep Sloan and himself from ramming into the dirt—Eragon lay with his arms folded at odd angles underneath his chest and stared with half-lidded eyes into the yellow flecks of citrine embedded within the small rock an inch or two from his nose. Sloan weighed on his back like a pile of iron ingots. Air seeped from Eragon's lungs, but none seemed to return. His vision darkened as if a cloud had covered the sun. A deadly lull separated each beat of his heart, and the throb, when it came, was no more than a faint flutter.

Eragon was no longer capable of coherent thought, but somewhere in the back of his brain he was aware that he was about to die. It did not frighten him; to the contrary, the prospect comforted him, for he was tired beyond belief, and death would free him from the battered shell of his flesh and allow him to rest for all of eternity.

From above and behind his head, there came a bumblebee as big as his thumb. It circled his ear, then hovered by the rock, probing the nodes of citrine, which were the same bright yellow as the field-stars that bloomed among the hills. The bumblebee's mane glowed in the morning light—each hair sharp and distinct to Eragon—and its blurred wings generated a gentle bombilation, like a tattoo played on a drum. Pollen powdered the bristles on its legs.

The bumblebee was so vibrant, so alive, and so beautiful, its presence renewed Eragon's will to survive. A world that contained a creature as amazing as that bumblebee was a world he wanted to live in.

By sheer force of will, he pushed his left hand free of his chest and grasped the woody stem of a nearby shrub. Like a leech or a tick or some other parasite, he extracted the life from the plant, leaving it limp and brown. The subsequent rush of energy that coursed through Eragon sharpened his wits. Now he was scared; having regained his desire to continue existing, he found nothing but terror in the blackness beyond.

Dragging himself forward, he seized another shrub and transferred its vitality into his body, then a third shrub and a fourth shrub, and so on until he once again possessed the full measure of his strength. He stood and looked back at the trail of brown plants that stretched out behind him; a bitter taste filled his mouth as he saw what he had wrought.

Eragon knew that he had been careless with the magic and that his reckless behavior would have doomed the Varden to certain defeat if he had died. In hindsight, his stupidity made him wince. *Brom would box my ears for getting into this mess,* he thought.

Returning to Sloan, Eragon hoisted the gaunt butcher off the ground. Then he turned east and loped away from Helgrind and into the concealment of a draw. Ten minutes later, when he paused to check for pursuers, he saw a cloud of dirt swirling at the base of Helgrind, which he took to mean that the horsemen had arrived at the dark tower of stone.

He smiled. Galbatorix's minions were too far away for any lesser magicians among their ranks to detect his or Sloan's minds. *By the time they discover the Ra'zac's bodies,* he thought, *I shall have run a league or more. I doubt they will be able to find me then. Besides, they will be searching for a dragon and her Rider, not a man traveling on foot.*

Satisfied that he did not have to worry about an imminent attack, Eragon resumed his previous pace: a steady, effortless stride that he could maintain for the entire day.

Above him, the sun gleamed gold and white. Before him, trackless wilderness extended for many leagues before lapping against the outbuildings of some village. And in his heart, a new joy and hope flared.

At last the Ra'zac were dead!

At last his quest for vengeance was complete. At last he had fulfilled his duty to Garrow and to Brom. And at last he had cast off the pall of fear and anger that he had labored beneath ever since the Ra'zac first appeared in Carvahall. Killing them had taken far longer than he expected, but now the deed was done, and a mighty deed it was. He allowed himself to revel in satisfaction over having accomplished such a difficult feat, albeit with assistance from Roran and Saphira.

Yet, to his surprise, his triumph was bittersweet, tainted by an unexpected sense of loss. His hunt for the Ra'zac had been one of his last ties to his life in Palancar Valley, and he was loath to relinquish that bond, gruesome as it was. Moreover, the task had given him a purpose in life when he had none; it was the reason why he had originally left his home. Without it, a hole gaped inside of him where he had nurtured his hate for the Ra'zac.

That he could mourn the end of such a terrible mission appalled Eragon, and he vowed to avoid making the same mistake twice. *I refuse to become so attached to my struggle against the Empire and Murtagh and Galbatorix that I won't want to move on to something else when, and if, the time comes—or, worse, that I'll try to prolong the conflict rather than adapt to whatever happens next* He chose then to push away his misbegotten regret and to concentrate instead on his relief: relief that he was free of the grim demands of his self-imposed quest and that his only remaining obligations were those born of his current position.

Elation lightened his steps. With the Ra'zac gone, Eragon felt as if he could finally make a life for himself based not on who he had been but on who he had become: a Dragon Rider.

He smiled at the uneven horizon and laughed as he ran, indifferent as to whether anyone might hear him. His voice rolled up and down the draw, and around him, everything seemed new and beautiful and full of promise.

To Walk the Land Alone

Eragon's stomach gurgled.

He was lying on his back, legs folded under at the knees—stretching his thighs after running farther and with more weight than he ever had before—when the loud, liquid rumble erupted from his innards.

The sound was so unexpected, Eragon bolted upright, groping for his staff.

Wind whistled across the empty land. The sun had set, and in its absence, everything was blue and purple. Nothing moved, save for the blades of grass that fluttered and Sloan, whose fingers slowly opened and closed in response to some vision in his enchanted slumber. A bone-biting cold heralded the arrival of true night.

Eragon relaxed and allowed himself a small smile.

His amusement soon vanished as he considered the source of his discomfort. Battling the Ra'zac, casting numerous spells, and bearing Sloan upon his shoulders for most of the day had left Eragon so ravenous, he imagined that if he could travel back in time, he could eat the entire feast the dwarves had cooked in his honor during his visit to Tarnag. The memory of how the roast Nagra, the giant boar, had smelled—hot, pungent, seasoned with honey and spices, and dripping with lard—was enough to make his mouth water.

The problem was, he had no supplies. Water was easy enough to come by; he could draw moisture from the soil whenever he wanted. Finding food in that desolate place, however, was not only far more difficult, it presented him with a moral dilemma that he had hoped to avoid.

Oromis had devoted many of his lessons to the various climates and geographic regions that existed throughout Alagaësia. Thus, when Eragon left their camp to investigate the surrounding area, he was able to identify most of the plants he encountered. Few were edible, and of those, none were large or bountiful enough for him to gather a meal for two grown men in a reasonable amount of time. The local animals were sure to have hidden away caches of seeds and fruit, but he had no idea where to begin searching for them. Nor did he think it was likely that a desert mouse would have amassed more than a few mouthfuls of food.

That left him with two options, neither of which appealed to him. He could—as he had before—drain the energy from the plants and insects around their camp. The price of doing so would be to leave a death-spot upon the earth, a blight where nothing, not even the tiny organisms in the soil, still lived. And while it might keep him and Sloan on their feet, transfusions of energy were far from satisfying, as they did nothing to fill one's stomach.

Or he could hunt.

Eragon scowled and twisted the butt of his staff into the ground. After sharing the thoughts and desires of numerous animals, it revolted him to consider eating one. Nevertheless, he was not about to weaken himself and perhaps allow the Empire to capture him just because he went without supper in order to spare the life of a rabbit. As both Saphira and Roran had pointed out, every living thing survived by eating something else. *Ours is a cruel world,* he thought, *and I cannot change how it is made. . . . The elves may be right to avoid flesh, but at the moment, my need is great. I refuse to feel guilty if circumstances drive me to this. It is not a crime to enjoy some bacon or a trout or what have you.*

He continued to reassure himself with various arguments, yet disgust at the concept still squirmed within his gut. For almost half an hour, he remained rooted to the spot, unable to do what logic told him was necessary. Then he became aware of how late it was and swore at himself for wasting time; he needed every minute of rest he could get.

Steeling himself, Eragon sent out tendrils from his mind and probed the land until he located two large lizards and, curled in a sandy den, a colony of rodents that reminded him of a cross between a rat, a rabbit, and a squirrel. "Deyja," said Eragon, and killed the lizards and one of the rodents. They died instantly and without pain, but he still gritted his teeth as he extinguished the bright flames of their minds.

The lizards he retrieved by hand, flipping over the rocks they had been hiding underneath. The rodent, however, he extracted from the den with magic. He was careful to not wake the other animals as he maneuvered the body up to the surface; it seemed cruel to terrify them with the knowledge that an invisible predator could kill them in their most secret havens.

He gutted, skinned, and otherwise cleaned the lizards and rodent, burying the offal deep enough to hide it from scavengers. Gathering thin, flat stones, he built a small oven, lit a fire within, and started the meat cooking. Without salt, he could not properly season any sort of food, but some of the native plants released a pleasant smell when he crushed them between his fingers, and those he rubbed over and packed into the carcasses.

The rodent was ready first, being smaller than the lizards. Lifting it off the top of the makeshift oven, Eragon held the meat in front of his mouth. He grimaced and would have remained locked in the grip of his revulsion, except that he had to continue tending the fire and the lizards. Those two activities distracted him enough that, without thinking, he obeyed the strident command of his hunger and ate.

The initial bite was the worst; it stuck in his throat, and the taste of hot grease threatened to make him sick. Then he shivered and dry-swallowed twice, and the urge passed. After that, it was easier. He was actually grateful the meat was rather bland, for the lack of flavor helped him to forget what he was chewing.

He consumed the entire rodent and then part of a lizard. Tearing the last bit of flesh off a thin leg bone, he heaved a sigh of contentment and then hesitated, chagrined to realize that, in spite of himself, he had enjoyed the meal. He was so hungry, the meager supper had seemed delicious once he overcame his inhibitions. *Perhaps,* he mused, *perhaps when I return . . . if I am at Nasuada's table, or King Orrin's, and meat is served . . . perhaps, if I feel like it and it would be rude to refuse, I might have a few bites. . . . I won't eat the way I used to, but neither shall I be as strict as the elves. Moderation is a wiser policy than zealotry, I think.*

By the light from the coals in the oven, Eragon studied Sloan's hands; the butcher lay a yard or two away, where Eragon had placed him. Dozens of thin white scars crisscrossed his long, bony fingers, with their oversized knuckles and long fingernails that, while they had been meticulous in Carvahall, were now ragged, torn, and blackened with accumulated filth. The scars testified to the relatively few mistakes Sloan had made during the decades he had spent wielding knives. His skin was wrinkled and weathered and bulged with wormlike veins, yet the muscles underneath were hard and lean.

Eragon sat on his haunches and crossed his arms over his knees. "I can't just let him go," he murmured. If he did, Sloan might track down Roran and Katrina, a prospect that Eragon considered unacceptable. Besides, even though he was not going to kill Sloan, he believed the butcher should be punished for his crimes.

Eragon had not been close friends with Byrd, but he had known him to be a good man, honest and steadfast, and he remembered Byrd's wife, Felda, and their children with some fondness, for Garrow, Roran, and Eragon had eaten and slept in their house on several occasions. Byrd's death, then, struck Eragon as being particularly cruel, and he felt the watchman's family deserved justice, even if they never learned about it.

What, however, would constitute proper punishment? *I refused to become an executioner,* thought Eragon, *only to make myself an arbiter. What do I know about the law?*

Rising to his feet, he walked over to Sloan and bent toward his ear and said, "Vakna."

With a jolt, Sloan woke, scrabbling at the ground with his sinewy hands. The remnants of his eyelids quivered as, by instinct, the butcher tried to lift them and look at his surroundings. Instead, he remained trapped in his own personal night.

Eragon said, "Here, eat this." He thrust the remaining half of his lizard toward Sloan, who, although he could not see it, surely must have smelled the food.

"Where am I?" asked Sloan. With trembling hands, he began to explore the rocks and plants in front of him. He touched his torn wrists and ankles and appeared confused to discover that his fetters were gone.

"The elves—and also the Riders in days gone by—called this place Mírnathor. The dwarves refer to it as Werghadn, and humans as the Gray Heath. If that does not answer your question, then perhaps it will if I say we are a number of leagues southeast of Helgrind, where you were imprisoned."

Sloan mouthed the word *Helgrind*. "You rescued me?"

"I did."

"What about—"

"Leave your questions. Eat this first."

His harsh tone acted like a whip on the butcher; Sloan cringed and reached with fumbling fingers for the lizard. Releasing it, Eragon retreated to his place next to the rock oven and scooped handfuls of dirt onto the coals, blotting out the glow so that it would not betray their presence in the unlikely event that anyone else was in the vicinity.

After an initial, tentative lick to determine what it was Eragon had given him, Sloan dug his teeth into the lizard and ripped a thick gobbet from the carcass. With each bite, he crammed as much flesh into his mouth as he could and only chewed once or twice before swallowing and repeating the process. He stripped each bone clean with the efficiency of a man who possessed an intimate understanding of how animals were constructed and what was the quickest way to disassemble them. The bones he dropped into a neat pile on his left. As the final morsel of meat from the lizard's tail vanished down Sloan's gullet, Eragon handed him the other reptile, which was yet whole. Sloan grunted in thanks and continued to gorge himself, making no attempt to wipe the fat from his mouth and chin.

The second lizard proved to be too large for Sloan to finish. He stopped two ribs above the bottom of the chest cavity and placed what was left of the carcass on the cairn of bones. Then he straightened his back, drew his hand across his lips, tucked his long hair behind his ears, and said, "Thank you, strange sir, for your hospitality. It has been so long since I had a proper meal, I think I prize your food even above my own freedom. . . . If I may ask, do you know of my daughter, Katrina, and what has happened to her? She was imprisoned with me in Helgrind." His voice contained a complex mixture of emotions: respect, fear, and submission in the presence of an unknown authority; hope and trepidation as to his daughter's fate; and determination as unyielding as the mountains of the Spine. The one element Eragon expected to hear but did not was the sneering disdain Sloan had used with him during their encounters in Carvahall.

"She is with Roran."

Sloan gaped. "Roran! How did he get here? Did the Ra'zac capture him as well? Or did—"

"The Ra'zac and their steeds are dead."

"You *killed* them? How? . . . Who—" For an instant, Sloan froze, as if he were stuttering with his entire body, and then his cheeks and mouth went slack and his shoulders caved in and he clutched at a bush to steady himself. He shook his head. "No, no, no. . . . *No.* . . . It can't be. The Ra'zac spoke of this; they demanded answers I didn't have, but I *thought* . . . That is, who would believe . . . ?" His sides heaved with such violence, Eragon wondered if he would hurt himself. In a gasping whisper, as if he were forced to speak after being punched in the middle, Sloan said, "You can't be *Eragon.*"

A sense of doom and destiny descended upon Eragon. He felt as if he were the instrument of those two merciless overlords, and he replied in accordance, slowing his speech so each word struck like a hammer blow and carried all the weight of his dignity, station, and anger. "I am Eragon and far more. I am Argetlam and Shadeslayer and Firesword. My dragon is Saphira, she who is also known as Bjartskular and Flametongue. We were taught by Brom, who was a Rider before us, and by the dwarves and by the elves. We have fought the Urgals and a Shade and Murtagh, who is Morzan's son. We serve the Varden and the peoples of Alagaësia. And I have brought you here, Sloan Aldensson, to pass judgment upon you for murdering Byrd and for betraying Carvahall to the Empire."

"You lie! You cannot be—"

"Lie?" roared Eragon. "I do not lie!" Thrusting out with his mind, he engulfed Sloan's consciousness in his own and forced the butcher to accept memories that confirmed the truth of his statements. He also wanted Sloan to feel the power that was now his and to realize that he was no longer entirely human. And while Eragon was reluctant to admit it, he enjoyed having control over a man who had often made trouble for him and also tormented him with gibes, insulting both him and his family. He withdrew a half minute later.

Sloan continued to quiver, but he did not collapse and grovel as Eragon thought he might. Instead, the butcher's demeanor became cold and flinty. "Blast you," he said. "I don't have to explain myself to you, Eragon Son of None. Understand this, though: I did what I did for Katrina's sake and nothing else."

"I know. That's the only reason you're still alive."

"Do what you want with me, then. I don't care, so long as she's safe. . . . Well, go on! What's it to be? A beating? A branding? They already had my eyes, so one of my hands? Or will you leave me to starve or to be recaptured by the Empire?"

"I have not decided yet."

Sloan nodded with a sharp motion and pulled his tattered clothes tight around his limbs to ward off the night cold. He sat with military precision, gazing with blank, empty eye sockets into the shadows that ringed their camp. He did not beg. He did not ask for mercy. He did not deny his acts or attempt to placate Eragon. He but sat and waited, armored by his perfect stoic fortitude.

His bravery impressed Eragon.

The dark landscape around them seemed immense beyond reckoning to Eragon, and he felt as if the entire hidden expanse was converging upon him, a notion that heightened his anxiety over the choice that confronted him. My *verdict will shape the rest of his life*, he thought.

Abandoning for the moment the question of punishment, Eragon considered what he knew about Sloan: the butcher's overriding love for Katrina—obsessive, selfish, and generally unhealthy as it was, although it had once been something wholesome—his hate and fear of the Spine, which were the offspring of his grief for his late wife, Ismira, who had fallen to her death among those cloud-rending peaks; his estrangement from the remaining branches of his family; his pride in his work; the stories Eragon had heard about Sloan's childhood; and Eragon's own knowledge of what it was like to live in Carvahall.

Eragon took that collection of scattered, fragmented insights and turned them over in his mind, pondering their significance. Like the pieces of a puzzle, he tried to fit them together. He rarely succeeded, but he persisted, and gradually he traced a myriad of connections between the events and emotions of Sloan's life, and thereby he wove a tangled web, the patterns of which represented who Sloan was. Throwing the last line of his web, Eragon felt as if he finally comprehended the reasons for Sloan's behavior. Because of that, he empathized with Sloan.

More than empathy, he felt he understood Sloan, that he had isolated the core elements of Sloan's personality, those things one could not remove without irrevocably changing the man. There occurred to him, then, three words in the ancient language that seemed to embody Sloan, and without thinking about it, Eragon whispered the words under his breath.

The sound could not have reached Sloan, yet he stirred—his

hands gripping his thighs—and his expression became one of un-ease.

A cold tingle crawled down Eragon's left side, and goosebumps appeared on his arms and legs as he watched the butcher. He considered a number of different explanations for Sloan's reaction, each more elaborate than the last, but only one seemed plausible, and even it struck him as being unlikely. He whispered the trio of words again. As before, Sloan shifted in place, and Eragon heard him mutter, ". . . someone walking on my grave."

Eragon released a shaky breath. It was difficult for him to believe, but his experiment left no room for doubt: he had, quite by accident, chanced upon Sloan's true name. The discovery left him rather bewildered. Knowing someone's true name was a weighty responsibility, for it granted you absolute power over that person. Because of the inherent risks, the elves rarely revealed their true names, and when they did, it was only to those whom they trusted without reservation.

Eragon had never learned anyone's true name before. He had always expected that if he did, it would be as a gift from someone he cared about a great deal. Gaining Sloan's true name without his consent was a turn of events Eragon was unprepared for and uncertain how to deal with. It dawned upon Eragon that in order to guess Sloan's true name, he must understand the butcher better than he did himself, for he had not the slightest inkling what his own might be.

The realization was an uncomfortable one. He suspected that—given the nature of his enemies—not knowing everything he could about himself might well prove fatal. He vowed, then, to devote more time to introspection and to uncovering his true name. *Perhaps Oromis and Glaedr could tell me what it is,* he thought.

Whatever the doubts and confusion Sloan's true name roused within him, it gave Eragon the beginning of an idea for how to deal with the butcher. Even once he had the basic concept, it still took him another ten minutes to thrash out the rest of his plan and make sure that it would work in the manner he intended.

Sloan tilted his head in Eragon's direction as Eragon rose and walked out of their camp into the starlit land beyond. "Where are you going?" asked Sloan.

Eragon remained silent.

He wandered through the wilderness until he found a low, broad rock covered with scabs of lichen and with a bowl-like hollow in the middle. "Adurna rïsa," said he. Around the rock, countless minuscule droplets of water filtered up through the soil and coalesced into flawless silver tubes that arched over the edge of the rock and down into the hollow. When the water started to overflow and return to the earth, only to be again ensnared by his spell, Eragon released the flow of magic.

He waited until the surface of the water became perfectly still—so that it acted like a mirror and he stood before what looked like a basin of stars—and then he said, "Draumr kópa," and many other words besides, reciting a spell that would allow him to not only see but speak with others at a distance. Oromis had taught him the variation on scrying two days before he and Saphira had left Ellesméra for Surda.

The water went completely black, as if someone had extinguished the stars like candles. A moment or two later, an oval shape brightened in the middle of the water and Eragon beheld the interior of a large white tent, illuminated by the flameless light from a red Erisdar, one of the elves' magical lanterns.

Normally, Eragon would be unable to scry a person or place he had not seen before, but the elves' seeing glass was enchanted to transmit an image of its surroundings to anyone who contacted the glass. Likewise, Eragon's spell would project an image of himself and his surroundings onto the surface of the glass. The arrangement allowed strangers to contact each other from any location in the world, which was an invaluable ability in times of war.

A tall elf with silver hair and battle-worn armor entered Eragon's field of vision, and he recognized Lord Däthedr, who advised Queen Islanzadí and was a friend of Arya's. If Däthedr was surprised to see

Eragon, he did not show it; he inclined his head, touched the first two fingers of his right hand to his lips, and said in his lilting voice, "Atra esterní ono thelduin, Eragon Shur'tugal."

Mentally making the shift to conversing in the ancient language, Eragon duplicated the gesture with his fingers and replied, "Atra du evarínya ono varda, Däthedr-vodhr."

Continuing in his native tongue, Däthedr said, "I am glad to know you are well, Shadeslayer. Arya Dröttningu informed us of your mission some days ago, and we have been much concerned on your behalf and Saphira's. I trust nothing has gone amiss?"

"No, but I encountered an unforeseen problem, and if I may, I would consult with Queen Islanzadí and seek her wisdom in this matter."

Däthedr's catlike eyes drifted nearly shut, becoming two angled slashes that gave him a fierce and unreadable expression. "I know you would not ask this unless it is important, Eragon-vodhr, but beware: a drawn bow may just as easily snap and injure the archer as it may send the arrow flying. . . . If it so please you, wait, and I shall inquire after the queen."

"I shall wait. Your assistance is most welcome, Däthedr-vodhr." As the elf turned away from the seeing glass, Eragon grimaced. He disliked the elves' formality, but most of all, he hated trying to interpret their enigmatic statements. *Was he warning me that scheming and plotting around the queen is a dangerous pastime or that Islanzadí is a drawn bow about to snap? Or did he mean something else entirely?*

At least I'm able to contact the elves, thought Eragon. The elves' wards prevented anything from entering Du Weldenvarden by magical means, including the far-sight of scrying. So long as elves remained in their cities, one could communicate with them only by sending messengers into their forest. But now that the elves were on the move and had left the shade of their black-needled pine trees, their great spells no longer protected them and it was possible to use devices such as the seeing glass.

Eragon became increasingly anxious as first one minute and then another trickled past. "Come on," he murmured. He quickly glanced around to make sure that no person or beast was creeping up on him while he gazed into the pool of water.

With a sound akin to ripping cloth, the entrance flap to the tent flew open as Queen Islanzadí thrust it aside and stormed toward the seeing glass. She wore a bright corselet of golden scale armor, augmented with mail and greaves and a beautifully decorated helm—set with opals and other precious gemstones—that held back her flowing black tresses. A red cape trimmed with white billowed from her shoulders; it reminded Eragon of a looming storm front. In her left hand, Islanzadí wielded a naked sword. Her right hand was empty, but it appeared gloved in crimson, and after a moment, Eragon realized that dripping blood coated her fingers and wrist.

Islanzadí's slanting eyebrows narrowed as she looked upon Eragon. With that expression, she bore a striking resemblance to Arya, although her stature and bearing were even more impressive than her daughter's. She was beautiful and terrible, like a frightful goddess of war.

Eragon touched his lips with his fingers, then twisted his right hand over his chest in the elves' gesture of loyalty and respect and recited the opening line of their traditional greeting, speaking first, as was proper when addressing one of higher rank. Islanzadí made the expected response, and in an attempt to please her and demonstrate his knowledge of their customs, Eragon concluded with the optional third line of the salutation: "And may peace live in your heart."

The ferocity of Islanzadí's pose diminished somewhat, and a faint smile touched her lips, as if to acknowledge his maneuver. "And yours as well, Shadeslayer." Her low, rich voice contained hints of rustling pine needles and gurgling brooks and music played on reed pipes. Sheathing her sword, she moved across the tent to the folding table and stood at an angle to Eragon as she washed the blood off her skin with water from a pitcher. "Peace is difficult to come by these days, I fear."

"The fighting is heavy, Your Majesty?"

"It will be soon. My people are massing along the western edge of Du Weldenvarden, where we may prepare to kill and be killed while we are close to the trees we love so much. We are a scattered race and do not march in rank and file like others do—on account of the damage it inflicts upon the land—and so it takes time for us to assemble from the distant reaches of the forest."

"I understand. Only . . ." He searched for a way to ask his question without being rude. "If the fighting has not started yet, I cannot help but wonder why your hand is dyed with gore."

Shaking water droplets off her fingers, Islanzadí lifted her perfect gold-brown forearm for Eragon's inspection, and he realized that she had been the model for the sculpture of two intertwined arms that stood in the entryway to his tree house in Ellesméra. "Dyed no more. The only stain blood leaves on a person is on her soul, not her body. I said the fighting would escalate in the near future, *not* that we had yet to start." She pulled the sleeve of her corselet and the tunic underneath back down to her wrist. From the jeweled belt wrapped around her slim waist, she removed a gauntlet stitched with silver thread and worked her hand into it. "We have been observing the city of Ceunon, for we intend to attack there first. Two days ago, our rangers spotted teams of men and mules traveling from Ceunon into Du Weldenvarden. We thought they wished to collect timber from the edge of the forest, as is often done. 'Tis a practice we tolerate, for the humans must have wood, and the trees within the fringe are young and nearly beyond our influence, and we have not wanted to expose ourselves before. The teams did not stop at the fringe, however. They burrowed far into Du Weldenvarden, following game trails they were obviously familiar with. They were searching for the tallest, thickest trees—trees as old as Alagaësia itself, trees that were already ancient and fully grown when the dwarves discovered Farthen Dûr. When they found them, they began to saw them down." Her voice rippled with rage. "From their remarks, we learned why they were here. Galbatorix wanted the largest trees he could acquire to replace the siege engines and battering rams he lost during the battle on the Burning Plains. If their motive had been pure and honest, we might have forgiven the loss of one monarch of our forest. Maybe even two. But not eight-and-twenty."

A chill crept through Eragon. "What did you do?" he asked, although he already suspected the answer.

Islanzadí lifted her chin, and her face grew hard. "I was present with two of our rangers. Together, we *corrected* the humans' mistake. In the past, the people of Ceunon knew better than to intrude upon our lands. Today we reminded them why that was so." Without seeming to notice, she rubbed her right hand, as if it pained her, and she gazed past the seeing glass, looking at some vision of her own. "You have learned what it is like, Eragon-finiarel, to touch the life force of the plants and animals around you. Imagine how you would cherish them if you had possessed that ability for centuries. We give of ourselves to sustain Du Weldenvarden, and the forest is an extension of our bodies and minds. Any hurt it suffers is our hurt as well. . . . We are a slow people to rouse, but once roused we are like the dragons: we go mad with anger. It has been over a hundred years since I, or most any elf, shed blood in battle. The world has forgotten what we are capable of. Our strength may have declined since the Riders' fall, but we shall still give a full reckoning of ourselves; to our enemies, it will seem as if even the elements have turned against them. We are an Elder Race, and our skill and knowledge far exceed that of mortal men. Let Galbatorix and his allies beware, for we elves are about to forsake our forest, and we shall return in triumph, or never again."

Eragon shivered. Even during his confrontations with Durza, he had never encountered such implacable determination and ruthlessness. *It's not human*, he thought, then laughed mockingly to himself. *Of course not. And I would do well to remember that. However much we may look alike—and in my case, nigh on identical—we are not the same.* "If you take Ceunon," he said, "how will you control the people there? They may hate the Empire more than death itself, but I doubt they will trust you, if only because they are humans and you are elves."

Islanzadí waved a hand. "That is unimportant. Once we are within the city walls, we have ways to ensure that no one will oppose us. This is not the first time we have fought your kind." She removed her helm then, and her hair fell forward and framed her face between raven locks. "I was not pleased to hear of your raid on Helgrind, but I take it the assault is already over and was successful?"

"Yes, Your Majesty."

"Then my objections are for naught. I warn you, however, Eragon Shur'tugal, do not imperil yourself on such needlessly dangerous ventures. It is a cruel thing I must say, but true nevertheless, and it is this: your life is more important than your cousin's happiness."

"I swore an oath to Roran that I would help him."

"Then you swore recklessly, without considering the consequences."

"Would you have me abandon those I care about? If I did that, I would become a man to despise and distrust: an ill-formed vehicle for the hopes of the people who believe I will, *somehow*, bring low Galbatorix. And also, while Katrina was Galbatorix's hostage, Roran was vulnerable to his manipulation."

The queen lifted one dagger-sharp eyebrow. "A vulnerability that you could have prevented Galbatorix from exploiting by tutoring Roran in certain oaths in this, the language of magic. . . . I do not counsel you to cast away your friends or family. That would be folly indeed. But keep you firmly in mind what is at stake: the entirety of Alagaësia. If we fail now, then Galbatorix's tyranny will extend over all the races, and his reign shall have no conceivable end. You are the tip of the spear that is our effort, and if the tip should break and be lost, then our spear shall bounce off the armor of our foe, and we too shall be lost."

Folds of lichen cracked underneath Eragon's fingers as he gripped the edge of the rock basin and suppressed the urge to make an impertinent remark about how any well-equipped warrior ought to have a sword or another weapon to rely upon besides a spear. He was frustrated by the direction the conversation had taken and eager to change the topic as quickly as he could; he had not contacted the queen so she could berate him as if he were a mere child. Nevertheless, allowing his impatience to dictate his actions would do nothing to further his cause, so he remained calm and replied, "Please believe me, Your Majesty, I take your concerns very, very seriously. I can only say that if I hadn't helped Roran, I would have been as miserable as he, and more so if he attempted to rescue Katrina by himself and died as a result. In either case, I would have been too upset to be of any use to you or anyone. Cannot we at least agree to differ on the subject? Neither of us shall convince the other."

"Very well," said Islanzadí. "We shall lay the matter to rest . . . for the present. But do not think you have escaped a proper investigation of your decision, Eragon Dragon Rider. It seems to me you display a frivolous attitude toward your larger responsibilities, and that is a serious matter. I shall discuss it with Oromis; he will decide what is to be done about you. Now tell me, why did you seek this audience?"

Eragon clenched his teeth several times before he could bring himself to, in a civil tone, explain the day's events, the reasons for his actions in regard to Sloan, and the punishment he envisioned for the butcher.

When he finished, Islanzadí whirled around and paced the circumference of the tent—her movements as lithe as a cat's—then stopped and said, "You chose to stay behind, in the middle of the Empire, to save the life of a murderer and a traitor. You are alone with this man, on foot, without supplies or weapons, save for magic, and your enemies are close behind. I see my earlier admonishments were more than justified. You—"

"Your Majesty, if you must be angry with me, be angry with me later. I want to resolve this quickly so I can get some rest before dawn; I have many miles to cover tomorrow."

The queen nodded. "Your survival is all that matters. I shall be furious after we are done speaking. . . . As for your request, such a thing is unprecedented in our history. If I had been in your place, I would have killed Sloan and rid myself of the problem then and there."

"I know you would have. I once watched Arya slay a gyrfalcon who was injured, for she said its death was inevitable, and by killing it, she saved the bird hours of suffering. Perhaps I should have done the same with Sloan, but I couldn't. I think it would have been a choice I would have regretted for the rest of my life, or worse, one that would have made it easier for me to kill in the future."

Islanzadí sighed, and suddenly she appeared tired. Eragon reminded himself that she too had been fighting that day. "Oromis may have been your proper teacher, but you have proved yourself Brom's heir, not Oromis's. Brom is the only other person who managed to entangle himself in as many predicaments as you. Like him, you seem compelled to find the deepest patch of quicksand and then dive into it."

Eragon hid a smile, pleased by the comparison. "What of Sloan?" he asked. "His fate rests with you now."

Slowly, Islanzadí sat upon a stool next to the folding table, placed her hands in her lap, and gazed to one side of the seeing glass. Her countenance became one of enigmatic observation: a beautiful mask that concealed her thoughts and feelings, and one that Eragon could not penetrate, no matter how hard he strove. When she spoke, she said, "As you have seen fit to save this man's life, at no little trouble and effort on your own part, I cannot refuse your request and thereby render your sacrifice meaningless. If Sloan survives the ordeal you have set before him, then Gilderien the Wise shall allow him to pass, and Sloan shall have a room and a bed and food to eat. More I cannot promise, for what happens afterward will depend on Sloan himself, but if the conditions you named are met, then yes, we shall light his darkness."

"Thank you, Your Majesty. You are most generous."

"No, not generous. This war does not allow me to be generous, only practical. Go and do what you must, and be you careful, Eragon Shadeslayer."

"Your Majesty." He bowed. "If I may ask one last favor: would you please refrain from telling Arya, Nasuada, or any of the Varden of my current situation? I don't want them to worry about me any longer than they have to, and they'll learn of it soon enough from Saphira."

"I shall consider your request."

Eragon waited, but when she remained silent and it became clear she had no intention of announcing her decision, he bowed a second time and again said, "Thank you."

The glowing image on the surface of the water flickered and then vanished into darkness as Eragon ended the spell he had used to create it. He leaned back on his heels and gazed up at the multitude of stars, allowing his eyes to readjust to the faint, glimmering light they provided. Then he left the crumbling rock with the pool of water and retraced his path across the grass and scrub to the camp, where Sloan still sat upright, rigid as cast iron.

Eragon struck a pebble with his foot, and the resulting noise revealed his presence to Sloan, who snapped his head around, quick as a bird. "Have you made up your mind?" demanded Sloan.

"I have," said Eragon. He stopped and squatted in front of the butcher, steadying himself with one hand on the ground. "Hear me well, for I don't intend to repeat myself. You did what you did because of your love for Katrina, or so you say. Whether you admit it or not, I believe you also had other, baser motives in wanting to separate her from Roran: anger . . . hate . . . vindictiveness . . . and your own hurt."

Sloan's lips hardened into thin white lines. "You wrong me."

"No, I don't think so. Since my conscience prevents me from killing you, your punishment is to be the most terrible I could invent short of death. I'm convinced that what you said before is true, that Katrina is more important to you than anything else. Therefore, your punishment is this: you shall not see, touch, or talk with your daughter again, even unto your dying day, and you shall live with the knowledge that she is with Roran and they are happy together, without you."

Sloan inhaled through his clenched teeth. "*That* is your punishment? Ha! You cannot enforce it; you have no prison to put me in."

"I'm not finished. I will enforce it by having you swear oaths in the elves' tongue—in the language of truth and magic—to abide by the terms of your sentence."

"You can't force me to give my word," Sloan growled. "Not even if you torture me."

"I can, and I won't torture you. Furthermore, I will lay upon you a compulsion to travel northward until you reach the elf city of Ellesméra, which stands deep in the heart of Du Weldenvarden. You can try to resist the urge if you want, but no matter how long you fight it, the spell will irritate you like an unscratched itch until you obey its demands and travel to the elves' realm."

"Don't you have the guts to kill me yourself?" asked Sloan. "You're too much of a coward to put a blade to my neck, so you'll make me wander the wilderness, blind and lost, until the weather or the beasts do me in?" He spat to the left of Eragon. "You're nothing but the yellow-bellied offspring of a canker-ridden bunter. You're a bastard, you are, and an unlicked cub; a dung-splattered, tallow-faced rock-gnasher; a puking villain and a noxious toad; the runty, mewling spawn of a greasy sow. I wouldn't give you my last crust if you were starving, or a drop of water if you were burning, or a beggar's grave if you were dead. You have pus for marrow and fungus for brains, and you're a scug-backed cheek-biter!"

There was, Eragon thought, something rather obscenely impressive about Sloan's swearing, although his admiration did not prevent him from wanting to strangle the butcher, or to at least respond in kind. What stayed his desire for retaliation, however, was his suspicion that Sloan was deliberately trying to infuriate him enough to strike down the older man and thus give him a quick and undeserved end.

Eragon said, "Bastard I may be, but not a murderer." Sloan drew a sharp breath. Before he could resume his torrent of abuse, Eragon added: "Wherever you go, you shall not want for food, nor will wild animals attack you. I will place certain enchantments around you that will keep men and beasts from troubling you and will cause animals to bring you sustenance when you need it."

"You can't do this," whispered Sloan. Even in the starlight, Eragon could see the last remnants of color drain from his skin, leaving him bone white. "You don't have the means. You don't have the right."

"I am a Dragon Rider. I have as much right as any king or queen."

Then Eragon, who had no interest in continuing to chastise Sloan, uttered the butcher's true name loud enough for him to hear. An expression of horror and revelation crawled across Sloan's face, and he threw his arms up before him and howled as if he had been stabbed. His cry was raw and jagged and desolate: the scream of a man condemned by his own nature to a fate he could not escape. He fell forward onto the palms of his hands and remained in that position and began to sob, his face obscured by shocks of hair.

Eragon watched, transfixed by Sloan's reaction. *Does learning your true name affect everyone like this? Would this happen to me as well?*

Hardening his heart to Sloan's misery, Eragon set about doing what he said he would. He repeated Sloan's true name and, word by word, schooled the butcher in the ancient language oaths that would ensure Sloan never met or contacted Katrina again. Sloan resisted with much weeping and wailing and grinding of his teeth, but no matter how vigorously he struggled, he had no choice but to obey whenever Eragon invoked his true name. And when they finished with the oaths, Eragon cast the five spells that would drive Sloan toward Ellesméra, would protect him from unprovoked violence, and would entice the birds and the beasts and the fish that dwelled in the rivers and lakes to feed him. Eragon fashioned the spells so they would derive their energy from Sloan and not himself.

Midnight was a fading memory by the time Eragon completed the final incantation. Drunk with weariness, he leaned against the hawthorn staff. Sloan lay curled at his feet.

"Finished," said Eragon.

A garbled moan drifted up from the figure below. It sounded as if Sloan were attempting to say something. Frowning, Eragon knelt beside him. Sloan's cheeks were red and bloody where he had scraped them with his fingers. His nose ran, and tears dripped from the corner of his left eye socket, which was the less mutilated of the two. Pity and guilt welled up inside of Eragon; it gave him no pleasure to see Sloan reduced to such a low state. He was a broken man, stripped of everything he valued in life, including his self-delusions, and Eragon was the one who had broken him. The accomplishment left Eragon feeling soiled, as if he had done something shameful. *It was necessary*, he thought, *but no one should have to do what I did.*

Another moan emanated from Sloan, and then he said, ". . . only a piece of rope. I didn't mean to . . . Ismira . . . No, no, please no . . ." The butcher's ramblings subsided, and in the intervening silence, Eragon placed his hand on Sloan's upper arm. Sloan stiffened at the contact. "Eragon . . . ," he whispered. "Eragon . . . I am blind, and you send me to walk the land . . . to walk the land alone. I am forsaken and forsworn. I know who I am and I cannot bear it. Help me; kill me! Free me of this agony."

On an impulse, Eragon pressed the hawthorn rod into Sloan's right hand and said, "Take my staff. Let it guide you on your journey."

"Kill me!"

"No."

A cracked shout burst from Sloan's throat, and he thrashed from side to side and pounded the earth with his fists. "Cruel, cruel you are!" His meager strength depleted, he curled into an even tighter ball, panting and whimpering.

Bending over him, Eragon placed his mouth close to Sloan's ear and whispered, "I am not without mercy, so I give you this hope: If you reach Ellesméra, you will find a home waiting for you. The elves will care for you and allow you to do whatever you want for the rest of your life, with one exception: once you enter Du Weldenvarden, you cannot leave. . . . Sloan, listen to me. When I was among the elves, I learned that a person's true name often changes as they age. Do you understand what that means? Who you are is not fixed for all of eternity. A man could forge himself anew if he so wanted."

Sloan made no reply.

Eragon left the staff next to Sloan and crossed to the other side of the camp and stretched out his full length on the ground. His eyes already closed, he mumbled a spell that would rouse him before dawn and then allowed himself to drift into the soothing embrace of his waking rest.

93

The Gray Heath was cold, dark, and inhospitable when a low buzz sounded inside Eragon's head. "Letta," he said, and the buzzing ceased. Groaning as he stretched sore muscles, he got to his feet and lifted his arms over his head, shaking them to get the blood flowing. His back felt so bruised, he hoped it would be a long while before he had to swing a weapon again. He lowered his arms and then looked for Sloan.

The butcher was gone.

Eragon smiled as he saw a set of tracks, accompanied by the round imprint of the staff, leading away from the camp. The trail was confused and meandering, and yet its general direction was northward, toward the great forest of the elves.

I want him to succeed, Eragon thought with mild surprise. *I want him to succeed, because it will mean we may all have a chance to redeem ourselves from our mistakes. And if Sloan can mend the flaws in his character and come to terms with the evil he wrought, he will find his plight is not so bleak as he believes.* For Eragon had not told Sloan that if the butcher demonstrated that he truly regretted his crimes, reformed his ways, and lived as a better person, Queen Islanzadí would have her spellweavers restore his vision. However, it was a reward Sloan had to earn without knowing about its existence, else he might seek to trick the elves into bestowing it prematurely.

Eragon stared at the footprints for a long while, then lifted his gaze to the horizon and said, "Good luck."

Tired, but also content, he turned his back on Sloan's trail and began to run across the Gray Heath. To the southwest, he knew there stood the ancient sandstone formations where Brom lay encased in his diamond tomb. He longed to divert his path and to go pay his respects but dared not, for if Galbatorix had discovered the site, he would send his agents there to look for Eragon.

"I'll return," he said. "I promise you, Brom: someday I'll return."

He sped onward.

✦ ✦ ✦

THE TRIAL OF THE LONG KNIVES

"**B**ut we are your people!"

Fadawar, a tall, high-nosed, black-skinned man, spoke with the same heavy emphasis and altered vowels Nasuada remembered hearing during her childhood in Farthen Dûr, when emissaries from her father's tribe would arrive and she would sit on Ajihad's lap and doze while they talked and smoked cardus weed.

Nasuada gazed up at Fadawar and wished she were six inches taller so that she could look the warlord and his four retainers straight in the eyes. Still, she was accustomed to men looming over her. She found it rather more disconcerting to be among a group of people who were as dark as she was. It was a novel experience not to be the object of people's curious stares and whispered comments.

She was standing in front of the carved chair where she held her audiences—one of the only solid chairs the Varden had brought with them on their campaign—inside her red command pavilion. The sun was close to setting, and its rays filtered through the right side of the pavilion as through stained glass and gave the contents a ruddy glow. A long, low table covered with scattered reports and maps occupied one-half of the pavilion.

Just outside the entrance to the large tent, she knew the six members of her personal guard—two humans, two dwarves, and two Urgals—were waiting with drawn weapons, ready to attack if they received the slightest indication she was in peril. Jörmundur, her oldest and most trusted commander, had saddled her with guards since the day Ajihad died, but never so many for so long. However, the day after the battle on the Burning Plains, Jörmundur expressed his deep and abiding concern for her safety, a concern, he said, that often kept him up nights with a burning stomach. As an assassin had tried to kill her in Aberon, and Murtagh had actually accomplished the deed in regard to King Hrothgar less than a week past, it was Jörmundur's opinion that Nasuada ought to create a force dedicated to her own defense. She had objected that such a measure would be an overreaction but had been unable to convince Jörmundur; he had threatened to abdicate his post if she refused to adopt what he considered to be proper precautions. Eventually, she acceded, only to spend the next hour haggling over how many guards she was to have. He had wanted twelve or more at all times. She wanted four or fewer. They settled on six, which still struck Nasuada as too many; she worried about appearing afraid or, worse, as if she were attempting to intimidate those she met. Again her protestations had failed to sway Jörmundur. When she accused him of being a stubborn old worrywart, he laughed and said, "Better a stubborn old worrywart than a foolhardy youngling dead before his time."

As the members of her guard changed every six hours, the total number of warriors assigned to protect Nasuada was four-and-thirty, including the ten additional warriors who remained in readiness to replace their comrades in case of sickness, injury, or death.

It was Nasuada who had insisted upon recruiting the force from each of the three mortal races arrayed against Galbatorix. By doing so, she hoped to foster greater solidarity among them, as well as to convey that she represented the interests of all the races under her command, not just the humans. She would have included the elves as well, but at the moment, Arya was the only elf who fought alongside the Varden and their allies, and the twelve spellcasters Islanzadí had sent to protect Eragon had yet to arrive. To Nasuada's disappointment, her human and dwarf guards had been hostile to the Urgals they served with, a reaction she anticipated but had been unable to avert or mitigate. It would, she knew, take more than one shared battle to ease the tensions between races that had fought and hated each other for more generations than she cared to count. Still, she viewed it as encouraging that the warriors chose to name their corps the Nighthawks, for the title was a play upon both her coloring and the fact that the Urgals invariably referred to her as Lady Nightstalker.

Although she would never admit it to Jörmundur, Nasuada had quickly come to appreciate the increased sense of security her guards provided. In addition to being masters of their chosen weapons—whether they were the humans' swords, the dwarves' axes, or the Urgals' eccentric collection of instruments—many of the warriors were skilled spellweavers. And they had all sworn their undying loyalty to her in the ancient language. Since the day the Nighthawks first assumed their duties, they had not left Nasuada alone with another person, save for Farica, her handmaid.

That was, until now.

Nasuada had sent them out of the pavilion because she knew her meeting with Fadawar might lead to the type of bloodshed the Nighthawks' sense of duty would require them to prevent. Even so, she was not entirely defenseless. She had a dagger hidden in the folds of her dress, and an even smaller knife in the bodice of her undergarments, and the prescient witch-child, Elva, was standing just behind the curtain that backed Nasuada's chair, ready to intercede if need be.

Fadawar tapped his four-foot-long scepter against the ground. The chased rod was made of solid gold, as was his fantastic array of jewelry: gold bangles covered his forearms; a breastplate of hammered gold armored his chest; long, thick chains of gold hung around his neck; embossed disks of white gold stretched the lobes of his ears; and upon the top of his head rested a resplendent gold crown of such huge proportions, Nasuada wondered how Fadawar's neck could support the weight without buckling and how such a monumental piece of architecture remained fixed in place. It seemed one would have to bolt the edifice, which was at least two and a half feet tall, to its bony bedrock in order to keep it from toppling over.

Fadawar's men were garbed in the same fashion, although less opulently. The gold they wore served to proclaim not only their wealth but also the status and deeds of each individual and the skill of their tribe's far-famed craftsmen. As either nomads or city dwellers, the dark-skinned peoples of Alagaësia had long been renowned for the quality of their jewelry, which at its best rivaled that of the dwarves.

Nasuada owned several pieces of her own, but she had chosen not to wear them. Her poor raiment could not compete with Fadawar's splendor. Also, she believed it would not be wise to affiliate herself with any one group, no matter how rich or influential, when she had to deal with and speak for all the differing factions of the Varden. If she displayed partiality toward one or another, her ability to control the whole lot of them would diminish.

Which was the basis of her argument with Fadawar.

Fadawar again jabbed his scepter into the ground. "Blood is the most important thing! First come your responsibilities to your family, then to your tribe, then to your warlord, then to the gods above and below, and only then to your king and to your nation, if you have them. That is how Unulukuna intended men to live, and that is how we should live if we want to be happy. Are you brave enough to spit on the shoes of the Old One? If a man does not help his family, whom can he depend upon to help him? Friends are fickle, but family is forever."

"You ask me," said Nasuada, "to give positions of power to your fellow kinsmen because you are my mother's cousin and because my father was born among you. This I would be happy to do if your kinsmen could fulfill those positions better than anyone else in the Varden, but nothing you have said thus far has convinced me that is so. And before you squander more of your gilt-tongued eloquence, you should know that appeals based upon our shared blood are meaningless to me. I would give your request greater consideration if ever you had done more to support my father than send trinkets and empty promises to Farthen Dûr. Only now that victory and influence are mine have you made yourself known to me. Well, my parents are dead, and I say I have no family but myself. You are my people, yes, but nothing more."

Fadawar narrowed his eyes and lifted his chin and said, "A woman's pride is always without sense. You shall fail without our support."

He had switched to his native language, which forced Nasuada to respond in kind. She hated him for it. Her halting speech and uncertain tones exposed her unfamiliarity with her birth tongue, emphasizing that she had not grown up in their tribe but was an outsider. The ploy undermined her authority. "I always welcome new allies," she said. "However, I cannot indulge in favoritism, nor should you have need of it. Your tribes are strong and well gifted. They should be able to rise quickly through the ranks of the Varden without having to rely upon the charity of others. Are you starving dogs to sit whining at my table, or are you men who can feed themselves? If you can, then I look forward to working with you to better the Varden's lot and to defeat Galbatorix."

"Bah!" exclaimed Fadawar. "Your offer is as false as you are. We shall not do servants' work; we are the chosen ones. You insult us, you do. You stand there and you smile, but your heart is full of scorpion's poison."

Stifling her anger, Nasuada attempted to calm the warlord. "It was not my intent to cause offense. I was only trying to explain my position. I have no enmity for the wandering tribes, nor have I any special love for them. Is that such a bad thing?"

"It is worse than bad, it is bald-faced treachery! Your father made certain requests of us based upon our relation, and now you ignore our service and turn us away like empty-handed beggars!"

A sense of resignation overwhelmed Nasuada. *So Elva was right — it is inevitable,* she thought. A thrill of fear and excitement coursed through her. *If it must be, then I have no reason to maintain this charade.* Allowing her voice to ring forth, she said, "Requests that you did not honor half the time."

"We did!"

"You did not. And even if you were telling the truth, the Varden's position is too precarious for me to give you something for nothing. You ask for favors, yet tell me, what do you offer in return? Will you help fund the Varden with your gold and jewels?"

"Not directly, but—"

"Will you give me the use of your craftsmen, free of charge?"

"We could not—"

"How, then, do you intend to earn these boons? You cannot pay with warriors; your men already fight for me, whether in the Varden or in King Orrin's army. Be content with what you have, Warlord, and do not seek more than is rightfully yours."

"You twist the truth to suit your own selfish goals. I seek what is rightfully ours! That is why I am here. You talk and you talk, yet your words are meaningless, for by your actions, you have betrayed us." The bangles on his arms clattered together as he gestured, as if before an audience of thousands. "You admit we are your people. Then do you still follow our customs and worship our gods?"

Here is the turning point, thought Nasuada. She could lie and claim she had abandoned the old ways, but if she did, the Varden would lose Fadawar's tribes, and other nomads besides, once they heard of her statement. *We need them. We need everyone we can get if we're to have the slightest chance of toppling Galbatorix.*

"I do," she said.

"Then I say you are unfit to lead the Varden, and as is my right, I challenge you to the Trial of the Long Knives. If you are triumphant, we shall bow to you and never again question your authority. But if you lose, then you shall step aside, and I shall take your place as head of the Varden."

Nasuada noted the spark of glee that lit Fadawar's eyes. *This is what he wanted all along,* she realized. *He would have invoked the trial even if I had complied with his demands.* She said, "Perhaps I am mistaken, but I thought it was tradition that whoever won assumed command of his rival's tribes, as well as his own. Is that not so?" She almost laughed at the expression of dismay that flashed across Fadawar's face. *You didn't expect me to know that, did you?*

"It is."

"I accept your challenge, then, with the understanding that should I win, your crown and scepter will be mine. Are we agreed?"

Fadawar scowled and nodded. "We are." He stabbed his scepter deep enough into the ground that it stood upright by itself, then grasped the first bangle on his left arm and began to work it down over his hand.

"Wait," said Nasuada. Going to the table that filled the other side of the pavilion, she picked up a small brass bell and rang it twice, paused, and then rang it four times.

Only a moment or two passed before Furica entered the tent. She cast a frank gaze at Nasuada's guests, then curtsied to the lot of them and said, "Yes, Mistress?"

Nasuada gave Fadawar a nod. "We may proceed." Then she addressed her handmaid: "Help me out of my dress; I don't want to ruin it."

The older woman looked shocked by the request. "Here, Ma'am? In front of these . . . men?"

"Yes, here. And be quick about it too! I shouldn't have to argue with my own servant." Nasuada was harsher than she meant to be, but her heart was racing and her skin was incredibly, terribly sensitive; the soft linen of her undergarments seemed as abrasive as canvas. Patience and courtesy were beyond her now. All she could concentrate on was her upcoming ordeal.

Nasuada stood motionless as Farica picked and pulled at the laces to her dress, which extended from her shoulder blades to the base of her spine. When the cords were loose enough, Farica lifted Nasuada's arms out of the sleeves, and the shell of bunched fabric dropped in a pile around Nasuada's feet, leaving her standing almost

naked in her white chemise. She fought back a shiver as the four
warriors examined her, feeling vulnerable beneath their covetous
looks. Ignoring them, she stepped forward, out of the dress, and
Farica snatched the garment out of the dirt.

Across from Nasuada, Fadawar had been busy removing the bangles from his forearms, revealing the embroidered sleeves of his
robes underneath. Finished, he lifted off his massive crown and
handed it to one of his retainers.

The sound of voices outside the pavilion delayed further progress.
Marching through the entrance, a message boy—Jarsha was his
name, Nasuada remembered—planted himself a foot or two inside
and proclaimed: "King Orrin of Surda, Jörmundur of the Varden,
Trianna of Du Vrangr Gata, and Naako and Ramusewa of the
Inapashunna tribe." Jarsha very pointedly kept his eyes fixed on the
ceiling while he spoke.

Snapping about, Jarsha departed and the congregation he had
announced entered, with Orrin at the vanguard. The king saw
Fadawar first and greeted him, saying, "Ah, Warlord, this *is* unexpected. I trust you and—" Astonishment suffused his youthful face
as he beheld Nasuada. "Why, Nasuada, what is the meaning of
this?"

"I should like to know that as well," rumbled Jörmundur. He
gripped the hilt of his sword and glowered at anyone who dared
stare at her too openly.

"I have summoned you here," she said, "to witness the Trial of the
Long Knives between Fadawar and myself and to afterward speak
the truth of the outcome to everyone who asks."

The two gray-haired tribesmen, Naako and Ramusewa, appeared
alarmed by her revelation; they leaned close together and began
to whisper. Trianna crossed her arms—baring the snake bracelet
coiled around one slim wrist—but otherwise betrayed no reaction.
Jörmundur swore and said, "Have you taken leave of your senses, my
Lady? This is madness. You cannot—"

"I can, and I will."

"My Lady, if you do, I—"

"Your concern is noted, but my decision is final. And I forbid anyone from interfering." She could tell he longed to disobey her order, but as much as he wanted to shield her from harm, loyalty had ever been Jörmundur's predominant trait.

"But, Nasuada," said King Orrin. "This trial, is not it where—"

"It is."

"Blast it, then; why don't you give up this mad venture? You would have to be addled to carry it out."

"I have already given my word to Fadawar."

The mood in the pavilion became even more somber. That she had given her word meant she could not rescind her promise without revealing herself to be an honorless oath-breaker that fair-minded men would have no choice but to curse and shun. Orrin faltered for a moment, but he persisted with his questions: "To what end? That is, if you should lose—"

"If I should lose, the Varden shall no longer answer to me, but to Fadawar."

Nasuada had expected a storm of protest. Instead, there came a silence, wherein the hot anger that animated King Orrin's visage cooled and sharpened and acquired a brittle temper. "I do not appreciate your choice to endanger our entire cause." To Fadawar, he said, "Will you not be reasonable and release Nasuada from her obligation? I will reward you richly if you agree to abandon this ill-conceived ambition of yours."

"I am rich already," said Fadawar. "I have no need for your tin-tainted gold. No, nothing but the Trial of the Long Knives can compensate me for the slander Nasuada has aimed at my people and me."

"Bear witness now," said Nasuada.

Orrin clenched tight the folds of his robes, but he bowed and said, "Aye, I will bear witness."

From within their voluminous sleeves, Fadawar's four warriors produced small, hairy goat-hide drums. Squatting, they placed the drums between their knees and struck up a furious beat, pounding so fast, their hands were sooty smudges in the air. The rough music obliterated all other sound, as well as the host of frantic thoughts that had been bedeviling Nasuada. Her heart felt as if it were keeping pace with the manic tempo that assaulted her ears.

Without missing a single note, the oldest of Fadawar's men reached inside his vest and, from there, drew two long, curved knives that he tossed toward the peak of the tent. Nasuada watched the knives tumble haft over blade, fascinated by the beauty of their motion.

When it was close enough, she lifted her arm and caught her knife. The opal-studded hilt stung her palm.

Fadawar successfully intercepted his weapon as well.

He then grasped the left cuff of his garment and pushed the sleeve past his elbow. Nasuada kept her eyes fixed upon Fadawar's forearm as he did. His limb was thick and muscled, but she deemed that of no importance; athletic gifts would not help him win their contest. What she looked for instead were the telltale ridges that, if they existed, would lie across the belly of his forearm.

She observed five of them.

Five! she thought. *So many.* Her confidence wavered as she contemplated the evidence of Fadawar's fortitude. The only thing that kept her from losing her nerve altogether was Elva's prediction: the girl had said that, in this, Nasuada would prevail. Nasuada clung to the memory as if it were her only child. *She said I can do this, so I must be able to outlast Fadawar. . . . I must be able to!*

As he was the one who had issued the challenge, Fadawar went first. He held his left arm straight out from his shoulder, palm-upward; placed the blade of his knife against his forearm, just below the crease of his elbow; and drew the mirror-polished edge across his flesh. His skin split like an overripe berry, blood welling from within the crimson crevice.

He locked gazes with Nasuada.

She smiled and set her own knife against her arm. The metal was as cold as ice. Theirs was a test of wills to discover who could withstand the most cuts. The belief was that whoever aspired to become the chief of a tribe, or even a warlord, should be willing to endure more pain than anyone else for the sake of his or her people. Otherwise, how could the tribes trust their leaders to place the concerns of the community before their own selfish desires? It was Nasuada's opinion that the practice encouraged extremism, but she also understood the ability of the gesture to earn people's trust. Although the Trial of the Long Knives was specific to the dark-skinned tribes, besting Fadawar would solidify her standing among the Varden and, she hoped, King Orrin's followers.

She offered a quick plea for strength to Gokukara, the praying mantis goddess, and then pulled on the knife. The sharpened steel slid through her skin so easily, she struggled to avoid cutting too deeply. She shuddered at the sensation. She wanted to fling the knife away and clutch her wound and scream.

She did none of those things. She kept her muscles slack; if she tensed, the process would hurt all the more. And she kept smiling as, slowly, the blade mutilated her body. The cut ended after only three seconds, but in those seconds, her outraged flesh delivered a thousand shrieking complaints, and each one nearly made her stop. As she lowered the knife, she noticed that while the tribesmen still beat upon their drums, she heard naught but the pounding of her pulse.

Then Fadawar slashed himself a second time. The cords in his neck stood in high relief, and his jugular vein bulged as if it would burst while the knife carved its bloody path.

Nasuada saw it was her turn again. Knowing what to expect only increased her fear. Her instinct for self-preservation—an instinct that had served her well on all other occasions—warred against the commands she sent to her arm and hand. Desperate, she concentrated upon her desire to preserve the Varden and overthrow Galbatorix: the two causes to which she had devoted her entire being. In her mind, she saw her father and Jörmundur and Eragon and the people of the Varden, and she thought, *For them! I do this for them. I was born to serve, and this is my service.*

She made the incision.

A moment later, Fadawar opened up a third gash on his forearm, as did Nasuada on her own.

The fourth cut followed soon thereafter.

And the fifth . . .

A strange lethargy overtook Nasuada. She was so very tired, and cold as well. It occurred to her then that tolerance of pain might not decide the trial, but rather who would faint first from loss of blood. Shifting streams of it ran across her wrist and down her fingers, splashing into the thick pool by her feet. A similar, if larger, puddle gathered around Fadawar's boots.

The row of gaping red slits on the warlord's arm reminded Nasuada of the gills of a fish, a thought that for some reason seemed incredibly funny to her; she had to bite her tongue to keep from giggling.

With a howl, Fadawar succeeded in completing his sixth cut. "Best that, you feckless witch!" he shouted over the noise of the drums, and dropped to one knee.

She did.

Fadawar trembled as he transferred his knife from his right hand to his left; tradition dictated a maximum of six cuts per arm, else you risked severing the veins and tendons close to the wrist. As Nasuada imitated his movement, King Orrin sprang between them and said, "Stop! I won't allow this to continue. You're going to kill yourselves."

He reached toward Nasuada, then jumped back as she stabbed at him. "Don't meddle," she growled between her teeth.

Now Fadawar started on his right forearm, releasing a spray of blood from his rigid muscles. *He's clenching,* she realized. She hoped the mistake would be enough to break him.

Nasuada could not help herself; she uttered a wordless cry when the knife parted her skin. The razor edge burned like a white-hot wire. Halfway through the cut, her traumatized left arm twitched. The knife swerved as a result, leaving her with a long, jagged laceration twice as deep as the others. Her breath stopped while she weathered the agony. *I can't go on*, she thought. *I can't . . . I can't! It's too much to bear. I'd rather die. . . . Oh please, let it end!* It gave her some relief to indulge in those and other desperate complaints, but in the depths of her heart, she knew she would never give up.

For the eighth time, Fadawar positioned his blade above one of his forearms, and there he held it, the pale metal suspended a quarter of an inch away from his sable skin. He remained thus as sweat dripped over his eyes and his wounds shed ruby tears. It appeared as though his courage might have failed him, but then he snarled and, with a quick yank, sliced his arm.

His hesitation bolstered Nasuada's flagging strength. A fierce exhilaration overtook her, transmuting her pain into an almost pleasurable sensation. She matched Fadawar's effort and then, spurred onward by her sudden, heedless disregard for her own well-being, brought the knife down again.

"Beat *that*," she whispered.

The prospect of having to make two cuts in a row—one to equal the number of Nasuada's and one to advance the contest—seemed to intimidate Fadawar. He blinked, licked his lips, and adjusted his grip on his knife three times before he raised the weapon over his arm.

His tongue darted out and moistened his lips again.

A spasm distorted his left hand, and the knife dropped from his contorted fingers, burying itself upright in the ground.

He picked it up. Underneath his robe, his chest rose and fell with frantic speed. Lifting the knife, he touched it to his arm; it promptly drew a small trickle of blood. Fadawar's jaw knotted and writhed, and then a shudder ran the length of his spine and he doubled over, pressing his injured arms against his belly. "I submit," he said.

The drums stopped.

The ensuing silence lasted for only an instant before King Orrin,

Jörmundur, and everyone else filled the pavilion with their overlapping exclamations.

Nasuada paid no attention to their remarks. Groping behind herself, she found her chair and sank into it, eager to take the weight off her legs before they gave way beneath her. She strove to remain conscious as her vision dimmed and flickered; the last thing she wanted to do was pass out in front of the tribesmen. A gentle pressure on her shoulder alerted her to the fact that Farica was standing next to her, holding a pile of bandages.

"My Lady, may I tend to you?" asked Farica, her expression both concerned and hesitant, as if she were uncertain how Nasuada would react.

Nasuada nodded her approval.

As Farica began to wind strips of linen around her arms, Naako and Ramusewa approached. They bowed, and Ramusewa said, "Never before has anyone endured so many cuts in the Trial of the Long Knives. Both you and Fadawar proved your mettle, but you are undoubtedly the victor. We shall tell our people of your achievement, and they shall give you their fealty."

"Thank you," said Nasuada. She closed her eyes as the throbbing in her arms increased.

"My Lady."

Around her, Nasuada heard a confused medley of sounds, which she made no effort to decipher, preferring instead to retreat deep inside herself, where her pain was no longer so immediate and menacing. She floated in the womb of a boundless black space, illuminated by formless blobs of ever-changing color.

Her respite was interrupted by the voice of Trianna as the sorceress said, "Leave off what you're doing, handmaid, and remove those bandages so I can heal your mistress."

Nasuada opened her eyes to see Jörmundur, King Orrin, and Trianna standing over her. Fadawar and his men had departed the pavilion. "No," said Nasuada.

The group looked at her with surprise, and then Jörmundur said,

"Nasuada, your thoughts are clouded. The trial is over. You don't have to live with these cuts any longer. In any event, we have to stanch your bleeding."

"Farica is doing that well enough as is. I shall have a healer stitch my wounds and make a poultice to reduce the swelling, and that is all."

"But why!"

"The Trial of the Long Knives requires participants to allow their wounds to heal at their natural pace. Otherwise, we won't have experienced the full measure of pain the trial entails. If I violate the rule, Fadawar will be declared the victor."

"Will you at least allow me to alleviate your suffering?" asked Trianna. "I know several spells that can eliminate any amount of pain. If you had consulted me beforehand, I could have arranged it so that you could lop off an entire limb without the slightest discomfort."

Nasuada laughed and allowed her head to loll to the side, feeling rather giddy. "My answer would have been the same then as it is now: trickery is dishonorable. I had to win the trial without deceit so no one can question my leadership in the future."

In a deadly soft tone, King Orrin said, "But what if you had lost?"

"I could not lose. Even if it meant my death, I never would have allowed Fadawar to gain control of the Varden."

Grave, Orrin studied her for a long while. "I believe you. Only, is the tribes' loyalty worth such a great sacrifice? You are not so common that we can easily replace you."

"The tribes' loyalty? No. But this will have an effect far beyond the tribes, as you must know. It should help unify our forces. And that is a prize valuable enough for me to willingly brave a host of unpleasant deaths."

"Pray tell, what would the Varden have gained if you *had* died today? No benefit would exist then. Your legacy would be discouragement, chaos, and likely ruin."

Whenever Nasuada drank wine, mead, and especially strong

spirits, she became most cautious with her speech and motions, for even if she did not notice it at once, she knew the alcohol degraded her judgment and coordination, and she had no desire to behave inappropriately or to give others an advantage in their dealings with her.

Pain-drunk as she was, she later realized she should have been as vigilant in her discussion with Orrin as if she had imbibed three tankards of the dwarves' blackberry-honey mead. If she had, her well-developed sense of courtesy would have prevented her from replying so: "You worry like an old man, Orrin. I had to do this, and it is done. 'Tis bootless to fret about it now. . . . I took a risk, yes. But we cannot defeat Galbatorix unless we dance along the very cliff edge of disaster. You are a king. You ought to understand that danger is the mantle a person assumes when he—or she—has the arrogance to decide the fates of other men."

"I understand well enough," growled Orrin. "My family and I have defended Surda against the Empire's encroachment every day of our lives for generations, while the Varden merely hid in Farthen Dûr and leeched off Hrothgar's generosity." His robes swirled about him as he turned and stalked out of the pavilion.

"That was badly handled, my Lady," observed Jörmundur.

Nasuada winced as Farica tugged on her bandages. "I know," she gasped. "I'll mend his broken pride tomorrow."

WINGED TIDINGS

A gap appeared then in Nasuada's memories: an absence of sensory information so complete, she only became aware of the missing time when it dawned upon her that Jörmundur was shaking her shoulder and saying something loudly. It took her several moments to decipher the sounds coming out of his mouth, and then she heard: ". . . keep looking at me, blast it! That's the thing! Don't go to sleep again. You won't wake up again if you do."

"You can let go of me, Jörmundur," she said, and mustered a weak smile. "I'm all right now."

"And my uncle Undset was an elf."

"Wasn't he?"

"Bah! You are the same as your father: always ignoring caution when it comes to your own safety. The tribes can rot in their bloody old customs, for all I care. Let a healer at you. You're in no condition to make decisions."

"That's why I waited until it was evening. See, the sun is almost down. I can rest tonight, and tomorrow I will be able to deal with the affairs that require my attention."

Farica appeared from the side and hovered over Nasuada. "Oh, Ma'am, you gave us quite a fright there."

"Still are, as a matter of fact," muttered Jörmundur.

"Well, I'm better now." Nasuada pushed herself upright in the chair, ignoring the heat from her forearms. "You can both go; I shall be fine. Jörmundur, send word to Fadawar that he may remain chief of his own tribe, so long as he swears loyalty to me as his warlord. He is too skilled a leader to waste. And, Farica, on your way back to your tent, please inform Angela the herbalist that I require her services. She agreed to mix some tonics and poultices for me."

"I won't leave you alone in this condition," declared Jörmundur.

Farica nodded. "Begging your pardon, my Lady, but I agree with him. It's not safe."

Nasuada glanced toward the entrance to the pavilion, to ensure none of the Nighthawks were close enough to overhear, and then dropped her voice into a low whisper. "I shall not *be* alone." Jörmundur's eyebrows shot up, and an alarmed expression crossed Farica's face. "I am *never* alone. Do you understand?"

"You have taken certain . . . precautions, my Lady?" asked Jörmundur.

"I have."

Both her caretakers appeared uneasy with her assurance, and Jörmundur said, "Nasuada, your safety is my responsibility; I need to know what additional protection you may have and who exactly has access to your person."

"No," she said gently. Seeing the hurt and indignation that appeared in Jörmundur's eyes, she continued. "It's not that I doubt your loyalty—far from it. Only, this I must have for myself. For the sake of my own peace of mind, I need to have a dagger no one else can see: a hidden weapon tucked up my sleeve, if you will. Consider it a flaw in my character, but do not torment yourself by imagining my choice is in any way a criticism of how you perform your duties."

"My Lady." Jörmundur bowed, a formality he almost never used with her.

Nasuada lifted her hand, indicating her permission for them to leave, and Jörmundur and Farica hurried from the red pavilion.

For a long minute, perhaps two, the only sound Nasuada heard was the harsh cry of gore-crows circling above the Varden's encampment. Then, from behind her, there came a slight rustling, like that of a mouse nosing about for food. Turning her head, she saw Elva slip out of her hiding place, emerging between two panels of fabric into the main chamber of the pavilion.

Nasuada studied her.

The girl's unnatural growth had continued. When Nasuada first met her but a short while ago, Elva had appeared between three and four years old. Now she looked closer to six. Her plain dress was black, with a few folds of purple around the neck and shoulders. Her long, straight hair was even darker: a liquid void that flowed down to the small of her back. Her sharp-angled face was bone white, for she rarely ventured outside. The dragon mark on her brow was silver. And her eyes, her violet eyes, contained a jaded, cynical air—the result of Eragon's blessing that was a curse, for it forced her to both endure other people's pain and also try to prevent it. The recent battle had almost killed her, what with the combined agony of thousands beating upon her mind, even though one of Du Vrangr Gata had placed her in an artificial slumber for the duration of the fighting, in an attempt to protect her. Only recently had the girl begun to speak and take interest in her surroundings again.

She wiped her rosebud mouth with the back of her hand, and Nasuada asked, "Were you ill?"

Elva shrugged. "The pain I'm used to, but it never gets any easier to resist Eragon's spell. . . . I am hard to impress, Nasuada, but you are a strong woman to withstand so many cuts."

Even though Nasuada had heard it many times, Elva's voice still inspired a thrill of alarm in her, for it was the bitter, mocking voice of a world-weary adult, not that of a child. She struggled to ignore it as she responded: "You are stronger. I did not have to suffer through Fadawar's pain as well. Thank you for staying with me. I know what it must have cost you, and I'm grateful."

"Grateful? Ha! There's an empty word for me, *Lady Nightstalker*." Elva's small lips twisted in a misshapen smile. "Have you anything to eat? I'm famished."

"Farica left some bread and wine behind those scrolls," said Nasuada, pointing across the pavilion. She watched the girl make her way to the food and begin wolfing down the bread, cramming large chunks into her mouth. "At least you won't have to live like this for much longer. As soon as Eragon returns, he'll remove the spell."

"Perhaps." After she had devoured half a loaf, Elva paused. "I lied about the Trial of the Long Knives."

"What do you mean?"

"I foresaw that you would lose, not win."

"What!"

"If I had allowed events to take their course, your nerve would have broken on the seventh cut and Fadawar would be sitting where you are now. So I told you what you needed to hear in order to prevail."

A chill crept over Nasuada. If what Elva said was true, then she was in the witch-child's debt more than ever. Still, she disliked being manipulated, even if it was for her own benefit. "I see. It seems I must thank you once again."

Elva laughed then, a brittle sound. "And you hate every moment of it, don't you? No matter. You need not worry about offending me, Nasuada. We are useful to each other, no more."

Nasuada was relieved when one of the dwarves guarding the pavilion, the captain of that particular watch, banged his hammer against his shield and proclaimed, "The herbalist Angela requests an audience with you, Lady Nightstalker."

"Granted," said Nasuada, raising her voice.

Angela bustled into the pavilion, carrying several bags and baskets looped over her arms. As always, her curly hair formed a stormy cloud around her face, which was pinched with concern. At her heels padded the werecat Solembum, in his animal form. He immediately angled toward Elva and began to rub against her legs, arching his back as he did.

Depositing her luggage on the ground, Angela rolled her shoulders and said, "Really! Between you and Eragon, I seem to spend most of my time among the Varden healing people too silly to realize they need to *avoid* getting chopped into tiny little pieces." While she spoke, the short herbalist marched over to Nasuada and began unwinding the bandages around her right forearm. She clucked with disapproval. "Normally, this is when the healer asks her patient how she is, and the patient lies through her teeth and says, 'Oh, not too bad,' and the healer says, 'Good, good. Be cheery and you'll make a fine recovery.' I think it's obvious, however, you're *not* about to start running around and leading charges against the Empire. Far from it."

"I will recover, won't I?" asked Nasuada.

"You would if I could use magic to seal up these wounds. Since I can't, it's a bit harder to tell. You'll have to muddle along like most people do and hope none of these cuts get infected." She paused in her work and gazed directly at Nasuada. "You do realize these will scar?"

"It will be what it will be."

"True enough."

Nasuada stifled a groan and gazed upward as Angela stitched each of her wounds and then covered them with a thick, wet mat of pulped plants. Out of the corner of her eye, she saw Solembum jump onto the table and sit next to Elva. Extending a large, shaggy paw, the werecat hooked a piece of bread off Elva's plate and nibbled on the morsel, his white fangs flashing. The black tassels on his oversized ears quivered as he swiveled his ears from side to side, listening to metal-clad warriors walking past the red pavilion.

"Barzûl," muttered Angela. "Only men would think of cutting themselves to determine who the pack leader is. Idiots!"

It hurt to laugh, but Nasuada could not help herself. "Indeed," she said after her fit subsided.

Just as Angela finished retying the last strip of cloth around Nasuada's arms, the dwarf captain outside the pavilion shouted, "Halt!" and there came a chorus of shimmering, bell-like notes as the human guards crossed their swords, barring the way to whoever sought entrance.

Without pausing to think, Nasuada drew the four-inch knife from the sheath sewn within the bodice of her chemise. It was difficult for her to grasp the hilt, as her fingers felt thick and clumsy and the muscles in her arm were slow to respond. It was as if the limb had fallen asleep, save for the sharp, burning lines scribed into her flesh.

Angela also pulled a dagger from somewhere in her clothes, and she placed herself before Nasuada and muttered a line of the ancient language. Leaping to the ground, Solembum crouched next to Angela. His fur stood on end, making him appear larger than most dogs. He growled low in his throat.

Elva continued eating, seemingly unperturbed by the commotion. She examined the morsel of bread she was holding between her thumb and index finger, as one might inspect a strange species of insect, and then dipped it into a goblet of wine and popped the bread into her mouth.

"My Lady!" shouted a man. "Eragon and Saphira fast approach from the northeast!"

Nasuada sheathed her knife. Pushing herself out of her chair, she said to Angela, "Help me dress."

Angela held the garment open in front of Nasuada, who stepped into it. Then Angela gently guided Nasuada's arms into the sleeves and, when they were in place, set about lacing up the back of the dress. Elva joined her. Together, they soon had Nasuada properly attired.

Nasuada surveyed her arms and saw no trace of her bandages. "Should I hide or reveal my injuries?" she asked.

"That depends," said Angela. "Do you think showing them will increase your standing or encourage your enemies, because they assume you are weak and vulnerable? The question is actually a rather philosophical one, predicated on whether when looking at a man who has lost a big toe, you say, 'Oh, he's a cripple' or 'Oh, he was smart or strong or lucky enough to escape worse injury.' "

"You make the strangest comparisons."

"Thank you."

"The Trial of the Long Knives is a contest of strength," said Elva.

"That is well known among the Varden and Surdans. Are you proud of your strength, Nasuada?"

"Cut off the sleeves," said Nasuada. When they hesitated, she said, "Go on! At the elbows. Don't mind the dress; I shall have it repaired later."

With a few deft movements, Angela removed the sections Nasuada had identified and dropped the excess fabric on the table.

Nasuada lifted her chin. "Elva, if you sense I'm about to faint, please tell Angela and have her catch me. Shall we, then?" The three of them gathered into a tight formation, with Nasuada at the lead. Solembum walked alone.

As they exited the red pavilion, the dwarf captain barked, "Stations!" and the six present members of the Nighthawks ranged themselves around Nasuada's group: the humans and dwarves fore and aft, and the hulking Kull—Urgals who stood eight feet and taller—on either side.

Dusk spread its gold and purple wings over the Varden's encampment, lending a sense of mystery to the rows of canvas tents that extended beyond the limits of Nasuada's sight. Deepening shadows presaged the advent of night, and countless torches and watchfires already glowed pure and bright in the warm twilight. The sky was clear to the east. South, a long, low cloud of black smoke hid the horizon and the Burning Plains, which were a league and a half away. West, a line of beeches and aspens marked the path of the Jiet River, upon which floated the *Dragon Wing*, the ship Jeod and Roran and the other villagers from Carvahall had pirated. But Nasuada had eyes only for the north, and the glittering shape of Saphira descending thence. Light from the fading sun still illuminated her, cloaking her in a blue halo. She appeared like a cluster of stars falling from the heavens.

The sight was so majestic, Nasuada stood transfixed for a moment, thankful she was fortunate enough to witness it. *They're safe!* she thought, and breathed a sigh of relief.

The warrior who had brought word of Saphira's arrival—a thin man with a large, untrimmed beard—bowed and then pointed. "My Lady, as you can see, I spoke the truth."

"Yes. You did well. You must have exceedingly sharp eyes to have spotted Saphira earlier. What is your name?"

"Fletcher, son of Harden, my Lady."

"You have my thanks, Fletcher. You may return to your post now."

With another bow, the man trotted off toward the edge of the camp.

Keeping her gaze fixed upon Saphira, Nasuada picked her way between the rows of tents toward the large clearing set aside as a place for Saphira to land and take off. Her guards and companions accompanied her, but she paid them little heed, eager as she was to rendezvous with Eragon and Saphira. She had spent much of the previous days worrying about them, both as the leader of the Varden and, somewhat to her surprise, as a friend.

Saphira flew as fast as any hawk or falcon Nasuada had seen, but she was still a number of miles away from the camp, and it took her almost ten minutes to traverse the remaining distance. In that time, a massive crowd of warriors gathered around the clearing: humans, dwarves, and even a contingent of gray-skinned Urgals, led by Nar Garzhvog, who spit at the men closest to them. Also in the congregation were King Orrin and his courtiers, who positioned themselves opposite Nasuada; Narheim, the dwarf ambassador who had assumed Orik's duties since Orik left for Farthen Dûr; Jörmundur; the other members of the Council of Elders; and Arya.

The tall elf woman wove her way through the crowd toward Nasuada. Even with Saphira nigh upon them, men and women alike tore their gaze from the sky to watch Arya's progress, she presented such a striking image. Dressed all in black, she wore leggings like a man, a sword on her hip, and a bow and quiver on her back. Her skin was the color of light honey. Her face was as angular as a cat's. And she moved with a slinking, muscular grace that bespoke her skill with a blade, and also her supernatural strength.

Her eccentric ensemble had always struck Nasuada as slightly indecent; it revealed so much of her form. But Nasuada had to admit that even if Arya donned a gown of rags, she would still appear more regal and dignified than any mortal-born noble.

Halting before Nasuada, Arya gestured with one elegant finger at Nasuada's wounds. "As the poet Earnë said, to place yourself in harm's way for the sake of the people and the country you love is the finest thing one can do. I have known every leader of the Varden, and they were all mighty men and women, and none so much as Ajihad. In this, though, I believe you have surpassed even him."

"You honor me, Arya, but I fear that if I burn so brightly, too few shall remember my father as he deserves."

"The deeds of the children are a testament of the upbringing they received from their parents. Burn like the sun, Nasuada, for the brighter you burn, the more people there shall be who will respect Ajihad for teaching you how to bear the responsibilities of command at such a tender age."

Nasuada dipped her head, taking to heart Arya's advice. Then she smiled and said, "A tender age? I'm a grown woman, by our reckoning."

Amusement gleamed in Arya's green eyes. "True. But if we judge by years, and not wisdom, no human would be considered an adult among my kind. Except for Galbatorix, that is."

"And me," Angela chimed in.

"Come now," said Nasuada, "you can't be much older than I am."

"Ha! You're confusing appearances with age. You ought to have more sense than that after being around Arya so long."

Before Nasuada could ask just how old Angela really was, she felt a hard tug on the back of her dress. Looking around, she saw that it was Elva who had taken such a liberty and that the girl was beckoning. Bending, Nasuada placed an ear close to Elva, who muttered, "Eragon's not on Saphira."

Nasuada's chest tightened, restricting her breathing. She peered upward: Saphira circled directly over the camp, some thousands of feet high. Her huge, batlike wings were black against the sky. Nasuada could see Saphira's underside, and her talons white against the lapped scales of her belly, but nothing of whoever might be riding her.

"How do you know?" she asked, keeping her voice low.

"I cannot feel his discomfort, nor his fears. Roran is there, and a woman I guess is Katrina. No one else."

Straightening, Nasuada clapped her hands and said, "Jörmundur!" allowing her voice to ring forth.

Jörmundur, who was almost a dozen yards away, came running, shoving aside those who got in his way; he was experienced enough to know when an emergency was at hand. "My Lady."

"Clear the field! Get everyone away from here before Saphira lands."

"Including Orrin and Narheim and Garzhvog?"

She grimaced. "No, but allow no one else to remain. Hurry!"

As Jörmundur began shouting orders, Arya and Angela converged upon Nasuada. They appeared as alarmed as she felt. Arya said, "Saphira would not be so calm if Eragon was hurt or dead."

"Where is he, then?" demanded Nasuada. "What trouble has he gotten himself into now?"

A raucous commotion filled the clearing as Jörmundur and his men directed the onlookers back to their tents, laying about them with swagger sticks whenever the reluctant warriors lingered or protested. Several scuffles broke out, but the captains under Jörmundur quickly overwhelmed the culprits, so as to prevent the violence from taking root and spreading. Fortunately, the Urgals, at the word of their war chief, Garzhvog, left without incident, although Garzhvog himself advanced toward Nasuada, as did King Orrin and the dwarf Narheim.

Nasuada felt the ground tremble under her feet as the eight-and-a-half-foot-tall Urgal approached her. He lifted his bony chin, baring his throat as was the custom of his race, and said, "What means this, Lady Nightstalker?" The shape of his jaws and teeth, coupled with his accent, made it difficult for Nasuada to understand him.

"Yes, I'd bloody well like an explanation myself," said Orrin. His face was red.

"And I," said Narheim.

It occurred to Nasuada, as she regarded them, that this was probably the first time in thousands of years that members of so many of the races of Alagaësia had gathered together in peace. The only ones missing were the Ra'zac and their mounts, and Nasuada knew no sane being would ever invite those foul creatures into their secret councils. She pointed at Saphira and said, "She shall provide the answers you desire."

Just as the last stragglers quit the clearing, a torrent of air rushed across Nasuada as Saphira swooped to the ground, raking her wings to slow herself before alighting upon her rear legs. She dropped to all fours, and a dull boom resounded across the camp. Unbuckling themselves from her saddle, Roran and Katrina quickly dismounted.

Striding forward, Nasuada examined Katrina. She was curious to see what kind of woman could inspire a man to undertake such extraordinary feats in order to rescue her. The young woman before her was strong-boned, with the pallid complexion of an invalid, a mane of copper hair, and a dress so torn and filthy, it was impossible to determine what it might have looked like originally. In spite of the toll her captivity had taken, it was apparent to Nasuada that Katrina was attractive enough, but not what the bards would call a great beauty. However, she possessed a certain force of gaze and bearing that made Nasuada think that if Roran had been the one captured, Katrina would have been just as capable of rousing the villagers of Carvahall, getting them south to Surda, fighting in the Battle of the Burning Plains, and then continuing on to Helgrind, all for the sake of her beloved. Even when she noticed Garzhvog, Katrina did not flinch or quail but remained standing where she was, next to Roran.

Roran bowed to Nasuada and, swiveling, also to King Orrin. "My Lady," he said, his face grave. "Your Majesty. If I may, this is my betrothed, Katrina." She curtsied to them both.

121

"Welcome to the Varden, Katrina," said Nasuada. "We have all heard your name here, on account of Roran's uncommon devotion. Songs of his love for you already spread across the land."

"You are most welcome," added Orrin. "Most welcome indeed."

Nasuada noticed that the king had eyes only for Katrina, as did every man present, including the dwarves, and Nasuada was certain they would be recounting tales of Katrina's charms to their comrades-in-arms before the night was out. What Roran had done on her behalf elevated her far above ordinary women; it made her an object of mystery, fascination, and allure to the warriors. That anyone should sacrifice so much for another person meant, by reason of the price paid, that person must be unusually precious.

Katrina blushed and smiled. "Thank you," she said. Along with her embarrassment at such attentions, a hint of pride colored her expression, as if she knew how remarkable Roran was and delighted in having captured his heart, of all the women in Alagaësia. He was hers, and that was all the status or treasure she desired.

A pang of loneliness shot through Nasuada. *I wish I had what they have,* she thought. Her responsibilities prevented her from entertaining girlish dreams of romance and marriage—and certainly children—unless she were to arrange a marriage of convenience for the good of the Varden. She had often considered doing that with Orrin, but her nerve always failed her. Still, she was content with her lot and did not begrudge Katrina and Roran their happiness. Her cause was what she cared about; defeating Galbatorix was far more important than something as trifling as marriage. Most everyone got married, but how many had the opportunity to oversee the birth of a new age?

I'm not myself this evening, realized Nasuada. *My wounds have set my thoughts ahumming like a nest of bees.* Shaking herself, she looked past Roran and Katrina to Saphira. Nasuada opened up the barriers she usually maintained around her mind so she might hear what Saphira had to say and then asked: "Where is he?"

With the dry rustle of scales sliding over scales, Saphira crept forward and lowered her neck so her head was directly in front of Nasuada, Arya, and Angela. The dragon's left eye sparkled with blue fire. She sniffed twice, and her crimson tongue darted out of her mouth. Hot, moist breath ruffled the lace collar on Nasuada's dress.

Nasuada swallowed as Saphira's consciousness brushed against her own. Saphira felt unlike any other being Nasuada had encountered: ancient, alien, and both ferocious and gentle. That, along with Saphira's imposing physical presence, always reminded Nasuada that if Saphira wanted to eat them, she could. It was impossible, Nasuada believed, to be complacent around a dragon.

I smell blood, said Saphira. *Who has hurt you, Nasuada? Name them, and I shall tear them from neck to groin and bring you their heads for trophies.*

"There's no need for you to tear anyone apart. Not yet, at least. I wielded the knife myself. However, this is the wrong time to delve into the matter. Right now, all I care about is Eragon's whereabouts."

Eragon, said Saphira, *decided to remain in the Empire.*

For a few seconds, Nasuada was unable to move or think. Then a mounting sense of doom replaced her stunned denial of Saphira's revelation. The others reacted in various ways as well, from which Nasuada deduced Saphira had spoken to them all at once.

"How . . . how could you allow him to stay?" she asked.

Small tongues of fire rippled in Saphira's nostrils as she snorted. *Eragon made his own choice. I could not stop him. He insists upon doing what he thinks is right, no matter the consequences for him or the rest of Alagaësia. . . . I could shake him like a hatchling, but I'm proud of him. Fear not; he can take care of himself. So far, no misfortune has befallen him. I would know if he was hurt.*

Arya spoke: "And why did he make this choice, Saphira?"

It would be faster for me to show you rather than explain with words. May I?

They all indicated their consent.

A river of Saphira's memories poured into Nasuada. She saw black Helgrind from above a layer of clouds; heard Eragon, Roran, and Saphira discussing how best to attack; watched them discover the Ra'zac's lair; and experienced Saphira's epic battle with the Lethrblaka. The procession of images fascinated Nasuada. She had been born in the Empire but could remember nothing of it; this was the first time as an adult that she had looked upon anything besides the wild fringes of Galbatorix's holdings.

Lastly came Eragon and his confrontation with Saphira. Saphira attempted to hide it, but the anguish she felt over leaving Eragon was still so raw and piercing, Nasuada had to dry her cheeks with the bandages on her forearms. However, the reasons Eragon gave for staying—killing the last Ra'zac and exploring the remainder of Helgrind—were reasons Nasuada deemed inadequate.

She frowned. *Eragon may be rash, but he's certainly not foolish enough to endanger everything we seek to accomplish merely so he could visit a few caves and drain the last bitter dregs of his revenge. There must be another explanation.* She wondered whether she should press Saphira for the truth, but she knew Saphira would not withhold such information on a whim. *Perhaps she wants to discuss it in private*, she thought.

"Blast it!" exclaimed King Orrin. "Eragon could not have picked a worse time to set off on his own. What matters a single Ra'zac when Galbatorix's entire army resides but a few miles from us? . . . We have to get him back."

Angela laughed. She was knitting a sock using five bone needles, which clicked and clacked and scraped against each other with a steady, if peculiar, rhythm. "How? He'll be traveling during the day, and Saphira daren't fly around searching for him when the sun's up and anyone might spot her and alert Galbatorix."

"Yes, but he's our Rider! We cannot sit by idly while he remains in the midst of our enemies."

"I agree," said Narheim. "However it is done, we must ensure his safe return. Grimstnzborith Hrothgar adopted Eragon into his family and clan—that is mine own clan, as you know—and we owe him the loyalty of our law and our blood."

Arya knelt and, to Nasuada's surprise, began to unlace and retie the upright sections of her boots. Holding one of the cords between her teeth, Arya said, "Saphira, where exactly was Eragon when you last touched his mind?"

In the entrance to Helgrind.

"And have you any idea what path he intended to follow?"

He did not yet know himself.

Springing to her feet, Arya said, "Then I shall have to look everywhere I can."

Like a deer, she bounded forward and ran across the clearing, vanishing among the tents beyond as she sped northward as fast and light as the wind itself.

"Arya, no!" shouted Nasuada, but the elf was already gone. Hopelessness threatened to engulf Nasuada as she stared after her. *The center is crumbling,* she thought.

Grasping the edges of the mismatched pieces of armor that covered his torso as if to tear them off, Garzhvog said to Nasuada, "Do you want me to follow, Lady Nightstalker? I cannot run as fast as little elves, but I can run as long."

"No . . . no, stay. Arya can pass for human at a distance, but soldiers would hunt you down the moment some farmer caught sight of you."

"I am used to being hunted."

"But not in the middle of the Empire, with hundreds of Galbatorix's men wandering the countryside. No, Arya will have to fend for herself. I pray that she can find Eragon and keep him safe, for without him, we are doomed."

125

❖ ❖ ❖

ESCAPE AND EVASION

Eragon's feet drummed against the ground.

The pounding beat of his stride originated in his heels and ran up his legs, through his hips, and along his spine until it terminated at the base of his skull, where the recurring impact jarred his teeth and exacerbated the headache that seemed to worsen with every passing mile. The monotonous music of his running had annoyed him at first, but before long, it lulled him into a trancelike state where he did not think, but moved.

As Eragon's boots descended, he heard brittle stalks of grass snap like twigs and glimpsed puffs of dirt rising from the cracked soil. He guessed it had been at least a month since it last rained in this part of Alagaësia. The dry air leached the moisture from his breath, leaving his throat raw. No matter how much he drank, he could not compensate for the amount of water the sun and the wind stole from him.

Thus his headache.

Helgrind was far behind him. However, he had made slower progress than he had hoped. Hundreds of Galbatorix's patrols—containing both soldiers and magicians—swarmed across the land, and he often had to hide in order to avoid them. That they were searching for him, he had no doubt. The previous evening, he had even spotted Thorn riding low on the western horizon. He had immediately shielded his mind, thrown himself into a ditch, and stayed there for half an hour, until Thorn dipped back down below the edge of the world.

Eragon had decided to travel on established roads and trails wherever possible. The events of the past week had pushed him to the limits of his physical and emotional endurance. He preferred to allow his body to rest and recover, rather than strain himself forging through brambles, over hills, and across muddy rivers. The time for desperate, violent exertion would come again, but now was not it.

So long as he held to the roads, he dared not run as fast as he was capable; indeed, it would be wiser to avoid running altogether. A fair number of villages and outbuildings were scattered throughout the area. If any of the inhabitants observed a lone man sprinting across the countryside as if a pack of wolves were chasing him, the spectacle would be sure to arouse curiosity and suspicion and might even inspire a frightened crofter to report the incident to the Empire. That could prove fatal for Eragon, whose greatest defense was the cloak of anonymity.

He only ran now because he had encountered no living creatures, except a long snake sunning itself, for over a league.

Returning to the Varden was Eragon's primary concern, and it rankled him to plod along like a common vagabond. Still, he appreciated the opportunity to be by himself. He had not been alone, truly alone, since he found Saphira's egg in the Spine. Always her thoughts had rubbed against his, or Brom or Murtagh or someone else had been at his side. In addition to the burden of constant companionship, Eragon had spent all the months since he had left Palancar Valley engaged in arduous training, breaking only for travel or to take part in the tumult of battle. Never before had he concentrated so intensely for so long or dealt with such huge amounts of worry and fear.

He welcomed his solitude, then, and the peace it brought. The absence of voices, including his own, was a sweet lullaby that, for a short while, washed away his fear of the future. He had no desire to scry Saphira—although they were too far apart to touch each other's minds, his bond with her would tell him if she was hurt—or to contact Arya or Nasuada and hear their angry words. Far better, he thought, to listen to the songs of the flitting birds and the sighing of the breeze through the grass and leafy branches.

The sound of jingling harnesses, clomping hooves, and men's voices jarred Eragon out of his reverie. Alarmed, he stopped and glanced around, trying to determine from what direction the men were approaching. A pair of cackling jackdaws spiraled upward from a nearby ravine.

The only cover close to Eragon was a small thicket of juniper trees. He sprinted toward it and dove under the drooping branches just as six soldiers emerged from the ravine and rode cantering out onto the thin dirt road not ten feet away. Normally, Eragon would have sensed their presence long before they got so close, but since Thorn's distant appearance, he had kept his mind walled off from his surroundings.

The soldiers reined in their horses and milled around in the middle of the road, arguing among themselves. "I'm telling you, I saw something!" one of them shouted. He was of medium height, with ruddy cheeks and a yellow beard.

His heart hammering, Eragon struggled to keep his breathing slow and quiet. He touched his brow to ensure the cloth strip he had tied around his head still covered his upswept eyebrows and pointed ears. *I wish I were still wearing my armor,* he thought. In order to avoid attracting unwanted attention, he had made himself a pack—using dead branches and a square of canvas he had bartered from a tinker—and placed his armor within it. Now he dared not remove and don his armor, for fear the soldiers would hear.

The soldier with the yellow beard climbed down from his bay charger and walked along the edge of the road, studying the ground and the juniper trees beyond. Like every member of Galbatorix's army, the soldier wore a red tunic embroidered with gold thread in the outline of a jagged tongue of fire. The thread sparkled as he moved. His armor was simple—a helmet, a tapered shield, and a leather brigandine—indicating he was little more than a mounted footman. As for arms, he bore a spear in his right hand and a longsword on his left hip.

As the soldier approached his location, spurs clinking, Eragon began to whisper a complex spell in the ancient language. The words poured off his tongue in an unbroken stream, until, to his alarm, he mispronounced a particularly difficult cluster of vowels and had to start the incantation anew.

The soldier took another step toward him.

And another.

Just as the soldier paused in front of him, Eragon completed the spell and felt his strength ebb as the magic took effect. He was an instant too late, however, to completely escape detection, for the soldier exclaimed, "Aha!" and brushed aside the branches, exposing Eragon.

Eragon did not move.

The soldier peered directly at him and frowned. "What the . . . ," he muttered. He jabbed his spear into the thicket, missing Eragon's face by less than an inch. Eragon dug his nails into his palms as a tremor racked his clenched muscles. "Ah, blast it," said the soldier, and released the branches, which sprang back to their original positions, hiding Eragon once more.

"What was it?" called another of the men.

"Nothing," said the soldier, returning to his companions. He removed his helmet and wiped his brow. "My eyes are playing tricks on me."

"What does that bastard Braethan expect of us? We've hardly gotten a wink of sleep these past two days."

"Aye. The king must be desperate to drive us so hard. . . . To be honest, I'd rather not find whoever it is we're searching for. It's not that I'm fainthearted, but anyone who gives Galbatorix pause is best avoided by the likes of us. Let Murtagh and his monster of a dragon catch our mysterious fugitive, eh?"

"Unless we be searching for Murtagh," suggested a third man. "You heard what Morzan's spawn said well as I did."

An uncomfortable silence settled over the soldiers. Then the one who was on the ground vaulted back onto his charger, wrapped the reins around his left hand, and said, "Keep your yap shut, Derwood. You talk too much."

With that, the group of six spurred their steeds forward and continued north on the road.

As the sound of the horses faded, Eragon ended the spell, then rubbed his eyes with his fists and rested his hands on his knees. A long, low laugh escaped him, and he shook his head, amused by how outlandish his predicament was compared with his upbringing in Palancar Valley. *I certainly never imagined this happening to me*, he thought.

The spell he had used contained two parts: the first bent rays of light around his body so he appeared invisible, and the second hopefully prevented other spellweavers from detecting his use of magic. The spell's main drawbacks were that it could not conceal footprints—therefore one had to remain stone-still while using it—and it often failed to completely eliminate a person's shadow.

Picking his way out of the thicket, Eragon stretched his arms high over his head and then faced the ravine from whence the soldiers had emerged. A single question occupied him as he resumed his journey:

What had Murtagh said?

"Ahh!"

The gauzelike illusion of Eragon's waking dreams vanished as he tore at the air with his hands. He twisted nearly in half as he rolled away from where he had been lying. Scrabbling backward, he pushed himself to his feet and raised his arms in front of himself to deflect oncoming blows.

The dark of night surrounded him. Above, the impartial stars continued to gyrate in their endless celestial dance. Below, not a creature stirred, nor could he hear anything but the gentle wind caressing the grass.

Eragon stabbed outward with his mind, convinced that someone was about to attack him. He extended himself over a thousand feet in every direction but found no one else in the vicinity.

At last he lowered his hands. His chest heaved, and his skin burned, and he stank of sweat. In his mind, a tempest roared: a whirlwind of flashing blades and severed limbs. For a moment, he thought he was in Farthen Dûr, fighting the Urgals, and then on the Burning Plains, crossing swords with men like himself. Each location was so real, he would have sworn some strange magic had transported him backward through space and time. He saw standing before him the men and the Urgals whom he had slain; they appeared so real, he wondered if they would speak. And while he no longer bore the scars of his wounds, his body remembered the many injuries he had suffered, and he shuddered as he again felt swords and arrows piercing his flesh.

With a shapeless howl, Eragon fell to his knees and wrapped his arms around his stomach, hugging himself as he rocked back and forth. *It's all right. . . . It's all right.* He pressed his forehead against the ground, curling into a hard, tight ball. His breath was hot against his belly.

"What's wrong with me?"

None of the epics Brom had recited in Carvahall mentioned that such visions had bedeviled the heroes of old. None of the warriors Eragon had met in the Varden seemed troubled by the blood they shed. And even though Roran admitted he disliked killing, he did not wake up screaming in the middle of the night.

I'm weak, thought Eragon. *A man should not feel like this. A Rider should not feel like this. Garrow or Brom would have been fine, I know. They did what needed to be done, and that was that. No crying about it, no endless worrying or gnashing of teeth. . . . I'm weak.*

Jumping up, he paced around his nest in the grass, trying to calm himself. After half an hour, when apprehension still clenched his chest in an iron grip and his skin itched as if a thousand ants crawled underneath it and he started at the slightest noise, Eragon grabbed his pack and set off at a dead run. He cared not what lay before him in the unknown darkness, nor who might notice his headlong flight.

He only sought to escape his nightmares. His mind had turned against him, and he could not rely upon rational thought to dispel his panic. His one recourse, then, was to trust in the ancient animal wisdom of his flesh, which told him to *move*. If he ran fast and hard enough, perhaps he could anchor himself in the moment. Perhaps the thrashing of his arms, the thudding of his feet on dirt, the slick chill of sweat under his arms, and a myriad of other sensations would, by their sheer weight and number, force him to forget.

Perhaps.

A flock of starlings darted across the afternoon sky, like fish through the ocean.

Eragon squinted at them. In Palancar Valley, when the starlings returned after winter, they often formed groups so large, they transformed day into night. This flock was not that large, yet it reminded him of evenings spent drinking mint tea with Garrow and Roran on the porch of their house, watching a rustling black cloud turn and twist overhead.

Lost in memory, he stopped and sat on a rock so he could retie the laces on his boots.

The weather had changed; it was cool now, and a gray smudge to the west hinted at the possibility of a storm. The vegetation was lusher, with moss and reeds and thick clumps of green grass. Several miles away, five hills dotted the otherwise smooth land. A stand of thick oak trees adorned the central hill. Above the hazy mounds of foliage, Eragon glimpsed the crumbling walls of a long-abandoned building, constructed by some race in ages past.

Curiosity aroused, he decided to break his fast among the ruins. They were sure to contain plentiful game, and foraging would provide him with an excuse to do a bit of exploring before continuing on his way.

Eragon arrived at the base of the first hill an hour later, where he found the remnants of an ancient road paved with squares of stone. He followed it toward the ruins, wondering at its strange construction, for it was unlike any human, elf, or dwarf work he was familiar with.

The shadows under the oak trees chilled Eragon as he climbed the central hill. Near the summit, the ground leveled off underneath his feet and the thicket opened up, and he entered a large glade. A broken tower stood there. The lower part of the tower was wide and ribbed, like the trunk of a tree. Then the structure narrowed and rose toward the sky for over thirty feet, ending in a sharp, jagged line. The upper half of the tower lay on the ground, shattered into innumerable fragments.

Excitement stirred within Eragon. He suspected that he had found an elven outpost, erected long before the destruction of the Riders. No other race had the skill or inclination to build such a structure.

Then he spotted the vegetable garden at the opposite side of the glade.

A single man sat hunched among the rows of plants, weeding a patch of snap peas. Shadows covered his downturned face. His gray beard was so long, it lay piled in his lap like a mound of uncombed wool.

Without looking up, the man said, "Well, are you going to help me finish these peas or not? There's a meal in it for you if you do."

Eragon hesitated, unsure what to do. Then he thought, *Why should I be afraid of an old hermit?* and walked over to the garden. "I'm Bergan. . . . Bergan, son of Garrow."

The man grunted. "Tenga, son of Ingvar."

The armor in Eragon's pack rattled as he dropped it to the ground. For the next hour, he labored in silence along with Tenga. He knew he should not stay for so long, but he enjoyed the task; it kept him from brooding. As he weeded, he allowed his mind to expand and touch the multitude of living things within the glade. He welcomed the sense of unity he shared with them.

When they had removed every last bit of grass, purslane, and dandelions from around the peas, Eragon followed Tenga to a narrow door set into the front of the tower, through which was a spacious kitchen and dining room. In the middle of the room, a circular staircase coiled up to the second story. Books, scrolls, and sheaves of loose-bound vellum covered every available surface, including a goodly portion of the floor.

Tenga pointed at the small pile of branches in the fireplace. With a pop and a crackle, the wood burst into flame. Eragon tensed, ready to grapple physically and mentally with Tenga.

The other man did not seem to notice his reaction but continued to bustle about the kitchen, procuring mugs, dishes, knives, and various leftovers for their lunch. He muttered to himself in an undertone while he did.

Every sense alert, Eragon sank onto the bare corner of a nearby chair. *He didn't utter the ancient language,* he thought. *Even if he said the spell in his head, he still risked death or worse to start a mere cookfire!* For as Oromis had taught Eragon, words were the means by which one controlled the release of magic. To cast a spell without the structure of language binding that motive power was to risk having a stray thought or emotion distort the result.

Eragon gazed around the chamber, searching for clues about his host. He spotted an open scroll that displayed columns of words from the ancient language and recognized it as a compendium of true names similar to those he had studied in Ellesméra. Magicians coveted such scrolls and books and would sacrifice almost anything to obtain them, for with them one could learn new words for a spell and also record therein words one had discovered. Few, however, were able to acquire a compendium, for they were exceedingly rare and those who already owned them almost never parted with them willingly.

It was unusual, then, for Tenga to possess one such compendium, but to Eragon's amazement, he saw six others throughout the room, in addition to writings on subjects ranging from history to mathematics to astronomy to botany.

A mug of ale and a plate with bread, cheese, and a slice of cold meat pie appeared in front of him as Tenga shoved the dishes under his nose.

"Thank you," said Eragon, accepting them.

Tenga ignored him and sat cross-legged next to the fireplace. He continued to grumble and mutter into his beard as he devoured his lunch.

After Eragon had scraped his plate clean and drained the last drops of the fine harvest ale, and Tenga had also nearly completed his repast, Eragon could not help but ask, "Did the elves build this tower?"

Tenga fixed him with a pointed gaze, as if the question made him doubt Eragon's intelligence. "Aye. The tricky elves built Edur Ithindra."

"What is it you do here? Are you all alone, or—"

"I search for the answer!" exclaimed Tenga. "A key to an unopened door, the secret of the trees and the plants. Fire, heat, lightning, light . . . Most do not know the question and wander in ignorance. Others know the question but fear what the answer will mean. Bah! For thousands of years we have lived like savages. Savages! I shall end that. I shall usher in the age of light, and all shall praise my deed."

"Pray tell, what exactly do you search for?"

A frown twisted Tenga's face. "You don't know the question? I thought you might. But no, I was mistaken. Still, I see you understand my search. You search for a different answer, but you search nevertheless. The same brand burns in your heart as burns in mine. Who else but a fellow pilgrim can appreciate what we must sacrifice to find the answer?"

"The answer to what?"

"To the question we choose."

He's mad, thought Eragon. Casting about for something with which he could distract Tenga, his gaze lit upon a row of small wood animal statues arranged on the sill below a teardrop-shaped window. "Those are beautiful," he said, indicating the statues. "Who made them?"

"*She* did . . . before she left. She was always making things." Tenga bounded upright and placed the tip of his left index finger on the first of the statues. "Here the squirrel with his waving tail, he so bright and swift and full of laughing gibes." His finger drifted to the next statue in line. "Here the savage boar, so deadly with his slashing tusks. . . . Here the raven with . . ."

Tenga paid no attention as Eragon backed away, nor when he lifted the latch to the door and slipped out of Edur Ithindra. Shouldering his pack, Eragon trotted down through the crown of oak trees and away from the cluster of five hills and the demented spellcaster who resided among them.

Throughout the rest of that day and the next, the number of people on the road increased until it seemed to Eragon as if a new group was always appearing over a hill. Most were refugees, although soldiers and other men of business were also present. Eragon avoided those he could and trudged along with his chin tucked against his collar the rest of the time.

That practice, however, forced him to spend the night in the village of Eastcroft, twenty miles north of Melian. He had intended to abandon the road long before he arrived at Eastcroft and find a sheltered hollow or cave where he might rest until morn, but because of his relative unfamiliarity with the land, he misjudged the distance and came upon the village while in the company of three men-at-arms. Leaving then, less than an hour from the safety of Eastcroft's walls and gates and the comfort of a warm bed, would have inspired even the slowest dullard to ask why he was trying to avoid the village. So Eragon set his teeth and silently rehearsed the stories he had concocted to explain his trip.

The bloated sun was two fingers above the horizon when Eragon first beheld Eastcroft, a medium-sized village enclosed by a tall palisade. It was almost dark by the time he finally arrived at the village and entered through the gate. Behind him, he heard a sentry ask the men-at-arms if anyone else had been close behind them on the road.

"Not that I could tell."

"That's good enough for me," replied the sentry. "If there are laggards, they'll have to wait until tomorrow to get in." To another man on the opposite side of the gate, he shouted, "Close it up!" Together they pushed the fifteen-foot-tall ironbound doors shut and barred them with four oak beams as thick as Eragon's chest.

They must expect a siege, thought Eragon, and then smiled at his own blindness. *Well, who doesn't expect trouble in these times?* A few months ago, he would have worried about being trapped in Eastcroft, but now he was confident he could scale the fortifications barehanded and, if he concealed himself with magic, escape unnoticed in the gloom of night. He chose to stay, however, for he was tired and casting a spell might attract the attention of nearby magicians, if there were any.

Before he took more than a few steps down the muddy lane that led to the town square, a watchman accosted him, thrusting a lantern toward his face. "Hold there! You've not been to Eastcroft before, have you?"

"This is my first visit," said Eragon.

The stubby watchman bobbed his head. "And have you family or friends here to welcome you?"

"No, I don't."

"What brings you to Eastcroft, then?"

"Nothing. I'm traveling south to fetch my sister's family and bring them back to Dras-Leona." Eragon's story seemed to have no effect on the watchman. *Perhaps he doesn't believe me*, Eragon speculated. *Or perhaps he's heard so many accounts like mine, they've ceased to matter to him.*

"Then you want the wayfarers' house, by the main well. Go there and you will find food and lodging. And while you stay here in Eastcroft, let me warn you, we don't tolerate murder, thievery, or lechery in these parts. We have sturdy stocks and gallows, and they have had their share of tenants. My meaning is clear?"

"Yes, sir."

"Then go, and be you of good fortune. But wait! What is your name, stranger?"

"Bergan."

With that, the watchman strode away, returning to his evening rounds. Eragon waited until the combined mass of several houses concealed the lantern the watchman carried before wandering over to the message board mounted to the left of the gates.

There, nailed over a half-dozen posters of various criminals, were two sheets of parchment almost three feet long. One depicted Eragon, one depicted Roran, and both labeled them traitors to the Crown. Eragon examined the posters with interest and marveled at the reward offered: an earldom apiece to whoever captured them. The drawing of Roran was a good likeness and even included the beard he had grown since fleeing Carvahall, but Eragon's portrait showed him as he had been before the Blood-oath Celebration, when he still appeared fully human.

How things have changed, thought Eragon.

Moving on, he slipped through the village until he located the wayfarers' house. The common room had a low ceiling with tar-stained timbers. Yellow tallow candles provided a soft, flickering light and thickened the air with intersecting layers of smoke. Sand and rushes covered the floor, and the mixture crunched underneath Eragon's boots. To his left were tables and chairs and a large fire-place, where an urchin turned a pig on a spit. Opposite this was a long bar, a fortress with raised drawbridges that protected casks of lager, ale, and stout from the horde of thirsty men who assailed it from all sides.

A good sixty people filled the room, crowding it to an uncomfortable level. The roar of conversation would have been startling enough to Eragon after his time on the road, but with his sensitive hearing, he felt as if he stood in the middle of a pounding waterfall. It was hard for him to concentrate upon any one voice. As soon as he caught hold of a word or a phrase, it was swept away by another utterance. Off in one corner, a trio of minstrels was singing and playing a comic version of "Sweet Aethrid o' Dauth," which did nothing to improve the clamor.

Wincing at the barrage of noise, Eragon wormed his way through the crowd until he reached the bar. He wanted to talk with the serving woman, but she was so busy, five minutes passed before she looked at him and asked, "Your pleasure?" Strands of hair hung over her sweaty face.

"Have you a room to let, or a corner where I could spend the night?"

"I wouldn't know. The mistress of the house is the one you should speak to about that. She'll be down directly," said the serving woman, and flicked a hand at a rank of gloomy stairs.

While he waited, Eragon rested against the bar and studied the people in the room. They were a motley assortment. About half he guessed were villagers from Eastcroft come to enjoy a night of drinking. Of the rest, the majority were men and women—families oftentimes—who were migrating to safer parts. It was easy for him to identify them by their frayed shirts and dirty pants and by how they huddled in their chairs and peered at anyone who came near. However, they studiously avoided looking at the last and smallest group of patrons in the wayfarers' house: Galbatorix's soldiers. The men in red tunics were louder than anyone else. They laughed and shouted and banged on tabletops with their armored fists while they quaffed beer and groped any maid foolish enough to walk by them.

Do they behave like that because they know no one dares oppose them and they enjoy demonstrating their power? wondered Eragon. *Or because they were forced to join Galbatorix's army and seek to dull their sense of shame and fear with their revels?*

Now the minstrels were singing:

> *So with her hair aflying, sweet Aethrid o' Dauth*
> *Ran to Lord Edel and cried, "Free my lover,*
> *Else a witch shall turn you into a woolly goat!"*
> *Lord Edel, he laughed and said, "No witch shall turn me*
> *   into a woolly goat!"*

The crowd shifted and granted Eragon a view of a table pushed against one wall. At it sat a lone woman, her face hidden by the drawn hood of her dark traveling cloak. Four men surrounded her, big, beefy farmers with leathery necks and cheeks flushed with the fever of alcohol. Two of them were leaning against the wall on either side of the woman, looming over her, while one sat grinning in a chair turned around backward and the fourth stood with his left foot on the edge of the table and was bent forward over his knee. The men spoke and gestured, their movements careless. Although Eragon could not hear or see what the woman said, it was obvious to him that her response angered the farmers, for they scowled and swelled their chests, puffing themselves up like roosters. One of them shook a finger at her.

To Eragon, they appeared decent, hardworking men who had lost their manners in the depths of their tankards, a mistake he had witnessed often enough on feast days in Carvahall. Garrow had had little respect for men who knew they could not hold their beer and yet insisted on embarrassing themselves in public. "It's unseemly," he had said. "What's more, if you drink to forget your lot in life and not for pleasure, you ought to do it where you won't disturb anyone."

The man to the left of the woman suddenly reached down and hooked a finger underneath the edge of her hood, as if to toss it back. So quickly that Eragon barely saw, the woman lifted her right hand and grasped the man's wrist, but then released it and returned to her previous position. Eragon doubted that anyone else in the common room, including the man she touched, had noticed her actions.

The hood collapsed around her neck, and Eragon stiffened, astounded. The woman was human, but she resembled Arya. The only differences between them were her eyes—which were round and level, not slanted like a cat's—and her ears, which lacked the pointed tips of an elf's. She was just as beautiful as the Arya Eragon knew, but in a less exotic, more familiar way.

Without hesitation, Eragon probed toward the woman with his mind. He had to know who she really was.

As soon as he touched her consciousness, a mental blow struck back at Eragon, destroying his concentration, and then in the confines of his skull, he heard a deafening voice exclaim, *Eragon!*

Arya?

Their eyes met for a moment before the crowd thickened again and hid her.

Eragon hurried across the room to her table, prying apart the bodies packed close together to clear himself a path. The farmers looked askance at him when he emerged from the press, and one said, "You're awful rude, barging in on us uninvited-like. Best make yourself scarce, eh?"

In as diplomatic a voice as he could muster, Eragon said, "It seems to me, gentlemen, that the lady would rather be left alone. Now, you wouldn't ignore the wishes of an honest woman, would you?"

"An honest woman?" laughed the nearest man. "No honest woman travels alone."

"Then let me set your concern to rest, for I am her brother, and we are going to live with our uncle in Dras-Leona."

The four men exchanged uneasy glances. Three of them began to edge away from Arya, but the largest planted himself a few inches in front of Eragon and, breathing upon his face, said, "I'm not sure I

believe you, *friend*. You're just trying to drive us away so you can be
with her yourself."

He's not far off, thought Eragon.

Speaking quietly enough that only that man could hear, Eragon
said, "I assure you, she *is* my sister. Please, sir, I have no quarrel with
you. Won't you go?"

"Not when I think you're a lying milksop."

"Sir, be reasonable. There's no need for this unpleasantness. The
night is young, and there's drink and music aplenty. Let's not quarrel about such a petty misunderstanding. It's beneath us."

To Eragon's relief, the other man relaxed after a few seconds and
uttered a scornful grunt. "I wouldn't want to fight a youngling like
you anyway," he said. Turning around, he lumbered toward the bar
with his friends.

Keeping his gaze fixed upon the crowd, Eragon slipped behind
the table and sat next to Arya. "What are you doing here?" he
asked, barely moving his lips.

"Searching for you."

Surprised, he glanced at her, and she raised a curved eyebrow. He
looked back at the throng of people and, pretending to smile, asked,
"Are you alone?"

"No longer. . . . Did you rent a bed for the night?"

He shook his head.

"Good. I already have a room. We can talk there."

They rose in unison, and he followed her to the stairs at the back
of the common room. The worn treads creaked under their feet as
they climbed to a hallway on the second story. A single candle illuminated the dingy, wood-paneled corridor. Arya led the way to the
last door on the right, and from within the voluminous sleeve of her
cloak, she produced an iron key. Unlocking the door, she entered
the room, waited for Eragon to cross the threshold after her, and
then closed and secured the door again.

A faint orange glow penetrated the lead-lined window across

from Eragon. The glow came from a lantern hanging on the other side of Eastcroft's town square. By it, he was able to make out the shape of an oil lamp on a low table to his right.

"Brisingr," whispered Eragon, and lit the wick with a spark from his finger.

Even with the lamp burning, the room was still dark. The chamber contained the same paneling as the hallway, and the chestnut-colored wood absorbed most of the light that struck it and made the room seem small and heavy, as if a great weight pressed inward. Aside from the table, the only other piece of furniture was a narrow bed with a single blanket thrown over the ticking. A small bag of supplies rested on the mattress.

Eragon and Arya stood facing each other. Then Eragon reached up and removed the cloth strip tied around his head, and Arya unfastened the brooch that held her cloak around her shoulders and placed the garment on the bed. She wore a forest-green dress, the first dress Eragon had seen her in.

It was a strange experience for Eragon to have their appearances reversed, so that he was the one who looked like an elf, and Arya a human. The change did nothing to diminish his regard for her, but it did make him more comfortable in her presence, for she was less alien to him now.

It was Arya who broke the silence. "Saphira said you stayed behind to kill the last Ra'zac and to explore the rest of Helgrind. Is that the truth?"

"It's part of the truth."

"And what is the whole truth?"

Eragon knew that nothing less would satisfy her. "Promise me that you won't share what I'm about to tell you with anyone unless I give you permission."

"I promise," she said in the ancient language.

Then he told her about finding Sloan, why he decided not to bring him back to the Varden, the curse he had laid upon the butcher, and the chance he had given Sloan to redeem himself—at least partially—and to regain his sight. Eragon finished by saying, "Whatever happens, Roran and Katrina can *never* learn that Sloan is still alive. If they do, there'll be no end of trouble."

Arya sat on the edge of the bed and, for a long while, stared at the lamp and its jumping flame. Then: "You should have killed him."

"Maybe, but I couldn't."

"Just because you find your task distasteful is no reason to shirk it. You were a coward."

Eragon bridled at her accusation. "Was I? Anyone with a knife could have killed Sloan. What I did was far harder."

"Physically, but not morally."

"I didn't kill him because I thought it was wrong." Eragon frowned with concentration as he searched for the words to explain himself. "I wasn't afraid . . . not that. Not after going into battle. . . . It was something else. I will kill in war. But I won't take it upon myself to decide who lives and who dies. I don't have the experience or the wisdom. . . . Every man has a line he won't cross, Arya, and I found mine when I looked upon Sloan. Even if I had Galbatorix as my captive, I would not kill him. I would take him to Nasuada and King Orrin, and if they condemned him to death, then I would happily lop off his head, but not before. Call it weakness if you will, but that is how I am made, and I won't apologize for it."

"You will be a tool, then, wielded by others?"

"I will serve the people as best I can. I've never aspired to lead. Alagaësia does not need another tyrant king."

Arya rubbed her temples. "Why does everything have to be so complicated with you, Eragon? No matter where you go, you seem to get yourself mired in difficult situations. It's as if you make an effort to walk through every bramble in the land."

"Your mother said much the same."

"I'm not surprised. . . . Very well, let it be. Neither of us is about to change our opinions, and we have more pressing concerns than arguing about justice and morality. In the future, though, you would do well to remember who you are and what you mean to the races of Alagaësia."

"I never forgot." Eragon paused, waiting for her response, but Arya let his statement pass unchallenged. Sitting on the edge of the table, he said, "You didn't have to come looking for me, you know. I was fine."

"Of course I did."

"How did you find me?"

"I guessed which route you would take from Helgrind. Luckily for me, my guess placed me forty miles west of here, and that was close enough for me to locate you by listening to the whispers of the land."

"I don't understand."

"A Rider does not walk unnoticed in this world, Eragon. Those who have the ears to hear and the eyes to see can interpret the signs easily enough. The birds sing of your coming, the beasts of the earth heed your scent, and the very trees and grass remember your touch. The bond between Rider and dragon is so powerful that those who are sensitive to the forces of nature can feel it."

"You'll have to teach that trick to me sometime."

"It is no trick, merely the art of paying attention to what is already around you."

"Why did you come to Eastcroft, though? It would have been safer to meet me outside the village."

"Circumstances forced me here, as I assume they did you. You did not come here willingly, no?"

"No. . . ." He rolled his shoulders, weary from the day's traveling. Pushing back sleep, he waved a hand at her dress and said, "Have you finally abandoned your shirt and trousers?"

A small smile appeared on Arya's face. "Only for the duration of this trip. I've lived among the Varden for more years than I care to recall, yet I still forget how humans insist upon separating their women from their men. I never could bring myself to adopt your customs, even if I did not conduct myself entirely as an elf. Who was to say yea or nay to me? My mother? She was on the other side of Alagaësia." Arya seemed to catch herself then, as if she had said more than she intended. She continued. "In any event, I had an unfortunate encounter with a pair of ox herders soon after I left the Varden, and I stole this dress directly afterward."

"It fits well."

"One of the advantages of being a spellcaster is that you never have to wait for a tailor."

Eragon laughed for a moment. Then he asked, "What now?"

"Now we rest. Tomorrow, before the sun rises, we shall slip out of Eastcroft, and no one shall be the wiser."

That night, Eragon lay in front of the door, while Arya took the bed. Their arrangement was not the result of deference or courtesy on Eragon's part—although he would have insisted on giving Arya the bed in any event—but rather caution. If anyone were to barge into the room, it would seem odd to find a woman on the floor.

As the empty hours crept by, Eragon stared at the beams above his head and traced the cracks in the wood, unable to calm his racing thoughts. He tried every method he knew to relax, but his mind kept returning to Arya, to his surprise at meeting her, to her comments about his treatment of Sloan, and, above all else, to the feelings he had for her. What those were exactly, he was unsure. He longed to be with her, but she had rejected his advances, and that tarnished his affection with hurt and anger, and also frustration, for while Eragon refused to accept that his suit was hopeless, he could not think of how to proceed.

An ache formed in his chest as he listened to the gentle rise and fall of Arya's breathing. It tormented him to be so close and yet be unable to approach her. He twisted the edge of his tunic between his fingers and wished there was something he could do instead of resigning himself to an unwelcome fate.

He wrestled with his unruly emotions deep into the night, until finally he succumbed to exhaustion and drifted into the waiting embrace of his waking dreams. There he wandered for a few fitful hours until the stars began to fade and it was time for him and Arya to leave Eastcroft.

Together, they opened the window and jumped from the sill to the ground twelve feet below, a small drop for one with an elf's abilities. As she fell, Arya grasped the skirt of her dress to keep it from billowing around her. They landed inches apart and then set off running between the houses toward the palisade.

"People will wonder where we went," said Eragon between strides. "Maybe we should have waited and left like normal travelers."

"It's riskier to stay. I paid for my room. That's all the innkeeper really cares about, not whether we snuck out early." The two of them parted for a few seconds as they circumvented a decrepit wagon, and then Arya added, "The most important thing is to keep moving. If we linger, the king will surely find us."

When they arrived at the outer wall, Arya ranged along it until she found a post that protruded somewhat. She wrapped her hands around it and pulled, testing the wood with her weight. The post swayed and rattled against its neighbors, but otherwise held.

"You first," said Arya.

"Please, after you."

With a sigh of impatience, she tapped her bodice. "A dress is somewhat breezier than a pair of leggings, Eragon."

Heat flooded his cheeks as he caught her meaning. Reaching above his head, he got a good grip and then began to climb the palisade, bracing himself with his knees and feet during the ascent. At the top, he stopped and balanced on the tips of the sharpened posts.

"Go on," whispered Arya.

"Not until you join me."

"Don't be so—"

"Watchman!" said Eragon, and pointed. A lantern floated in the darkness between a pair of nearby houses. As the light approached, the gilded outline of a man emerged from the gloom. He carried a naked sword in one hand.

Silent as a specter, Arya grasped the post and, using only the strength of her arms, pulled herself hand over hand toward Eragon. She seemed to glide upward, as if by magic. When she was close enough, Eragon seized her right forearm and lifted her above the remainder of the posts, setting her down next to him. Like two strange birds, they perched on the palisade, motionless and breathless as the watchman walked underneath them. He swung the lantern in either direction, searching for intruders.

Don't look at the ground, pleaded Eragon. *And don't look up.*

A moment later, the watchman sheathed his sword and continued on his rounds, humming to himself.

Without a word, Eragon and Arya dropped to the other side of the palisade. The armor in Eragon's pack rattled as he struck the grass-covered bank below and rolled to dissipate the force of the impact. Springing to his feet, he bent low and dashed away from Eastcroft over the gray landscape, Arya close behind. They kept to hollows and dry streambeds as they skirted the farms that surrounded the village. A half-dozen times, indignant dogs ran out to protest the invasion of their territories. Eragon tried to calm them with his mind, but the only way he found to stop the dogs from barking was to assure them that their terrible teeth and claws had scared him and Arya away. Pleased with their success, the dogs pranced with wagging tails back to the barns, sheds, and porches where they had been standing guard over their fiefdoms. Their smug confidence amused Eragon.

Five miles from Eastcroft, when it became apparent they were utterly alone and no one was trailing them, Eragon and Arya drew to a halt by a charred stump. Kneeling, Arya scooped several handfuls of dirt from the ground in front of her. "Adurna rïsa," she said. With a faint trickle, water welled out of the surrounding soil and poured into the hole she had dug. Arya waited until the water filled the cavity and then said, "Letta," and the flow ceased.

She intoned a spell of scrying, and Nasuada's face appeared upon the surface of the still water. Arya greeted her. "My Lady," Eragon said, and bowed.

"Eragon," she replied. She appeared tired, hollow-cheeked, as if she had suffered a long illness. A lock snapped free of her bun and coiled itself into a tight knot at her hairline. Eragon glimpsed a row of bulky bandages on her arm as she slid a hand over her head, pressing the rebellious hair flat. "You are safe, thank Gokukara. We were so worried."

"I'm sorry I upset you, but I had my reasons."

"You must explain them to me when you arrive."

"As you wish," he said. "How were you hurt? Did someone attack you? Why haven't any of Du Vrangr Gata healed you?"

"I ordered them to leave me alone. And that I will explain when you arrive." Thoroughly puzzled, Eragon nodded and swallowed his questions. To Arya, Nasuada said, "I'm impressed; you found him. I wasn't sure you could."

"Fortune smiled upon me."

"Perhaps, but I tend to believe your skill was as important as Fortune's generosity. How long until you rejoin us?"

"Two, three days, unless we encounter unforeseen difficulties."

"Good. I will expect you then. From now on, I want you to contact me at least once before noon and once before nightfall. If I fail to hear from you, I'll assume you've been captured, and I'll send Saphira with a rescue force."

"We may not always have the privacy we need to work magic."

"Find a way to get it. I need to know where you two are and whether you're safe."

Arya considered for a moment and then said, "If I can, I will do as you ask, but not if it puts Eragon in danger."

"Agreed."

Taking advantage of the ensuing pause in the conversation, Eragon said, "Nasuada, is Saphira near at hand? I would like to talk to her. . . . We haven't spoken since Helgrind."

"She left an hour ago to scout our perimeter. Can you maintain this spell while I find out if she has returned?"

"Go," said Arya.

A single step carried Nasuada out of their field of view, leaving behind a static image of the table and chairs inside her red pavilion. For a good while, Eragon appraised the contents of the tent, but then restlessness overtook him and he allowed his eyes to drift from the pool of water to the back of Arya's neck. Her thick black hair fell to one side, exposing a strip of smooth skin just above the collar of her dress. That transfixed him for the better part of a minute, and then he stirred and leaned against the charred stump.

There came the sound of breaking wood, and then a field of sparkling blue scales covered the pool as Saphira forced herself into the pavilion. It was hard for Eragon to tell what part of her he saw, it was such a small part. The scales slid past the pool and he glimpsed the underside of a thigh, a spike on her tail, the baggy membrane of a folded wing, and then the gleaming tip of a tooth as she turned and twisted, trying to find a position from which she could comfortably view the mirror Nasuada used for arcane communications. From the alarming noises that originated behind Saphira, Eragon guessed she was crushing most of the furniture. At last she settled in place, brought her head close to the mirror—so that one large sapphire eye occupied the entire pool—and peered out at Eragon.

They looked at each other for a full minute, neither of them moving. It surprised Eragon how relieved he was to see her. He had not truly felt safe since he and she had separated.

"I missed you," he whispered.

She blinked once.

"Nasuada, are you still there?"

The muffled answer floated toward him from somewhere to the right of Saphira: "Yes, barely."

"Would you be so kind as to relay Saphira's comments to me?"

"I'm more than happy to, but at the moment, I'm caught between a wing and a pole, and there's no path free, so far as I can tell. You may have difficulty hearing me. If you're willing to bear with me, though, I'll give it a try."

"Please do."

Nasuada was quiet for several heartbeats, and then in a tone so like Saphira's that Eragon almost laughed, she said, "You are well?"

"I'm healthy as an ox. And you?"

"To compare myself with a bovine would be both ridiculous and insulting, but I'm as fit as ever, if that is what you are asking. I'm pleased Arya is with you. It's good for you to have someone sensible around to watch your back."

"I agree. Help is always welcome when you're in danger." While Eragon was grateful that he and Saphira were able to talk, albeit in a roundabout fashion, he found the spoken word a poor substitute for the free exchange of thoughts and emotions they enjoyed when in close proximity. Furthermore, with Arya and Nasuada privy to their conversation, Eragon was reluctant to address topics of a more personal nature, such as whether Saphira had forgiven him for forcing her to leave him in Helgrind. Saphira must have shared in his reluctance, for she too refrained from broaching the subject. They chatted about other, inconsequential happenings and then bade each other farewell. Before he stepped away from the pool, Eragon touched his fingers to his lips and silently mouthed, *I'm sorry.*

A sliver of space appeared around each of the small scales that rimmed Saphira's eye as the underlying flesh softened. She blinked long and slow, and he knew she understood his message and that she bore him no ill will.

After Eragon and Arya took their leave of Nasuada, Arya

151

terminated her spell and stood. With the back of her hand, she knocked the dirt from her dress.

While she did, Eragon fidgeted, impatient as he had not been before; right then he wanted nothing else but to run straight to Saphira and curl up with her in front of a campfire.

"Let us be off," he said, already moving.

✦ ✦ ✦

A DELICATE MATTER

The muscles of Roran's back popped and rippled as he heaved the boulder off the ground.

He rested the large rock on his thighs for an instant and then, grunting, pressed it overhead and locked his arms straight. For a full minute, he held the crushing weight in the air. When his shoulders were trembling and about to fail, he threw the boulder onto the ground in front of him. It landed with a dull thud, leaving an indentation several inches deep in the dirt.

On either side of Roran, twenty of the Varden's warriors struggled to lift boulders of similar size. Only two succeeded; the rest returned to the lighter rocks they were accustomed to. It pleased Roran that the months he had spent in Horst's forge and the years of farmwork before had given him the strength to hold his own with men who had drilled with their weapons every day since they turned twelve.

Roran shook the fire from his arms and took several deep breaths, the air cool against his bare chest. Reaching up, he massaged his right shoulder, cupping the round ball of muscle and exploring it with his fingers, confirming once again that no trace remained of the injury he had suffered when the Ra'zac had bitten him. He grinned, glad to be whole and sound again, being as it had seemed no likelier to him than a cow dancing a jig.

A yelp of pain caused him to look over at Albriech and Baldor, who were sparring with Lang, a swarthy, battle-scarred veteran who taught the arts of war. Even two against one, Lang held his own, and with his wooden practice sword, he had disarmed Baldor, knocked him across the ribs, and jabbed Albriech so hard in the leg, he fell sprawling, all in the span of a few seconds. Roran empathized with them; he had just finished his own session with Lang, and it had left him with several new bruises to go with his faded ones from Helgrind. For the most part, he preferred his hammer over a sword, but he thought he should still be able to handle a blade if the occasion called for it. Swords required more finesse than he felt most fights deserved: bash a swordsman on the wrist and, armored or not, he would be too preoccupied with his broken bones to defend himself.

After the Battle of the Burning Plains, Nasuada had invited the villagers from Carvahall to join the Varden. They had all accepted her offer. Those who would have refused had already elected to stay in Surda when the villagers stopped in Dauth on their way to the Burning Plains. Every able-bodied man from Carvahall had taken up proper arms—discarding their makeshift spears and shields—and had worked to become warriors equal to any in Alagaësia. The people of Palancar Valley were accustomed to a hard life. Swinging a sword was no worse than chopping wood, and it was a far sight easier than breaking sod or hoeing acres of beets in the heat of summer. Those who knew a useful trade continued to ply their craft in service to the Varden, but in their spare time they still strove to master the weapons given to them, for every man was expected to fight when the call to battle sounded.

Roran had devoted himself to the training with unwavering dedication since returning from Helgrind. Helping the Varden defeat the Empire and, ultimately, Galbatorix was the one thing he could do to protect the villagers and Katrina. He was not arrogant enough to believe that he alone could tip the balance of the war, but he was confident in his ability to shape the world and knew that if he applied himself, he could increase the Varden's chances of victory. He had to stay alive, though, and that meant conditioning his body and mastering the tools and techniques of slaughter so as to avoid falling to a more experienced warrior.

As he crossed the practice field, on his way back to the tent he shared with Baldor, Roran passed a strip of grass sixty feet long whereon lay a twenty-foot log stripped of its bark and polished smooth by the thousands of hands that rubbed against it every day. Without breaking his stride, Roran turned, slipped his fingers under the thick end of the log, lifted it, and, grunting from the strain, walked it upright. He gave the log a push then, and it toppled over. Grabbing the thin end, he repeated the process twice more.

Unable to muster the energy to flip the log again, Roran left the field and trotted through the surrounding maze of gray canvas tents, waving to Loring and Fisk and others he recognized, as well as a half-dozen or so strangers who greeted him. "Hail, Stronghammer!" they cried in warm tones.

"Hail!" he replied. *It is a strange thing*, he thought, *to be known to people whom you have not met before*. A minute later, he arrived at the tent that had become his home and, ducking inside, stored away the bow, the quiver of arrows, and the short sword the Varden had given him.

He snared his waterskin from beside his bedding, then hurried back into the bright sunlight and, unstoppering the skin, poured the contents over his back and shoulders. Baths tended to be sporadic and infrequent events for Roran, but today was an important day, and he wanted to be fresh and clean for what was to come. With the sharp edge of a polished stick, he scraped the grime off his arms and legs and out from under his fingernails and then combed his hair and trimmed his beard.

Satisfied that he was presentable, he pulled on his freshly washed tunic, stuck his hammer through his belt, and was about to head off through the camp when he became aware of Birgit watching him from behind the corner of the tent. She clenched a sheathed dagger with both hands.

Roran froze, ready to draw his hammer at the slightest provocation. He knew that he was in mortal danger, and despite his prowess, he was not confident of defeating Birgit if she attacked, for like him, she pursued her enemies with single-minded determination.

"You once asked me to help you," said Birgit, "and I agreed

because I wanted to find the Ra'zac and kill them for eating my husband. Have I not upheld my bargain?"

"You have."

"And do you remember I promised that once the Ra'zac were dead, I would have my compensation from you for your role in Quimby's death?"

"I do."

Birgit twisted the dagger with increasing urgency, the back of her fists ridged with tendons. The dagger rose out of its sheath a full inch, baring the bright steel, and then slowly sank into darkness again. "Good," she said. "I would not want your memory to fail you. I *will* have my compensation, Garrowsson. Never you doubt that." With a swift, firm step, she departed, the dagger hidden among the folds of her dress.

Releasing his breath, Roran sat on a nearby stool and rubbed his throat, convinced that he had narrowly escaped being gutted by Birgit. Her visit had alarmed him but it did not surprise him; he had been aware of her intentions for months, since before they left Carvahall, and he knew that one day he would have to settle his debt with her.

A raven soared overhead, and as he tracked it, his mood lightened and he smiled. "Well," he said to himself. *A man rarely knows the day and hour when he will die. I could be killed at any moment, and there's not a blasted thing I can do about it. What will happen will happen, and I won't waste the time I have aboveground worrying. Misfortune always comes to those who wait. The trick is to find happiness in the brief gaps between disasters. Birgit will do what her conscience tells her to, and I will deal with it when I must.*

By his left foot, he noticed a yellowish stone, which he picked up and rolled between his fingers. Concentrating on it as hard as he could, he said, "Stenr rïsa." The stone ignored his command and remained immobile between his thumb and forefinger. With a snort, he tossed it away.

Standing, he strode north between the rows of tents. While he walked, he tried to untangle a knot in the lacing at his collar, but it resisted his efforts, and he gave up on it when he arrived at Horst's tent, which was twice as large as most. "Hello in there," he said, and knocked on the pole between the two entrance flaps.

Katrina burst out of the tent, copper hair flying, and wrapped her arms around him. Laughing, he lifted her by the waist and spun her in a circle, all the world a blur except her face, then gently set her down. She pecked him on the lips, once, twice, three times. Growing still, he gazed into her eyes, more happy than he could ever remember being.

"You smell nice," she said.

"How are you?" The only flaw in his joy was seeing how thin and pale imprisonment had left her. It made him want to resurrect the Ra'zac so they could endure the same suffering they had inflicted upon her and his father.

"Every day you ask me, and every day I tell you, 'Better.' Be patient; I will recover, but it will take time. . . . The best remedy for what ails me is being with you here under the sun. It does me more good than I can tell you."

"That was not all I was asking."

Crimson spots appeared on Katrina's cheeks, and she tilted her head back, her lips curving in a mischievous smile. "My, you are bold, dear sir. Most bold indeed. I'm not sure I should be alone with you, for fear you might take liberties with me."

The spirit of her reply set his concern to rest. "Liberties, eh? Well, since you already consider me a scoundrel, I might as well enjoy some of these *liberties*." And he kissed her until she broke the contact, although she remained in his embrace.

"Oh," she said, out of breath. "You're a hard man to argue with, Roran Stronghammer."

"That I am." Nodding toward the tent behind her, he lowered his voice and asked, "Does Elain know?"

"She would if she weren't so preoccupied with her pregnancy. I think the stress of the trip from Carvahall may cause her to lose the child. She's sick a good part of the day, and she has pains that . . . well, of an unfortunate nature. Gertrude has been tending her, but she can't do much to ease her discomfort. All the same, the sooner Eragon returns, the better. I'm not sure how long I can keep this secret."

"You'll do fine, I'm sure." He released her then and tugged on the hem of his tunic to smooth out the wrinkles. "How do I look?"

Katrina studied him with a critical eye and then wet the tips of her fingers and ran them through his hair, pushing it back off his forehead. Spotting the knot at his collar, she began to pick at it, saying, "You ought to pay closer attention to your clothes."

"Clothes haven't been trying to kill me."

"Well, things are different now. You're the cousin of a Dragon Rider, and you should look the part. People expect it of you."

He allowed her to continue fussing with him until she was pleased with his appearance. Kissing her goodbye, he walked the half mile to the center of the Varden's massive camp, where Nasuada's red command pavilion stood. The pennant mounted on the top bore a black shield and two parallel swords slanting underneath, and it whipped and snapped in a warm wind from the east.

The six guards outside the pavilion—two humans, two dwarves, and two Urgals—lowered their weapons as Roran approached, and one of the Urgals, a thickset brute with yellow teeth, challenged him, saying, "Who goes there?" His accent was nearly unintelligible.

"Roran Stronghammer, son of Garrow. Nasuada sent for me."

Pounding his breastplate with one fist, which produced a loud crash, the Urgal announced, "Roran Stronghammer requests an audience with you, Lady Nightstalker."

"You may admit him," came the answer from inside.

The warriors lifted their blades, and Roran carefully made his way past. They watched him, and he them, with the detached air of men who might have to fight each other at a moment's notice.

Inside the pavilion, Roran was alarmed to see that most of the furniture was broken and overturned. The only pieces that seemed unharmed were a mirror mounted on a pole and the grand chair in which Nasuada was sitting. Ignoring their surroundings, he knelt and bowed to her.

Nasuada's features and bearing were so different from those of the women Roran had grown up with, he was not sure how to act. She appeared strange and imperious, with her embroidered dress and the gold chains in her hair and her dusky skin, which at the moment had a reddish cast, due to the color of the fabric walls. In stark contrast to the rest of her apparel, linen bandages encased her forearms, a testament to her astounding courage during the Trial of the Long Knives. Her feat had been a topic of constant discussion among the Varden ever since Roran had returned with Katrina. It was the one aspect of her he felt as if he understood, for he too would make any sacrifice in order to protect those he cared about. It just so happened that she cared about a group of thousands, while he was committed to his family and his village.

"Please, rise," said Nasuada. He did as he was instructed and rested a hand on the head of his hammer, then waited while she inspected him. "My position rarely allows me the luxury of clear, direct speech, Roran, but I will be blunt with you today. You seem to be a man who appreciates candor, and we have much to discuss in a small amount of time."

"Thank you, my Lady. I have never enjoyed playing word games."

"Excellent. To be blunt, then, you have presented me with two difficulties, neither of which I can easily resolve."

He frowned. "What sort of difficulties?"

"One of character, and one of politics. Your deeds in Palancar Valley and during your flight thence with your fellow villagers are nigh on incredible. They tell me that you have a daring mind and that you are skilled at combat, strategy, and inspiring people to follow you with unquestioning loyalty."

"They may have followed me, but they certainly never stopped questioning me."

A smile touched her lips. "Perhaps. But you still got them here, didn't you? You possess valuable talents, Roran, and the Varden could use you. I assume you wish to be of service?"

"I do."

"As you know, Galbatorix has divided his army and sent troops south to reinforce the city of Aroughs, west toward Feinster, and north toward Belatona. He hopes to drag out this fight, to bleed us dry through slow attrition. Jörmundur and I cannot be in a dozen locations at once. We need captains whom we can trust to deal with the myriad conflicts springing up around us. In this, you could prove your worth to us. But . . ." Her voice faded.

"But you do not yet know if you can rely upon me."

"Indeed. Protecting one's friends and family stiffens a person's spine, but I wonder how you will fare without them. Will your nerve hold? And while you can lead, can you also obey orders? I cast no aspersions on your character, Roran, but the fate of Alagaësia is at stake, and I cannot risk putting someone incompetent in charge of my men. This war does not forgive such errors. Nor would it be fair to the men already with the Varden to place you over them without just cause. You must earn your responsibilities with us."

"I understand. What would you have me do, then?"

"Ah, but it's not that easy, for you and Eragon are practically brothers, and that complicates things immeasurably. As I'm sure you are aware, Eragon is the keystone of our hopes. It is important, then, to shelter him from distractions so he may concentrate upon the task before him. If I send you into battle and you die as a result, grief and anger might very well unbalance him. I've seen it happen before. Moreover, I must take great care with whom I allow you to serve, for there are those who will seek to influence you because of your relation to Eragon. So now you have a fair idea of the scope of my concerns. What have you to say about them?"

"If the land itself is at stake and this war is as hotly contested as you imply, then I say you cannot afford to let me sit idle. Employing me as a common swordsman would be just as much a waste. But I think you know that already. As for politics . . ." He shrugged. "I don't care one whit whom you put me with. No one shall get to Eragon through me. My only concern is breaking the Empire so that my kith and kin can return to our home and live in peace."

"You are determined."

"Very. Could you not allow me to remain in charge of the men from Carvahall? We are as close as family, and we work well together. Test me that way. The Varden would not suffer, then, if I failed."

She shook her head. "No. Perhaps in the future, but not yet. They require proper instruction, and I cannot judge your performance when you are surrounded by a group of people who are so loyal that at your urging they abandoned their homes and traversed the width of Alagaësia."

She considers me a threat, he realized. *My ability to influence the villagers makes her wary of me.* In an attempt to disarm her, he said, "They had their own sense to guide them. They knew it was folly to stay in the valley."

"You cannot explain away their behavior, Roran."

"What do you want of me, Lady? Will you let me serve or not? And if so, how?"

"Here is my offer. This morning, my magicians detected a patrol of twenty-three of Galbatorix's soldiers due east. I am sending out a contingent under the command of Martland Redbeard, the Earl of Thun, to destroy them and to do some scouting besides. If you are agreeable, you will serve under Martland. You will listen to and obey him and hopefully learn from him. He, in turn, will watch you and report to me whether he believes you are suitable for advancement. Martland is very experienced, and I have every confidence in his opinion. Does this strike you as fair, Roran Stronghammer?"

"It does. Only, when would I leave, and how long would I be gone?"

"You would leave today and return within a fortnight."

"Then I must ask, could you wait and send me on a different

expedition, in a few days? I would like to be here when Eragon returns."

"Your concern for your cousin is admirable, but events move apace, and we cannot delay. As soon as I know Eragon's fate, I will have one of Du Vrangr Gata contact you with the tidings, whether they be good or ill."

Roran rubbed his thumb along the sharp edges of his hammer as he tried to compose a reply that would convince Nasuada to change her mind and yet would not betray the secret he held. At last he abandoned the task as impossible and resigned himself to revealing the truth. "You're right. I am worried about Eragon, but of all people he can fend for himself. Seeing him safe and sound isn't why I want to stay."

"Why, then?"

"Because Katrina and I wish to be married, and we would like Eragon to perform the ceremony."

There was a cascade of sharp clicks as Nasuada tapped her fingernails against the arms of her chair. "If you believe I will allow you to loll about when you could be helping the Varden, just so you and Katrina can enjoy your wedding night a few days earlier, then you are sorely mistaken."

"It is a matter of some urgency, Lady Nightstalker."

Nasuada's fingers paused in midair, and her eyes narrowed. "How urgent?"

"The sooner we are wed, the better it will be for Katrina's honor. If you understand me at all, know that I would never ask favors for myself."

Light shifted on Nasuada's skin as she tilted her head. "I see. . . . Why Eragon? Why do you want him to perform the ceremony? Why not someone else: an elder from your village perhaps?"

"Because he is my cousin and I care for him, and because he is a Rider. Katrina lost nearly everything on my account—her home, her father, and her dowry. I cannot replace those things, but I at least want to give her a wedding worth remembering. Without gold or livestock, I cannot pay for a lavish ceremony, so I must find some other means besides wealth to make our wedding memorable, and it seems to me nothing could be more grand than having a Dragon Rider marry us."

Nasuada held her peace for so long, Roran began to wonder if she expected him to leave. Then: "It would indeed be an honor to have a Dragon Rider marry you, but it would be a sorry day if Katrina had to accept your hand without a proper dowry. The dwarves furnished me with many presents of gold and jewelry when I lived in Tronjheim. Some I have already sold to fund the Varden, but what I have left would still keep a woman clothed in mink and satin for many years to come. They shall be Katrina's, if you are amenable."

Startled, Roran bowed again. "Thank you. Your generosity is overwhelming. I don't know how I can ever repay you."

"Repay me by fighting for the Varden as you fought for Carvahall."

"I will, I swear it. Galbatorix will curse the day he ever sent the Ra'zac after me."

"I'm sure he already does. Now go. You may remain in camp until Eragon returns and marries you to Katrina, but then I expect you to be in the saddle the following morning."

✦ ✦ ✦

BLOODWOLF

What a proud man, thought Nasuada as she watched Roran leave the pavilion. *It's interesting; he and Eragon are alike in so many ways, and yet their personalities are fundamentally different. Eragon may be one of the most deadly warriors in Alagaësia, but he isn't a hard or cruel person. Roran, however, is made of sterner stuff. I hope that he never crosses me; I would have to destroy him in order to stop him.*

She checked her bandages and, satisfied that they were still fresh, rang for Farica and ordered her to bring a meal. After her handmaid delivered the food and then retired from the tent, Nasuada signaled Elva, who emerged from her hiding place behind the false panel at the rear of the pavilion. Together, the two of them shared a mid-morning repast.

Nasuada spent the next few hours reviewing the Varden's latest inventory reports, calculating the number of wagon trains she would need to move the Varden farther north, and adding and subtracting rows of figures that represented the finances of her army. She sent messages to the dwarves and Urgals, ordered the blade-smiths to increase their production of spearheads, threatened the Council of Elders with dissolution—as she did most every week—and otherwise attended to the Varden's business. Then, with Elva at her side, Nasuada rode out on her stallion, Battle-storm, and met with Trianna, who had captured and was busy interrogating a member of Galbatorix's spy network, the Black Hand.

As she and Elva left Trianna's tent, Nasuada became aware of a commotion to the north. She heard shouts and cheers, then a man appeared from among the tents, sprinting toward her. Without a word, her guards formed a tight circle around her, save for one of the Urgals, who planted himself in the path of the runner and hefted his club. The man slowed to a stop before the Urgal and, gasping, shouted, "Lady Nasuada! The elves are here! The elves have arrived!"

For a wild, improbable moment, Nasuada thought he meant Queen Islanzadí and her army, but then she remembered Islanzadí was near Ceunon; not even the elves could move a host across the width of Alagaësia in less than a week. *It must be the twelve spell-weavers Islanzadí sent to protect Eragon.*

"Quick, my horse," she said, and snapped her fingers. Her forearms burned as she swung herself onto Battle-storm. She waited only long enough for the nearest Urgal to hand her Elva, then drove her heels into the stallion. His muscles surged beneath her as he sprang into a gallop. Bending low over his neck, she steered him down a crude lane between two rows of tents, dodging men and animals and jumping a rain barrel that barred her way. The men did not seem to take offense; they laughed and scrambled after her so they could see the elves with their own eyes.

When she arrived at the northern entrance to the camp, she and Elva dismounted and scanned the horizon for motion.

"There," said Elva, and pointed.

Nearly two miles away, twelve long, lean figures emerged from behind a stand of juniper trees, their outlines wavering in the morning heat. The elves ran in unison, so light and fast, their feet raised no dust and they appeared to fly over the countryside. Nasuada's scalp prickled. Their speed was both beautiful and unnatural. They reminded her of a pack of predators chasing their prey. She felt the same sense of danger as when she had seen a Shrrg, a giant wolf, in the Beor Mountains.

"Awe-inspiring, aren't they?"

Nasuada started to find Angela next to her. She was annoyed and mystified by how the herbalist had been able to sneak up on her. She wished Elva had warned her of Angela's approach. "How is it you always manage to be present when something interesting is about to occur?"

"Oh well, I like to know what's going on, and being there is so much faster than waiting for someone to tell me about it afterward. Besides, people always leave out important pieces of information, like whether someone's ring finger is longer than their index finger, or whether they have magical shields protecting them, or whether the donkey they are riding happens to have a bald patch in the shape of a rooster's head. Don't you agree?"

Nasuada frowned. "You never reveal your secrets, do you?"

"Now, what good would that do? Everyone would get all excited over some piffle of a spell, and then I'd have to spend hours trying to explain, and in the end, King Orrin would want to chop off my head and I would have to fight off half your spellcasters during my escape. It's just not worth the effort, if you ask me."

"Your answer hardly inspires confidence. But—"

"That's because you are too serious, Lady Nightstalker."

"But tell me," Nasuada persisted, "why would you want to know if someone is riding a donkey with a bald patch shaped like a rooster's head?"

"Ah, that. Well, the man who owns that particular donkey cheated me at a game of knucklebones out of three buttons and a rather interesting shard of enchanted crystal."

"Cheated *you?*"

Angela pursed her lips, obviously irked. "The knucklebones were loaded. I switched them on him, but then he replaced them with a set of his own when I was distracted. . . . I'm still not quite sure how he tricked me."

"So you were both cheating."

"It was a valuable crystal! Besides, how can you cheat a cheater?"

Before Nasuada could respond, the six Nighthawks came pounding out of the camp and took up positions around her. She hid her distaste as the heat and smell of their bodies assailed her. The odor of the two Urgals was especially pungent. Then, somewhat to her surprise, the captain of the shift, a burly man with a crooked nose and the name of Garven, accosted her. "My Lady, may I have a word with you in private?" He spoke through close-set teeth, as if struggling to contain a great emotion.

Angela and Elva looked at Nasuada for confirmation that she wanted them to withdraw. She nodded, and they began walking west, toward the Jiet River. Once Nasuada was confident they were out of hearing, she began to speak, but Garven overrode her, exclaiming, "Blast it, Lady Nasuada, you shouldn't have left us as you did!"

"Peace, Captain," she replied. "It was a small enough risk, and I felt it was important to be here in time to greet the elves."

Garven's mail rustled as he struck his leg with a bunched fist. "A small risk? Not an hour ago, you received proof that Galbatorix still has agents hidden among us. He has been able to infiltrate us again and again, and yet you see fit to abandon your escort and go racing through a host of potential assassins! Have you forgotten the attack in Aberon, or how the Twins slew your father?"

"Captain Garven! You go too far."

"I'll go even further if it means ensuring your well-being."

The elves, Nasuada observed, had halved the distance between them and the camp. Angry, and eager to end the conversation, she said, "I am not without my own protection, Captain."

Flicking his eyes toward Elva, Garven said, "We have suspected as much, Lady." A pause followed, as if he were hoping she would volunteer more information. When she remained silent, he forged onward: "If you were actually safe, then I was wrong to accuse you of recklessness, and I apologize. Still, safety and the appearance of safety are two different things. For the Nighthawks to be effective, we have to be the smartest, toughest, meanest warriors in the land, and people have to *believe* that we're the smartest, the toughest, and the meanest. They have to believe that if they try to stab you or shoot you with a crossbow or use magic against you, that we *will* stop them. If they believe they have about as much chance of killing you as a mouse does a dragon, then they may very well give up the idea as hopeless, and we will have averted an attack without ever having to lift a finger.

"We cannot fight all your enemies, Lady Nasuada. That would take an army. Even Eragon couldn't save you if all who want you dead had the courage to act upon their hatred. You might survive a hundred attempts on your life or a thousand, but eventually one would succeed. The only way to keep that from happening is to convince the majority of your enemies that they will *never* get past the Nighthawks. Our reputation can protect you just as surely as our swords and our armor. It does us no good, then, for people to see you riding off without us. No doubt we looked a right bunch of fools back there, frantically trying to catch up. After all, if you do not respect us, Lady, why should anyone else?"

Garven moved closer, dropping his voice. "We will gladly die for you if we must. All we ask in return is that you allow us to perform our duties. It is a small favor, considering. And the day may come when you are grateful we are here. Your other protection is human, and therefore fallible, whatever her arcane powers may be. She has not sworn the same oaths in the ancient language that we of the Nighthawks have. Her sympathies could shift, and you would do well to ponder your fate if she turned against you. The Nighthawks, however, will never betray you. We are yours, Lady Nasuada, fully and completely. So please, let the Nighthawks do what they are supposed to do. . . . Let us protect you."

Initially, Nasuada was indifferent to his arguments, but his eloquence and the clarity of his reasoning impressed her. He was, she thought, a man she might have use for elsewhere. "I see Jörmundur has surrounded me with warriors as skilled with their tongues as they are with their swords," she said with a smile.

"My Lady."

"You are right. I should not have left you and your men behind, and I am sorry. It was careless and inconsiderate. I am still unaccustomed to having guards with me at all hours of the day, and sometimes I forget I cannot move about with the freedom I once did. You have my word of honor, Captain Garven, it shall not happen again. I do not wish to cripple the Nighthawks any more than you."

"Thank you, my Lady."

Nasuada turned back toward the elves, but they were hidden from sight below the bank of a dry stream a quarter of a mile away. "It strikes me, Garven, that you may have invented a motto for the Nighthawks a moment ago."

"Did I? If so, I cannot recall."

"You did. 'The smartest, the toughest, and the meanest,' you said. That would be a fine motto, although perhaps without the *and*. If the other Nighthawks approve of it, you should have Trianna translate the phrase into the ancient language, and I will have it inscribed on your shields and embroidered on your standards."

"You are most generous, my Lady. When we return to our tents, I shall discuss the matter with Jörmundur and my fellow captains. Only . . ."

He hesitated then, and guessing at what troubled him, Nasuada said, "But you are worried that such a motto may be too vulgar for men of your position, and you would prefer something more noble and high-minded, am I right?"

"Exactly, my Lady," he said with a relieved expression.

"It's a valid concern, I suppose. The Nighthawks represent the Varden, and you must interact with notables of every race and rank in the course of your duty. It would be regrettable if you were to convey the wrong impression. . . . Very well, I leave it to you and your compatriots to devise an appropriate motto. I am confident you will do an excellent job."

At that moment, the twelve elves emerged from the dry streambed, and Garven, after murmuring additional thanks, moved a discreet distance from Nasuada. Composing herself for a state visit, Nasuada signaled Angela and Elva to return.

When he was still several hundred feet away, the lead elf appeared soot-black from head to toe. At first Nasuada assumed he was dark-skinned, like herself, and wearing dark attire, but as he drew closer, she saw that the elf wore only a loincloth and a braided fabric belt with a small pouch attached. The rest of him was covered with midnight-blue fur that glistened with a healthy sheen under the glare of the sun. On average, the fur was a quarter-inch long—a smooth, flexible armor that mirrored the shape and movement of the underlying muscles—but on his ankles and the undersides of his forearms, it extended a full two inches, and between his shoulder blades, there was a ruffled mane that stuck out a handsbreadth from his body and tapered down along his back to the base of his spine. Jagged bangs shadowed his brow, and catlike tufts sprouted from the tips of his pointed ears, but otherwise the fur on his face was so short and flat, only its color betrayed its presence. His eyes were bright yellow. Instead of fingernails, a claw protruded from each of his middle fingers. And as he slowed to a stop before her, Nasuada noticed that a certain odor surrounded him: a salty musk reminiscent of dry juniper wood, oiled leather, and smoke. It was such a strong smell, and so obviously masculine, Nasuada felt her skin go hot and cold and crawl with anticipation, and she blushed and was glad it would not show.

The rest of the elves were more as she had expected, of the same general build and complexion as Arya, with short tunics of dusky orange and pine-needle green. Six were men, and six were women. They all had raven hair, save for two of the women whose hair was like starlight. It was impossible to determine their ages, for their faces were smooth and unlined. They were the first elves besides Arya that Nasuada had met in person, and she was eager to find out if Arya was representative of her race.

Touching his first two fingers to his lips, the lead elf bowed, as did his companions, and then twisted his right hand against his chest and said, "Greetings and felicitations, Nasuada, daughter of Ajihad. Atra esterní onto thelduin." His accent was more pronounced than Arya's: a lilting cadence that gave his words music.

"Atra du evarínya ono varda," replied Nasuada, as Arya had taught her.

The elf smiled, revealing teeth that were sharper than normal. "I am Blödhgarm, son of Ildrid the Beautiful." He introduced the other elves in turn before continuing. "We bring you glad tidings from Queen Islanzadí; last night our spellcasters succeeded in destroying the gates of Ceunon. Even as we speak, our forces advance through the streets toward the tower where Lord Tarrant has barricaded himself. Some few still resist us, but the city has fallen, and soon we shall have complete control over Ceunon."

Nasuada's guards and the Varden gathered behind her burst into cheers at the news. She too rejoiced at the victory, but then a sense of foreboding and disquiet tempered her celebratory mood as she pictured elves—especially ones as strong as Blödhgarm—invading human homes. *What unearthly forces have I unleashed?* she wondered. "These are glad tidings indeed," she said, "and I am well pleased to hear them. With Ceunon captured, we are that much closer to Urû'baen, and thus to Galbatorix and the fulfillment of our goals." In a more private voice, she said, "I trust that Queen Islanzadí will be gentle with the people of Ceunon, with those who have no love for Galbatorix but lack the means or the courage to oppose the Empire."

"Queen Islanzadí is both kind and merciful to her subjects, even if they are her unwilling subjects, but if anyone dares oppose us, we shall sweep them aside like dead leaves before an autumn storm."

"I would expect nothing less from a race as old and mighty as yours," Nasuada replied. After satisfying the demands of courtesy with several more polite exchanges of increasing triviality, Nasuada deemed it appropriate to address the reason for the elves' visit. She ordered the assembled crowd to disperse, then said, "Your purpose here, as I understand it, is to protect Eragon and Saphira. Am I right?"

"You are, Nasuada Svit-kona. And we are aware that Eragon is still inside the Empire but that he will return soon."

"Are you also aware that Arya left in search of him and that they are now traveling together?"

Blödhgarm flicked his ears. "We were informed of that as well. It is unfortunate that they should both be in such danger, but hopefully no harm will befall them."

"What do you intend to do, then? Will you seek them out and escort them back to the Varden? Or will you stay and wait and trust that Eragon and Arya can defend themselves against Galbatorix's minions?"

"We will remain as your guests, Nasuada, daughter of Ajihad. Eragon and Arya are safe enough as long as they avoid detection. Joining them in the Empire could very well attract unwanted attention. Under the circumstances, it seems best to bide our time where we can yet do some good. Galbatorix is most likely to strike here, at the Varden, and if he does, and if Thorn and Murtagh should reappear, Saphira will need all our help to drive them off."

Nasuada was surprised. "Eragon said you were among the strongest spellcasters of your race, but do you really have the wherewithal to thwart that accursed pair? Like Galbatorix, they have powers far beyond those of ordinary Riders."

"With Saphira helping us, yes, we believe that we can match or overcome Thorn and Murtagh. We know what the Forsworn were capable of, and while Galbatorix has probably made Thorn and Murtagh stronger than any individual member of the Forsworn, he certainly won't have made them his equals. In that regard, at least, his fear of treachery is to our benefit. Even three of the Forsworn could not conquer the twelve of us and a dragon. Therefore, we are confident that we can hold our own against all but Galbatorix."

"That is heartening. Since Eragon's defeat at the hands of Murtagh, I have been wondering if we should retreat and hide until Eragon's strength increases. Your assurances convince me that we are not entirely without hope. We may have no idea how to kill Galbatorix himself, but until we batter down the gates of his citadel in Urû'baen, or until he chooses to fly out on Shruikan and confront us on the field of battle, nothing shall stop us." She paused. "You have given me no reason to distrust you, Blödhgarm, but before you enter our camp, I must ask that you allow one of my men to touch each of your minds to confirm that you are actually elves, and not humans Galbatorix has sent here in disguise. It pains me to make such a request, but we have been plagued by spies and traitors, and we dare not take you, or anyone else, at their word. It is not my intention to cause offense, but war has taught us these precautions are necessary. Surely you, who have ringed the entire leafy expanse of Du Weldenvarden with protective spells, can understand my reasons. So I ask, will you agree to this?"

Blödhgarm's eyes were feral and his teeth were alarmingly sharp as he said, "For the most part, the trees of Du Weldenvarden have needles, not leaves. Test us if you must, but I warn you, whomever you assign the task should take great care he does not delve too deeply into our minds, else he may find himself stripped of his reason. It is perilous for mortals to wander among our thoughts; they can easily become lost and be unable to return to their bodies. Nor are our secrets available for general inspection."

Nasuada understood. The elves would destroy anyone who ventured into forbidden territory. "Captain Garven," she said.

Stepping forward with the expression of a man approaching his doom, Garven stood opposite Blödhgarm, closed his eyes, and frowned intensely as he searched out Blödhgarm's consciousness. Nasuada bit the inside of her lip as she watched. When she was a child, a one-legged man by the name of Hargrove had taught her how to conceal her thoughts from telepaths and how to block and divert the stabbing lances of a mental attack. At both those skills she excelled, and although she had never succeeded at initiating contact with the mind of another, she was thoroughly familiar with the principles involved. She empathized, then, with the difficulty and the delicacy of what Garven was trying to do, a trial only made harder by the strange nature of the elves.

Leaning toward her, Angela whispered, "You should have had me check the elves. It would have been safer."

"Perhaps," said Nasuada. Despite all the help the herbalist had given her and the Varden, she still felt uncomfortable relying upon her for official business.

For a few moments longer, Garven continued his efforts, and then his eyes snapped open and he released his breath in an explosive burst. His neck and face were mottled from the strain, and his pupils were dilated, as if it were night. In contrast, Blödhgarm appeared undisturbed; his fur was smooth, his breathing regular, and a faint smile of amusement flickered about the corners of his lips.

"Well?" asked Nasuada.

It seemed to take Garven a longish while to hear her question, and then the burly captain with the crooked nose said, "He is not human, my Lady. Of that I have no doubt. No doubt whatsoever."

Pleased and disturbed, for there was something uncomfortably remote about his reply, Nasuada said, "Very well. Proceed." Thereafter, Garven required less and less time to examine each elf, spending no more than a half-dozen seconds on the very last of the group. Nasuada kept a close eye on him throughout the process, and she saw how his fingers became white and bloodless, and the skin at his temples sank into his skull like the eardrums of a frog, and he acquired the languid appearance of a person swimming deep underwater.

Having completed his assignment, Garven returned to his post beside Nasuada. He was, she thought, a changed man. His original determination and fierceness of spirit had faded into the dreamy air of a sleepwalker, and while he looked at her when she asked if he was well, and he answered in an even enough tone, she felt as if his spirit was far away, ambling among dusty, sunlit glades somewhere in the elves' mysterious forest. Nasuada hoped he would soon recover. If he did not, she would ask Eragon or Angela, or perhaps the two of them together, to attend to Garven. Until such time as his condition improved, she decided that he should no longer serve as an active member of the Nighthawks; Jörmundur would give him something simple to do, so she would not suffer guilt at causing him any further injury, and he might at least have the pleasure of enjoying whatever visions his contact with the elves had left him with.

Bitter at her loss, and furious with herself, with the elves, and with Galbatorix and the Empire for making such a sacrifice necessary, she had difficulty maintaining a soft tongue and good manners. "When you spoke of peril, Blödhgarm, you would have done well to mention that even those who return to their bodies do not escape entirely unscathed."

"My Lady, I am fine," said Garven. His protestation was so weak and ineffectual, hardly anyone noticed, and it only served to strengthen Nasuada's sense of outrage.

The fur on Blödhgarm's nape rippled and stiffened. "If I failed to explain myself clearly enough before, then I apologize. However, do not blame us for what has happened; we cannot help our nature. And do not blame yourself either, for we live in an age of suspicion. To allow us to pass unchallenged would have been negligent on your part. It is regrettable that such an unpleasant incident should mar this historic meeting between us, but at least now you may rest easy, confident that you have established our origins and that we are what we seem to be: elves of Du Weldenvarden."

A fresh cloud of his musk drifted over Nasuada, and even though she was hard with anger, her joints weakened and she was assailed by thoughts of bowers draped in silk, goblets of cherry wine, and the mournful dwarf songs she had often heard echoing through the empty halls of Tronjheim. Distracted, she said, "I would Eragon or Arya were here, for they could have looked at your minds without fear of losing their sanity."

Again she succumbed to the wanton attraction of Blödhgarm's odor, imagining what it would feel like to run her hands through his mane. She only returned to herself when Elva pulled on her left arm, forcing her to bend over and place her ear close to the witch-child's mouth. In a low, harsh voice, Elva said, "Horehound. Concentrate upon the taste of horehound."

Following her advice, Nasuada summoned a memory from the previous year, when she had eaten horehound candy during one of King Hrothgar's feasts. Just thinking about the acrid flavor of the candy dried out her mouth and counteracted the seductive qualities of Blödhgarm's musk. She attempted to conceal her lapse in concentration by saying, "My young companion here is wondering why you look so different from other elves. I must confess to some curiosity on the subject as well. Your appearance is not what we have come to expect from your race. Would you be so kind as to share with us the reason for your more *animalistic* features?"

A shiny ripple flowed through Blödhgarm's fur as he shrugged. "This shape pleased me," he said. "Some write poems about the sun and the moon, others grow flowers or build great structures or compose music. As much as I appreciate those various art forms, I believe that true beauty only exists in the fang of a wolf, in the pelt of the forest cat, in the eye of an eagle. So I adopted those attributes for myself. In another hundred years, I may lose interest in the beasts of the land and instead decide that the beasts of the sea embody all that is good, and then I will cover myself with scales, transform my hands into fins and my feet into a tail, and I will vanish beneath the surface of the waves and never again be seen in Alagaësia."

If he was jesting, as Nasuada believed, he showed no indication of it. Quite to the contrary, he was so serious, she wondered if he was mocking her. "Most interesting," she said. "I hope the urge to become a fish does not strike you in the near future, for we have need of you on dry ground. Of course, if Galbatorix should decide to also enslave the sharks and the rockfish, why, then, a spellcaster who can breathe underwater may be of some use."

Without warning, the twelve elves filled the air with their clear, bright laughter, and birds for over a mile in every direction burst into song. The sound of their mirth was like water falling on crystal. Nasuada smiled without meaning to, and around her she saw similar expressions on the faces of her guards. Even the two Urgals seemed giddy with joy. And when the elves fell silent and the world became mundane again, Nasuada felt the sadness of a fading dream. A film of tears obscured her vision for a clutch of heartbeats, and then that too was gone.

Smiling for the first time, and thereby presenting a visage both handsome and terrifying, Blödhgarm said, "It will be an honor to serve alongside a woman as intelligent, capable, and witty as yourself, Lady Nasuada. One of these days, when your duties permit, I would be delighted to teach you our game of Runes. You would make a formidable opponent, I'm sure."

The elves' sudden shift in behavior reminded her of a word she had occasionally heard the dwarves use to describe them: *capricious*. It had seemed a harmless enough description when she was a girl— it reinforced her concept of the elves as creatures who flitted from one delight to another, like fairies in a garden of flowers—but she now recognized that what the dwarves really meant was *Beware! Beware, for you never know what an elf will do.* She sighed to herself, depressed by the prospect of having to contend with another group of beings intent on controlling her for their own ends. *Is life always this complicated?* she wondered. *Or do I bring it upon myself?*

From within the camp, she saw King Orrin riding toward them at the head of a massive train of nobles, courtiers, functionaries major and minor, advisers, assistants, servants, men-at-arms, and a plethora of other species she did not bother identifying, while from the west, rapidly descending on outstretched wings, she saw Saphira. Girding herself for the loud tedium about to engulf them, she said, "It may be some months before I have the opportunity to accept your offer, Blödhgarm, but I appreciate it nevertheless. I would enjoy the distraction of a game after the work of a long day. For the present, however, it must remain a deferred pleasure. The entire weight of human society is about to crash down upon you. I suggest you prepare yourselves for an avalanche of names, questions, and requests. We humans are a curious lot, and none of us have seen so many elves before."

"We are prepared for this, Lady Nasuada," said Blödhgarm.

As King Orrin's thundering cavalcade drew near and Saphira prepared to land, flattening the grass with the wind from her wings, Nasuada's last thought was, *Oh dear. I'll have to put a battalion around Blödhgarm to keep him from being torn apart by the women in the camp. And even that might not solve the problem!*

◆ ◆ ◆

MERCY, DRAGON RIDER

It was midafternoon the day after they had left Eastcroft when Eragon sensed the patrol of fifteen soldiers ahead of them.

He mentioned it to Arya, and she nodded. "I noticed them as well." Neither he nor she voiced any concerns, but worry began to gnaw at Eragon's belly, and he saw how Arya's eyebrows lowered into a fierce frown.

The land around them was open and flat, devoid of any cover. They had encountered groups of soldiers before, but always in the company of other travelers. Now they were alone on the faint trail of a road.

"We could dig a hole with magic, cover the top with brush, and hide in it until they leave," said Eragon.

Arya shook her head without breaking stride. "What would we do with the excess dirt? They'd think they had discovered the biggest badger den in existence. Besides, I would rather save our energy for running."

Eragon grunted. *I'm not sure how many more miles I have left in me.* He was not winded, but the relentless pounding was wearing him down. His knees hurt, his ankles were sore, his left big toe was red and swollen, and blisters continued to break out on his heels, no matter how tightly he bound them. The previous night, he had healed several of the aches and pains troubling him, and while that had provided a measure of relief, the spells only exacerbated his exhaustion.

The patrol was visible as a plume of dust for half an hour before Eragon was able to make out the shapes of the men and the horses at the base of the yellow cloud. Since he and Arya had keener eyesight than most humans, it was unlikely the horsemen could see them at that distance, so they continued to run for another ten minutes. Then they stopped. Arya removed her skirt from her pack and tied it over the leggings she wore while running, and Eragon stored Brom's ring in his own pack and smeared dirt over his right palm to hide his silvery gedwëy ignasia. They resumed their journey with bowed heads, hunched shoulders, and dragging feet. If all went well, the soldiers would assume they were just another pair of refugees.

Although Eragon could feel the rumble of approaching hoofbeats and hear the cries of the men driving their steeds, it still took the better part of an hour for their two groups to meet on the vast plain. When they did, Eragon and Arya moved off the road and stood looking down between their feet. Eragon caught a glimpse of horse legs from under the edge of his brow as the first few riders pounded past, but then the choking dust billowed over him, obscuring the rest of the patrol. The dirt in the air was so thick, he had to close his eyes. Listening carefully, he counted until he was sure that more than half the patrol had gone by. *They're not going to bother questioning us!* he thought.

His elation was short-lived. A moment later, someone in the swirling blizzard of dust shouted, "Company, halt!" A chorus of *Whoas*, *Steady theres*, and *Hey there, Nells* rang out as the fifteen men coaxed their mounts to form a circle around Eragon and Arya. Before the soldiers completed their maneuver and the air cleared, Eragon pawed the ground for a large pebble, then stood back up.

"Be still!" hissed Arya.

While he waited for the soldiers to make their intentions known, Eragon strove to calm his racing heart by rehearsing the story he and Arya had concocted to explain their presence so close to the border with Surda. His efforts failed, for notwithstanding his strength, his training, the knowledge of the battles he had won, and the half-dozen wards protecting him, his flesh remained convinced that imminent injury or death awaited him. His gut twisted, his throat constricted, and his limbs were light and unsteady. *Oh, get on with it!* he thought. He longed to tear something apart with his hands, as if an act of destruction would relieve the pressure building inside of him, but the urge only heightened his frustration, for he dared not move. The one thing that steadied him was Arya's presence. He would sooner cut off a hand than have her consider him a coward. And although she was a mighty warrior in her own right, he still felt the desire to defend her.

The voice that had ordered the patrol to halt again issued forth. "Let me see your faces." Raising his head, Eragon saw a man sitting before them on a roan charger, his gloved hands folded over the pommel of his saddle. Upon his upper lip there sprouted an enormous curly mustache that, after descending to the corners of his mouth, extended a good nine inches in either direction and was in stark contrast to the straight hair that fell to his shoulders. How such a massive piece of sculpted foliage supported its own weight puzzled Eragon, especially since it was dull and lusterless and obviously had not been impregnated with warm beeswax.

The other soldiers held spears pointed at Eragon and Arya. So much dirt covered them, it was impossible to see the flames stitched on their tunics.

"Now then," said the man, and his mustache wobbled like an unbalanced set of scales. "Who are you? Where are you going? And what is your business in the king's lands?" Then he waved a hand. "No, don't bother answering. It doesn't matter. Nothing matters nowadays. The world is coming to an end, and we waste our days interrogating peasants. Bah! Superstitious vermin who scurry from place to place, devouring all the food in the land and reproducing at a ghastly rate. At my family's estate near Urû'baen, we would have the likes of you flogged if we caught you wandering around without permission, and if we learned that you had stolen from your master, why, then we'd hang you. Whatever you want to tell me is lies. It always is. . . .

"What have you got in that pack of yours, eh? Food and blankets, yes, but maybe a pair of gold candlesticks, eh? Silverware from the locked chest? Secret letters for the Varden? Eh? Cat got your tongue? Well, we'll soon sort the matter out. Langward, why don't you see what treasures you can excavate from yonder knapsack, there's a good boy."

Eragon staggered forward as one of the soldiers struck him across the back with the haft of a spear. He had wrapped his armor in rags to keep the pieces from rubbing against each other. The rags, however, were too thin to entirely absorb the force of the blow and muffle the clang of metal.

"Oho!" exclaimed the man with the mustache.

Grabbing Eragon from behind, the soldier unlaced the top of his pack and pulled out his hauberk, saying, "Look, sir!"

The man with the mustache broke out in a delighted grin. "Armor! And of fine make as well. Very fine, I should say. Well, you *are* full of surprises. Going to join the Varden, were you? Intent on treason and sedition, mmh?" His expression soured. "Or are you one of those who generally give honest soldiers a bad name? If so, you are a most incompetent mercenary; you don't even have a weapon. Was it too much trouble to cut yourself a staff or a club, eh? Well, how about it? Answer me!"

"No, sir."

"No, sir? Didn't occur to you, I suppose. It's a pity we have to accept such slow-minded wretches, but that's what this blasted war has reduced us to, scrounging for leftovers."

"Accept me where, sir?"

"Silence, you insolent rascal! No one gave you permission to speak!" His mustache quivering, the man gestured. Red lights exploded across Eragon's field of vision as the soldier behind him bashed him on the head. "Whether you are a thief, a traitor, a mercenary, or merely a fool, your fate will be the same. Once you swear the oath of service, you will have no choice but to obey Galbatorix and those who speak for him. We are the first army in history to be free of dissent. No mindless blathering about what we should do. Only orders, clear and direct. You too shall join our cause, and you shall have the privilege of helping to make real the glorious future our great king has foreseen. As for your lovely companion, there are other ways she can be of use to the Empire, eh? Now tie them up!"

Eragon knew then what he had to do. Glancing over, he found Arya already looking at him, her eyes hard and bright. He blinked once. She blinked in return. His hand tightened around the pebble.

Most of the soldiers Eragon had fought on the Burning Plains had possessed certain rudimentary wards intended to shield them from magical attacks, and he suspected these men were likewise equipped. He was confident he could break or circumvent any spells Galbatorix's magicians invented, but it would require more time than he now had. Instead, he cocked his arm and, with a flick of his wrist, threw the pebble at the man with the mustache.

The pebble punctured the side of his helm.

Before the soldiers could react, Eragon twisted around, yanked the spear from the hands of the man who had been tormenting him, and used it to knock him off his horse. As the man landed, Eragon stabbed him through the heart, breaking the blade of the spear on the metal plates of the soldier's gambeson. Releasing the spear, Eragon dove backward, his body parallel with the ground as he passed underneath seven spears that were flying toward where he had been. The lethal shafts seemed to float above him as he fell.

The instant Eragon had released the pebble, Arya bounded up the side of the horse nearest her, jumping from stirrup to saddle, and kicked the head of the oblivious soldier who was perched on the mare. He went hurtling more than thirty feet. Then Arya leaped from the back of horse to horse, killing the soldiers with her knees, her feet, and her hands in an incredible display of grace and balance.

Jagged rocks tore at Eragon's stomach as he tumbled to a stop. Grimacing, he sprang upright. Four soldiers who had dismounted confronted him with drawn swords. They charged. Dodging to the right, he caught the first soldier's wrist as the man swung his sword and punched him in the armpit. The man collapsed and was still. Eragon dispatched his next opponents by twisting their heads until their spines snapped. The fourth soldier was so close by then, running at him with sword held high, Eragon could not evade him.

Trapped, he did the one thing he could: he struck the man in the chest with all his might. A fount of blood and sweat erupted as his fist connected. The blow staved in the man's ribs and propelled him more than a dozen feet over the grass, where he fetched up against another corpse.

Eragon gasped and doubled over, cradling his throbbing hand. Four of his knuckles were disjointed, and white cartilage showed through his mangled skin. *Blast,* he thought as hot blood poured from the wounds. His fingers refused to move when he ordered them to; he realized that his hand would be useless until he could heal it. Fearing another attack, he looked around for Arya and the rest of the soldiers.

The horses had scattered. Only three soldiers remained alive. Arya was grappling with two of them some distance away while the

third and final soldier fled south along the road. Gathering his strength, Eragon pursued him. As he narrowed the gap between them, the man began to plead for mercy, promising he would tell no one about the massacre and holding out his hands to show they were empty. When Eragon was within arm's reach, the man veered to the side and then a few steps later changed direction again, darting back and forth across the countryside like a frightened jackrabbit. All the while, the man continued to beg, tears streaming down his cheeks, saying that he was too young to die, that he had yet to marry and father a child, that his parents would miss him, and that he had been pressed into the army and this was only his fifth mission and why couldn't Eragon leave him alone? "What have you against me?" he sobbed. "I only did what I had to. I'm a good person!"

Eragon paused and forced himself to say: "You can't keep up with us. We can't leave you; you'll catch a horse and betray us."

"No, I won't!"

"People will ask what happened here. Your oath to Galbatorix and the Empire won't let you lie. I'm sorry, but I don't know how to release you from your bond, except . . ."

"Why are you doing this? You're a monster!" screamed the man. With an expression of pure terror, he made an attempt to dash around Eragon and return to the road. Eragon overtook him in less than ten feet, and as the man was still crying and asking for clemency, Eragon wrapped his left hand around his neck and squeezed. When he relaxed his grip, the soldier fell across his feet, dead.

Bile coated Eragon's tongue as he stared down at the man's slack face. *Whenever we kill, we kill a part of ourselves*, he thought. Shaking with a combination of shock, pain, and self-loathing, he walked back to where the fight had begun. Arya was kneeling beside a body, washing her hands and arms with water from a tin flask one of the soldiers had been carrying.

"How is it," asked Arya, "you could kill that man, but you could not bring yourself to lay a finger on Sloan?" She stood and faced him, her gaze frank.

Devoid of emotion, he shrugged. "He was a threat. Sloan wasn't. Isn't it obvious?"

Arya was quiet for a while. "It ought to be, but it isn't. . . . I am ashamed to be instructed in morality by one with so much less experience. Perhaps I have been too certain, too confident of my own choices."

Eragon heard her speak, but the words meant nothing to him as his gaze drifted over the corpses. *Is this all my life has become?* he wondered. *A never-ending series of battles?* "I feel like a murderer."

"I understand how difficult this is," said Arya. "Remember, Eragon, you have experienced only a small part of what it means to be a Dragon Rider. Eventually, this war will end, and you will see that your duties encompass more than violence. The Riders were not just warriors, they were teachers, healers, and scholars."

His jaw muscles knotted for a moment. "Why are we fighting these men, Arya?"

"Because they stand between us and Galbatorix."

"Then we should find a way to strike at Galbatorix directly."

"None exist. We cannot march to Urû'baen until we defeat his forces. And we cannot enter his castle until we disarm almost a century's worth of traps, magical and otherwise."

"There has to be a way," he muttered. He remained where he was as Arya strode forward and picked up a spear. But when she placed the tip of the spear under the chin of a slain soldier and thrust it into his skull, Eragon sprang toward her and pushed her away from the body. "What are you doing?" he shouted.

Anger flashed across Arya's face. "I will forgive that only because you are distraught and not of your right mind. Think, Eragon! It is too late in the day for anyone to be coddling you. Why is this necessary?"

The answer presented itself to him, and he grudgingly said, "If we don't, the Empire will notice that most of the men were killed by hand."

"Exactly! The only ones capable of such a feat are elves, Riders, and Kull. And since even an imbecile could figure out a Kull was not responsible for this, they'll soon know we are in the area, and in less than a day, Thorn and Murtagh will be flying overhead, searching for us." There was a wet squelch as she pulled the spear out of the body. She held it out to him until he accepted it. "I find this as repulsive as you do, so you might as well make yourself useful and help."

Eragon nodded. Then Arya scavenged a sword, and together they set out to make it appear as if a troop of ordinary warriors had killed the soldiers. It was grisly work, but it went quickly, for they both knew exactly what kinds of wounds the soldiers should have to ensure the success of the deception, and neither of them wished to linger. When they came to the man whose chest Eragon had destroyed, Arya said, "There's little we can do to disguise an injury like that. We will have to leave it as is and hope people assume a horse stepped on him." They moved on. The last soldier they dealt with was the commander of the patrol. His mustache was now limp and torn and had lost most of its former splendor.

After enlarging the pebble hole so it more closely resembled the triangular pit left by the spike of a war hammer, Eragon rested for a moment, contemplating the commander's sad mustache, then said, "He was right, you know."

"About what?"

"I need a weapon, a proper weapon. I need a sword." Wiping his palms on the edge of his tunic, he surveyed the plain around them, counting the bodies. "That's it, then, isn't it? We're done." He went and collected his scattered armor, rewrapped it in cloth, and returned it to the bottom of his pack. Then he joined Arya on the low hillock she had climbed.

"We had best avoid the roads from now on," she said. "We cannot risk another encounter with Galbatorix's men." Indicating his deformed right hand, which stained his tunic with blood, she said, "You should tend to that before we set forth." She gave him no time to respond but grasped his paralyzed fingers and said, "Waíse heill."

An involuntary groan escaped him as his fingers popped back into their sockets, and as his abraded tendons and crushed cartilage regained the fullness of their proper shapes, and as the flaps of skin hanging from his knuckles again covered the raw flesh below. When the spell ended, he opened and closed his hand to confirm that it was fully cured. "Thank you," he said. It surprised him that she had taken the initiative when he was perfectly capable of healing his own wounds.

Arya seemed embarrassed. Looking away, out over the plains, she said, "I am glad you were by my side today, Eragon."

"And you by mine."

She favored him with a quick, uncertain smile. They lingered on the hillock for another minute, neither of them eager to resume their journey. Then Arya sighed and said, "We should be off. The shadows lengthen, and someone else is bound to appear and raise a hue and cry when they discover this crows' feast."

Abandoning the hillock, they orientated themselves in a south-westerly direction, angling away from the road, and loped out across the uneven sea of grass. Behind them, the first of the carrion eaters dropped from the sky.

SHADOWS OF THE PAST

That night, Eragon sat staring at their meager fire, chewing on a dandelion leaf. Their dinner had consisted of an assortment of roots, seeds, and greens that Arya had gathered from the surrounding countryside. Eaten uncooked and unseasoned, they were hardly appetizing, but he had refrained from augmenting the meal with a bird or rabbit, of which there was an abundance in the immediate vicinity, for he did not wish Arya to regard him with disapproval. Moreover, after their fight with the soldiers, the thought of taking another life, even an animal's, sickened him.

It was late, and they would have to get an early start the next morning, but he made no move to retire, nor did Arya. She was situated at right angles to him, her legs pulled up, with her arms wrapped around them and her chin resting on her knees. The skirt of her dress spread outward, like the wind-battered petals of a flower.

His chin sunk low against his chest, Eragon massaged his right hand with his left, trying to dispel a deep-seated ache. *I need a sword,* he thought. *Short of that, I could use some sort of protection for my hands so I don't cripple myself whenever I hit something. The problem is, I'm so strong now, I would have to wear gloves with several inches of padding, which is ridiculous. They would be too bulky, too hot, and what's more, I can't go around with gloves on for the rest of my life.* He frowned. Pushing the bones of his hand out of their normal positions, he studied how they altered the play of light over his skin, fascinated by the malleability of his body. *And what happens if I get in a fight while I'm wearing Brom's ring? It's of elvish make, so I probably don't have to worry about breaking the sapphire. But if I hit anything with the ring on my finger, I won't just dislocate a few joints, I'll splinter every bone in my hand. . . . I might not even be able to repair the damage. . . .* He tightened his hands into fists and slowly turned them from side to side, watching the shadows deepen and fade between his knuckles. *I could invent a spell that would stop any object that was moving at a dangerous speed from touching my hands. No, wait, that's no good. What if it was a boulder? What if it was a mountain? I'd kill myself trying to stop it.*

Well, if gloves and magic won't work, I'd like to have a set of the dwarves' Ascûdgamln, their "fists of steel." With a smile, he remembered how the dwarf Shrrgnien had a steel spike threaded into a metal base that was embedded in each of his knuckles, excluding those on his thumbs. The spikes allowed Shrrgnien to hit whatever he wanted with little fear of pain, and they were convenient too, for he could remove them at will. The concept appealed to Eragon, but he was not about to start drilling holes in his knuckles. *Besides,* he thought, *my bones are thinner than dwarf bones, too thin, perhaps, to attach the base and still have the joints function as they should. . . . So Ascûdgamln are a bad idea, but maybe instead I can . . .*

Bending low over his hands, he whispered, "Thaefathan."

The backs of his hands began to crawl and prickle as if he had fallen into a patch of stinging nettles. The sensation was so intense and so unpleasant, he longed to jump up and scratch himself as hard as he could. With an effort of will, he stayed where he was and watched as the skin on his knuckles bulged, forming a flat, whitish callus half an inch thick over each joint. They reminded him of the hornlike deposits that appear on the inside of horses' legs. When he was pleased with the size and density of the knobs, he released the flow of magic and set about exploring, by touch and sight, the mountainous new terrain that loomed over his fingers.

His hands were heavier and stiffer than before, but he could still move his fingers through their full range of motion. *It may be ugly,* he thought, rubbing the rough protuberances on his right hand against the palm of his left, *and people may laugh and sneer if*

*they notice, but I don't care, for it will serve its purpose and may keep
me alive.*

Brimming with silent excitement, he struck the top of a domed
rock that rose out of the ground between his legs. The impact jarred
his arm and produced a muted thud but caused him no more discomfort than it would have to punch a board covered with several
layers of cloth. Emboldened, he retrieved Brom's ring from his pack
and slipped on the cool gold band, checking that the adjacent callus was higher than the face of the ring. He tested his observation by
again ramming his fist against the rock. The only resulting sound
was that of dry, compacted skin colliding with unyielding stone.

"What are you doing?" asked Arya, peering at him through a veil
of her black hair.

"Nothing." Then he held out his hands. "I thought it would be a
good idea, since I'll probably have to hit someone again."

Arya studied his knuckles. "You are going to have difficulty wearing gloves."

"I can always cut them open to make room."

She nodded and returned to gazing at the fire.

Eragon leaned back on his elbows and stretched out his legs, content that he was prepared for whatever fights might await him in the
immediate future. Beyond that, he dared not speculate, for if he did,
he would begin to ask himself how he and Saphira could possibly
defeat Murtagh or Galbatorix, and then panic would sink its icy
claws into him.

He fixed his gaze on the flickering depths of the fire. There, in
that writhing inferno, he sought to forget his cares and responsibilities. But the constant motion of the flames soon lulled him into a
passive state where unrelated fragments of thoughts, sounds, images, and emotions drifted through him like snowflakes falling from
a calm winter's sky. And amid that flurry, there appeared the face of
the soldier who had begged for his life. Again Eragon saw him crying, and again he heard his desperate pleas, and again he felt how
his neck snapped like a wet branch of wood.

Tormented by the memories, Eragon clenched his teeth and breathed hard through flared nostrils. Cold sweat sprang up over his entire body. He shifted in place and strove to dispel the soldier's unfriendly ghost, but to no avail. *Go away!* he shouted. *It wasn't my fault. Galbatorix is the one you should blame, not me. I didn't want to kill you!*

Somewhere in the darkness surrounding them, a wolf howled. From various locations across the plains, a score of other wolves answered, raising their voices in a discordant melody. The eerie singing made Eragon's scalp tingle and goosebumps break out on his arms. Then, for a brief moment, the howls coalesced into a single tone that was similar to the battle-cry of a charging Kull.

Eragon shifted, uneasy.

"What's wrong?" asked Arya. "Is it the wolves? They shall not bother us, you know. They are teaching their pups how to hunt, and they won't allow their younglings near creatures who smell as strangely as we do."

"It's not the wolves out there," said Eragon, hugging himself. "It's the wolves in here." He tapped the middle of his forehead.

Arya nodded, a sharp, birdlike motion that betrayed the fact she was not human, even though she had assumed the shape of one. "It is always thus. The monsters of the mind are far worse than those that actually exist. Fear, doubt, and hate have hamstrung more people than beasts ever have."

"And love," he pointed out.

"And love," she admitted. "Also greed and jealousy and every other obsessive urge the sentient races are susceptible to."

Eragon thought of Tenga alone, in the ruined elf outpost of Edur Ithindra, hunched over his precious hoard of tomes, searching, always searching, for his elusive "answer." He refrained from mentioning the hermit to Arya, for it was not in him to discuss that curious encounter at the present. Instead, he asked, "Does it bother you when you kill?"

Arya's green eyes narrowed. "Neither I nor the rest of my people eat the flesh of animals because we cannot bear to hurt another creature to satisfy our hunger, and you have the effrontery to ask if killing disturbs us? Do you really understand so little of us that you believe we are coldhearted murderers?"

"No, of course not," he protested. "That's not what I meant."

"Then say what you mean, and do not give insult unless it is your intention."

Choosing his words with greater care now, Eragon said, "I asked this of Roran before we attacked Helgrind, or a question very like it. What I want to know is, how do you feel when you kill? How are you supposed to feel?" He scowled at the fire. "Do you see the warriors you have vanquished staring back at you, as real as you are before me?"

Arya tightened her arms around her legs, her gaze pensive. A flame jetted upward as the fire incinerated one of the moths circling the camp. "Gánga," she murmured, and motioned with a finger. With a flutter of downy wings, the moths departed. Never lifting her eyes from the clump of burning branches, she said, "Nine months after I became an ambassador, my mother's only ambassador, if truth be told, I traveled from the Varden in Farthen Dûr to the capital of Surda, which was still a new country in those days. Soon after my companions and I left the Beor Mountains, we encountered a band of roving Urgals. We were content to keep our swords in their sheaths and continue on our way, but as is their wont, the Urgals insisted on trying to win honor and glory to better their standing within their tribes. Our force was larger than theirs—for Weldon, the man who succeeded Brom as leader of the Varden, was with us—and it was easy for us to drive them off. . . . That day was the first time I took a life. It troubled me for weeks afterward, until I realized I would go mad if I continued to dwell upon it. Many do, and they become so angry, so grief-ridden, they can no longer be relied upon, or their hearts turn to stone and they lose the ability to distinguish right from wrong."

"How did you come to terms with what you had done?"

"I examined my reasons for killing to determine if they were just. Satisfied they were, I asked myself if our cause was important enough to continue supporting it, even though it would probably require me to kill again. Then I decided that whenever I began to think of the dead, I would picture myself in the gardens of Tialdarí Hall."

"Did it work?"

Brushing her hair out of her face, she tucked it behind one round ear. "It did. The only antidote for the corrosive poison of violence is finding peace within yourself. It's a difficult cure to obtain, but well worth the effort." She paused and then added, "Breathing helps too."

"Breathing?"

"Slow, regular breathing, as if you were meditating. It is one of the most effective methods for calming yourself."

Following her advice, Eragon began to consciously inhale and exhale, taking care to maintain a steady tempo and to expel all the air from his lungs with each breath. Within a minute, the knot inside his gut loosened, his frown eased, and the presence of his fallen enemies no longer seemed quite so tangible. . . . The wolves howled again, and after an initial burst of trepidation, he listened without fear, for their baying had lost the power to unsettle him. "Thank you," he said. Arya responded with a gracious tilt of her chin.

Silence reigned for a quarter of an hour until Eragon said, "Urgals." He let the statement stand for a while, a verbal monolith of ambivalence. "What do you think about Nasuada allowing them to join the Varden?"

Arya picked up a twig by the edge of her splayed dress and rolled it between her aquiline fingers, studying the crooked piece of wood as if it contained a secret. "It was a courageous decision, and I admire her for it. She always acts in the best interests of the Varden, no matter what the cost may be."

"She upset many of the Varden when she accepted Nar Garzhvog's offer of support."

"And she won back their loyalty with the Trial of the Long Knives. Nasuada is very clever when it comes to maintaining her position." Arya flicked the twig into the fire. "I have no love for Urgals, but neither do I hate them. Unlike the Ra'zac, they are not inherently evil, merely overfond of war. It is an important distinction, even if it can provide no consolation to the families of their victims. We elves have treated with Urgals before, and we shall again when the need arises. It is a futile prospect, however."

She did not have to explain why. Many of the scrolls Oromis had assigned Eragon to read were devoted to the subject of Urgals, and one in particular, *The Travels of Gnaevaldrskald*, had taught him that the Urgals' entire culture was based upon feats of combat. Male Urgals could only improve their standing by raiding another village—whether Urgal, human, elf, or dwarf mattered little—or by fighting their rivals one on one, sometimes to the death. And when it came to picking a mate, Urgal females refused to consider a ram eligible unless he had defeated at least three opponents. As a result, each new generation of Urgals had no choice but to challenge their peers, challenge their elders, and scour the land for opportunities to prove their valor. The tradition was so deeply ingrained, every attempt to suppress it had failed. *At least they are true to who they are*, mused Eragon. *That's more than most humans can claim.*

"How is it," he asked, "that Durza was able to ambush you, Glenwing, and Fäolin with Urgals? Didn't you have wards to protect yourself against physical attacks?"

"The arrows were enchanted."

"Were the Urgals spellcasters, then?"

Closing her eyes, Arya sighed and shook her head. "No. It was some dark magic of Durza's invention. He gloated about it when I was in Gil'ead."

"I don't know how you managed to resist him for so long. I saw what he did to you."

"It . . . it was not easy. I viewed the torments he inflicted on me as a test of my commitment, as a chance to demonstrate that I had not made a mistake and I was indeed worthy of the yawë symbol. As such, I welcomed the ordeal."

"But still, even elves are not immune to pain. It's amazing you could keep the location of Ellesméra hidden from him all those months."

A touch of pride colored her voice. "Not just the location of Ellesméra but also where I had sent Saphira's egg, my vocabulary in the ancient language, and everything else that might be of use to Galbatorix."

The conversation lapsed, and then Eragon said, "Do you think about it much, what you went through in Gil'ead?" When she did not respond, he added, "You never talk about it. You recount the facts of your imprisonment readily enough, but you never mention what it was like for you, nor how you feel about it now."

"Pain is pain," she said. "It needs no description."

"True, but ignoring it can cause more harm than the original injury. . . . No one can live through something like that and escape unscathed. Not on the inside, at least."

"Why do you assume I have not already confided in someone?"

"Who?"

"Does it matter? Ajihad, my mother, a friend in Ellesméra."

"Perhaps I am wrong," he said, "but you do not seem that close to anyone. Where you walk, you walk alone, even among your own people."

Arya's countenance remained impassive. Her lack of expression was so complete, Eragon began to wonder if she would deign to respond, a doubt that had just transformed into conviction when she whispered, "It was not always so."

Alert, Eragon waited without moving, afraid that whatever he might do would stop her from saying more.

"Once, I had someone to talk to, someone who understood what I was and where I came from. Once . . . He was older than I, but we were kindred spirits, both curious about the world outside our forest, eager to explore and eager to strike against Galbatorix. Neither of us could bear to stay in Du Weldenvarden—studying, working magic, pursuing our own personal projects—when we knew the Dragon Killer, the bane of the Riders, was searching for a way to conquer our race. He came to that conclusion later than I—decades after I assumed my position as ambassador and a few years before Hefring stole Saphira's egg—but the moment he did, he volunteered to accompany me wherever Islanzadí's orders might take me." She blinked, and her throat convulsed. "I wasn't going to let him, but the queen liked the idea, and he was so very convincing. . . ." She pursed her lips and blinked again, her eyes brighter than normal.

As gently as he could, Eragon asked, "Was it Fäolin?"

"Yes," she said, releasing the confirmation almost as a gasp.

"Did you love him?"

Casting back her head, Arya gazed up at the twinkling sky, her long neck gold with firelight, her face pale with the radiance of the heavens. "Do you ask out of friendly concern or your own self-interest?" She gave an abrupt, choked laugh, the sound of water falling over cold rocks. "Never mind. The night air has addled me. It has undone my sense of courtesy and left me free to say the most spiteful things that occur to me."

"No matter."

"It does matter, because I regret it, and I shall not tolerate it. Did I love Fäolin? How would you define love? For over twenty years, we traveled together, the only immortals to walk among the short-lived races. We were companions . . . and friends."

A pang of jealousy afflicted Eragon. He wrestled with it, subdued it, and tried to eliminate it but was not altogether successful. A slight remnant of the feeling continued to aggravate him, like a splinter burrowing underneath his skin.

"Over twenty years," repeated Arya. Persisting in her survey of the constellations, she rocked back and forth, seemingly oblivious to Eragon. "And then in a single instant, Durza tore that away from me. Fäolin and Glenwing were the first elves to die in combat for nearly a century. When I saw Fäolin fall, I understood then that the true agony of war isn't being wounded yourself, it's having to watch those you care about being hurt. It was a lesson I thought I had already learned during my time with the Varden when, one after another, the men and women I had come to respect died from swords, arrows, poison, accidents, and old age. The loss had never been so personal, however, and when it happened, I thought, 'Now I must surely die as well.' For whatever danger we had encountered before, Fäolin and I had always survived it together, and if he could not escape, then why should I?"

Eragon realized she was crying, thick tears rolling from the outer corners of her eyes, down her temples, and into her hair. By the stars, her tears appeared like rivers of silvered glass. The intensity of her distress startled him. He had not thought it was possible to elicit such a reaction from her, nor had he intended to.

"Then Gil'ead," she said. "Those days were the longest of my life. Fäolin was gone, I did not know whether Saphira's egg was safe or if I had inadvertently returned her to Galbatorix, and Durza . . . Durza sated the bloodlust of the spirits that controlled him by doing the most horrible things he could imagine to me. Sometimes, if he went too far, he would heal me so he could begin anew the following morning. If he had given me a chance to collect my wits, I might have been able to fool my jailer, as you did, and avoid consuming the drug that kept me from using magic, but I never had more than a few hours' respite.

"Durza needed sleep no more than you or I, and he kept at me whenever I was conscious and his other duties permitted. While he worked on me, every second was an hour, every hour a week, and every day an eternity. He was careful not to drive me mad—Galbatorix would have been displeased with that—but he came close. He came very, very close. I began to hear birdsong where no birds could fly and to see things that could not exist. Once, when I was in my cell, gold light flooded the room and I grew warm all over. When I looked up, I found myself lying on a branch high in a tree

198

near the center of Ellesméra. The sun was about to set, and the whole city glowed as if it were on fire. The Äthalvard were chanting on the path below, and everything was so calm, so peaceful . . . so beautiful, I would have stayed there forever. But then the light faded, and I was again on my cot. . . . I had forgotten, but once there was a soldier who left a white rose in my cell. It was the only kindness anyone ever showed me in Gil'ead. That night, the flower took root and matured into a huge rosebush that climbed the wall, forced its way between the blocks of stone in the ceiling, breaking them, and pushed its way out of the dungeon and into the open. It continued to ascend until it touched the moon and stood as a great, twisting tower that promised escape if I could but lift myself off the floor. I tried with every ounce of my remaining strength, but it was beyond me, and when I glanced away, the rosebush vanished. . . . That was my state of mind when you dreamed of me and I felt your presence hovering over me. Small wonder I disregarded the sensation as another delusion."

She gave him a wan smile. "And then you came, Eragon. You and Saphira. After hope had deserted me and I was about to be taken to Galbatorix in Urû'baen, a Rider appeared to rescue me. A Rider and dragon!"

"And Morzan's son," he said. "*Both* of Morzan's sons."

"Describe it how you will, it was such an improbable rescue, I occasionally think that I did go mad and that I've imagined everything since."

"Would you have imagined me causing so much trouble by staying behind at Helgrind?"

"No," she said. "I suppose not." With the cuff of her left sleeve, she dabbed her eyes, drying them. "When I awoke in Farthen Dûr, there was too much that needed doing for me to dwell on the past. But events of late have been dark and bloody, and increasingly I have found myself remembering that which I should not. It makes me grim and out of sorts, without patience for the ordinary delays of life." She shifted into a kneeling position and placed her hands on the ground on either side of her, as if to steady herself. "You say I walk alone. Elves do not incline toward the open displays of friendship humans and dwarves favor, and I have ever been of a solitary disposition. But if you had known me before Gil'ead, if you had known me as I was, you would not have considered me so aloof. Then I could sing and dance and not feel threatened by a sense of impending doom."

Reaching out, Eragon placed his right hand over her left. "The stories about the heroes of old never mention that this is the price you pay when you grapple with the monsters of the dark and the monsters of the mind. Keep thinking about the gardens of Tialdarí Hall, and I'm sure you will be fine."

Arya permitted the contact between them to endure for almost a minute, a time not of heat or passion for Eragon, but rather of quiet companionship. He made no attempt to press his suit with her, for he cherished her trust more than anything besides his bond with Saphira and he would sooner march into battle than endanger it. Then, with a slight lift of her arm, Arya let him know the moment had passed, and without complaint he withdrew his hand.

Eager to lighten her burden however he could, Eragon glanced about the ground nearest him and then murmured so softly as to be inaudible, "Loivissa." Guided by the power of the true name, he sifted through the earth by his feet until his fingers closed upon what he sought: a thin, papery disk half the size of his smallest fingernail. Holding his breath, he deposited it in his right palm, centering it over his gedwëy ignasia with as much delicacy as he could muster. He reviewed what Oromis had taught him concerning the sort of spell he was about to cast to ensure he would not make a mistake, and then he began to sing after the fashion of the elves, smooth and flowing:

Eldhrimner O Loivissa nuanen, dautr abr deloi,
Eldhrimner nen ono weohnataí medh solus un thringa,

Eldhrimner un fortha onr fëon vara,
Wiol allr sjon.

Eldhrimner O Loivissa nuanen . . .

Again and again, Eragon repeated the same four lines, directing them toward the brown flake in his hand. The flake trembled and then swelled and bulged, becoming spherical. White tendrils an inch or two long sprouted from the bottom of the peeling globe, tickling Eragon, while a thin green stem poked its way out of the tip and, at his urging, shot nearly a foot in the air. A single leaf, broad and flat, grew from the side of the stem. Then the tip of the stem thickened, drooped, and, after a moment of seeming inactivity, split into five segments that expanded outward to reveal the waxy petals of a deep-throated lily. The flower was pale blue and shaped like a bell.

When it reached its full size, Eragon released the magic and examined his handiwork. Singing plants into shape was a skill most every elf mastered at an early age, but it was one Eragon had practiced only a few times, and he had been uncertain whether his efforts would meet with success. The spell had exacted a heavy toll from him; the lily required a surprising amount of energy to feed what was the equivalent of a year and a half of growth.

Satisfied with what he had wrought, he handed the lily to Arya. "It's not a white rose, but . . ." He smiled and shrugged.

"You should not have," she said. "But I am glad you did." She caressed the underside of the blossom and lifted it to smell. The lines on her face eased. For several minutes, she admired the lily. Then she scooped a hole in the soil next to her and planted the bulb, pressing down the soil with the flat of her hand. She touched the petals again and kept glancing at the lily as she said, "Thank you. Giving flowers is a custom both our races share, but we elves attach greater importance to the practice than do humans. It signifies all that is good: life, beauty, rebirth, friendship, and more. I explain so you understand how much this means to me. You did not know, but—"

"I knew."

Arya regarded him with a solemn countenance, as if to decide what he was about. "Forgive me. That is twice now I have forgotten the extent of your education. I shall not make the mistake again."

She repeated her thanks in the ancient language, and—joining her in her native tongue—Eragon replied that it was his pleasure and he was happy she enjoyed his gift. He shivered, hungry despite the meal they had just eaten. Noticing, Arya said, "You used too much of your strength. If you have any energy left in Aren, use it to steady yourself."

It took Eragon a moment to remember that Aren was the name of Brom's ring; he had heard it uttered only once before, from Islanzadí, on the day he arrived in Ellesméra. *My ring now,* he told himself. *I have to stop thinking of it as Brom's.* He cast a critical gaze at

the large sapphire that sparkled in its gold setting on his finger. "I don't know if there *is* any energy in Aren. I've never stored any there myself, and I never checked if Brom had." Even as he spoke, he extended his consciousness toward the sapphire. The instant his mind came into contact with the gem, he felt the presence of a vast, swirling pool of energy. To his inner eye, the sapphire thrummed with power. He wondered that it did not explode from the amount of force contained within the boundaries of its sharp-edged facets. After he used the energy to wash away his aches and pains and re-store strength to his limbs, the treasure trove inside Aren was hardly diminished.

His skin tingling, Eragon severed his link with the gem. Delighted by his discovery and his sudden sense of well-being, he laughed out loud, then told Arya what he had found. "Brom must have squirreled away every bit of energy he could spare the whole time he was hiding in Carvahall." He laughed again, marveling. "All those years . . . With what's in Aren, I could tear apart an en-tire castle with a single spell."

"He knew he would need it to keep the new Rider safe when Saphira hatched," observed Arya. "Also, I am sure Aren was a way for him to protect himself if he had to fight a Shade or some other similarly powerful opponent. It was not by accident that he managed to frustrate his enemies for the better part of a century. . . . If I were you, I would save the energy he left you for your hour of greatest need, and I would add to it whenever I could. It is an incredibly valuable resource. You should not squander it."

No, thought Eragon, *that I will not.* He twirled the ring around his finger, admiring how it gleamed in the firelight. *Since Murtagh stole Zar'roc, this, Saphira's saddle, and Snowfire are the only things I have of Brom, and even though the dwarves brought Snowfire from Farthen Dûr, I rarely ride him nowadays. Aren is really all I have to remember him by. . . . My only legacy of him. My only inheritance. I wish he were still alive! I never had a chance to talk with him about Oromis, Murtagh, my father. . . . Oh, the list is endless. What would he have said about my feelings for Arya?* Eragon snorted to himself. *I know what he would have said: he would have berated me for being a love-struck fool and for wasting my energy on a hopeless cause. . . . And he would have been right too, I suppose, but, ah, how can I help it? She is the only woman I wish to be with.*

The fire cracked. A flurry of sparks flew upward. Eragon watched with half-closed eyes, contemplating Arya's revelations. Then his mind returned to a question that had been bothering him ever since the battle on the Burning Plains. "Arya, do male dragons grow any faster than female dragons?"

"No. Why do you ask?"

"Because of Thorn. He's only a few months old, and yet he's already nearly as big as Saphira. I don't understand it."

Picking a dry blade of grass, Arya began sketching in the loose soil, tracing the curved shapes of glyphs from the elves' script, the Liduen Kvaedhí. "Most likely Galbatorix accelerated his growth so Thorn would be large enough to hold his own with Saphira."

"Ah. . . . Isn't that dangerous, though? Oromis told me that if he used magic to give me the strength, speed, endurance, and other skills I needed, I would not understand my new abilities as well as if I had gained them the ordinary way: by hard work. He was right too. Even now, the changes the dragons made to my body during the Agaetí Blödhren still sometimes catch me by surprise."

Arya nodded and continued sketching glyphs in the dirt. "It is possible to reduce the undesirable side effects by certain spells, but it is a long and arduous process. If you wish to achieve true mastery of your body, it is still best to do so through normal means. The transformation Galbatorix has forced upon Thorn must be incredibly confusing for him. Thorn now has the body of a nearly grown dragon, and yet his mind is still that of a youngling."

Eragon fingered the newly formed calluses on his knuckles. "Do you also know why Murtagh is so powerful . . . more powerful than I am?"

"If I did, no doubt I would also understand how Galbatorix has managed to increase his own strength to such unnatural heights, but alas, I do not."

But Oromis does, Eragon thought. Or at least the elf had hinted as much. However, he had yet to share the information with Eragon and Saphira. As soon as they were able to return to Du Weldenvarden, Eragon intended to ask the elder Rider for the truth of the matter. *He has to tell us now! Because of our ignorance, Murtagh defeated us, and he could have easily taken us to Galbatorix.* Eragon almost mentioned Oromis's comments to Arya but held his tongue, for he realized that Oromis would not have concealed such an important fact for over a hundred years unless secrecy was of the utmost importance.

Arya signed a stop to the sentence she had been writing on the ground. Bending over, Eragon read, *Adrift upon the sea of time, the lonely god wanders from shore to distant shore, upholding the laws of the stars above.*

"What does it mean?"

"I don't know," she said, and smoothed out the line with a sweep of her arm.

"Why is it," he asked, speaking slowly as he organized his thoughts, "that no one ever refers to the dragons of the Forsworn by name? We say 'Morzan's dragon' or 'Kialandí's dragon,' but we never actually name the dragon. Surely they were as important as their Riders! I don't even remember seeing their names in the scrolls Oromis gave me . . . although they *must* have been there. . . . Yes, I'm certain they were, but for some reason, they don't stick in my head. Isn't that strange?" Arya started to answer, but before she could do more than open her mouth, he said, "For once I'm glad Saphira's not here. I'm ashamed I haven't noticed this before. Even you, Arya, and Oromis and every other elf I've met refuse to call them by name, as if they were dumb animals, undeserving of the honor. Do you do it on purpose? Is it because they were your enemies?"

"Did none of your lessons speak of this?" asked Arya. She seemed genuinely surprised.

"I think," he said, "Glaedr mentioned something about it to Saphira, but I'm not exactly sure. I was in the middle of a backbend during the Dance of Snake and Crane, so I wasn't really paying attention to what Saphira was doing." He laughed a little, embarrassed by his lapse and feeling as if he had to explain himself. "It got confusing at times. Oromis would be talking to me while I was listening to Saphira's thoughts while she and Glaedr communicated with their minds. What's worse, Glaedr rarely uses a recognizable language with Saphira; he tends to use images, smells, and feelings, rather than words. Instead of names, he sends impressions of the people and objects he means."

"Do you recall nothing of what he said, whether with words or not?"

Eragon hesitated. "Only that it concerned a name that was no name, or some such. I couldn't make heads or tails out of it."

"What he spoke of," said Arya, "was Du Namar Aurboda, The Banishing of the Names."

"The Banishing of the Names?"

Touching her dry blade of grass to the ground, she resumed writing in the dirt. "It is one of the most significant events that happened during the fighting between the Riders and the Forsworn. When the dragons realized that thirteen of their own had betrayed them—that those thirteen were helping Galbatorix to eradicate the rest of their race and that it was unlikely anyone could stop their rampage—the dragons grew so angry, every dragon not of the Forsworn combined their strength and wrought one of their inexplicable pieces of magic. Together, they stripped the thirteen of their names."

Awe crawled over Eragon. "How is that possible?"

"Did I not just say it was inexplicable? All we know is that after the dragons cast their spell, no one could utter the names of the thirteen; those who remembered the names soon forgot them; and while you can read the names in scrolls and letters where they are recorded and even copy them if you look at only one glyph at a time, they are as gibberish. The dragons spared Jarnunvösk, Galbatorix's first dragon, for it was not his fault he was killed by Urgals, and also Shruikan, for he did not choose to serve Galbatorix but was forced to by Galbatorix and Morzan."

What a horrible fate, to lose one's name, thought Eragon. He shivered. *If there's one thing I've learned since becoming a Rider, it's that you never, ever want to have a dragon for an enemy.* "What about their true names?" he asked. "Did they erase those as well?"

Arya nodded. "True names, birth names, nicknames, family names, titles. Everything. And as a result, the thirteen were reduced to little more than animals. No longer could they say, 'I like this' or 'I dislike that' or 'I have green scales,' for to say that would be to name themselves. They could not even call themselves dragons. Word by word, the spell obliterated everything that defined them as thinking creatures, and the Forsworn had no choice but to watch in silent misery as their dragons descended into complete ignorance. The experience was so disturbing, at least five of the thirteen, and several of the Forsworn, went mad as a result." Arya paused, considering the outline of a glyph, then rubbed it out and redrew it. "The Banishing of the Names is the main reason so many people now believe that dragons were nothing more than animals to ride from one place to another."

"They wouldn't believe that if they had met Saphira," said Eragon.

Arya smiled. "No." With a flourish, she completed the latest sentence she had been working on. He tilted his head and sidled closer in order to decipher the glyphs she had inscribed. They read: *The trickster, the riddler, the keeper of the balance, he of the many faces who finds life in death and who fears no evil; he who walks through doors.*

"What prompted you to write this?"

"The thought that many things are not what they appear." Dust billowed around her hand as she patted the ground, effacing the glyphs from the surface of the earth.

"Has anyone tried to guess Galbatorix's true name?" Eragon asked. "It seems as if that would be the fastest way to end this war. To be honest, I think it might be the only hope we have of vanquishing him in battle."

"Were you not being honest with me before?" asked Arya, a gleam in her eyes.

Her question forced him to chuckle. "Of course not. It's just a figure of speech."

"And a poor one at that," she said. "Unless you happen to be in the habit of lying."

Eragon floundered for a moment before he caught hold of his thread of speech again and could say, "I know it would be hard to find Galbatorix's true name, but if all the elves and all the members of the Varden who know the ancient language searched for it, we could not help but succeed."

Like a pale, sun-bleached pennant, the dry blade of grass hung from between Arya's left thumb and forefinger. It trembled in sympathy with each surge of blood through her veins. Pinching it at the top with her other hand, she tore the leaf in half lengthwise, then did the same with each of the resulting strips, quartering the leaf. Then she began to plait the strips, forming a stiff braided rod. She said, "Galbatorix's true name is no great secret. Three different elves—one a Rider, and two ordinary spellcasters—discovered it on their own and many years apart."

"They did!" exclaimed Eragon.

Unperturbed, Arya picked another blade of grass, tore it into strips, inserted the pieces into the gaps in her braided rod, and continued plaiting in a different direction. "We can only speculate whether Galbatorix himself knows his true name. I am of the opinion that he does not, for whatever it is, his true name must be so terrible, he could not go on living if he heard it."

"Unless he is so evil or so demented, the truth about his actions has no power to disturb him."

"Perhaps." Her nimble fingers flew so fast, twisting, braiding, weaving, that they were nearly invisible. She picked two more blades of grass. "Either way, Galbatorix is certainly aware that he has a true name, like all creatures and things, and that it is a potential weakness. At some point before he embarked upon his campaign against the Riders, he cast a spell that kills whoever uses his true name. And since we do not know exactly how this spell kills, we cannot shield ourselves from it. You see, then, why we have all but abandoned that line of inquiry. Oromis is one of the few who are brave enough to continue seeking out Galbatorix's name, albeit in a roundabout manner." With a pleased expression, she held out her hands, palms-upward. Resting on them was an exquisite ship made of green and white grass. It was no more than four inches long, but so detailed, Eragon descried benches for rowers, tiny railings along the edge of the deck, and portholes the size of raspberry seeds. The curved prow was shaped somewhat like the head and neck of a rearing dragon. There was a single mast.

"It's beautiful," he said.

Arya leaned forward and murmured, "Flauga." She gently blew upon the ship, and it rose from her hands and sailed around the fire and then, gathering speed, slanted upward and glided off into the sparkling depths of the night sky.

"How far will it go?"

"Forever," she said. "It takes the energy to stay aloft from the plants below. Wherever there are plants, it can fly."

The idea bemused Eragon, but he also found it rather sad to think of the pretty grass ship wandering among the clouds for the rest of eternity, with none but birds for company. "Imagine the stories people will tell about it in years to come."

Arya knit her long fingers together, as if to keep them from making something else. "Many such oddities exist in the world. The longer you live and the farther you travel, the more of them you will see."

Eragon gazed at the pulsing fire for a while, then said, "If it's so important to protect your true name, should I cast a spell to keep Galbatorix from using my true name against me?"

"You can if you wish to," said Arya, "but I doubt it's necessary. True names are not so easy to find as you think. Galbatorix does not know you well enough to guess your name, and if he were inside your mind and able to examine your every thought and memory, you would be already lost to him, true name or no. If it is any comfort, I doubt that even I could divine your true name."

"Couldn't you?" he asked. He was both pleased and displeased that she believed any part of him was a mystery to her.

She glanced at him and then lowered her eyes. "No, I do not think so. Could you guess mine?"

"No."

Silence enveloped their camp. Above, the stars gleamed cold and white. A wind sprang up from the east and raced across the plains, battering the grass and wailing with a long, thin voice, as if lamenting the loss of a loved one. As it struck, the coals burst into flame again and a twisting mane of sparks trailed off to the west. Eragon hunched his shoulders and pulled the collar of his tunic close around his neck. There was something unfriendly about the wind; it bit at him with unusual ferocity, and it seemed to isolate him and Arya from the rest of the world. They sat motionless, marooned on their tiny island of light and heat, while the massive river of air rushed past, howling its angry sorrows into the empty expanse of land.

When the gusts became more violent and began to carry the sparks farther away from the bare patch where Eragon had built the fire, Arya poured a handful of dirt over the wood. Moving forward onto his knees, Eragon joined her, scooping the dirt with both hands to speed the process. With the fire extinguished, he had difficulty seeing; the countryside had become a ghost of itself, full of writhing shadows, indistinct shapes, and silvery leaves.

Arya made as if to stand, then stopped in a half crouch, arms outstretched for balance, her expression alert. Eragon felt it as well: the air prickled and hummed, as if a bolt of lightning were about to strike. The hair on the back of his hands rose from his skin and waved freely in the wind.

"What is it?" he asked.

"We are being watched. Whatever happens, don't use magic or you may get us killed."

"Who—"

"Shh."

Casting about, he found a fist-sized rock, pried it out of the ground, and hefted it, testing its weight.

In the distance, a cluster of glowing multicolored lights appeared. They darted toward the camp, flying low over the grass. As they drew near, he saw that the lights were constantly changing in size—ranging from an orb no larger than a pearl to one several feet in diameter—and that their colors also varied, cycling through every hue in the rainbow. A crackling nimbus surrounded each orb, a halo of liquid tendrils that whipped and lashed, as if hungry to entangle something in their grasp. The lights moved so fast, he could not determine exactly how many there were, but he guessed it was about two dozen.

The lights hurtled into the camp and formed a whirling wall around him and Arya. The speed with which they spun, combined with the barrage of pulsing colors, made Eragon dizzy. He put a hand on the ground to steady himself. The humming was so loud now, his teeth vibrated against one another. He tasted metal, and his hair stood on end. Arya's did the same, despite its additional length, and when he glanced at her, he found the sight so ridiculous, he had to resist the urge to laugh.

"What do they want?" shouted Eragon, but she did not answer.

A single orb detached itself from the wall and hung before Arya at eye level. It shrank and expanded like a throbbing heart, alternating between royal blue and emerald green, with occasional flashes of red. One of its tendrils caught hold of a strand of Arya's hair. There was a sharp *pop*, and for an instant, the strand shone like a fragment of the sun, then it vanished. The smell of burnt hair drifted toward Eragon.

Arya did not flinch or otherwise betray alarm. Her face calm, she lifted an arm and, before Eragon could leap forward and stop her, laid her hand upon the lambent orb. The orb turned gold and white, and it swelled until it was over three feet across. Arya closed her eyes and tilted her head back, radiant joy suffusing her features. Her lips moved, but whatever she said, Eragon could not hear. When she finished, the orb flushed blood-red and then in quick succession shifted from red to green to purple to a ruddy orange to a blue so bright he had to avert his gaze and then to pure black fringed with a corona of twisting white tendrils, like the sun during an eclipse. Its appearance ceased to fluctuate then, as if only the absence of color could adequately convey its mood.

Drifting away from Arya, it approached Eragon, a hole in the fabric of the world, encircled by a crown of flames. It hovered in front of him, humming with such intensity, his eyes watered. His tongue seemed plated with copper, his skin crawled, and short filaments of electricity danced on the tips of his fingers. Somewhat frightened, he wondered whether he should touch the orb as Arya had. He looked at her for advice. She nodded and gestured for him to proceed.

He extended his right hand toward the void that was the orb. To his surprise, he encountered resistance. The orb was incorporeal, but it pushed against his hand the way a swift stream of water might. The closer he got, the harder it pushed. With an effort, he reached across the last few inches and came into contact with the center of the creature's being.

Bluish rays shot out from between Eragon's palm and the surface of the orb, a dazzling, fanlike display that overwhelmed the light from the other orbs and bleached everything a pale blue white. Eragon shouted with pain as the rays stabbed at his eyes, and he ducked his head, squinting. Then something moved inside the orb, like a sleeping dragon uncoiling, and a *presence* entered his mind, brushing aside his defenses as if they were dry leaves in an autumn storm. He gasped. Transcendent joy filled him; whatever the orb was, it seemed to be composed of distilled happiness. It enjoyed being alive, and everything around it pleased it to a greater or lesser degree. Eragon would have wept with sheer gladness, but he no longer had control of his body. The creature held him in place, the shimmering rays still blazing from underneath his hand while it flitted through his bones and muscles, lingering at the sites where he had been injured, and then returned to his mind. Euphoric as Eragon was, the creature's presence was so strange and so unearthly, he wanted to flee from it, but inside his consciousness, there was nowhere to hide. He had to remain in intimate contact with the fiery soul of the creature while it scoured his memories, dashing from one to the next with the speed of an elvish arrow. He wondered how it could comprehend so much information so quickly. While it searched, he tried to probe the orb's mind in return, to learn what he could about its nature and its origins, but it defied his attempts to understand it. The few impressions he gleaned were so different from those he had found in the minds of other beings, they were incomprehensible.

After a final, nearly instantaneous circuit through his body, the creature withdrew. The contact between them broke like a twisted cable under too much tension. The panoply of rays outlining Eragon's hand faded into oblivion, leaving behind lurid pink afterimages streaked across his field of vision.

Again changing colors, the orb in front of Eragon shrank to the size of an apple and rejoined its companions in the swirling vortex of light that encircled him and Arya. The humming increased to an almost unbearable pitch, and then the vortex exploded outward as the blazing orbs scattered in every direction. They regrouped a hundred feet or so from the dim camp, tumbling over each other like wrestling kittens, then raced off to the south and disappeared, as if they had never existed in the first place. The wind subsided to a gentle breeze.

Eragon fell to his knees, arm outstretched toward where the orbs had gone, feeling empty without the bliss they had given him. "What," he asked, and then had to cough and start over again, his throat was so dry. "What are they?"

"Spirits," said Arya. She sat.

"They didn't look like the ones that came out of Durza when I killed him."

"Spirits can assume many different guises, dictated by their whim."

He blinked several times and wiped the corners of his eyes with the back of a finger. "How can anyone bear to enslave them with magic? It's monstrous. I would be ashamed to call myself a sorcerer. Gah! And Trianna boasts of being one. I'll have her stop using spirits or I'll expel her from Du Vrangr Gata and ask Nasuada to banish her from the Varden."

"I would not be so hasty."

"Surely you don't think it's right for magicians to force spirits to obey their will. . . . They are so beautiful that—" He broke off and shook his head, overcome with emotion. "Anyone who harms them ought to be thrashed within an inch of their life."

With a hint of a smile, Arya said, "I take it Oromis had yet to address the topic when you and Saphira left Ellesméra."

"If you mean spirits, he mentioned them several times."

"But not in any great detail, I dare say."

"Perhaps not."

In the darkness, the outline of her shape moved as she leaned to one side. "Spirits always induce a sense of rapture when they choose to communicate with we who are made of matter, but do not allow them to deceive you. They are not as benevolent, content, or cheerful as they would have you believe. Pleasing those they interact with is their way of defending themselves. They hate to be bound in one place, and they realized long ago that if the person they are dealing with is happy, then he or she will be less likely to detain the spirits and keep them as servants."

"I don't know," said Eragon. "They make you feel so good, I can understand why someone would want to keep them nearby, instead of releasing them."

Her shoulders rose and fell. "Spirits have as much difficulty predicting our behavior as we do theirs. They share so little in common with the other races of Alagaësia, conversing with them in even the simplest terms is a challenging prospect, and any meeting is fraught with peril, for one never knows how they will react."

"None of which explains why I shouldn't order Trianna to abandon sorcery."

"Have you ever seen her summon spirits to do her bidding?"

"No."

"I thought not. Trianna has been with the Varden for nigh on six years, and in that time she has demonstrated her mastery of sorcery exactly once, and that after much coaxing on Ajihad's part and much consternation and preparation on Trianna's. She has the necessary skills—she is no charlatan—but summoning spirits is exceedingly dangerous, and one does not embark upon it lightly."

Eragon rubbed his shining palm with his left thumb. The hue of light changed as blood rushed to the surface of his skin, but his efforts did nothing to reduce the amount of light radiating from his hand. He scratched at the gedwëy ignasia with his fingernails. *This had better not last more than a few hours. I can't go around shining like a lantern. It could get me killed. And it's silly too. Whoever heard of a Dragon Rider with a glowing body part?*

Eragon considered what Brom had told him. "They aren't human spirits, are they? Nor elf, nor dwarf, nor those of any other creature. That is, they aren't ghosts. We don't become them after we die."

"No. And please do not ask me, as I know you are about to, what, then, they really are. It is a question for Oromis to answer, not me. The study of sorcery, if properly conducted, is long and arduous and should be approached with care. I do not want to say anything that may interfere with the lessons Oromis has planned for you, and I certainly don't want you to hurt yourself trying something I mentioned when you lack the proper instruction."

"And when am I supposed to return to Ellesméra?" he demanded. "I can't leave the Varden again, not like this, not while Thorn and Murtagh are still alive. Until we defeat the Empire, or the Empire defeats us, Saphira and I have to support Nasuada. If Oromis and Glaedr really want to finish our training, they should join us, and Galbatorix be blasted!"

"Please, Eragon," she said. "This war shall not end as quickly as you think. The Empire is large, and we have but pricked its hide. As long as Galbatorix does not know about Oromis and Glaedr, we have an advantage."

"Is it an advantage if they never make full use of themselves?" he grumbled. She did not answer, and after a moment, he felt childish for complaining. Oromis and Glaedr wanted more than anyone else to destroy Galbatorix, and if they chose to bide their time in

Ellesméra, it was because they had excellent reasons for doing so. Eragon could even name several of them if he was so inclined, the most prominent being Oromis's inability to cast spells that required large amounts of energy.

Cold, Eragon pulled his sleeves down over his hands and crossed his arms. "What was it you said to the spirit?"

"It was curious why we had been using magic; that was what brought us to their attention. I explained, and I also explained that you were the one who freed the spirits trapped inside of Durza. That seemed to please them a great deal." Silence crept between them, and then she sidled toward the lily and touched it again. "Oh!" she said. "They were indeed grateful. Naina!"

At her command, a wash of soft light illuminated the camp. By it, he saw that the leaf and stem of the lily were solid gold, the petals were a whitish metal he failed to recognize, and the heart of the flower, as Arya revealed by tilting the blossom upward, appeared to have been carved out of rubies and diamonds. Amazed, Eragon ran a finger over the curved leaf, the tiny wire hairs on it tickling him. Bending forward, he discerned the same collection of bumps, grooves, pits, veins, and other minute details with which he had adorned the original version of the plant; the only difference was they were now made of gold.

"It's a perfect copy!" he said.

"And it is still alive."

"No!" Concentrating, he searched for the faint signs of warmth and movement that would indicate the lily was more than an inanimate object. He located them, strong as they ever were in a plant during the night. Fingering the leaf again, he said, "This is beyond everything I know of magic. By all rights, this lily ought to be dead. Instead, it is thriving. I cannot even imagine what would be involved in turning a plant into living metal. Perhaps Saphira could do it, but she would never be able to teach the spell to anyone else."

"The real question," said Arya, "is whether this flower will produce seeds that are fertile."

"It could spread?"

"I would not be surprised if it does. Numerous examples of self-perpetuating magic exist throughout Alagaësia, such as the floating crystal on the island of Eoam and the dream well in Mani's Caves. This would be no more improbable than either of those phenomena."

"Unfortunately, if anyone discovers this flower or the offspring it may have, they will dig them all up. Every fortune hunter in the land would come here to pick the golden lilies."

"They will not be so easy to destroy, I think, but only time will tell for sure."

A laugh bubbled up inside of Eragon. With barely contained glee, he said, "I've heard the expression 'to gild the lily' before, but the spirits actually did it! They gilded the lily!" And he fell to laughing, letting his voice boom across the empty plain.

Arya's lips twitched. "Well, their intentions were noble. We cannot fault them for being ignorant of human sayings."

"No, but . . . oh, ha, ha, ha!"

Arya snapped her fingers, and the wash of light faded into oblivion. "We have talked away most of the night. It is time we rested. Dawn is fast approaching, and we must depart soon thereafter."

Eragon stretched himself out on a rock-free expanse of the ground, still chuckling as he drifted into his waking dreams.

AMID THE RESTLESS CROWD

It was midafternoon when the Varden finally came into sight.

Eragon and Arya stopped on the crest of a low hill and studied the sprawling city of gray tents that lay before them, teeming as it was with thousands of men, horses, and smoking cookfires. To the west of the tents, there wound the tree-lined Jiet River. Half a mile to the east was a second, smaller camp—like an island floating close off the shore of its mother continent—where the Urgals led by Nar Garzhvog resided. Ranging for several miles around the perimeter of the Varden were numerous groups of horsemen. Some were riding patrol, others were banner-carrying messengers, and others were raiding parties either setting out on or returning from a mission. Two of the patrols spotted Eragon and Arya and, after sounding signal horns, galloped toward them with all possible speed.

A broad smile stretched Eragon's face, and he laughed, relieved. "We made it!" he exclaimed. "Murtagh, Thorn, hundreds of soldiers, Galbatorix's pet magicians, the Ra'zac—none of them could catch us. Ha! How's that for taunting the king? This'll tweak his beard for sure when he hears of it."

"He will be twice as dangerous then," warned Arya.

"I know," he said, grinning even wider. "Maybe he'll get so angry, he'll forget to pay his troops and they will all throw away their uniforms and join the Varden."

"You are in fine fettle today."

"And why shouldn't I be?" he demanded. Bouncing on the tips of his toes, he opened his mind as wide as he could and, gathering his strength, shouted, *Saphira!* sending the thought flying over the countryside like a spear.

A response was not long in coming:

Eragon!

They embraced with their minds, smothering each other with warm waves of love, joy, and concern. They exchanged memories of their time apart, and Saphira comforted Eragon over the soldiers he had killed, drawing off the pain and anger that had accumulated within him since the incident. He smiled. With Saphira so close, everything seemed right in the world.

I missed you, he said.

And I you, little one. Then she sent him an image of the soldiers he and Arya had fought and said, *Without fail, every time I leave you, you get yourself in trouble. Every time! I hate to so much as turn tail on you for fear you will be locked in mortal combat the moment I take my eyes off you.*

Be fair: I've gotten into plenty of trouble when I am with you. It's not something that just happens when I'm alone. We seem to be lodestones for unexpected events.

No, you are a lodestone for unexpected events, she sniffed. *Nothing out of the ordinary ever occurs to me when I'm by myself. But you attract duels, ambushes, immortal enemies, obscure creatures such as the Ra'zac, long-lost family members, and mysterious acts of magic as if they were starving weasels and you were a rabbit that wandered into their den.*

What about the time you spent as Galbatorix's possession? Was that an ordinary event?

I had not hatched yet, she said. *You cannot count that. The difference between you and me is that things happen to you, whereas I cause things to happen.*

Maybe, but that's because I'm still learning. Give me a few years, and I'll be as good as Brom at getting things done, eh? You can't say I didn't seize the initiative with Sloan.

Mmh. We still have to talk about that. If you ever surprise me like that again, I will pin you on the ground and lick you from head to toe.

Eragon shivered. Her tongue was covered with hooked barbs that could strip hair, hide, and meat off a deer with a single swipe. I *know, but I wasn't sure myself whether I was going to kill Sloan or let him go free until I was standing in front of him. Besides, if I had told you I was going to stay behind, you would have insisted on stopping me.*

He sensed a faint growl as it rumbled through her chest. She said, *You should have trusted me to do the right thing. If we cannot talk openly, how are we supposed to function as dragon and Rider?*

Would doing the right thing have involved taking me from Helgrind, regardless of my wishes?

It might not *have,* she said with a hint of defensiveness.

He smiled. *You're right, though. I should have discussed my plan with you. I'm sorry. From now on, I promise I will consult with you before I do anything you don't expect. Is that acceptable?*

Only if it involves weapons, magic, kings, or family members, she said.

Or flowers.

Or flowers, she agreed. *I don't need to know if you decide to eat some bread and cheese in the middle of the night.*

Unless a man with a very long knife is waiting for me outside of my tent.

If you could not defeat a single man with a very long knife, you would be a poor excuse for a Rider indeed.

Not to mention dead.

Well . . .

By your own argument, you should take comfort in the fact that while I may attract more trouble than most people, I am perfectly capable of escaping from situations that would kill most anyone else.

Even the greatest warriors can fall prey to bad luck, she said. *Remember the dwarf king Kaga, who was killed by a novice swordsman— swordsdwarf?—when he tripped on a rock. You should always remain cautious, for no matter your skills, you cannot anticipate and prevent every misfortune fate directs your way.*

Agreed. Now, can we please abandon such weighty conversation? I have become thoroughly exhausted with thoughts of fate, destiny, justice, and other, equally gloomy topics over the past few days. As far as I am concerned, philosophic questioning is just as likely to make you confused and depressed as it is to improve your condition. Swiveling his head, Eragon surveyed the plain and sky, searching for the distinctive blue glitter of Saphira's scales. *Where are you? I can feel you are nearby, but I can't see you.*

Right above you!

With a bugle of joy, Saphira dove out of the belly of a cloud several thousand feet overhead, spiraling toward the ground with her wings tucked close to her body. Opening her fearsome jaws, she released a billow of fire, which streamed back over her head and neck like a burning mane. Eragon laughed and held his arms outstretched to her. The horses of the patrol galloping toward him and Arya shied at the sight and sound of Saphira and bolted in the opposite direction while their riders frantically tried to rein them in.

"I had hoped we could enter the camp without attracting undue attention," Arya said, "but I suppose I should have realized we could not be unobtrusive with Saphira around. A dragon is hard to ignore."

I heard that, said Saphira, spreading her wings and landing with a thunderous crash. Her massive thighs and shoulders rippled as she absorbed the force of the impact. A blast of air struck Eragon's face, and the earth shuddered underneath him. He flexed his knees to maintain his balance. Folding her wings so they lay flat upon her back, she said, *I can be stealthy if I want.* Then she cocked her head and blinked, the tip of her tail whipping from side to side. *But I don't want to be stealthy today! Today I am a dragon, not a frightened pigeon trying to avoid being seen by a hunting falcon.*

When are you not a dragon? asked Eragon as he ran toward her. Light as a feather, he leaped from her left foreleg to her shoulder and thence to the hollow at the base of her neck that was his usual seat. Settling into place, he put his hands on either side of her warm neck, feeling the rise and fall of her banded muscles as she breathed.

He smiled again, with a profound sense of contentment. *This is where I belong, here with you.* His legs vibrated as Saphira hummed with satisfaction, her deep rumbling following a strange, subtle melody he did not recognize.

"Greetings, Saphira," said Arya, and twisted her hand over her chest in the elves' gesture of respect.

Crouching low and bending her long neck, Saphira touched Arya upon the brow with the tip of her snout, as she had when she blessed Elva in Farthen Dûr, and said, *Greetings, älfa-kona. Welcome, and may the wind rise under your wings.* She spoke to Arya with the same tone of affection that, until then, she had reserved for Eragon, as if she now considered Arya part of their small family and worthy of the same regard and intimacy as they shared. Her gesture surprised Eragon, but after an initial flare of jealousy, he approved. Saphira continued speaking: *I am grateful to you for helping Eragon to return without harm. If he had been captured, I do not know what I would have done!*

222

"Your gratitude means much to me," said Arya, and bowed. "As for what you would have done if Galbatorix had seized Eragon, why, you would have rescued him, and I would have accompanied you, even if it was to Urû'baen itself."

Yes, I like to think I would have rescued you, Eragon, said Saphira, turning her neck to look at him, *but I worry that I would have surrendered to the Empire in order to save you, no matter the consequences for Alagaësia.* Then she shook her head and kneaded the soil with her claws. *Ah, these are pointless meanderings. You are here and safe, and that is the true shape of the world. To while away the day contemplating evils that might have been is to poison the happiness we already have. . . .*

At that moment, a patrol galloped toward them and, halting thirty yards away because of their nervous horses, asked if they might escort the three to Nasuada. One of the men dismounted and gave his steed to Arya, and then as a group, they advanced toward the sea of tents to the southwest. Saphira set the pace: a leisurely crawl that allowed her and Eragon to enjoy the pleasure of each other's company before they immersed themselves in the noise and chaos that were sure to assault them once they neared the camp.

Eragon inquired after Roran and Katrina, then said, *Have you been eating enough fireweed? Your breath seems stronger than usual.*

Of course I have. You only notice it because you have been gone for many days. I smell exactly as a dragon should smell, and I'll thank you not to make disparaging comments about it unless you want me to drop you on your head. Besides, you humans have nothing to brag about, sweaty, greasy, pungent things that you are. The only creatures in the wild as smelly as humans are male goats and hibernating bears. Compared to you, the scent of a dragon is a perfume as delightful as a meadow of mountain flowers.

Come now, don't exaggerate. Although, he said, wrinkling his nose, *since the Agaetí Blödhren, I have noticed that humans tend to be rather smelly. But you cannot lump me in with the rest, for I am no longer entirely human.*

Perhaps not, but you still need a bath!

As they crossed the plain, more and more men congregated around Eragon and Saphira, providing them with a wholly unnecessary but very impressive honor guard. After so long spent in the wilds of Alagaësia, the dense press of bodies, the cacophony of high, excited voices, the storm of unguarded thoughts and emotions, and the confused motion of flailing arms and prancing horses were overwhelming for Eragon.

He retreated deep within himself, where the discordant mental chorus was no louder than the distant thunder of crashing waves. Even through the layers of barriers, he sensed the approach of twelve elves, running in formation from the other side of the camp, swift and lean as yellow-eyed mountain cats. Wanting to make a favorable impression, Eragon combed his hair with his fingers and squared his shoulders, but he also tightened the armor around his consciousness so that no one but Saphira could hear his thoughts.

The elves had come to protect him and Saphira, but ultimately their allegiance belonged to Queen Islanzadí. While he was grateful for their presence, and he doubted their inherent politeness would allow them to eavesdrop on him, he did not want to provide the queen of the elves with any opportunity to learn the secrets of the Varden, nor to gain a hold over him. If she could wrest him away from Nasuada, he knew she would. On the whole, the elves did not trust humans, not after Galbatorix's betrayal, and for that and other reasons, he was sure Islanzadí would prefer to have him and Saphira under her direct command. And of the potentates he had met, he trusted Islanzadí the least. She was too imperious and too erratic.

The twelve elves halted before Saphira. They bowed and twisted their hands as Arya had done and, one by one, introduced themselves to Eragon with the initial phrase of the elves' traditional greeting, to which he replied with the appropriate lines. Then the lead elf, a tall, handsome male with glossy blue-black fur covering his entire body, proclaimed the purpose of their mission to everyone within earshot and formally asked Eragon and Saphira if the twelve might assume their duties.

"You may," said Eragon.

You may, said Saphira.

Then Eragon asked, "Blödhgarm-vodhr, did I perchance see you at the Agaetí Blödhren?" For he remembered watching an elf with a similar pelt gamboling among the trees during the festivities.

Blödhgarm smiled, exposing the fangs of an animal. "I believe you met my cousin Liotha. We share a most striking family resemblance, although her fur is brown and flecked, whereas mine is dark blue."

"I would have sworn it was you."

"Unfortunately, I was otherwise engaged at the time and was unable to attend the celebration. Perhaps I shall have the opportunity when next the occasion occurs, a hundred years from now."

Would you not agree, Saphira said to Eragon, *that he has a pleasant aroma?*

Eragon sniffed the air. *I don't smell anything. And I would if there was anything to smell.*

That's odd. She provided him then with the range of odors she had detected, and at once he realized what she meant. Blödhgarm's musk surrounded him like a cloud, thick and heady, a warm, smoky scent that contained hints of crushed juniper berries and that set Saphira's nostrils to tingling. *All the women in the Varden seem to have fallen in love with him,* she said. *They stalk him wherever he goes, desperate to talk with him but too shy to utter so much as a squeak when he looks at them.*

Maybe only females can smell him. He cast a concerned glance at Arya. *She does not seem to be affected.*

She has protection against magical influences.

I hope so. . . . Do you think we should put a stop to Blödhgarm? What he is doing is a sneaky, underhanded way of gaining a woman's heart.

Is it any more underhanded than adorning yourself with fine clothing to catch the eye of your beloved? Blödhgarm has not taken advantage of the women who are fascinated by him, and it seems improbable that he would have composed the notes of his scent to appeal specifically to human women. Rather, I would guess it is an unintended consequence and that he created it to serve another purpose altogether. Unless he discards all semblance of decency, I think we should refrain from interfering.

What about Nasuada? Is she vulnerable to his charms?

Nasuada is wise and wary. She had Trianna place a ward around her that protects her against Blödhgarm's influence.

Good.

When they arrived at the tents, the crowd swelled in size until half the Varden appeared to be gathered around Saphira. Eragon raised his hand in response as people shouted, "Argetlam!" and "Shadeslayer!" and he heard others say, "Where have you been, Shadeslayer? Tell us of your adventures!" A fair number referred to him as the Bane of the Ra'zac, which he found so immensely satisfying, he repeated the phrase four times to himself under his breath.

People also shouted blessings upon his health and Saphira's too, and invitations to dine, and offers of gold and jewelry, and piteous requests for aid: would he please heal a son who had been born blind, or would he remove a growth that was killing a man's wife, or would he fix a horse's broken leg or repair a bent sword, for as the man bellowed, "It was my grandfather's!" Twice a woman's voice cried out, "Shadeslayer, will you marry me?" and while he looked, he was unable to identify the source.

Throughout the commotion, the twelve elves hovered close. The knowledge that they were watching for that which he could not see and listening for that which he could not hear was a comfort to Eragon and allowed him to interact with the massed Varden with an ease that had escaped him in the past.

Then from between the curving rows of woolen tents, the former villagers of Carvahall began to appear. Dismounting, Eragon walked among the friends and acquaintances of his childhood, shaking hands, slapping shoulders, and laughing at jokes that would be incomprehensible to anyone who had not grown up around Carvahall. Horst was there, and Eragon grasped the smith's brawny forearm. "Welcome back, Eragon. Well done. We're in your debt for avenging us on the monsters that drove us from our homes. I'm glad to see you are still in one piece, eh?"

"The Ra'zac would have had to move a sight faster to chop any parts off of me!" said Eragon. Then he found himself greeting Horst's sons, Albriech and Baldor; and then Loring the shoemaker and his three sons; Tara and Morn, who had owned Carvahall's tavern; Fisk; Felda; Calitha; Delwin and Lenna; and then fierce-eyed Birgit, who said, "I thank you, Eragon Son of None. I thank you for ensuring that the creatures who ate my husband were properly punished. My hearth is yours, now and forever."

Before Eragon could respond, the crowd swept them apart. *Son of None?* he thought. *Ha! I have a father, and everyone hates him.*

Then to his delight, Roran shouldered his way out of the throng,

Katrina beside him. He and Roran embraced, and Roran growled, "That was a fool thing to do, staying behind. I ought to knock your block off for abandoning us like that. Next time, give me advance warning before you traipse off on your own. It's getting to be a habit with you. And you should have seen how upset Saphira was on the flight back."

Eragon put a hand on Saphira's left foreleg and said, "I'm sorry I could not tell you beforehand that I planned to stay, but I did not realize it was necessary until the very last moment."

"And why was it exactly you remained in those foul caverns?"

"Because there was something I had to investigate."

When he failed to expand upon his answer, Roran's broad face hardened, and for a moment Eragon feared he would insist upon a more satisfactory explanation. But then Roran said, "Well, what hope has an ordinary man like myself of understanding the whys and wherefores of a Dragon Rider, even if he is my cousin? All that matters is that you helped free Katrina and you are here now, safe and sound." He craned his neck, as if he were trying to see what lay on top of Saphira, then he looked at Arya, who was several yards behind them, and said, "You lost my staff! I crossed the entire breadth of Alagaësia with that staff. Couldn't you manage to hold on to it for more than a few days?"

"It went to a man who needed it more than I," said Eragon.

"Oh, stop nipping at him," Katrina said to Roran, and after a moment's hesitation, she hugged Eragon. "He is really very glad to see you, you know. He just has difficulty finding the words to say it."

With a sheepish grin, Roran shrugged. "She's right about me, as always." The two of them exchanged a loving glance.

Eragon studied Katrina closely. Her copper hair had regained its original luster, and for the most part, the marks left by her ordeal had faded away, although she was still thinner and paler than normal.

Moving closer to him, so none of the Varden clustered around them could overhear, she said, "I never thought that I would owe you so much, Eragon. That *we* would owe you so much. Since Saphira brought us here, I have learned what you risked to rescue me, and I am most grateful. If I had spent another week in Helgrind, it would have killed me or stripped me of reason, which is a living death. For saving me from that fate, and for repairing Roran's shoulder, you have my utmost thanks, but more than that, you have my thanks for bringing the two of us back together again. If not for you, we never would have been reunited."

"Somehow I think Roran would have found a way to extricate you from Helgrind, even without me," commented Eragon. "He has a silver tongue when roused. He would have convinced another spellcaster to help him—Angela the herbalist, perhaps—and he would have succeeded all the same."

"Angela the herbalist?" scoffed Roran. "That prating girl would have been no match for the Ra'zac."

"You would be surprised. She's more than she appears . . . or

sounds." Then Eragon dared to do something that he never would have attempted when he was living in Palancar Valley but that he felt was appropriate in his role as a Rider: he kissed Katrina upon her brow, and then he kissed Roran upon his, and he said, "Roran, you are as a brother to me. And, Katrina, you are as a sister to me. If ever you are in trouble, send for me, and whether you need Eragon the farmer or Eragon the Rider, everything I am shall be at your disposal."

"And likewise," said Roran, "if ever you are in trouble, you have but to send for us, and we shall rush to your aid."

Eragon nodded, acknowledging his offer, and refrained from mentioning that the troubles he was most likely to encounter would not be of a sort either of them could assist him with. He gripped them both by the shoulders and said, "May you live long, may you always be together and happy, and may you have many children." Katrina's smile faltered for a moment, and Eragon wondered at it.

At Saphira's urging, they resumed walking toward Nasuada's red pavilion in the center of the encampment. In due time, they and the host of cheering Varden arrived at its threshold, where Nasuada stood waiting, King Orrin to her left and scores of nobles and other notables gathered behind a double row of guards on either side.

Nasuada was garbed in a green silk dress that shimmered in the sun, like the feathers on the breast of a hummingbird, in bright contrast to the sable shade of her skin. The sleeves of the dress ended in lace ruffs at her elbows. White linen bandages covered the rest of her arms to her narrow wrists. Of all the men and women assembled before her, she was the most distinguished, like an emerald resting on a bed of brown autumn leaves. Only Saphira could compete with the brilliance of her appearance.

Eragon and Arya presented themselves to Nasuada and then to King Orrin. Nasuada gave them formal welcome on behalf of the Varden and praised them for their bravery. She finished by saying, "Aye, Galbatorix may have a Rider and dragon who fight for him even as Eragon and Saphira fight for us. He may have an army so large that it darkens the land. And he may be adept at strange and terrible magics, abominations of the spellcaster's art. But for all his wicked power, he could not stop Eragon and Saphira from invading his realm and killing four of his most favored servants, nor Eragon from crossing the Empire with impunity. The pretender's arm has grown weak indeed when he cannot defend his borders, nor protect his foul agents within their hidden fortress."

Amid the Varden's enthusiastic cheering, Eragon allowed himself a secret smile at how well Nasuada played upon their emotions, inspiring confidence, loyalty, and high spirits in spite of a reality that was far less optimistic than she portrayed it. She did not lie to them—to his knowledge, she did not lie, not even when dealing with the Council of Elders or other of her political rivals. What she did was report the truths that best supported her position and her arguments. In that regard, he thought, she was like the elves.

When the Varden's outpouring of excitement had subsided, King

Orrin greeted Eragon and Arya as Nasuada had. His delivery was staid compared with hers, and while the crowd listened politely and applauded afterward, it was obvious to Eragon that however much the people respected Orrin, they did not love him as they loved Nasuada, nor could he fire their imagination as Nasuada fired it. The smooth-faced king was gifted with a superior intellect. But his personality was too rarefied, too eccentric, and too subdued for him to be a receptacle for the desperate hopes of the humans that opposed Galbatorix.

If we overthrow Galbatorix, Eragon said to Saphira, *Orrin should not replace him in Urû'baen. He would not be able to unite the land as Nasuada has united the Varden.*

Agreed.

At length, King Orrin concluded. Nasuada whispered to Eragon, "Now it is your turn to address those who have assembled to catch a glimpse of the renowned Dragon Rider." Her eyes twinkled with suppressed merriment.

"Me!"

"It is expected."

Then Eragon turned and faced the multitude, his tongue dry as sand. His mind was blank, and for a handful of panic-stricken seconds, he thought the use of language would continue to elude him and he would embarrass himself in front of the entire Varden. Somewhere a horse nickered, but otherwise the camp seemed frightfully quiet. It was Saphira who broke his paralysis by nudging his elbow with her snout and saying, *Tell them how honored you are to have their support and how happy you are to be back among them.* With her encouragement, he managed to find a few fumbling words, and then, as soon as it was acceptable, he bowed and retreated a step.

Forcing a smile while the Varden clapped and cheered and beat their swords against their shields, he exclaimed, *That was horrible! I would rather fight a Shade than do that again.*

Really! It was not that hard, Eragon.

Yes, it was!

A puff of smoke drifted up from her nostrils as she snorted with amusement. *A fine Dragon Rider you are, afraid of talking to a large group! If only Galbatorix knew, he could have you at his mercy if he but asked you to make a speech to his troops. Ha!*

It's not funny, he grumbled, but she still continued to chuckle.

231

TO ANSWER A KING

After Eragon gave his address to the Varden, Nasuada gestured and Jörmundur leaped to her side. "Have everyone here return to their posts. If we were attacked now, we would be overwhelmed."

"Yes, my Lady."

Beckoning to Eragon and Arya, Nasuada placed her left hand on King Orrin's arm and, with him, entered the pavilion.

What about you? Eragon asked Saphira as he followed. Then he stepped inside the pavilion and saw that a panel at the back had been rolled up and tied to the wooden frame above so that Saphira might insert her head and participate in the goings-on. He had to wait but a moment before her glittering head and neck swung into view around the edge of the opening, darkening the interior as she settled into place. Purple flecks of light adorned the walls, projected by her blue scales onto the red fabric.

Eragon examined the rest of the tent. It was barren compared with when he had last visited, a result of the destruction Saphira had caused when she crawled into the pavilion to see Eragon in Nasuada's mirror. With only four pieces of furniture, the tent was austere even by military standards. There was the polished high-backed chair where Nasuada was sitting, King Orrin standing next to her; the selfsame mirror, which was mounted at eye level on a carved brass pole; a folding chair; and a low table strewn with maps and other documents of import. An intricately knotted dwarf rug covered the ground. Besides Arya and himself, a score of people were already gathered before Nasuada. They were all looking at him. Among them he recognized Narheim, the current commander of the dwarf troops; Trianna and other spellcasters from Du Vrangr Gata; Sabrae, Umérth, and the rest of the Council of Elders, save for Jörmundur; and a random assortment of nobles and functionaries from King Orrin's court. Those who were strangers to him he assumed also held positions of distinction in one of the many factions that made up the Varden's army. Six of Nasuada's guards were present—two stationed by the entrance and four behind Nasuada—and Eragon detected the convoluted pattern of Elva's dark and twisted thoughts from where the witch-child was hidden at the far end of the pavilion.

"Eragon," said Nasuada, "you have not met before, but let me introduce Sagabato-no Inapashunna Fadawar, chief of the Inapashunna tribe. He is a brave man."

For the next hour, Eragon endured what seemed like an endless procession of introductions, congratulations, and questions that he could not answer forthrightly without revealing secrets that were better left unsaid. When all of the guests had conversed with him, Nasuada bade them take their leave. As they filed out of the pavilion, she clapped her hands and the guards outside ushered in a second group and then, when the second group had enjoyed the dubious fruits of their visitation with him, a third. Eragon smiled the whole while. He shook hand after hand. He exchanged meaningless pleasantries and strove to memorize the plethora of names and titles that besieged him and otherwise acted with perfect civility the role he was expected to play. He knew that they honored him not because he was their friend but because of the chance of victory he embodied for the free peoples of Alagaësia, because of his power, and because of what they hoped to gain by him. In his heart, he howled with frustration and longed to break free of the stifling constraints of good manners and polite conduct and to climb on Saphira and fly away to somewhere peaceful.

The one part of the process Eragon enjoyed was watching how the supplicants reacted to the two Urgals who loomed behind Nasuada's chair. Some pretended to ignore the horned warriors—

although from the quickness of their motions and the shrill tones of their voices, Eragon could tell that the creatures unnerved them—while others glared at the Urgals and kept their hands on the pommels of their swords or daggers, and still others affected a false bravado and belittled the Urgals' notorious strength and boasted of their own. Only a few people truly seemed unaffected by the sight of the Urgals. Foremost among them was Nasuada, but their number also included King Orrin, Trianna, and an earl who said he had seen Morzan and his dragon lay waste to an entire town when he had been but a boy.

When Eragon could bear no more, Saphira swelled her chest and released a low, humming growl, so deep that it shook the mirror in its frame. The pavilion became as silent as a tomb. Her growl was not overtly threatening, but it captured everyone's attention and proclaimed her impatience with the proceedings. None of the guests were foolish enough to test her forbearance. With hurried excuses, they gathered their things and filed out of the pavilion, quickening their pace when Saphira tapped the tips of her claws against the ground.

Nasuada sighed as the entrance flap swung closed behind the last visitor. "Thank you, Saphira. I am sorry that I had to subject you to the misery of public presentation, Eragon, but as I am sure you are aware, you occupy an exalted position among the Varden, and I cannot keep you to myself anymore. You belong to the people now. They demand that you recognize them and that you give them what they consider their rightful share of your time. Neither you nor Orrin nor I can refuse the wishes of the crowd. Even Galbatorix in his dark seat of power at Urû'baen fears the fickle crowd, although he may deny it to everyone, including himself."

With the guests departed, King Orrin abandoned the guise of royal decorum. His stern expression relaxed into one of more human relief, irritation, and ferocious curiosity. Rolling his shoulders beneath his stiff robes, he looked at Nasuada and said, "I do not think we require your Nighthawks to wait on us any longer."

"Agreed." Nasuada clapped her hands, dismissing the six guards from the inside of the tent.

Dragging the spare chair over to Nasuada's, King Orrin seated himself in a tangle of sprawling limbs and billowing fabric. "Now," he said, switching his gaze between Eragon and Arya, "let us have a full account of your doings, Eragon Shadeslayer. I have heard only vague explanations for why you chose to delay at Helgrind, and I have had my fill of evasions and deceptive answers. I am determined to know the truth of the matter, so I warn you, do not attempt to conceal what actually transpired while you were in the Empire. Until I am satisfied you have told me everything there is to tell, none of us shall so much as step outside of this tent."

Her voice cold, Nasuada said, "You assume too much . . . Your Majesty. You do not have the authority to bind me in place; nor Eragon, who is my vassal; nor Saphira; nor Arya, who answers to no mortal lord but rather to one more powerful than the two of us combined. Nor do we have the authority to bind you. The five of us are as close to equals as any of us is likely to find in Alagaësia. You would do well to remember that."

King Orrin's response was equally flinty. "Do I exceed the bounds of my sovereignty? Well, perhaps I do. You are right: I have no hold over you. However, if we are equals, I have yet to see evidence of it in your treatment of me. Eragon answers to you and only you. By the Trial of the Long Knives, you have gained dominion over the wandering tribes, many of which I have long counted among my subjects. And you command as you will both the Varden and the men of Surda, who have long served my family with bravery and determination beyond that of ordinary men."

"It was you yourself who asked me to orchestrate this campaign," said Nasuada. "I have not deposed you."

"Aye, it was at my request you assumed command of our disparate forces. I am not ashamed to admit you have had more experience and success than I in waging war. Our prospects are too precarious for you, me, or any of us to indulge in false pride. However, since your investiture, you seem to have forgotten that I am still the king of Surda, and we of the Langfeld family can trace our line back to Thanebrand the Ring Giver himself, he who succeeded old, mad Palancar and who was the first of our race to sit on the throne in what is now Urû'baen.

"Considering our heritage and the assistance the House of Langfeld has rendered you in this cause, it is insulting of you to ignore the rights of my office. You act as if yours was the only verdict of moment and the opinions of others are of no account, to be trampled over in pursuit of whatever goal you have already determined is best for the portion of free humanity that is fortunate enough to have you as their leader. You negotiate treaties and alliances, such as that with the Urgals, of your own initiative and expect me, and others, to abide by your decisions, as if you speak for us all. You arrange preemptive visits of state, such as that with Blödhgarm-vodhr, and do not trouble to alert me of his arrival, nor wait for me to join you so we might greet his embassy together as equals. And when I have the temerity to ask why Eragon—the man whose very existence is the reason I have staked my country in this venture— when I have the temerity to ask *why* this all-important person has elected to endanger the lives of Surdans and those of every creature who opposes Galbatorix by tarrying in the midst of our enemies, how is it you respond? By treating me as if I were no more than an overzealous, overinquisitive underling whose childish concerns distracted you from more pressing matters. Bah! I will not have it, I tell you. If you cannot bring yourself to respect my station and to accept a fair division of responsibility, as two allies ought to, then it is my opinion that you are unfit to command a coalition such as ours, and I shall set myself against you however I may."

What a long-winded fellow, Saphira observed.

Alarmed by the direction the conversation had taken, Eragon said, *What should I do? I had not intended to tell anyone else about Sloan, except for Nasuada. The fewer people who know he's alive, the better.*

236

A flickering sea-blue shimmer ran from the base of Saphira's head to the crest of her shoulders as the tips of the sharp, diamond-shaped scales along the sides of her neck rose a fraction of an inch from the underlying skin. The jagged layers of projecting scales gave her a fierce, ruffled appearance. *I cannot tell you what is best, Eragon. In this, you must rely upon your own judgment. Listen closely to what your heart says and perhaps it will become clear how to win free of these treacherous downdrafts.*

In response to King Orrin's sally, Nasuada clasped her hands in her lap, her bandages startling white against the green of her dress, and in a calm, even voice said, "If I have slighted you, Sire, then it was due to my own hasty carelessness and not to any desire on my part to diminish you or your house. Please forgive my lapses. They shall not happen again; that I promise you. As you have pointed out, I have but recently ascended to this post, and I have yet to master all of the accompanying niceties."

Orrin inclined his head in a cool but gracious acceptance of her words.

"As for Eragon and his activities in the Empire, I could not have provided you with specific details, for I have had no further intelligence myself. It was not, as I am sure you can appreciate, a situation that I wished to advertise."

"No, of course not."

"Therefore, it seems to me that the swiftest cure for the dispute that afflicts us is to allow Eragon to lay bare the facts of his trip that we may apprehend the full scope of this event and render judgment upon it."

"Of its own, that is not a cure," said King Orrin. "But it is the beginning of a cure, and I will gladly listen."

"Then let us tarry no longer," said Nasuada. "Let us begin this beginning and have done with our suspense. Eragon, it is time for your tale."

With Nasuada and the others gazing at him with wondering eyes, Eragon made his choice. Lifting his chin, he said, "What I tell you,

I tell you in confidence. I know I cannot expect either you, King Orrin, or you, Lady Nasuada, to swear that you will keep this secret bound within your hearts from now until the day you die, but I beg you to act as if you had. It could cause a great deal of grief if this knowledge were to be whispered in the wrong ears."

"A king does not remain king for long unless he appreciates the value of silence," said Orrin.

Without further ado, Eragon described everything that had happened to him in Helgrind and in the days that had followed. Afterward, Arya explained how she had gone about locating Eragon and then corroborated his account of their travels by providing several facts and observations of her own. When they had both said their fill, the pavilion was quiet as Orrin and Nasuada sat motionless upon their chairs. Eragon felt as if he were a child again, waiting for Garrow to tell him what his punishment would be for doing something foolish on their farm.

Orrin and Nasuada remained lost deep in reflection for several minutes, then Nasuada smoothed the front of her dress and said, "King Orrin may be of a different opinion, and if so, I look forward to hearing his reasons, but for my part, I believe that you did the right thing, Eragon."

"As do I," said Orrin, surprising them all.

"You do!" exclaimed Eragon. He hesitated. "I don't mean to sound impertinent, for I'm glad you approve, but I didn't expect you to look kindly upon my decision to spare Sloan's life. If I may ask, why—"

King Orrin interrupted. "Why do we approve? The rule of law must be upheld. If you had appointed yourself Sloan's executioner, Eragon, you would have taken for yourself the power that Nasuada and I wield. For he who has the audacity to determine who should live and who should die no longer serves the law but dictates the law. And however benevolent you might be, that would be no good thing for our species. Nasuada and I, at least, answer to the one lord even kings must kneel before. We answer to Angvard, in his realm of eternal twilight. We answer to the Gray Man on his gray horse. Death. We could be the worst tyrants in the whole of history, and given enough time, Angvard would bring us to heel. . . . But not you. Humans are a short-lived race, and we should not be governed by one of the Undying. We do not need another Galbatorix." A strange laugh escaped from Orrin then, and his mouth twisted in a humorless smile. "Do you understand, Eragon? You are so dangerous, we are forced to acknowledge the danger to your face and hope that you are one of the few people able to resist the lure of power."

King Orrin laced his fingers together underneath his chin and gazed at a fold in his robes. "I have said more than I intended. . . . So, for all those reasons, and others besides, I agree with Nasuada. You were right to stay your hand when you discovered this Sloan in Helgrind. As inconvenient as this episode has been, it would have been far worse, and for you as well, if you had killed to please yourself and not in self-defense or in service to others."

Nasuada nodded. "That was well spoken."

Throughout, Arya listened with an inscrutable expression. Whatever her own thoughts on the matter were, she did not divulge them.

Orrin and Nasuada pressed Eragon with a number of questions about the oaths he had laid upon Sloan, as well as queries about the remainder of his trip. The interrogation continued for so long, Nasuada had a tray of cooled cider, fruit, and meat pies brought into the pavilion, along with the haunch of a steer for Saphira. Nasuada and Orrin had ample opportunity to eat between questions; however, they kept Eragon so busy talking, he managed to consume only two bites of fruit and a few sips of cider to wet his throat.

At long last King Orrin bade them farewell and departed to review the status of his cavalry. Arya left a minute later, explaining that she needed to report to Queen Islanzadí and to, as she said, "heat a tub of water, wash the sand from my skin, and return my features to their usual shape. I do not feel myself, with the tips of my ears missing, my eyes round and level, and the bones of my face in the wrong places."

When she was alone with Eragon and Saphira, Nasuada sighed and leaned her head against the back of the chair. Eragon was shocked by how tired she appeared. Gone were her previous vitality and strength of presence. Gone was the fire from her eyes. She had, he realized, been pretending to be stronger than she was in order to avoid tempting her enemies and demoralizing the Varden with the spectacle of her weakness.

"Are you ill?" he asked.

She nodded toward her arms. "Not exactly. It's taking me longer to recuperate than I had anticipated. . . . Some days are worse than others."

"If you want, I can—"

"No. Thank you, but no. Do not tempt me. One rule of the Trial of the Long Knives is that you must allow your wounds to heal at their own pace, without magic. Otherwise, the contestants will not have endured the full measure of pain from their cuts."

"That's barbaric!"

A slow smile touched her lips. "Maybe so, but it is what it is, and I would not fail so late in the trial merely because I could not withstand a bit of an ache."

"What if your wounds fester?"

"Then they fester, and I shall pay the price for my mistake. But I doubt they will while Angela ministers to me. She has an amazing storehouse of knowledge where medicinal plants are concerned. I half believe she could tell you the true name of every species of grass on the plains east of here merely by feeling their leaves."

Saphira, who had been so still she appeared asleep, now yawned—nearly touching the floor and the ceiling with the tips of her open jaws—and shook her head and neck, sending the flecks of light reflected by her scales spinning about the tent with dizzying speed.

Straightening in her seat, Nasuada said, "Ah, I am sorry. I know this has been tedious. You have both been very patient. Thank you."

Eragon knelt and placed his right hand over hers. "You do not need to worry about me, Nasuada. I know my duty. I have never aspired to rule; that is not my destiny. And if ever I am offered the chance to sit upon a throne, I shall refuse and see that it goes to someone who is better suited than I to lead our race."

"You are a good person, Eragon," murmured Nasuada, and pressed his hand between hers. Then she chuckled. "What with you, Roran, and Murtagh, I seem to spend most of my time worrying about members of your family."

Eragon bridled at the statement. "Murtagh is no family of mine."

"Of course. Forgive me. But still, you must admit it's startling how much bother the three of you have caused both the Empire *and the* Varden."

"It's a talent of ours," joked Eragon.

It runs in their blood, said Saphira. *Wherever they go, they get themselves entangled in the worst danger possible.* She nudged Eragon in the arm. *Especially this one. What else can you expect of people from Palancar Valley? Descendants all of a mad king.*

"But not mad themselves," said Nasuada. "At least I don't think so. It's hard to tell at times." She laughed. "If you, Roran, and Murtagh were locked in the same cell, I'm not sure who would survive."

Eragon laughed as well. "Roran. He's not about to let a little thing like death stand between him and Katrina."

Nasuada's smile became slightly strained. "No, I suppose he wouldn't at that." For a score of heartbeats, she was silent, then: "Goodness me, how selfish I am. The day is almost done, and here I am detaining you merely so I can enjoy a minute or two of idle conversation."

"The pleasure is mine."

"Yes, but there are better places than this for talk among friends. After what you have been through, I expect you would like a wash, a change, and a hearty meal, no? You must be famished!" Eragon glanced at the apple he still held and regretfully concluded it would be impolite to continue eating it when his audience with Nasuada was drawing to a close. Nasuada caught his look and said, "Your face answers for you, Shadeslayer. You have the guise of a winter-starved wolf. Well, I shall not torment you any longer. Go and bathe and garb yourself in your finest tunic. When you are presentable, I would be most pleased if you would consent to join me for my evening meal. Understand, you would not be my only guest, for the affairs of the Varden demand my constant attention, but you would brighten the proceedings considerably for me if you chose to attend."

Eragon fought back a grimace at the thought of having to spend hours more parrying verbal thrusts from those who sought to use him for their own advantage or to satisfy their curiosity about Riders and dragons. Still, Nasuada was not to be denied, so he bowed and agreed to her request.

A FEAST WITH FRIENDS

Eragon and Saphira left Nasuada's crimson pavilion with the contingent of elves ranged about them and walked to the small tent that had been assigned to him when they had joined the Varden at the Burning Plains. There he found a hogshead of boiling water waiting for him, the coils of steam opalescent in the oblique light from the large evening sun. Ignoring it for the moment, he ducked inside the tent.

After checking to ensure that none of his few possessions had been disturbed during his absence, Eragon unburdened himself of his pack and carefully removed his armor, storing it beneath his cot. It needed to be wiped and oiled, but that was a task that would have to wait. Then he reached even farther underneath the cot, his fingers scraping the fabric wall beyond, and groped in the darkness until his hand came into contact with a long, hard object. Grasping it, he lay the heavy cloth-wrapped bundle across his knees. He picked apart the knots in the wrapping, and then, starting at the thickest end of the bundle, began to unwind the coarse strips of canvas.

Inch by inch, the scuffed leather hilt of Murtagh's hand-and-a-half sword came into view. Eragon stopped when he had exposed the hilt, the crossguard, and a fair expanse of the gleaming blade, which was as jagged as a saw from where Murtagh had blocked Eragon's blows with Zar'roc.

Eragon sat and stared at the weapon, conflicted. He did not know what had prompted him, but the day after the battle, he had returned to the plateau and retrieved the sword from the morass of trampled dirt where Murtagh had dropped it. Even after only a single night exposed to the elements, the steel had acquired a mottled veil of rust. With a word, he had dispelled the scrim of corrosion. Perhaps it was because Murtagh had stolen his own sword that Eragon felt compelled to take up Murtagh's, as if the exchange, unequal and involuntary though it was, minimized his loss. Perhaps it was because he wished to claim a memento of that bloody conflict. And perhaps it was because he still harbored a sense of latent affection for Murtagh, despite the grim circumstances that had turned them against each other. No matter how much Eragon abhorred what Murtagh had become, and pitied him for it too, he could not deny the connection that existed between them. Theirs was a shared fate. If not for an accident of birth, he would have been raised in Urû'baen, and Murtagh in Palancar Valley, and then their current positions might well have been reversed. Their lives were inexorably intertwined.

As he gazed at the silver steel, Eragon composed a spell that would smooth the wrinkles from the blade, close the wedge-shaped gaps along the edges, and restore the strength of the temper. He wondered, however, if he ought to. The scar that Durza had given him he had kept as a reminder of their encounter, at least until the dragons erased it during the Agaetí Blödhren. Should he keep this scar as well, then? Would it be healthy for him to carry such a painful memory on his hip? And what sort of message would it send to the rest of the Varden if he chose to wield the blade of another betrayer? Zar'roc had been a gift from Brom; Eragon could not have refused to accept it, nor was he sorry he had. But he was under no such compulsion to claim as his own the nameless blade that rested upon his thighs.

I need a sword, he thought. *But not this sword.*

He wrapped the blade again in its shroud of canvas and slid it back under the cot. Then, with a fresh shirt and tunic tucked under his elbow, he left the tent and went to bathe.

When he was clean and garbed in the fine lámarae shirt and tunic, he set out to meet with Nasuada near the tents of the healers, as she had requested. Saphira flew, for as she said, *It is too cramped for*

me on the ground; I keep knocking over tents. Besides, if I walk with you,
such a herd of people will gather around us, we will hardly be able to
move.

Nasuada was waiting for him by a row of three flagpoles, upon which a half-dozen gaudy pennants hung limp in the cooling air. She had changed since they had parted and now wore a light summer frock, the color of pale straw. Her dense, mosslike hair she had piled high on her head in an intricate mass of knots and braids. A single white ribbon held the arrangement in place.

She smiled at Eragon. He smiled in return and quickened his pace. As he drew close, his guards mingled with her guards with a conspicuous display of suspicion on the part of the Nighthawks and studied indifference on the part of the elves.

Nasuada took his arm and, while they spoke in comfortable tones, guided his steps as they ambled through the sea of tents. Above, Saphira circled the camp, content to wait until they arrived at their destination before she went to the effort of landing. Eragon and Nasuada spoke of many things. Little of consequence passed between their lips, but her wit, her gaiety, and the thoughtfulness of her remarks charmed him. It was easy for him to talk to her and easier to listen, and that very ease caused him to realize how much he cared for her. Her hold on him far exceeded that of a liegelord over her vassal. It was a new feeling for him, their bond. Aside from his aunt Marian, of whom he had but faint memories, he had grown up in a world of men and boys, and he had never had the opportunity to be friends with a woman. His inexperience made him uncertain, and his uncertainty made him awkward, but Nasuada did not seem to notice.

She stopped him before a tent that glowed from within with the light of many candles and that hummed with a multitude of unintelligible voices. "Now we must dive into the swamp of politics again. Prepare yourself."

She swept back the entrance flap to the tent, and Eragon jumped as a host of people shouted, "Surprise!" A wide trestle table laden with food dominated the center of the tent, and at the table were sitting Roran and Katrina, twenty or so of the villagers from Carvahall—including Horst and his family—Angela the herbalist, Jeod and his wife, Helen, and several people Eragon did not recognize but who had the look of sailors. A half-dozen children had been playing on the ground next to the table; they paused in their games and stared at Nasuada and Eragon with open mouths, seemingly unable to decide which of these two strange figures deserved more of their attention.

Eragon grinned, overwhelmed. Before he could think of what to say, Angela raised her flagon and piped, "Well, don't just stand there gaping! Come in, sit down. I'm hungry!"

As everyone laughed, Nasuada pulled Eragon toward the two empty chairs next to Roran. Eragon helped Nasuada to her seat, and as she sank into the chair, he asked, "Did *you* arrange this?"

"Roran suggested whom you might want to attend, but yes, the original idea was mine. And I made a few additions of my own to the table, as you can see."

"Thank you," said Eragon, humbled. "Thank you so much."

He saw Elva sitting cross-legged in the far-left corner of the tent, a platter of food on her lap. The other children shunned her—Eragon could not imagine they had much in common—and none of the adults, save Angela, seemed comfortable in her presence. The small, narrow-shouldered girl gazed up at him from under her black bangs with her horrible violet eyes and mouthed what he guessed was "Greetings, Shadeslayer."

"Greetings, Farseer," he mouthed in return. Her small pink lips parted in what would have been a charming smile if not for the fell orbs that burned above them.

Eragon gripped the arms of his chair as the table shook, the dishes rattled, and the walls of the tent flapped. Then the back of the tent bulged and parted as Saphira pushed her head inside. *Meat!* she said. *I smell meat!*

For the next few hours, Eragon lost himself in a blur of food, drink, and the pleasure of good company. It was like returning home. The wine flowed like water, and after they had drained their cups once or twice, the villagers forgot their deference and treated him as one of their own, which was the greatest gift they could give. They were equally generous with Nasuada, although they refrained from making jokes at her expense, as they sometimes did with Eragon. Pale smoke filled the tent as the candles consumed themselves. Beside him, Eragon heard the boom of Roran's laughter ring forth again and again, and across the table the even deeper boom of Horst's laugh. Muttering an incantation, Angela set to dancing a small man she had fashioned from a crust of sourdough bread, much to everyone's amusement. The children gradually overcame their fear of Saphira and dared to walk up to her and pet her snout. Soon they were clambering over her neck, hanging from her spikes, and tugging at the crests above her eyes. Eragon laughed as he watched. Jeod entertained the crowd with a song he had learned from a book long ago. Tara danced a jig. Nasuada's teeth flashed as she tossed her head back. And Eragon, by popular request, recounted several of his adventures, including a detailed description of his flight from Carvahall with Brom, which was of special interest to his listeners.

247

"To think," said Gertrude, the round-faced healer tugging on her shawl, "we had a dragon in our valley and we never even knew it." With a pair of knitting needles produced from within her sleeves, she pointed at Eragon. "To think I nursed you when your legs had been scraped from flying on Saphira and I never suspected the cause." Shaking her head and clucking her tongue, she cast on with brown wool yarn and began to knit with speed born of decades of practice.

Elain was the first to leave the party, pleading exhaustion brought on by her advanced stage of pregnancy; one of her sons, Baldor, went with her. Half an hour later, Nasuada also made to leave, explaining that the demands of her position prevented her from staying as long as she would like but that she wished them health and happiness and hoped they would continue to support her in her fight against the Empire.

As she moved away from the table, Nasuada beckoned to Eragon. He joined her by the entrance. Turning her shoulder to the rest of the tent, she said, "Eragon, I know that you need time to recover from your journey and that you have affairs of your own that you must tend to. Therefore, tomorrow and the day after are yours to spend as you will. But on the morning of the third day, present your-self at my pavilion and we shall talk about your future. I have a most important mission for you."

"My Lady." Then he said, "You keep Elva close at hand wherever you go, do you not?"

"Aye, she is my safeguard against any danger that might slip past the Nighthawks. Also, her ability to divine what it is that pains people has proved enormously helpful. It is so much easier to obtain someone's cooperation when you are privy to all of their secret hurts."

"Are you willing to give that up?"

She studied him with a piercing gaze. "You intend to remove your curse from Elva?"

"I intend to try. Remember, I promised her I would."

"Yes, I was there." The crash of a falling chair distracted her for an instant, then she said, "Your promises will be the death of us. . . . Elva is irreplaceable; no one else has her skill. And the service she provides, as I just testified, is worth more than a mountain of gold. I have even thought that, of all of us, she alone might be able to de-feat Galbatorix. She would be able to anticipate his every attack, and your spell would show her how to counter them, and as long as countering them did not require her to sacrifice her life, she would prevail. . . . For the good of the Varden, Eragon, for the good of everyone in Alagaësia, couldn't you feign your attempt to cure Elva?"

"No," he said, biting off the word as if it offended him. "I would not do it even if I could. It would be wrong. If we force Elva to remain as she is, she will turn against us, and I do not want her as an enemy." He paused, then at Nasuada's expression added, "Besides, there is a good chance I may not succeed. Removing such a vaguely worded spell is a difficult prospect at best. . . . If I may make a suggestion?"

"What?"

"Be honest with Elva. Explain to her what she means to the Varden, and ask her if she will continue to carry her burden for the sake of all free people. She may refuse; she has every right to, but if she does, her character is not one we would want to rely upon anyway. And if she accepts, then it shall be of her own free will."

With a slight frown, Nasuada nodded. "I shall speak with her tomorrow. You should be present as well, to help me persuade her and to lift your curse if we fail. Be at my pavilion three hours after dawn." And with that, she swept into the torch-lit night outside.

Much later, when the candles guttered in their sockets and the villagers began to disperse in twos and threes, Roran grasped Eragon's arm by the elbow and drew him through the back of the tent to stand by Saphira's side, where the others could not hear. "What you said earlier about Helgrind, was that all of it?" asked Roran. His grip was like a pair of iron pincers clamped around Eragon's flesh. His eyes were hard and questioning, and also unusually vulnerable.

Eragon held his gaze. "If you trust me, Roran, never ask me that question again. It's not something you want to know." Even as he spoke, Eragon felt a deep sense of unease over having to conceal Sloan's existence from Roran and Katrina. He knew the deception was necessary, but it still made him uncomfortable to lie to his family. For a moment, Eragon considered telling Roran the truth, but then he remembered all the reasons he had decided not to and held his tongue.

Roran hesitated, his face troubled, then he set his jaw and released Eragon. "I trust you. That's what family is for, after all, eh? Trust."

"That and killing each other."

Roran laughed and rubbed his nose with a thumb. "That too." He rolled his thick, round shoulders and reached up to massage his right one, a habit he had fallen into since the Ra'zac had bitten him. "I have another question."

"Oh?"

"It is a boon . . . a favor I seek of you." A wry smile touched his lips, and he shrugged. "I never thought I would speak to you of this. You're younger than I, you've barely reached your manhood, and you're my cousin to boot."

"Speak of what? Stop beating around the bush."

"Of marriage," said Roran, and lifted his chin. "Will you marry Katrina and me? It would please me if you would, and while I have refrained from mentioning it to her until I had your answer, I know Katrina would be honored and delighted if you would consent to join us as man and wife."

Astonished, Eragon was at a loss for words. At last he managed to stammer, "Me?" Then he hastened to say, "I would be happy to do it, of course, but . . . *me*? Is that really what you want? I'm sure Nasuada would agree to marry the two of you. . . . You could have King Orrin, a real king! He would leap at the chance to preside over the ceremony if it would help him earn my favor."

"I want you, Eragon," said Roran, and clapped him on the shoulder. "You are a Rider, and you are the only other living person who shares my blood; Murtagh does not count. I cannot think of anyone else I would rather have tie the knot around my wrist and hers."

"Then," said Eragon, "I shall." The air whooshed out of him as Roran embraced him and squeezed with all of his prodigious strength. He gasped slightly when Roran released him and then, once his breath had returned, said, "When? Nasuada has a mission planned for me. I don't know what it is yet, but I'm guessing it will keep me busy for some time. So . . . maybe early next month, if events allow?"

Roran's shoulders bunched and knotted. He shook his head like a bull sweeping its horns through a clump of brambles. "What about the day after tomorrow?"

"So soon? Isn't that rushing it a bit? There would hardly be any time to prepare. People will think it's unseemly."

Roran's shoulders rose, and the veins on his hands bulged as he opened and closed his fists. "It can't wait. If we're not married and quick, the old women will have something far more interesting to gossip about than my impatience. Do you understand?"

It took Eragon a moment to grasp Roran's meaning, but once he did, Eragon could not stop a broad smile from spreading across his face. *Roran's going to be a father!* he thought. Still smiling, he said, "I think so. The day after tomorrow it is." Eragon grunted as Roran hugged him again, pounding him on the back. With some difficulty, he freed himself.

Grinning, Roran said, "I'm in your debt. Thank you. Now I must go share the news with Katrina, and we must do what we can to ready a wedding feast. I will let you know the exact hour once we decide on it."

"That sounds fine."

Roran began walking toward the tent, then he spun around and threw his arms out in the air as if he would gather the entire world to his breast. "Eragon, I'm going to be married!"

With a laugh, Eragon waved his hand. "Go on, you fool. She's waiting for you."

Eragon climbed onto Saphira as the flaps of the tent closed over Roran. "Blödhgarm?" he called. Quiet as a shadow, the elf glided into the light, his yellow eyes glowing like coals. "Saphira and I are going to fly for a little while. We will meet you at my tent."

"Shadeslayer," said Blödhgarm, and tilted his head.

Then Saphira raised her massive wings, ran forward three steps, and launched herself over the rows of tents, battering them with wind as she flapped hard and fast. The movements of her body beneath him shook Eragon, and he gripped the spike in front of him for support. Saphira spiraled upward above the twinkling camp until it was an inconsequential patch of light dwarfed by the dark landscape that surrounded it. There she remained, floating between the heavens and the earth, and all was silent.

Eragon lay his head on her neck and stared up at the glittering band of dust that spanned the sky.

Rest if you want, little one, said Saphira. *I shall not let you fall.*

And he rested, and visions beset him of a circular stone city that stood in the center of an endless plain and of a small girl who wandered among the narrow, winding alleys within and who sang a haunting melody.

And the night wore on toward morning.

INTERSECTING SAGAS

It was just after dawn and Eragon was sitting on his cot, oiling his mail hauberk, when one of the Varden's archers came to him and begged him to heal his wife, who was suffering from a malignant tumor. Even though he was supposed to be at Nasuada's pavilion in less than an hour, Eragon agreed and accompanied the man to his tent. Eragon found his wife much weakened from the growth, and it took all of his skill to extract the insidious tendrils from her flesh. The effort left him tired, but he was pleased that he was able to save the woman from a long and painful death.

Afterward, Eragon rejoined Saphira outside of the archer's tent and stood with her for a few minutes, rubbing the muscles near the base of her neck. Humming, Saphira flicked her sinuous tail and twisted her head and shoulders so that he had better access to her smooth plated underside. She said, *While you were occupied in there, other petitioners came to seek an audience with you, but Blödhgarm and his ilk turned them away, for their requests were not urgent.*

Is that so? He dug his fingers under the edge of one of her large neck scales, scratching even harder. *Perhaps I should emulate Nasuada.*

How so?

On the sixth day of every week, from morning until noon, she grants an audience to everyone who wishes to bring requests or disputes before her. I could do the same.

I like the idea, said Saphira. *Only, you will have to be careful that you do not expend too much of your energy on people's demands. We must be ready to fight the Empire at a moment's notice.* She pushed her neck against his hand, humming even louder.

I need a sword, Eragon said.

Then get one.

Mmh. . . .

Eragon continued to scratch her until she pulled away and said, *You will be late for Nasuada unless you hurry.*

Together, they started toward the center of the camp and Nasuada's pavilion. It was less than a quarter of a mile away, so Saphira walked with him instead of soaring among the clouds, as she had before.

About a hundred feet from the pavilion, they chanced upon Angela the herbalist. She was kneeling between two tents, pointing at a square of leather draped across a low, flat rock. On the leather lay a jumbled pile of finger-length bones branded with a different symbol on each facet: the knucklebones of a dragon, with which she had read Eragon's future in Teirm.

Opposite Angela sat a tall woman with broad shoulders; tanned, weather-beaten skin; black hair braided in a long, thick rope down her back; and a face that was still handsome despite the hard lines that the years had carved around her mouth. She wore a russet dress that had been made for a shorter woman; her wrists stuck out several inches from the ends of her sleeves. She had tied a strip of dark cloth around each wrist, but the strip on the left had loosened and slipped toward her elbow. Eragon saw thick layers of scars where it had been. They were the sort of scars one could only get from the constant chafing of manacles. At some point, he realized, she had been captured by her enemies, and she had fought—fought until she had torn open her wrists to the bone, if her scars were anything to judge by. He wondered whether she had been a criminal or a slave, and he felt his countenance darken as he considered the thought of someone being so cruel as to allow such harm to befall a prisoner under his control, even if it was self-inflicted.

Next to the woman was a serious-looking teenage girl just entering into the full bloom of her adult beauty. The muscles of her forearms were unusually large, as if she had been an apprentice to a

254

smith or a swordsman, which was highly improbable for a girl, no matter how strong she might be.

Angela had just finished saying something to the woman and her companion when Eragon and Saphira halted behind the curly-haired witch. With a single motion, Angela gathered up the knuckle-bones in the leather square and tucked them under the yellow sash at her waist. Standing, she flashed Eragon and Saphira a brilliant smile. "My, you both have the most impeccable sense of timing. You always seem to turn up whenever the drop spindle of fate begins to spin."

"The drop spindle of fate?" questioned Eragon.

She shrugged. "What? You can't expect brilliance all the time, not even from me." She gestured at the two strangers, who had also stood, and said, "Eragon, will you consent to give them your bless-ing? They have endured many dangers, and a hard road yet lies be-fore them. I am sure they would appreciate whatever protection the benediction of a Dragon Rider may convey."

Eragon hesitated. He knew that Angela rarely cast the dragon bones for the people who sought her services—usually only for those whom Solembum deigned to speak with—as such a prognos-tication was no false act of magic but rather a true foretelling that could reveal the mysteries of the future. That Angela had chosen to do this for the handsome woman with the scars on her wrists and the teenage girl with the forearms of a swordfighter told him they were people of note, people who had had, and would have, impor-tant roles in shaping the Alagaësia to be. As if to confirm his suspi-cions, he spotted Solembum in his usual form of a cat with large, tufted ears lurking behind the corner of a nearby tent, watching the proceedings with enigmatic yellow eyes. And yet Eragon still hesi-tated, haunted by the memory of the first and last blessing he had bestowed—how, because of his relative unfamiliarity with the an-cient language, he had distorted the life of an innocent child.

Saphira? he asked.

Her tail whipped through the air. *Do not be so reluctant. You have*

learned from your mistake, and you shall not make it again. Why, then,
should you withhold your blessing from those who may benefit from it?
Bless them, I say, and do it properly this time.

"What are your names?" he asked.

"If it please you, Shadeslayer," said the tall, black-haired woman, with a hint of an accent he could not place, "names have power, and we would prefer ours remain unknown." She kept her gaze angled slightly downward, but her tone was firm and unyielding. The girl uttered a small gasp, as if shocked by the woman's effrontery.

Eragon nodded, neither upset nor surprised, although the woman's reticence had piqued his curiosity even more. He would have liked to know their names, but they were not essential for what he was about to do. Pulling the glove off his right hand, he placed his palm on the middle of the woman's warm forehead. She flinched at the contact but did not retreat. Her nostrils flared, the corners of her mouth thinned, a crease appeared between her eyebrows, and he felt her tremble, as if his touch pained her and she were fighting the urge to knock aside his arm. In the background, Eragon was vaguely aware of Blödhgarm stalking closer, ready to pounce on the woman should she prove to be hostile.

Disconcerted by her reaction, Eragon broached the barrier in his mind, immersed himself in the flow of magic, and, with the full power of the ancient language, said, "Atra guliä un ilian tauthr ono un atra ono waíse sköliro fra rauthr." By imbuing the phrase with energy, as he would the words of a spell, he ensured that it would shape the course of events and thereby improve the woman's lot in life. He was careful to limit the amount of energy he transferred into the blessing, for unless he put checks on it, a spell of that sort would feed off his body until it absorbed all of his vitality, leaving him an empty husk. Despite his caution, the drop in his strength was more than he expected; his vision dimmed and his legs wobbled and threatened to collapse underneath him.

A moment later, he recovered.

It was with a sense of relief that he lifted his hand from the woman's brow, a sentiment that she seemed to share, for she stepped back and rubbed her arms. She looked to him like a person trying to cleanse herself of some foul substance.

Moving on, Eragon repeated the procedure with the teenage girl. Her face widened as he released the spell, as if she could feel it becoming part of her body. She curtsied. "Thank you, Shadeslayer. We are in your debt. I hope that you succeed in defeating Galbatorix and the Empire."

She turned to leave but stopped when Saphira snorted and snaked her head past Eragon and Angela, so she loomed above the two women. Bending her neck, Saphira breathed first upon the face of the older woman and then upon the face of the younger, and projecting her thoughts with such force as to overwhelm all but the thickest defenses—for she and Eragon had noticed that the black-haired woman had a well-armored mind—she said, *Good hunting, O Wild Ones. May the wind rise under your wings, may the sun always be at your backs, and may you catch your prey napping. And, Wolf-Eyes, I hope that when you find the one who left your paws in his traps, you do not kill him too quickly.*

Both women stiffened when Saphira began to speak. Afterward, the elder clapped her fists against her chest and said, "That I shall not, O Beautiful Huntress." Then she bowed to Angela, saying, "Train hard, strike first, Seer."

"Bladesinger."

With a swirl of skirts, she and the teenager strode away and soon were lost from sight in the maze of identical gray tents.

What, no marks upon their foreheads? Eragon asked Saphira.

Elva was unique. I shall not brand anyone else in a like manner. What happened in Farthen Dûr just . . . happened. Instinct drove me. Beyond that, I cannot explain.

As the three of them walked toward Nasuada's pavilion, Eragon glanced at Angela. "Who were they?"

Her lips quirked. "Pilgrims on their own quest."

"That is hardly an answer," he complained.

"It is not my habit to hand out secrets like candied nuts on winter solstice. Especially not when they belong to others."

He was silent for a few paces. Then: "When someone refuses to tell me a certain piece of information, it only makes me that much more determined to find out the truth. I hate being ignorant. For me, a question unanswered is like a thorn in my side that pains me every time I move until I can pluck it out."

"You have my sympathy."

"Why is that?"

"Because if that is so, you must spend every waking hour in mortal agony, for life is full of unanswerable questions."

Sixty feet from Nasuada's pavilion, a contingent of pikemen marching through camp blocked their way. While they waited for the warriors to file past, Eragon shivered and blew on his hands. "I wish we had time for a meal."

Quick as ever, Angela said, "It's the magic, isn't it? It has worn you down." He nodded. Sticking a hand into one of the pouches that hung from her sash, Angela pulled out a hard brown lump flecked with shiny flaxseeds. "Here, this will hold you until lunch."

"What is it?"

She thrust it at him, insistent. "Eat it. You'll like it. Trust me." As he took the oily lump from between her fingers, she grasped his wrist with her other hand and held him in place while she inspected the half-inch-high calluses on his knuckles. "How very clever of you," she said. "They are as ugly as the warts on a toad, but who cares if they help keep your skin intact, eh? I like this. I like this quite a lot. Were you inspired by the dwarves' Ascûdgamln?"

"Nothing escapes you, does it?" he asked.

"Let it escape. I only concern myself with things that exist." Eragon blinked, thrown as he often was by her verbal trickery. She tapped a callus with the tip of one of her short fingernails. "I would do this myself, except that it would catch on the wool when I'm spinning or knitting."

"You knit with your own yarn?" he said, surprised that she would engage in anything so ordinary.

"Of course! It's a wonderful way to relax. Besides, if I didn't, where would I get a sweater with Dvalar's ward against mad rabbits knit in the Liduen Kvaedhí across the inside of the chest, or a snood that was dyed yellow, green, and bright pink?"

"Mad rabbits—"

She tossed her thick curls. "You would be amazed how many magicians have died after being bitten by mad rabbits. It's far more common than you might think."

Eragon stared at her. *Do you think she's jesting?* he asked Saphira.

Ask her and find out.

She would only answer with another riddle.

The pikemen having gone, Eragon, Saphira, and Angela continued toward the pavilion, accompanied by Solembum, who had joined them without Eragon noticing. Picking her way around piles of dung left by the horses of King Orrin's cavalry, Angela said, "So tell me: aside from your fight with the Ra'zac, did anything terribly interesting happen to you during your trip? You know how I love to hear about *interesting things.*"

Eragon smiled, thinking of the spirits that had visited him and Arya. However, he did not want to discuss them, so instead he said, "Since you ask, quite a few interesting things happened. For example, I met a hermit named Tenga living in the ruins of an elf tower. He possessed the most amazing library. In it were seven—"

Angela stopped so abruptly, Eragon kept walking another three paces before he caught himself and turned back. The witch seemed stunned, as if she had taken a hard knock to her head. Padding toward her, Solembum leaned against her legs and gazed upward. Angela wet her lips, then said, "Are . . ." She coughed once. "Are you sure his name was Tenga?"

"Have you met him?"

Solembum hissed, and the hair on his back stood straight out.

Eragon edged away from the werecat, eager to escape the reach of his claws.

"Met him?" With a bitter laugh, Angela planted her hands on her hips. "Met him? Why, I did better than that! I was his apprentice for . . . for an unfortunate number of years."

Eragon had never expected Angela to willingly reveal anything about her past. Eager to learn more, he asked, "When did you meet him? And where?"

"Long ago and far away. However, we parted badly, and I have not seen him for many, many years." Angela frowned. "In fact, I thought he was already dead."

Saphira spoke then, saying, *Since you were Tenga's apprentice, do you know what question he's trying to answer?*

"I have not the slightest idea. Tenga always had a question he was trying to answer. If he succeeded, he immediately chose another one, and so on. He may have answered a hundred questions since I last saw him, or he may still be gnashing his teeth over the same conundrum as when I left him."

Which was?

"Whether the phases of the moon influence the number and quality of the opals that form in the roots of the Beor Mountains, as is commonly held among the dwarves."

"But how could you prove that?" objected Eragon.

Angela shrugged. "If anyone could, it would be Tenga. He may be deranged, but his brilliance is none the less for it."

He is a man who kicks at cats, said Solembum, as if that summed up Tenga's entire character.

Then Angela clapped her hands together and said, "No more! Eat your sweet, Eragon, and let us go to Nasuada."

MAKING AMENDS

"Y ou are late," said Nasuada as Eragon and Angela found seats in the row of chairs arranged in a semicircle before Nasuada's high-backed throne. Also seated in the semi-circle were Elva and her caretaker, Greta, the old woman who had pleaded with Eragon in Farthen Dûr to bless her charge. As before, Saphira lay outside the pavilion and stuck her head through an opening at one end so that she could participate in the meeting. Solembum had curled up in a ball next to her head. He appeared to be sound asleep, except for occasional flicks of his tail.

Along with Angela, Eragon made his apologies for their tardiness, and then he listened as Nasuada explained to Elva the value of her abilities to the Varden—*As if she doesn't already know*, Eragon commented to Saphira—and entreated her to release Eragon from his promise to try to undo the effects of his blessing. She said she understood that what she was asking of Elva was difficult, but the fate of the entire land was at stake, and was it not worth sacrificing one's own comfort to help rescue Alagaësia from Galbatorix's evil clutches? It was a magnificent speech: eloquent, impassioned, and full of arguments intended to appeal to Elva's more noble sentiments.

Elva, who had been resting her small, pointed chin on her fists, raised her head and said, "No." Shocked silence pervaded the pavilion. Transferring her unblinking gaze from one person to the next, she elaborated: "Eragon, Angela, you both know what it is like to share someone's thoughts and emotions as they die. You know how horrible, how wrenching it is, how it feels as if part of yourself has vanished forever. And that is only from the death of one person.

Neither of you has to endure the experience unless you want to, whereas I . . . I have no choice but to share them all. I feel every death around me. Even now I can feel the life ebbing out of Sefton, one of your swordsmen, Nasuada, who was wounded on the Burning Plains, and I know what words I could say to him that would lessen his terror of obliteration. His fear is so great, oh, it makes me tremble!" With an incoherent cry, she cast up her arms before her face, as if to ward off a blow. Then: "Ah, he has gone. But there are others. There are always others. The line of dead never ends." The bitter mocking quality of her voice intensified, a travesty of a child's normal speech. "Do you truly understand, Nasuada, Lady Nightstalker . . . She Who Would Be Queen of the World? Do you truly understand? I am privy to all of the agony around me, whether physical or mental. I feel it as if it were my own, and Eragon's magic drives me to alleviate the discomfort of those who suffer, regardless of the cost to myself. And if I resist the urge, as I am this very moment, my body rebels against me: my stomach turns acid, my head throbs as if a dwarf is hammering on it, and I find it hard to move, much less think. Is this what you would wish on me, Nasuada?

"Night and day I have no respite from the pain of the world. Since Eragon *blessed* me, I have known nothing but hurt and fear, never happiness or pleasure. The lighter side of life, the things that make this existence bearable, these are denied me. Never do I see them. Never do I share in them. Only darkness. Only the combined misery of all the men, women, and children within a mile, battering at me like a midnight storm. This *blessing* has deprived me of the opportunity to be like other children. It has forced my body to mature faster than normal, and my mind even faster still. Eragon may be able to remove this ghastly ability of mine and the compulsion that accompanies it, but he cannot return me to what I was, nor what I should be, not without destroying who I have become. I am a freak, neither a child nor an adult, forever doomed to stand apart. I am not blind, you know. I see how you recoil when you hear me speak." She shook her head. "No, this is too much to ask of me. I will not continue like this for the sake of you, Nasuada, nor the Varden, nor the whole of Alagaësia, nor even for my dear mother, were she still alive today. It is not worth it, not for anything. I could go live by myself, so that I would be free of other people's afflictions, but I do not want to live like that. No, the only solution is for Eragon to attempt to correct his mistake." Her lips curved in a sly smile. "And if you disagree with me, if you think I am being stupid and selfish, why, then, you would do well to remember that I am hardly more than a swaddling babe and have yet to celebrate my second birthday. Only fools expect an infant to martyr herself for the greater good. But infant or not, I have made my decision, and nothing you can say will convince me otherwise. In this, I am as iron."

Nasuada reasoned with her further, but as Elva had promised, it proved to be a futile prospect. At last Nasuada asked Angela, Eragon, and Saphira to intervene. Angela refused on the grounds that she could not improve on Nasuada's words and that she believed Elva's choice was a personal one and therefore the girl ought to be able to do as she wished without being harried like an eagle by a flock of jays. Eragon was of a similar opinion, but he consented to say, "Elva, I cannot tell you what you should do—only you can determine that—but do not reject Nasuada's request out of hand. She is trying to save us all from Galbatorix, and she needs our support if we are to have any chance of success. The future is hidden to me, but I believe that your ability might be the perfect weapon against Galbatorix. You could predict his every attack. You could tell us exactly how to counteract his wards. And above all else, you would be able to sense where Galbatorix is vulnerable, where he is most weak, and what we could do to hurt him."

"You will have to do better than that, Rider, if you want to change my mind."

"I don't want to change your mind," said Eragon. "I only want to make sure you have given due consideration to the implications of your decision and that you are not being overly hasty."

The girl shifted but did not respond.

Then Saphira asked: *What is in your heart, O Shining Brow?*

Elva answered in a soft tone, with no trace of malice. "I have spoken my heart, Saphira. Any other words would be redundant."

If Nasuada was frustrated by Elva's obstinacy, she did not allow it to show, although her expression was stern, as befitted the discussion. She said, "I do not agree with your choice, Elva, but we will abide by it, for it is obvious that we cannot sway you. I suppose I cannot fault you, as I have no experience with the suffering you are exposed to on a daily basis, and if I were in your position, it is possible I would act no differently. Eragon, if you will . . ."

At her bidding, Eragon knelt in front of Elva. Her lustrous violet eyes bored into him as he placed her small hands between his larger ones. Her flesh burned against his as if she had a fever.

"Will it hurt, Shadeslayer?" Greta asked, the old woman's voice quavering.

"It shouldn't, but I do not know for sure. Removing spells is a much more inexact art than casting them. Magicians rarely if ever attempt it because of the challenges it poses."

The wrinkles on her face contorted with worry, Greta patted Elva on the head, saying, "Oh, be brave, my plum. Be brave." She did not seem to notice the look of irritation Elva directed at her.

Eragon ignored the interruption. "Elva, listen to me. There are two different methods for breaking an enchantment. One is for the magician who originally cast the spell to open himself to the energy that fuels our magic—"

"That's the part I always had difficulty with," said Angela. "It's why I rely more upon potions and plants and objects that are magical in and of themselves than upon incantations."

"*If* you don't mind . . ."

Her cheeks dimpling, Angela said, "I'm sorry. Proceed."

"Right," growled Eragon. "One is for the original magician to open himself—"

"Or herself," Angela interjected.

"Will you please let me finish?"

"Sorry."

Eragon saw Nasuada fight back a smile. "He opens himself to the flow of energy within his body and, speaking in the ancient language, recants not only the words of his spell but also the intention behind it. This can be quite difficult, as you might imagine. Unless the magician has the right intent, he will end up altering the original spell instead of lifting it. And then he would have to unsay *two* intertwined spells.

"The other method is to cast a spell that directly counteracts the effects of the original spell. It does not eliminate the original spell, but if done properly, it renders it harmless. With your permission, this is the method I intend to use."

"A most elegant solution," Angela proclaimed, "but who, pray tell, provides the continuous stream of energy needed to maintain this counterspell? And since someone must ask, what can go wrong with this particular method?"

Eragon kept his gaze fixed on Elva. "The energy will have to come from you," he told her, pressing her hands with his. "It won't be much, but it will still reduce your stamina by a certain amount. If I do this, you will never be able to run as far or lift as many pieces of firewood as someone who does not have a similar incantation leeching off them."

"Why can't you provide the energy?" asked Elva, arching an eyebrow. "You are the one who is responsible for my predicament, after all."

"I would, but the farther away I got from you, the harder it would be to send the energy to you. And if I went too far—a mile, say, or maybe a bit more—the effort would kill me. As for what can go wrong, the only risk is that I will word the counterspell improperly and it won't block all of my blessing. If that happens, I will simply cast another counterspell."

"And if that falls short as well?"

He paused. "Then I can always resort to the first method I explained. I would prefer to avoid that, however. It is the only way

265

to completely do away with a spell, but if the attempt were to go amiss, and it very well might, you could end up worse off than you are now."

Elva nodded. "I understand."

"Have I your permission to proceed, then?"

When she dipped her chin again, Eragon took a deep breath, readying himself. His eyes half closed from the strength of his concentration, he began to speak in the ancient language. Each word fell from his tongue with the weight of a hammer blow. He was careful to enunciate every syllable, every sound that was foreign to his own language, so as to avoid a potentially tragic mishap. The counterspell was burned into his memory. He had spent many hours during his trip from Helgrind inventing it, agonizing over it, challenging himself to devise better alternatives, all in anticipation of the day he would attempt to atone for the harm he had caused Elva. As he spoke, Saphira channeled her strength into him, and he felt

her supporting him and watching closely, ready to intervene if she saw in his mind that he was about to mangle the incantation. The counterspell was very long and very complicated, for he had sought to address every reasonable interpretation of his blessing. As a result, a full five minutes passed before Eragon uttered the last sentence, word, and then syllable.

In the silence that followed, Elva's face clouded with disappointment. "I can still sense them," she said.

Nasuada leaned forward in her seat. "Who?"

"You, him, her, everyone who's in pain. They haven't gone away! The urge to help them, that's gone, but this agony still courses through me."

Nasuada leaned forward in her throne. "Eragon?"

He frowned. "I must have missed something. Give me a little while to think, and I'll put together another spell that may do the trick. There are a few other possibilities I considered, but . . ." He trailed off, troubled by the fact that the counterspell had not performed as expected. Moreover, deploying a spell specifically to block the pain Elva was feeling would be far more difficult than trying to undo the blessing as a whole. One wrong word, one poorly constructed phrase, and he might destroy her sense of empathy, or preclude her from ever learning how to communicate with her mind, or inhibit her own sense of pain, so she would not immediately notice when she was injured.

Eragon was in the midst of consulting with Saphira when Elva said, "No!"

Puzzled, he looked at her.

An ecstatic glow seemed to emanate from Elva. Her round, pearl-like teeth gleamed as she smiled, her eyes flashing with triumphant joy. "No, don't try again."

"But, Elva, why would—"

"Because I don't want any more spells feeding off me. And because I just realized *I can ignore them!*" She gripped the arms of her chair, trembling with excitement. "Without the urge to aid everyone who is suffering, I can ignore their troubles, and it doesn't make me sick! I can ignore the man with the amputated leg, I can ignore the woman who just scalded her hand, I can ignore them all, and I feel no worse for it! It's true I can't block them perfectly, not yet at least, but oh, what a relief! Silence. Blessed silence! No more cuts, scrapes, bruises, or broken bones. No more petty worries of air-headed youths. No more anguish of abandoned wives or cuckolded husbands. No more the thousands of unbearable injuries of an entire war. No more the gut-wrenching panic that precedes the final darkness." With tears starting down her cheeks, she laughed, a husky warble that set Eragon's scalp atingle.

What madness is this? asked Saphira. *Even if you can put it out of your mind, why remain shackled to the pain of others when Eragon may yet be able to free you of it?*

Elva's eyes glowed with unsavory glee. "I will never be like ordinary people. If I must be different, then let me keep that which sets me apart. As long as I can control this power, as it seems I now can, I have no objection to carrying this burden, for it shall be by my choice and not forced upon me by your magic, Eragon. Ha! From now on, I shall answer to no one and no thing. If I help anyone, it will be because I want to. If I serve the Varden, it will be because my conscience tells me I should and not because you ask me to, Nasuada, or because I'll throw up if I don't. I will do as I please, and woe unto those who oppose me, for I know all their fears and shall not hesitate to play upon them in order to fulfill my wishes."

"Elva!" exclaimed Greta. "Do not say such terrible things! You cannot mean them!"

The girl turned toward her so sharply, her hair fanned out behind her. "Ah yes, I had forgotten about you, my nursemaid. Ever faithful. Always fussing. I am grateful to you for adopting me after my mother died, and for the care you've given me since Farthen Dûr, but I do not require your assistance anymore. I will live alone, tend to myself, and be beholden to no one." Cowed, the old woman covered her mouth with the hem of a sleeve and shrank back.

What Elva said appalled Eragon. He decided that he could not allow her to retain her ability if she was going to abuse it. With Saphira's assistance, for she agreed with him, he picked the most promising of the new counterspells he had been contemplating earlier and opened his mouth to deliver the lines.

Quick as a snake, Elva clamped a hand over his lips, preventing him from speaking. The pavilion shook as Saphira snarled, nearly deafening Eragon, with his enhanced hearing. As everyone reeled, save for Elva, who kept her hand pressed against Eragon's face, Saphira said, *Let him go, hatchling!*

Drawn by Saphira's snarl, Nasuada's six guards charged inside, brandishing their weapons, while Blödhgarm and the other elves ran up to Saphira and stationed themselves on either side of her shoulders, pulling back the wall of the tent so they could all see what was happening. Nasuada gestured, and the Nighthawks lowered their weapons, but the elves remained poised for action. Their blades gleamed like ice.

Neither the commotion she had engendered nor the swords

leveled at her seemed to perturb Elva. She cocked her head and gazed at Eragon as if he were an unusual beetle she had found crawling along the edge of her chair, and then she smiled with such a sweet, innocent expression, he wondered why he did not have greater faith in her character. In a voice like warm honey, she said, "Eragon, cease. If you cast that spell, you will hurt me as you hurt me once before. You do not want that. Every night when you lay yourself down to sleep, you will think of me, and the memory of the wrong you have committed will torment you. What you were about to do was evil, Eragon. Are you the judge of the world? Will you condemn me in the absence of wrongdoing merely because you do not approve of me? That way lies the depraved pleasure of controlling others for your own satisfaction. Galbatorix would approve."

She released him then, but Eragon was too troubled to move. She had struck at his very core, and he had no counterarguments with which to defend himself, for her questions and observations were the very ones he directed at himself. Her understanding of him sent a chill crawling down his spine. "I am grateful to you also, Eragon, for coming here today to correct your mistake. Not everyone is as willing to acknowledge and confront their shortcomings. However, you have earned no favor with me today. You have righted the scales as best you could, but that is only what any decent person ought to have done. You have not compensated me for what I have endured, nor can you. So when next we cross paths, Eragon Shadeslayer, count me not as a friend or foe. I am ambivalent toward you, Rider; I am just as prepared to hate you as I am to love you. The outcome is yours alone to decide. . . . Saphira, you gave me the star upon my brow, and you have always been kind to me. I am and shall always remain your faithful servant."

Lifting her chin to maximize her three-and-a-half-foot height, Elva surveyed the interior of the pavilion. "Eragon, Saphira, Nasuada . . . Angela. Good day." And with that, she swept off toward the entrance. The Nighthawks parted ranks as she passed between them and went outside.

Eragon stood, feeling unsteady. "What sort of monster have I created?" The two Urgal Nighthawks touched the tip of each of their horns, which he knew was how they warded off evil. To Nasuada, he said, "I'm sorry. I seem to have only made things worse for you—for all of us."

Calm as a mountain lake, Nasuada arranged her robes before answering: "No matter. The game has gotten a little more complicated, that is all. It is to be expected the closer we get to Urû'baen and Galbatorix."

A moment later, Eragon heard the sound of an object rushing through the air toward him. He flinched, but fast as he was, he was too slow to avoid a stinging slap that knocked his head to one side and sent him staggering against a chair. He rolled across the seat of the chair and sprang upright, his left arm lifted to ward off an oncoming blow, his right arm pulled back, ready to stab with the hunting knife he had snatched from his belt during the maneuver. To his astonishment, he saw that it was Angela who had struck him. The elves were gathered inches behind the fortuneteller, ready to subdue her if she should attack him again or to escort her away should Eragon order it. Solembum was at her feet, teeth and claws bared, and his hair standing on end.

Right then, Eragon could care less about the elves. "What did you do that for?" he demanded. He winced as his split lower lip stretched, tearing the flesh farther apart. Warm, metallic-tasting blood trickled down his throat.

Angela tossed her head. "Now I'm going to have to spend the next ten years teaching Elva how to behave! That's *not* what I had in mind for the next decade!"

"Teach her?" exclaimed Eragon. "She won't let you. She'll stop you as easily as she stopped me."

"Humph. Not likely. She doesn't know what bothers me, nor what might be about to hurt me. I saw to that the day she and I first met."

"Would you share this spell with us?" Nasuada asked. "After how

270

this has turned out, it seems prudent for us to have a means of protecting ourselves from Elva."

"No, I don't think I will," said Angela. Then she too marched out of the pavilion, and Solembum stalked after her, waving his tail ever so gracefully.

The elves sheathed their blades and retreated to a discreet distance from the tent.

Nasuada rubbed her temples with a circular motion. "Magic," she cursed.

"Magic," agreed Eragon.

The pair of them started as Greta cast herself upon the ground and began to weep and wail while pulling at her thin hair, beating herself on the face, and ripping at her bodice. "Oh, my poor dear! I've lost my lamb! Lost! What will become of her, all alone? Oh, woe is me, my own little blossom rejecting me. It's a shameful reward it is for the work I've done, bending my back like a slave I have. What a cruel, hard world, always stealing your happiness from you." She groaned. "My plum. My rose. My pretty sweet pea. Gone! And no one to look after her. . . . Shadeslayer! Will you watch over her?"

Eragon grasped her by the arm and helped her to her feet, consoling her with assurances that he and Saphira would keep a close eye on Elva. *If only*, as Saphira said to Eragon, *because she might attempt to slip a knife between our ribs.*

GIFTS OF GOLD

Eragon stood next to Saphira, fifty yards from Nasuada's crimson pavilion. Glad to be free of all the commotion that had surrounded Elva, he gazed up at the clear azure sky and rolled his shoulders, already tired from the events of the day. Saphira intended to fly out to the Jiet River and bathe herself in its deep, slow-moving water, but his own intentions were less definite. He still needed to finish oiling his armor, prepare for Roran and Katrina's wedding, visit with Jeod, locate a proper sword for himself, and also . . . He scratched his chin.

How long will you be gone? he asked.

Saphira unfurled her wings in preparation for flight. *A few hours. I'm hungry. Once I am clean, I am going to catch two or three of those plump deer I've seen nibbling the grass on the western bank of the river. The Varden have shot so many of them, though, I may have to fly a half-dozen leagues toward the Spine before I find any game worth hunting.*

Don't go too far, he cautioned, *else you might encounter the Empire.*

I won't, but if I happen upon a lone group of soldiers . . . She licked her chops. *I would enjoy a quick fight. Besides, humans taste just as good as deer.*

Saphira, you wouldn't!

Her eyes sparkled. *Maybe, maybe not. It depends on whether they are wearing armor. I hate biting through metal, and scooping my food out of a shell is just as annoying.*

I see. He glanced over at the nearest elf, a tall, silver-haired woman. *The elves won't want you to go alone. Will you allow a couple of them to ride on you? Otherwise, it will be impossible for them to keep pace.*

Not today. Today, I hunt alone! With a sweep of her wings, she took off, soaring high overhead. As she turned west, toward the Jiet River, her voice sounded in his mind, fainter than before because of the distance between them. *When I return, we will fly together, won't we, Eragon?*

Yes, when you return, we will fly together, just the two of us. Her pleasure at that caused him to smile as he watched her arrow away toward the west.

Eragon lowered his gaze as Blödhgarm ran up to him, lithe as a forest cat. The elf asked where Saphira was going and seemed displeased with Eragon's explanation, but if he had any objections, he kept them to himself.

"Right," Eragon said to himself as Blödhgarm rejoined his companions. "First things first."

He strode through the camp until he found a large square of open space where thirty-some Varden were practicing with a wide assortment of weapons. To his relief, they were too busy training to notice his presence. Crouching, he lay his right hand palm-upward on the trampled earth. He chose the words he would need from the ancient language, then murmured, "Kuldr, rïsa lam iet un malthinae unin böllr."

The soil beside his hand appeared unchanged, although he could feel the spell sifting through the dirt for hundreds of feet in every direction. Not more than five seconds later, the surface of the earth began to boil like a pot of water left to sit for too long over a high flame, and it acquired a bright yellow sheen. Eragon had learned from Oromis that wherever one went, the land was sure to contain minute particles of nearly every element, and while they would be too small and scattered to mine with traditional methods, a knowledgeable magician could, with great effort, extract them.

From the center of the yellow patch, a fountain of sparkling dust arched up and over, landing in the middle of Eragon's palm. There each glittering mote melded into the next, until three spheres of pure gold, each the size of a large hazelnut, rested on his hand.

273

"Letta," said Eragon, and released the magic. He sat back on his heels and braced himself against the ground as a wave of weariness washed over him. His head drooped forward, and his eyelids descended halfway as his vision flickered and dimmed. Taking a deep breath, he admired the mirror-smooth orbs in his hand while he waited for his strength to return. *So pretty*, he thought. *If only I could have done this when we were living in Palancar Valley. . . . It would almost be easier to mine the gold, though. A spell hasn't taken so much out of me since I carried Sloan down from the top of Helgrind.*

He pocketed the gold and set out again through the camp. He found a cook tent and ate a large lunch, which he needed after casting so many arduous spells, then headed toward the area where the villagers from Carvahall were staying. As he approached, he heard the ring of metal striking metal. Curious, he turned in that direction.

Eragon stepped around a line of three wagons parked across the mouth of the lane and saw Horst standing in a thirty-foot gap between the tents, holding one end of a five-foot-long bar of steel. The other end of the bar was bright cherry red and rested on the face of a massive two-hundred-pound anvil that was staked to the top of a low, wide stump. On either side of the anvil, Horst's burly sons, Albriech and Baldor, alternated striking the steel with sledgehammers, which they swung over their heads in huge circular blows. A makeshift forge glowed several feet behind the anvil.

The hammering was so loud, Eragon kept his distance until Albriech and Baldor had finished spreading the steel and Horst had returned the bar to the forge. Waving his free arm, Horst said, "Ho, Eragon!" Then he held up a finger, forestalling Eragon's reply, and pulled a plug of felted wool out of his left ear. "Ah, now I can hear again. What brings you about, Eragon?" While he spoke, his sons scooped more charcoal into the forge from a bucket and set about tidying up the tongs, hammers, dies, and other tools that lay on the ground. All three men gleamed with sweat.

"I wanted to know what was causing such a commotion," said

Eragon. "I should have guessed it was you. No one else can create as big an uproar as someone from Carvahall."

Horst laughed, his thick, spade-shaped beard pointed up toward the sky until his mirth was exhausted. "Ah, that tickles my pride, it does. And aren't you the living truth of it, eh?"

"We all are," Eragon replied. "You, me, Roran, everyone from Carvahall. Alagaësia will never be the same once the lot of us are done." He gestured at the forge and the other equipment. "Why are you here? I thought that all the smiths were—"

"So they are, Eragon. So they are. However, I convinced the captain who's in charge of this part of the camp to let me work closer to our tent." Horst tugged at the end of his beard. "It's on account of Elain, you know. This child, it goes hard with her, and no wonder, considering what we went through to get here. She's always been delicate, and now I worry that . . . well . . ." He shook himself like a bear ridding itself of flies. "Maybe you could look in on her when you get a chance and see if you can ease her discomfort."

"I'll do that," Eragon promised.

With a satisfied grunt, Horst lifted the bar partway out of the coals to better judge the color of the steel. Plunging the bar back into the center of the fire, he jerked his beard toward Albriech. "Here now, give it some air. It's almost ready." As Albriech began to pump the leather bellows, Horst grinned at Eragon. "When I told the Varden I was a smith, they were so happy, you would have thought I was another Dragon Rider. They don't have enough metalworkers, you see. And they gave me what tools I was missing, including that anvil. When we left Carvahall, I wept at the prospect that I would not have the opportunity to practice my craft again. I am no swordsmith, but here, ah, here there is enough work to keep Albriech, Baldor, and me busy for the next fifty years. It doesn't pay very well, but at least we're not stretched out on a rack in Galbatorix's dungeons."

"Or the Ra'zac could be nibbling on our bones," observed Baldor.

"Aye, that too." Horst motioned for his sons to take up the

275

sledgehammers again and then, holding the felt plug beside his left ear, said, "Is there anything else you wish of us, Eragon? The steel is ready, and I cannot leave it in the fire any longer without weakening it."

"Do you know where Gedric is?"

"Gedric?" The furrow between Horst's eyebrows deepened. "He should be practicing the sword and spear along with the rest of the men, thataway about a quarter of a mile." Horst pointed with a thumb.

Eragon thanked him and departed in the direction Horst had indicated. The repetitive ring of metal striking metal resumed, clear as the peals of a bell and as sharp and piercing as a glass needle stabbing the air. Eragon covered his ears and smiled. It comforted him that Horst had retained his strength of purpose and that, despite the loss of his wealth and home, he was still the same person he had been in Carvahall. Somehow the smith's consistency and resiliency renewed Eragon's faith that if only they could overthrow Galbatorix, everything would be all right in the end, and his life and those of the villagers from Carvahall would regain a semblance of normalcy.

Eragon soon arrived at the field where the men of Carvahall were drilling with their new weapons. Gedric was there, as Horst had suggested he would be, sparring with Fisk, Darmmen, and Morn. A quick word on the part of Eragon with the one-armed veteran who was leading the drills was sufficient to secure Gedric's temporary release.

The tanner ran over to Eragon and stood before him, his gaze lowered. He was short and swarthy, with a jaw like a mastiff's, heavy eyebrows, and arms thick and gnarled from stirring the foul-smelling vats where he had cured his hides. Although he was far from handsome, Eragon knew him to be a kind and honest man.

"What can I do for you, Shadeslayer?" Gedric mumbled.

"You have already done it. And I have come here to thank and repay you."

"I? How have I helped you, Shadeslayer?" He spoke slowly, cautiously, as if afraid Eragon were setting a trap for him.

"Soon after I ran away from Carvahall, you discovered that someone had stolen three ox hides from the drying hut by the vats. Am I right?"

Gedric's face darkened with embarrassment, and he shuffled his feet. "Ah, well now, I didn't lock that hut, you know. Anyone might have snuck in and carried those hides off. Besides, given what's happened since, I can't see as it's much important. I destroyed most of my stock before we trooped into the Spine, to keep the Empire and those filthy Ra'zac from getting their claws on anything of use. Whoever took those hides saved me from having to destroy three more. So let bygones be bygones, I say."

"Perhaps," said Eragon, "but I still feel honor-bound to tell you that it was I who stole your hides."

Gedric met his gaze then, looking at him as if he were an ordinary person, without fear, awe, or undue respect, as if the tanner were reevaluating his opinion of Eragon.

"I stole them, and I'm not proud of it, but I needed the hides. Without them, I doubt I would have survived long enough to reach the elves in Du Weldenvarden. I always preferred to think that I had borrowed the hides, but the truth is, I stole them, for I had no intention of returning them. Therefore, you have my apologies. And since I am keeping the hides, or what is left of them, it seems only right to pay you for them." From within his belt, Eragon removed one of the spheres of gold—hard, round, and warm from the heat of his flesh—and handed it to Gedric.

Gedric stared at the shiny metal pearl, his massive jaw clamped shut, the lines around his thin-lipped mouth harsh and unyielding. He did not insult Eragon by weighing the gold in his hand, nor by biting it, but when he spoke, he said, "I cannot accept this, Eragon. I was a good tanner, but the leather I made was not worth this much. Your generosity does you credit, but it would bother me to keep this gold. I would feel as if I hadn't earned it."

Unsurprised, Eragon said, "You would not deny another man the opportunity to haggle for a fair price, would you?"

"No."

"Good. Then you cannot deny me this. Most people haggle downward. In this case, I have chosen to haggle upward, but I will still haggle as fiercely as if I were trying to save myself a handful of coins. To me, the hides are worth every ounce of that gold, and I would not pay you a copper less, not even if you held a knife to my throat."

Gedric's thick fingers closed around the gold orb. "Since you insist, I will not be so churlish as to keep refusing you. No one can say that Gedric Ostvensson allowed good fortune to pass him by because he was too busy protesting his own unworthiness. My thanks, Shadeslayer." He placed the orb in a pouch on his belt, wrapping the gold in a patch of wool cloth to protect it from scratches. "Garrow did right by you, Eragon. He did right by both you and Roran. He may have been sharp as vinegar and as hard and dry as a winter rutabaga, but he raised the two of you well. He would be proud of you, I think."

Unexpected emotion clogged Eragon's chest.

As Gedric turned to rejoin the other villagers, he paused. "If I may ask, Eragon, why were those hides worth so much to you? What did you use them for?"

Eragon chuckled. "Use them for? Why, with Brom's help, I made a saddle for Saphira out of them. She doesn't wear it as often as she used to—not since the elves gave us a proper dragon's saddle—but it served us well through many a scrape and fight, and even the Battle of Farthen Dûr."

Astonishment raised Gedric's eyebrows, exposing pale skin that normally lay hidden in deep folds. Like a split in blue-gray granite, a wide grin spread across his jaw, transforming his features. "A saddle!" he breathed. "Imagine, me tanning the leather for a Rider's saddle! And without a hint of what I was doing at the time, no less! No, not *a* Rider, *the* Rider. He who will finally cast down the black tyrant himself! If only my father could see me now!" Kicking up his heels, Gedric danced an impromptu jig. With his grin undiminished, he bowed to Eragon and trotted back to his place among the villagers, where he began to relate his tale to everyone within earshot.

Eager to escape before the lot of them could descend upon him, Eragon slipped away between the rows of tents, pleased with what he had accomplished. *It might take me a while*, he thought, *but I always settle my debts.*

Before long, he arrived at another tent, close to the eastern edge of the camp. He knocked on the pole between the two front flaps.

With a sharp sound, the entrance was yanked aside to reveal Jeod's wife, Helen, standing in the opening. She regarded Eragon with a cold expression. "You've come to talk with *him*, I suppose."

"If he's here." Which Eragon knew perfectly well he was, for he could sense Jeod's mind as clearly as Helen's.

For a moment, Eragon thought Helen might deny the presence of her husband, but then she shrugged and moved aside. "You might as well come in, then."

Eragon found Jeod sitting on a stool, poring over an assortment of scrolls, books, and sheaves of loose papers that were piled high on a cot bare of blankets. A thin shock of hair hung across Jeod's forehead, mimicking the curve of the scar that stretched from his scalp to his left temple.

"Eragon!" he cried as he saw him, the lines of concentration on his face clearing. "Welcome, welcome!" He shook Eragon's hand and then offered him the stool. "Here, I shall sit on the corner of the bed. No, please, you are our guest. Would you care for some food or drink? Nasuada gives us an extra ration, so do not restrain yourself for fear that we will go hungry on your account. It is poor fare compared with what we served you in Teirm, but then no one should go to war and expect to eat well, not even a king."

"A cup of tea would be nice," said Eragon.

"Tea and biscuits it is." Jeod glanced at Helen.

Snatching the kettle off the ground, Helen braced it against her hip, fit the nipple of a waterskin in the end of the spout, and squeezed. The kettle reverberated with a dull roar as a stream of water struck the bottom. Helen's fingers tightened around the neck of the waterskin, restricting the flow to a languorous trickle. She remained thus, with the detached look of a person performing an unpleasant task, while the water droplets drummed out a maddening beat against the inside of the kettle.

An apologetic smile flickered across Jeod's face. He stared at a scrap of paper beside his knee as he waited for Helen to finish. Eragon studied a wrinkle in the side of the tent.

The bombastic trickle continued for over three minutes.

When the kettle was finally full, Helen removed the deflated waterskin from the spout, hung it on a hook on the center pole of the tent, and stormed out.

Eragon raised an eyebrow at Jeod.

Jeod spread his hands. "My position with the Varden is not as prominent as she had hoped, and she blames me for the fact. She agreed to flee Teirm with me, expecting, or so I believe, that Nasuada would vault me into the inner circle of her advisers, or grant me lands and riches fit for a lord, or some other extravagant reward for my help stealing Saphira's egg those many years ago. What Helen did not bargain on was the unglamorous life of a common swordsman: sleeping in a tent, fixing her own food, washing her own clothes, and so on. It's not that wealth and status are her only concerns, but you have to understand, she was born into one of the richest shipping families of Teirm, and for most of our marriage, I was not unsuccessful in my own ventures. She is unused to such privations as these, and she has yet to reconcile herself to them." His shoulders rose and fell a fraction of an inch. "My own hope was that this adventure—if it deserves such a romantic term—would narrow the rifts that have opened between us in recent years, but as always, nothing is ever as simple as it seems."

"Do *you* feel that the Varden ought to show you greater consideration?" asked Eragon.

"For myself, no. For Helen . . ." Jeod hesitated. "I want her to be happy. My reward was in escaping from Gil'ead with my life when Brom and I were attacked by Morzan, his dragon, and his men; in the satisfaction of knowing that I had helped strike a crippling blow against Galbatorix; in being able to return to my previous life and yet still help further the Varden's cause; and in being able to marry Helen. Those were my rewards, and I am more than content with them. Any doubts I had vanished the instant I saw Saphira fly out of the smoke of the Burning Plains. I do not know what to do about Helen, though. But I forget myself. These are not your troubles, and I should not lay them upon you."

Eragon touched a scroll with the tip of his index finger. "Then tell me, why so many papers? Have you become a copyist?"

The question amused Jeod. "Hardly, although the work is often as tedious. Since it was I who discovered the hidden passageway into Galbatorix's castle, in Urû'baen, and I was able to bring with me some of the rare books from my library in Teirm, Nasuada has set me to searching for similar weaknesses in the other cities of the Empire. If I could find mention of a tunnel that led underneath the walls of Dras-Leona, for example, it might save us a great deal of bloodshed."

"Where are you looking?"

"Everywhere I can." Jeod brushed back the lock of hair that was hanging over his forehead. "Histories; myths; legends; poems; songs; religious tracts; the writings of Riders, magicians, wanderers, madmen, obscure potentates, various generals, anyone who might have knowledge of a hidden door or a secret mechanism or something of that ilk that we might turn to our advantage. The amount of material I have to sift through is immense, for all of the cities have stood for hundreds of years, and some antedate the arrival of humans in Alagaësia."

"Is it likely you will actually find anything?"

"No, not likely. It is never likely that you will succeed in ferreting out the secrets of the past. But I may still prevail, given enough time. I have no doubt that what I am searching for exists in each of the cities; they are too old *not* to contain surreptitious ways in and out through their walls. However, it is another question entirely whether *records* of those ways exist and whether we possess those records. People who know about concealed trapdoors and the like usually want to keep the information to themselves." Jeod grasped a handful of the papers next to him on the cot and brought them closer to his face, then snorted and tossed the papers away. "I'm trying to solve riddles invented by people who didn't want them to be solved."

He and Eragon continued talking about other, less important matters until Helen reappeared, carrying three mugs of steaming-hot red-clover tea. As Eragon accepted his mug, he noted that her earlier anger seemed to have subsided, and he wondered if she had been listening outside to what Jeod had said about her. She handed Jeod his mug and, from somewhere behind Eragon, procured a tin plate laden with flat biscuits and a small clay pot of honey. Then she withdrew a few feet and stood leaning against the center pole, blowing on her own mug.

As was polite, Jeod waited until Eragon had taken a biscuit from the plate and consumed a bite of it before saying, "To what do I owe the pleasure of your company, Eragon? Unless I am mistaken, this is no idle visit."

Eragon sipped his tea. "After the Battle of the Burning Plains, I promised I would tell you how Brom died. That is why I have come."

A gray pallor replaced the color in Jeod's cheeks. "Oh."

"I don't have to, if that's not what you want," Eragon quickly pointed out.

With an effort, Jeod shook his head. "No, I do. You merely caught me by surprise."

When Jeod did not ask Helen to leave, Eragon was uncertain

whether he should continue, but then he decided that it did not matter if Helen or anyone else heard his story. In a slow, deliberate voice, Eragon began to recount the events that had transpired since he and Brom had left Jeod's house. He described their encounter with the band of Urgals, their search for the Ra'zac in Dras-Leona, how the Ra'zac had ambushed them outside the city, and how the Ra'zac had stabbed Brom as they fled from Murtagh's attack.

Eragon's throat constricted as he spoke of Brom's last hours, of the cool sandstone cave where he had lain, of the feelings of help-lessness that had assailed Eragon as he watched Brom slipping away, of the smell of death that had pervaded the dry air, of Brom's final words, of the sandstone tomb Eragon had made with magic, and of how Saphira had transformed it into pure diamond.

"If only I had known what I know now," Eragon said, "then I could have saved him. Instead . . ." Unable to summon words past the tightness in his throat, he wiped his eyes and gulped at his tea. He wished it were something stronger.

A sigh escaped Jeod. "And so ended Brom. Alas, we are all far worse off without him. If he could have chosen the means of his death, though, I think he would have chosen to die like this, in the service of the Varden, defending the last free Dragon Rider."

"Were you aware that he had been a Rider himself?"

Jeod nodded. "The Varden told me before I met him."

"He seemed as it he was a man who revealed little about himself," observed Helen.

Jeod and Eragon laughed. "That he was," said Jeod. "I still have not recovered from the shock of seeing him and you, Eragon, stand-ing on our doorstep. Brom always kept his own counsel, but we be-came close friends when we were traveling together, and I cannot understand why he let me believe he was dead for what, sixteen, seventeen years? Too long. What's more, since it was Brom who de-livered Saphira's egg to the Varden after he slew Morzan in Gil'ead, the Varden couldn't very well tell me they had her egg without re-vealing that Brom was still alive. So I've spent the better part of two decades convinced that the one great adventure of my life had ended in failure and that, as a result, we had lost our only hope of having a Dragon Rider to help us overthrow Galbatorix. The knowledge was no easy burden, I can assure you. . . ."

With one hand, Jeod rubbed his brow. "When I opened our front door and realized whom I was looking at, I thought that the ghosts of my past had come to haunt me. Brom said he kept himself hidden to ensure that he would still be alive to train the new Rider when he or she should appear, but his explanation has never entirely satisfied me. Why was it necessary for him to cut himself off from nearly everyone he knew or cared about? What was he afraid of? What was he protecting?"

Jeod fingered the handle of his mug. "I cannot prove it, but it seems to me that Brom must have discovered something in Gil'ead when he was fighting Morzan and his dragon, something so momentous, it moved Brom to abandon everything that was his life up until then. It's a fanciful conjecture, I admit, but I cannot account for Brom's actions except by postulating that there was a piece of information he never shared with me nor another living soul."

Again Jeod sighed, and he drew a hand down his long face. "After so many years apart, I had hoped Brom and I might ride together once more, but fate had other ideas, it seems. And then to lose him a second time but a few weeks after discovering he was still alive was a cruel joke for the world to play." Helen swept past Eragon and went to stand by Jeod, touching him on the shoulder. He offered her a wan smile and wrapped an arm around her narrow waist. "I'm glad that you and Saphira gave Brom a tomb even a dwarf king might envy. He deserved that and more for all he did for Alagaësia. Although once people discover his grave, I have a horrible suspicion they will not hesitate to break it apart for the diamond."

"If they do, they will regret it," muttered Eragon. He resolved to return to the site at the earliest opportunity and place wards around Brom's tomb to protect it from grave robbers. "Besides, they will be too busy hunting gold lilies to bother Brom."

"What?"

"Nothing. It's not important." The three of them sipped their tea. Helen nibbled on a biscuit. Then Eragon asked, "You met Morzan, didn't you?"

"They were not the friendliest of occasions, but yes, I met him."

"What was he like?"

"As a person? I really couldn't say, although I'm well acquainted with tales of his atrocities. Every time Brom and I crossed paths with him, he was trying to kill us. Or rather, capture, torture, and *then* kill us, none of which are conducive to establishing a close relationship." Eragon was too intent to respond to Jeod's humor. Jeod shifted on the bed. "As a warrior, Morzan was terrifying. We spent a great deal of time running away from him, I seem to remember— him and his dragon, that is. Few things are as frightening as having an enraged dragon chasing you."

"How did he look?"

"You seem inordinately interested in him."

Eragon blinked once. "I'm curious. He was the last of the Forsworn to die, and Brom was the one who slew him. And now Morzan's son is my mortal enemy."

"Let me see, then," said Jeod. "He was tall, he had broad shoulders, his hair was dark like a raven's feathers, and his eyes were different colors. One was blue and one was black. His chin was bare, and he was missing the tip of one of his fingers; I forget which. Handsome he was, in a cruel, haughty manner, and when he spoke, he was most charismatic. His armor was always polished bright, whether mail or a breastplate, as if he had no fear of being spotted by his enemies, which I suppose he hadn't. When he laughed, it sounded as if he were in pain."

"What of his companion, the woman Selena? Did you meet her as well?"

Jeod laughed. "If I had, I would not be here today. Morzan may have been a fearsome swordsman, a formidable magician, and a murderous traitor, but it was that woman of his who inspired the most terror in people. Morzan only used her for missions that were so repugnant, difficult, or secretive that no one else would agree to undertake them. She was his Black Hand, and her presence always signaled imminent death, torture, betrayal, or some other horror." Eragon felt sick hearing his mother described thusly. "She was utterly ruthless, devoid of either pity or compassion. It was said that when she asked Morzan to enter his service, he tested her by teaching her the word for *heal* in the ancient language—for she was a spellcaster as well as a common fighter—and then pitting her against twelve of his finest swordsmen."

"How did she defeat them?"

"She healed them of their fear and their hate and all the things that drive a man to kill. And then while they stood grinning at each other like idiot sheep, she went up to the men and cut their throats. . . . Are you feeling well, Eragon? You are as pale as a corpse."

"I'm fine. What else do you remember?"

Jeod tapped the side of his mug. "Precious little concerning Selena. She was always somewhat of an enigma. No one besides Morzan even knew her real name until just a few months before Morzan's death. To the public at large, she has never been anything other than the Black Hand; the Black Hand we have now—the collection of spies, assassins, and magicians who carry out Galbatorix's low skulduggery—is Galbatorix's attempt to re-create Selena's usefulness to Morzan. Even among the Varden, only a handful of people were privy to her name, and most of them are moldering in graves now. As I recall, it was Brom who discovered her true identity. Before I went to the Varden with the information concerning the secret passageway into Castle Ilirea—which the elves built millennia ago and which Galbatorix expanded upon to form the black citadel that now dominates Urû'baen—before I went to them, Brom had spent a rather significant length of time spying on Morzan's estate in the hope he might unearth a hitherto unsuspected weakness of Morzan's. . . . I believe Brom gained admittance to Morzan's hall by disguising himself as a member of the serving staff. It was then that he found out what he did about Selena. Still, we never did learn why she was so attached to Morzan. Perhaps she loved him. In any event, she was utterly loyal to him, even to the point of death. Soon after Brom killed Morzan, word reached the Varden that sickness had taken her. It is as if the trained hawk was so fond of her master, she could not live without him."

She was not entirely loyal, thought Eragon. *She defied Morzan when it came to me, even though she lost her life as a result. If only she could have rescued Murtagh as well.* As for Jeod's accounts of her misdeeds, Eragon chose to believe that Morzan had perverted her essentially good nature. For the sake of his own sanity, Eragon could not accept that both his parents had been evil.

"She loved him," he said, staring at the murky dregs at the bottom of his mug. "In the beginning, she loved him; maybe not so much later. Murtagh is her son."

Jeod raised an eyebrow. "Indeed? You have it from Murtagh himself, I suppose?" Eragon nodded. "Well, that explains a number of questions I always had. Murtagh's mother . . . I'm surprised that Brom didn't uncover that particular secret."

"Morzan did everything he could to conceal Murtagh's existence, even from the other members of the Forsworn."

"Knowing the history of those power-hungry, backstabbing knaves, he probably saved Murtagh's life. More's the pity too."

Silence crept among them then, like a shy animal ready to flee at the slightest motion. Eragon continued to gaze into his mug. A host of questions bedeviled him, but he knew that Jeod could not answer them and it was unlikely anyone else could either: Why had Brom hidden himself in Carvahall? To keep watch over Eragon, the son of his most hated foe? Had it been some cruel joke giving Eragon Zar'roc, his father's blade? And why had Brom not told him the truth about his parentage? He tightened his grip on the mug and, without meaning to, shattered the clay.

The three of them started at the unexpected noise.

"Here, let me help you with that," said Helen, bustling forward and dabbing at his tunic with a rag. Embarrassed, Eragon apologized several times, to which both Jeod and Helen responded by assuring him it was a small mishap and not to worry himself about it.

While Helen picked up the shards of fire-hardened clay, Jeod began to dig through the layers of books, scrolls, and loose papers that covered the bed, saying, "Ah, it had nearly slipped my mind. I have something for you, Eragon, that might prove useful. If only I can find it here. . . ." With a pleased exclamation, he straightened, flourishing a book, which he handed to Eragon.

It was *Domia abr Wyrda*, the *Dominance of Fate*, a complete history of Alagaësia written by Heslant the Monk. Eragon had first seen it in Jeod's library in Teirm. He had not expected that he would ever get a chance to examine it again. Savoring the feeling, he ran his hands over the carved leather on the front cover, which was shiny with age, then opened the book and admired the neat rows of runes within, lettered in glossy red ink. Awed by the size of the knowledge hoard he held, Eragon said, "You wish me to have this?"

"I do," asserted Jeod. He moved out of the way as Helen retrieved a fragment of the mug from under the bed. "I think you might profit by it. You are engaged in historic events, Eragon, and the roots of the difficulties you face lie in happenings from decades, centuries, and millennia ago. If I were you, I would study at every opportunity the lessons history has to teach us, for they may help you with the problems of today. In my own life, reading the record of the past has often provided me with the courage and the insight to choose the correct path."

Eragon longed to accept the gift, but still he hesitated. "Brom said that *Domia abr Wyrda* was the most valuable thing in your house. And rare as well. . . . Besides, what of your work? Don't you need this for your research?"

"*Domia abr Wyrda* is valuable and it is rare," said Jeod, "but only in the Empire, where Galbatorix burns every copy he finds and hangs their unfortunate owners. Here in the camp, I have already had six copies foisted upon me by members of King Orrin's court, and this is hardly what one would call a great center of learning. However, I do not part with it lightly, and only because you can put it to better use than I can. Books should go where they will be most appreciated, and not sit unread, gathering dust on a forgotten shelf, don't you agree?"

"I do." Eragon closed *Domia abr Wyrda* and again traced the intricate patterns on the front with his fingers, fascinated by the swirling designs that had been chiseled into the leather. "Thank you. I shall treasure it for as long as it is mine to watch over." Jeod dipped his head and leaned back against the wall of the tent, appearing satisfied. Turning the book on its edge, Eragon examined the lettering on the spine. "What was Heslant a monk of?"

"A small, secretive sect called the Arcaena that originated in the area by Kuasta. Their order, which has endured for at least five hundred years, believes that all knowledge is sacred." A hint of a smile lent Jeod's features a mysterious cast. "They have dedicated themselves to collecting every piece of information in the world and preserving it against a time when they believe an unspecified catastrophe will destroy all the civilizations in Alagaësia."

"It seems a strange religion," Eragon said.

"Are not all religions strange to those who stand outside of them?" countered Jeod.

Eragon said, "I have a gift for you as well, or rather, for you, Helen." She tilted her head, a quizzical frown on her face. "Your family was a merchant family, yes?" She jerked her chin in an affirmative. "Were you very familiar with the business yourself?"

Lightning sparked in Helen's eyes. "If I had not married him"— she motioned with a shoulder—"I would have taken over the family affairs when my father died. I was an only child, and my father taught me everything he knew."

That was what Eragon had hoped to hear. To Jeod, he said, "You claimed that you are content with your lot here with the Varden."

"And so I am. Mostly."

"I understand. However, you risked a great deal to help Brom and me, and you risked even more to help Roran and everyone else from Carvahall."

"The Palancar Pirates."

Eragon chuckled and continued. "Without your assistance, the Empire would surely have captured them. And because of your act of rebellion, you both lost all that was dear to you in Teirm."

"We would have lost it anyway. I was bankrupt and the Twins had betrayed me to the Empire. It was only a matter of time before Lord Risthart had me arrested."

"Maybe, but you still helped Roran. Who can blame you if you were protecting your own necks at the same time? The fact remains that you abandoned your lives in Teirm in order to steal the *Dragon Wing* along with Roran and the villagers. And for your sacrifice, I will always be grateful. So this is part of my thanks. . . ."

Sliding a finger underneath his belt, Eragon removed the second of the three gold orbs and presented it to Helen. She cradled it as gently as if it were a baby robin. While she gazed at it with wonder, and Jeod craned his neck to see over the edge of her hand, Eragon said, "It's not a fortune, but if you are clever, you should be able to make it grow. What Nasuada did with lace taught me that there is a great deal of opportunity for a person to prosper in war."

"Oh yes," breathed Helen. "War is a merchant's delight."

"For one, Nasuada mentioned to me last night at dinner that the dwarves are running low on mead, and as you might suspect, they have the means to buy as many casks as they want, even if the price were a thousandfold of what it was before the war. But then, that's just a suggestion. You may find others who are more desperate to trade if you look for yourself."

Eragon staggered back a step as Helen rushed at him and embraced him. Her hair tickled his chin. She released him, suddenly shy, then her excitement burst forth again and she lifted the honey-colored globe in front of her nose and said, "Thank you, Eragon! Oh, thank you!" She pointed at the gold. "This I can use. I know I can. With it, I'll build an empire even larger than my father's." The shiny orb disappeared within her clenched fist. "You believe my ambition exceeds my abilities? It shall be as I have said. I shall not fail!"

Eragon bowed to her. "I hope that you succeed and that your success benefits us all."

Eragon noticed that hard cords stood out in Helen's neck as she curtsied and said, "You are most generous, Shadeslayer. Again I thank you."

"Yes, thank you," said Jeod, rising from the bed. "I cannot think that we deserve this"—Helen shot him a furious look, which he ignored—"but it is most welcome nevertheless."

Improvising, Eragon added, "And for you, Jeod, your gift is not from me, but Saphira. She has agreed to let you fly on her when you both have a spare hour or two." It pained Eragon to share Saphira, and he knew that she would be upset he had not consulted her before volunteering her services, but after giving Helen the gold, he would have felt guilty about not giving Jeod something of equal value.

A film of tears glazed Jeod's eyes. He grasped Eragon's hand and shook it and, still holding it, said, "I cannot imagine a higher honor. Thank you. You don't know how much you have done for us."

Extricating himself from Jeod's grip, Eragon edged toward the entrance to the tent while excusing himself as gracefully as he could and making his farewells. Finally, after yet another round of thanks on their part and a self-deprecating "It was nothing," he managed to escape outdoors.

Eragon hefted *Domia abr Wyrda* and then glanced at the sun. It would not be long until Saphira returned, but he still had time to attend to one other thing. First, though, he would have to stop by his tent; he did not want to risk damaging *Domia abr Wyrda* by carrying it with him across the camp.

I own a book, he thought, delighted.

He set off at a trot, clasping the book against his chest, as Blödhgarm and the other elves followed close behind.

I NEED A SWORD!

Once *Domia abr Wyrda* was safely ensconced in his tent, Eragon went to the Varden's armory, a large open pavilion filled with racks of spears, swords, pikes, bows, and crossbows. Mounds of shields and leather armor filled slatted crates. The more expensive mail, tunics, coifs, and leggings hung on wooden stands. Hundreds of conical helmets gleamed like polished silver. Bales of arrows lined the pavilion, and among them sat a score or more fletchers, busy refurbishing arrows whose feathers had been damaged during the Battle of the Burning Plains. A constant stream of men rushed in and out of the pavilion: some bringing weapons and armor to be repaired, others new recruits coming to be outfitted, and still others ferrying equipment to different parts of the camp. Everyone seemed to be shouting at the top of their lungs. And in the center of the commotion stood the man Eragon had hoped to see: Fredric, the Varden's weapon master.

Blödhgarm accompanied Eragon as he strode into the pavilion toward Fredric. As soon as they stepped underneath the cloth roof, the men inside fell silent, their eyes fixed on the two of them. Then they resumed their activities, albeit with quicker steps and quieter voices.

Raising an arm in welcome, Fredric hurried to meet them. As always, he wore his suit of hairy oxhide armor—which smelled nearly as offensive as the animal must have in its original form—as well as a massive two-handed sword hung crosswise over his back, the hilt projecting above his right shoulder. "Shadeslayer!" he rumbled. "How can I help you this fine afternoon?"

"I need a sword."

Fredric's smile broke through his beard. "Ah, I wondered if you'd be visiting me about that. When you set out for Helgrind without a blade in hand, I thought, well, maybe you're beyond such things now. Maybe you can do all your fighting with magic."

"No, not yet."

"Well, I can't say as I'm sorry. Everyone needs a good sword, no matter how skilled they may be with conjuring. In the end, it always comes down to steel against steel. Just you watch, that's how this fight with the Empire will be resolved, with the point of a sword being driven through Galbatorix's accursed heart. Heh, I'd wager a year's wages that even Galbatorix has a sword of his own and that he *uses* it too, despite him being able to gut you like a fish with a flick of his finger. Nothing can quite compare to the feel of fine steel in your fist."

While he spoke, Fredric led them toward a rack of swords that stood apart from the others. "What kind of sword are you looking for?" he asked. "That Zar'roc you had was a one-handed sword, if I remember rightly. With a blade about two thumbs wide—two of my thumbs, in any case—and of a shape equally suited for both the cut and thrust, yes?" Eragon indicated that was so, and the weapon master grunted and began to pull swords off the rack and swing them through the air, only to replace them with seeming dissatisfaction. "Elf blades tend to be thinner and lighter than ours or the dwarves', on account of the enchantments they forge into the steel. If we made ours as delicate as theirs, the swords wouldn't last more than a minute in a battle before bending, breaking, or chipping so badly, you couldn't cut soft cheese with them." His eyes darted toward Blödhgarm. "Isn't that so, elf?"

"Even as you say, human," responded Blödhgarm in a perfectly modulated voice.

Fredric nodded and examined the edge of another sword, then snorted and dropped it back on the rack. "Which means whatever sword you choose will probably be heavier than you're used to. That shouldn't pose much difficulty for you, Shadeslayer, but the extra weight may still upset the timing of your blows."

"I appreciate the warning," said Eragon.

"Not at all," said Fredric. "That's what I'm here for: to keep as many of the Varden from getting killed as I can and to help them kill as many of Galbatorix's blasted soldiers as I can. It's a good job." Leaving the rack, he lumbered over to another one, hidden behind a pile of rectangular shields. "Finding the right sword for someone is an art unto itself. A sword should feel like an extension of your arm, as if it had grown out of your very flesh. You shouldn't have to think about how you want it to move; you should simply move it as instinctively as an egret his beak or a dragon her claws. The perfect sword is intent incarnate: what you want, so it does."

"You sound like a poet."

With a modest expression, Fredric half shrugged. "I've been picking weapons for men who are about to march into combat for twenty-six years. It seeps into your bones after a while, turns your mind to thoughts of fate and destiny and whether that young fellow I sent off with a billed pike would still be alive if I had given him a mace instead." Fredric paused with a hand hovering over the middle sword on the rack and looked at Eragon. "Do you prefer to fight with or without a shield?"

"With," Eragon said. "But I can't carry one around with me all the time. And there never seems to be one handy when I'm attacked."

Fredric tapped the hilt of the sword and gnawed on the edge of his beard. "Humph. So you need a sword you can use by itself but that's not too long to use with every kind of shield from a buckler to a wall shield. That means a sword of medium length, easy to wield with one arm. It has to be a blade you can wear at all occasions, elegant enough for a coronation and tough enough to fend off a band of Kull." He grimaced. "It's not natural, what Nasuada's done, allying us with those monsters. It can't last. The likes of us and them were never meant to mix. . . ." He shook himself. "It's a pity you only want a single sword. Or am I mistaken?"

"No. Saphira and I travel far too much to be lugging around a half-dozen blades."

"I suppose you're right. Besides, a warrior like you isn't expected to have more than one weapon. The curse of the named blade, I call it."

"What's that?"

"Every great warrior," said Fredric, "wields a sword—it's usually a sword—that has a name. Either he names it himself or, once he proves his prowess with some extraordinary feat, the bards name it for him. Thereafter, he *has* to use that sword. It's expected of him. If he shows up to a battle without it, his fellow warriors will ask where it is, and they will wonder if he is ashamed of his success and if he is insulting them by rejecting the acclaim they have bestowed upon him, and even his enemies may insist upon waiting to fight until he fetches his famed blade. Just you watch; as soon as you fight Murtagh or do anything else memorable with your new sword, the Varden will insist upon giving it a title. And they will look to see it on your hip from then on." He continued speaking while he proceeded to a third rack: "I never thought I would be fortunate enough to help a Rider choose his weapon. What an opportunity! It feels as if this is a culmination of my work with the Varden."

Plucking a sword from the rack, Fredric handed it to Eragon. Eragon tilted the tip of the sword up and down, then shook his head; the shape of the hilt was wrong for his hand. The weapon master did not seem disappointed. To the contrary, Eragon's rejection seemed to invigorate him, as if he relished the challenge Eragon posed. He presented another sword to Eragon, and again Eragon shook his head; the balance was too far forward for his liking.

"What worries me," Fredric said, returning to the rack, "is that any sword I give you will have to withstand impacts that would destroy an ordinary blade. What you need is dwarf-work. Their smiths are the finest besides the elves', and sometimes they even exceed them." Fredric peered at Eragon. "Hold now, I've been asking the wrong questions! How was it you were taught to block and parry? Was it edge on edge? I seem to recall you doing something of the kind when you dueled Arya in Farthen Dûr."

Eragon frowned. "What of it?"

"What of it?" Fredric guffawed. "Not to be disrespectful, Shadeslayer, but if you hit the edge of a sword against that of another, you will cause grave damage to both. That might not have been a problem with an enchanted blade like Zar'roc, but you can't do it with any of the swords I have here, not unless you want to replace your sword after every battle."

An image flashed in Eragon's mind of the chipped edges of Murtagh's sword, and he felt irritated with himself for having forgotten something so obvious. He had become accustomed to Zar'roc, which never dulled, never showed signs of wear, and, so far as he knew, was impervious to most spells. He was not even sure it was possible to destroy a Rider's sword. "You need not worry about that; I will protect the sword with magic. Must I wait all day for a weapon?"

"One more question, Shadeslayer. Will your magic last forever?"

Eragon's frown deepened. "Since you ask, no. Only one elf understands the making of a Rider's sword, and she has not shared her secrets with me. What I *can* do is transfer a certain amount of energy into a sword. The energy will keep it from getting damaged until the blows that *would* have damaged the sword exhaust the store of energy, at which point the sword will revert to its original state and, odds are, shatter in my grip the next time I close with my opponent."

Fredric scratched his beard. "I'll take your word for it, Shadeslayer. The point being, if you hammer on soldiers long enough, you'll wear out your spells, and the harder you hammer, the sooner the spells will vanish. Eh?"

"Exactly."

"Then you should still avoid going edge on edge, as it will wear out your spells faster than most any other move."

"I don't have time for this," Eragon snapped, his impatience overflowing. "I don't have the time to learn a completely different way of fighting. The Empire might attack at any moment. I have to concentrate on practicing what I *do* know, not trying to master a whole new set of forms."

Fredric clapped his hands. "I know just the thing for you, then!" Going to a crate filled with arms, he began digging through it, talking to himself as he did. "First *this*, then *that*, and then we'll see where we stand." From the bottom of the crate, he pulled out a large black mace with a flanged head.

Fredric rapped a knuckle against the mace. "You can break swords with this. You can split mail and batter in helms, and you won't do it the slightest bit of harm, no matter what you hit."

"It's a club," Eragon protested. "A metal club."

"What of it? With your strength, you can swing it as if it were light as a reed. You'll be a terror on the battlefield with this, you will."

Eragon shook his head. "No. Smashing things isn't how I prefer to fight. Besides, I would never have been able to kill Durza by stabbing him through the heart if I had been carrying a mace instead of a sword."

"Then I have only one more suggestion, unless you insist upon a traditional blade." From another part of the pavilion, Fredric brought Eragon a weapon he identified as a falchion. It was a sword, but not a type of sword Eragon was accustomed to, although he had seen them among the Varden before. The falchion had a polished, disk-shaped pommel, bright as a silver coin; a short grip made of wood covered with black leather; a curved crossguard carved with a line of dwarf runes; and a single-edged blade that was as long as his outstretched arm and had a thin fuller on either side, close to the spine. The falchion was straight until about six inches from the end, where the back of the blade flared upward in a small peak before gently curving down to the needle-sharp tip. This widening of the blade reduced the likelihood that the point would bend or snap when driven through armor and lent the end of the falchion a fanglike appearance. Unlike a double-edged sword, the falchion was made to be held with the blade and crossguard perpendicular to the ground. The most curious aspect of the falchion, though, was the bottom half inch of the blade, including the edge, which was pearly gray and substantially darker than the mirror-smooth steel above. The boundary between the two areas was wavy, like a silk scarf rippling in the wind.

Eragon pointed at the gray band. "I've not seen that before. What is it?"

"The thriknzdal," said Fredric. "The dwarves invented it. They temper the edge and the spine separately. The edge they make hard, harder than we dare with the whole of our blades. The middle of the blade and the spine they anneal so that the back of the falchion is softer than the edge, soft enough to bend and flex and survive the stress of battle without fracturing like a frost-ridden file."

"Do the dwarves treat all their blades thusly?"

Fredric shook his head. "Only their single-edged swords and the finest of their double-edged swords." He hesitated, and uncertainty crept into his gaze. "You understand why I chose this for you, Shadeslayer, yes?"

Eragon understood. With the blade of the falchion at right angles to the ground, unless he deliberately tilted his wrist, any blows he caught on the sword would strike the flat of the blade, saving the edge for attacks of his own. Wielding the falchion would require only a small adjustment to his fighting style.

Striding out of the pavilion, he assumed a ready position with the falchion. Swinging it over his head, he brought it down upon the head of an imaginary foe, then twisted and lunged, beat aside an invisible spear, sprang six yards to his left, and, in a brilliant but impractical move, spun the blade behind his back, passing it from one hand to the next as he did so. His breathing and heartbeat calm as ever, he returned to where Fredric and Blödhgarm were waiting. The speed and balance of the falchion had impressed Eragon. It was not the equal of Zar'roc, but it was still a superb sword.

"You chose well," he said.

Fredric detected the reticence in his bearing, however, for he said, "And yet you are not entirely pleased, Shadeslayer."

Eragon twirled the falchion in a circle, then grimaced. "I just wish it didn't look so much like a big skinning knife. I feel rather ridiculous with it."

"Ah, pay no heed if your enemies laugh. They'll not be able to once you lop off their heads."

Amused, Eragon nodded. "I'll take it."

"One moment, then," said Fredric, and disappeared into the pavilion, returning with a black leather scabbard decorated with silver scrollwork. He handed the scabbard to Eragon and asked, "Did you ever learn how to sharpen a sword, Shadeslayer? You wouldn't have had need with Zar'roc, would you?"

"No," Eragon admitted, "but I am a fair hand with a whetstone. I can hone a knife until it is so keen, it will cut a thread draped over it. Besides, I can always true up the edge with magic if I have to."

Fredric groaned and slapped his thighs, knocking loose a dozen or so hairs from his oxhide leggings. "No, no, a razor-thin edge is just what you *don't* want on a sword. The bevel has to be thick, thick and strong. A warrior has to be able to maintain his equipment properly, and that includes knowing how to sharpen his sword!"

Fredric insisted, then, on procuring a new whetstone for Eragon and showing him exactly how to put a battle-ready edge on the falchion while they sat in the dirt beside the pavilion. Once he was satisfied that Eragon could grind an entirely new edge on the sword, he said, "You can fight with rusty armor. You can fight with a dented helmet. But if you want to see the sun rise again, never fight with a dull sword. If you've just survived a battle and you're tired as a man who has climbed one of the Beor Mountains and your sword isn't sharp as it is now, it doesn't matter how you feel, you plunk yourself down the first chance you get and pull out your whetstone and strop. Just as you would see to your horse, or to Saphira, before you attended to your own needs, so too you should care for your sword before yourself. Because without it, you're no more than helpless prey for your enemies."

They had been sitting out in the late-afternoon sun for over an hour by the time the weapon master finally finished his instructions. As he did, a cool shadow slid over them and Saphira landed close by.

You waited, said Eragon. *You deliberately waited! You could have rescued me ages ago, but instead you left me here to listen to Fredric go on about water stones, oil stones, and whether linseed oil is better than rendered fat for protecting metal from water.*

And is it?

Not really. It's just not as smelly. But that's irrelevant! Why did you leave me to this doom?

One of her thick eyelids drooped in a lazy wink. *Don't exaggerate. Doom? You and I have far worse dooms to look forward to if we are not properly prepared. What the man with the smelly clothes was saying seemed important for you to know.*

Well, perhaps it was, he conceded. She arched her neck and licked the claws on her right foreleg.

After thanking Fredric and bidding him farewell, and agreeing upon a meeting place with Blödhgarm, Eragon fastened the falchion to the belt of Beloth the Wise and clambered onto Saphira's back. He whooped and she roared as she raised her wings and surged up into the sky.

Giddy, Eragon clung to the spike in front of him and watched the people and tents below dwindle away into flat, miniature versions of themselves. From above, the camp was a grid of gray, triangular peaks, the eastern faces of which were deep in shadow, giving the whole region a checkered appearance. The fortifications that encircled the camp bristled like a hedgehog, the white tips of the distant poles bright in the slanted sunlight. King Orrin's cavalry was a mass of milling dots in the northwestern quadrant of the camp. To the east was the Urgals' camp, low and dark on the rolling plain.

They soared higher.

The cold, pure air stung Eragon's checks and burned in his lungs. He took only shallow breaths. Beside them floated a thick column of clouds, looking as solid as whipped cream. Saphira spiraled around it, her ragged shadow racing across the plume. A lone scrap of moisture struck Eragon, blinding him for a few seconds and filling his nose and mouth with frigid droplets. He gasped and wiped his face.

They rose above the clouds.

A red eagle screeched at them as it flew past.

Saphira's flapping became labored, and Eragon began to feel light-headed. Stilling her wings, Saphira glided from one thermal to the next, maintaining her altitude but ascending no farther.

Eragon looked down. They were so high, height had ceased to matter and things on the ground no longer seemed real. The Varden's camp was an irregularly shaped playing board covered with tiny gray and black rectangles. The Jiet River was a silver rope fringed with green tassels. To the south, the sulfurous clouds rising from the Burning Plains formed a range of glowing orange mountains, home to shadowy monsters that flickered in and out of existence. Eragon quickly averted his gaze.

For perhaps half an hour, he and Saphira drifted with the wind, relaxing in the silent comfort of each other's company. An inaudible spell served to insulate Eragon from the chill. At last they were alone together, alone as they had been in Palancar Valley before the Empire had intruded upon their life.

Saphira was the first to speak. *We are the rulers of the sky.*

Here at the ceiling of the world. Eragon reached up, as if from where he sat he could brush the stars.

Banking to the left, Saphira caught a gust of warmer air from below, then leveled off again. *You will marry Roran and Katrina tomorrow.*

What a strange thought that is. Strange Roran should marry, and strange I should be the one to perform the ceremony. . . . Roran married. Thinking about it makes me feel older. Even we, who were boys but a short while ago, cannot escape the inexorable progress of time. So the generations pass, and soon it will be our turn to send our children out into the land to do the work that needs to be done.

But not unless we can survive the next few months.

Aye, there is that.

Saphira wobbled as turbulence buffeted them. Then she looked back at him and asked: Ready?

Go!

Tilting forward, she pulled her wings close against her sides and plummeted toward the ground, faster than a speeding arrow. Eragon laughed as the sensation of weightlessness overtook him. He tightened his legs around Saphira to keep himself from drifting away from her, then, overtaken by a surge of recklessness, released his grip and held his hands over his head. The disk of land below spun like a wheel as Saphira augered through the air. Slowing and then stopping her rotation, she rolled to the right until she was falling upside down.

"Saphira!" cried Eragon, and pounded her shoulder.

A ribbon of smoke streaming from her nostrils, she righted herself and again pointed herself at the fast-approaching ground. Eragon's ears popped, and he worked his jaw as the pressure increased. Less than a thousand feet above the Varden's camp, and only a few seconds from crashing into the tents and excavating a large and bloody crater, Saphira allowed the wind to catch her wings. The subsequent jolt threw Eragon forward, and the spike he had been holding nearly stabbed him in the eye.

With three powerful flaps, Saphira brought them to a complete halt. Locking her wings outstretched, she then began to gently circle downward.

Now that was fun! exclaimed Eragon.

There is no more exciting sport than flying, for if you lose, you die.

Ah, but I have complete confidence in your abilities; you would never *run us into the ground.* Her pleasure at his compliment radiated from her.

Angling toward his tent, she shook her head, jostling him, and said, *I ought to be accustomed to it by now, but every time I come out of a dive like that, it makes my chest and wing arms so sore, the next morning I can barely move.*

He patted her. *Well, you shouldn't have to fly tomorrow. The wedding is our only obligation, and you can walk to it.* She grunted and landed amid a billow of dust, knocking over an empty tent with her tail in the process.

Dismounting, Eragon left her grooming herself with six of the elves standing nearby, and with the other six, he trotted through the camp until he located the healer Gertrude. From her he learned the marriage rites he would need the following day, and he practiced them with her that he might avoid an embarrassing blunder when the moment arrived.

Then Eragon returned to his tent and washed his face and changed his clothes before going with Saphira to dine with King Orrin and his entourage, as promised.

Late that night, when the feast was finally over, Eragon and Saphira walked back to his tent, gazing at the stars and talking about what had been and what yet might be. And they were happy. When they arrived at their destination, Eragon paused and looked up at Saphira, and his heart was so full of love, he thought it might stop beating.

Good night, Saphira.

Good night, little one.

UNEXPECTED GUESTS

The next morning, Eragon went behind his tent, removed his heavy outer clothes, and began to glide through the poses of the second level of the Rimgar, the series of exercises the elves had invented. Soon his initial chill vanished. He began to pant from the effort, and sweat coated his limbs, which made it difficult for him to keep hold of his feet or his hands when contorted into a position that felt as if it were going to tear the muscles from his bones.

An hour later, he finished the Rimgar. Drying his palms on the corner of his tent, he drew the falchion and practiced his swordsmanship for another thirty minutes. He would have preferred to continue familiarizing himself with the sword for the rest of the day—for he knew his life might depend upon his skill with it—but Roran's wedding was fast approaching, and the villagers could use all the help they could get if they were to complete the preparations in time.

Refreshed, Eragon bathed in cold water and dressed, and then he and Saphira walked to where Elain was overseeing the cooking of Roran and Katrina's wedding feast. Blödhgarm and his companions followed a dozen or so yards behind, slipping between the tents with stealthy ease.

"Ah, good, Eragon," Elain said. "I had hoped you would come." She stood with both her hands pressed into the small of her back to relieve the weight of her pregnancy. Pointing with her chin past a row of spits and cauldrons suspended over a bed of coals, past a clump of men butchering a hog, past three makeshift ovens built of mud and stone, and past a pile of kegs toward a line of planks set on stumps that six women were using as a counter, she said, "There are still twenty loaves of bread dough that have to be kneaded. Will you see to it, please?" Then she frowned at the calluses on his knuckles. "And try not to get those in the dough, won't you?"

The six women standing at the planks, which included Felda and Birgit, fell silent when Eragon took his place among them. His few attempts to restart the conversation failed, but after a while, when he had given up on putting them at ease and was concentrating on his kneading, they resumed talking of their own accord. They spoke about Roran and Katrina and how lucky the two of them were and of the villagers' life in the camp and of their journey thence, and then without preamble, Felda looked over at Eragon and said, "Your dough looks a little sticky. Shouldn't you add some flour?"

Eragon checked the consistency. "You're right. Thank you." Felda smiled, and after that, the women included him in their conversation.

While Eragon worked the warm dough, Saphira lay basking on a nearby patch of grass. The children from Carvahall played on and around her; laughing shrieks punctuated the deeper thrum of the adults' voices. When a pair of mangy dogs started barking at Saphira, she lifted her head off the ground and growled at them. They ran away yipping.

Everyone in the clearing was someone Eragon had known while growing up. Horst and Fisk were on the other side of the spits, constructing tables for the feast. Kiselt was wiping the hog's blood off his forearms. Albriech, Baldor, Mandel, and several other of the younger men were carrying poles wound with ribbons toward the hill where Roran and Katrina wished to be married. The tavern-keeper Morn was off mixing the wedding drink, with his wife, Tara, holding three flagons and a cask for him. A few hundred feet away, Roran was shouting something at a mule-driver who was attempting to run his charges through the clearing. Loring, Delwin, and the boy Nolfavrell stood clustered nearby, watching. With a loud curse,

Roran grabbed the lead mule's harness and struggled to turn the animals around. The sight amused Eragon; he had never known Roran to get so flustered, nor to be so short-tempered.

"The mighty warrior is nervous ere his contest," observed Isold, one of the six women next to Eragon. The group laughed.

"Perhaps," Birgit said, stirring water into flour, "he is worried his sword may bend in the battle." Gales of merriment swept the women. Eragon's cheeks flushed. He kept his gaze fixed on the dough in front of him and increased the speed of his kneading. Bawdy jokes were common at weddings, and he had enjoyed his share before, but hearing them directed at his cousin disconcerted him.

The people who would not be able to attend the wedding were as much on Eragon's mind as those who could. He thought of Byrd, Quimby, Parr, Hida, young Elmund, Kelby, and the others who had died because of the Empire. But most of all, he thought of Garrow and wished his uncle were still alive to see his only son acclaimed a hero by the villagers and the Varden alike and to see him take Katrina's hand and finally become a man in full.

Closing his eyes, Eragon turned his face toward the noonday sun and smiled up at the sky, content. The weather was pleasant. The aroma of yeast, flour, roasting meat, freshly poured wine, boiling soups, sweet pastries, and melted candies suffused the clearing. His friends and family were gathered around him for celebration and not for mourning. And for the moment, he was safe and Saphira was safe. *This is how life ought to be.*

A single horn rang out across the land, unnaturally loud.

Then again.

And again.

Everyone froze, uncertain what the three notes signified.

For a brief interval, the entire camp was silent, except for the animals, then the Varden's war-drums began to beat. Chaos erupted. Mothers ran for their children and cooks dampened their fires while the rest of the men and women scrambled after their weapons.

Eragon sprinted toward Saphira even as she surged to her feet.

Reaching out with his mind, he found Blödhgarm and, once the elf lowered his defenses somewhat, said, *Meet us at the north entrance.*

We hear and obey, Shadeslayer.

Eragon flung himself onto Saphira. The instant he got a leg over her neck, she jumped four rows of tents, landed, and then jumped a second time, her wings half furled, not flying but rather bounding through the camp like a mountain cat crossing a fast-flowing river. The impact of each landing jarred Eragon's teeth and spine and threatened to knock him off his perch. As they rose and fell, frightened warriors dodging out of their path, Eragon contacted Trianna and the other members of Du Vrangr Gata, identifying the location of each spellcaster and organizing them for battle.

Someone who was not of Du Vrangr Gata touched his thoughts. He recoiled, slamming walls up around his consciousness, before he realized that it was Angela the herbalist and allowed the contact. She said, *I am with Nasuada and Elva. Nasuada wants you and Saphira to meet her at the north entrance—*

As soon as we can. Yes, yes, we're on our way. What of Elva? Does she sense anything?

Pain. Great pain. Yours. The Varden's. The others'. I'm sorry, she's not very coherent right now. It's too much for her to cope with. I'm going to put her to sleep until the violence is at an end. Angela severed the connection.

Like a carpenter laying out and examining his tools before beginning a new project, Eragon reviewed the wards he had placed around himself, Saphira, Nasuada, Arya, and Roran. They all seemed to be in order.

Saphira slid to a stop before his tent, furrowing the packed earth with her talons. He leaped off her back, rolling as he struck the ground. Bouncing upright, he dashed inside, undoing his sword belt as he went. He dropped the belt and the attached falchion into the dirt and, scrabbling under his cot, retrieved his armor. The cold, heavy rings of the mail hauberk slid over his head and settled on his shoulders with a sound like falling coins. He tied on his arming cap, placed the coif over it, and then jammed his head into his helm. Snatching up the belt, he refastened it around his waist. With his greaves and his bracers in his left hand, he hooked his little finger through the arm strap of his shield, grabbed Saphira's heavy saddle with his right hand, and burst out of the tent.

Releasing his armor in a noisy clatter, he threw the saddle onto the mound of Saphira's shoulders and climbed after it. In his haste and excitement, and his apprehension, he had trouble buckling the straps.

Saphira shifted her stance. *Hurry. You're taking too long.*

Yes! I'm moving as fast as I can! It doesn't help you're so blasted big!

She growled.

The camp swarmed with activity, men and dwarves streaming in jangling rivers toward the north, rushing to answer the summons of the war-drums.

Eragon collected his abandoned armor off the ground, mounted Saphira, and settled into the saddle. With a flash of down-swept wings, a jolt of acceleration, a blast of swirling air, and the bitter complaint of bracers scraping against shield, Saphira took to the air. While they sped toward the northern edge of the camp, Eragon strapped the greaves to his shins, holding himself on Saphira merely with the strength of his legs. The bracers he wedged between his belly and the front of the saddle. The shield he hung from a neck spike. When the greaves were secure, he slid his legs through the row of leather loops on either side of the saddle, then tightened the slipknot on each loop.

Eragon's hand brushed against the belt of Beloth the Wise. He groaned, remembering that he had emptied the belt while healing Saphira in Helgrind. *Argh! I should have stored some energy in it.*

We'll be fine, said Saphira.

He was just fitting on the bracers when Saphira arched her wings, cupping the air with the translucent membranes, and reared, stalling to a standstill as she alighted upon the crest of one of the embankments that ringed the camp. Nasuada was already there, sitting upon her massive charger, Battle-storm. Beside her was Jörmundur, also mounted; Arya, on foot; and the current watch of the Nighthawks, led by Khagra, one of the Urgals Eragon had met on the Burning Plains. Blödhgarm and the other elves emerged from the forest of tents behind them and stationed themselves close to Eragon and Saphira. From a different part of the camp galloped King Orrin and his retinue, reining in their prancing steeds as they drew near Nasuada. Close upon their heels came Narheim, chief of the dwarves, and three of his warriors, the group of them riding ponies clad with leather and mail armor. Nar Garzhvog ran out of the fields to the east, the Kull's thudding footsteps preceding his arrival by several seconds. Nasuada shouted an order, and the guards at the north entrance pulled aside the crude wooden gate to allow Garzhvog inside the camp, although if he had wanted, the Kull probably could have knocked open the gate by himself.

"Who challenges?" growled Garzhvog, scaling the embankment with four inhumanly long strides. The horses shied away from the gigantic Urgal.

"Look." Nasuada pointed.

Eragon was already studying their enemies. Roughly two miles away, five sleek boats, black as pitch, had landed upon the near bank of the Jiet River. From the boats there issued a swarm of men garbed in the livery of Galbatorix's army. The host glittered like wind-whipped water under a summer sun as swords, spears, shields, helmets, and mail ringlets caught and reflected the light.

Arya shaded her eyes with a hand and squinted at the soldiers. "I put their number between two hundred seventy and three hundred."

"Why so few?" wondered Jörmundur.

King Orrin scowled. "Galbatorix cannot be mad enough to believe he can destroy us with such a paltry force!" Orrin pulled off his helm, which was in the shape of a crown, and dabbed his brow with the corner of his tunic. "We could obliterate that entire group and not lose a man."

"Maybe," said Nasuada. "Maybe not."

Gnawing on the words, Garzhvog added, "The Dragon King is a false-tongued traitor, a rogue ram, but his mind is not feeble. He is cunning like a blood-hungry weasel."

The soldiers assembled themselves in orderly ranks and then began marching toward the Varden.

A messenger boy ran up to Nasuada. She bent in her saddle to listen, then dismissed him. "Nar Garzhvog, your people are safe within our camp. They are gathered near the east gate, ready for you to lead them."

Garzhvog grunted but remained where he was.

Looking back at the approaching soldiers, Nasuada said, "I can think of no reason to engage them in the open. We can pick them off with archers once they are within range. And when they reach our breastwork, they will break themselves against the trenches and the staves. Not a single one will escape alive," she concluded with evident satisfaction.

"When they have committed themselves," said Orrin, "my horsemen and I could ride out and attack them from the rear. They will be so surprised, they will not even have a chance to defend themselves."

"The tide of battle may—" Nasuada was replying when the brazen horn that had announced the arrival of the soldiers sounded once more, so loudly that Eragon, Arya, and the rest of the elves covered their ears. Eragon winced with pain from the blast.

Where is that coming from? he asked Saphira.

A more important question, I think, is why the soldiers would want to warn us of their attack, if they are indeed responsible for this baying.

Maybe it's a diversion or—

Eragon forgot what he was going to say as he saw a stir of motion on the far side of the Jiet River, behind a veil of sorrowful willow trees. Red as a ruby dipped in blood, red as iron hot to forge, red as a burning ember of hate and anger, Thorn appeared above the languishing trees. And upon the back of the glittering dragon, there sat Murtagh in his bright steel armor, thrusting Zar'roc high over his head.

They have come for us, said Saphira. Eragon's gut twisted, and he felt Saphira's own dread like a current of bilious water running through his mind.

FIRE IN THE SKY

s Eragon watched Thorn and Murtagh rise high in the northern sky, he heard Narheim whisper, "Barzûl," and then curse Murtagh for killing Hrothgar, the king of the dwarves.

Arya spun away from the sight. "Nasuada, Your Majesty," she said, her eyes flicking toward Orrin, "you have to stop the soldiers before they reach the camp. You cannot allow them to attack our defenses. If they do, they will sweep over these ramparts like a storm-driven wave and wreak untold havoc in our midst, among the tents, where we cannot maneuver effectively."

"Untold havoc?" Orrin scoffed. "Have you so little confidence in our prowess, Ambassador? Humans and dwarves may not be as gifted as elves, but we shall have no difficulty in disposing of these miserable wretches, I can assure you."

The lines of Arya's face tightened. "Your prowess is without compare, Your Majesty. I do not doubt it. But listen: this is a trap set for Eragon and Saphira. *They*"—she flung an arm toward the rising figures of Thorn and Murtagh—"have come to capture Eragon and Saphira and spirit them away to Urû'baen. Galbatorix would not have sent so few men unless he was confident they could keep the Varden occupied long enough for Murtagh to overwhelm Eragon. Galbatorix *must* have placed spells on those men, spells to aid them in their mission. What those enchantments might be, I do not know, but of this I am certain: the soldiers are more than they appear, and we must prevent them from entering this camp."

Emerging from his initial shock, Eragon said, "You don't want to let Thorn fly over the camp; he could set fire to half of it with a single pass."

Nasuada clasped her hands over the pommel of her saddle, seemingly oblivious to Murtagh and Thorn and to the soldiers, who were now less than a mile away. "But why not attack us while we were unawares?" she asked. "Why alert us to their presence?"

It was Narheim who answered. "Because they would not want Eragon and Saphira to get caught up in the fighting on the ground. No, unless I am mistaken, their plan is for Eragon and Saphira to meet Thorn and Murtagh in the air while the soldiers assail our position here."

"Is it wise, then, to accommodate their wishes, to willingly send Eragon and Saphira into this trap?" Nasuada raised an eyebrow.

"Yes," insisted Arya, "for we have an advantage they could not suspect." She pointed at Blödhgarm. "This time Eragon shall not face Murtagh alone. He will have the combined strength of thirteen elves supporting him. Murtagh will not be expecting that. Stop the soldiers before they reach us, and you will have frustrated part of Galbatorix's design. Send Saphira and Eragon up with the mightiest spellcasters of my race bolstering their efforts, and you will disrupt the remainder of Galbatorix's scheme."

"You have convinced me," said Nasuada. "However, the soldiers are too close for us to intercept them any distance from the camp with men on foot. Orrin—"

Before she finished, the king had turned his horse around and was racing toward the north gate of the camp. One of his retinue winded a trumpet, a signal for the rest of Orrin's cavalry to assemble for a charge.

To Garzhvog, Nasuada said, "King Orrin will require assistance. Send your rams to join him."

"Lady Nightstalker." Throwing back his massive horned head, Garzhvog loosed a wild wailing bellow. The skin on the back of Eragon's arms and neck prickled as he listened to the Urgal's savage howl. With a snap of his jaws, Garzhvog ceased his belling and then grunted, "They will come." The Kull broke into an earth-shattering trot and ran toward the gate where King Orrin and his horsemen were gathered.

Four of the Varden dragged open the gate. King Orrin raised his sword, shouted, and galloped out of the camp, leading his men toward the soldiers in their gold-stitched tunics. A plume of cream-colored dust billowed out from underneath the hooves of the horses, obscuring the arrowhead-shaped formation from view.

"Jörmundur," said Nasuada.

"Yes, my Lady?"

"Order two hundred swordsmen and a hundred spearmen after them. And have fifty archers station themselves seventy to eighty yards away from the fighting. I want these soldiers crushed, Jörmundur, obliterated, ground out of existence. The men are to understand that no quarter is to be given or accepted."

Jörmundur bowed.

"And tell them that although I cannot join them in this battle, on account of my arms, my spirit marches with them."

"My Lady."

As Jörmundur hurried off, Narheim urged his pony closer to Nasuada. "What of mine own people, Nasuada? What role shall we play?"

Nasuada frowned at the thick, choking dust that drifted across the rolling expanse of grass. "You can help guard our perimeter. If the soldiers should somehow win free of—" She was forced to pause as four hundred Urgals—more had arrived since the Battle of the Burning Plains—pounded out of the center of the camp, through the gate, and onto the field beyond, roaring incomprehensible war-cries the whole while. As they vanished into the dust, Nasuada resumed speaking: "If the soldiers should win free, your axes will be most welcome in the lines."

The wind gusted toward them, carrying with it the screams of dying men and horses, the shivery sound of metal sliding over metal, the clink of swords glancing off helmets, the dull impact of spears on shields, and, underlying it all, a horrible humorless laughter that issued from a multitude of throats and continued without pause throughout the mayhem. It was, Eragon thought, the laughter of the insane.

Narheim pounded his fist against his hip. "By Morgothal, we are not ones to stand by idly when there is a fight to be had! Release us, Nasuada, and let us hew a few necks for you!"

"No!" exclaimed Nasuada. "No, no, and no! I have given you my orders, and I expect you to abide by them. This is a battle of horses and men and Urgals and perhaps even dragons. It is not a fit place for dwarves. You would be trampled like children." At Narheim's outraged oath, she raised a hand. "I am well aware you are fearsome warriors. No one knows that better than I, who fought beside you in Farthen Dûr. However, not to put too fine a point on it, you are short by our standards, and I would rather not risk your warriors in a fray such as this, where your stature might be your undoing. Better to wait here, on the high ground, where you stand taller than anyone who tries to climb this berm, and let the soldiers come to you. If any soldiers do reach us, they shall be warriors of such tremendous skill, I want you and your people there to repel them, for one might as well try to uproot a mountain as defeat a dwarf."

Still displeased, Narheim grumbled some response, but whatever he said was lost as the Varden Nasuada had deployed filed through the cleft in the embankment where the gate had been. The noise of tramping feet and clattering equipment faded as the men drew away from the camp. Then the wind stiffened into a steady breeze, and from the direction of the fighting, the grim giggle again wafted toward them.

A moment later, a mental shout of incredible strength overwhelmed Eragon's defenses and tore through his consciousness, filling him with agony as he heard a man say, *Ah, no, help me! They won't die! Angvard take them, they won't die!* The link between their minds vanished then, and Eragon swallowed hard as he realized that the man had been killed.

Nasuada shifted in her saddle, her expression strained. "Who was that?"

"You heard him too?"

"It seems we all did," said Arya.

"I think it was Barden, one of the spellcasters who rides with King Orrin, but—"

"Eragon!"

Thorn had been circling higher and higher while King Orrin and his men engaged the soldiers, but now the dragon hung motionless in the sky, halfway between the soldiers and the camp, and Murtagh's voice, augmented with magic, echoed forth across the land: *"Eragon! I see you there, hiding behind Nasuada's skirts. Come fight me, Eragon! It is your destiny. Or are you a coward, Shadeslayer?"*

Saphira answered for Eragon by lifting her head and roaring even louder than Murtagh's thunderous speech, then discharging a twenty-foot-long jet of crackling blue fire. The horses close to Saphira, including Nasuada's, bolted away, leaving Saphira and Eragon alone on the embankment with the elves.

Walking over to Saphira, Arya placed a hand on Eragon's left leg and looked up at him with her slanted green eyes. "Accept this from me, Shur'tugal," she said. And he felt a surge of energy flow into him.

"Eka elrun ono," he murmured to her.

Also in the ancient language, she said, "Be careful, Eragon. I would not want to see you broken by Murtagh. I . . ." It seemed as if she were going to say more, but she hesitated, then removed her hand from his leg and retreated to stand by Blödhgarm.

"Fly well, Bjartskular!" the elves sang out as Saphira launched herself off the embankment.

As Saphira winged her way toward Thorn, Eragon joined his

mind first with her and then with Arya and, through Arya, with Blödhgarm and the eleven other elves. By having Arya serve as the focal point for the elves, Eragon was able to concentrate on the thoughts of Arya and Saphira; he knew them so well that their reactions would not distract him in the middle of a fight.

Eragon grasped the shield with his left hand and unsheathed his falchion, holding it upraised so he would not accidentally stab Saphira's wings as she flapped, nor slash her shoulders nor her neck, which were in constant motion. *I'm glad I took the time last night to reinforce the falchion with magic*, he said to Saphira and Arya.

Let us hope your spells hold, Saphira answered.

Remember, said Arya, *remain as close to us as you can. The more distance you place between us, the harder it is for us to maintain this bond with you.*

Thorn did not dive at Saphira or otherwise attack her as she neared him, but rather slid away on rigid wings, allowing her to rise to his level unmolested. The two dragons balanced upon the thermals, facing each other across a gap of fifty yards, the tips of their barbed tails twitching, both of their muzzles wrinkled with ferocious snarls.

He's bigger, observed Saphira. *It's not been two weeks since we last fought and he has grown another four feet, if not more.*

She was right. Thorn was longer from head to tail, and deeper in the chest, than he had been when they first clashed over the Burning Plains. He was barely older than a hatchling, but he was already nearly as large as Saphira.

Eragon reluctantly shifted his gaze from the dragon to the Rider.

Murtagh was bareheaded, and his long black hair billowed behind him like a sleek mane. His face was hard, harder than Eragon had ever seen before, and Eragon knew that this time Murtagh would not, could not, show him mercy. The volume of his voice substantially reduced, but still louder than normal, Murtagh said, "You and Saphira have caused us a great deal of pain, Eragon. Galbatorix was furious with us for letting you go. And after the two of you killed the Ra'zac, he was so angry, he slew five of his servants and then turned his wrath upon Thorn and me. We have both suffered horribly on account of you. We shall not do so again." He drew back his arm, as if Thorn were about to lunge forward and Murtagh were preparing to slash at Eragon and Saphira.

"Wait!" cried Eragon. "I know of a way you can both free yourselves of your oaths to Galbatorix."

An expression of desperate longing transformed Murtagh's features, and he lowered Zar'roc a few inches. Then he scowled and spat toward the ground and shouted, "I don't believe you! It's not possible!"

"It is! Just let me explain."

Murtagh seemed to be struggling with himself, and for a while Eragon thought he might refuse. Swinging his head around, Thorn looked back at Murtagh, and something passed between them. "Blast you, Eragon," said Murtagh, and lay Zar'roc across the front of his saddle. "Blast you for baiting us with this. We had already made peace with our lot, and you have to tantalize us with the specter of a hope we had abandoned. If this proves to be a false hope, *brother,* I swear I'll cut off your right hand before we present you to Galbatorix. . . . You won't need it for what you will be doing in Urû'baen."

A threat of his own occurred to Eragon, but he suppressed it. Lowering the falchion, he said, "Galbatorix would not have told you, but when I was among the elves—"

Eragon, do not reveal anything more about us! exclaimed Arya.

"—I learned that if your personality changes, so does your true name in the ancient language. Who you are isn't cast in iron, Murtagh! If you and Thorn can change something about yourselves, your oaths will no longer bind you, and Galbatorix will lose his hold on you."

Thorn drifted several yards closer to Saphira. "Why didn't you mention this before?" Murtagh demanded.

"I was too confused at the time."

A scant fifty feet separated Thorn and Saphira by then. The red dragon's snarl had subsided to a faint warning curl of his upper lip, and in his sparkling crimson eyes appeared a vast, puzzled sadness, as if he hoped Saphira or Eragon might know why he had been brought into the world merely so Galbatorix could enslave him, abuse him, and force him to destroy other beings' lives. The tip of Thorn's nose twitched as he sniffed at Saphira. She sniffed him in return, and her tongue darted out of her mouth as she tasted his scent. Pity for Thorn welled up inside Eragon and Saphira together, and they wished they could speak with him directly, but they dared not open their minds to him.

With so little distance between them, Eragon noticed the bundles of cords that ridged Murtagh's neck and the forked vein that pulsed in the middle of his forehead.

"I am not evil!" said Murtagh. "I've done the best I could under the circumstances. I doubt you would have survived as well as I did if our mother had seen fit to leave *you* in Urû'baen and hide *me* in Carvahall."

"Perhaps not."

Murtagh banged his breastplate with his fist. "Aha! Then how am I supposed to follow your advice? If I am already a good man, if I have already done as well as could be expected, how can I change? Must I become worse than I am? Must I embrace Galbatorix's darkness in order to free myself of it? That hardly seems like a reasonable solution. If I succeeded in so altering my identity, you would not like who I had become, and you would curse me as strongly as you curse Galbatorix now."

Frustrated, Eragon said, "Yes, but you do not have to become better or worse than you are now, only different. There are many kinds of people in the world and many ways to behave honorably. Look at someone whom you admire but who has chosen paths other than your own through life and model your actions upon his. It may take a while, but if you can shift your personality enough, you can leave Galbatorix, and you can leave the Empire, and you and Thorn could join us in the Varden, where you would be free to do as you wish."

What of your own oaths to avenge Hrothgar's death? Saphira asked. Eragon ignored her.

Murtagh sneered at him. "So you are asking me to be that which I am not. If Thorn and I are to save ourselves, we must destroy our current identities. Your cure is worse than our affliction."

"I'm asking you to allow yourself to grow into something other than you are now. It's a difficult thing to do, I know, but people re-make themselves all the time. Let go of your anger, for one, and you can turn your back on Galbatorix once and for all."

"Let go of my anger?" Murtagh laughed. "I'll let go of my anger when you forget yours over the Empire's role in the death of your uncle and the razing of your farm. Anger defines us, Eragon, and without it, you and I would be a feast for maggots. Still . . ." His eyes half lidded, Murtagh tapped Zar'roc's crossguard, the cords in his neck softening, although the vein that split his forehead remained swollen as ever. "The concept is intriguing, I admit. Perhaps we can work on it together when we are in Urû'baen. That is, if the king permits us to be alone with each other. Of course, he may decide to keep us permanently separated. I would if I were in his position."

Eragon tightened his fingers around the hilt of the falchion. "You seem to think we will accompany you to the capital."

"Oh, but you will, brother." A crooked smile stretched Murtagh's mouth. "Even if we wanted to, Thorn and I could not change who we are in an instant. Until such time as we may have that opportunity, we shall remain beholden to Galbatorix, and he has ordered us, in no uncertain terms, to bring him the two of you. Neither of us is willing to brave the king's displeasure again. We defeated you once before. It will be no great achievement to do so again."

A spurt of flame escaped from between Saphira's teeth, and Eragon had to stifle a similar response in words. If he lost control of his temper now, bloodshed would be unavoidable. "Please,

Murtagh, Thorn, will you not at least try what I've suggested? Have you no desire to resist Galbatorix? You will never cast off your chains unless you are willing to defy him."

"You underestimate Galbatorix, Eragon," growled Murtagh. "He has been creating name-slaves for over a hundred years, ever since he recruited our father. Do you think he is unaware that a person's true name may vary over the course of his life? He is sure to have taken precautions against that eventuality. If my true name were to change this very moment, or Thorn's, most likely it would trigger a spell that would alert Galbatorix to the change and force us to return to him in Urû'baen so he could bind us to him again."

"But only if he could guess your new names."

"He is most adept at the practice." Murtagh raised Zar'roc off the saddle. "We may make use of your suggestion in the future, but only after careful study and preparation, so that Thorn and I do not regain our freedom only to have Galbatorix steal it back from us directly afterward." He hefted Zar'roc, the sword's iridescent blade shimmering. "Therefore, we have no choice but to take you with us to Urû'baen. Will you go peacefully?"

Unable to contain himself any longer, Eragon said, "I would sooner tear out my own heart!"

"Better to tear out my hearts," Murtagh replied, then stabbed Zar'roc overhead and shouted a wild war cry.

Roaring in unison, Thorn flapped twice, fast, to climb above Saphira. He twisted in a half circle as he rose, so his head would be over Saphira's neck, where he could immobilize her with a single bite at the base of her skull.

Saphira did not wait for him. She tipped forward, rotating her wings in their shoulder sockets, so that, for the span of a heartbeat, she pointed straight down, her wings still parallel with the dust-smeared ground, supporting her entire unstable weight. Then she pulled in her right wing and swung her head to the left and her tail to the right, spinning in a clockwise direction. Her muscular tail struck Thorn across his left side just as he sailed over her, breaking his wing in five separate places. The jagged ends of Thorn's hollow flight bones pierced his hide and stuck out between his flashing scales. Globules of steaming dragon blood rained down upon Eragon and Saphira. A droplet splashed against the back of Eragon's coif and seeped through the mail to his bare skin. It burned like hot oil. He scrabbled at his neck, trying to wipe off the blood.

His roar converting into a whine of pain, Thorn tumbled past Saphira, unable to stay aloft.

"Well done!" Eragon shouted to Saphira as she righted herself.

Eragon watched from above as Murtagh removed a small round object from his belt and pressed it against Thorn's shoulder. Eragon sensed no surge of magic from Murtagh, but the object in his hand flared and Thorn's broken wing jerked as his bones snapped back in place and muscles and tendons rippled and the tears in them vanished. Lastly, the wounds in Thorn's hide sealed over.

How did he do that? Eragon exclaimed.

Arya answered, *He must have imbued the item with a spell of healing beforehand.*

We should have thought of that ourselves.

His injuries mended, Thorn halted his fall and began to ascend toward Saphira with prodigious speed, searing the air in front of him with a boiling spear of sullen red fire. Saphira dove at him, spiraling around the tower of flame. She snapped at Thorn's neck—causing him to shy away—and raked his shoulders and chest with her front claws and buffeted him with her huge wings. The edge of her right wing clipped Murtagh, knocking him sideways in his saddle. He recovered quickly and slashed at Saphira, opening up a three-foot rent in the membrane of her wing.

Hissing, Saphira kicked Thorn away with her hind legs and released a jet of fire, which split and passed harmlessly on either side of Thorn.

Eragon felt through Saphira the throbbing of her wound. He stared at the bloody gash, thoughts racing. If they had been fighting any magician besides Murtagh, he would not dare to cast a spell while engaged in hostilities, for the magician would most likely believe he or she was about to die and would counter with a desperate, all-out magical attack.

It was different with Murtagh. Eragon knew Galbatorix had ordered Murtagh to capture, not kill, him and Saphira. *No matter what I do*, Eragon thought, *he will not attempt to slay me*. It was safe, then, Eragon decided, to heal Saphira. And, he belatedly realized, he could attack Murtagh with any spells he desired and Murtagh would not be able to respond with deadly force. But he wondered why Murtagh had used an enchanted object to cure Thorn's hurts instead of casting the spell himself.

Saphira said, *Perhaps he wants to preserve his strength. Or perhaps he wanted to avoid frightening you. It would not please Galbatorix if, by using magic, Murtagh caused you to panic and you killed yourself or Thorn or Murtagh as a result. Remember, the king's great ambition is to have all four of us under his command, not dead, where we are beyond his reach.*

That must be it, Eragon agreed.

As he prepared to mend Saphira's wing, Arya said, *Wait. Do not.*

What? Why? Can't you feel Saphira's pain?

Let my brethren and I tend to her. It will confuse Murtagh, and this way, the effort shall not weaken you.

Aren't you too far away to work such a change?

Not when the lot of us pool our resources. And, Eragon? We recommend you refrain from striking at Murtagh with magic until he attacks with mind or magic himself. He may yet be stronger than you, even with the thirteen of us lending our strength. We do not know. It is better not to test yourself against him until there is no other alternative.

And if I cannot prevail?

All of Alagaësia will fall to Galbatorix.

Eragon sensed Arya concentrating, then the cut in Saphira's wing ceased weeping tears of blood and the raw edges of the delicate cerulean membrane flowed together without a scab or a scar. Saphira's relief was palpable. With a tinge of fatigue, Arya said, *Guard yourself better if you can. This was not easy.*

After Saphira had kicked him, Thorn flailed and lost altitude. He must have assumed that Saphira meant to harry him downward, where it would be harder for him to evade her attacks, because he fled west a quarter of a mile. When he finally noticed that Saphira was not pursuing him, he circled up and around until he was a good thousand feet higher than she was.

Drawing in his wings, Thorn hurtled toward Saphira, flames flickering in his open maw, his ivory talons outstretched, Murtagh brandishing Zar'roc on his back.

Eragon nearly lost his grip on the falchion as Saphira folded one wing and flipped upside down with a dizzying wrench, then extended the wing again to slow her descent. If he craned his head backward, Eragon could see the ground below them. Or was it above them? He gritted his teeth and concentrated on maintaining his hold on the saddle.

Thorn and Saphira collided, and to Eragon, it was as if Saphira had crashed into the side of a mountain. The force of the impact drove him forward, and he banged his helmet against the neck spike in front of him, denting the thick steel. Dazed, he hung loose from the saddle and watched as the disks of the heavens and the earth reversed themselves, spinning without a discernible pattern. He felt Saphira shudder as Thorn battered her exposed belly. Eragon wished there had been time to dress her in the armor the dwarves had given her.

A glittering ruby leg appeared around Saphira's shoulder, mauling her with bloody claws. Without thinking, Eragon hacked at it, shattering a line of scales and severing a bundle of tendons. Three of the toes on the foot went limp. Eragon hacked again.

Snarling, Thorn disengaged from Saphira. He arched his neck, and Eragon heard an inrush of air as the stocky dragon filled his lungs. Eragon ducked, burying his face in the corner of his elbow. A ravening inferno engulfed Saphira. The heat of the fire could not harm them—Eragon's wards prevented that—but the torrent of incandescent flames was still blinding.

Saphira veered to the left, out of the churning fire. By then, Murtagh had repaired the damage to Thorn's leg, and Thorn again flung himself at Saphira, grappling with her as they plummeted in sickening lurches toward the gray tents of the Varden. Saphira managed to clamp her teeth on the horned crest that projected from the rear of Thorn's head, despite the points of bone that punctured her tongue. Thorn bellowed and thrashed like a hooked fish, trying to pull away, but he was no match for the iron muscles of Saphira's jaws. The two dragons drifted downward side by side, like a pair of interlocked leaves.

Eragon leaned over and slashed crosswise at Murtagh's right shoulder, not intending to kill him but rather to injure him severely enough to end the fight. Unlike during their clash over the Burning Plains, Eragon was well rested; with his arm as fast as an elf's, he was confident Murtagh would be defenseless before him.

Murtagh lifted his shield and blocked the falchion.

His reaction was so unexpected, Eragon faltered, then barely had time to recoil and parry as Murtagh retaliated, swinging Zar'roc at him, the blade humming through the air with inordinate speed. The stroke jarred Eragon's shoulder. Pressing the attack, Murtagh struck at Eragon's wrist and then, when Eragon dashed aside Zar'roc, thrust underneath Eragon's shield and stabbed through the fringe of his mail hauberk and his tunic and the waist of his breeches and into his left hip. The tip of Zar'roc embedded itself in bone.

The pain shocked Eragon like a splash of frigid water, but it also lent his thoughts a preternatural clarity and sent a burst of uncommon strength coursing through his limbs.

As Murtagh withdrew Zar'roc, Eragon yelled and lunged at Murtagh, who, with a flip of his wrist, trapped the falchion beneath Zar'roc. Murtagh bared his teeth in a sinister smile. Without pause, Eragon yanked the falchion free, feinted toward Murtagh's right knee, then whipped the falchion in the opposite direction and sliced Murtagh across the cheek.

"You should have worn a helmet," said Eragon.

They were so close to the ground then—only a few hundred feet—that Saphira had to release Thorn, and the two dragons separated before Eragon and Murtagh could exchange any more blows.

As Saphira and Thorn spiraled upward, racing each other toward a pearl-white cloud gathering over the tents of the Varden, Eragon lifted his hauberk and tunic and examined his hip. A fist-sized patch of skin was discolored where Zar'roc had crushed the mail against his flesh. In the middle of the patch was a thin red line, two inches long, where Zar'roc had pierced him. Blood oozed from the wound, soaking the top of his breeches.

Being hurt by Zar'roc—a sword that had never failed him in moments of danger and that he still regarded as rightfully his— unsettled him. To have his own weapon turned against him was *wrong*. It was a warping of the world, and his every instinct rebelled against it.

Saphira wobbled as she flew through an eddy of air, and Eragon winced, renewed pain lancing up his side. It was fortunate, he concluded, that they were not fighting on foot, for he did not think his hip would bear his weight.

Arya, he said, *do you want to heal me, or shall I do it myself and let Murtagh stop me if he can?*

We shall attend to it for you, Arya said. *You may be able to catch Murtagh by surprise if he believes you are still wounded.*

Oh, wait.

Why?

I have to give you permission. Otherwise, my wards will block the spell. The phrase did not leap into Eragon's mind at first, but eventually he remembered the construction of the safeguard and, in the ancient language, whispered, "I agree to let Arya, daughter of Islanzadí, cast a spell on me."

We shall have to talk about your wards when you are not so distracted. What if you were unconscious? How could we minister to you then?

It seemed like a good idea after the Burning Plains. Murtagh immobi-

lized us both with magic. *I don't want him or anyone else to be able to cast spells on us without our consent.*

Nor should they, but there are more elegant solutions than yours.

Eragon squirmed in the saddle as the elves' magic took effect and his hip began to tingle and itch as if covered with flea bites. When the itching ceased, he slid a hand under his tunic and was delighted to feel nothing but smooth skin.

Right, he said, rolling his shoulders. *Let us teach them to fear our names!*

The pearl-white cloud looming large before them, Saphira twisted to the left and then, while Thorn was struggling to turn, plunged into the heart of the cloud. Everything went cold and damp and white, then Saphira shot out of the far side, exiting only a few feet above and behind Thorn.

Roaring with triumph, Saphira dropped upon Thorn and seized him by the flanks, sinking her claws deep into his thighs and along his spine. She snaked her head forward, caught Thorn's left wing in her mouth, and clamped down with the *snick* of razor teeth cutting through meat.

Thorn writhed and screamed, a horrible sound Eragon had not suspected dragons were capable of producing.

I have him, said Saphira. *I can tear off his wing, but I would rather not. Whatever you are going to do, do it before we fall too far.*

His face pale beneath smeared gore, Murtagh pointed at Eragon with Zar'roc—the sword trembling in the air—and a mental ray of immense power invaded Eragon's consciousness. The foreign presence groped after his thoughts, seeking to grab ahold and subdue them and subject them to Murtagh's approval. As on the Burning Plains, Eragon noticed that Murtagh's mind felt as if it contained multitudes, as if a confused chorus of voices was murmuring beneath the turmoil of Murtagh's own thoughts.

Eragon wondered if Murtagh had a group of magicians assisting him, even as the elves were him.

Difficult as it was, Eragon emptied his mind of everything but an image of Zar'roc. He concentrated on the sword with all his might, smoothing the plane of his consciousness into the calm of meditation so Murtagh would find no purchase with which to establish a foothold in Eragon's being. And when Thorn flailed underneath them and Murtagh's attention wavered for an instant, Eragon launched a furious counterattack, clutching at Murtagh's consciousness.

The two of them strove against each other in grim silence while they fell, wrestling back and forth in the confines of their minds. Sometimes Eragon seemed to gain the upper hand, sometimes Murtagh, but neither could defeat the other. Eragon glanced at the ground rushing up at them and realized that their contest would have to be decided by other means.

Lowering the falchion so it was level with Murtagh, Eragon shouted, "Letta!"—the same spell Murtagh had used on him during their previous confrontation. It was a simple piece of magic—it would do nothing more than hold Murtagh's arms and torso in place—but it would allow them to test themselves directly against one another and determine which of them had the most energy at their disposal.

Murtagh mouthed a counterspell, the words lost in Thorn's snarling and in the howling of the wind.

Eragon's pulse raced as the strength ebbed from his limbs. When he had nearly depleted his reserves and was faint from the effort, Saphira and the elves poured the energy from their bodies into his, maintaining the spell for him. Across from him, Murtagh had originally appeared smug and confident, but as Eragon continued to restrain him, Murtagh's scowl deepened, and he pulled back his lips, baring his teeth. And the whole while, they besieged each other's minds.

Eragon felt the energy Arya was funneling into him decrease once, then twice, and he assumed that two of the spellweavers under Blödhgarm's command had fainted. *Murtagh* can't *hold out much longer*, he thought, and then had to struggle to regain control of his mind, for his lapse of concentration had granted Murtagh entry.

The force from Arya and the other elves declined by half, and even Saphira began to shake with exhaustion. Just as Eragon became convinced Murtagh would prevail, Murtagh uttered an anguished shout, and a great weight seemed to lift off Eragon as Murtagh's resistance vanished. Murtagh appeared astonished by Eragon's success.

What now? Eragon asked Arya and Saphira. *Do we take them as hostages? Can we?*

Now, said Saphira, *I must fly.* She released Thorn and pushed herself away from him, raising her wings and laboriously flapping as she endeavored to keep them aloft. Eragon looked over her shoulder and had a brief impression of horses and sun-streaked grass hurtling toward them; then it was as if a giant struck him from underneath and his sight went black.

The next thing Eragon saw was a swath of Saphira's neck scales an inch or two in front of his nose. The scales shone like cobalt-blue ice. Eragon was dimly aware of someone reaching out to his mind from across a great distance, their consciousness projecting an intense sense of urgency. As his faculties returned, he recognized the other person as Arya. She said: *End the spell, Eragon! It will kill us all if you keep it up. End it; Murtagh is too far away! Wake up, Eragon, or you will pass into the void.*

With a jolt, Eragon sat upright in the saddle, barely noticing that Saphira was crouched amid a circle of King Orrin's horsemen. Arya was nowhere to be seen. Now that he was alert again, Eragon could feel the spell he had cast on Murtagh still draining his strength, and in ever-increasing amounts. If not for the aid of Saphira and Arya and the other elves, he would have already died.

Eragon released the magic, then looked for Thorn and Murtagh on the ground.

There, said Saphira, and motioned with her snout. Low in the northwestern sky, Eragon saw Thorn's glittering shape, the dragon winging his way up the Jiet River, fleeing toward Galbatorix's army some miles distant.

How?

Murtagh healed Thorn again, and Thorn was lucky enough to land on the slope of a hill. He ran down it, then took off before you regained consciousness.

From across the rolling landscape, Murtagh's magnified voice boomed: "Do not think you have won, Eragon, Saphira. We shall meet again, I promise, and Thorn and I shall defeat you then, for we shall be even stronger than we are now!"

Eragon clenched his shield and his falchion so tightly, he bled from underneath his fingernails. *Do you think you can overtake him?*

I could, but the elves would not be able to help you from so far away, and I doubt we could prevail without their support.

We might be able— Eragon stopped and pounded his leg in frustration. *Blast it, I'm an idiot! I forgot about Aren. We could have used the energy in Brom's ring to help defeat them.*

You had other things on your mind. Anyone might have made the same mistake.

Maybe, but I still wish I had thought of Aren sooner. We could still use it to capture Thorn and Murtagh.

And then what? asked Saphira. *How could we keep them as prisoners? Would you drug them like Durza drugged you in Gil'ead? Or do you just want to kill them?*

I don't know! We could help them to change their true names, to break their oaths to Galbatorix. Letting them wander around unchecked, though, is too dangerous.

Arya said, *In theory, you are right, Eragon, but you are tired, Saphira is tired, and I would rather Thorn and Murtagh escape than we lose the two of you because you were not at your best.*

But—

But we do not have the capabilities to safely detain a dragon and Rider for an extended period, and I do not think killing Thorn and Murtagh would be as easy as you assume, Eragon. Be grateful we have driven them off, and rest easy knowing we can do so again when next they dare to confront us. So saying, she withdrew from his mind.

Eragon watched until Thorn and Murtagh had vanished from sight, then he sighed and rubbed Saphira's neck. *I could sleep for a fortnight.*

As could I.

You should be proud; you outflew Thorn at nearly every turn.

Yes, I did, didn't I? She preened. *It was hardly a fair competition. Thorn does not have my experience.*

Nor your talent, I should think.

Twisting her neck, she licked the upper part of his right arm, the mail hauberk tinkling, and then gazed down at him with sparkling eyes.

He managed a ghost of a smile. *I suppose I should have expected it, but it still surprised me that Murtagh was as fast as me. More magic on the part of Galbatorix, no doubt.*

Why did your wards fail to deflect Zar'roc, though? They saved you from worse blows when we fought the Ra'zac.

I'm not sure. Murtagh or Galbatorix might have invented a spell I had not thought to guard against. Or it could just be that Zar'roc is a Rider's blade, and as Glaedr said—

—the swords Rhunön forged excel at—

—cutting through enchantments of every kind, and—

—it is only rarely they are—

—affected by magic. Exactly. Eragon stared at the streaks of dragon blood on the flat of the falchion, weary. *When will we be able to defeat our enemies on our own? I couldn't have killed Durza if Arya hadn't broken the star sapphire. And we were only able to prevail over Murtagh and Thorn with the help of Arya and twelve others.*

We must become more powerful.

Yes, but how? How has Galbatorix amassed his strength? Has he found a way to feed off the bodies of his slaves even when he is hundreds of miles away? Garr! I don't know.

A runnel of sweat coursed down Eragon's brow and into the corner of his right eye. He wiped off the perspiration with the palm of his hand, then blinked and again noticed the horsemen gathered around him and Saphira. *What are they doing here?* Looking beyond, he realized Saphira had landed close to where King Orrin had intercepted the soldiers from the boats. Not far off to her left, hundreds of men, Urgals, and horses milled about in panic and confusion. Occasionally, the clatter of swords or the scream of a wounded man broke through the uproar, accompanied by snatches of demented laughter.

I think they are here to protect us, said Saphira.

Us! From what? Why haven't they killed the soldiers yet? Where— Eragon abandoned his question as Arya, Blödhgarm, and four other haggard-looking elves sprinted up to Saphira from the direction of the camp. Raising a hand in greeting, Eragon called, "Arya! What's happened? No one seems to be in command."

To Eragon's alarm, Arya was breathing so hard, she was unable to speak for a few moments. Then: "The soldiers proved more dangerous than we anticipated. We do not know how. Du Vrangr Gata has heard nothing but gibberish from Orrin's spellcasters." Regaining her breath, Arya started examining Saphira's cuts and bruises.

Before Eragon could ask more, a collection of excited cries from within the maelstrom of warriors drowned out the rest of the tumult, and he heard King Orrin shout, "Back, back, all of you! Archers, hold the line! Blast you, no one move, we have him!"

Saphira had the same thought as Eragon. Gathering her legs under her, she leaped over the ring of horsemen—startling the horses so they bucked and ran—and made her way across the corpse-strewn battlefield toward the sound of King Orrin's voice, brushing aside men and Urgals alike as if they were so many stalks of grass. The rest of the elves hurried to keep up, swords and bows in hand.

Saphira found Orrin sitting on his charger at the leading edge of the tightly packed warriors, staring at a lone man forty feet away. The king was flushed and wild-eyed, his armor besmirched with filth from combat. He had been wounded under his left arm, and the shaft of a spear protruded several inches from his right thigh. When Saphira's approach caught his attention, his face registered sudden relief.

"Good, good, you're here," he muttered as Saphira crawled abreast of his charger. "We needed you, Saphira, and you, Shadeslayer." One of the archers edged forward a few inches. Orrin waved his sword at him and yelled, "Back! I'll have the head of anyone who doesn't remain where he is, I swear by Angvard's crown!" Then Orrin resumed glaring at the lone man.

Eragon followed his gaze. The man was a soldier of medium height, with a purple birthmark on his neck and brown hair plastered flat by the helmet he had been wearing. His shield was a splintered ruin. His sword was notched, bent, and broken, missing the last six inches. River mud caked his mail hose. Blood sheeted from a gash along his ribs. An arrow fletched with white swan feathers had impaled his right foot and pinned it to the ground, three-quarters of the shaft buried in the hard dirt. From the man's throat, a horrid gurgling laugh emanated. It rose and fell with a drunken cadence, pitching from note to note as if the man were about to begin shrieking with horror.

"What are you?" shouted King Orrin. When the soldier did not immediately respond, the king cursed and said, "Answer me, or I'll let my spellcasters at you. Be you man or beast or some ill-spawned demon? In what foul pit did Galbatorix find you and your brothers? Are you kin of the Ra'zac?"

The king's last question acted like a needle driven into Eragon; he straightened bolt upright, every sense tingling.

The laughter paused for a moment. "Man. I am a man."

"You are like no man I know."

"I wanted to assure the future of my family. Is that so foreign to you, Surdan?"

"Give me no riddles, you fork-tongued wretch! Tell me how you became as you are, and speak honestly, lest you convince me to pour boiling lead down your throat and see if *that* pains you."

The unbalanced chuckles intensified, then the soldier said, "You cannot hurt me, Surdan. No one can. The king himself made us impervious to pain. In return, our families will live in comfort for the rest of their lives. You can hide from us, but we will never stop pursuing you, even when ordinary men would drop dead from exhaustion. You can fight us, but we will continue killing you as long as we have an arm to swing. You cannot even surrender to us, for we take no prisoners. You can do nothing but die and return this land to peace."

With a gruesome grimace, the soldier wrapped his mangled shield hand around the arrow and, with the sound of tearing flesh, pulled the shaft out of his foot. Lumps of crimson meat clung to the arrowhead as it came free. The soldier shook the arrow at them, then threw the missile at one of the archers, wounding him in the hand. His laugh louder than ever, the soldier lurched forward, dragging his injured foot behind him. He raised his sword, as if he intended to attack.

"Shoot him!" shouted Orrin.

Bowstrings twanged like badly tuned lutes, then a score of spinning arrows leaped toward the soldier and, an instant later, struck him in the torso. Two of the arrows bounced off his gambeson; the remainder penetrated his rib cage. His laughter reduced to a wheezing chuckle as blood seeped into his lungs, the soldier continued moving forward, painting the grass underneath him bright scarlet. The archers shot again, and arrows sprouted from the man's shoulders and arms, but he did not stop. Another volley of arrows followed close upon the last. The soldier stumbled and fell as an arrow split his left kneecap and others skewered his upper legs and one passed entirely through his neck—punching a hole in his birthmark—and whistled out across the field, trailing a spray of blood. And still the soldier refused to die. He began to crawl, dragging himself forward with his arms, grinning and giggling as if the whole world were an obscene joke that only he could appreciate.

A cold tingle shivered down Eragon's spine as he watched.

King Orrin swore violently, and Eragon detected a hint of hysteria in his voice. Jumping off his charger, Orrin threw his sword and his shield into the dirt and then pointed at the nearest Urgal. "Give me your ax." Startled, the gray-skinned Urgal hesitated, then surrendered his weapon.

King Orrin limped over to the soldier, raised the heavy ax with both hands, and, with a single blow, chopped off the soldier's head.

The giggling ceased.

The soldier's eyes rolled and his mouth worked for another few seconds, and then he was still.

Orrin grasped the head by the hair and lifted it so all could see. "They *can* be killed," he declared. "Spread the word that the only sure way of stopping these abominations is to behead them. That or bash in their skulls with a mace or shoot them in the eye from a safe distance. . . . Graytooth, where are you?" A stout, middle-aged horseman urged his mount forward. Orrin threw him the head, which he caught. "Mount that on a pole by the north gate of the camp. Mount *all* of their heads. Let them serve as a message to Galbatorix that we do not fear his underhanded tricks and we shall prevail in spite of them." Striding back to his charger, Orrin returned the ax to the Urgal, then picked up his own weapons.

A few yards away, Eragon spotted Nar Garzhvog standing among a cluster of Kull. Eragon spoke a few words to Saphira, and she sidled over to the Urgals. After exchanging nods, Eragon asked Garzhvog, "Were all the soldiers like that?" He gestured toward the arrow-riddled corpse.

"All men with no pain. You hit them and you think them dead, turn your back and they hamstring you." Garzhvog scowled. "I lost many rams today. We have fought droves of humans, Firesword, but never before these laughing ghouls. It is not natural. It makes us think they are possessed by hornless spirits, that maybe the gods themselves have turned against us."

"Nonsense," scoffed Eragon. "It is merely a spell by Galbatorix, and we shall soon have a way to protect ourselves against it."

Notwithstanding his outer confidence, the concept of fighting enemies who felt no pain unsettled him as much as it did the Urgals. Moreover, from what Garzhvog had said, he guessed that maintaining morale among the Varden was going to be even more difficult for Nasuada once everyone learned about the soldiers.

While the Varden and the Urgals set about collecting their fallen comrades, stripping the dead of useful equipment, and beheading the soldiers and dragging their truncated bodies into piles to burn, Eragon, Saphira, and King Orrin returned to the camp, accompanied by Arya and the other elves.

Along the way, Eragon offered to heal Orrin's leg, but the king refused, saying, "I have my own physicians, Shadeslayer."

Nasuada and Jörmundur were waiting for them by the north gate. Accosting Orrin, Nasuada said, "What went wrong?"

Eragon closed his eyes as Orrin explained how at first the attack on the soldiers had seemed to go well. The horsemen had swept through their ranks, dealing what they had thought were death-blows left and right, and had suffered only one casualty during their charge. When they had engaged the remaining soldiers, however, many of those they had struck down before rose up and rejoined the fight. Orrin shuddered. "We lost our nerve then. Any man would have. We did not know if the soldiers were invincible, or if they were even men at all. When you see an enemy coming at you with bone sticking out of his calf, a javelin through his belly, and half his face sheared away, and he *laughs* at you, it's a rare man who can stand his ground. My warriors panicked. They broke formation. It was utter confusion. Slaughter. When the Urgals and your warriors, Nasuada, reached us, they became caught up in the madness." He shook his head. "I've never seen the like of it, not even on the Burning Plains."

Nasuada's face had grown pale, even with her dark skin. She looked at Eragon and then Arya. "How could Galbatorix have done this?"

It was Arya who answered, "Block most, but not all, of a person's ability to feel pain. Leave just enough sensation so they know where they are and what they are doing, but not so much that pain can incapacitate them. The spell would require only a small amount of energy."

Nasuada wet her lips. Again speaking to Orrin, she said, "Do you know how many we lost?"

A tremor racked Orrin. He doubled over, pressed a hand against his leg, gritted his teeth, and growled, "Three hundred soldiers against . . . What was the size of the force you sent?"

"Two hundred swordsmen. A hundred spearmen. Fifty archers."

"Those, plus the Urgals, plus my cavalry . . . Say around a thousand strong. Against three hundred foot soldiers on an open field. We slew every last one of the soldiers. What it cost us, though . . ." The king shook his head. "We won't know for sure until we count the dead, but it looked to me as if three-quarters of your swordsmen are gone. More of the spearmen. Some archers. Of my cavalry, few remain: fifty, seventy. Many of them were my friends. Perhaps a hundred, a hundred and fifty Urgals dead. Overall? Five or six hundred to bury, and the better part of the survivors wounded. I don't know . . . I don't know. I don't—" His jaw going slack, Orrin slumped to the side and would have fallen off his horse if Arya had not sprung forward and caught him.

Nasuada snapped her fingers, summoning two of the Varden from among the tents, and ordered them to take Orrin to his pavilion and then to fetch the king his healers.

"We have suffered a grievous defeat, no matter that we exterminated the soldiers," Nasuada murmured. She pressed her lips together, sorrow and despair mixed in equal portions in her expression. Her eyes glimmered with unshed tears. Stiffening her back, she fixed Eragon and Saphira with an iron gaze. "How fared it with the two of you?" She listened without moving while Eragon described their encounter with Murtagh and Thorn. Afterward, she nodded. "That you would be able to escape their clutches was all we dared hope. However, you accomplished more than that. You proved that Galbatorix has not made Murtagh so powerful that we have no hope of defeating him. With a few more spellcasters to help you, Murtagh would have been yours to do with as you pleased. For that reason, he will not dare confront Queen Islanzadí's army by himself, I think. If we can gather enough spellcasters around you, Eragon, I believe we can finally kill Murtagh and Thorn the next time they come to abduct the pair of you."

"Don't you want to capture them?" Eragon asked.

"I want a great number of things, but I doubt I shall receive very many of them. Murtagh and Thorn may not be trying to kill you, but if the opportunity presents itself, we must kill them without hesitation. Or do you see it otherwise?"

". . . No."

Shifting her attention to Arya, Nasuada asked, "Did any of your spellweavers die during the contest?"

"Some fainted, but they have all recovered, thank you."

Nasuada took a deep breath and looked northward, her eyes focused on infinity. "Eragon, please inform Trianna that I want Du Vrangr Gata to figure out how to replicate Galbatorix's spell. Despicable as it is, we must imitate Galbatorix in this. We cannot afford not to. It won't be practical for all of us to be unable to feel pain—we would hurt ourselves far too easily—but we should have a few hundred swordsmen, volunteers, who are immune to physical suffering."

"My Lady."

"So many dead," said Nasuada. She twisted her reins in her hands. "We have remained in one place for too long. It is time we force the Empire onto the defensive again." She spurred Battlestorm away from the carnage that lay before the camp, the stallion tossing his head and gnawing on his bit. "Your cousin, Eragon, begged me to allow him to take part in today's fighting. I refused, on account of his impending marriage, which pleased him not— although I suspect his betrothed feels otherwise. Would you do me the favor of notifying me if they still intend to proceed with the ceremony today? After so much bloodshed, it would hearten the Varden to attend a marriage."

"I will let you know as soon as I find out."

"Thank you. You may go now, Eragon."

The first thing Eragon and Saphira did upon leaving Nasuada was to visit the elves who had fainted during their battle with Murtagh and Thorn and thank them and their companions for their assistance. Then Eragon, Arya, and Blödhgarm attended to the hurts Thorn had dealt Saphira, mending her cuts and scratches and a few of her bruises. When they finished, Eragon located Trianna with his mind and conveyed Nasuada's instructions.

Only then did he and Saphira seek out Roran. Blödhgarm and his elves accompanied them; Arya left to attend to business of her own.

Roran and Katrina were arguing quietly and intensely when Eragon spotted them standing by the corner of Horst's tent. They fell silent as Eragon and Saphira drew near. Katrina crossed her arms and stared away from Roran, while Roran gripped the top of his hammer thrust through his belt and scuffed the heel of his boot against a rock.

Stopping in front of them, Eragon waited a few moments, hoping they would explain the reason for their quarrel, but instead Katrina said, "Are either of you injured?" Her eyes flicked from him to Saphira and back.

"We were, but no longer."

"That is so . . . strange. We heard tales of magic in Carvahall, but I never really believed them. They seemed so impossible. But here, there are magicians everywhere. . . . Did you wound Murtagh and Thorn badly? Is that why they fled?"

"We bested them, but we caused them no permanent harm." Eragon paused, and when neither Roran nor Katrina spoke, he asked if they still wanted to get married that day. "Nasuada suggested you proceed, but it might be better to wait. The dead have yet to be buried, and there is much that needs doing. Tomorrow would be more convenient . . . and more seemly."

"No," said Roran, and ground the tip of his boot against the rock. "The Empire could attack again at any moment. Tomorrow might be too late. If . . . if somehow I died before we were wed, what would become of Katrina or our . . ." He faltered and his cheeks reddened.

Her expression softening, Katrina turned to Roran and took his hand. She said, "Besides, the food has been cooked, the decorations have been hung, and our friends have gathered for our marriage. It would be a pity if all those preparations were for nothing." Reaching up, she stroked Roran's beard, and he smiled at her and placed an arm around her.

I don't understand half of what goes on between them, Eragon complained to Saphira. "When shall the ceremony take place, then?"

"In an hour," said Roran.

MAN AND WIFE

Four hours later, Eragon stood on the crest of a low hill dotted with yellow wildflowers.

Surrounding the hill was a lush meadow that bordered the Jiet River, which rushed past a hundred feet to Eragon's right. The sky was bright and clear; sunshine bathed the land with a soft radiance. The air was cool and calm and smelled fresh, as if it had just rained.

Gathered in front of the hill were the villagers from Carvahall, none of whom had been injured during the fighting, and what seemed to be half of the men of the Varden. Many of the warriors held long spears mounted with embroidered pennants of every color. Various horses, including Snowfire, were picketed at the far end of the meadow. Despite Nasuada's best efforts, organizing the assembly had taken longer than anyone had reckoned.

Wind tousled Eragon's hair, which was still wet from washing, as Saphira glided over the congregation and alighted next to him, fanning her wings. He smiled and touched her on the shoulder.

Little one.

Under normal circumstances, Eragon would have been nervous about speaking in front of so many people and performing such a solemn and important ceremony, but after the earlier fighting, everything had assumed an air of unreality, as if it were no more than a particularly vivid dream.

At the base of the hill stood Nasuada, Arya, Narheim, Jörmundur, Angela, Elva, and others of importance. King Orrin was absent, as his wounds had proved to be more serious than they had first appeared and his healers were still laboring over him in his pavilion. The king's prime minister, Irwin, was attending in his stead.

The only Urgals present were the two in Nasuada's private guard. Eragon had been there when Nasuada had invited Nar Garzhvog to the event, and he had been relieved when Garzhvog had had the good sense to decline. The villagers would never have tolerated a large group of Urgals at the wedding. As it was, Nasuada had difficulty convincing them to allow her guards to remain.

With a rustle of cloth, the villagers and the Varden parted, forming a long, open path from the hill to the edge of the crowd. Then, joining their voices, the villagers began to sing the ancient wedding songs of Palancar Valley. The well-worn verses spoke of the cycle of the seasons, of the warm earth that gave birth to a new crop each year, of the spring calving, of nesting robins and spawning fish, and of how it was the destiny of the young to replace the old. One of Blödhgarm's spellcasters, a female elf with silver hair, withdrew a small gold harp from a velvet case and accompanied the villagers with notes of her own, embellishing upon the simple themes of their melodies, lending the familiar music a wistful mood.

With slow, steady steps, Roran and Katrina emerged from either side of the crowd at the far end of the path, turned toward the hill, and, without touching, began to advance toward Eragon. Roran wore a new tunic he had borrowed from one of the Varden. His hair was brushed, his beard was trimmed, and his boots were clean. His face beamed with inexpressible joy. All in all, he seemed very handsome and distinguished to Eragon. However, it was Katrina who commanded Eragon's attention. Her dress was light blue, as befitted a bride at her first wedding, of a simple cut but with a lace train that was twenty feet long and carried by two girls. Against the pale fabric, her free-flowing locks glowed like polished copper. In her hands was a posy of wildflowers. She was proud, serene, and beautiful.

Eragon heard gasps from some of the women as they beheld Katrina's train. He resolved to thank Nasuada for having Du Vrangr

Gata make the dress for Katrina, for he assumed it was she who was responsible for the gift.

Three paces behind Roran walked Horst. And at a similar distance behind Katrina walked Birgit, careful to avoid stepping on the train.

When Roran and Katrina were halfway to the hill, a pair of white doves flew out from the willow trees lining the Jiet River. The doves carried a circlet of yellow daffodils clutched in their feet. Katrina slowed and stopped as they approached her. The birds circled her three times, north to east, and then dipped down and laid the circlet upon the crown of her head before returning to the river.

"Did you arrange that?" Eragon murmured to Arya.

She smiled.

At the top of the hill, Roran and Katrina stood motionless before Eragon while they waited for the villagers to finish singing. As the final refrain faded into oblivion, Eragon raised his hands and said, "Welcome, one and all. Today we have come together to celebrate the union between the families of Roran Garrowsson and Katrina Ismirasdaughter. They are both of good reputation, and to the best of my knowledge, no one else has a claim upon their hands. If that not be the case, however, or if any other reason exists that they should not become man and wife, then make your objections known before these witnesses, that we may judge the merit of your arguments." Eragon paused for an appropriate interval, then continued. "Who here speaks for Roran Garrowsson?"

343

Horst stepped forward. "Roran has neither father nor uncle, so I, Horst Ostrecsson, speak for him as my blood."

"And who here speaks for Katrina Ismirasdaughter?"

Birgit stepped forward. "Katrina has neither mother nor aunt, so I, Birgit Mardrasdaughter, speak for her as my blood." Despite her vendetta against Roran, by tradition it was Birgit's right and responsibility to represent Katrina, as she had been a close friend of Katrina's mother.

"It is right and proper. What, then, does Roran Garrowsson bring to this marriage, that both he and his wife may prosper?"

"He brings his name," said Horst. "He brings his hammer. He brings the strength of his hands. And he brings the promise of a farm in Carvahall, where they may both live in peace."

Astonishment rippled through the crowd as people realized what Roran was doing: he was declaring in the most public and binding way possible that the Empire would not stop him from returning home with Katrina and providing her with the life she would have had if not for Galbatorix's murderous interference. Roran was staking his honor, as a man and a husband, on the downfall of the Empire.

"Do you accept this offer, Birgit Mardrasdaughter?" Eragon asked.

Birgit nodded. "I do."

"And what does Katrina Ismirasdaughter bring to this marriage, that both she and her husband may prosper?"

"She brings her love and devotion, with which she shall serve Roran Garrowsson. She brings her skills at running a household. And she brings a dowry." Surprised, Eragon watched as Birgit motioned and two men who were standing next to Nasuada came forward, carrying a metal casket between them. Birgit undid the clasp to the casket, then lifted open the lid and showed Eragon the contents. He gaped as he beheld the mound of jewelry inside. "She brings with her a gold necklace studded with diamonds. She brings a brooch set with red coral from the Southern Sea and a pearl net to hold her hair. She brings five rings of gold and electrum. The first ring—" As Birgit described each item, she lifted it from the casket so all might see she spoke the truth.

Bewildered, Eragon glanced at Nasuada and noted the pleased smile she wore.

After Birgit had finished her litany and closed the casket and fastened the lock again, Eragon asked, "Do you accept this offer, Horst Ostrecsson?"

"I do."

"Thus your families become one, in accordance with the law of the land." Then, for the first time, Eragon addressed Roran and Katrina directly: "Those who speak for you have agreed upon the terms of your marriage. Roran, are you pleased with how Horst Ostrecsson has negotiated on your behalf?"

"I am."

"And, Katrina, are you pleased with how Birgit Mardrasdaughter has negotiated on your behalf?"

"I am."

"Roran Stronghammer, son of Garrow, do you swear then, by your name and by your lineage, that you shall protect and provide for Katrina Ismirasdaughter while you both yet live?"

"I, Roran Stronghammer, son of Garrow, do swear, by my name and by my lineage, that I shall protect and provide for Katrina Ismirasdaughter while we both yet live."

"Do you swear to uphold her honor, to remain steadfast and faithful to her in the years to come, and to treat her with the proper respect, dignity, and gentleness?"

"I swear I shall uphold her honor, remain steadfast and faithful to her in the years to come, and treat her with the proper respect, dignity, and gentleness."

"And do you swear to give her the keys to your holdings, such as they may be, and to your strongbox where you keep your coin, by sunset tomorrow, so she may tend to your affairs as a wife should?"

Roran swore he would.

"Katrina, daughter of Ismira, do you swear, by your name and by your lineage, that you shall serve and provide for Roran Garrowsson while you both yet live?"

"I, Katrina, daughter of Ismira, do swear, by my name and by my lineage, that I shall serve and provide for Roran Garrowsson while we both yet live."

"Do you swear to uphold his honor, to remain steadfast and faithful to him in the years to come, to bear his children while you may, and to be a caring mother for them?"

"I swear I shall uphold his honor, remain steadfast and faithful to him in the years to come, bear his children while I may, and be a caring mother for them."

"And do you swear to assume charge of his wealth and his possessions, and to manage them responsibly, so he may concentrate upon those duties that are his alone?"

Katrina swore she would.

Smiling, Eragon drew a red ribbon from his sleeve and said, "Cross your wrists." Roran and Katrina extended their left and right arms, respectively, and did as he instructed. Laying the middle of the ribbon across their wrists, Eragon wound the strip of satin three times around and then tied the ends together with a bowknot. "As is my right as a Dragon Rider, I now declare you man and wife!"

The crowd erupted into cheers. Leaning toward each other, Roran and Katrina kissed, and the crowd redoubled their cheering.

Saphira dipped her head toward the beaming couple and, as Roran and Katrina separated, she touched each of them on the brow with the tip of her snout. *Live long, and may your love deepen with every passing year,* she said.

Roran and Katrina turned toward the crowd and raised their joined arms skyward. "Let the feast begin!" Roran declared.

Eragon followed the pair as they descended from the hill and walked through the press of shouting people toward two chairs that had been set at the forefront of a row of tables. There Roran and Katrina sat, as the king and queen of their wedding.

Then the guests lined up to offer their congratulations and present gifts. Eragon was first. His grin as large as theirs, he shook Roran's free hand and inclined his head toward Katrina.

"Thank you, Eragon," Katrina said.

"Yes, thank you," Roran added.

"The honor was mine." He looked at both of them, then burst out laughing.

"What?" demanded Roran.

"You! The two of you are as happy as fools."

Eyes sparkling, Katrina laughed and hugged Roran. "That we are!"

Growing sober, Eragon said, "You must know how fortunate you are to be here today, together. Roran, if you had not been able to rally everyone and travel to the Burning Plains, and if the Ra'zac had taken you, Katrina, to Urû'baen, neither of you would have—"

"Yes, but I did, and they didn't," interrupted Roran. "Let us not darken this day with unpleasant thoughts about what might have been."

"That is not why I mention it." Eragon glanced at the line of people waiting behind him, making sure they were not close enough to eavesdrop. "All three of us are enemies of the Empire. And as today has demonstrated, we are not safe, even here among the Varden. If Galbatorix can, he will strike at any one of us, including you, Katrina, in order to hurt the others. So I made these for you." From the pouch at his belt, Eragon withdrew two plain gold rings, polished until they shone. The previous night, he had molded them out of the last of the gold orbs he had extracted from the earth. He handed the larger one to Roran and the smaller one to Katrina.

Roran turned his ring, examining it, then held it up against the sky, squinting at the glyphs in the ancient language carved into the inside of the band. "It's very nice, but how can these help protect us?"

"I enchanted them to do three things," said Eragon. "If you ever need my help, or Saphira's, twist the ring once around your finger and say, 'Help me, Shadeslayer; help me, Brightscales,' and we will hear you, and we will come as fast as we can. Also, if either of you is close to death, your ring will alert us and you, Roran, or you, Katrina, depending on who is in peril. And so long as the rings are touching your skin, you will always know how to find each other, no matter how far apart you may be." He hesitated, then added, "I hope you will agree to wear them."

"Of course we will," said Katrina.

Roran's chest swelled, and his voice became husky. "Thank you," he said. "Thank you. I wish we had had these before she and I were separated in Carvahall."

Since they only had one free hand apiece, Katrina slid Roran's ring on for him, placing it on the third finger of his right hand, and he slid Katrina's on for her, placing it on the third finger of her left hand.

"I have another gift for you as well," said Eragon. Turning, he whistled and waved. Pushing his way through the crowd, a groom hurried toward them, leading Snowfire by the bridle. The groom handed Eragon the reins to the stallion, then bowed and withdrew. Eragon said, "Roran, you will need a good steed. This is Snowfire. He was Brom's to begin with, then mine, and now I am giving him to you."

Roran ran his eyes over Snowfire. "He's a magnificent beast."

"The finest. Will you accept him?"

"With pleasure."

Eragon summoned back the groom and returned Snowfire to his care, instructing him that Roran was the stallion's new owner. As the man and horse left, Eragon looked at the people in line who were carrying presents for Roran and Katrina. Laughing, he said, "The two of you may have been poor this morning, but you'll be rich by this evening. If Saphira and I ever have a chance to settle down, we'll have to come live with you in the giant hall you will build for all of your children."

"Whatever we build, it will hardly be large enough for Saphira, I think," said Roran.

"But you will always be welcome with us," said Katrina. "Both of you."

After congratulating them once more, Eragon ensconced himself at the end of a table and amused himself by throwing scraps of roast chicken toward Saphira and watching her snap them out of the air. He remained there until Nasuada had spoken with Roran and Katrina, handing them something small he could not see. Then he intercepted Nasuada as she was departing the festivities.

"What is it, Eragon?" she asked. "I cannot linger."

"Was it you who gave Katrina her dress and her dowry?"

"Aye. Do you disapprove?"

"I am grateful you were so kind to my family, but I wonder . . ."

"Yes?"

"Isn't the Varden desperate for gold?"

"We are," Nasuada said, "but not so desperate as before. Since my scheme with the lace, and since I triumphed in the Trial of the Long Knives and the wandering tribes swore absolute fealty to me and granted me access to their riches, we are less likely to starve to death and more likely to die because we don't have a shield or a spear." Her lips twitched in a smile. "What I gave Katrina is insignificant compared with the vast sums this army requires to function. And I do not believe I have squandered my gold. Rather, I believe I have made a valuable purchase. I have purchased prestige and self-respect for Katrina, and by extension, I have purchased Roran's goodwill. I may be overly optimistic, but I suspect his loyalty will prove far more valuable than a hundred shields or a hundred spears."

349

"You are always seeking to improve the Varden's prospects, aren't you?" Eragon said.

"Always. As you should be." Nasuada started to walk away from him, then returned and said, "Sometime before sunset, come to my pavilion, and we will visit the men who were wounded today. There are many we cannot heal, you know. It will do them good to see that we care about their welfare and that we appreciate their sacrifice."

Eragon nodded. "I will be there."

"Good."

Hours passed as Eragon laughed and ate and drank and traded stories with old friends. Mead flowed like water, and the wedding feast became ever more boisterous. Clearing a space between the tables, the men tested their prowess against one another with feats of wrestling and archery and bouts with quarterstaves. Two of the elves, a man and a woman, demonstrated their skill with swordplay—awing the onlookers with the speed and grace of their dancing blades—and even Arya consented to perform a song, which sent shivers down Eragon's spine.

Throughout, Roran and Katrina said little, preferring to sit and gaze at each other, oblivious to their surroundings.

When the bottom of the orange sun touched the distant horizon, however, Eragon reluctantly excused himself. With Saphira by his side, he left the sounds of revelry behind and walked to Nasuada's pavilion, breathing deeply of the cool evening air to clear his head. Nasuada was waiting for him in front of her red command tent, the Nighthawks gathered close around. Without saying a word, she, Eragon, and Saphira made their way across the camp to the tents of the healers, where the injured warriors lay.

For over an hour, Nasuada and Eragon visited with the men who had lost their limbs or their eyes or had contracted an incurable infection in the course of fighting the Empire. Some of the warriors had been injured that morning. Others, as Eragon discovered, had been wounded on the Burning Plains and had yet to recover, despite all the herbs and spells lavished upon them. Before they had set forth among the rows of blanket-covered men, Nasuada had warned Eragon not to tire himself further by attempting to heal everyone he met, but he could not help muttering a spell here and there to ease pain or to drain an abscess or to reshape a broken bone or to remove an unsightly scar.

One of the men Eragon met had lost his left leg below the knee, as well as two fingers on his right hand. His beard was short and gray, and his eyes were covered with a strip of black cloth. When Eragon greeted him and asked how he fared, the man reached out and grasped Eragon by the elbow with the three fingers of his right hand. In a hoarse voice, the man said, "Ah, Shadeslayer. I knew you would come. I have been waiting for you ever since the light."

"What do you mean?"

"The light that illuminated the flesh of the world. In a single instant, I saw every living thing around me, from the largest to the smallest. I saw my bones shining through my arms. I saw the worms in the earth and the gore-crows in the sky and the mites on the wings of the crows. The gods have touched me, Shadeslayer. They gave me this vision for a reason. I saw you on the field of battle, you and your dragon, and you were like a blazing sun among a forest of dim candles. And I saw your brother, your brother and his dragon, and they too were like a sun."

The nape of Eragon's neck prickled as he listened. "I have no brother," he said.

The maimed swordsman cackled. "You cannot fool me, Shade-slayer. I know better. The world burns around me, and from the fire, I hear the whisper of minds, and I learn things from the whispers. You hide yourself from me now, but I can still see you, a man of yellow flame with twelve stars floating around your waist and another star, brighter than the others, upon your right hand."

Eragon pressed his palm against the belt of Beloth the Wise, checking that the twelve diamonds sewn within were still concealed. They were.

"Listen to me, Shadeslayer," whispered the man, pulling Eragon toward his lined face. "I saw your brother, and he burned. But he did not burn like you. Oh no. The light from his soul shone *through* him, as if it came from somewhere else. He, *he* was a void, a shape of a man. And through that shape came the brilliance that burned. Do you understand? *Others* illuminated him."

"Where were these others? Did you see them as well?"

The warrior hesitated. "I could feel them close at hand, raging at the world as if they hated everything in it, but their bodies were hidden from my sight. They were there and not there. I cannot explain better than that. . . . I would not want to get any closer to those creatures, Shadeslayer. They aren't human, of that I'm sure, and their hate, it was like the largest thunderstorm you've ever seen crammed into a tiny glass bottle."

"And when the bottle breaks . . . ," Eragon murmured.

"Exactly, Shadeslayer. Sometimes I wonder if Galbatorix has managed to capture the gods themselves and make them his slaves, but then I laugh and call myself a fool."

"Whose gods, though? The dwarves'? Those of the wandering tribes?"

"Does it matter, Shadeslayer? A god is a god, regardless of where he comes from."

Eragon grunted. "Perhaps you're right."

As he left the man's pallet, one of the healers pulled Eragon aside. She said, "Forgive him, my Lord. The shock of his wounds has driven him quite mad. He's always ranting about suns and stars and glowing lights he claims to see. Sometimes it seems as if he knows things he shouldn't, but don't you be deceived, he gets them from the other patients. They gossip all the time, you know. It's all they have to do, poor things."

"I am not a lord," Eragon said, "and he is not mad. I'm not sure what he is, but he has an uncommon ability. If he gets better or worse, please inform one of Du Vrangr Gata."

The healer curtsied. "As you wish, Shadeslayer. I'm sorry for my mistake, Shadeslayer."

"How was he hurt?"

"A soldier cut off his fingers when he tried to block a sword with his hand. Later, one of the missiles from the Empire's catapults landed upon his leg, crushing it beyond repair. We had to amputate. The men who were beside him said that when the missile struck, he immediately began screaming about the light, and when they picked him up, they noticed that his eyes had turned pure white. Even his pupils have disappeared."

"Ah. You have been most helpful. Thank you."

It was dark when Eragon and Nasuada finally left the healers' tents. Nasuada sighed and said, "Now I could use a mug of mead." Eragon nodded, staring down between his feet. They started back to her pavilion, and after a while, she asked, "What are you thinking, Eragon?"

"That we live in a strange world, and I'll be lucky if I ever understand more than a small portion of it." Then he recounted his conversation with the man, which she found as interesting as he had.

"You should tell Arya about this," said Nasuada. "She might know what these 'others' could be."

They parted at her pavilion, Nasuada going inside to finish reading a report, while Eragon and Saphira continued on to Eragon's tent. There Saphira curled up on the ground and prepared to sleep as Eragon sat next to her and gazed at the stars, a parade of wounded men marching before his eyes.

What many of them had told him continued to reverberate through his mind: *We fought for you, Shadeslayer.*

✦ ✦ ✦

WHISPERS IN THE NIGHT

Roran opened his eyes and stared at the drooping canvas overhead.

A thin gray light pervaded the tent, leaching objects of their color, rendering everything a pale shadow of its daylight self. He shivered. The blankets had slid down to his waist, exposing his torso to the cold night air. As he pulled them back up, he noticed that Katrina was no longer by his side.

He saw her sitting by the entrance to the tent, staring up at the sky. She had a cloak wrapped over her shift. Her hair fell to the small of her back, a dark tangled bramble.

A lump formed in Roran's throat as he studied her.

Dragging the blankets with him, he sat beside her. He placed an arm around her shoulders, and she leaned against him, her head and neck warm against his chest. He kissed her on the brow. For a long while, he contemplated the glimmering stars with her and listened to the regular pattern of her breathing, the only sound besides his own in the sleeping world.

Then she whispered, "The constellations are shaped differently here. Have you noticed?"

"Aye." He shifted his arm, fitting it against the curve of her waist and feeling the slight bulge of her growing belly. "What woke you?"

She shivered. "I was thinking."

"Oh."

Starlight gleamed in her eyes as she twisted in his arms and gazed at him. "I was thinking about you and us . . . and our future together."

"Those are heavy thoughts for so late at night."

"Now that we are married, how do you plan to care for me and for our child?"

"Is that what worries you?" He smiled. "You won't starve; we have gold enough to assure that. Besides, the Varden will always see to it that Eragon's cousins have food and shelter. Even if something were to happen to me, they would continue to provide for you and the baby."

"Yes, but what do you intend to *do*?"

Puzzled, he searched her face for the source of her agitation. "I am going to help Eragon end this war so we can return to Palancar Valley and settle down without fear of soldiers dragging us off to Urû'baen. What else would I do?"

"You will fight with the Varden, then?"

"You know I will."

"As you would have fought today if Nasuada had let you?"

"Yes."

"What of our baby, though? An army on the march is no place to raise a child."

"We cannot run away and hide from the Empire, Katrina. Unless the Varden win, Galbatorix will find and kill us, or he will find and kill our children, or our children's children. And I do not think the Varden will achieve victory unless everyone does their utmost to help them."

She placed a finger over his lips. "You are my only love. No other man shall ever capture my heart. I will do everything I can to lighten your burden. I will cook your meals, mend your clothes, and clean your armor. . . . But once I give birth, I will leave this army."

"Leave!" He went rigid. "That's nonsense! Where would you go?"

"Dauth, perhaps. Remember, Lady Alarice offered us sanctuary, and some of our people are still there. I would not be alone."

"If you think I'm going to let you and our newborn child go tramping across Alagaësia by yourselves, then—"

"You don't need to shout."

"I'm not—"

"Yes, you are." Clasping his hand between hers and pressing it against her heart, she said, "It's not safe here. If it were only the two of us, I could accept the danger, but not when it is our baby who might die. I love you, Roran, I love you so much, but our child has to come before anything we want for ourselves. Otherwise, we do not deserve to be called parents." Tears shone in her eyes, and he felt his own eyes dampen. "It was you, after all, who convinced me to leave Carvahall and hide in the Spine when the soldiers attacked. This is no different."

The stars swam before Roran as his vision blurred. "I would rather lose an arm than be parted from you again."

Katrina began to cry then, her quiet sobs shaking his body. "I don't want to leave you either."

He tightened his embrace and rocked back and forth with her. When her weeping subsided, he whispered in her ear, "I would rather lose an arm than be parted from you, but I would rather die than allow anyone to hurt you . . . or our child. If you are going to leave, you should leave now, while it's still easy for you to travel."

She shook her head. "No. I want Gertrude as my midwife. She's the only one I trust. Besides, if I have any difficulty, I would rather be here, where there are magicians trained in healing."

"Nothing will go wrong," he said. "As soon as our child is born, you will go to Aberon, not Dauth; it is less likely to be attacked. And if Aberon becomes too dangerous, then you will go to the Beor Mountains and live with the dwarves. And if Galbatorix strikes at the dwarves, then you will go to the elves in Du Weldenvarden."

"And if Galbatorix attacks Du Weldenvarden, I will fly to the moon and raise our child among the spirits who inhabit the heavens."

"And they will bow down to you and make you their queen, as you deserve."

She snuggled closer to him.

Together, they sat and watched as, one by one, the stars vanished from the sky, obscured by the glow spreading in the east. When only the morning star remained, Roran said, "You know what this means, don't you?"

"What?"

"I'll just have to ensure we kill every last one of Galbatorix's soldiers, capture all the cities in the Empire, defeat Murtagh and Thorn, and behead Galbatorix and his turncoat dragon before your time comes. That way, there will be no need for you to go away."

She was silent for a moment, then said, "If you could, I would be very happy."

They were about to return to their cot when, out of the glimmering sky, there sailed a miniature ship, woven of dry strips of grass. The ship hovered in front of their tent, rocking upon invisible waves of air, and almost seemed to be looking at them with its dragon-head-shaped prow.

Roran froze, as did Katrina.

Like a living creature, the ship darted across the path before their tent, then it swooped up and around, chasing an errant moth. When the moth escaped, the ship glided back toward the tent, stopping only inches from Katrina's face.

357

Before Roran could decide if he should snatch the ship out of the air, it turned and flew off toward the morning star, vanishing once more into the endless ocean of the sky, leaving them to gaze after it in wonder.

✦ ✦ ✦

ORDERS

Late that night, visions of death and violence gathered along the edges of Eragon's dreams, threatening to overwhelm him with panic. He stirred with unease, wanting to break free but unable to do so. Brief, disjointed images of stabbing swords and screaming men and Murtagh's angry face flashed before his eyes.

Then Eragon felt Saphira enter his mind. She swept through his dreams like a great wind, brushing aside his looming nightmare. In the silence that followed, she whispered, *All is well, little one. Rest easy; you are safe, and I am with you. . . . Rest easy.*

A sense of profound peace crept over Eragon. He rolled over and drifted off into happier memories, comforted by his awareness of Saphira's presence.

When Eragon opened his eyes, an hour before sunrise, he found himself lying underneath one of Saphira's vein-webbed wings. She had her tail wrapped around him, and her side was warm against his head. He smiled and crawled out from under her wing even as she lifted her head and yawned.

Good morning, he said.

She yawned again and stretched like a cat.

Eragon bathed, shaved with magic, cleaned the falchion's scabbard of dried blood from the previous day, and then dressed in one of his elf tunics.

Once he was satisfied he was presentable, and Saphira had finished her tongue bath, they walked to Nasuada's pavilion. All six of the current shift of Nighthawks were standing outside, their seamed faces set into their usual grim expressions. Eragon waited while a stocky dwarf announced them. Then he entered the tent, and Saphira crawled around to the open panel where she could insert her head and participate in the discussion.

Eragon bowed to Nasuada where she sat in her high-backed chair carved with blooming thistles. "My Lady, you asked me to come here to talk about my future; you said you had a most important mission for me."

"I did, and I do," said Nasuada. "Please, be seated." She indicated a folding chair next to Eragon. Tilting the sword at his waist so it would not catch, he settled into the chair. "As you know, Galbatorix has sent battalions to the cities of Aroughs, Feinster, and Belatona in an attempt to prevent us from taking them by siege or, failing that, to slow our progress and force us to divide our own troops so we would be more vulnerable to the depredations of the soldiers who were camped north of us. After yesterday's battle, our scouts reported that the last of Galbatorix's men withdrew to parts unknown. I was going to strike at those soldiers days ago, but I had to refrain since you were absent. Without you, Murtagh and Thorn could have slaughtered our warriors with impunity, and we had no way of discovering whether the two of them were among the soldiers. Now that you are with us again, our position is somewhat improved, although not as much as I had hoped, given that we must now also contend with Galbatorix's latest artifice, these men without pain. Our only encouragement is that the two of you, along with Islanzadí's spellcasters, have proved you can fend off Murtagh and Thorn. Upon that hope depends our plan for victory."

That red runt is no match for me, said Saphira. *If he did not have Murtagh protecting him, I would trap him against the ground and shake him by the neck until he submitted to me and acknowledged me as leader of the hunt.*

"I am sure you would," said Nasuada, smiling.

Eragon asked, "What course of action have you decided upon, then?"

"I have decided upon several courses, and we must undertake

them all simultaneously if any are to be successful. First, we cannot push farther into the Empire, leaving cities behind us that Galbatorix still controls. To do that would be to expose ourselves to attacks from both the front and the rear and to invite Galbatorix to invade and seize Surda while we were absent. So I have already ordered the Varden to march north, to the nearest place where we can safely cross the Jiet River. Once we are on the other side of the river, I will send warriors south to capture Aroughs while King Orrin and I continue with the remainder of our forces to Feinster, which, with your help and Saphira's, should fall before us without too much trouble.

"While we are engaged in the tedious business of tramping across the countryside, I have other responsibilities for you, Eragon." She leaned forward in her seat. "We need the full help of the dwarves. The elves are fighting for us in the north of Alagaësia, the Surdans have joined with us body and mind, and even the Urgals have allied themselves with us. But we need the dwarves. We cannot succeed without them. Especially now that we must contend with soldiers who cannot feel pain."

"Have the dwarves chosen a new king or queen yet?"

Nasuada grimaced. "Narheim assures me that the process is moving apace, but like the elves, dwarves take a longer view of time than we do. *Apace* for them might mean months of deliberations."

"Don't they realize the urgency of the situation?"

"Some do, but many oppose helping us in this war, and they seek to delay the proceedings as long as possible and to install one of their own upon the marble throne in Tronjheim. The dwarves have lived in hiding for so long, they have become dangerously suspicious of outsiders. If someone hostile to our aims wins the throne, we shall lose the dwarves. We cannot allow that to happen. Nor can we wait for the dwarves to resolve their differences at their usual pace. *But*"—she raised a finger—"from so far away, I cannot effectively intervene in their politics. Even if I were in Tronjheim, I could not ensure a favorable outcome; the dwarves do not take kindly to anyone who is not of their clans meddling in their government. So I want you, Eragon, to travel to Tronjheim in my stead and do what you can to ensure that the dwarves choose a new monarch in an expeditious manner—and that they choose a monarch who is sympathetic to our cause."

"Me! But—"

"King Hrothgar adopted you into Dûrgrimst Ingeitum. According to their laws and customs, you *are* a dwarf, Eragon. You have a legal right to participate in the hallmeets of the Ingeitum, and as Orik is set to become their chief, and as he is your foster brother and a friend of the Varden's, I am sure he will agree to let you accompany him into the secret councils of the thirteen clans where they elect their rulers."

Her proposal seemed preposterous to Eragon. "What about Murtagh and Thorn? When they return, as they surely will, Saphira and I are the only ones who can hold our own against them, albeit with some assistance. If we are not here, no one will be able to stop them from killing you or Arya or Orrin or the rest of the Varden."

The gap between Nasuada's eyebrows narrowed. "You dealt Murtagh a stinging defeat yesterday. Most likely, he and Thorn are winging their way back to Urû'baen even as we speak so Galbatorix may interrogate them about the battle and chastise them for their failure. He will not send them to attack us again until he is confident that they can overwhelm you. Murtagh is surely uncertain about the true limits of your strength now, so that unhappy event may yet be some while off. Between now and then, I believe you will have enough time to travel back and forth between Farthen Dûr."

"You could be wrong," argued Eragon. "Besides, how would you keep Galbatorix from learning about our absence and attacking while we are gone? I doubt you have found all of the spies he has seeded among us."

Nasuada tapped her fingers on the arms of her chair. "I said I wanted you to go to Farthen Dûr, Eragon. I did not say I wanted Saphira to go as well." Turning her head, Saphira released a small puff of smoke that drifted toward the peak of the tent.

"I'm not about to—"

"Let me finish, please, Eragon."

He clamped shut his jaw and glared at her, his left hand tight around the pommel of the falchion.

"You are not beholden to me, Saphira, but my hope is that you will agree to stay here while Eragon journeys to the dwarves so that we can deceive the Empire and the Varden as to Eragon's whereabouts. If we can hide your departure"—she gestured at Eragon—"from the masses, no one will have any reason to suspect you are not still here. We will only have to devise a suitable excuse, then, to account for your sudden desire to remain in your tent during the day—perhaps that you and Saphira are flying sorties into enemy territory at night and so must rest while the sun is up.

362   "In order for the ruse to work, however, Blödhgarm and his companions will have to stay here as well, both to avoid arousing suspicion and for reasons of defense. If Murtagh and Thorn reappear while you are gone, Arya can take your place on Saphira. Between her, Blödhgarm's spellcasters, and the magicians of Du Vrangr Gata, we should have a fair chance of thwarting Murtagh."

In a harsh voice, Eragon said, "If Saphira doesn't fly me to Farthen Dûr, then how am I supposed to travel there in a timely fashion?"

"By running. You told me yourself you ran much of the distance from Helgrind. I expect that without having to hide from soldiers or peasants you can traverse many more leagues each day on the way to Farthen Dûr than you were able to in the Empire." Again Nasuada drummed the polished wood of her chair. "Of course, it would be foolish to go alone. Even a powerful magician can die of a simple accident in the far reaches of the wilderness if he has no one to help him. Shepherding you through the Beor Mountains would be a waste of Arya's talents, and people would notice if one of Blödhgarm's elves disappeared without explanation. Therefore, I have decided that a Kull should accompany you, as they are the only other creatures capable of matching your pace."

"A Kull!" exclaimed Eragon, unable to contain himself any longer. "You would send me among the dwarves with a Kull by my side? I cannot think of any race the dwarves hate more than the Urgals. They make bows out of their horns! If I walked into Farthen Dûr with an Urgal, the dwarves would not pay heed to anything I had to say."

"I am well aware of that," said Nasuada. "Which is why you will not go directly to Farthen Dûr. Instead, you will first stop at Bregan Hold on Mount Thardûr, which is the ancestral home of the Ingeitum. There you will find Orik, and there you can leave the Kull while you continue on to Farthen Dûr in Orik's company."

Staring somewhat beyond Nasuada, Eragon said, "And what if I do not agree with the path you have chosen? What if I believe there are other, safer ways to accomplish what you desire?"

"What ways would those be, pray tell?" asked Nasuada, her fingers pausing in midair.

"I would have to think about it, but I am sure they exist."

"I *have* thought about it, Eragon, and at great length. Having you act as my emissary is our only hope of influencing the succession of the dwarves. I was raised among dwarves, remember, and I have a better understanding of them than most humans."

"I still believe it's a mistake," he growled. "Send Jörmundur instead, or one of your other commanders. I won't go, not while—"

"You *won't?*" said Nasuada, her voice rising. "A vassal who disobeys his lord is no better than a warrior who ignores his captain on the field of battle and may be punished similarly. As your liegelord, then, Eragon, I order you to run to Farthen Dûr, whether you want to or not, and to oversee the choosing of the next ruler of the dwarves."

Furious, Eragon breathed heavily through his nose, gripping and regripping the pommel of his falchion.

In a softer, although still guarded, tone, Nasuada said, "What will it be, Eragon? Will you do as I ask, or will you dispossess me and lead the Varden yourself? Those are your only options."

Shocked, he said, "No, I can reason with you. I can convince you otherwise."

"You cannot, because you cannot provide me with an alternative that is as likely to succeed."

He met her gaze. "I could refuse your order and let you punish me however you deem fit."

His suggestion startled her. Then she said, "To see you lashed to a whipping post would do irreparable harm to the Varden. And it would destroy my authority, for people would know you could defy me whenever you wanted, with the only consequence being a handful of stripes that you could heal an instant later, for we cannot execute you, as we would any other warrior who disobeyed a superior. I would rather abdicate my post and grant you command of the Varden than allow such a thing to occur. If you believe you are better suited for the task, then take my position, take my chair, and declare yourself master of this army! But so long as I speak for the Varden, I have the right to make these decisions. If they be mistakes, then that is my responsibility as well."

"Will you listen to no advice?" Eragon asked, troubled. "Will you dictate the course of the Varden regardless of what those around you counsel?"

Nasuada's middle fingernail clacked against the polished wood of her chair. "I do listen to advice. I listen to a continuous stream of advice every waking hour of my life, but sometimes my conclusions do not match those of my underlings. Now, you must decide whether you will uphold your oath of fealty and abide by my decision, even though you may not agree with it, or if you will set yourself up as a mirror image of Galbatorix."

"I only want what is best for the Varden," he said.

"As do I."

"You leave me no choice but one I dislike."

"Sometimes it is harder to follow than it is to lead."

"May I have a moment to think?"

"You may."

Saphira? he asked.

Flecks of purple light danced around the interior of the pavilion as she twisted her neck and fixed her eyes upon Eragon's. *Little one?*

Should I go?

I think you must.

He pressed his lips together in a rigid line. *And what of you?*

You know I hate to be separated from you, but Nasuada's arguments are well reasoned. If I can help keep Murtagh and Thorn away by remaining with the Varden, then perhaps I should.

His emotions and hers washed between their minds, tidal surges in a shared pool of anger, anticipation, reluctance, and tenderness. From him flowed the anger and reluctance; from her other, gentler sentiments—as rich in scope as his own—that moderated his choleric passion and lent him perspectives he would not otherwise have. Nevertheless, he clung with stubborn insistence to his opposition to Nasuada's scheme. *If you flew me to Farthen Dûr, I would not be gone for as long, meaning Galbatorix would have less of an opportunity to mount a new assault.*

But his spies would tell him the Varden were vulnerable the moment we left.

I do not want to part with you again so soon after Helgrind.

Our own desires cannot take precedence over the needs of the Varden, but no, I do not want to part with you either. Still, remember what Oromis said, that the prowess of a dragon and Rider is measured not only by how well they work together but also by how well they can function when apart. We are both mature enough to operate independently of each other, Eragon, however much we may dislike the prospect. You proved that yourself during your trip from Helgrind.

Would it bother you fighting with Arya on your back, as Nasuada mentioned?

Her I would mind least of all. We have fought together before, and it was she who ferried me across Alagaësia for nigh on twenty years when I was in my egg. You know that, little one. Why pose this question? Are you jealous?

What if I am?

An amused twinkle lit her sapphire eyes. She flicked her tongue at him. *Then it is very sweet of you. . . . Would you I should stay or go?*

It is your choice to make, not mine.

But it affects us both.

Eragon dug at the ground with the tip of his boot. Then he said, *If we must participate in this mad scheme, we should do everything we can to help it succeed. Stay, and see if you can keep Nasuada from losing her head over this thrice-blasted plan of hers.*

Be of good cheer, little one. Run fast, and we shall be reunited in short order.

Eragon looked up at Nasuada. "Very well," he said, "I will go."

Nasuada's posture relaxed somewhat. "Thank you. And you, Saphira? Will you stay or go?"

Projecting her thoughts to include Nasuada as well as Eragon, Saphira said, *I will stay, Nightstalker.*

Nasuada inclined her head. "Thank you, Saphira. I am most grateful for your support."

"Have you spoken to Blödhgarm of this?" asked Eragon. "Has he agreed to it?"

"No, I assumed you would inform him of the details."

Eragon doubted the elves would be pleased by the prospect of him traveling to Farthen Dûr with only an Urgal for company. He said, "If I might make a suggestion?"

"You know I welcome your suggestions."

That stopped him for a moment. "A suggestion and a request, then." Nasuada lifted a finger, motioning for him to continue. "When the dwarves have chosen their new king or queen, Saphira should join me in Farthen Dûr, both to honor the dwarves' new ruler and to fulfill the promise she made to King Hrothgar after the battle for Tronjheim."

Nasuada's expression sharpened into that of a hunting wildcat. "What promise was this?" she asked. "You have not told me of this before."

"That Saphira would mend the star sapphire, Isidar Mithrim, as recompense for Arya breaking it."

Her eyes wide with astonishment, Nasuada looked at Saphira and said, "You are capable of such a feat?"

I am, but I do not know if I will be able to summon the magic I will need when I am standing before Isidar Mithrim. My ability to cast spells is not subject to my own desires. At times, it is as if I have gained a new sense and I can feel the pulse of energy within my own flesh, and by directing it with my will, I can reshape the world as I wish. The rest of my life, however, I can no more cast a spell than a fish can fly. If I could mend Isidar Mithrim, though, it would go a long way toward earning us the goodwill of all the dwarves, not just a select few who have the breadth of knowledge to appreciate the importance of their cooperation with us.

"It would do more than you imagine," said Nasuada. "The star sapphire holds a special place in the hearts of dwarves. Every dwarf has a love of gemstones, but Isidar Mithrim they love and cherish above all others, because of its beauty, and most of all because of its immense size. Restore it to its previous glory and you will restore the pride of their race."

Eragon said, "Even if Saphira failed to repair Isidar Mithrim, she should be present for the coronation of the dwarves' new ruler. You could conceal her absence for a few days by letting it be known among the Varden that she and I have left on a brief trip to Aberon, or some such. By the time Galbatorix's spies realized you had deceived them, it would be too late for the Empire to organize an attack before we returned."

Nasuada nodded. "It is a good idea. Contact me as soon as the dwarves set a date for the coronation."

"I shall."

"You have made your suggestion, now out with your request. What is it you wish of me?"

"Since you insist I must make this trip, with your permission, I would like to fly with Saphira from Tronjheim to Ellesméra, after the coronation."

"For what purpose?"

"To consult with the ones who taught us during our last visit to Du Weldenvarden. We promised them that as soon as events allowed, we would return to Ellesméra to complete our training."

The line between Nasuada's eyebrows deepened. "There is not the time for you to spend weeks or months in Ellesméra continuing your education."

"No, but perhaps we have the time for a brief visit."

Nasuada leaned her head against the back of her carved chair and gazed down at Eragon from underneath heavy lids. "And who exactly are your teachers? I have noticed you always evade direct questions about them. Who was it that taught the two of you in Ellesméra, Eragon?"

Fingering his ring, Aren, Eragon said, "We swore an oath to Islanzadí that we would not reveal their identity without permission from her, Arya, or whoever may succeed Islanzadí to her throne."

"By all the demons above and below, how many oaths have you and Saphira sworn?" demanded Nasuada. "You seem to bind yourself to everyone you meet."

Feeling somewhat sheepish, Eragon shrugged and had opened his mouth to speak when Saphira said to Nasuada, *We do not seek them out, but how can we avoid pledging ourselves when we cannot topple Galbatorix and the Empire without the support of every race in Alagaësia? Oaths are the price we pay for winning the aid of those in power.*

"Mmh," said Nasuada. "So I must ask Arya for the truth of the matter?"

"Aye, but I doubt she will tell you; the elves consider the identity of our teachers to be one of their most precious secrets. They will not risk sharing it unless absolutely necessary, to keep word of it from reaching Galbatorix." Eragon stared at the royal-blue gemstone set in his ring, wondering how much more information his oath and his honor would allow him to divulge, then said, "Know this, though: we are not so alone as we once assumed."

Nasuada's expression sharpened. "I see. That is good to know, Eragon. . . . I only wish the elves were more forthcoming with me." After pursing her lips for a brief moment, Nasuada continued. "Why must you travel all the way to Ellesméra? Have you no means to communicate with your tutors directly?"

Eragon spread his hands in a gesture of helplessness. "If only we could. Alas, the spell has yet to be invented that can broach the wards that encircle Du Weldenvarden."

"The elves did not even leave an opening they themselves can exploit?"

"If they had, Arya would have contacted Queen Islanzadí as soon as she was revived in Farthen Dûr, rather than physically going to Du Weldenvarden."

"I suppose you are right. But then how was it you were able to consult Islanzadí about Sloan's fate? You implied that when you spoke with her, the elves' army was still situated within Du Weldenvarden."

"They were," he said, "but only in the fringe, beyond the protective measures of the wards."

The silence between them was palpable as Nasuada considered his request. Outside the tent, Eragon heard the Nighthawks arguing among themselves about whether a bill or a halberd was better suited for fighting large numbers of men on foot and, beyond them, the creak of a passing oxcart, the jangle of armor on men trotting in the opposite direction, and hundreds of other indistinct sounds that drifted through the camp.

When Nasuada spoke, she said, "What exactly do you hope to gain from such a visit?"

"I don't know!" growled Eragon. He struck the pommel of the

falchion with his fist. "And that's the heart of the problem: we don't know enough. It might accomplish nothing, but on the other hand, we might learn something that could help us vanquish Murtagh and Galbatorix once and for all. We barely won yesterday, Nasuada. Barely! And I fear that when we again face Thorn and Murtagh, Murtagh will be even stronger than before, and frost coats my bones when I consider the fact that Galbatorix's abilities far exceed Murtagh's, despite the vast amount of power he has already bestowed upon my *brother*. The elf who taught me, he . . ." Eragon hesitated, considering the wisdom of what he was about to say, then forged onward: "He hinted that he knows how it is Galbatorix's strength has been increasing every year, but he refused to reveal more at the time because we were not advanced enough in our training. Now, after our encounters with Thorn and Murtagh, I think he will share his knowledge with us. Moreover, there are entire branches of magic we have yet to explore, and any one of them might provide the means to defeat Galbatorix. If we are going to gamble upon this trip, Nasuada, then let us not gamble to maintain our current position; let us gamble to increase our standing and so win this game of chance."

Nasuada sat motionless for over a minute. "I cannot make this decision until after the dwarves hold their coronation. Whether you go to Du Weldenvarden will depend on the movements of the Empire then and on what our spies report about Murtagh and Thorn's activities."

Over the course of the next two hours, Nasuada instructed Eragon about the thirteen dwarf clans. She schooled him in their history and their politics; in the products upon which each clan based the majority of its trade; in the names, families, and personalities of the clan chiefs; in the list of important tunnels excavated and controlled by each clan; and in what she felt would be the best way to coax the dwarves to elect a king or queen friendly to the goals of the Varden.

"Ideally, Orik would be the one to take the throne," she said.

"King Hrothgar was highly regarded by most of his subjects, and Dûrgrimst Ingeitum remains one of the richest and most influential of clans, all of which is to Orik's benefit. Orik is devoted to our cause. He has served as one of the Varden, you and I both count him as a friend, and he is your foster brother. I believe he has the skills to become an excellent king for the dwarves." Amusement kindled in her expression. "Small matter, that. However, he is young by the standards of the dwarves, and his association with us may prove to be an insurmountable barrier for the other clan chiefs. Another obstacle is that the other great clans—Dûrgrimst Feldûnost and Dûrgrimst Knurlcarathn, to name but two—are eager, after over a hundred years of rule by the Ingeitum, to see the crown go to a different clan. By all means, support Orik if it can help him onto the throne, but if it becomes obvious that his attempt is doomed and your backing could guarantee the success of another clan chief who favors the Varden, then transfer your support, even if doing so will offend Orik. You cannot allow friendship to interfere with politics, not now."

When Nasuada finished her lecture on the dwarf clans, she, Eragon, and Saphira spent several minutes figuring out how Eragon could slip out of the camp without being noticed. After they had finally hammered out the details of the plan, Eragon and Saphira returned to their tent and told Blödhgarm what they had decided.

To Eragon's surprise, the fur-covered elf did not object. Curious, Eragon asked, "Do you approve?"

"It is not my place to say whether I approve or not," Blödhgarm replied, his voice a low purr. "But since Nasuada's stratagem does not seem to put either of you in unreasonable danger, and by means of this you may have the opportunity to further your learning in Ellesméra, neither I nor my brethren shall object." He inclined his head. "If you will excuse me, Bjartskular, Argetlam." Skirting Saphira, the elf exited the tent, allowing a bright flash of light to pierce the darkness inside as he pushed aside the entrance flap.

For a handful of minutes, Eragon and Saphira sat in silence, then

Eragon put his hand on the top of her head. *Say what you will, I will miss you.*

And I you, little one.

Be careful. If anything happened to you, I would . . .

And you as well.

He sighed. *We've been together only a few days, and already we must part again. I find it hard to forgive Nasuada for that.*

Do not condemn her for doing what she must.

No, but it leaves a bitter taste in my mouth.

Move swiftly then, so I may soon join you in Farthen Dûr.

I wouldn't mind being so far away from you if only I could still touch your mind. That's the worst part of it: the horrible sense of emptiness. We dare not even speak to each other through the mirror in Nasuada's tent, for people would wonder why you kept visiting her without me.

Saphira blinked and flicked out her tongue, and he sensed a strange shift in her emotions.

What? he asked.

I . . . She blinked again. *I agree. I wish we could remain in mental contact when we were at great distances from each other. It would reduce our worry and trouble and would allow us to confound the Empire more easily.* She hummed with satisfaction as he sat next to her and began to scratch the small scales behind the corner of her jaw.

FOOTPRINTS OF SHADOW

With a series of giddy leaps, Saphira carried Eragon through the camp to Roran and Katrina's tent. Outside the tent, Katrina was washing a shift in a bucket of soapy water, scrubbing the white fabric against a board of ridged wood. She lifted a hand to shield her eyes as a cloud of dust from Saphira's landing drifted over her.

Roran stepped out of the tent, buckling on his belt. He coughed and squinted in the dust. "What brings you here?" he asked as Eragon dismounted.

Speaking quickly, Eragon told them of his impending departure and impressed upon them the importance of keeping his absence a secret from the rest of the villagers. "No matter how slighted they feel because I supposedly refuse to see them, you cannot reveal the truth to them, not even to Horst or Elain. Let them think I have become a rude and ungrateful lout before you so much as utter a word about Nasuada's scheme. This I ask of you, for the sake of everyone who has pitted themselves against the Empire. Will you do it?"

"We would never betray you, Eragon," said Katrina. "Of that, you need have no doubts."

Then Roran said that he too was leaving.

"Where?" exclaimed Eragon.

"I just received my assignment a few minutes ago. We are going to raid the Empire's supply trains, somewhere well north of us, behind enemy lines."

Eragon gazed at the three of them in turn. First Roran, serious and determined, already tense with anticipation of battle; then Katrina, worried and trying to conceal it; and then Saphira, whose nostrils flickered with small tongues of flame, which sputtered as she breathed. "So we are all going our separate ways." What he did not say, but which hung over them like a shroud, was that they might never again see each other alive.

Grasping Eragon by the forearm, Roran pulled him close and hugged him for a moment. He released Eragon and stared deep into his eyes. "Guard your back, brother. Galbatorix isn't the only one who would like to slip a knife between your ribs when you aren't looking."

"Do the same yourself. And if you find yourself facing a spellcaster, run in the opposite direction. The wards I placed around you won't last forever."

Katrina hugged Eragon and whispered, "Don't take too long."

"I won't."

Together, Roran and Katrina went to Saphira and touched their foreheads to her long, bony snout. Her chest vibrated as she produced a pure bass note deep within her throat. *Remember, Roran,* she said, *do not make the mistake of leaving your enemies alive. And, Katrina? Do not dwell on that which you cannot change. It will only worsen your distress.* With a rustle of skin and scales, Saphira unfolded her wings and enveloped Roran, Katrina, and Eragon in a warm embrace, isolating them from the world.

As Saphira lifted her wings, Roran and Katrina stepped away while Eragon climbed onto her back. He waved at the newlywed couple, a lump in his throat, and continued waving even as Saphira took to the air. Blinking to clear his eyes, Eragon leaned against the spike behind him and gazed up at the tilting sky.

To the cook tents now? asked Saphira.

Aye.

Saphira climbed a few hundred feet before she aimed herself at the southwestern quadrant of the camp, where pillars of smoke drifted up from rows of ovens and large, wide pit fires. A thin stream of wind slipped past her and Eragon as she glided downward toward a clear patch of ground between two open-walled tents, each fifty feet long. Breakfast was over, so the tents were empty of men when Saphira landed with a loud thump.

Eragon hurried toward the fires beyond the plank tables, Saphira beside him. The many hundreds of men who were busy tending the fires, carving meat, cracking eggs, kneading dough, stirring cast-iron kettles full of mysterious liquids, scrubbing clean enormous piles of dirty pots and pans, and who were otherwise engaged in the enormous and never-ending task of preparing food for the Varden did not pause to gawk at Eragon and Saphira. For what importance was a dragon and Rider compared with the merciless demands of the ravenous many-mouthed creature whose hunger they were striving to sate?

A stout man with a close-cropped beard of white and black, who was almost short enough to pass for a dwarf trotted over to Eragon and Saphira and gave a curt bow. "I'm Quoth Merrinsson. How can I help you? If you want, Shadeslayer, we have some bread that just finished baking." He gestured toward a double row of sourdough loaves resting on a platter on a nearby table.

"I might have half a loaf, if you can spare it," said Eragon. "However, my hunger isn't the reason for our visit. Saphira would like something to eat, and we haven't time for her to hunt as she usually does."

Quoth looked past him and eyed Saphira's bulk, and his face grew pale. "How much does she normally . . . Ah, that is, how much do *you* normally eat, Saphira? I can have six sides of roast beef brought over immediately, and another six will be ready in about fifteen minutes. Will that be enough, or . . . ?" The knob in his throat jumped as he swallowed.

Saphira emitted a soft, rippling growl, which caused Quoth to squeak and hop backward. "She would prefer a live animal, if that's convenient," Eragon said.

In a high-pitched voice, Quoth said, "Convenient? Oh yes, it's convenient." He bobbed his head, twisting at his apron with his grease-stained hands. "Most convenient indeed, Shadeslayer,

Dragon Saphira. King Orrin's table will not be lacking this afternoon, then, oh no."

And a barrel of mead, Saphira said to Eragon.

White circles appeared around Quoth's irises as Eragon repeated
her request. "I—I am afraid that the dwarves have purchased most
of our stocks of m-m-mead. We have only a few barrels left, and
those are reserved for King—" Quoth flinched as a four-foot-long
flame leaped out of Saphira's nostrils and singed the grass in front
of him. Snarled lines of smoke drifted up from the blackened
stalks. "I—I—I will have a barrel brought to you at once. If you will
f-follow me, I will take y-you to the livestock, where you may have
whatever beast you like."

Skirting the fires and tables and groups of harried men, the cook
led them to a collection of large wooden pens, which contained
pigs, cattle, geese, goats, sheep, rabbits, and a number of wild deer
the Varden's foragers had captured during their forays into the surrounding wilderness. Close to the pens were coops full of chickens,
ducks, doves, quail, grouse, and other birds. Their squawking, chirp-
ing, cooing, and crowing formed a cacophony so harsh, it made
Eragon grit his teeth with annoyance. In order to avoid being overwhelmed by the thoughts and feelings of so many creatures, he was
careful to keep his mind closed to all but Saphira.

The three of them stopped over a hundred feet from the pens so
Saphira's presence would not panic the imprisoned animals. "Is
there any here catches your fancy?" Quoth asked, gazing up at her
and rubbing his hands with nervous dexterity.

As she surveyed the pens, Saphira sniffed and said to Eragon,
*What pitiful prey. . . . I'm not really that hungry, you know. I went
hunting only the day before yesterday, and I'm still digesting the bones of
the deer I ate.*

You're still growing quickly. The food will do you good.

Not if I can't stomach it.

Pick something small, then. A pig, maybe.

That would hardly be of any help to you. No . . . I'll take that one.

From Saphira, Eragon received the image of a cow of medium stature with a splattering of white splotches on her left flank.

After Eragon pointed out the cow, Quoth shouted at a line of men idling by the pens. Two of them separated the cow from the rest of the herd, slipped a rope over its head, and pulled the reluctant animal toward Saphira. Thirty feet from Saphira, the cow balked and lowed with terror and tried to shake free of the rope and flee. Before the animal could escape, Saphira pounced, leaping across the distance separating them. The two men who were pulling on the rope threw themselves flat as Saphira rushed toward them, her jaws gaping.

Saphira struck the cow broadside as it turned to run, knocking the animal over and holding it in place with her splayed feet. It uttered a single, terrified bleat before Saphira's jaws closed over its neck. With a ferocious shake of her head, she snapped its spine. She paused then, crouched low over her kill, and looked expectantly at Eragon.

Closing his eyes, Eragon reached out with his mind toward the cow. The animal's consciousness had already faded into darkness, but its body was still alive, its flesh thrumming with motive energy, which was all the more intense for the fear that had coursed through it moments before. Repugnance for what he was about to do filled Eragon, but he ignored it and, placing a hand over the belt of Beloth the Wise, transferred what energy he could from the body of the cow into the twelve diamonds hidden around his waist. The process took only a few seconds.

He nodded to Saphira. *I'm done.*

Eragon thanked the men for their assistance, and then the two of them left him and Saphira alone.

While Saphira gorged herself, Eragon sat against the barrel of mead and watched the cooks go about their business. Every time they or one of their assistants beheaded a chicken or cut the throat of a pig or a goat or any other animal, he transferred the energy from the dying animal into the belt of Beloth the Wise. It was grim work, for most of the animals were still aware when he touched their consciousness and the howling storm of their fear and confusion and pain battered at him until his heart pounded and sweat beaded his brow and he wished nothing more than to heal the suffering creatures. However, he knew it was their doom to die, lest the Varden should starve. He had depleted his reserve of energy during the past few battles, and Eragon wanted to replenish it before setting out on a long and potentially hazardous journey. If Nasuada had allowed him to remain with the Varden for another week, he could have stocked the diamonds with energy from his own body and still had time to recuperate before running to Farthen Dûr, but he could not in the few hours he had. And even if he had done nothing but lie in bed and pour the fire from his limbs into the gems, he would not have been able to garner as much force as he did then from the multitude of animals.

The diamonds in the belt of Beloth the Wise seemed to be able to absorb an almost unlimited amount of energy, so he stopped when he was unable to bear the prospect of immersing himself in the death throes of another animal. Shaking and dripping with sweat from head to toe, he leaned forward, his hands on his knees, and gazed at the ground between his feet, struggling not to be ill. Memories not his own intruded upon his thoughts, memories of Saphira soaring over Leona Lake with him on her back, of them plunging into the clear, cool water, a cloud of white bubbles swarming past them, of their shared delight in flying and swimming and playing together.

His breathing calmed, and he looked at Saphira where she sat among the remnants of her kill, chewing on the cow's skull. He smiled and sent her his gratitude for her help.

We can go now, he said.

Swallowing, she replied, *Take my strength as well. You may need it.*

No.

This is one argument you will not win. I insist.

And I insist otherwise. I won't leave you here weakened and unfit for battle. *What if Murtagh and Thorn attack later today? We both need to be ready to fight at any moment. You'll be in more danger than I will because Galbatorix and the whole of the Empire will still believe I'm with you.*

Yes, but you will be alone with a Kull in the middle of the wilderness.

I am as accustomed to the wilderness as you. Being away from civilization does not frighten me. As for a Kull, well, I don't know if I could beat one at a wrestling match, but my wards will protect me from any treachery. . . . I have enough energy, Saphira. You don't need to give me more.

She eyed him, considering his words, then lifted a paw and started licking it clean of blood. *Very well, I will keep myself . . . to myself?* The corners of her mouth seemed to lift with amusement. Lowering her paw, she said, *Would you be so kind as to roll that barrel over to me?* With a grunt, he got to his feet and did as she asked. She extended a single talon and punched two holes in the top of the barrel, which released the sweet smell of apple-honey mead. Arching her neck so her head was directly above the barrel, she grasped it between her massive jaws, then lifted it skyward and poured the gurgling contents down her gullet. The empty barrel shattered against the ground when she dropped it, and one of the iron hoops rolled several yards away. Her upper lip wrinkled, Saphira shook her head, then her breath hitched and she sneezed so hard that her nose struck the ground and a gout of fire erupted from both her mouth and her nostrils.

Eragon yelped with surprise and jumped sideways, batting at the smoking hem of his tunic. The right side of his face felt seared raw by the heat of the fire. *Saphira, be more careful!* he exclaimed.

Oops. She lowered her head and rubbed her dust-caked snout against the edge of one foreleg, scratching at her nostrils. *The mead tickles.*

Really, you ought to know better by now, he grumbled as he climbed onto her back.

After rubbing her snout against her foreleg once more, Saphira leaped high into the air and, gliding over the Varden's camp, returned Eragon to his tent. He slid off her, then stood looking up at Saphira. For a time, they said nothing, allowing their shared emotions to speak for them.

Saphira blinked, and he thought her eyes glistened more than normal. *This is a test*, she said. *If we pass it, we shall be the stronger for it, as dragon and Rider.*

We must be able to function by ourselves if necessary, else we will forever be at a disadvantage compared with others.

Yes. She gouged the earth with her clenching claws. *Knowing that does nothing to ease my pain, however.* A shiver ran the length of her sinuous body. She shuffled her wings. *May the wind rise under your wings and the sun always be at your back. Travel well and travel fast, little one.*

Goodbye, he said.

Eragon felt that if he remained with her any longer, he would never leave, so he whirled around and, without a backward glance, plunged into the dark interior of his tent. The connection between them—which had become as integral to him as the structure of his own flesh—he severed completely. They would soon be too far apart to sense each other's minds anyway, and he had no desire to prolong the agony of their parting. He stood where he was for a moment, gripping the hilt of the falchion and swaying as if he were dizzy. Already the dull ache of loneliness suffused him, and he felt small and isolated without the comforting presence of Saphira's consciousness. *I did this before, and I can do this again*, he thought, and forced himself to square his shoulders and lift his chin.

From underneath his cot, he removed the pack he had made during his trip from Helgrind. Into it he placed the carved wooden tube wrapped in cloth that contained the scroll of the poem he had written for the Agaetí Blödhren, which Oromis had copied for him in his finest calligraphy; the flask of enchanted faelnirv and the small soapstone box of nalgask that were also gifts from Oromis; the thick book, *Domia abr Wyrda*, which was Jeod's present; his whetstone and his strop; and, after some hesitation, the many pieces of his armor, for he reasoned, *If the occasion arises where I need it, I will be more happy to have it than I will be miserable carrying it all the way to Farthen Dûr.* Or so he hoped. The book and the scroll he took because—after having done so much traveling—he had concluded that the best way to avoid losing the objects he cared about was to keep them with him wherever he went.

The only extra clothes he decided to bring were a pair of gloves, which he stuffed inside his helmet, and his heavy woolen cloak, in case it got cold when they stopped nights. All the rest, he left rolled up in Saphira's saddlebags. *If I really am a member of Dûrgrimst Ingeitum,* he thought, *they will clothe me properly when I arrive at Bregan Hold.*

Cinching off the pack, he lay his unstrung bow and quiver across the top and lashed them to the frame. He was about to do the same with the falchion when he realized that if he leaned to the side, the sword could slide out of the sheath. Therefore, he tied the sword flat against the rear of the pack, angling it so the hilt would ride between his neck and his right shoulder, where he could still draw it if need be.

Eragon donned the pack and then stabbed through the barrier in his mind, feeling the energy surging in his body and in the twelve diamonds mounted on the belt of Beloth the Wise. Tapping into that flow of force, he murmured the spell he had cast but once before: that which bent rays of light around him and rendered him invisible. A slight pall of fatigue weakened his limbs as he released the spell.

He glanced downward and had the disconcerting experience of looking through where he knew his torso and legs to be and seeing the imprint of his boots on the dirt below. *Now for the difficult part,* he thought.

Going to the rear of the tent, he slit the taut fabric with his hunting knife and slipped through the opening. Sleek as a well-fed cat, Blödhgarm was waiting for him outside. He inclined his head in the general direction of Eragon and murmured, "Shadeslayer," then devoted his attention to mending the hole, which he did with a half-dozen short words in the ancient language.

Eragon drifted down the path between two rows of tents, using his knowledge of woodcraft to make as little noise as possible. Whenever anyone approached, Eragon darted off the path and stood motionless, hoping they would not notice the footprints of shadow in the dirt or on the grass. He cursed the fact that the land was so dry; his boots tended to raise small puffs of dust no matter how gently he lowered them. To his surprise, being invisible degraded his sense of balance; without the ability to see where his hands or his feet were, he kept misjudging distances and bumping into things, almost as if he had consumed too much ale.

Despite his uncertain progress, he reached the edge of the camp in fairly good time and without arousing any suspicion. He paused behind a rain barrel, hiding his footprints in its thick shadow, and studied the packed-earth ramparts and ditches lined with sharpened stakes that protected the Varden's eastern flank. If he had been trying to enter the camp, it would have been extremely difficult to escape detection by one of the many sentinels who patrolled the ramparts, even while invisible. But since the trenches and the ramparts had been designed to repel attackers and not imprison the defenders, crossing them from the opposite direction was a far easier task.

Eragon waited until the two closest sentinels had their backs turned toward him, and then he sprinted forward, pumping his arms with all his might. Within seconds, he traversed the hundred or so feet that separated the rain barrel from the slope of the rampart and dashed up the embankment so fast, he felt as if he were a stone skipping across water. At the crest of the embankment, he drove his legs into the ground and, arms flailing, leaped out over the lines of the Varden's defenses. For three silent heartbeats, he flew, then landed with a bone-jarring impact.

As soon as he regained his balance, Eragon pressed himself flat against the ground and held his breath. One of the sentinels paused in his rounds, but he did not seem to notice anything out of the ordinary, and after a moment he resumed his pacing. Eragon released his breath and whispered, "Du deloi lunaea," and felt as the spell smoothed out the impressions his boots had left in the embankment.

Still invisible, he stood and trotted away from the camp, careful to step only on clumps of grass so he would not kick up more dust. The farther he got from the sentinels, the faster he ran, until he sped over the land more quickly than a galloping horse.

Almost an hour later, he danced down the steep side of a narrow draw that the wind and rain had etched into the surface of the grasslands. At the bottom was a trickle of water lined with rushes and cattails. He continued downstream, staying well away from the soft ground next to the water—in an attempt to avoid leaving traces of his passage—until the creek widened into a small pond, and there by the edge, he saw the bulk of a bare-chested Kull sitting on a boulder.

As Eragon pushed his way through a stand of cattails, the sound of rustling leaves and stalks alerted the Kull of his presence. The creature turned his massive horned head toward Eragon, sniffing at the air. It was Nar Garzhvog, leader of the Urgals who had allied themselves with the Varden.

"You!" exclaimed Eragon, becoming visible once more.

"Greetings, Firesword," Garzhvog rumbled. Heaving up his thick limbs and giant torso, the Urgal rose to his full eight and a half feet, his gray-skinned muscles rippling in the light of the noonday sun.

"Greetings, Nar Garzhvog," said Eragon. Confused, he asked, "What of your rams? Who will lead them if you go with me?"

"My blood brother, Skgahgrezh, will lead. He is not Kull, but he has long horns and a thick neck. He is a fine war chief."

"I see. . . . Why did *you* want to come, though?"

The Urgal lifted his square chin, baring his throat. "You are

Firesword. You must not die, or the Urgralgra—the Urgals, as you name us—will not have our revenge against Galbatorix, and our race will die in this land. Therefore, I will run with you. I am the best of our fighters. I have defeated forty-two rams in single combat."

Eragon nodded, not displeased by the turn of events. Of all the Urgals, he trusted Garzhvog the most, for he had probed the Kull's consciousness before the Battle of the Burning Plains and had discovered that, by the standards of his race, Garzhvog was honest and reliable. *As long as he doesn't decide that his honor requires him to challenge me to a duel, we should have no cause for conflict.*

"Very well, Nar Garzhvog," he said, tightening the strap of the pack around his waist, "let us run together, you and I, as has not happened in the whole of recorded history."

Garzhvog chuckled deep in his chest. "Let us run, Firesword."

Together they faced east, and together they set forth for the Beor Mountains, Eragon running light and swift, and Garzhvog loping beside him, taking one stride for every two of Eragon's, the earth shuddering beneath the burden of his weight. Above them, swollen thunderheads gathered along the horizon, portending a torrential storm, and circling hawks uttered lonesome cries as they hunted their prey.

OVER HILL AND MOUNTAIN

Eragon and Nar Garzhvog ran for the rest of the day, through the night, and through the following day, stopping only to drink and to relieve themselves.

At the end of the second day, Garzhvog said, "Firesword, I must eat, and I must sleep."

Eragon leaned against a nearby stump, panting, and nodded. He had not wanted to speak first, but he was just as hungry and exhausted as the Kull. Soon after leaving the Varden, he had discovered that while he was faster than Garzhvog at distances of up to five miles, beyond that, Garzhvog's endurance was equal to or greater than his own.

"I will help you hunt," he said.

"That is not needed. Make us a big fire, and I will bring us food."

"Fine."

As Garzhvog strode off toward a thicket of beech trees north of them, Eragon untied the strap around his waist and, with a sigh of relief, dropped his pack next to the stump. "Blasted armor," he muttered. Even in the Empire, he had not run so far while carrying such a load. He had not anticipated how arduous it would be. His feet hurt, his legs hurt, his back hurt, and when he tried to crouch, his knees refused to bend properly.

Trying to ignore his discomfort, he set about gathering grass and dead branches for a fire, which he piled on a patch of dry, rocky ground.

He and Garzhvog were somewhere just east of the southern tip of Lake Tüdosten. The land was wet and lush, with fields of grass that stood six feet high, through which there roamed herds of deer, gazelles, and wild oxen with black hides and wide, backswept horns. The riches of the area were due, Eragon knew, to the Beor Mountains, which caused the formation of huge banks of clouds that drifted for many leagues over the plains beyond, bringing rain to places that would otherwise have been as dry as the Hadarac Desert.

Although the two of them had already run an enormous number of leagues, Eragon was disappointed by their progress. Between the Jiet River and Lake Tüdosten, they had lost several hours while hiding and taking detours to avoid being seen. Now that Lake Tüdosten was behind them, he hoped that their pace would increase. *Nasuada didn't foresee this delay, now did she? Oh no. She thought I could run flat out from there to Farthen Dûr. Ha!* Kicking at a branch that was in his way, he continued to gather wood, grumbling to himself the entire time.

When Garzhvog returned an hour later, Eragon had built a fire a yard long and two feet wide and was sitting in front of it, staring at the flames and fighting the urge to slip into the waking dreams that were his rest. His neck cracked as he looked up.

Garzhvog strode toward him, holding the carcass of a plump doe under his left arm. As if it weighed no more than a sack of rags, he lifted the doe and wedged its head in the fork of a tree twenty yards from the fire. Then he drew a knife and began to clean the carcass.

Eragon stood, feeling as if his joints had turned to stone, and stumbled toward Garzhvog.

"How did you kill it?" he asked.

"With my sling," rumbled Garzhvog.

"Do you intend to cook it on a spit? Or do Urgals eat their meat raw?"

Garzhvog turned his head and gazed through the coil of his left horn at Eragon, a deep-set yellow eye gleaming with some enigmatic emotion. "We are not beasts, Firesword."

"I did not say you were."

With a grunt, the Urgal returned to his work.

"It will take too long to cook on a spit," said Eragon.

"I thought a stew, and we can fry what is left on a rock."

"Stew? How? We don't have a pot."

Reaching down, Garzhvog scrubbed his right hand clean on the ground, then removed a square of folded material from the pouch at his belt and tossed it at Eragon.

Eragon tried to catch it but was so tired he missed, and the object struck the ground. It looked like an exceptionally large piece of vellum. As he picked it up, the square fell open, and he saw it had the shape of a bag, perhaps a foot and a half wide and three feet deep. The rim was reinforced with a thick strip of leather, upon which were sewn metal rings. He turned the container over, amazed by its softness and the fact that it had no seams.

"What is it?" he asked.

"The stomach of the cave bear I killed the year I first got my horns. Hang it from a frame or put it in a hole, then fill it with water and drop hot stones in it. Stones heat water, and stew tastes good."

"Won't the stones burn through the stomach?"

"They have not yet."

"Is it enchanted?"

"No magic. Strong stomach." Garzhvog's breath huffed out as he grasped the deer's hips on either side and, with a single movement, broke its pelvis in two. The sternum he split using his knife.

"It must have been a big bear," Eragon said.

Garzhvog made a *ruk-ruk* sound deep in his throat. "It was bigger than I am now, Shadeslayer."

"Did you kill it with your sling as well?"

"I choked him to death with my hands. No weapons are allowed when you come of age and must prove your courage." Garzhvog paused for a moment, his knife buried to the hilt in the carcass. "Most do not try to kill a cave bear. Most hunt wolves or mountain goats. That is why I became war chief and others did not."

Eragon left him preparing the meat and went to the fire. Next to it, he dug a hole, which he lined with the bear stomach, pushing stakes through the metal rings to hold the stomach in place. He gathered a dozen apple-sized rocks from the surrounding field and tossed them into the center of the fire. While he waited for the rocks to heat, he used magic to fill the bear stomach two-thirds with water, and then he fashioned a pair of tongs out of a sapling willow and a piece of knotted rawhide.

When the rocks were cherry red, he shouted, "They're ready!"

"Put them in," Garzhvog replied.

Using the tongs, Eragon extracted the nearest stone from the fire and lowered it into the container. The surface of the water exploded into steam as the stone touched it. He deposited two more stones in the bear stomach, which brought the water to a rolling boil.

Garzhvog lumbered over and poured a double handful of meat into the water, then seasoned the stew with large pinches of salt from the pouch at his belt and several sprigs of rosemary, thyme, and other wild greens he had chanced upon while hunting. Then he placed a flat piece of shale across one side of the fire. When the stone was hot, he fried strips of meat on it.

While the food cooked, Eragon and Garzhvog carved themselves spoons from the stump where Eragon had dropped his pack.

Hunger made it seem longer to Eragon, but it was not many more minutes before the stew was done, and he and Garzhvog ate, ravenous as wolves. Eragon devoured twice as much as he thought he ever had before, and what he did not consume, Garzhvog did, eating enough for six large men.

Afterward, Eragon lay back, propping himself up on his elbows, and stared at the flashing fireflies that had appeared along the edge of the beech trees, swirling in abstract patterns as they chased one another. Somewhere an owl hooted, soft and throaty. The first few stars speckled the purple sky.

Eragon stared without seeing and thought of Saphira and then of Arya and then of Arya and Saphira, and then he closed his eyes, a dull throb forming behind his temples. He heard a cracking sound and, opening his eyes once more, saw that on the other side of the empty bear stomach, Garzhvog was cleaning his teeth with the pointed end of a broken thighbone. Eragon dropped his gaze to the bottom of the Urgal's bare feet—Garzhvog having removed his sandals before they began their meal—and to his surprise noticed that the Urgal had seven toes on each foot.

"The dwarves have the same number of toes as you do," he said.

Garzhvog spat a piece of meat into the coals of the fire. "I did not know that. I have never wanted to look at the feet of a dwarf."

"Don't you find it curious that Urgals and dwarves should both have fourteen toes, while elves and humans have ten?"

Garzhvog's thick lips lifted in a snarl. "We share no blood with those hornless mountain rats, Firesword. They have fourteen toes, and we have fourteen toes. It pleased the gods to shape us so when they created the world. There is no other explanation."

Eragon grunted in response and returned to watching the fireflies. Then: "Tell me a story your race is fond of, Nar Garzhvog."

The Kull pondered for a moment, then removed the bone from his mouth. He said, "Long ago, there lived a young Urgralgra, and her name was Maghara. She had horns that shone like polished stone, hair that hung past her waist, and a laugh that could charm the birds out of the trees. But she was not pretty. She was ugly. Now, in her village, there also lived a ram who was very strong. He had killed four rams in wrestling matches and had defeated twenty-three others besides. But although his feats had won him wide renown, he had yet to choose a brood-mate. Maghara wished to be his brood-mate, but he would not look at her, for she was ugly, and because of her ugliness, he did not see her bright horns, nor her long hair, and he did not hear her pleasant laugh. Sick at heart that he would not look at her, Maghara climbed the tallest mountain in the Spine, and she called out to Rahna to help her. Rahna is mother of us all, and it was she who invented weaving and farming and she who raised the Beor Mountains when she was fleeing the great dragon.

Rahna, She of the Gilded Horns, she answered Maghara, and she asked why Maghara had summoned her. 'Make me pretty, Honored Mother, so I can attract the ram I want,' said Maghara. And Rahna answered, 'You do not need to be pretty, Maghara. You have bright horns and long hair and a pleasant laugh. With those, you can catch a ram who is not so foolish as to look at only a female's face.' And Maghara, she threw herself down upon the ground and said, 'I will not be happy unless I can have this ram, Honored Mother. Please, make me pretty.' Rahna, she smiled then and said, 'If I do this, child, how will you repay me for this favor?' And Maghara said, 'I will give you anything you want.'

"Rahna was well pleased with her offer, and so she made Maghara pretty then, and Maghara returned to her village, and everyone wondered at her beauty. With her new face, Maghara became the brood-mate of the ram she wanted, and they had many children, and they lived in happiness for seven years. Then Rahna came to

Maghara, and Rahna said, 'You have had seven years with the ram you wanted. Have you enjoyed them?' And Maghara said, 'I have.' And Rahna said, 'Then I have come for my payment.' And she looked around their house of stone, and she seized hold of Maghara's eldest son and said, 'I will have him.' Maghara begged She of the Gilded Horns not to take her eldest son, but Rahna would not relent. At last, Maghara took her brood-mate's club, and she struck at Rahna, but the club shattered in her hands. In punishment, Rahna stripped Maghara's beauty from her, and then Rahna left with Maghara's son for her hall where the four winds dwell, and she named the boy Hegraz and raised him to be one of the mightiest warriors who has ever walked this land. And so one should learn from Maghara to never fight one's fate, for you will lose that which you hold most dear."

Eragon watched the glowing rim of the crescent moon appear above the eastern horizon. "Tell me something about your villages."

"What?"

"Anything. I experienced hundreds of memories when I was in your mind and in Khagra's and in Otvek's, but I can recall only a handful of them, and those imperfectly. I am trying to make sense of what I saw."

"There is much I could tell you," rumbled Garzhvog. His heavy eyes pensive, he worked his makeshift toothpick around one of his fangs and then said, "We take logs, and we carve them with faces of the animals of the mountains, and these we bury upright by our houses so they will frighten away the spirits of the wild. Sometimes the poles almost seem to be alive. When you walk into one of our villages, you can feel the eyes of all the carved animals watching you. . . ." The bone paused in the Urgal's fingers, then resumed its back-and-forth motion. "By the doorway of each hut, we hang the namna. It is a strip of cloth as wide as my outstretched hand. The namna are brightly colored, and the patterns on them depict the history of the family that lives in that hut. Only the oldest and most skilled weavers are allowed to add to a namna or to reweave one if it becomes damaged. . . ." The bone disappeared inside of Garzhvog's fist. "During the months of winter, those who have mates work with them on their hearth rug. It takes at least five years to finish such a rug, so by the time it is done, you know whether you have made a good choice of mate."

"I've never seen one of your villages," said Eragon. "They must be very well hidden."

"Well hidden and well defended. Few who see our homes live to tell of it."

Focusing on the Kull and allowing an edge to creep into his voice, Eragon said, "How is it you learned this language, Garzhvog? Was there a human who lived among you? Did you keep any of us as slaves?"

Garzhvog returned Eragon's gaze without flinching. "We have no slaves, Firesword. I tore the knowledge from the minds of the men I fought, and I shared it with the rest of my tribe."

"You have killed many humans, haven't you?"

"You have killed many Urgralgra, Firesword. It is why we must be allies, or my race will not survive."

Eragon crossed his arms. "When Brom and I were tracking the Ra'zac, we passed through Yazuac, a village by the Ninor River. We found all of the people piled in the center of the village, dead, with a baby stuck on a spear at the top of the pile. It was the worst thing I've ever seen. And it was Urgals who killed them."

"Before I got my horns," said Garzhvog, "my father took me to visit one of our villages along the western fringes of the Spine. We found our people tortured, burnt, and slaughtered. The men of Narda had learned of our presence, and they had surprised the village with many soldiers. Not one of our tribe escaped. . . . It is true we love war more than other races, Firesword, and that has been our downfall many times before. Our women will not consider a ram for a mate unless he has proven himself in battle and killed at least three foes himself. And there is a joy in battle unlike any other joy. But though we love feats of arms, that does not mean we are not aware of our faults. If our race cannot change, Galbatorix will kill us all if he defeats the Varden, and you and Nasuada will kill us all if you overthrow that snake-tongued betrayer. Am I not right, Firesword?"

Eragon jerked his chin in a nod. "Aye."

"It does no good, then, to dwell upon past wrongs. If we cannot overlook what each of our races has done, there will never be peace between humans and the Urgralgra."

"How should we treat you, though, if we defeat Galbatorix and Nasuada gives your race the land you have asked for and, twenty years from now, your children begin to kill and plunder so they can win mates? If you know your own history, Garzhvog, then you know it has always been so when Urgals sign peace accords."

With a thick sigh, Garzhvog said, "Then we will hope that there are still Urgralgra across the sea and that they are wiser than us, for we will be no more in this land."

Neither of them spoke again that night. Garzhvog curled up on his side and slept with his massive head resting on the ground, while Eragon wrapped himself in his cloak and sat against the stump and gazed at the slowly turning stars, drifting in and out of his waking dreams.

By the end of the next day, they had come into sight of the Beor Mountains. At first the mountains were nothing more than ghostly shapes on the horizon, angled panes of white and purple, but as evening drew nigh, the distant range acquired substance, and Eragon was able to make out the dark band of trees along the base and, above that, the even wider band of gleaming snow and ice and, still higher yet, the peaks themselves, which were gray, bare stone, for they were so tall, no plants grew upon them and no snow fell upon them. As when he had first seen them, the sheer size of the Beor Mountains overwhelmed Eragon. His every instinct insisted that nothing that large could exist, and yet he knew his eyes did not deceive him. The mountains averaged ten miles high, and many were even taller.

Eragon and Garzhvog did not stop that night but continued running through the hours of darkness and through the day thereafter. When morning arrived, the sky grew bright, but because of the Beor Mountains, it was almost noon before the sun burst forth between two peaks and rays of light as wide as the mountains themselves streamed out over the land that was still caught in the strange twilight of shadow. Eragon paused then, on the bank of a brook, and contemplated the sight in silent wonderment for several minutes.

As they skirted the vast range of mountains, their journey began to seem to Eragon uncomfortably similar to his flight from Gil'ead to Farthen Dûr with Murtagh, Saphira, and Arya. He even thought he recognized the place where they had camped after crossing the Hadarac Desert.

The long days and longer nights slipped by with both excruciating slowness and surprising speed, for every hour was identical to the last, which made Eragon feel not only as if their ordeal would never end but also as if large portions of it had never taken place.

When he and Garzhvog arrived at the mouth of the great rift that split the range of mountains for many leagues from north to south, they turned to their right and passed between the cold and indifferent peaks. Arriving at the Beartooth River—which flowed out of the narrow valley that led to Farthen Dûr—they forded the frigid waters and continued southward.

That night, before they ventured east into the mountains proper, they camped by a small pond and rested their limbs. Garzhvog killed another deer with his sling, this time a buck, and they both ate their fill.

His hunger sated, Eragon was hunched over, mending a hole in the side of his boot, when he heard an eerie howl that set his pulse racing. He glanced around the darkened landscape, and to his alarm, he saw the silhouette of a huge beast loping around the pebble-lined shore of the pond.

"Garzhvog," said Eragon in a low voice, and reached over to his pack and drew his falchion.

Taking a fist-sized rock from the ground, the Kull placed it in the leather pocket of his sling, and then rising to his full height, he opened his maw and bellowed into the night until the land rang with echoes of his defiant challenge.

The beast paused, then proceeded at a slower pace, sniffing at the ground here and there. As it entered the circle of firelight, Eragon's breath caught in his throat. Standing before them was a gray-backed wolf as big as a horse, with fangs like sabers and burning yellow eyes that followed their every movement. The wolf's feet were the size of bucklers.

A *Shrrg!* thought Eragon.

As the giant wolf circled their camp, moving almost silently despite his great bulk, Eragon thought of the elves and how they would deal with a wild animal, and in the ancient language, he said, "Brother Wolf, we mean you no harm. Tonight our pack rests and does not hunt. You are welcome to share our food and the warmth of our den until morning." The Shrrg paused, and his ears swiveled forward while Eragon spoke in the ancient language.

"Firesword, what are you doing?" growled Garzhvog.

"Don't attack unless he does."

The heavy-shouldered beast slowly entered their camp, the tip of his huge wet nose twitching the whole while. The wolf poked his shaggy head toward the fire, seemingly curious about the writhing flames, then moved over to the scraps of meat and viscera scattered over the ground where Garzhvog had butchered the buck. Crouching, the wolf snapped up the gobbets of flesh, then rose and, without a backward glance, padded off into the depths of the night.

Eragon relaxed and sheathed the falchion. Garzhvog, however, remained standing where he was, his lips pulled back in a snarl, looking and listening for anything out of the ordinary in the surrounding darkness.

At dawn's first light, Eragon and Garzhvog left their camp, and running eastward, entered the valley that would lead them to Mount Thardûr.

As they passed underneath the boughs of the dense forest that guarded the interior of the mountain range, the air became noticeably cooler and the soft bed of needles on the ground muffled their footsteps. The tall, dark, grim trees that loomed over them seemed to be watching as they made their way between the thick trunks and around the twisted roots that knuckled up out of the moist earth, standing two, three, and often four feet high. Large black squirrels scampered among the branches, chattering loudly. A thick layer of moss blanketed the corpses of trees that had fallen. Ferns and thimbleberries and other green leafy plants flourished alongside mushrooms of every shape, size, and color.

The world narrowed once Eragon and Garzhvog were fully inside the long valley. The gigantic mountains pressed close on either side, oppressive with their bulk, and the sky was a distant, unreachable strip of sea blue, the highest sky Eragon had ever seen. A few thin clouds grazed the shoulders of the mountains.

An hour or so after noon, Eragon and Garzhvog slowed as a series of terrible roars echoed among the trees. Eragon pulled his sword from its sheath, and Garzhvog plucked a smooth river rock from the ground and fit it in the pocket of his sling.

"It is a cave bear," said Garzhvog. A furious, high-pitched squeal, similar to metal scraping over metal, punctuated his statement. "And Nagra. We must be careful, Firesword."

They proceeded at a slow pace and soon spotted the animals several hundred feet up the side of a mountain. A drove of reddish boars with thick, slashing tusks milled in squealing confusion before a huge mass of silver-brown fur, hooked claws, and snapping teeth that moved with deadly speed. At first the distance fooled Eragon, but then he compared the animals to the trees next to them and realized that each boar would have dwarfed a Shrrg and that the bear was nearly as large as his house in Palancar Valley. The boars had bloodied the cave bear's flanks, but that seemed to only enrage the beast. Rearing on his hind legs, the bear bellowed and swatted one of the boars with a massive paw, knocking it aside and tearing open its hide. Three more times the boar attempted to rise, and three more times the cave bear struck at it, until at last the boar gave up and lay still. As the bear bent to feed, the rest of the squealing pigs fled back under the trees, heading higher up the mountain and away from the bear.

Awed by the bear's strength, Eragon followed Garzhvog as the Urgal slowly walked across the bear's field of vision. Lifting his crimson snout from the belly of his kill, the bear watched them with small, beady eyes, then apparently decided they were no threat to him and resumed eating.

"I think even Saphira might not be able to overcome such a monster," Eragon murmured.

Garzhvog uttered a small grunt. "She can breathe fire. A bear cannot."

Neither of them looked away from the bear until trees hid it from view, and even then they kept their weapons at readiness, not knowing what other dangers they might encounter.

The day had passed into late afternoon when they became conscious of another sound: laughter. Eragon and Garzhvog halted, and then Garzhvog raised a finger and, with surprising stealth, crept through a wall of brush toward the laughter. Placing his feet with care, Eragon went with the Kull, holding his breath for fear his breathing would betray their presence.

Peering through a cluster of dogwood leaves, Eragon saw that there was now a well-worn path at the bottom of the valley, and next to the path, three dwarf children were playing, throwing sticks at each other and shrieking with laughter. No adults were visible. Eragon withdrew to a safe distance, exhaled, and studied the sky, where he spotted several plumes of white smoke perhaps a mile farther up the valley.

A branch snapped as Garzhvog squatted next to him, so that they were about level. Garzhvog said, "Firesword, here we part."

"You will not come to Bregan Hold with me?"

"No. My task was to keep you safe. If I go with you, the dwarves will not trust you as they should. Thardûr mountain is close at hand, and I am confident no one will dare hurt you between here and there."

Eragon rubbed the back of his neck and looked back and forth between Garzhvog and the smoke east of them. "Are you going to run straight back to the Varden?"

With a low chuckle, Garzhvog said, "Aye, but maybe not so fast as we did coming here."

Unsure of what to say, Eragon pushed at the rotten end of a log with the tip of his boot, exposing a clutch of white larvae squirming in the tunnels they had excavated. "Don't let a Shrrg or a bear eat you, eh? Then I would have to track down the beast and kill him, and I don't have the time for that."

Garzhvog pressed both his fists against his bony forehead. "May your enemies cower before you, Firesword." Standing and turning, Garzhvog loped away from Eragon. The forest soon hid the Kull's bulky form.

Eragon filled his lungs with the fresh mountain air, then pushed his way through the wall of brush. As he emerged from the thicket of brakes and dogwood, the tiny dwarf children froze, the expressions on their round-cheeked faces wary. Holding his hands out to his sides, Eragon said, "I am Eragon Shadeslayer, Son of None. I seek Orik, Thrifk's son, at Bregan Hold. Can you take me to him?" When the children did not respond, he realized they understood nothing of his own language. "I am a Dragon Rider," he said, speaking slowly and emphasizing the words. "Eka eddyr aí Shur'tugal . . . Shur'tugal . . . Argetlam."

At that, the children's eyes brightened, and their mouths formed round shapes of amazement. "Argetlam!" they exclaimed. "Argetlam!" And they ran over and threw themselves at him, wrapping their short arms around his legs and tugging at his clothes, shouting with merriment the entire time. Eragon stared down at them, feeling a foolish grin spread across his face. The children grasped his hands, and he allowed them to pull him down the path. Even though he could not understand, the children kept up a continuous stream of Dwarvish, telling him about what he knew not, but he enjoyed listening to their speech.

When one of the children—a girl, he thought—held her arms out toward him, he picked her up and placed her on his shoulders, wincing as she grasped fistfuls of his hair. She laughed, high and sweet, which made him smile again. Thus accoutered and accompanied, Eragon made his way toward Mount Thardûr and there to Bregan Hold and his foster brother, Orik.

✦ ✦ ✦

FOR MY LOVE

oran stared at the round, flat stone he held cupped in his hands. His eyebrows met in a scowl of frustration.

"Stenr rïsa!" he growled under his breath.

The stone refused to budge.

"What are you up to, Stronghammer?" asked Carn, dropping onto the log where Roran sat.

Slipping the stone into his belt, Roran accepted the bread and cheese Carn had brought him and said, "Nothing. Just woolgathering."

Carn nodded. "Most do before a mission."

As he ate, Roran allowed his gaze to drift over the men he found himself with. Their group was thirty strong, himself included. They were all hardened warriors. Everyone carried a bow, and most also wore a sword, although a few chose to fight with a spear, or with a mace or a hammer. Of the thirty men, he guessed that seven or eight were close to his own age, while the rest were several years older. The eldest among them was their captain, Martland Redbeard, the deposed earl of Thun, who had seen enough winters that his famed beard had become frosted with silver hairs.

When Roran had first joined Martland's command, he had presented himself to Martland in his tent. The earl was a short man, with powerful limbs from a lifetime of riding horses and wielding swords. His titular beard was thick and well groomed and hung to the middle of his sternum. After looking Roran over, the earl had said, "Lady Nasuada has told me great things about you, my boy, and I have heard much else from the stories my men tell, rumors, gossip, hearsay, and the like. You know how it is. No doubt, you have accomplished notable feats; bearding the Ra'zac in their own den, for example, now there was a tricky piece of work. Of course, you had your cousin to help you, didn't you, hmm? . . . You may be accustomed to having your way with the people from your village, but you are part of the Varden now, my boy. More specifically, you are one of my warriors. We are not your family. We are not your neighbors. We are not even necessarily your friends. Our duty is to carry out Nasuada's orders, and carry them out we will, no matter how any one of us might feel about it. While you serve under me, you will do what I tell you, when I tell you, and how I tell you, or I swear upon the bones of my blessed mother—may she rest in peace— I will personally whip the skin off your back, no matter to whom you may be related. Do you understand?"

"Yes, sir!"

"Very good. If you behave yourself and show you have some common sense, and if you can manage to stay alive, it is possible for a man of determination to advance quickly among the Varden. Whether you do or not, however, depends entirely on if I deem you fit to command men of your own. But don't you believe, not for one moment, not *one* blasted moment, that you can flatter me into a good opinion of you. I don't care whether you like or hate me. My only concern is whether you can do what needs to be done."

"I understand perfectly, sir!"

"Yes, well, maybe you do at that, Stronghammer. We shall know soon enough. Leave and report to Ulhart, my right-hand man."

Roran swallowed the last of his bread and washed it down with a swig of wine from the skin he carried. He wished they could have had a hot dinner that night, but they were deep in the Empire's territory, and soldiers might have spotted a fire. With a sigh, he stretched out his legs. His knees were sore from riding Snowfire from dusk until dawn for the past three days.

In the back of his mind, Roran felt a faint but constant pressure, a mental itch that, night or day, pointed him in the same direction: the direction of Katrina. The source of the sensation was the ring

Eragon had given him, and it was a comfort to Roran knowing that, because of it, he and Katrina could find each other anywhere in Alagaësia, even if they were both blind and deaf.

Beside him, he heard Carn muttering phrases in the ancient language, and he smiled. Carn was their spellcaster, sent to ensure that an enemy magician could not kill them all with a wave of his hand. From some of the other men, Roran had gathered that Carn was not a particularly strong magician—he struggled to cast every spell—but that he compensated for his weakness by inventing extraordinarily clever spells and by excelling at worming his way into his opponents' minds. Carn was thin of face and thin of body, with drooping eyes and a nervous, excitable air. Roran had taken an immediate liking to him.

Across from Roran, two of the men, Halmar and Ferth, were sitting in front of their tent, and Halmar was telling Ferth, ". . . so when the soldiers came for him, he pulled all his men inside his estate and set fire to the pools of oil his servants had poured earlier, trapping the soldiers and making it appear to those who came later as if the whole lot of them had burned to death. Can you believe it? Five hundred soldiers he killed at one go, without even drawing a blade!"

"How did he escape?" Ferth asked.

"Redbeard's grandfather was a cunning bastard, he was. He had a tunnel dug all the way from the family hall to the nearest river. With it, Redbeard was able to get his family and all their servants out alive. He took them to Surda then, where King Larkin sheltered them. It was quite a number of years before Galbatorix learned they were still alive. We're lucky to be under Redbeard, to be sure. He's lost only two battles, and those because of magic."

Halmar fell silent as Ulhart stepped into the middle of the row of sixteen tents. The grim-faced veteran stood with his legs spread, immovable as a deep-rooted oak tree, and surveyed the tents, checking that everyone was present. He said, "Sun's down, get to sleep. We ride out two hours before first light. Convoy should be seven miles northwest of us. Make good time, we strike just as they start moving. Kill everyone, burn everything, an' we go back. You know how it goes. Stronghammer, you ride with me. Mess up, an' I'll gut you with a dull fishhook." The men chuckled. "Right, get to sleep."

Wind whipped Roran's face. The thunder of pulsing blood filled his ears, drowning out every other sound. Snowfire surged between his legs, galloping. Roran's vision had narrowed; he saw nothing but the two soldiers sitting on brown mares next to the second-to-last wagon of the supply train.

Raising his hammer overhead, Roran howled with all his might.

The two soldiers started and fumbled with their weapons and shields. One of them dropped his spear and bent to recover it.

Pulling on Snowfire's reins to slow him, Roran stood upright in his stirrups and, drawing abreast of the first soldier, struck him on the shoulder, splitting his mail hauberk. The man screamed, his arm going limp. Roran finished him off with a backhand blow.

The other soldier had retrieved his spear, and he jabbed at Roran, aiming at his neck. Roran ducked behind his round shield, the spear jarring him each time it buried itself in the wood. He pressed his legs against Snowfire's sides, and the stallion reared, neighing and pawing at the air with iron-shod hooves. One hoof caught the soldier in the chest, tearing his red tunic. As Snowfire dropped to all fours again, Roran swung his hammer sideways and crushed the man's throat.

Leaving the soldier thrashing on the ground, Roran spurred Snowfire toward the next wagon in the convoy, where Ulhart was battling three soldiers of his own. Four oxen pulled each wagon, and as Snowfire passed the wagon Roran had just captured, the lead ox tossed his head, and the tip of his left horn caught Roran in the lower part of his right leg. Roran gasped. He felt as if a red-hot iron had been laid against his shin. He glanced down and saw a flap of his boot hanging loose, along with a layer of his skin and muscle.

With another battle-cry, Roran rode up to the closest of the three soldiers Ulhart was fighting and felled him with a single swipe of his hammer. The next man evaded Roran's subsequent attack, then turned his horse and galloped away.

"Get him!" Ulhart shouted, but Roran was already in pursuit.

The fleeing soldier dug his spurs into the belly of his horse until the animal bled, but despite his desperate cruelty, his steed could not outrun Snowfire. Roran bent low over Snowfire's neck as the stallion extended himself, flying over the ground with incredible speed. Realizing flight was hopeless, the soldier reined in his mount, wheeled about, and slashed at Roran with a saber. Roran lifted his hammer and barely managed to deflect the razor-sharp blade. He immediately retaliated with a looping overhead attack, but the soldier parried and then slashed at Roran's arms and legs twice more. In his mind, Roran cursed. The soldier was obviously more experienced with swordplay than he was; if he could not win the engagement in the next few seconds, the soldier would kill him.

The soldier must have sensed his advantage, for he pressed the attack, forcing Snowfire to prance backward. On three occasions, Roran was sure the soldier was about to wound him, but the man's saber twisted at the last moment and missed Roran, diverted by an unseen force. Roran was thankful for Eragon's wards then.

Having no other recourse, Roran resorted to the unexpected: he stuck his head and neck out and shouted, "Bah!" just as he would if he were trying to scare someone in a dark hallway. The soldier flinched, and as he flinched, Roran leaned over and brought his hammer down on the man's left knee. The man's face went white with pain. Before he could recover, Roran struck him in the small of his back, and then as the soldier screamed and arched his spine, Roran ended his misery with a quick blow to the head.

Roran sat panting for a moment, then tugged on Snowfire's reins and spurred him into a canter as they returned to the convoy. His eyes darting from place to place, drawn by any flicker of motion, Roran took stock of the battle. Most of the soldiers were already dead, as were the men who had been driving the wagons. By the lead wagon, Carn stood facing a tall man in robes, the two of them rigid except for occasional twitches, the only sign of their invisible duel. Even as Roran watched, Carn's opponent pitched forward and lay motionless on the ground.

By the middle of the convoy, however, five enterprising soldiers had cut the oxen loose from three wagons and had pulled the wagons into a triangle, from within which they were able to hold off Martland Redbeard and ten other Varden. Four of the soldiers poked spears between the wagons, while the fifth fired arrows at the Varden, forcing them to retreat behind the nearest wagon for cover. The archer had already wounded several of the Varden, some of whom had fallen off their horses, others of whom had kept their saddles long enough to find cover.

Roran frowned. They could not afford to linger out in the open on one of the Empire's main roads while they slowly picked off the entrenched soldiers. Time was against them.

All the soldiers were facing west, the direction from which the Varden had attacked. Aside from Roran, none of the Varden had crossed to the other side of the convoy. Thus, the soldiers were unaware that he was bearing down on them from the east.

A plan occurred to Roran. In any other circumstances, he would have dismissed it as ludicrous and impractical, but as it was, he accepted the plan as the only course of action that could resolve the standoff without further delay. He did not bother to consider the danger to himself; he had abandoned all fear of death and injury the moment their charge had begun.

Roran urged Snowfire into a full gallop. He placed his left hand on the front of his saddle, edged his boots almost out of the stirrups, and gathered his muscles in preparation. When Snowfire was fifty feet away from the triangle of wagons, he pressed downward with his hand and, lifting himself, placed his feet on the saddle and stood crouched on Snowfire. It took all his skill and concentration to maintain his balance. As Roran had expected, Snowfire lessened his speed and started to veer to the side as the cluster of wagons loomed large before them.

Roran released the reins just as Snowfire turned, and jumped off the horse's back, leaping high over the east-facing wagon of the triangle. His stomach lurched. He caught a glimpse of the archer's upturned face, the soldier's eyes round and edged with white, then slammed into the man, and they both crashed to the ground. Roran landed on top, the soldier's body cushioning his fall. Pushing himself onto his knees, Roran raised his shield and drove its rim through the gap between the soldier's helm and his tunic, breaking his neck. Then Roran shoved himself upright.

The other four soldiers were slow to react. The one to Roran's left made the mistake of trying to pull his spear inside the triangle of wagons, but in his haste, he wedged the spear between the rear of one wagon and the front wheel of another, and the shaft splintered in his hands. Roran lunged toward him. The soldier tried to retreat, but the wagons blocked his way. Swinging the hammer in an underhand blow, Roran caught the soldier beneath his chin.

The second soldier was smarter. He let go of his spear and reached for the sword at his belt but only succeeded in drawing the blade halfway out of the sheath before Roran staved in his chest.

The third and fourth soldiers were ready for Roran by then. They converged on him, naked blades outstretched, snarls on their faces. Roran tried to sidestep them, but his torn leg failed him, and he stumbled and fell to one knee. The closest soldier slashed downward. With his shield, Roran blocked the blow, then dove forward and crushed the soldier's foot with the flat end of his hammer. Cursing, the soldier toppled to the ground. Roran promptly smashed the soldier's face, then flipped onto his back, knowing that the last soldier was directly behind him.

Roran froze, his arms and legs splayed to either side.

The soldier stood over him, holding his sword extended, the tip of the gleaming blade less than an inch away from Roran's throat.

So this is how it ends, thought Roran.

Then a thick arm appeared around the soldier's neck, yanking him backward, and the soldier uttered a choked cry as a sword blade sprouted from the middle of his chest, along with a spray of blood. The soldier collapsed into a limp pile, and in his place, there stood Martland Redbeard. The earl was breathing heavily, and his beard and chest were splattered with gore.

Martland stuck his sword in the dirt, leaned on the pommel, and surveyed the carnage within the triangle of wagons. He nodded. "You'll do, I think."

Roran sat on the end of a wagon, biting his tongue as Carn cut off the rest of his boot. Trying to ignore the stabs of agony from his leg, Roran gazed up at the vultures circling overhead and concentrated on memories of his home in Palancar Valley.

He grunted as Carn probed especially deep into the gash.

"Sorry," said Carn. "I have to inspect the wound."

Roran kept staring at the vultures and did not answer. After a minute, Carn uttered a number of words in the ancient language, and a few seconds later, the pain in Roran's leg subsided to a dull ache. Looking down, Roran saw his leg was whole once more.

The effort of healing Roran and the two other men before him had left Carn gray-faced and shaking. The magician slumped against the wagon, wrapping his arms around his middle, his expression queasy.

"Are you all right?" Roran asked.

Carn lifted his shoulders in a minuscule shrug. "I just need a moment to recover. . . . The ox scratched the outer bone of your lower leg. I repaired the scratch, but I didn't have the strength to completely heal the rest of your injury. I stitched together your skin and muscle, so it won't bleed or pain you overmuch, but only lightly. The flesh there won't hold much more than your weight, not until it mends on its own, that is."

"How long will that take?"

"A week, perhaps two."

Roran pulled on the remains of his boot. "Eragon cast wards around me to protect me from injury. They saved my life several times today. Why didn't they protect me from the ox's horn, though?"

"I don't know, Roran," Carn said, sighing. "No one can prepare for every eventuality. That's one reason magic is so perilous. If you overlook a single facet of a spell, it may do nothing but weaken you, or worse, it may do some horrible thing you never intended. It happens to even the best magicians. There must be a flaw in your cousin's wards—a misplaced word or a poorly reasoned statement— that allowed the ox to gore you."

Easing himself off the wagon, Roran limped toward the head of the convoy, assessing the result of the battle. Five of the Varden had been wounded during the fighting, including himself, and two others had died: one a man Roran had barely met, the other Ferth, whom he had spoken with on several occasions. Of the soldiers and the men who steered the wagons, none remained alive.

Roran paused by the first two soldiers he had killed and studied their corpses. His saliva turned bitter, and his gut roiled with revulsion. *Now I have killed . . . I don't know how many.* He realized that during the madness of the Battle of the Burning Plains, he had lost count of the number of men he had slain. That he had sent so many to their deaths he could not remember the full number unsettled him. *Must I slaughter entire fields of men in order to regain what the Empire stole from me?* An even more disconcerting thought occurred to him: *And if I do, how could I return to Palancar Valley and live in peace when my soul was stained black with the blood of hundreds?*

Closing his eyes, Roran consciously relaxed all the muscles in his body, seeking to calm himself. *I kill for my love. I kill for my love of Katrina, and for my love of Eragon and everyone from Carvahall, and also for my love of the Varden, and my love of this land of ours. For my love, I will wade through an ocean of blood, even if it destroys me.*

"Never seen the likes o' that before, Stronghammer," said Ulhart. Roran opened his eyes to find the grizzled warrior standing in front of him, holding Snowfire by the reins. "No one else crazy enough to try a trick like that, jumping over the wagons, none that lived to tell the tale, nohow. Good job, that. Watch yourself, though. Can't go around leaping off horses an' taking on five men yourself an' expect to see another summer, eh? Bit of caution if you're wise."

"I'll keep that in mind," said Roran as he accepted Snowfire's reins from Ulhart.

In the minutes since Roran had disposed of the last of the soldiers, the uninjured warriors had been going to each of the wagons in the convoy, cutting open their bundles of cargo, and reporting the contents to Martland, who recorded what they found so Nasuada could study the information and perhaps gather from it some indication of Galbatorix's plans. Roran watched as the men examined the last few wagons, which contained bags of wheat and stacks of uniforms. That finished, the men slit the throats of the remaining oxen, soaking the road with blood. Killing the beasts bothered Roran, but he understood the importance of denying them to the Empire and would have wielded the knife himself if asked. They would have taken the oxen back to the Varden, but the animals were too slow and cumbersome. The soldiers' horses, however, could keep pace as they fled enemy territory, so they captured as many as they could and tied them behind their own steeds.

Then one of the men took a resin-soaked torch from his saddlebags and, after a few seconds of work with his flint and steel, lit it. Riding up and down the convoy, he pressed the torch against each wagon until it caught fire and then tossed the torch into the back of the last wagon.

"Mount up!" shouted Martland.

Roran's leg throbbed as he pulled himself onto Snowfire. He spurred the stallion over next to Carn as the surviving men assembled on their steeds in a double line behind Martland. The horses snorted and pawed at the ground, impatient to put distance between themselves and the fire.

Martland started forward at a swift trot, and the rest of the group followed, leaving behind them the line of burning wagons, like so many glowing beads strung out upon the lonely road.

A FOREST OF STONE

cheer went up from the crowd.

Eragon was sitting in the wooden stands that the dwarves had built along the base of the outer ramparts of Bregan Hold. The hold sat on a rounded shoulder of Thardûr mountain, over a mile above the floor of the mist-laden valley, and from it one could see for leagues in either direction, or until the ridged mountains obscured the view. Like Tronjheim and the other dwarf cities Eragon had visited, Bregan Hold was made entirely of quarried stone—in this case, a reddish granite that lent a sense of warmth to the rooms and corridors within. The hold itself was a thick, solid building that rose five stories to an open bell tower, which was topped by a teardrop of glass that was as large around as two dwarves and was held in place by four granite ribs that joined together to form a pointed capstone. The teardrop, as Orik had told Eragon, was a larger version of the dwarves' flameless lanterns, and during notable occasions or emergencies, it could be used to illuminate the entire valley with a golden light. The dwarves called it Az Sindriznarrvel, or The Gem of Sindri. Clustered around the flanks of the hold were numerous outbuildings, living quarters for the servants and warriors of Dûrgrimst Ingeitum, as well as other structures, such as stables, forges, and a church devoted to Morgothal, the dwarves' god of fire and their patron god of smiths. Below the high, smooth walls of Bregan Hold were dozens of farms scattered about clearings in the forest, coils of smoke drifting up from the stone houses.

All that and more, Orik had shown and explained to Eragon after the three dwarf children had escorted Eragon into the courtyard of Bregan Hold, shouting, "Argetlam!" to everyone within earshot.

Orik had greeted Eragon like a brother and then had taken him to the baths and, when he was clean, saw to it that he was garbed in a robe of deep purple, with a gold circlet for his brow.

Afterward, Orik surprised Eragon by introducing him to Hvedra, a bright-eyed, apple-faced dwarf woman with long hair, and proudly announcing that they had been married but two days past. While Eragon expressed his astonishment and congratulations, Orik shifted from foot to foot before replying, "It pained me that you were not able to attend the ceremony, Eragon. I had one of our spellcasters contact Nasuada, and I asked her if she would give you and Saphira my invitation, but she refused to mention it to you; she feared the offer might distract you from the task at hand. I cannot blame her, but I wish that this war would have allowed you to be at our wedding, and us at your cousin's, for we are all related now, by law if not by blood."

In her thick accent, Hvedra said, "Please, consider me as your kin now, Shadeslayer. So long as it is within mine power, you shall always be treated as family at Bregan Hold, and you may claim sanctuary of us whenever you need, even if it is Galbatorix who hunts you."

Eragon bowed, touched by her offer. "You are most kind." Then he asked, "If you don't mind my curiosity, why did you and Orik choose to marry now?"

"We had planned to join hands this spring, but . . ."

"But," Orik continued in his gruff manner, "the Urgals attacked Farthen Dûr, and then Hrothgar sent me traipsing off with you to Ellesméra. When I returned here and the families of the clan accepted me as their new grimstborith, we thought it the perfect time to consummate our betrothal and become husband and wife. None of us may survive the year, so why tarry?"

"So you did become clan chief," Eragon said.

"Aye. Choosing the next leader of Dûrgrimst Ingeitum was a contentious business—we were hard at it for over a week—but in the end, most of the families agreed that I should follow in

Hrothgar's footsteps and inherit his position since I was his only named heir."

Now Eragon sat next to Orik and Hvedra, devouring the bread and mutton the dwarves had brought him and watching the contest taking place in front of the stands. It was customary, Orik had said, for a dwarf family, if they had the gold, to stage games for the entertainment of their wedding guests. Hrothgar's family was so wealthy, the current games had already lasted for three days and were scheduled to continue for another four. The games consisted of many events: wrestling, archery, swordsmanship, feats of strength, and the current event, the Ghastgar.

From opposite ends of a grassy field, two dwarves rode toward each other on white Feldûnost. The horned mountain goats bounded across the sward, each leap over seventy feet long. The dwarf on the right had a small buckler strapped to his left arm but carried no weapons. The dwarf on the left had no shield, but in his right hand, he held a javelin poised to throw.

412

Eragon held his breath as the distance between the Feldûnost narrowed. When they were less than thirty feet apart, the dwarf with the spear whipped his arm through the air and launched the missile at his opponent. The other dwarf did not cover himself with his shield, but rather reached out and, with amazing dexterity, caught the spear by the shaft. He brandished it over his head. The crowd gathered around the lists let out a resounding cheer, which Eragon joined in, clapping vigorously.

"That was skillfully done!" exclaimed Orik. He laughed and drained his tankard of mead, his polished coat of mail sparkling in the early-evening light. He wore a helm embellished with gold, silver, and rubies and, on his fingers, five large rings. At his waist hung his ever-present ax. Hvedra was attired even more richly, with strips of embroidered cloth upon her sumptuous dress, strands of pearls and twisted gold around her neck, and in her hair, an ivory comb set with an emerald as large as Eragon's thumb.

A line of dwarves stood and winded a set of curved horns, the brassy notes echoing off the mountains. Then a barrel-chested dwarf stepped forward and, in Dwarvish, announced the winner of the last contest, as well as the names of the next pair to compete in the Ghastgar.

When the master of ceremonies finished speaking, Eragon bent over and asked, "Will you be accompanying us to Farthen Dûr, Hvedra?"

She shook her head and smiled widely. "I cannot. I must stay here and tend to the affairs of the Ingeitum while Orik is gone, so he does not return to find our warriors starving and all our gold spent."

Chuckling, Orik held out his tankard toward one of the servants standing several yards away. As the dwarf hurried over and refilled it with mead from a pitcher, Orik said to Eragon with obvious pride, "Hvedra does not boast. She is not only my wife, she is the . . . Ach, you have no word for it. She is the grimstcarvlorss of Dûrgrimst Ingeitum. *Grimstcarvlorss* means . . . 'the keeper of the house,' 'the arranger of the house.' It is her duty to ensure that the families of our clan pay their agreed-upon tithes to Bregan Hold, that our herds are driven to the proper fields at the proper times, that our stocks of feed and grain do not fall too low, that the women of the Ingeitum weave enough fabric, that our warriors are well equipped, that our smiths always have ore to smelt into iron, and in short, that our clan is well managed and will prosper and thrive. There is a saying among our people: a good grimstcarvlorss can make a clan—"

"And a bad grimstcarvlorss will destroy a clan," said Hvedra.

Orik smiled and clasped one of her hands in his. "And Hvedra is the best of grimstcarvlorssn. It is not an inherited title. You must prove that you are worthy of the post if you are to hold it. It is rare for the wife of a grimstborith to be grimstcarvlorss as well. I am most fortunate in that regard." Bending their heads together, he and Hvedra rubbed noses. Eragon glanced away, feeling lonely and excluded. Leaning back, Orik took a draught of mead, then said, "There have been many famous grimstcarvlorssn in our history. It is often said that the only thing we clan leaders are good for is declaring war on each other and that the grimstcarvlorssn prefer we spend our time squabbling among ourselves so we do not have the time to interfere in the workings of the clan."

"Come now, Skilfz Delva," chided Hvedra. "You know that is not truth. Or it shall not be truth with us."

"Mmm," said Orik, and touched his forehead to Hvedra's. They rubbed noses again.

Eragon returned his attention to the crowd below as it erupted in a frenzy of hissing and jeering. He saw that one of the dwarves competing in the Ghastgar had lost his nerve and, at the last moment, had yanked his Feldûnost off to one side and even then was attempting to flee his opponent. The dwarf with the javelin pursued him twice around the lists. When they were close enough, he rose up in his stirrups and cast the spear, striking the cowardly dwarf in the back of his left shoulder. With a howl, the dwarf fell off his steed and lay on his side, clutching at the blade and shaft embedded in his flesh. A healer rushed toward him. After a moment, everyone turned their backs on the spectacle.

Orik's upper lip curved with disgust. "Bah! It will be many years before his family is able to erase the stain of their son's dishonor. I am sorry you have had to witness this contemptible act, Eragon."

"It's never enjoyable watching someone shame themselves."

The three of them sat in silence through the next two contests, then Orik startled Eragon by grasping him by the shoulder and asking, "How would you like to see a forest of stone, Eragon?"

"No such thing exists, unless it is carved."

Orik shook his head, his eyes twinkling. "It is not carved, and it does exist. So I ask again, would you like to see a forest of stone?"

"If you are not jesting . . . yes, I would."

"Ah, I am glad you accepted. I do not jest, and I promise you that tomorrow you and I shall walk among trees of granite. It is one of the wonders of the Beor Mountains. Everyone who is a guest of Dûrgrimst Ingeitum should have an opportunity to visit it."

* * *

The following morning, Eragon rose from his too-small bed in his stone room with its low ceiling and half-sized furniture, washed his face in a basin of cold water, and, out of habit, reached with his mind toward Saphira. He felt only the thoughts of the dwarves and the animals in and around the hold. Eragon faltered and leaned forward, gripping the rim of the basin, overcome by his sense of isolation. He remained in that position, unable to move or think, until his vision turned crimson and flashing spots floated in front of his eyes. With a gasp, he exhaled and refilled his lungs.

I missed her during the trip from Helgrind, he thought, *but at least I knew I was returning to her as fast as I could. Now I am traveling away from her, and I do not know when we will be reunited.*

Shaking himself, he dressed and made his way through the winding corridors of Bregan Hold, bowing to the dwarves he passed, who for their part greeted him with energetic reiterations of "Argetlam!"

He found Orik and twelve other dwarves in the courtyard of the hold, saddling a line of sturdy ponies, whose breath formed white plumes in the cold air. Eragon felt like a giant as the short, burly men moved about him.

Orik hailed him. "We have a donkey in our stables, if you would like to ride."

"No, I'll continue on foot, if it's all the same to you."

Orik shrugged. "As you wish."

When they were ready to depart, Hvedra descended the broad stone steps from the entrance to the main hall of Bregan Hold, her dress trailing behind her, and presented to Orik an ivory horn clad with gold filigree around the mouth and bell. She said, "This was mine father's when he rode with Grimstborith Aldhrim. I give it to you so you may remember me in the days to come." She said more in Dwarvish, so softly Eragon could not hear, and then she and Orik touched foreheads. Straightening in his saddle, Orik placed the horn to his lips and winded it. A deep, rousing note rang forth, increasing in volume until the air within the courtyard seemed to vibrate like a wind-sawed rope. A pair of black ravens rose from the tower above, cawing. The sound of the horn made Eragon's blood tingle. He shifted in place, eager to be gone.

Lifting the horn over his head and with a final look at Hvedra, Orik spurred his pony forward, trotted out of the main gates of Bregan Hold, and turned east, toward the head of the valley. Eragon and the twelve other dwarves followed close behind.

For three hours, they followed a well-worn trail across the side of Thardûr mountain, climbing ever higher above the valley floor. The dwarves drove the ponies as fast as they could without injuring the animals, but their pace was still only a fraction of Eragon's speed when he was free to run unchecked. Although he was frustrated, Eragon refrained from complaining, for he realized that it was inevitable he would have to travel slower with any but elves or Kull.

He shivered and pulled his cloak closer around himself. The sun had yet to appear over the Beor Mountains, and a damp chill pervaded the valley, even though noon was only a few hours away.

Then they came upon a flat expanse of granite over a thousand feet wide, bordered on the right by a slanting cliff of naturally formed octagonal pillars. Curtains of shifting mist obscured the far end of the stone field.

Orik raised a hand and said, "Behold, Az Knurldrâthn."

Eragon frowned. Stare as he might, he could discern nothing of interest in the barren location. "I see no forest of stone."

Clambering down from his pony, Orik handed the reins to the warrior behind him and said, "Walk with me, if you would, Eragon."

Together they strode toward the twisting bank of fog, Eragon shortening his steps to match Orik's. The mist kissed Eragon's face, cool and moist. The vapor became so thick that it obscured the rest of the valley, enveloping them in a featureless gray landscape where even up and down seemed arbitrary. Undaunted, Orik proceeded with a confident gait. Eragon, however, felt disoriented and slightly unsteady, and he walked with a hand held out in front of him, in case he should bump into anything hidden within the fog.

Orik stopped at the edge of a thin crack that defaced the granite they stood on and said, "What see you now?"

Squinting, Eragon swept his gaze back and forth, but the fog seemed as monotonous as ever. He opened his mouth to say as much but then noticed a slight irregularity in the texture of the mist to his right, a faint pattern of light and dark that held its shape even while the mist drifted past. He became aware of other areas that were static as well: strange, abstract patches of contrast that formed no recognizable objects.

"I don't . . . ," he started to say when a breath of wind ruffled his hair. Under the gentle encouragement of the newborn breeze, the fog thinned and the disjoined patterns of shade resolved into the boles of large, ash-colored trees with bare and broken limbs. Dozens of the trees surrounded him and Orik, the pale skeletons of an ancient forest. Eragon pressed his palm against a trunk. The bark was as cold and hard as a boulder. Blotches of pallid lichen clung to the surface of the tree. The back of Eragon's neck prickled. Although he did not consider himself overly superstitious, the ghostly mist and the eerie half-light and the appearance of the trees themselves— grim and foreboding and mysterious—ignited a spark of fear inside of him.

He wet his lips and asked, "How did these come to be?"

Orik shrugged. "Some claim that Gûntera must have placed them here when he created Alagaësia out of nothingness. Others claim Helzvog made them, for stone is his favorite element, and would not the god of stone have trees of stone for his garden? And still others say no, that once these were trees like any others, and a great catastrophe eons ago must have buried them in the ground, and that over time, wood became dirt, and dirt became stone."

"Is that possible?"

"Only the gods know for certain. Who besides them can hope to understand the whys and wherefores of the world?" Orik shifted his position. "Our ancestors discovered the first of the trees while quarrying granite here, over a thousand years ago. The then grimst-borith of Dûrgrimst Ingeitum, Hvalmar Lackhand, stopped the mining and, instead, had his masons chisel out the trees from the surrounding stone. When they had excavated nigh on fifty trees, Hvalmar realized that there might be hundreds, or even thousands, of stone trees entombed within the side of Mount Thardûr, and so he ordered his men to abandon the project. This place, however, captured the imagination of our race, and ever since, knurlan from every clan have traveled here and labored to extricate more trees from the grip of the granite. There are even knurlan who have ded-icated their lives to the task. It has also become a tradition to send troublesome offspring here to chisel out a tree or two while under the supervision of a master mason."

"That sounds tedious."

"It gives them time to repent of their ways." With one hand, Orik stroked his braided beard. "I spent some months here myself when I was a rambunctious lad of four-and-thirty."

"And did you repent of your ways?"

"Eta. No. It was too . . . *tedious*. After all those weeks, I had freed only a single branch from the granite, so I ran away and fell in with a group of Vrenshrrgn—"

"Dwarves from the clan Vrenshrrgn?"

"Yes, knurlagn of the clan Vrenshrrgn, War Wolves, Wolves of War, however you might say it in this tongue. I fell in with them, became drunk on ale, and as they were hunting Nagran, decided that I too should kill a boar and bring it to Hrothgar to appease his anger at me. It wasn't the wisest thing I have done. Even our most skilled warriors fear to hunt Nagran, and I was still more boy than man. Once my mind cleared, I cursed myself for a fool, but I had sworn I would, so I had no choice but to fulfill my oath."

When Orik paused, Eragon asked, "What happened?"

"Oh, I killed a Nagra, with help from the Vrenshrrgn, but the boar gored me in the shoulder and tossed me into the branches of a nearby tree. The Vrenshrrgn had to carry the both of us, the Nagra and me, back to Bregan Hold. The boar pleased Hrothgar, and I . . . I, despite the ministrations of our best healers, I had to spend the next month resting in bed, which Hrothgar said was punishment enough for defying his orders."

Eragon watched the dwarf for a while. "You miss him."

Orik stood for a moment with his chin tucked against his stocky chest. Lifting his ax, he struck the granite with the end of the haft, producing a sharp clack that echoed among the trees. "It has been nigh on two centuries since the last dûrgrimstvren, the last clan war, racked our nation, Eragon. But by Morgothal's black beard, we stand on the brink of another one now."

"Now, of all times?" exclaimed Eragon, appalled. "Is it really that bad?"

Orik scowled. "It is worse. Tensions between the clans are higher than they have ever been in living memory. Hrothgar's death and Nasuada's invasion of the Empire have served to inflame passions, aggravate old rivalries, and lend strength to those who believe it is folly to cast our lot with the Varden."

"How can they believe that when Galbatorix has already attacked Tronjheim with the Urgals?"

"Because," said Orik, "they are convinced it is impossible to defeat Galbatorix, and their argument holds much sway with our people. Can you honestly tell me, Eragon, that if Galbatorix were to confront you and Saphira this very instant, that the two of you could best him?"

Eragon's throat tightened. "No."

"I thought not. Those who are opposed to the Varden have blinded themselves to Galbatorix's threat. They say that if we had refused shelter to the Varden, if we had not accepted you and Saphira into fair Tronjheim, then Galbatorix would have had no reason to make war on us. They say that if we just keep to ourselves and remain hidden in our caves and tunnels, we shall have nothing to fear from Galbatorix. They do not realize that Galbatorix's hunger for power is insatiable and that he will not rest until all of

Alagaësia lies at his feet." Orik shook his head, and the muscles in his forearms bunched and knotted as he pinched the ax blade between his wide fingers. "I will not allow our race to cower in tunnels like frightened rabbits until the wolf outside digs his way in and eats us all. We must continue fighting out of the hope that somehow we can find a way to kill Galbatorix. And I will not allow our nation to disintegrate into a clan war. With circumstances as they are, another dûrgrimstvren would destroy our civilization and possibly doom the Varden as well." His jaw set, Orik turned toward Eragon. "For the good of my people, I intend to seek the throne myself. Dûrgrimstn Gedthrall, Ledwonnû, and Nagra have already pledged their support to me. However, there are many who stand between me and the crown; it will not be easy to garner enough votes to become king. I need to know, Eragon, will you back me in this?"

Crossing his arms, Eragon walked from one tree to the next and then back again. "If I do, my support might turn the other clans against you. Not only will you be asking your people to ally themselves with the Varden, you will be asking them to accept a Dragon Rider as one of their own, which they have never done before and I doubt they will want to now."

"Aye, it may turn some against me," said Orik, "but it may also gain me the votes of others. Let me be the judge of that. All I wish to know is, Will you back me? . . . Eragon, why do you hesitate?"

Eragon stared at a gnarled root that rose out of the granite by his feet, avoiding Orik's eyes. "You are concerned about the good of your people, and rightly so. But my concerns are broader; they encompass the good of the Varden and the elves and everyone else who opposes Galbatorix. If . . . if it is not likely you can win the crown, and there is another clan chief who could, and who is not unsympathetic to the Varden—"

"No one would be a more sympathetic grimstnzborith than I!"

"I'm not questioning your friendship," Eragon protested. "But if what I said came to pass and my support might ensure that such a clan chief won the throne, for the good of your people and for the good of the rest of Alagaësia, shouldn't I back the dwarf who has the best chance of succeeding?"

In a deadly quiet voice, Orik said, "You swore a blood-oath on the Knurlnien, Eragon. By every law of our realm, you are a member of Dûrgrimst Ingeitum, no matter how greatly others may disapprove. What Hrothgar did by adopting you has no precedent in all of our history, and it cannot be undone unless, as grimstborith, I banish you from our clan. If you turn against me, Eragon, you will shame me in front of our entire race and none will ever trust my leadership again. Moreover, you will prove to your detractors that we cannot trust a Dragon Rider. Clan members do not betray each other to other clans, Eragon. It is not done, not unless you wish to wake up one night with a dagger buried in your heart."

"Are you threatening me?" asked Eragon, just as quietly.

Orik swore and banged his ax against the granite again. "No! I would never lift a hand against you, Eragon! You are my foster brother, you are the only Rider free of Galbatorix's influence, and blast it if I have not become fond of you during our travels together. But even though I would not harm you, that does not mean the rest of the Ingeitum would be so forbearing. I say that not as a threat but as a statement of fact. You must understand this, Eragon. If the clan hears you have given your support to another, I may not be able to restrain them. Even though you are our guest and the rules of hospitality protect you, if you speak out against the Ingeitum, the clan will see you as having betrayed them, and it is not our custom to allow traitors to remain within our midst. Do you understand me, Eragon?"

"What do you expect of me?" shouted Eragon. He flung his arms outward and paced back and forth in front of Orik. "I swore an oath to Nasuada as well, and those were the orders she gave me."

"And you also pledged yourself to Dûrgrimst Ingeitum!" roared Orik.

Eragon stopped and stared at the dwarf. "Would you have me doom all of Alagaësia just so you can maintain your standing among the clans?"

"Do not insult me!"

"Then don't ask the impossible of me! I will back you if it seems likely you can ascend to the throne, and if not, then I won't. You worry about Dûrgrimst Ingeitum and your race as a whole, while it is my duty to worry about them and all of Alagaësia as well." Eragon slumped against the cold trunk of a tree. "And I cannot afford to offend you or your—I mean, *our*—clan or the rest of dwarfdom."

In a kinder tone, Orik said, "There is another way, Eragon. It would be more difficult for you, but it would resolve your quandary."

"Oh? What wondrous solution would this be?"

Sliding his ax back under his belt, Orik walked over to Eragon, grasped him by the forearms, and gazed up at him through bushy eyebrows. "Trust me to do the right thing, Eragon Shadeslayer. Give me the same loyalty you would if you were indeed born of Dûrgrimst Ingeitum. Those under me would never presume to speak out against their own grimstborith in favor of another clan. If a grimstborith strikes the rock wrong, it is his responsibility alone, but that does not mean I am oblivious to your concerns." He glanced down for a moment, then said, "If I cannot be king, trust me not to be so blinded by the prospect of power that I cannot recognize when my bid has failed. If that should happen—not that I believe it shall—then I will, of my own volition, lend my support to one of the other candidates, for I have no more desire than you to see a grimstnzborith elected who is hostile to the Varden. And if I should help promote another to the throne, the status and prestige I will place at the service of that clan chief shall, of its very nature, include your own, since you are Ingeitum. Will you trust me, Eragon? Will you accept me as your grimstborith, as the rest of my hall-sworn subjects do?"

Eragon groaned and leaned his head against the rough tree and peered up at the crooked, bone-white branches wreathed in mist. *Trust.* Of all the things Orik could have asked of him, that was the most difficult to grant. Eragon liked Orik, but to subordinate himself to the dwarf's authority when so much was at stake would be to relinquish even more of his freedom, a prospect he loathed. And along with his freedom, he would also be relinquishing part of his responsibility for the fate of Alagaësia. Eragon felt as if he were hanging off the edge of a precipice and Orik was trying to convince him there was a ledge only a few feet below him, but Eragon could not bring himself to release his grip, for fear he would fall to his doom.

He said, "I would not be a mindless servant for you to order about. When it came to matters of Dûrgrimst Ingeitum, I would defer to you, but in all else, you would have no hold over me."

Orik nodded, his face serious. "I'm not worried about what mission Nasuada might send you on, nor whom you might kill while fighting the Empire. No, what gives me restless nights when I ought to be sleeping sound as Arghen in his cave is imagining you attempting to influence the clanmeet's voting. Your intentions are noble, I know, but noble or not, you are unfamiliar with our politics, no matter how well Nasuada may have schooled you. This is mine area of expertise, Eragon. Let me conduct it in the manner I deem appropriate. It is what Hrothgar groomed me for my entire life."

Eragon sighed, and with a sensation of falling, he said, "Very well. I will do as you think best about the succession, Grimstborith Orik."

A broad smile spread across Orik's face. He tightened his grip on Eragon's forearms, then released him, saying, "Ah, thank you, Eragon. You don't know what this means to me. It is good of you, very good of you, and I won't forget it, not if I live to be two hundred years old and my beard grows so long, it drags in the dirt."

Despite himself, Eragon chuckled. "Well, I hope it doesn't grow that long. You would trip over it all the time!"

"Perhaps I would at that," said Orik, laughing. "Besides, I rather think Hvedra would cut it short once it reached my knees. She has very definite opinions about the proper length of a beard."

✳ ✳ ✳

Orik led the way as the two of them departed the forest of stone trees, striding through the colorless mist that swirled among the calcified trunks. They rejoined Orik's twelve warriors, then began to descend the side of Mount Thardûr. At the bottom of the valley, they continued in a straight line to the other side, and there the dwarves brought Eragon to a tunnel hidden so cleverly within the rock face, he never would have found the entrance on his own.

It was with regret that Eragon left behind the pale sunshine and fresh mountain air for the darkness of the tunnel. The passageway was eight feet wide and six feet high—which made it feel quite low to Eragon—and like all the dwarf tunnels he had visited, it was as straight as an arrow for as far as he could see. He looked back over his shoulder just in time to see the dwarf Farr swing closed the hinged slab of granite that served as a door to the tunnel, plunging their party into night. A moment later, fourteen glowing orbs of differing colors appeared as the dwarves removed flameless lanterns from their saddlebags. Orik handed one to Eragon.

Then they started forward under the roots of the mountain, and the ponies' hooves filled the tunnel with clashing echoes that seemed to shout at them like angry wraiths. Eragon grimaced, knowing they would have to listen to the din all the way to Farthen Dûr, for that was where the tunnel ended, many leagues thence. He hunched his shoulders and tightened his grip on the straps of his pack and wished he were with Saphira, flying high above the ground.

✦ ✦ ✦

THE LAUGHING DEAD

Roran squatted and gazed through the latticework of willow branches.

Two hundred yards away, fifty-three soldiers and wagon drivers sat around three separate cookfires, eating their dinner as dusk rapidly settled over the land. The men had stopped for the night on the broad, grass-covered bank next to a nameless river. The wagons full of supplies for Galbatorix's troops were parked in a rough half circle around the fires. Scores of hobbled oxen grazed behind the camp, lowing occasionally to each other. Twenty yards or so downstream, however, a soft earth shelf reared high out of the ground, which prevented any attack or escape from that quarter.

What were they thinking? Roran wondered. It was only prudent, when in hostile territory, to camp in a defensible location, which usually meant finding a natural formation to protect your back. Even so, you had to be careful to choose a resting place you could flee from if ambushed. As it was, it would be childishly easy for Roran and the other warriors under Martland's command to sweep out of the brush where they were hiding and pin the men of the Empire in the tip of the V formed by the earthen shelf and the river, where they could pick off the soldiers and drivers at their leisure. It puzzled Roran that trained soldiers would make such an obvious mistake. *Maybe they are from a city,* he thought. *Or maybe they are merely inexperienced.* He frowned. *Then why would they be entrusted with such a crucial mission?*

"Have you detected any traps?" he asked. He did not have to turn his head to know that Carn was close beside him, as well as Halmar and two other men. Save the four swordsmen who had joined Martland's company to replace those who had died or been irreparably wounded during their last engagement, Roran had fought alongside all of the men in their group. While he did not like every single one, he trusted them with his life, as he knew they trusted him. It was a bond that transcended age or upbringing. After his first battle, Roran had been surprised by how close he felt to his companions, as well as by how warm they were to him in turn.

"None that I can tell," murmured Carn. "But then—"

"They may have invented new spells you cannot detect, yes, yes. Is there a magician with them, though?"

"I can't tell for sure, but no, I don't think so."

Roran pushed away a shock of narrow willow leaves to better see the layout of the wagons. "I don't like it," he grumbled. "A magician accompanied the other convoy. Why not this one?"

"There are fewer of us than you might imagine."

426 "Mmh." Roran scratched his beard, still bothered by the soldiers' apparent disregard of common sense. *Could they be trying to invite an attack? They don't seem prepared for one, but appearances are hardly everything. What sort of trap could they have prepared for us? No one else is within thirty leagues, and Murtagh and Thorn were last spotted flying north from Feinster.* "Send the signal," he said. "But tell Martland it bothers me they camped here. Either they're idiots or they have some sort of defense invisible to us: magic or other trickery of the king."

Silence, then: "I sent it. Martland says he shares your concern, but unless you want to run back to Nasuada with your tail tucked between your legs, we try our luck."

Roran grunted and turned away from the soldiers. He gestured with his chin, and the other men scampered with him on hands and knees to where they had left their horses.

Standing, Roran mounted Snowfire.

"Whoa, steady, boy," he whispered, petting Snowfire as the stallion tossed his head. In the dim light, Snowfire's mane and hide gleamed like silver. Not for the first time, Roran wished his horse were a less visible shade, a nice bay or chestnut perhaps.

Taking his shield from where it hung by his saddle, Roran fit his left arm through the straps, then pulled his hammer from his belt.

He dry-swallowed, a familiar tightness between his shoulders, and readjusted his grip on the hammer.

When the five men were ready, Carn raised a finger and his eyelids drifted half closed and his lips twitched, as if he were talking with himself. A cricket sounded nearby.

Carn's eyelids snapped open. "Remember, keep your gaze directed downward until your vision adjusts, and even then, don't look at the sky." Then he began to chant in the ancient language, incomprehensible words that shivered with power.

Roran covered himself with his shield and squinted at his saddle as a pure white light, bright as the noonday sun, illuminated the landscape. The stark glow originated from a point somewhere above the camp; Roran resisted the temptation to see exactly where.

Shouting, he kicked Snowfire in the ribs and hunched over the horse's neck as his steed leaped forward. On either side, Carn and the other warriors did the same, brandishing their weapons. Branches tore at Roran's head and shoulders, and then Snowfire broke free of the trees and raced toward the camp at full gallop.

Two other groups of horsemen also thundered toward the camp, one led by Martland, the other Ulhart.

The soldiers and drivers cried out in alarm and covered their eyes. Staggering about like blind men, they scrabbled after their weapons while trying to position themselves to repel the attack.

Roran made no attempt to slow Snowfire. Spurring the stallion once more, he rose high in the stirrups and held on with all his strength as Snowfire jumped over the slight gap between two wagons. His teeth clattered as they landed. Snowfire kicked dirt into one of the fires, sending up a burst of sparks.

The rest of Roran's group jumped the wagons as well. Knowing they would attend to the soldiers behind him, Roran concentrated on those in front. Aiming Snowfire at one of the men, he jabbed at the soldier with the end of his hammer and broke the man's nose, splashing crimson blood across his face. Roran dispatched the man with a second blow to the head, then parried a sword from another soldier.

Farther down the curved line of wagons, Martland, Ulhart, and their men also jumped into the camp, alighting with a clack of hooves and a jangle of armor and weapons. A horse screamed and fell as a soldier wounded it with a spear.

Roran blocked the soldier's sword a second time, then rapped the man's sword hand, breaking bones and forcing the man to drop his weapon. Without pause, Roran struck the man in the center of his red tunic, cracking his sternum and felling the gasping, mortally wounded soldier.

Roran twisted in the saddle, searching the camp for his next opponent. His muscles vibrated with frantic excitement; every detail around him was as sharp and clear as if it were etched in glass. He felt invincible, invulnerable. Time itself seemed to stretch and slow, so that a confused moth that fluttered past him appeared to be flying through honey instead of air.

Then a pair of hands clamped down on the back of his mail hauberk and yanked him off Snowfire and slammed him into the hard ground, knocking the breath out of him. Roran's sight flickered and went black for a moment. When he recovered, he saw that the first soldier he had attacked was sitting on his chest, choking him. The soldier blotted out the source of light Carn had created in the sky. A white halo surrounded his head and shoulders, casting his features in such deep shadow, Roran could make out nothing of his face but the flash of bared teeth.

The soldier tightened his fingers around Roran's throat as Roran gasped for air. Roran groped after his hammer, which he had dropped, but it was not within reach. Tensing his neck to keep the soldier from crushing the life out of him, he drew his dagger from his belt and drove it through the soldier's hauberk, through his gambeson, and between the ribs on the soldier's left side.

The soldier did not even flinch, nor did his grip relax.

A continuous stream of gurgling laughter emanated from the soldier. The lurching, heart-stopping chuckle, hideous in the extreme, turned Roran's stomach cold with fear. He remembered the sound from before; he had heard it while watching the Varden fight the men who felt no pain on the grassy field beside the Jiet River. In a flash, he understood why the soldiers had chosen such a poor campsite: *They do not care if they are trapped or not, for we cannot hurt them.*

Roran's vision turned red, and yellow stars danced before his eyes. Teetering on the edge of unconsciousness, he yanked the dagger free and stabbed upward, into the soldier's armpit, twisting the blade in the wound. Gouts of hot blood spurted over his hand, but the soldier did not seem to notice. The world exploded in blotches of pulsing colors as the soldier smashed Roran's head against the ground. Once. Twice. Three times. Roran bucked his hips, trying without success to throw the man off. Blind and desperate, he slashed at where he guessed the man's face to be and felt the dagger catch in soft flesh. He pulled the dagger back slightly, then lunged in that direction, feeling the impact as the tip of the blade struck bone.

The pressure around Roran's neck vanished.

Roran lay where he was, his chest heaving, then rolled over and vomited, throat burning. Still gasping and coughing, he staggered upright and saw the soldier sprawled motionless next to him, the dagger protruding from the man's left nostril.

"Go for the head!" shouted Roran, despite his raw throat. "The head!"

He left the dagger buried in the soldier's nostril and retrieved his hammer from the trampled ground where it had fallen, pausing long enough to also grab an abandoned spear, which he held with his shield hand. Jumping over the fallen soldier, he ran toward Halmar, who was on foot as well and dueling three soldiers at once. Before the soldiers noticed him, Roran bashed the two closest ones in the head so hard, he split their helms. The third he left to Halmar, instead bounding over to the soldier whose sternum he had broken and whom he had left for dead. He found the man sitting against the wheel of a wagon, spitting up clotted blood and struggling to string a bow.

Roran gored him through an eye with the spear. Pieces of gray flesh clung to the blade of the spear as he pulled it free.

An idea occurred to Roran then. He threw the spear at a man in a red tunic on the other side of the nearest fire—impaling him through the torso—then slid the haft of his hammer under his belt and strung the soldier's bow. Placing his back against a wagon, Roran began to shoot the soldiers rushing about the encampment, attempting either to kill them with a lucky shot to the face, the throat, or the heart or to cripple them so his companions could more easily dispatch them. If nothing else, he reasoned that an injured soldier might bleed to death before the fight ended.

The initial confidence of the attack had faded into confusion. The Varden were scattered and dismayed, some on their steeds, some on foot, and most bloodied. At least five, so far as Roran could tell, had died when soldiers they had thought slain had returned to assail them. How many soldiers were left, it was impossible to tell in the throng of flailing bodies, but Roran could see that they still outnumbered the scant twenty-five or so of the remaining Varden. *They could tear us into pieces with their bare hands while we try to hack them apart,* he realized. He searched with his eyes among the frenzy for Snowfire and saw that the white horse had run farther down the river, where he now stood by a willow tree, nostrils flared and ears plastered flat against his skull.

With the bow, Roran killed four more soldiers and wounded over a score. When he had only two arrows left, he spotted Carn standing on the other side of the camp, dueling a soldier by the corner of a burning tent. Drawing the bow until the fletching on the arrow tickled his ear, Roran shot the soldier in the chest. The soldier stumbled, and Carn decapitated him.

Roran tossed the bow aside and, hammer in hand, ran over to Carn and shouted, "Can't you kill them with magic?"

For a moment, Carn could only pant, then he shook his head and said, "Every spell I cast was blocked." The light from the burning tent gilded the side of his face.

Roran cursed. "Together then!" he cried, and hefted his shield.

Shoulder to shoulder, the two of them advanced upon the nearest group of soldiers: a cluster of eight men surrounding three of the Varden. The next few minutes were a spasm of flashing weapons, tearing flesh, and sudden pains for Roran. The soldiers tired more slowly than ordinary men, and they never shirked from an attack, nor did they slacken in their efforts even when suffering from the most horrific injuries. The exertion of the fight was so great, Roran's nausea returned, and after the eighth soldier fell, he leaned over and vomited again. He spat to clear his mouth of bile.

One of the Varden they had sought to rescue had died in the struggle, slain by a knife in the kidneys, but the two who were still standing joined forces with Roran and Carn, and with them, they charged the next batch of soldiers.

"Drive them toward the river!" Roran shouted. The water and the mud would limit the soldiers' movement and perhaps allow the Varden to gain the upper hand.

Not far away, Martland had succeeded in rallying the twelve of the Varden who were still on their horses, and they were already doing what Roran had suggested: herding the soldiers back toward the shining water.

The soldiers and the few drivers who were still alive resisted. They shoved their shields against the men on foot. They jabbed spears at the horses. But in spite of their violent opposition, the Varden forced them to retreat a step at a time until the men in the crimson tunics stood knee-deep in the fast-flowing water, half blinded by the uncanny light shining down on them.

"Hold the line!" shouted Martland, dismounting and planting himself with spread legs on the edge of the riverbank. "Don't let them regain the shore!"

Roran dropped into a half crouch, ground his heels into the soft earth until he was comfortable with his stance, and waited for the large soldier standing in the cold water several feet in front of him to attack. With a roar, the soldier splashed out of the shallows, swinging his sword at Roran, which Roran caught on his shield. Roran retaliated with a stroke of his hammer, but the soldier blocked him with his own shield and then cut at Roran's legs. For several seconds, they exchanged blows, but neither wounded the other. Then Roran shattered the man's left forearm, knocking him back several paces. The soldier merely smiled and uttered a mirthless, soul-chilling laugh.

Roran wondered whether he or any of his companions would survive the night. *They're harder to kill than snakes. We can cut them to ribbons, and they'll still keep coming at us unless we hit something vital.* His next thought vanished as the soldier rushed at him again, his notched sword flickering in the pale light like a tongue of flame.

Thereafter, the battle assumed a nightmarish quality for Roran. The strange, baleful light gave the water and the soldiers an unearthly aspect, bleaching them of color and projecting long, thin, razor-sharp shadows across the shifting water, while beyond and all around, the fullness of night prevailed. Again and again, he repelled the soldiers who stumbled out of the water to kill him, hammering at them until they were barely recognizable as human, and yet they would not die. With every blow, medallions of black blood stained the surface of the river, like blots of spilled ink, and drifted away on the current. The deadly sameness of each clash numbed and horrified Roran. No matter how hard he strove, there was always another mutilated soldier there to slash and stab at him. And always the demented giggling of men who knew they were dead and yet continued to maintain a semblance of life even while the Varden destroyed their bodies.

And then silence.

Roran remained crouched behind his shield with his hammer half raised, gasping and drenched with sweat and blood. A minute passed before it dawned on him that no one stood in the water before him. He glanced left and right three times, unable to grasp that the soldiers were finally, blessedly, irrevocably dead. A corpse floated past him in the glittering water.

An inarticulate bellow escaped him as a hand gripped his right arm. He whipped around, snarling and pulling away, only to see Carn next to him. The wan, gore-smeared spellcaster was speaking. "We won, Roran! Eh? They're gone! We vanquished them!"

Roran let his arms drop and tilted his head back, too tired even to sit. He felt . . . he felt as if his senses were abnormally sharp, and yet his emotions were dull, muted things, tamped down somewhere deep inside of himself. He was glad it was so; otherwise, he thought he would go mad.

"Gather up and inspect the wagons!" shouted Martland. "The sooner you bestir yourselves, the sooner we can leave this accursed place! Carn, attend to Welmar. I don't like the look of that gash."

With an enormous effort of will, Roran turned and trudged across the bank to the nearest wagon. Blinking away the sweat that dripped from his brow, he saw that of their original force, only nine were still fit to stand. He pushed the observation out of his mind. *Mourn later, not now.*

As Martland Redbeard walked across the corpse-strewn encampment, a soldier who Roran had assumed was dead flipped over and, from the ground, lopped off the earl's right hand. With a movement so graceful it appeared practiced, Martland kicked the sword out of the soldier's grip, then knelt on the soldier's throat and, using his left hand, drew a dagger from his belt and stabbed the man through one of his ears, killing him. His face flushed and strained, Martland shoved the stump of his wrist under his left armpit and waved away everyone who rushed over to him. "Leave me alone! It's hardly a wound at all. Get to those wagons! Unless you wastrels hurry up, we'll be here so long, my beard will turn white as snow. Go on!" When Carn refused to budge, however, Martland scowled and shouted, "Begone with you, or I'll have you flogged for insubordination, I will!"

Carn held up Martland's wayward hand. "I might be able to re-attach it, but I'll need a few minutes."

"Ah, confound it, give me that!" exclaimed Martland, and snatched his hand away from Carn. He tucked it inside his tunic. "Stop fretting about me and save Welmar and Lindel if you can. You can try reattaching it once we've put a few leagues between us and these monsters."

"It might be too late then," said Carn.

"That was an order, spellcaster, not a request!" thundered Martland. As Carn retreated, the earl used his teeth to tie off the sleeve of his tunic over the stump of his arm, which he again stuck in his left armpit. Sweat beaded his face. "Right, then! What misbegotten items are hidden in those confounded wagons?"

"Rope!" someone shouted.

"Whiskey!" shouted someone else.

Martland grunted. "Ulhart, you record the figures for me."

Roran helped the others as they rifled through each of the wagons, calling out the contents to Ulhart. Afterward, they slaughtered the teams of oxen and lit the wagons on fire, as before. Then they rounded up their horses and mounted them, tying the injured into their saddles.

When they were ready to depart, Carn gestured toward the flare of light in the sky and murmured a long, tangled word. Night enveloped the world. Glancing up, Roran beheld a throbbing after-image of Carn's face superimposed over the faint stars, and then as he became accustomed to the darkness, he beheld the soft gray shapes of thousands of disoriented moths scattering across the sky like the shades of men's souls.

His heart heavy within him, Roran touched his heels to Snowfire's flanks and rode away from the remnants of the convoy.

✦   ✦   ✦

BLOOD ON THE ROCKS

Frustrated, Eragon stormed out of the circular chamber buried deep under the center of Tronjheim. The oak door slammed shut behind him with a hollow boom.

Eragon stood with his hands on his hips in the middle of the arched corridor outside the chamber and glared at the floor, which was tessellated with rectangles of agate and jade. Since he and Orik had arrived in Tronjheim, three days ago, the thirteen chiefs of the dwarf clans had done nothing but argue about issues that Eragon considered inconsequential, such as which clans had the right to graze their flocks in certain disputed pastures. As he listened to the clan chiefs debate obscure points of their legal code, Eragon often felt like shouting that they were being blind fools who were going to doom all of Alagaësia to Galbatorix's rule unless they put aside their petty concerns and chose a new ruler without further delay.

Still lost in thought, Eragon slowly walked down the corridor, barely noticing the four guards who followed him—as they did wherever he went—nor the dwarves he passed in the hall, who greeted him with variations of "Argetlam." *The worst one is Íorûnn*, Eragon decided. The dwarf woman was the grimstborith of Dûrgrimst Vrenshrrgn, a powerful, warlike clan, and she had made it clear, from the very beginning of the deliberations, that she intended to have the throne for herself. Only one other clan, the Urzhad, had openly pledged themselves to her cause, but as she had demonstrated on multiple occasions during the meetings between the clan chiefs, she was clever, cunning, and able to twist most any situation to her advantage. *She might make an excellent queen*, Eragon admitted to himself, *but she's so devious, it's impossible to know whether she would support the Varden once she was enthroned.* He allowed himself a wry smile. Talking with Íorûnn was always awkward for him. The dwarves considered her a great beauty, and even by the standards of humans, she cut a striking figure. Besides which, she seemed to have developed a fascination with Eragon that he was unable to fathom. In every conversation they had, she insisted upon making allusions to the dwarves' history and mythology that Eragon did not understand but that seemed to amuse Orik and the other dwarves to no end.

In addition to Íorûnn, two other clan chiefs had emerged as rivals for the throne: Gannel, chief of Dûrgrimst Quan, and Nado, chief of Dûrgrimst Knurlcarathn. As the custodians of the dwarves' religion, the Quan wielded enormous influence among their race, but so far, Gannel had obtained the support of but two other clans, Dûrgrimst Ragni Hefthyn and Dûrgrimst Ebardac—a clan primarily devoted to scholarly research. In contrast, Nado had forged a larger coalition, consisting of the clans Feldûnost, Fanghur, and Az Sweldn rak Anhûin.

Whereas Íorûnn seemed to want the throne merely for the power she would gain thereafter, and Gannel did not seem inherently hostile to the Varden—although neither was he friendly toward them—Nado was openly and vehemently opposed to any involvement with Eragon, Nasuada, the Empire, Galbatorix, Queen Islanzadí, or, so far as Eragon could tell, any living being outside of the Beor Mountains. The Knurlcarathn were the stoneworkers' clan and, in men and material goods, they had no equal, for every other clan depended upon their expertise for the tunneling and the building of their abodes, and even the Ingeitum needed them to mine the ore for their smiths. And if Nado's bid for the crown should falter, Eragon knew that many of the other, lesser clan chiefs who shared his views would leap up to take his place. Az Sweldn rak Anhûin, for example—whom Galbatorix and the Forsworn had nearly obliterated during their uprising—had declared themselves Eragon's blood enemies during his visit to the city of Tarnag and, in every action of theirs at the clanmeet, had demonstrated their implacable hatred of Eragon, Saphira, and all things to do with dragons and those who rode them. They had objected to Eragon's very presence at the meetings of the clan chiefs, even though it was perfectly legal by dwarf law, and forced a vote on the issue, thereby delaying the proceedings another six unnecessary hours.

One of these days, thought Eragon, *I will have to find a way to make peace with them. That or I'll have to finish what Galbatorix started. I refuse to live my entire life in fear of Az Sweldn rak Anhûin.* Again, as he had done so often in the past few days, he waited a moment for Saphira's response, and when it was not forthcoming, a familiar pang of unhappiness lanced his heart.

How secure the alliances between any of the clans were, however, was a question of some uncertainty. Neither Orik nor Íorûnn nor Gannel nor Nado had enough support to win a popular vote, so they were all actively engaged in trying to retain the loyalties of the clans who had already promised to help them while at the same time trying to poach their opponents' backers. Despite the importance of the process, Eragon found it exceedingly tedious and frustrating.

Based upon Orik's explanation, it was Eragon's understanding that before the clan chiefs could elect a ruler, they had to vote on whether they were *prepared* to choose a new king or queen and that the preliminary election had to garner at least nine votes in its favor if it was to pass. As of yet, none of the clan chiefs, Orik included, felt secure enough in their positions to bring the matter to a head and proceed to the final election. It was, as Orik had said, the most delicate part of the process and, in some instances, had been known to drag on for a frustratingly long time.

As he pondered the situation, Eragon wandered aimlessly through the warren of chambers below Tronjheim until he found himself in a dry, dusty room lined with five black arches on one side and a bas-relief carving of a snarling bear twenty feet high on the other. The bear had gold teeth and round, faceted rubies for eyes.

"Where are we, Kvîstor?" asked Eragon, glancing at his guards. His voice spawned hollow echoes in the room. Eragon could sense the minds of many of the dwarves in the levels above them, but he had no idea how to reach them.

The lead guard, a youngish dwarf no older than sixty, stepped forward. "These rooms were cleared millennia ago by Grimstnzborith Korgan, when Tronjheim was under construction. We have not used them much since, except when our entire race congregates in Farthen Dûr."

Eragon nodded. "Can you lead me back to the surface?"

"Of course, Argetlam."

Several minutes of brisk walking brought them to a broad staircase with shallow, dwarf-sized steps that climbed out of the ground to a passageway somewhere in the southwestern quadrant of Tronjheim's base. From there Kvîstor guided Eragon to the southern branch of the four mile-long hallways that divided Tronjheim along the cardinal compass points.

It was the same hallway through which Eragon and Saphira had first entered Tronjheim several months ago, and Eragon walked down it, toward the center of the city-mountain, with a strange sense of nostalgia. He felt as if he had aged several years in the interim.

The four-story-high avenue thronged with dwarves from every clan. All of them noticed Eragon, of that he was sure, but not all deigned to acknowledge him, for which he was grateful, as it saved him the effort of having to return even more greetings.

Eragon stiffened as he saw a line of Az Sweldn rak Anhûin cross the hallway. As one, the dwarves turned their heads and looked at him, their expressions obscured behind the purple veils those of their clan always wore in public. The last dwarf in line spat on the floor toward Eragon before filing through an archway and out of the hall along with his or her brethren.

If Saphira were here, they would not dare to be so rude, thought Eragon.

A half hour later, he reached the end of the majestic hallway, and although he had been there many times before, a sense of awe and wonder overwhelmed him as he stepped between the pillars of black onyx topped with yellow zircons thrice the size of a man and entered the circular chamber in the heart of Tronjheim.

The chamber was a thousand feet from side to side, with a floor of polished carnelian etched with a hammer surrounded by twelve pentacles, which was the crest of Dûrgrimst Ingeitum and of the dwarves' first king, Korgan, who had discovered Farthen Dûr while mining for gold. Opposite Eragon and to either side were the openings to the three other halls that radiated out through the city-mountain. The chamber had no ceiling but ascended all the way to the top of Tronjheim, a mile overhead. There it opened to the dragonhold where Eragon and Saphira had resided before Arya broke the star sapphire, and then to the sky beyond: a rich blue disk that seemed unimaginably distant, ringed as it was by the open mouth of Farthen Dûr, the hollow ten-mile-high mountain that sheltered Tronjheim from the rest of the world.

Only a scant amount of daylight filtered down to the base of Tronjheim. The City of Eternal Twilight, the elves called it. Since so little of the sun's radiance entered the city-mountain—except for a dazzling half hour before and after noon during the height of summer—the dwarves illuminated the interior with uncounted numbers of their flameless lanterns. Thousands of them were on glorious display in the chamber. A bright lantern hung from the outside of every other pillar of the curved arcades that lined each level of the city-mountain, and even more lanterns were mounted within the arcades, marking the entrances to strange and unknown rooms, as well as the path of Vol Turin, the Endless Staircase, which spiraled around the chamber from top to bottom. The effect was both moody and spectacular. The lanterns were of many different colors, making it appear as if the interior of the chamber were dotted with glowing jewels.

Their glory, however, paled beside the splendor of a real jewel, the greatest jewel of them all: Isidar Mithrim. On the floor of the chamber, the dwarves had built a wooden scaffold sixty feet in diameter, and within the enclosure of fitted oak beams, they were, piece by precious piece, reassembling the shattered star sapphire with the utmost care and delicacy. The shards they had yet to place they had stored in open-topped boxes padded with nests of raw wool, each box labeled with a line of spidery runes. The boxes were spread out across a large portion of the western side of the vast room. Perhaps three hundred dwarves sat hunched over them, intent on their work as they strove to fit the shards together into a cohesive whole. Another group bustled about the scaffolding, tending to the fragmented gem within, as well as building additional structures.

Eragon watched them at their labor for several minutes, then wandered over to the section of the floor Durza had broken when he and his Urgal warriors had entered Tronjheim from the tunnels below. With the tip of his boot, Eragon tapped the polished stone in front of him. No trace of the damage Durza had wrought remained. The dwarves had done a marvelous job of erasing the marks left by the Battle of Farthen Dûr, although Eragon hoped they would commemorate the battle with a memorial of some sort, for he felt it was important that future generations not forget the cost in blood the dwarves and the Varden had paid during the course of their struggle against Galbatorix.

As Eragon walked toward the scaffolding, he nodded at Skeg, who was standing on a platform overlooking the star sapphire. Eragon had met the thin, quick-fingered dwarf before. Skeg was of Dûrgrimst Gedthrall, and it was to him King Hrothgar had entrusted the restoration of the dwarves' most valuable treasure.

Skeg gestured for Eragon to climb up onto the platform. A sparkling vista of slanting, needle-sharp spires, glittering, paper-thin edges, and rippling surfaces confronted Eragon as he heaved himself onto the rough-hewn planks. The top of the star sapphire reminded him of the ice on the Anora River in Palancar Valley at the end of winter, when the ice had melted and refrozen multiple times and was treacherous to walk over, on account of the bumps and ridges the swings in temperature had cast up. Only instead of blue, white, or clear, the remnants of the star sapphire were a soft, rosy pink, shot through with traces of dusky orange.

"How goes it?" asked Eragon.

Skeg shrugged and fluttered his hands in the air like a pair of butterflies. "It goes as it does, Argetlam. You cannot hurry perfection."

"It looks to me as if you are making quick progress."

With a bony forefinger, Skeg tapped the side of his broad, flat nose. "The top of Isidar Mithrim, what is now the bottom, Arya broke it into large pieces, which are easy to fit together. The bottom of Isidar Mithrim, though, what is now the top . . ." Skeg shook his head, his lined face doleful. "The force of the break, all the pieces pushing against the face of the gem, pushing away from Arya and the dragon Saphira, pushing down toward you and that black-hearted Shade . . . it cracked the petals of the rose into ever-smaller fragments. And the rose, Argetlam, the rose is the key to the gem. It is the most complex, the most beautiful part of Isidar Mithrim. And it is in the most pieces. Unless we can reassemble it, every last speck where it ought to be, we might as well give the gem to our jewelers and have them grind it into rings for our mothers." The words spilled out of Skeg like water from an overflowing beaker. He shouted in Dwarvish at a dwarf carrying a box across the chamber, then tugged at his white beard and asked, "Have you ever heard recounted, Argetlam, the tale of how Isidar Mithrim was carved, in the Age of Herran?"

Eragon hesitated, thinking back to his history lessons in Ellesméra. "I know it was Dûrok who carved it."

"Aye," said Skeg, "it was Dûrok Ornthrond—Eagle-eye, as you say in this tongue. It was not he who discovered Isidar Mithrim, but it was he alone who extracted it from the surrounding stone, he who carved it, and he who polished it. Fifty-seven years he spent working on the Star Rose. The gem enthralled him as nothing else.

Every night he sat crouched over Isidar Mithrim until the wee hours of the morning, as he was determined that the Star Rose should be not just art but something that would touch the hearts of all who gazed upon it and would earn him a seat of honor at the table of the gods. His devotion was such that, in the thirty-second year of his labors, when his wife told him that either he had to share the burden of the project with his apprentices or she would leave his hall, Dûrok said not a word but turned his shoulder to her and continued grinding the contours of the petal he had begun earlier that year.

"Dûrok worked on Isidar Mithrim until he was pleased with its every line and curve. Then he dropped his polishing cloth, took one step back from the Star Rose, said, 'Gûntera, protect me; it is done,' and fell dead on the floor." Skeg tapped his chest, producing a hollow thump. "His heart gave out, for what else did he have to live for? . . . That is what we are trying to reconstruct, Argetlam: fifty-seven years of ceaseless concentration by one of the finest artists our race has known. Unless we can put Isidar Mithrim back together *exactly* the way it was, we shall diminish Dûrok's accomplishment for all who have yet to see the Star Rose." Knotting his right hand into a fist, Skeg bounced it off his thigh to emphasize his words.

Eragon leaned against the hip-high railing in front of him and watched as five dwarves on the opposite side of the gem lowered a sixth dwarf, who was bound in a rope harness, until he hung inches above the sharp edges of the fractured sapphire. Reaching inside his tunic, the suspended dwarf removed a sliver of Isidar Mithrim from a leather wallet and, grasping the sliver with a minuscule set of pincers, fit it into a small gap in the gem below.

"If the coronation were held three days from now," said Eragon, "could you have Isidar Mithrim ready by then?"

Skeg drummed the railing with all ten of his fingers, tapping out a melody Eragon failed to recognize. The dwarf said, "We would not rush so with Isidar Mithrim if not for the offer of your dragon. This haste is foreign to us, Argetlam. It is not our nature, as it is humans', to rush about like agitated ants. Still, we shall do our best to have Isidar Mithrim ready in time for the coronation. If that should be three days from now . . . well, I should not be too hopeful of our prospects. But if it were later in the week, I think we might be finished."

Eragon thanked Skeg for his prediction, then took his leave. With his guards trailing after him, Eragon walked to one of the many common eating halls in the city-mountain, a long, low room with stone tables arranged in rows on one side and dwarves busying themselves about soapstone ovens on the other.

There Eragon dined on sourdough bread, fish with white meat that the dwarves caught in underground lakes, mushrooms, and some sort of mashed tuber that he had eaten before in Tronjheim but whose provenance he had yet to learn. Before he began eating, though, he was careful to test the food for poison, using the spells Oromis had taught him.

As Eragon washed down the last crust of bread with a sip of thin, watered-down breakfast beer, Orik and his contingent of ten warriors entered the hall. The warriors sat at their own tables, positioning themselves where they could watch both entrances, while Orik joined Eragon, lowering himself onto the stone bench opposite him with a weary sigh. He placed his elbows on the table and rubbed his face with his hands.

Eragon cast several spells to prevent anyone from eavesdropping, then asked, "Did we suffer another setback?"

"No, no setback. Only, these deliberations are trying in the extreme."

"I noticed."

"And everyone noticed your frustration," said Orik. "You must control yourself better hereafter, Eragon. Revealing weakness of any sort to our opponents does nothing but further their cause. I—" Orik fell silent as a portly dwarf waddled up and deposited a plate of steaming food in front of him.

Eragon scowled at the edge of the table. "But are you any closer to the throne? Have we gained any ground with all of this long-winded prattle?"

Orik raised a finger while he chewed on a mouthful of bread. "We have gained a great deal. Do not be so gloomy! After you left, Havard agreed to lower the tax on the salt Dûrgrimst Fanghur sells to the Ingeitum, in exchange for summer access to our tunnel to Nalsvrid-mérna, so they may hunt the red deer that gather around the lake during the warm months of the year. You should have seen how Nado gritted his teeth when Havard accepted my offer!"

"Bah," spat Eragon. "Taxes, deer—what does any of it have to do with who succeeds Hrothgar as ruler? Be honest with me, Orik. What is your position compared with the other clan chiefs? And how much longer is this likely to drag on? With every day that passes, it becomes more likely that the Empire will discover our ruse and Galbatorix will strike at the Varden when I am not there to fend off Murtagh and Thorn."

Orik wiped his mouth on the corner of the tablecloth. "My position is sound enough. None of the grimstborithn have the support to call a vote, but Nado and I command the greatest followings. If either of us can win over, say, another two or three clans, the balance will quickly tip in that person's favor. Havard is already wavering. It won't take too much more encouragement, I think, to convince him to defect to our camp. Tonight we will break bread with him, and I will see what I can do toward providing that encouragement." Orik devoured a piece of roast mushroom, then said, "As for when the clanmeet will end, maybe after another week if we are lucky, and maybe two if we're not."

Eragon cursed in an undertone. He was so tense, his stomach churned and rumbled and threatened to reject the meal he had just eaten.

Reaching across the table, Orik caught Eragon by the wrist. "There is nothing you or I can do to further hasten the clanmeet's decision, so do not let it upset you overmuch. Worry about what you can change, and leave the rest to sort itself out, eh?" He released Eragon.

Eragon slowly exhaled and leaned on his forearms against the table. "I know. It's only that we have so little time, and if we fail . . ."

"What will be will be," said Orik. He smiled, but his eyes were sad and hollow. "No one can escape fate's design."

"Couldn't you seize the throne by force? I know you don't have that many troops in Tronjheim, but with my support, who could stand against you?"

Orik paused with his knife halfway between his plate and his mouth, then shook his head and resumed eating. Between mouthfuls, he said, "Such a ploy would prove disastrous."

"Why?"

"Must I explain? Our entire race would turn against us, and instead of seizing control of our nation, I would inherit an empty title. If that came to pass, I would not bet a broken sword we would live to see out the year."

"Ah."

Orik said nothing more until the food on his plate was gone. Then he downed a mouthful of beer, belched, and resumed the conversation: "We are balanced upon a windy mountain path with a mile-high drop on either side. So many of my race hate and fear Dragon Riders because of the crimes Galbatorix, the Forsworn, and now Murtagh have committed against us. And so many of them fear the world beyond the mountains and the tunnels and caverns wherein we hide." He turned his mug around on the table. "Nado and Az Sweldn rak Anhûin are only worsening the situation. They play upon people's fears and poison their minds against you, the Varden, and King Orrin. . . . Az Sweldn rak Anhûin is the epitome of what we must overcome if I am to be king. Somehow we must needs find a way to allay their concerns and the concerns of those like them, for even if I am king, I will have to give them a fair hearing if I am to retain the support of the clans. A dwarf king or queen is always at the mercy of the clans, no matter how strong a ruler they may be, just as the grimstborithn are at the mercy of the families of their clan." Tilting back his head, Orik drained the last of the beer from his mug, then set it down with a sharp clack.

"Is there anything I could do, any custom or ceremony of yours I could perform, that would appease Vermûnd and his followers?" asked Eragon, naming the current grimstborith of Az Sweldn rak Anhûin. "There must be *something* I can do to put their suspicions to rest and bring this feud to an end."

Orik laughed and stood from the table. "You could die."

Early the next morning, Eragon sat with his back against the curved wall of the round room set deep below the center of Tronjheim, along with a select group of warriors, advisers, servants, and family members of the clan chiefs who were privileged enough to attend the clanmeet. The clan chiefs themselves were seated in heavy, carved chairs arranged around the edge of a circular table, which like most objects of note in the lower levels of the city-mountain bore the crest of Korgan and the Ingeitum.

At the moment, Gáldhiem, grimstborith of Dûrgrimst Feldûnost, was speaking. He was short, even for a dwarf—hardly more than two feet in height—and wore patterned robes of gold, russet, and midnight blue. Unlike the dwarves of the Ingeitum, he did not trim or braid his beard, and it tumbled across his chest like a tangled bramble. Standing on the seat of his chair, he pounded the polished table with his gloved fist and roared, ". . . Eta! Narho ûdim etal os isû vond! Narho ûdim etal os formvn mendûnost brakn, az Varden, hrestvog dûr grimstnzhadn! Az Jurgenvren qathrid né dômar oen etal—"

". . . No," Eragon's translator, a dwarf named Hûndfast, whispered in his ear. "I will not let that happen. I will not let these beardless fools, the Varden, destroy our country. The Dragon War left us weak and not—"

Eragon stifled a yawn, bored. He allowed his gaze to drift around the granite table, from Gáldhiem to Nado, a round-faced dwarf with flaxen hair who was nodding with approval at Gáldhiem's thundering speech; to Havard, who was using a dagger to clean under the fingernails of the two remaining fingers on his right hand; to Vermûnd, heavy-browed but otherwise inscrutable behind his purple veil; to Gannel and Ûndin, who sat leaning toward each other, whispering, while Hadfala, an elderly dwarf woman who was the clan chief of Dûrgrimst Ebardac and the third member of Gannel's alliance, frowned at the sheaf of rune-covered parchment she brought with her to every meeting; and then to the chief of Dûrgrimst Ledwonnû, Manndrâth, who sat in profile to Eragon, displaying his long, drooping nose to good effect; to Thordris, grimstborith of Dûrgrimst Nagra, of whom he could see little but her wavy auburn hair, which fell past her shoulders and lay coiled on the floor in a braid twice as long as she was tall; to the back of Orik's head as he slouched to one side in his chair; to Freowin, grimstborith of Dûrgrimst Gedthrall, an immensely corpulent dwarf who kept his eyes fixed upon the block of wood he was busy carving into the likeness of a hunched raven; and then to Hreidamar, grimstborith of Dûrgrimst Urzhad, who, in contrast with Freowin, was fit and compact, with corded forearms, and who wore a mail hauberk and helm to every gathering; and finally to Íorûnn, she of the nut-brown skin marred only by a thin, crescent-shaped scar high upon her left cheekbone, she of the satin-bright hair bound underneath a silver helm wrought in the shape of a snarling wolf's head, she of the vermilion dress and the necklace of flashing emeralds set in squares of gold carved with lines of arcane runes.

Íorûnn noticed Eragon looking at her. A lazy smile appeared on her lips. With voluptuous ease, she winked at Eragon, obscuring one of her almond-shaped eyes for a pair of heartbeats.

Eragon's cheeks stung as blood suffused them, and the tips of his ears burned. He shifted his gaze and returned it to Gáldhiem, who was still busy pontificating, his chest puffed out like that of a strutting pigeon.

As Orik had asked, Eragon remained impassive throughout the meeting, concealing his reactions from those who were watching. When the clanmeet broke for their midday meal, he hastened over to Orik and, bending so that no one else could hear, said, "Do not look for me at your table. I have had my fill of sitting and talking. I am going to explore the tunnels for a bit."

Orik nodded, appearing distracted, and murmured in reply, "Do as you wish, only be sure you are here when we resume; it would not be meet for you to play truant, no matter how tedious these talks be."

"As you say."

Eragon edged out of the conference room, along with the press of dwarves eager to have their lunches, and rejoined his four guards in the hallway outside, where they had been playing dice with idle warriors from other clans. With his guards in tow, Eragon struck out in a random direction, allowing his feet to carry him where they would while he pondered methods of welding the dwarves' contentious factions into a whole united against Galbatorix. To his exasperation, the only methods he could envision were so far-fetched, it was absurd to imagine they might succeed.

Eragon paid little attention to the dwarves he met in the tunnels—aside from mumbled greetings that courtesy occasionally demanded—nor even to his exact surroundings, trusting that Kvîstor could guide him back to the conference room. Although Eragon did not study his surroundings in any great detail visually, he kept track of the minds of every living creature he was able to sense within a radius of several hundred feet, even down to the smallest spider crouched behind its web in the corner of a room, for Eragon had no desire to be surprised by anyone who might have cause to seek him out.

When at last he stopped, he was surprised to find himself in the same dusty room he had discovered during his wanderings the previous day. There to his left were the same five black arches that led to caverns unknown, while there to his right was the same bas-relief carving of the head and shoulders of a snarling bear. Bemused by the coincidence, Eragon sauntered over to the bronze sculpture and gazed up at the bear's gleaming fangs, wondering what had drawn him back.

After a moment, he went to the middle of the five archways and gazed through it. The narrow hallway beyond was devoid of lanterns and soon faded into the soft oblivion of shadow. Reaching out with his consciousness, Eragon probed the length of the tunnel and several of the abandoned chambers it opened to. A half-dozen spiders and a sparse collection of moths, millipedes, and blind crickets were the only inhabitants. "Hello!" called Eragon, and listened as the hall returned his voice to him with ever-decreasing volume. "Kvîstor," said Eragon, looking at him, "does no one at all live in these ancient parts?"

The fresh-faced dwarf answered, "Some do. A few strange knurlan, those to whom empty solitude is more pleasing than the touch of their wife's hand or the sound of their friends' voices. It was one such knurlag who warned us of the approach of the Urgal army, if you remember, Argetlam. Also, although we do not speak of it often, there are those who have broken the laws of our land and whom their clan chiefs have banished on pain of death for a term of years or, if the offense is severe, for the remainder of their lives. All such are as the walking dead to us; we shun them if we meet them outside of our lands and hang them if we catch them within our borders."

When Kvîstor had finished speaking, Eragon indicated that he was ready to leave. Kvîstor took the lead, and Eragon followed him out the doorway through which they had entered, the three other dwarves close behind. They had gone no more than twenty feet when Eragon heard a faint scuffing from the rear, so faint Kvîstor did not seem to notice.

Eragon glanced back. By the amber light cast by the flameless lanterns mounted on either side of the passageway, he saw seven dwarves garbed entirely in black, their faces masked with dark cloth and their feet muffled with rags, running toward his group with a speed that Eragon had assumed was the sole province of elves, Shades, and other creatures whose blood hummed with magic. In their right hands, the dwarves held long, sharp daggers with pale blades that flickered with prismatic colors, while in their left, each carried a metal buckler with a sharpened spike protruding from the boss. Their minds, like those of the Ra'zac, were hidden from Eragon.

Saphira! was Eragon's first thought. Then he remembered he was alone.

Twisting to face the black-garbed dwarves, Eragon reached for the hilt of his falchion while opening his mouth to shout a warning.

He was too late.

As the first word rang in his throat, three of the strange dwarves grabbed the hindmost of Eragon's guards and lifted their glimmering daggers to stab him. Faster than speech or conscious thought, Eragon plunged his whole being into the flow of magic and, without relying upon the ancient language to structure his spell, rewove the fabric of the world into a pattern more pleasing to him. The three guards who stood between him and the attackers flew toward him, as if yanked by invisible strings, and landed upon their feet beside him, unharmed but disoriented.

Eragon winced at the sudden decrease in his strength.

Two of the black-garbed dwarves rushed him, stabbing at his belly with their blood-hungry daggers. Sword in hand, Eragon parried both blows, stunned by the dwarves' speed and ferocity. One of his guards leaped forward, shouting and swinging his ax at the would-be assassins. Before Eragon could grab the dwarf's hauberk and yank him back to safety, a white blade, writhing as with spectral flame, pierced the dwarf's corded neck. As the dwarf fell, Eragon glimpsed his contorted face and was shocked to see Kvîstor—and that his throat was glowing molten red as it disintegrated around the dagger.

I can't let them so much as scratch me, Eragon thought.

Enraged by Kvîstor's death, Eragon stabbed at his killer so quickly, the black-garbed dwarf had no opportunity to evade the blow and dropped lifeless at Eragon's feet.

With all his strength, Eragon shouted, "Stay behind me!"

Thin cracks split the floors and walls, and flakes of stone fell from the ceiling as his voice reverberated through the corridor. The attacking dwarves faltered at the unbridled power of his voice, then resumed their offensive.

Eragon retreated several yards to give himself room to maneuver free of the corpses and settled into a low crouch, waving the falchion to and fro, like a snake preparing to strike. His heart was racing at twice its normal rate, and although the fight had just begun, he was already gasping for breath.

The hallway was eight feet wide, which was wide enough for three of his six remaining enemies to attack him at once. They spread out, two attempting to flank him on the right and the left, while the third charged straight at him, slashing with frenzied speed at Eragon's arms and legs.

Afraid to duel with the dwarves as he would have if they wielded normal blades, Eragon drove his legs against the floor and jumped up and forward. He spun halfway around and struck the ceiling feet-first. He pushed off, spun halfway around again, and landed on his hands and feet a yard behind the three dwarves. Even as they whirled toward him, he stepped forward and beheaded the lot of them with a single backhand blow.

Their daggers clattered against the floor an instant before their heads.

Leaping over their truncated bodies, Eragon twisted in midair and landed on the spot he had started from.

He was not a moment too soon.

A breath of wind tickled his neck as the tip of a dagger whipped past his throat. Another blade tugged at the cuff of his leggings, cutting them open. He flinched and swung the falchion, trying to gain space to fight. *My wards should have turned their blades away!* he thought, bewildered.

An involuntary cry escaped his throat as his foot struck a patch of slick blood and he lost his balance and toppled over backward.

With a sickening crunch, his head collided with the stone floor. Blue lights flashed before his eyes. He gasped.

His three remaining guards sprang over him and swung their axes in unison, clearing the air above Eragon and saving him from the bite of the flashing daggers.

That was all the time Eragon needed to recover. He flipped upright and, berating himself for not trying this sooner, shouted a spell laced with nine of the twelve death-words Oromis had taught him. However, the moment after he loosed his magic he abandoned the spell, for the black-garbed dwarves were protected by numerous wards. Given a few minutes, he might have been able to evade or defeat the wards, but minutes might as well have been days in a battle such as theirs, where every second was as long as an hour. Having failed with magic, Eragon hardened his thoughts into an iron-hard spear and launched it at where the consciousness of one of the black-garbed dwarves ought to be. The spear skated off mental armor of a sort Eragon had not encountered before: smooth and seamless, seemingly unbroken by the concerns natural to mortal creatures engaged in a struggle to the death.

Someone else is protecting them, Eragon realized. *There are more behind this attack than just these seven.*

Pivoting on one foot, Eragon lunged forward and with his falchion impaled his leftmost attacker in a knee, drawing blood. The dwarf stumbled, and Eragon's guards converged upon him, grasping the dwarf's arms so he could not swing his dire blade and hacking at him with their curved axes.

The nearest of the last two attackers raised his shield in anticipation of the blow Eragon was about to direct at him. Summoning the full measure of his might, Eragon cut at the shield, intending to shear it and the arm underneath in half, as he had often done with Zar'roc. In the fever of battle, though, he forgot to account for the dwarf's inexplicable speed. As the falchion neared its target, the dwarf tilted his shield, so as to deflect the blow to the side.

Two plumes of sparks erupted from the surface of the shield as the falchion glanced off the upper part and then the steel spike mounted in the center. Momentum carried the falchion farther than Eragon had intended, and it continued flying through the air until it struck edge-first against a wall, jarring Eragon's arm. With a crystalline sound, the blade of the falchion shattered into a dozen pieces, leaving him with a six-inch spike of jagged metal protruding from the hilt.

Dismayed, Eragon dropped the broken sword and gripped the rim of the dwarf's buckler, wresting with him back and forth and struggling to keep the shield between him and the dagger graced with a halo of translucent colors. The dwarf was incredibly tough; he matched Eragon's efforts and even succeeded in pushing him back a step. Releasing the buckler with his right hand but still holding on with his left, Eragon drew back his arm and struck the shield as hard as he could, punching through the tempered steel as easily as if it were made of rotten wood. Because of the calluses on his knuckles, he felt no pain from the impact.

The force of the blow threw the dwarf against the opposite wall. His head lolling upon a boneless neck, the dwarf dropped to the ground, like a puppet whose strings had been severed.

Eragon pulled his hand back through the jagged hole in the shield, scratching himself on the torn metal, and drew his hunting knife.

Then the last of the black-garbed dwarves was upon him. Eragon parried his dagger twice . . . thrice . . . and then cut through the dwarf's padded sleeve and scored his dagger arm from the elbow to the wrist. The dwarf hissed with pain, blue eyes furious above his cloth mask. He initiated a series of blows, the dagger whistling through the air faster than the eye could follow, which forced Eragon to hop away to avoid the deadly edge. The dwarf pressed the attack. For several yards, Eragon succeeded in evading him, until his heel struck a body and, in attempting to step around it, he stumbled and fell against a wall, bruising his shoulder.

With an evil laugh, the dwarf pounced, stabbing downward

453

toward Eragon's exposed chest. Throwing up an arm in a futile attempt to protect himself, Eragon rolled farther down the hallway, knowing that this time his luck had run out and he would not be able to escape.

As he completed a revolution and his face was momentarily turned toward the dwarf again, Eragon glimpsed the pale dagger descending toward his flesh, like a bolt of lightning from on high. Then, to his astonishment, the tip of the dagger caught on one of the flameless lanterns mounted on the wall. Eragon whirled away before he could see more, but an instant later, a burning hot hand seemed to strike him from behind, throwing him a good twenty feet through the hall, until he fetched up against the edge of an open archway, instantly accumulating a new collection of scrapes and bruises. A booming report deafened him. Feeling as if someone were driving splinters into his eardrums, Eragon clapped his hands over his ears and curled into a ball, howling.

When the noise and the pain had subsided, he lowered his hands and staggered to his feet, clenching his teeth as his injuries announced their presence with a myriad of unpleasant sensations. Groggy and confused, he gazed upon the site of the explosion.

The blast had blackened a ten-foot length of the hallway with soot. Soft flakes of ash tumbled through the air, which was as hot as the air from a heated forge. The dwarf who had been about to strike Eragon lay on the ground, thrashing, his body covered with burns. After a few more convulsions, he grew still. Eragon's three remaining guards lay at the edge of the soot, where the explosion had thrown them. Even as he watched, they staggered upright, blood dripping from their ears and gaping mouths, their beards singed and in disarray. The links along the fringe of their hauberks glowed red, but their leather under-armor seemed to have protected them from the worst of the heat.

Eragon took a single step forward, then stopped and groaned as a patch of agony bloomed between his shoulder blades. He tried to twist his arm around to feel the extent of the wound, but as his skin stretched, the pain became too great to continue. Nearly losing consciousness, he leaned against the wall for support. He glanced at the burnt dwarf again. *I must have suffered similar injuries on my back.*

Forcing himself to concentrate, he recited two of the spells designed to heal burns that Brom had taught him during their travels. As they took effect, it felt as if cool, soothing water were flowing across his back. He sighed with relief and straightened.

"Are you hurt?" he asked as his guards hobbled over.

The lead dwarf frowned, tapped his right ear, and shook his head.

Eragon muttered a curse and only then did he notice he could not hear his own voice. Again drawing upon the reserves of energy within his body, he cast a spell to repair the inner mechanisms of his ears and of theirs. As the incantation concluded, an irritating itch squirmed inside his ears, then faded along with the spell.

"Are you hurt?"

The dwarf on the right, a burly fellow with a forked beard, coughed and spat out a glob of congealed blood, then growled, "Nothing that time won't mend. What of you, Shadeslayer?"

"I'll live."

Testing the floor with every step, Eragon entered the soot-blackened area and knelt beside Kvîstor, hoping that he might still save the dwarf from the clutches of death. As soon as he beheld Kvîstor's wound again, he knew it was not to be.

Eragon bowed his head, the memory of recent and former bloodshed bitter to his soul. He stood. "Why did the lantern explode?"

"They are filled with heat and light, Argetlam," one of his guards replied. "If they are broken, all of it escapes at once and then it is better to be far away."

Gesturing at the crumpled corpses of their attackers, Eragon asked, "Do you know of which clan they are?"

The dwarf with the forked beard rifled through the clothes of several of the black-garbed dwarves, then said, "Barzûl! They carry no marks upon them such as you would recognize, Argetlam, but they carry this." He held up a bracelet made of braided horsehair set with polished cabochons of amethyst.

"What does it mean?"

"This amethyst," said the dwarf, and tapped one of the cabochons with a soot-streaked fingernail, "this particular variety of amethyst, it grows in only four parts of the Beor Mountains, and three of them belong to Az Sweldn rak Anhûin."

Eragon frowned. "Grimstborith Vermûnd ordered this attack?"

"I cannot say for sure, Argetlam. Another clan might have left the bracelet for us to find. They might want us to think it was Az Sweldn rak Anhûin so we do not realize who our foes really are. But . . . if I had to wager, Argetlam, I would wager a cartload of gold that it is Az Sweldn rak Anhûin who is responsible."

"Blast them," Eragon murmured. "Whoever it was, blast them." He clenched his fists to stop them from shaking. With the side of his boot, he nudged one of the prismatic daggers the assassins had wielded. "The spells on these weapons and on the . . . on the men"—he motioned with his chin—"men, dwarves, be as it may, they must have required an incredible amount of energy, and I cannot even imagine how complex their wording was. Casting them would have been hard and dangerous. . . ." Eragon looked at each of his guards in turn and said, "As you are my witnesses, I swear I shall not let this attack, nor Kvîstor's death, go unpunished. Whichever clan or clans sent these dung-faced killers, when I learn their names, they will wish they had never thought to strike at me and, by striking at me, strike at Dûrgrimst Ingeitum. This I swear to you, as a Dragon Rider and as a fellow member of Dûrgrimst Ingeitum, and if any ask you of it, repeat my promise to them as I have given it to you."

The dwarves bowed before him, and he with the forked beard replied, "As you command, so we shall obey, Argetlam. You honor Hrothgar's memory by your words."

Then another of the dwarves said, "Whichever clan it was, they have violated the law of hospitality; they have attacked a guest.

They are not even so high as rats; they are *menknurlan*." He spat on the floor, and the other dwarves spat with him.

Eragon walked to where the remains of his falchion lay. He knelt in the soot and, with the tip of a finger, touched one of the pieces of metal, tracing its ragged edges. *I must have hit the shield and the wall so hard, I overwhelmed the spells I used to reinforce the steel,* he thought.

Then he thought, *I need a sword.*

I need a Rider's sword.

A MATTER OF PERSPECTIVE

The wind-of-morning-heat-above-flat-land, which was different from the wind-of-morning-heat-above-hills, shifted.

Saphira adjusted the angle of her wings to compensate for the changes in the speed and pressure of the air that supported her weight thousands of feet above the sun-bathed land below. She closed her double eyelids for a moment, luxuriating in the soft bed of the wind, as well as the warmth of the morning rays beating down upon her sinewy length. She imagined how the light must make her scales sparkle and how those who saw her circling in the sky must marvel at the sight, and she hummed with pleasure, content in the knowledge that she was the most beautiful creature in Alagaësia, for who could hope to match the glory of her scales; and her long, tapering tail; and her wings, so fair and well formed; and her curved claws; and her long white fangs, with which she could sever the neck of a wild ox with a single bite? Not Glaedr-of-the-gold-scales, who had lost a leg during the fall of the Riders. Nor could Thorn or Shruikan, for they were both slaves to Galbatorix, and their forced servitude had twisted their minds. A dragon who was not free to do as he or she wished was not a dragon at all. Besides, they were males, and while males might appear majestic, they could not embody the beauty she did. No, she was the most stunning creature in Alagaësia, and that was as it should be.

Saphira wriggled with satisfaction all the way from the base of her head to the tip of her tail. Today was a perfect day. The heat of the sun made her feel as if she were lying in a nest of coals. Her belly was full, the sky was clear, and there was nothing she needed to attend to, besides watching for foes who might wish to fight, which she did anyway, as a matter of habit.

Her happiness had only one flaw, but it was a profound flaw, and the longer she considered it, the more discontented she grew, until she realized she was no longer satisfied; she wished Eragon were there to share the day with her. She growled and loosed a brief jet of blue flame from between her jaws, searing the air in front of her, then constricted her throat, cutting off the stream of liquid fire. Her tongue tingled from the flames that had run over it. When was Eragon, partner-of-her-mind-and-heart-Eragon, going to contact Nasuada from Tronjheim and ask for her, Saphira, to join him? She had urged him to obey Nasuada and travel to the mountains-higher-than-she-could-fly, but now too long had passed, and Saphira felt cold and empty in her gut.

There is a shadow in the world, she thought. *That is what has upset me. Something is wrong with Eragon. He is in danger, or he was in danger recently. And I cannot help him.* She was not a wild dragon. Since she had hatched, she had shared her entire life with Eragon, and without him, she was only half herself. If he died because she was not there to protect him, she would have no reason to continue living, save for revenge. She knew she would tear his killers apart and then she would fly on the black city of the egg-breaker-traitor who had kept her imprisoned for so many decades, and she would do her best to slay him, no matter that it would mean certain death for her.

Saphira growled again and snapped at a tiny sparrow that was foolish enough to fly within range of her teeth. She missed, and the sparrow darted past and continued on its way unmolested, which only exacerbated her foul mood. For a moment, she considered chasing the sparrow but then decided it was not worth bothering herself over such an inconsequential speck of bones and feathers. It would not even make a good snack.

Tilting on the wind and swinging her tail in the opposite direction to facilitate her turn, she wheeled around, studying the ground far below and all the small scurrying things that strove to hide from her hunter's eyes. Even from her height of thousands of feet, she could count the number of feathers on the back of a chicken hawk that was skimming the fields of planted wheat west of the Jiet River. She could see the blur of brown fur as a rabbit dashed to the safety of its warren. She could pick out the small herd of deer cowering underneath the branches of the currant bushes clustered along a tributary of the Jiet River. And she could hear the high-pitched squeaks of frightened animals warning their brethren of her presence. Their wavering cries gratified her; it was only right that her food should fear her. If ever she should fear it, she would know it was her time to die.

A league farther upstream, the Varden were packed against the Jiet River like a herd of red deer against the edge of a cliff. The Varden had arrived at the crossing yesterday, and since then, perhaps a third of the men-who-were-friends and the Urgals-who-were-friends and the horses-she-must-not-eat had forded the river. The army moved so slowly, she sometimes wondered how humans ever had time to do anything other than travel, considering how short their lives were. *It would be much more convenient if they could fly*, she thought, and wondered why they did not choose to. Flying was so easy, it never ceased to puzzle her why any creature would remain earthbound. Even Eragon retained his attachment to the soft-hard-ground, when she knew he could join her in the sky at any time merely by uttering a few words in the ancient language. But then, she did not always understand the actions of those who tottered about on two legs, whether they had round ears, pointed ears, or horns or were so short she could squash them under her feet.

A flicker of movement to the northeast caught her attention, and she angled toward it, curious. She saw a line of five-and-forty weary horses trudging toward the Varden. Most of the horses were riderless; therefore, it did not occur to her until another half hour had elapsed and she could make out the faces of the men in the saddles that the group might be Roran's returning from their raid. She wondered what had happened to so reduce their numbers and felt a momentary twinge of unease. She was not bonded to Roran, but Eragon cared for him, and that was reason enough for her to worry about his well-being.

Pushing her consciousness down toward the disorganized Varden, she searched until she found the music of Arya's mind, and once the elf acknowledged her and allowed access to her thoughts, Saphira said, *Roran shall be here by late afternoon. However, his company is sore diminished. Some great evil befell them this trip.*

Thank you, Saphira, said Arya. *I shall inform Nasuada.*

As Saphira withdrew from Arya's mind, she felt the questing touch of black-blue-wolf-hair-Blödhgarm. *I am not a hatchling,* she snapped. *You need not check on my health every few minutes.*

You have my most humble apologies, Bjartskular, only you have been gone for quite some time now, and if any are watching, they will begin to wonder why you and—

Yes, I know, she growled. Shortening her wingspan, she tilted downward, the sensation of weight leaving her, and gyrated in slow spirals as she dove toward the turgid river. *I shall be there shortly.*

A thousand feet above the water, she flared her wings and felt the strain in her flight membranes as the wind pressed against them with immense force. She slowed to a near standstill, then spilled air from her wings and accelerated once more, gliding to within a hundred feet of the brown not-good-to-drink-water. With an occasional flap to maintain her altitude, she flew up the Jiet River, alert for the sudden changes of pressure that plagued cool-air-above-flowing-water and that could push her in an unexpected direction or, worse, into sharp-pointy-trees or the break-bone-ground.

She swept high above the Varden gathered next to the river, high enough that her arrival would not unduly frighten the silly horses. Then, drifting downward upon still wings, she landed in a clearing among the tents—a clearing Nasuada had ordered set aside just for her—and crawled through the camp to Eragon's empty tent, where Blödhgarm and the eleven other elves he commanded were waiting for her. She greeted them with a blink of her eyes and a flick of her tongue and then curled up in front of Eragon's tent, resigned to dozing and waiting for dark as she would if Eragon were actually in the tent and he and she were flying missions at night. It was dull, tedious work, lying there day after day, but it was necessary in order to maintain the deception that Eragon was still with the Varden, so Saphira did not complain, even if after twelve or more hours spent on the rough-hard-ground dirtying her scales, she felt like fighting a thousand soldiers, or razing a forest with tooth and claw and fire, or leaping up and flying until she could fly no more or until she reached the end of earth, water, and air.

Growling to herself, she kneaded the ground with her claws, softening it, then lay her head across her forelegs and closed her inner eyelids so she could rest and still watch those who walked by. A dragonfly buzzed over her head, and not for the first time she wondered what could have possibly inspired some feebleminded runtling to name the insect after her race. *It looks nothing like a dragon*, she grumbled, then drifted off into a light sleep.

The big-round-fire-in-the-sky was close to the horizon when Saphira heard the shouts and cries of welcome that meant Roran and his fellow warriors had reached the camp. She roused herself. As he had before, Blödhgarm half sang, half whispered a spell that created an insubstantial likeness of Eragon, which the elf caused to walk out of the tent and climb onto Saphira's back, where it sat looking around in a perfect imitation of independent life. Visually, the apparition was flawless, but it had no mind of its own, and if any of Galbatorix's agents tried to eavesdrop upon Eragon's thoughts, they would discover the deceit forthwith. Therefore, the success of the ploy depended upon Saphira ferrying the apparition through the camp and out of sight as quickly as possible, and upon the hope that Eragon's reputation was so formidable, it would discourage clandestine observers from attempting to glean information about the Varden from his consciousness, for fear of his vengeance.

Saphira started up and bounded through the camp, the twelve elves running in formation around her. Men leaped out of their path, shouting, "Hail, Shadeslayer!" and "Hail, Saphira!" which kindled a warm glow in her belly.

When she arrived at Nasuada's folded-wing-red-butterfly-chrysalis-tent, she crouched and stuck her head inside the dark gap along one wall, where Nasuada's guards had pulled aside a panel of fabric to allow her access. Blödhgarm resumed his soft singing then, and the Eragon-wraith climbed down off Saphira, entered the crimson tent, and, once it was out of sight of the gawking onlookers outside, dissolved into nothingness.

"Do you think our ruse was discovered?" Nasuada asked from her high-backed chair.

Blödhgarm bowed with an elegant gesture. "Again, Lady Nasuada, I cannot say for sure. We will have to wait and see if the Empire moves to take advantage of Eragon's absence before we will know the answer to that question."

"Thank you, Blödhgarm. That will be all."

With another bow, the elf withdrew from the tent and took up a position several yards behind Saphira, guarding her flank.

Saphira settled down onto her underside and began to lick clean the scales around the third claw on her left forefoot, between which there had accumulated unsightly lines of the dry white clay she remembered standing in when she ate her last kill.

Not a minute later, Martland Redbeard, Roran, and a man-with-round-ears, whom she did not recognize, entered the red tent and bowed to Nasuada. Saphira paused in her cleaning to taste the air with her tongue and discerned the tang of dried blood, the bitter-sour musk of sweat, the scent of horse and leather intermingled, and, faint but unmistakable, the sharp spike of man-fear. She examined the trio again and saw that the red-long-beard-man had lost his right hand, then returned to excavating the clay from around her scales.

She continued licking her foot, restoring every scale to pristine

463

brilliance, while first Martland, then the man-with-round-ears-who-was-Ulhart, then Roran, told a tale of blood and fire and of laughing men who refused to die at their allotted times but insisted upon continuing to fight long past when Angvard had called their names. As was her wont, Saphira held her peace while others—specifically Nasuada and her adviser, long-man-gaunt-face-Jörmundur—questioned the warriors about the details of their ill-fated mission. Saphira knew it sometimes puzzled Eragon why she did not participate more in conversations. Her reasons for silence were simple: save for Arya or Glaedr, she felt most comfortable communicating only with Eragon, and in her opinion, most conversations were nothing more than pointless dithering. Whether round-ear, pointed-ear, horned, or short, two-legs seemed addicted to dithering. Brom had not dithered, which was something Saphira had liked about him. For her, choices were simple; either there was an action she could take to improve the situation, in which case she took it, or there was not, and everything else said on the subject was so much meaningless noise. In any event, she did not worry herself about the future, except where Eragon was concerned. Him, she always worried about.

When the questions were finished, Nasuada expressed her condolences to Martland for his lost hand, then dismissed Martland and Ulhart, but not Roran, to whom she said, "You have demonstrated your prowess once again, Stronghammer. I am well pleased with your abilities."

"Thank you, my Lady."

"Our best healers will attend to him, but Martland will still need time to recover from his injury. Even once he does, he cannot lead raids such as these with only one hand. From now on, he will have to serve the Varden from the back of the army, not the front. I think, perhaps, that I shall promote him and make him one of my battle advisers. Jörmundur, what think you of that idea?"

"I think it an excellent idea, my Lady."

Nasuada nodded, appearing satisfied. "This means, however, that I must find another captain for you to serve under, Roran."

Then Roran said, "My Lady, what of my own command? Have I not proven myself to your satisfaction with these two raids, as well as with my past accomplishments?"

"If you continue to distinguish yourself as you have, Stronghammer, you will win your command soon enough. However, you must be patient and abide awhile longer. Two missions alone, however impressive, may not reveal the full scope of a man's character. I am a cautious person when it comes to entrusting my people to others, Stronghammer. In this, you must humor me."

Roran gripped the head of the hammer stuck through his belt, veins and tendons standing out on his hand, but his tone remained polite. "Of course, Lady Nasuada."

"Very good. A page will bring you your new assignment later today. Oh, and see to it that you have a large meal once you and Katrina finish celebrating your reunion. That's an order, Stronghammer. You look as if you're about to fall over."

"My Lady."

As Roran started to leave, Nasuada raised a hand and said, "Roran." He paused. "Now that you have fought these men who feel no pain, do you believe that having similar protection from the agonies of the flesh would make it easier to defeat them?"

Roran hesitated, then shook his head. "Their strength is their weakness. They do not shield themselves as they would if they feared the bite of a sword or the stab of an arrow, and thus they are careless with their lives. It is true they can continue fighting long past when an ordinary man would have dropped dead, and that is no small advantage in battle, but they also die in greater numbers, because they do not protect their bodies as they ought. In their numb confidence, they will walk into traps and peril we would go to great lengths to avoid. As long as the Varden's spirits remain high, I believe that with the right tactics we can prevail against these laughing monsters. If we were like them, though, we would hack each other into oblivion, and neither of us would care, since we would have no thought for self-preservation. Those are my thoughts."

"Thank you, Roran."

When Roran had gone, Saphira said, *Nothing yet from Eragon?*

Nasuada shook her head. "No, nothing yet from him, and his silence is beginning to concern me. If he has not contacted us by the day after tomorrow, I will have Arya send a message to one of Orik's spellcasters demanding a report from him. If Eragon is unable to hasten the end of the dwarves' clanmeet, then I fear we will no longer be able to count on the dwarves as allies during the battles to come. The only good of such a disastrous outcome would be that Eragon could return to us without further delay."

When Saphira was ready to leave the red-chrysalis-tent, Blödhgarm again summoned up the apparition of Eragon and placed it on Saphira's back. Then Saphira withdrew her head from the confines of the tent and, as she had before, bounded through the camp, the lithe elves keeping step with her the entire way.

Once she reached Eragon's tent and the colored-shadow-Eragon disappeared inside it, Saphira lowered herself to the ground and resigned herself to waiting out the remainder of the day in unrelieved monotony. Before she resumed her reluctant nap, however, she extended her mind toward Roran and Katrina's tent and pressed against Roran's mind until he lowered the barriers around his consciousness.

Saphira? he asked.

Do you know another such as me?

Of course not. You just surprised me. I am . . . ah, somewhat occupied at the moment.

She studied the color of his emotions, as well as those of Katrina, and was amused by her findings. *I only wished to welcome you back. I am glad you were not injured.*

Roran's thoughts flashed quick-hot-muddled-cold, and he seemed to have difficulty forming a coherent answer. Eventually, he said, *That's very kind of you, Saphira.*

If you can, come visit me tomorrow, when we may speak at greater length. I grow restless sitting here day after day. Perhaps you could tell me more about how Eragon was before I hatched for him.

It . . . it would be my honor.

Satisfied she had fulfilled the demands of round-ears-two-legs courtesy by welcoming Roran, and heartened by the knowledge that the following day would not be as boring—for it was unthinkable anyone would dare ignore her request for an audience—Saphira made herself as comfortable as she could on the bare earth, wishing as she often did for the soft nest that was hers in Eragon's wind-rocked-tree-house in Ellesméra. A puff of smoke escaped her as she sighed and fell asleep and dreamed that she flew higher than she ever had before.

She flapped and she flapped until she rose above the unreachable peaks of the Beor Mountains. There she circled for a time, gazing down at the whole of Alagaësia laid out before her. Then an uncontrollable desire entered her to climb even higher and see what she might, and so she began flapping again, and in what seemed like the blink of an eye, she soared past the glaring moon, until only she and the silver stars hung in the black sky. She drifted among the heavens for an indeterminate period, queen of the bright, jewel-like world below, but then disquiet entered her soul, and she cried out with her thoughts:

Eragon, where are you!

✦ ✦ ✦

KISS ME SWEET

Waking, Roran extricated himself from Katrina's smooth arms and sat bare-chested on the edge of the cot they shared. He yawned and rubbed his eyes, then gazed at the pale strip of firelight that glowed between the two entrance flaps, feeling dull and stupid with accumulated exhaustion. A chill crept over him, but he remained where he was, motionless.

"Roran?" Katrina asked in a sleep-smeared voice. She propped herself up on one arm and reached for him with the other. He did not react as she touched him, sliding her hand across his upper back and rubbing his neck. "Sleep. You need your rest. You'll be gone again before long."

He shook his head, not looking at her.

"What is it?" she asked. Sitting upright, she pulled a blanket over his shoulders, then leaned against him, her cheek warm against his arm. "Are you worried about your new captain or where Nasuada may send you next?"

"No."

She was silent for a while. "Every time you leave, I feel as if less of you returns to me. You have become so grim and quiet. . . . If you want to tell me about what is troubling you, you can, you know, no matter how terrible it is. I am the daughter of a butcher, and I have seen my share of men fall in battle."

"Want!" Roran exclaimed, choking on the word. "I don't ever want to think about it again." He clenched his fists, his breathing uncertain. "A true warrior would not feel as I do."

"A true warrior," she said, "does not fight because he wishes to but because he has to. A man who yearns for war, a man who *enjoys* his killing, he is a brute and a monster. No matter how much glory he wins on the battlefield, that cannot erase the fact that he is no better than a rabid wolf who will turn on his friends and family as soon as his foes." She brushed his hair away from his brow and stroked the top of his head, light and slow. "You once told me that 'The Song of Gerand' was your favorite of Brom's stories, that it was why you fight with a hammer instead of a blade. Remember how Gerand disliked killing and how reluctant he was to take up arms again?"

"Aye."

"And yet he was considered the greatest warrior of his age." She cupped his cheek in her hand and turned his face toward her so that he was forced to gaze into her solemn eyes. "And you are the greatest warrior I know of, Roran, here or anywhere."

With a dry mouth, he said, "What of Eragon or—"

"They are not half so valorous as you. Eragon, Murtagh, Galbatorix, the elves . . . all of them march into battle with spells upon their lips and might that far exceeds ours. But you"—she kissed him on the nose—"you are no more than a man. You face your foes on your own two feet. You are not a magician, and yet you slew the Twins. You are only as fast and as strong as a human may be, and yet you did not shirk from attacking the Ra'zac in their lair and freeing me from their dungeon."

He swallowed. "I had wards from Eragon to protect me."

"But no longer. Besides, you did not have any wards in Carvahall either, and did you flee from the Ra'zac then?" When he was unresponsive, she said, "You are no more than a man, but you have done things not even Eragon or Murtagh could have. To me, that makes you the greatest warrior in Alagaësia. . . . I cannot think of anyone else in Carvahall who would have gone to the lengths you did to rescue me."

"Your father would have," he said.

He felt her shiver against him. "Yes, he would have," she whispered. "But he never would have been able to convince others to follow him, as you did." She tightened her arm around him. "Whatever you have seen or done, you will always have me."

"That is all I will ever need," he said, and clasped her in his arms and held her for a span. Then he sighed. "Still, I wish this war were at an end. I wish I could till a field again and sow my crops and harvest them when they ripened. Farming is backbreaking work, but at least it is honest labor. This killing isn't honest. It is thievery . . . the thievery of men's lives, and no right-minded person should aspire to it."

"As I said."

"As you said." Difficult as it was, he made himself smile. "I have forgotten myself. Here I am burdening you with my troubles when you have worries enough of your own." And he placed a hand over her rounding womb.

"Your troubles shall always be my troubles, so long as we are married," she murmured, and nuzzled his arm.

"Some troubles," he said, "no one else should have to endure, especially not those you love."

She withdrew an inch or two from him, and he saw her eyes become bleak and listless, as they did whenever she fell to brooding over the time she had spent imprisoned in Helgrind. "No," she whispered, "some troubles no one else should have to endure."

"Ah, do not be sad." He pulled her closer and rocked back and forth with her and wished with all his might that Eragon had not found Saphira's egg in the Spine. After a while, when Katrina had grown soft in his arms again, and even he no longer felt quite so tense, he caressed the curve of her neck. "Come, kiss me sweet, and then let us return to bed, for I am tired, and I would sleep."

She laughed at him then, and kissed him most sweetly, and then they lay upon the cot as they had before, and outside the tent all was still and quiet except for the Jiet River, which flowed past the camp, never pausing, never stopping, and poured itself into Roran's dreams, where he imagined himself standing at the prow of a ship, Katrina by his side, and gazing into the maw of the giant whirlpool, the Boar's Eye.

And he thought, *How can we hope to escape?*

GLÛMRA

undreds of feet below Tronjheim, the stone opened up into a cavern thousands of feet long with a still black lake of unknown depth along one side and a marble shore on the other. Brown and ivory stalactites dripped from the ceiling, while stalagmites stabbed upward from the ground, and in places the two joined to form bulging pillars thicker around than even the largest trees in Du Weldenvarden. Scattered among the pillars were mounds of compost studded with mushrooms, as well as three-and-twenty low stone huts. A flameless lantern glowed iron red next to each of their doors. Beyond the reach of the lanterns, shadows abounded.

Inside one of the huts, Eragon sat in a chair that was too small for him, at a granite table no higher than his knees. The smell of soft goat cheese, sliced mushrooms, yeast, stew, pigeon eggs, and coal dust pervaded the air. Across from him, Glûmra, a dwarf woman of the Family of Mord, she who was the mother of Kvîstor, Eragon's slain guard, wailed and tore at her hair and beat at her breast with her fists. Glistening tracks marked where her tears had rolled down her plump face.

The two of them were alone in the hut. Eragon's four guards—their numbers replenished by Thrand, a warrior from Orik's retinue—were waiting outside, along with Hûndfast, Eragon's translator, whom Eragon had dismissed from the hut once he learned that Glûmra could speak his language.

After the attempt on his life, Eragon had contacted Orik with his mind, whereupon Orik insisted Eragon run as fast as he could to the chambers of the Ingeitum, where he would be safe from any more assassins. Eragon had obeyed, and there he had remained while

Orik forced the clanmeet to adjourn until the following morning, on the grounds that an emergency had arisen within his clan that required his immediate attention. Then Orik marched with his stoutest warriors and most adept spellcaster to the site of the ambush, which they studied and recorded with means both magical and mundane. Once Orik was satisfied they had learned all they could, he had hurried back to his chambers, where he said to Eragon, "We have much to do and little time in which to do it. Before the clanmeet resumes upon the third morning hour of tomorrow, we must attempt to establish beyond all doubt who ordered the attack. If we can, then we will have leverage to use against them. If not, then we will be flailing in the dark, uncertain of our enemies. We can keep the attack a secret until the clanmeet, but no longer. Knurlan will have heard echoes of your fight throughout the tunnels under Tronjheim, and even now, I know they will be searching for the source of the disturbance, for fear there may have been a cave-in or similar catastrophe that might undermine the city above." Orik stamped his feet and cursed the ancestors of whoever had sent the assassins, then planted his fists on his hips and said, "A clan war was already threatening us, but now it stands upon our very threshold. We must move quickly if we are to avert that dread fate. There are knurlan to find, questions to ask, threats to make, bribes to offer, and scrolls to steal—and all before morn."

"What of me?" Eragon asked.

"You should remain here until we know if Az Sweldn rak Anhûin or some other clan has a larger force massed elsewhere to kill you. Also, as long as we can hide from your attackers whether you are alive, dead, or wounded, the longer we may keep them uncertain as to the safety of the rock beneath their feet."

At first Eragon agreed with Orik's proposal, but as he watched the dwarf bustle about issuing orders, he felt increasingly uneasy and helpless. Finally, he caught Orik by the arm and said, "If I have to sit here and stare at the wall while you search for the villains who did this, I'll grind my teeth down to nubs. There must be something I can do to help. . . . What of Kvîstor? Do any of his family live in Tronjheim? Has anyone told them of his death yet? Because if not, I would be the one to bring them the tidings, for it was me he died defending."

Orik inquired of his guards, and from them they learned that Kvîstor did indeed have family in Tronjheim, or more accurately, underneath Tronjheim. When he heard, Orik frowned and muttered a strange word in Dwarvish. "They are deep dwellers," he said, "knurlan who have forsaken the surface of the land for the world below, except for occasional forays above. More of them live here, below Tronjheim and Farthen Dûr, than anywhere else, because they can come out in Farthen Dûr and not feel as if they are actually outside, which most of them cannot bear, they are so accustomed to closed-in spaces. I had not known Kvîstor was of their number."

"Would you mind if I go to visit his family?" Eragon asked. "Among these rooms, there are stairs that lead below, am I right? We could leave without anyone being the wiser."

Orik thought for a moment, then nodded. "You're right. The path is safe enough, and no one would think to look for you among the deep dwellers. They would come here first, and here they would otherwise find you. . . . Go, and do not return until I send a messenger for you, even if the Family of Mord turns you away and you must sit on a stalagmite until morn. But, Eragon, be you careful; the deep dwellers keep to themselves for the most part, and they are prickly to an extreme about their honor, and they have strange customs of their own. Tread carefully, as if you were on rotten shale, eh?"

And so, with Thrand added to his guards, and Hûndfast accompanying them—and with a short dwarf sword belted around his waist—Eragon went to the nearest staircase leading downward, and following it, he descended farther into the bowels of the earth than ever he had before. And in due time, he found Glûmra and informed her of Kvîstor's demise, and now he sat listening as she grieved for her slain child, alternating between wordless howls and scraps of Dwarvish sung in a haunting, dissonant key.

Discomfited by the strength of her sorrow, Eragon glanced away from her face. He looked at the green soapstone stove that stood against one wall and the worn carvings of geometric design that adorned its edges. He studied the green and brown rug that lay before the hearth, and the churn in the corner, and the provisions hanging from the beams of the ceiling. He gazed at the heavy-timbered loom that stood underneath a round window with panes of lavender glass.

Then, at the height of her wailing, Glûmra caught Eragon's eye as she rose from the table, went to the counter, and placed her left hand on the cutting board. Before Eragon could stop her, she took a carving knife and cut off the first joint of her little finger. She groaned and doubled over.

Eragon sprang halfway up with an involuntary exclamation. He wondered what madness had overcome the dwarf woman and whether he should attempt to restrain her, lest she should do herself additional harm. He opened his mouth to ask if she wanted him to heal the wound, but then he thought better of it, remembering Orik's admonishments about the deep dwellers' strange customs and strong sense of honor. *She might consider the offer an insult*, he realized. Closing his mouth, he sank back into his too-small chair.

After a minute, Glûmra straightened out of her hunched position, took a deep breath, and then quietly and calmly washed the raw end of her finger with brandy, smeared it with a yellow salve, and bandaged the wound. Her moon-face still pale from the shock, she lowered herself into the chair opposite Eragon. "I thank you, Shadeslayer, for bringing me news of mine son's fate yourself. I am glad to know that he died proudly, as a warrior ought to."

"He was most brave," Eragon said. "He could see that our enemies were as fast as elves, and yet he still leaped forward to protect me. His sacrifice bought me time to escape their blades and also revealed the danger of the enchantments they had placed on their weapons. If not for his actions, I doubt I would be here now."

Glûmra nodded slowly, eyes downcast, and smoothed the front of

475

her dress. "Do you know who was responsible for this attack on our clan, Shadeslayer?"

"We have only suspicions. Grimstborith Orik is trying to determine the truth of the matter even as we speak."

"Was it Az Sweldn rak Anhûin?" Glûmra asked, surprising Eragon with the astuteness of her guess. He did his best to conceal his reaction. When he remained silent, she said, "We all know of their blood feud with you, Argetlam; every knurla within these mountains knows. Some of us have looked with favor upon their opposition of you, but if they thought to actually kill you, then they have misjudged the lay of the rock and doomed themselves because of it."

Eragon raised an eyebrow, interested. "Doomed? How?"

"It was you, Shadeslayer, who slew Durza and so allowed us to save Tronjheim and the dwellings below from the clutches of Galbatorix. Our race shall never forget that so long as Tronjheim remains standing. And then there is word come by the tunnels that your dragon shall make whole again Isidar Mithrim?"

Eragon nodded.

"That is good of you, Shadeslayer. You have done much for our race, and whichever clan it was attacked you, we shall turn against them and have our vengeance."

"I swore before witnesses," Eragon said, "and I swear to you as well, that I will punish whoever sent those backstabbing murderers and that I'll make them wish they had never thought of such a foul deed. However—"

"Thank you, Shadeslayer."

Eragon hesitated, then inclined his head. "However, we must not do anything that would ignite a clan war. Not now. If force is to be used, it should be Grimstborith Orik who decides when and where we draw our swords, don't you agree?"

"I will think upon what you have said, Shadeslayer," Glûmra replied. "Orik is . . ." Whatever she was going to say next caught in her mouth. Her thick eyelids drooped and she sagged forward for a moment, pressing her maimed hand against her abdomen. When the bout passed, she pushed herself upright and held the back of the hand against her opposite cheek and swayed from side to side, moaning, "Oh, mine son . . . mine beautiful son."

Standing, she staggered around the table, heading toward a small collection of swords and axes mounted on the wall behind Eragon, next to an alcove covered by a curtain of red silk. Afraid that she intended to cause herself further injury, Eragon leaped to his feet, knocking over the oak chair in his haste. He reached for her and then saw that she was walking toward the curtained alcove, not the weapons, and he snatched his arm back before he caused offense.

The brass rings sewn on top of the silk drapery clattered against one another as Glûmra swept aside the cloth to expose a deep, shadowed shelf carved with runes and shapes of such fantastic detail, Eragon thought he could stare at them for hours and still not grasp them in their entirety. On the low shelf rested statues of the six major dwarf gods, as well as nine other entities Eragon was unfamiliar with, all carved with exaggerated features and postures to better convey the character of the being portrayed.

Glûmra removed an amulet of gold and silver from within her bodice, which she kissed and then held against the hollow of her throat as she knelt before the alcove. Her voice rising and falling in the strange patterns of dwarf music, she began to croon a dirge in her native language. The melody brought tears to Eragon's eyes. For several minutes, Glûmra sang, and then she fell silent and continued to gaze at the figurines, and as she gazed, the lines of her grief-ravaged face softened, and where before Eragon had perceived only anger, distress, and hopelessness, her countenance assumed an air of calm acceptance, of peacefulness, and of sublime transcendence. A soft glow seemed to emanate from her features. So complete was Glûmra's transformation, Eragon almost did not recognize her.

She said, "Tonight Kvîstor will dine in Morgothal's hall. That I know." She kissed her amulet again. "I wish I might break bread with him, along with mine husband, Bauden, but it is not mine time to sleep in the catacombs of Tronjheim, and Morgothal refuses entry to his hall to those who quicken their arrival. But in time, our family shall be reunited, including all of our ancestors since Gûntera created the world from darkness. That I know."

Eragon knelt next to her, and in a hoarse voice, he asked, "How do you know this?"

"I know because it is so." Her movements slow and respectful, Glûmra touched the chiseled feet of each of the gods with the tips of her fingers. "How could it be otherwise? Since the world could not have created itself any more than a sword or a helm might, and since the only beings with the wherewithal to forge the earth and the heavens into shape are those with divine power, it is to the gods we must look for our answers. Them I trust to ensure the rightness of the world, and by mine trust, I free myself of the burdens of mine flesh."

She spoke with such conviction, Eragon felt a sudden desire to share in her belief. He longed to toss aside his doubts and fears and to know that, however horrible the world might seem at times, life was not mere confusion. He wished to know for certain that who he was would not end if a sword should shear off his head and that one day he would meet again with Brom, Garrow, and everyone else he had cared for and lost. A desperate yearning for hope and comfort filled him, confused him, left him unsteady upon the face of the earth.

And yet.

Part of himself held back and would not allow him to commit to the dwarf gods and bind his identity and his sense of well-being to something he did not understand. He also had difficulty accepting that if gods did exist, the dwarf gods were the only ones. Eragon was certain that if he asked Nar Garzhvog or a member of the nomad tribes, or even the black priests of Helgrind, if their gods were real, they would uphold the supremacy of their deities just as vigorously as Glûmra would uphold hers. *How am I supposed to know which religion is the true religion?* he wondered. *Just because someone follows a certain faith does not necessarily mean it is the right path. . . . Perhaps no one religion contains all of the truth of the world. Perhaps every religion contains fragments of the truth and it is our responsibility to identify those fragments and piece them together. Or perhaps the elves are right and there are no gods. But how can I know for sure?*

With a long sigh, Glûmra murmured a phrase in Dwarvish, then rose from her knees and drew closed the silk curtain over the alcove. Eragon likewise stood, wincing as his battle-sore muscles stretched, and followed her to the table, where he returned to his chair. From a stone cupboard set into the wall, the dwarf woman took two pewter mugs, then retrieved a bladder full of wine from where it hung from the ceiling and poured a drink for both her and Eragon. She raised her mug and uttered a toast in Dwarvish, which Eragon struggled to imitate, and then they drank.

"It is good," said Glûmra, "to know that Kvîstor still lives on, to know that even now he is garbed in robes fit for a king while he enjoys the evening feast in Morgothal's hall. May he win much honor in the service of the gods!" And she drank again.

Once he had emptied his mug, Eragon began to bid farewell to Glûmra, but she forestalled him with a motion of her hand. "Have you a place to stay, Shadeslayer, safe from those who wish you dead?" Whereupon Eragon told her how he was supposed to remain hidden underneath Tronjheim until Orik sent a messenger for him. Glûmra nodded with a short, definitive jerk of her chin and said, "Then you and your companions must wait here until the messenger arrives, Shadeslayer. I insist upon it." Eragon started to protest, but she shook her head. "I could not allow the men who fought with mine son to languish in the damp and the dark of the caves while I yet have life in mine bones. Summon your companions, and we shall eat and be merry this gloomy night."

Eragon realized that he could not leave without upsetting Glûmra, so he called to his guards and his translator. Together, they helped Glûmra to prepare a dinner of bread, meat, and pie, and when it was ready, the lot of them ate and drank and talked late into the night. Glûmra was particularly lively; she drank the most, laughed the loudest, and was always the first to make a witty remark. At first Eragon was shocked by her behavior, but then he noticed how her smiles never reached her eyes and how, if she thought no one was looking, the mirth would drain from her face and her expression would become one of somber quietude. Entertaining them, he concluded, was her way of celebrating her son's memory, as well as fending off her grief at Kvîstor's death.

I have never met anyone like you before, he thought as he watched her.

Long after midnight, someone knocked on the door of the hut. Hûndfast ushered in a dwarf who was garbed in full armor and who seemed edgy and ill at ease; he kept glancing at the doors and windows and shadowed corners. With a series of phrases in the ancient language, he convinced Eragon that he was Orik's messenger, and then he said, "I am Farn, son of Flosi. . . . Argetlam, Orik bids you return with all possible haste. He has most important tidings concerning the events of today."

At the doorway, Glûmra grasped Eragon's left forearm with fingers like steel, and as he gazed down into her flinty eyes, she said, "Remember your oath, Shadeslayer, and do not let the killers of mine son escape without retribution!"

"That I shall not," he promised.

CLANMEET

The dwarves standing watch outside of Orik's chambers threw open the double doors that led inside as Eragon strode toward them.

The entryway beyond was long and ornate, furnished with three circular seats upholstered with red fabric set in a line down the middle of the room. Embroidered hangings decorated the walls, along with the dwarves' ubiquitous flameless lanterns, while the ceiling had been carved to depict a famous battle from dwarven history.

Orik stood consulting with a group of his warriors and several gray-bearded dwarves of Dûrgrimst Ingeitum. As Eragon approached, Orik turned toward him, his face grim. "Good, you did not delay! Hûndfast, you may retire to your quarters now. We must needs speak in private."

Eragon's translator bowed and disappeared through an archway to the left, his footsteps echoing on the polished agate floor. Once he was out of hearing, Eragon said, "You don't trust him?"

Orik shrugged. "I do not know whom to trust at the moment; the fewer people who know what we have discovered, the better. We cannot risk the news escaping to another clan before tomorrow. If it does, it will certainly mean a clan war." The dwarves behind him muttered among themselves, appearing disconcerted.

"What is your news, though?" asked Eragon, worried.

The warriors gathered behind Orik moved aside as he gestured at them, revealing as they did so three bound and bloodied dwarves stacked on top of one another in the corner. The dwarf on the bottom groaned and kicked his feet in the air but was unable to extricate himself from under his fellow prisoners.

"Who are they?" asked Eragon.

Orik replied, "I had several of our smiths examine the daggers your attackers carried. They identified the craftsmanship as that of one Kiefna Long-nose, a bladesmith of our clan who has achieved great renown among our people."

"So he can tell us who bought the daggers and thus who our enemies are?"

A brusque laugh shook Orik's chest. "Hardly, but we were able to track the daggers from Kiefna to an armorer in Dalgon, many leagues from here, who sold them to a knurlaf with—"

"A knurlaf?" Eragon asked.

Orik scowled. "A woman. A woman with seven fingers on each hand bought the daggers two months ago."

"And did you find her? There can't be very many women with that number of fingers."

"Actually, the condition is fairly common among our people," said Orik. "Be that as it may, after quite a bit of difficulty, we managed to locate the woman in Dalgon. My warriors there questioned her most closely. She is of Dûrgrimst Nagra, but so far as we can determine, she was acting of her own accord, and not under orders from the leaders of her clan. From her, we learned that a dwarf had engaged her to buy the daggers and then to deliver them to a wine merchant who would take them with him from Dalgon. The woman's employer did not tell her where the daggers were destined, but by asking among the merchants of the city, we discovered that he traveled directly from Dalgon to one of the cities held by Dûrgrimst Az Sweldn rak Anhûin."

"So it *was* them!" Eragon exclaimed.

"That or it could have been someone who wished us to think it was them. We needed more evidence before we could establish Az Sweldn rak Anhûin's guilt for certain." A twinkle appeared in Orik's eyes, and he raised a finger. "So, by means of a very, very clever spell, we retraced the path of the assassins back through the tunnels and caves and up to a deserted area on the twelfth level of

Tronjheim, off the subadjunct auxiliary hall of the southern spoke, in the western quadrant, along the . . . ah, well, it does not matter. But someday I will have to teach you how the rooms are arranged in Tronjheim, so that if ever you need to find a place within the city by yourself, you can. In any event, the trail led us to an abandoned storeroom where those three"—he gestured toward the bound dwarves—"had been staying. They were not expecting us, and so we were able to capture them alive, although they tried to kill themselves. It was not easy, but we broke the minds of two of them— leaving the third for the other grimstborithn to interrogate at their pleasure—and we took from them everything they knew about this matter." Orik pointed at the prisoners again. "It was they who equipped the assassins for the attack, gave them the daggers and their black clothes, and fed and sheltered them last night."

"Who are they?" asked Eragon.

"Bah!" exclaimed Orik, and spat on the floor. "They are Vargrimstn, warriors who have disgraced themselves and are now clanless. No one deals with such filth unless they are engaged in villainy themselves and do not wish others to know of it. And so it was with those three. They took their orders directly from Grimstborith Vermûnd of Az Sweldn rak Anhûin."

"There is no doubt?"

Orik shook his head. "There is no doubt; it is Az Sweldn rak Anhûin who tried to kill you, Eragon. We will probably never know if any other clans joined them in the attempt, but if we expose Az Sweldn rak Anhûin's treachery, it will force everyone else who might have been involved in the plot to disparage their former confederates; to abandon, or at least delay, further attacks on Dûrgrimst Ingeitum; and, if this is handled properly, to give me their vote for king."

An image flashed in Eragon's mind of the prismatic blade emerging from the back of Kvîstor's neck and of the dwarf's agonized expression as he had fallen to the floor, dying. "How will we punish Az Sweldn rak Anhûin for this crime? Should we kill Vermûnd?"

"Ah, leave that to me," said Orik, and tapped the side of his nose. "I have a plan. But we must tread carefully, for this is a situation of the utmost delicacy. Such a betrayal has not occurred in many long years. As an outsider, you cannot know how abhorrent we find it that one of our own should attack a guest. You being the only free Rider left to oppose Galbatorix only worsens the offense. Further bloodshed may yet be necessary, but at the moment, it would only bring about another clan war."

"A clan war might be the only way to deal with Az Sweldn rak Anhûin," Eragon pointed out.

"I think not, but if I am mistaken and war is unavoidable, we must ensure it is a war between the rest of the clans and Az Sweldn rak Anhûin. That would not be so bad. Together, we could crush them inside of a week. A war with the clans split into two or three factions, however, would destroy our country. It is crucial, then, that before we draw our swords, we convince the other clans of what Az Sweldn rak Anhûin has done. Toward that end, will you allow magicians from different clans to examine your memories of the attack so they may see it happened as we shall say it did and that we did not stage it for our own benefit?"

Eragon hesitated, reluctant to open his mind to strangers, then nodded toward the three dwarves stacked on top of one another. "What about them? Won't their memories be enough to convince the clans of Az Sweldn rak Anhûin's guilt?"

Orik grimaced. "They ought to be, but in order to be thorough, the clan chiefs will insist upon verifying their memories against yours, and if you refuse, Az Sweldn rak Anhûin will claim we are hiding something from the clanmeet and that our accusations are nothing more than slanderous fiction."

"Very well," said Eragon. "If I must, I must. But if any of the magicians stray where they are not supposed to, even if by accident, I will have no choice but to burn what they have seen out of their minds. There are some things I cannot allow to become common knowledge."

Nodding, Orik said, "Aye, I can think of at least one three-legged piece of information that would cause us some consternation if it were to be trumpeted throughout the land, eh? I am sure the clan chiefs will accept your conditions—for they all have secrets of their own they would not want bandied about—just as I am sure they will order their magicians to proceed, regardless of the danger. This attack has the potential to incite such turmoil among our race, the grimstborithn will feel compelled to determine the truth about it, though it may cost them their most skilled spellcasters."

Drawing himself upright then, to the full extent of his limited height, Orik ordered the prisoners removed from the ornate entryway and dismissed all of his vassals, save for Eragon and a contingent of twenty-six of his finest warriors. With a graceful flourish, Orik grasped Eragon's left elbow and conducted him toward the inner rooms of his chambers. "Tonight you must remain here, with me, where Az Sweldn rak Anhûin will not dare to strike."

"If you intend to sleep," said Eragon, "I must warn you, I cannot rest, not tonight. My blood still churns from the tumult of the fight, and my thoughts are likewise uneasy."

Orik replied, "Rest or not as you will; you shall not disturb my slumber, for I shall pull a thick woolen cap low over my eyes. I urge you to try and calm yourself, however—perhaps with some of the techniques the elves taught you—and recover what strength you may. The new day is already upon us, and but a few hours remain until the clanmeet shall be assembled. We should both be as fresh as possible for what is to come. What we do and say today shall determine the ultimate fate of mine people, mine country, and the rest of Alagaësia. . . . Ah, do not look so grim about the mouth! Think of this instead: whether success or failure awaits us, and I surely hope we prevail, our names shall be remembered until the end of time for how we comport ourselves at this clanmeet. That at least is an accomplishment to fill your belly with pride! The gods are fickle, and the only immortality we can count on is that which we win through our deeds. Fame or infamy, either one is preferable to being forgotten when you have passed from this realm."

Later that night, in the dead hours before morning, Eragon's thoughts wandered as he sat slumped within the embrace of the padded arms of a dwarf couch, and the frame of his consciousness dissolved into the disordered fantasy of his waking dreams. Yet conscious of the mosaic of colored stones mounted upon the wall opposite him, he also beheld, as if a glowing scrim draped over the mosaic, scenes of his life in Palancar Valley before momentous and bloody fate had intervened in his existence. The scenes diverged from established fact, however, and immersed him in imaginary situations constructed piecemeal from fragments of what had actually been. In the last few moments before he roused himself from his stupor, his vision flickered and the images acquired a sense of heightened reality.

He was standing in Horst's workshop, the doors of which hung open, loose upon their hinges, like an idiot's slackjaw grin. Outside was a starless night, and the all-consuming darkness seemed to press against the edges of the dull red light cast by the coals, as if eager to devour everything within the scope of that ruddy sphere. Next to the forge, Horst loomed like a giant, the shifting shadows upon his face and beard fearsome to behold. His burly arm rose and fell, and a bell-like clang shivered the air as the hammer he wielded struck the end of a yellow-glowing bar of steel. A burst of sparks extinguished itself on the ground. Four more times the smith smote the metal; then he lifted the bar from his anvil and plunged it into a barrel of oil. Wraithlike flames, blue and gossamer, flickered across the surface of the oil and then vanished with small shrieks of fury. Removing the bar from the barrel, Horst turned toward Eragon and frowned at him. He said, "Why have you come here, Eragon?"

"I need a Dragon Rider's sword."

"Begone with you. I have no time to forge you a Rider's sword. Cannot you see I am working on a pothook for Elain? She must have it for the battle. Are you alone?"

"I do not know."

"Where is your father? Where is your mother?"

"I do not know."

Then a new voice sounded, a well-polished voice of strength and power, and it said, "Good smith, he is not alone. He came with me."

"And who might you be?" demanded Horst.

"I am his father."

Between the gaping doors, a huge figure rimmed with pale light emerged from the clotted darkness and stood upon the threshold of the workshop. A red cape billowed from shoulders wider than a Kull's. In the man's left hand gleamed Zar'roc, sharp as pain. Through the slits of his brightly polished helm, his blue eyes bored into Eragon, pinning him into place, like an arrow through a rabbit. He lifted his free hand and held it out toward Eragon. "My son, come with me. Together, we can destroy the Varden, kill Galbatorix, and conquer all of Alagaësia. But give me your heart, and we shall be invincible.

"Give me your heart, my son."

With a strangled exclamation, Eragon leaped out of the couch and stood staring at the floor, his fists clenched, his chest heaving. Orik's guards gave him inquisitive glances, but he ignored them, too upset to explain his outburst.

The hour was still early, so after a time, Eragon settled back onto the couch, but thereafter, he remained alert and did not allow himself to sink into the land of dreams, for fear of what manifestations might torment him.

Eragon stood with his back to the wall, his hand on the pommel of his dwarf sword, as he watched the various clan chiefs file into the round conference room buried beneath Tronjheim. He kept an especially close eye on Vermûnd, the grimstborith of Az Sweldn rak Anhûin, but if the purple-veiled dwarf was surprised to see Eragon alive and well, he did not show it.

Eragon felt Orik's boot nudge his own. Without looking away from Vermûnd, Eragon leaned over toward Orik and heard him whisper, "Remember, to the left and three doorways down," referring to the place where Orik had stationed a hundred of his warriors without the other clan chiefs knowing.

Whispering as well, Eragon said, "If blood is shed, should I seize the opportunity to kill that snake, Vermûnd?"

"Unless he is attempting the same with you or me, please do not." A low chuckle emanated from Orik. "It would hardly *endear* you to the other grimstborithn. . . . Ah, I must go now. Pray to Sindri for luck, would you? We are about to venture into a lava field none have dared cross before."

And Eragon prayed.

When all of the clan chiefs were seated around the table in the center of the room, those watching from the perimeter, including Eragon, took their own seats from among the ring of chairs set against the curving wall. Eragon did not relax into his, however, as many of the dwarves did, but sat upon the edge, ready to fight at the slightest hint of danger.

As Gannel, the black-eyed warrior-priest of Dûrgrimst Quan, rose from the table and began to speak in Dwarvish, Hûndfast sidled closer to Eragon's right side and murmured a continuous translation. The dwarf said, "Greetings again, mine fellow clan chiefs. But whether 'tis well met or not, I am undecided, for certain disturbing rumors—rumors of rumors, if truth be told—have reached mine ears. I have no information beyond these vague and worrisome mutterings, nor proof upon which to found an accusation of misdeeds. However, as today is mine day to preside over this, our congregation, I propose that we delay our most serious debates for the moment, and if you are agreeable, allow me to pose a few questions to the meet."

The clan chiefs muttered among themselves, and then Íorûnn, bright, dimpling Íorûnn, said, "I have no objection, Grimstborith Gannel. You have aroused mine curiosity with these cryptic insinuations. Let us hear what questions you have."

"Aye, let us hear them," said Nado.

"Let us hear them," agreed Manndrâth and all the rest of the clan chiefs, including Vermûnd.

Having received the permission he sought, Gannel rested his knuckles upon the table and was silent for a span, garnering the attention of everyone in the room. Then he spoke. "Yesterday, while we were lunching in our chosen places of repast, knurlan throughout the tunnels underneath the southern quadrant of Tronjheim heard a noise. Reports of its loudness differ, but that so many noticed it over so large an area proves that it was no small disturbance. Like you, I received the usual warnings of a possible cave-in. What you may not be aware of, however, is that just two hours past—"

Hûndfast hesitated, and quickly whispered, "The word is difficult to render in this tongue. *Runners-of-the-tunnels*, I think." And then he resumed translating as before:

"—runners-of-the-tunnels discovered evidence of a mighty fight within one of the ancient tunnels that our famed forefather, Korgan Longbeard, excavated. The floor was painted with blood, the walls were dark with soot from a lantern a warrior of careless blade did breach, cracks split the surrounding stone, and sprawled throughout were seven charred and mangled bodies, with signs that others may have been removed. Nor were these the remnants of some obscure skirmish from the Battle of Farthen Dûr. No! For the blood had yet to dry, the soot was soft, the cracks were most obviously freshly broken, and, I am told, the residue of powerful magics could still be detected within the area. Even now, several of our most accomplished spellcasters are attempting to reconstruct a pictorial facsimile of what occurred, but they have little hope of success, as those involved were wrapped about with such devious enchantments. So my first question for the meet is this: do any of you possess further knowledge of this mysterious action?"

As Gannel concluded his speech, Eragon tensed his legs, ready to spring up if the purple-veiled dwarves of Az Sweldn rak Anhûin should reach for their blades.

Orik cleared his throat and said, "I believe that I can satisfy some

489

of your curiosity upon that point, Gannel. However, since my answer must of necessity be a lengthy one, I suggest you ask your other questions before I begin."

A frown darkened Gannel's brow. Rapping his knuckles against the table, he said, "Very well. . . . In what is undoubtedly related to the clash of arms in Korgan's tunnels, I have had reports of numerous knurlan moving through Tronjheim and, with furtive intent, gathering here and there into large bands of armed men. My agents were unable to ascertain the clan of the warriors, but that any of this council should attempt to surreptitiously marshal their forces whilst we are engaged in a meet to decide who should succeed King Hrothgar suggests motives of the darkest kind. So my second question for the meet is this: who is responsible for this ill-thought-of maneuvering? And if none are willing to admit their misconduct, I move most strongly that we order all warriors, regardless of their clan, expelled from Tronjheim for the duration of the meet and that we immediately appoint a reader-of-law to investigate these doings and determine whom we should censure."

Gannel's revelation, question, and subsequent proposal aroused a flurry of heated conversation among the clan chiefs, with the dwarves hurling accusations, denials, and counteraccusations at each other with increasing vitriol, until, at last, when an infuriated Thordris was shouting at a red-faced Gáldhiem, Orik cleared his throat again, causing everyone to stop and stare at him.

In a mild tone, Orik said, "This too I believe I can explain to you, Gannel, at least in part. I cannot speak to the activities of the other clans, but several hundred of the warriors who have been hurrying through the servants' halls in Tronjheim have been of Dûrgrimst Ingeitum. This I freely admit."

All was silent until Íorûnn said, "And what explanation have you for this belligerent behavior, Orik, Thrifk's son?"

"As I said before, fair Íorûnn, my answer must of necessity be a lengthy one, so if you, Gannel, have any other questions to ask, I suggest you proceed forthwith."

Gannel's frown deepened until his projecting eyebrows nearly touched. He said, "I will withhold mine other questions for the time being, for they all pertain to those I have already put to the meet, and it seems we must wait upon your pleasure to learn any more of those subjects. However, since you are involved fist and foot with these doubtful activities, a new question has occurred to me that I would ask of you specifically, Grimstborith Orik. For what reason did you desert yesterday's meet? And let me warn you, I will brook no evasions. You have already intimated you have knowledge of these affairs. Well, time is for you to provide a full accounting of yourself, Grimstborith Orik."

Orik stood even as Gannel sat, and he said, "It shall be mine pleasure."

Lowering his bearded chin until it rested upon his chest, Orik paused for a brief span and then began to speak in a sonorous voice, but he did not begin as Eragon had expected, nor, Eragon surmised, as the rest of the congregation had expected. Instead of describing the attempt on Eragon's life, and thus explaining why he had terminated the previous clanmeet prematurely, Orik commenced by recounting how, at the dawn of history, the race of dwarves had migrated from the once-verdant fields of the Hadarac Desert to the Beor Mountains, where they had excavated their uncounted miles of tunnels, built their magnificent cities both above and below the ground, and waged lusty war between their various factions, as well as with the dragons, whom, for thousands of years, the dwarves had regarded with a combination of hate, fear, and reluctant awe.

Then Orik spoke of the elves' arrival in Alagaësia and of how the elves had fought with the dragons until they nearly destroyed each other and of how, as a result, the two races had agreed to create the Dragon Riders to maintain the peace thereafter.

"And what was our response when we learned of their intentions?" demanded Orik, his voice ringing loud in the chamber. "Did we ask to be included in their pact? Did we aspire to share in the power that would be the Dragon Riders'? No! We clung to our old ways, our old hatreds, and we rejected the very thought of bonding with the dragons or allowing anyone outside our realm to police us. To preserve our authority, we sacrificed our future, for I am convinced that if some of the Dragon Riders had been knurlan, Galbatorix might have never risen to power. Even if I am wrong— and I mean not to belittle Eragon, who has proven himself a fine Rider—the dragon Saphira might have hatched for one of our race and not a human. And then what glory might have been ours?

"Instead, our importance in Alagaësia has diminished ever since Queen Tarmunora and Eragon's namesake made peace with the dragons. At first our lessened status was not so bitter a draught to swallow, and often it was easier to deny than to accept. But then came the Urgals, and then the humans, and the elves amended their spells so humans might be Riders as well. And then did we seek to be included in their accord, as well we might have . . . as was our right?" Orik shook his head. "Our pride would not allow it. Why should we, the oldest race in the land, beg the elves for the favor of their magic? We did not need to chain our fate to the dragons' in order to save our race from destruction, as had the elves and humans. We ignored, of course, the battles we waged among ourselves. Those, we reasoned, were private affairs and of no concern to anyone else."

The listening clan chiefs stirred. Many of them bore expressions of dissatisfaction at Orik's criticism, whereas the rest seemed more receptive to his comments and were thoughtful of countenance.

Orik continued: "While the Riders watched over Alagaësia, we enjoyed the greatest period of prosperity ever recorded in the annals of our realm. We flourished as never before, and yet we had no share in the cause of it: the Dragon Riders. When the Riders fell, our fortunes faltered, but again we had no share in the cause of it: the Riders. Neither state of affairs is, I deem, fitting for a race of our stature. We are not a country of vassals subject to the whims of foreign masters. Nor should those who are not the descendants of Odgar and Hlordis dictate our fate."

This line of reasoning was more to the liking of the clan chiefs; they nodded and smiled, and Havard even clapped a few times at the final line.

"Consider now our present era," said Orik. "Galbatorix is ascendant, and every race fights to remain free of his rule. He has grown so powerful, the only reason we are not already his slaves is that, so far, he has not chosen to fly out upon his black dragon and attack us directly. If he did, we would fall before him like saplings before an avalanche. Fortunately, he seems content to wait for us to slaughter our way to the gates of his citadel in Urû'baen. Now, I remind you that before Eragon and Saphira turned up wet and bedraggled on our front doorstep, with a hundred yammering Kull hard upon their heels, our only hope of defeating Galbatorix was that someday, somewhere, Saphira would hatch for her chosen Rider and that this unknown person would, perhaps, perchance, if we were luckier than every gambler who has ever won a toss of dice, be able to overthrow Galbatorix. Hope? Ha! We did not even have hope; we had a hope of a hope. When Eragon first presented himself, many of us were dismayed by his appearance, myself included. 'He is but a boy,' we said. 'It would have been better if he had been an elf,' we said. But lo, he has shown himself to be the embodiment of our every hope! He slew Durza, and so allowed us to save our most beloved city, Tronjheim. His dragon, Saphira, has promised to restore the Star Rose to its former glory. During the Battle of the Burning Plains, he drove off Murtagh and Thorn, and so allowed us to win the day. And look! He even now wears the semblance of an elf, and through their strange magics, he has acquired their speed and their strength."

Orik raised a finger for emphasis. "Moreover, King Hrothgar, in his wisdom, did what no other king or grimstborith has ever done; he offered to adopt Eragon into Dûrgrimst Ingeitum and to make him a member of his own family. Eragon was under no obligation to accept this offer. Indeed, he was aware that many of the families of the Ingeitum objected to it and that, in general, many knurlan would not regard it with favor. Yet in spite of that discouragement, and in spite of the fact that he was already bound in fealty to Nasuada, Eragon accepted Hrothgar's gift, knowing full well that it would only make his life harder. As he has told me himself, Eragon swore the hall-oath upon the Heart of Stone because of the sense of obligation he feels toward all the races of Alagaësia, and especially toward us, since we, by the actions of Hrothgar, showed him and Saphira such kindness. Because of Hrothgar's genius, the last free Rider of Alagaësia, and our one and only hope against Galbatorix, freely chose to become a knurla in all but blood. Since then, Eragon has abided by our laws and traditions to the best of his knowledge, and he has sought to learn ever more about our culture so that he may honor the true meaning of his oath. When Hrothgar fell, struck down by the traitor Murtagh, Eragon swore to me upon every stone in Alagaësia, and also as a member of Dûrgrimst Ingeitum, that he would strive to avenge Hrothgar's death. He has given me the respect and obedience I am due as grimstborith, and I am proud to regard him as mine foster brother."

Eragon glanced downward, his cheeks and the tips of his ears burning. He wished Orik were not so free with his praise; it would only make his position harder to maintain in the future.

Sweeping his arms out to include the other clan chiefs, Orik exclaimed, "Everything we could have ever wished for in a Dragon Rider we have received in Eragon! He exists! He is powerful! And he has embraced our people as no other Dragon Rider ever has!" Then Orik lowered his arms and, with them, the volume of his voice, until Eragon had to strain to hear his words. "How have we responded to his friendship, though? In the main, with sneers and slights and surly resentment. We are an ungrateful race, I say, and our memories are too long for our own good. . . . There are even those who have become so filled with festering hatred, they have turned to violence to slake the thirst of their anger. Perhaps they still believe they are doing what is best for our people, but if so, then their minds are as moldy as a lump of year-old cheese. Otherwise, why would they try to kill Eragon?"

The listening clan chiefs became perfectly still, their eyes riveted to Orik's face. So intense was their concentration, the corpulent grimstborith, Freowin, had set aside his carving of a raven and folded his hands on top of his ample belly, appearing for all the world like one of the dwarves' statues.

As they gazed at him with unblinking eyes, Orik related to the clanmeet how the seven black-clad dwarves had attacked Eragon and his guards while they were meandering among the tunnels underneath Tronjheim. Then Orik told them of the braided horsehair bracelet set with amethyst cabochons that Eragon's guards had found upon one of the corpses.

"Do not think to blame this attack upon mine clan based upon such paltry evidence!" exclaimed Vermûnd, bolting upright. "One can buy similar trinkets in most every market of our realm!"

"Quite so," said Orik, and inclined his head toward Vermûnd. In a dispassionate voice, and with a quick pace, Orik proceeded to tell his audience, as he had told Eragon the previous night, how his subjects in Dalgon had confirmed for him that the strange flickering daggers the assassins had wielded had been forged by the smith Kiefna, and also how his subjects had discovered that the dwarf who had bought the weapons had arranged for them to be transported from Dalgon to one of the cities held by Az Sweldn rak Anhûin.

Uttering a low, growling oath, Vermûnd leaped to his feet again. "Those daggers might never have reached our city, and even if they did, you can draw no conclusions from that fact! Knurlan of many clans stay within our walls, as they do within the walls of Bregan Hold, for example. It signifies *nothing*. Be careful what you say next, Grimstborith Orik, for you have no grounds upon which to level accusations against mine clan."

"I was of the same opinion as you, Grimstborith Vermûnd," Orik replied. "Therefore, last night, my spellcasters and I retraced the assassins' path back to their place of origin, and on the twelfth level of Tronjheim, we captured three knurlan who were hiding in a dusty storeroom. We broke the minds of two of them and, from them, we learned they provisioned the assassins for their attack. And," said Orik, his voice growing harsh and terrible, "from them we learned the identity of their master. I name you, Grimstborith Vermûnd! I name you Murderer and Oath-breaker. I name you an enemy of Dûrgrimst Ingeitum, and I name you a traitor to your kind, for it was you and your clan who attempted to kill Eragon!"

The clanmeet erupted into chaos as every clan chief except Orik and Vermûnd began to shout and wave their hands and otherwise attempt to dominate the conversation. Eragon stood and loosened his borrowed sword in its sheath, drawing it out a half inch, so he could respond with all possible speed if Vermûnd or one of his dwarves chose that moment to attack. Vermûnd did not move, however, nor did Orik; they stared at each other like rival wolves and paid no attention to the commotion around them.

When at last Gannel succeeded in restoring order, he said, "Grimstborith Vermûnd, can you refute these charges?"

In a flat, emotionless voice, Vermûnd replied, "I deny them with every bone in my body, and I challenge anyone to prove them to the satisfaction of a reader-of-law."

Gannel turned toward Orik. "Present your evidence, then, Grimstborith Orik, that we may judge whether it is valid or not. There are five readers-of-law here today, if I am not mistaken." He motioned toward the wall, where five white-bearded dwarves stood and bowed. "They will ensure that we do not stray beyond the boundaries of the law in our investigation. Are we agreed?"

"I am agreed," said Ûndin.

"I am agreed," said Hadfala and all the rest of the clan chiefs after her save Vermûnd.

First, Orik placed the amethyst bracelet upon the table. Every clan chief had one of their magicians examine it, and all agreed that as evidence it was inconclusive.

Then Orik had an aide bring in a mirror mounted on a bronze tripod. One of the magicians within his retinue cast a spell, and upon the glossy surface of the mirror there appeared the image of a small, book-filled room. A moment passed, and then a dwarf rushed into the room and bowed toward the clanmeet from within the mirror. In a breathless voice, he introduced himself as Rimmar, and after swearing oaths in the ancient language to ensure his honesty, he told the clanmeet how he and his assistants had made their discoveries concerning the daggers Eragon's attackers had wielded.

When the clan chiefs finished questioning Rimmar, Orik had his warriors bring in the three dwarves the Ingeitum had captured. Gannel ordered them to swear the oaths of truthfulness in the ancient language, but they cursed at him and spat on the floor and refused. Then magicians from all of the different clans joined their thoughts, invaded the prisoners' minds, and wrested from them the information the clanmeet desired. Without exception, the magicians confirmed what Orik had already said.

Lastly, Orik called upon Eragon to testify. Eragon felt nervous as he walked over to the table and the thirteen grim clan chiefs stared at him. He gazed across the room at a small whorl of color on a marble pillar and tried to ignore his discomfort. He repeated the oaths of truthfulness as one of the dwarf magicians gave them to him, and then, speaking no more than was necessary, Eragon told the clan chiefs how he and his guards had been attacked. Afterward, he answered the dwarves' inevitable questions and then allowed two of the magicians—whom Gannel chose at random from among those assembled—to examine his memories of the event. As Eragon lowered the barriers around his mind, he noted that the two magicians appeared apprehensive, and he drew some comfort from the observation. *Good*, he thought. *They will be less likely to wander where they should not if they fear me.*

To Eragon's relief, the inspection went without incident, and the magicians corroborated his account to the clan chiefs.

Gannel rose from his chair and addressed the readers-of-law, asking them: "Are you satisfied with the quality of the evidence Grimstborith Orik and Eragon Shadeslayer have shown us?"

The five white-bearded dwarves bowed, and the middle dwarf said, "We are, Grimstborith Gannel."

Gannel grunted, seeming unsurprised. "Grimstborith Vermûnd, you are responsible for the death of Kvîstor, son of Bauden, and you attempted to kill a guest. By doing so, you have brought shame upon our entire race. What say you to this?"

The clan chief of Az Sweldn rak Anhûin pressed his hands flat against the table, veins bulging underneath his tanned skin. "If this *Dragon Rider* is a knurla in all but blood, then he is no guest and we may treat him as we would any of our enemies from a different clan."

"Why, that's preposterous!" exclaimed Orik, almost sputtering with outrage. "You can't say he—"

"Still your tongue, if you please, Orik," said Gannel. "Shout-

ing will not settle this point. Orik, Nado, Íorûnn, if you will come with me."

Worry began to gnaw at Eragon as the four dwarves went and conferred with the readers-of-law for several minutes. *Surely they won't let Vermûnd escape punishment just because of some verbal trickery!* he thought.

Returning to the table, Íorûnn said, "The readers-of-law are unanimous. Even though Eragon is a sworn member of Dûrgrimst Ingeitum, he also holds positions of importance beyond our realm: namely, that of Dragon Rider, but also that of an official envoy of the Varden, sent by Nasuada to witness the coronation of our next ruler, and also that of a friend of high influence with Queen Islanzadí and her race as a whole. For those reasons, Eragon is due the same hospitality we would extend to any visiting ambassador, prince, monarch, or other person of significance." The dwarf woman glanced sidelong at Eragon, her dark, flashing eyes bold upon his limbs. "In short, he is our honored guest, and we should treat him as such . . . which every knurla who is not cave-mad ought to know."

"Aye, he is our guest," concurred Nado. His lips were pinched and white and his cheeks drawn, as if he had just bitten into an apple only to discover it was not yet ripe.

"What say you now, Vermûnd?" demanded Gannel.

Rising from his seat, the purple-veiled dwarf looked around the table, gazing at each of the clan chiefs in turn. "I say this, and hear me well, grimstborithn: if any clan turns their ax against Az Sweldn rak Anhûin because of these false accusations, we shall consider it an act of war, and we shall respond appropriately. If you imprison me, that too we shall consider an act of war, and we shall respond appropriately." Eragon saw Vermûnd's veil twitch, and he thought the dwarf might have smiled underneath. "If you strike at us in any possible way, whether with steel or with words, no matter how mild your rebuke, we shall consider it an act of war, and we shall respond appropriately. Unless you are eager to rend our country into a thou-sand bloody scraps, I suggest you let the wind waft away this morn-ing's discussion and, in its place, fill your minds with thoughts of who should next rule from upon the granite throne."

The clan chiefs sat in silence for a long while.

Eragon had to bite his tongue to keep from jumping onto the table and railing against Vermûnd until the dwarves agreed to hang him for his crimes. He reminded himself that he had promised Orik that he would follow Orik's lead when dealing with the clanmeet. *Orik is my clan chief, and I must let him respond to this as he sees fit.*

Freowin unfolded his hands and slapped the table with a meaty palm. With his hoarse baritone voice, which carried throughout the room, although it seemed no louder than a whisper, the corpulent dwarf said, "You have shamed our race, Vermûnd. We cannot retain our honor as knurlan and ignore your trespass."

The elderly dwarf woman, Hadfala, shuffled her sheaf of rune-covered pages and said, "What did you think to accomplish, besides our doom, by killing Eragon? Even if the Varden could unseat Galbatorix without him, what of the sorrow the dragon Saphira would rain down upon us if we slew her Rider? She would fill Farthen Dûr with a sea of our own blood."

Not a word came from Vermûnd.

Laughter broke the quiet. The sound was so unexpected, at first Eragon did not realize it was coming from Orik. His mirth subsiding, Orik said, "If we move against you or Az Sweldn rak Anhûin, you will consider it an act of war, Vermûnd? Very well, then we shall not move against you, not at all."

Vermûnd's brow beetled. "How can this provide you with a source of amusement?"

Orik chuckled again. "Because I have thought of something you have not, Vermûnd. You wish us to leave you and your clan alone? Then I propose to the clanmeet that we do as Vermûnd wishes. If Vermûnd had acted upon his own and not as a grimstborith, he would be banished for his offenses upon pain of death. Therefore, let us treat the clan as we would treat the person; let us banish Az Sweldn rak Anhûin from our hearts and minds until they choose to replace Vermûnd with a grimstborith of a more moderate temperament and until they acknowledge their villainy and repent of it to the clanmeet, even if we must wait a thousand years."

The wrinkled skin around Vermûnd's eyes went pale. "You would not dare."

Orik smiled. "Ah, but we would not lay a finger upon you or your kind. We will simply ignore you and refuse to trade with Az Sweldn rak Anhûin. Will you declare war upon us for doing nothing, Vermûnd? For if the meet agrees with me, that is exactly what we shall do: *nothing*. Will you force us at swordpoint to buy your honey and your cloth and your amethyst jewelry? You have not the warriors to compel us so." Turning to the rest of the table, Orik asked, "What say the rest of you?"

The clanmeet did not take long to decide. One by one, the clan chiefs stood and voted to banish Az Sweldn rak Anhûin.

Even Nado, Gáldhiem, and Havard—Vermûnd's erstwhile allies—supported Orik's proposal. With every vote of affirmation, what skin was visible of Vermûnd's face grew ever whiter, until he appeared like a ghost dressed in the clothes of his former life.

When the vote was finished, Gannel pointed toward the door and said, "Begone, Vargrimstn Vermûnd. Leave Tronjheim this very day and may none of Az Sweldn rak Anhûin trouble the clanmeet until they have fulfilled the conditions we have set forth. Until such time as that happens, we shall shun every member of Az Sweldn rak Anhûin. Know this, however: while your clan may absolve themselves of their dishonor, you, Vermûnd, shall always remain Vargrimstn, even unto your dying day. Such is the will of the clanmeet." His declaration concluded, Gannel sat.

Vermûnd remained where he was, his shoulders quivering with an emotion Eragon could not identify. "It is you who have shamed and betrayed our race," he growled. "The Dragon Riders killed all of our clan, save Anhûin and her guards. You expect us to forget this? You expect us to forgive this? Bah! I spit on the graves of your ancestors. We at least have not lost our beards. We shall not cavort with this puppet of the elves while our dead family members still cry out for vengeance."

Outrage gripped Eragon when none of the other clan chiefs replied, and he was about to answer Vermûnd's tirade with harsh words of his own when Orik glanced over at him and shook his head ever so slightly. Difficult as it was, Eragon kept his anger in check, although he wondered why Orik would allow such dire insults to pass uncontested.

It is almost as if . . . Oh.

Pushing himself away from the table, Vermûnd stood, his hands balled into fists and his shoulders hunched high. He resumed speaking, berating and disparaging the clan chiefs with increasing passion until he was shouting at the top of his lungs.

No matter how vile Vermûnd's imprecations were, however, the clan chiefs did not respond. They gazed into the distance, as if pondering complex dilemmas, and their eyes slid over Vermûnd without pause. When, in his fury, Vermûnd grasped Hreidamar by the front of his mail hauberk, three of Hreidamar's guards jumped forward and pulled Vermûnd away, but as they did, Eragon noticed their expressions remained bland and unchanging, as if they were merely helping Hreidamar to straighten his hauberk. Once they released Vermûnd, the guards did not look at him again.

A chill crept up Eragon's spine. The dwarves acted as if Vermûnd had ceased to exist. *So this is what it means to be banished among the dwarves.* Eragon thought he would rather be killed than suffer such a fate, and for a moment, he felt a stir of pity for Vermûnd, but his pity vanished an instant later as he remembered Kvîstor's dying expression.

With a final oath, Vermûnd strode out of the room, followed by those of his clan who had accompanied him to the meet.

The mood among the remaining clan chiefs eased as the doors swung shut behind Vermûnd. Once again the dwarves gazed around without restriction, and they resumed talking in loud voices, discussing what else they would need to do with regard to Az Sweldn rak Anhûin.

Then Orik rapped the pommel of his dagger against the table, and everyone turned to hear what he had to say. "Now that we have dealt with Vermûnd, there is another issue I wish the meet to consider. Our purpose in assembling here is to elect Hrothgar's successor. We have all had much to say upon the topic, but now I believe the time is ripe to put words behind us and allow our actions to speak for us. So I call upon the meet to decide whether we are ready—and we are more than ready, in mine opinion—to proceed to the final vote three days hence, as is our law. My vote, as I cast it, is aye."

Freowin looked at Hadfala, who looked at Gannel, who looked at Manndrâth, who tugged on his drooping nose and looked at Nado, sunk low in his chair and biting the inside of his cheek.

"Aye," said Íorûnn.

"Aye," said Ûndin.

". . . Aye," said Nado, and so did the eight other clan chiefs.

Hours later, when the clanmeet broke for lunch, Orik and Eragon returned to Orik's chambers to eat. Neither of them spoke until they entered his rooms, which were proofed against eavesdroppers. There Eragon allowed himself to smile. "You planned all along to banish Az Sweldn rak Anhûin, didn't you?"

A satisfied expression on his face, Orik smiled as well and slapped his stomach. "That I did. It was the only action I could take that would not inevitably lead to a clan war. We may still have a clan war, but it shall not be of our making. I doubt such a calamity will come to pass, though. As much as they hate you, most of Az Sweldn rak Anhûin will be appalled by what Vermûnd has done in their name. He will not remain grimstborith for long, I think."

"And now you have ensured that the vote for the new king—"

"Or queen."

"—or queen shall take place." Eragon hesitated, reluctant to tarnish Orik's enjoyment of his triumph, but then he asked, "Do you really have the support you need to win the throne?"

Orik shrugged. "Before this morning, no one had the support they needed. Now the balance has shifted, and for the time being, sympathies lie with us. We might as well strike while the iron is hot; we shall never have a better opportunity than this. In any case, we cannot allow the clanmeet to drag on any longer. If you do not return to the Varden soon, all may be lost."

"What shall we do while we wait for the vote?"

"First, we shall celebrate our success with a feast," Orik declared. "Then, when we are sated, we shall continue as before: attempting to gather additional votes while defending those we have already won." Orik's teeth flashed white underneath the fringe of his beard as he smiled again. "But before we consume so much as a single sip of mead, there is something you must attend to, which you have forgotten."

"What?" asked Eragon, puzzled by Orik's obvious delight.

"Why, you must summon Saphira to Tronjheim, of course! Whether I become king or not, we shall crown a new monarch in three days' time. If Saphira is to attend the ceremony, she will need to fly quickly in order to arrive here before then."

With a wordless exclamation, Eragon ran to find a mirror.

INSUBORDINATION

The rich black soil was cool against Roran's hand.

He picked up a loose clod and crumbled it between his fingers, noting with approval that it was moist and full of decomposing leaves, stems, moss, and other organic matter that would provide excellent food for crops. He pressed it to his lips and tongue. The soil tasted alive, full of hundreds of flavors, from pulverized mountains to beetles and punky wood and the tender tips of grass roots.

This is good farmland, thought Roran. He cast his mind back to Palancar Valley, and again he saw the autumn sun streaming through the field of barley outside his family's house—neat rows of golden stalks shifting in the breeze—with the Anora River to the west and the snowcapped mountains rising high on either side of the valley. *That is where I should be, plowing the earth and raising a family with Katrina, not watering the ground with the sap of men's limbs.*

"Ho there!" cried Captain Edric, pointing toward Roran from on his horse. "Have an end to your dawdling, Stronghammer, lest I change my mind about you and leave you to stand guard with the archers!"

Dusting his hands on his leggings, Roran rose from a kneeling position. "Yes, sir! As you wish, sir!" he said, suppressing his dislike for Edric. Since he had joined Edric's company, Roran had attempted to learn what he could of the man's history. From what he heard, Roran had concluded Edric was a competent commander—Nasuada never would have put him in charge of such an important mission otherwise—but he had an abrasive personality, and he disciplined his warriors for even the slightest deviation from established practice, as Roran had learned to his chagrin upon three separate occasions during his first day with Edric's company. It was, Roran believed, a style of command that undermined a man's morale, as well as discouraged creativity and invention from those underneath you. *Perhaps Nasuada gave me to him for those very reasons*, thought Roran. *Or perhaps this is another test of hers. Perhaps she wants to know whether I can swallow my pride long enough to work with a man like Edric.*

Getting back onto Snowfire, Roran rode to the front of the column of two hundred and fifty men. Their mission was simple; since Nasuada and King Orrin had withdrawn the bulk of their forces from Surda, Galbatorix had apparently decided to take advantage of their absence and wreak havoc throughout the defenseless country, sacking towns and villages and burning the crops needed to sustain the invasion of the Empire. The easiest way to eliminate the soldiers would have been for Saphira to fly out and tear them to pieces, but unless she was winging her way toward Eragon, everyone agreed it would be too dangerous for the Varden to be without her for so long. So Nasuada had sent Edric's company to repel the soldiers, whose number her spies had initially estimated to be around three hundred. However, two days ago, Roran and the rest of the warriors had been dismayed when they came across tracks that indicated the size of Galbatorix's force was closer to seven hundred.

Roran reined in Snowfire next to Carn on his dappled mare and scratched his chin while he studied the lay of the land. Before them was a vast expanse of undulating grass, dotted with occasional stands of willow and cottonwood trees. Hawks hunted above, while below, the grass was full of squeaking mice, rabbits, burrowing rodents, and other wildlife. The only evidence that men had ever visited the place before was the swath of trampled vegetation that led toward the eastern horizon, marking the soldiers' trail.

Carn glanced up at the noonday sun, the skin pulling tight around his drooping eyes as he squinted. "We should overtake them before our shadows are longer than we are tall."

"And then we'll discover whether there are enough of us to drive them away," muttered Roran, "or whether they will just massacre us. For once I'd like to outnumber our enemies."

A grim smile appeared on Carn's face. "It is always thus with the Varden."

"Form up!" shouted Edric, and spurred his horse down the trail trampled through the grass. Roran clamped his jaw shut and touched his heels to Snowfire's flanks as the company followed their captain.

Six hours later, Roran sat on Snowfire, hidden within a cluster of beech trees that grew along the edge of a small, flat stream clotted with rushes and strands of floating algae. Through the net of branches that hung before him, Roran gazed upon a crumbling, gray-sided village of no more than twenty houses. Roran had watched with ever-increasing fury as the villagers had spotted the soldiers advancing from the west and then had gathered up a few bundles of possessions and fled south, toward the heart of Surda. If it had been up to him, Roran would have revealed their presence to the villagers and assured them they were not about to lose their houses, not if he and the rest of his companions could prevent it, for he well remembered the pain and desperation and sense of hopelessness that abandoning Carvahall had caused him, and he would have spared them that if he could. Also, he would have asked the men of the village to fight with them. Another ten or twenty sets of arms might mean the difference between victory or defeat, and Roran knew better than most the fervor with which people would fight to defend their homes. However, Edric had rejected the idea and insisted that the Varden remain concealed in the hills southeast of the village.

"We're lucky they're on foot," murmured Carn, indicating the red column of soldiers marching toward the village. "We would not have been able to get here first otherwise."

Roran glanced back at the men gathered behind them. Edric

had given him temporary command over eighty-one warriors. They consisted of swordsmen, spearmen, and a half-dozen archers. One of Edric's familiars, Sand, led another eighty-one of the company, while Edric headed the rest himself. All three groups were pressed against one another among the beech trees, which Roran thought was a mistake; the time it took to organize themselves once they broke from cover would be extra time the soldiers would have to marshal their defenses.

Leaning over toward Carn, Roran said, "I don't see any of them with missing hands or legs or other injuries of note, but that proves nothing one way or another. Can you tell if any of them are men who cannot feel pain?"

Carn sighed. "I wish I could. Your cousin might be able to, for Murtagh and Galbatorix are the only spellcasters Eragon need fear, but I am a poor magician, and I dare not test the soldiers. If there are any magicians disguised among the soldiers, they would know of my spying, and there is every chance I would not be able to break their minds before they alerted their companions we are here."

"We seem to have this discussion every time we are about to fight," Roran observed, studying the soldiers' armaments and trying to decide how best to deploy his men.

With a laugh, Carn said, "That's all right. I only hope we keep having it, because if not—"

"One or both of us will be dead—"

"Or Nasuada will have reassigned us to different captains—"

"And then we might as well be dead, because no one else will guard our backs as well," Roran concluded. A smile touched his lips. It had become an old joke between them. He drew his hammer from his belt and then winced as his right leg twinged where the ox had ripped his flesh with its horn. Scowling, he reached down and massaged the location of the wound.

Carn saw and asked, "Are you well?"

"It won't kill me," said Roran, then reconsidered his words.

"Well, maybe it will, but I'll be blasted if I'm going to wait here while you go off and cut those bumbling oafs to pieces."

When the soldiers reached the village, they marched straight through it, pausing only to break down the door to each house and tramp through the rooms to see if anyone was hiding inside. A dog ran out from behind a rain barrel, his ruff standing on end, and began barking at the soldiers. One of the men stepped forward and threw his spear at the dog, killing it.

As the first of the soldiers reached the far side of the village, Roran tightened his hand around the haft of his hammer in preparation for the charge, but then he heard a series of high-pitched screams, and a sense of dread gripped him. A squad of soldiers emerged from the second-to-last house, dragging three struggling people: a lanky, white-haired man, a young woman with a torn blouse, and a boy no older than eleven.

Sweat sprang up on Roran's brow. In a low, slow monotone, he began to swear, cursing the three captives for not having fled with their neighbors, cursing the soldiers for what they had done and might yet do, cursing Galbatorix, and cursing whatever whim of fate had resulted in the situation as it was. Behind him, he was aware of his men shifting and muttering with anger, eager to punish the soldiers for their brutality.

Having searched all of the houses, the mass of soldiers retraced their steps to the center of the village and formed a rough semicircle around their prisoners.

Yes! crowed Roran to himself as the soldiers turned their backs to the Varden. Edric's plan had been to wait for them to do just that. In anticipation of the order to charge, Roran rose up several inches above his saddle, his entire body tense. He tried to swallow, but his throat was too dry.

The officer in charge of the soldiers, who was the only man among them on a horse, dismounted his steed and exchanged a few inaudible words with the white-haired villager. Without warning, the officer drew his saber and decapitated the man, then hopped backward to avoid the resulting spray of blood. The young woman screamed even louder than before.

"Charge," said Edric.

It took Roran a half second to comprehend that the word Edric had uttered so calmly was the command he had been waiting for.

"Charge!" shouted Sand on the other side of Edric, and galloped out of the copse of beech trees along with his men.

"Charge!" shouted Roran, and dug his heels into Snowfire's sides. He ducked behind his shield as Snowfire carried him through the net of branches, then lowered it again when they were in the open, flying down the side of the hill, with the thunder of hoofbeats surrounding them. Desperate to save the woman and the boy, Roran urged Snowfire to the limit of his speed. Looking back, he was heartened to see that his contingent of men had separated from the rest of the Varden without too much trouble; aside from a few stragglers, the majority were in a single bunch not thirty feet behind him.

Roran glimpsed Carn riding at the vanguard of Edric's men, his gray cloak flapping in the wind. Once again, Roran wished Edric had allowed them to remain in the same group.

As were his orders, Roran did not enter the village head-on, but rather veered to the left and rode around the buildings, so as to flank the soldiers and attack them from another direction. Sand did the same on the right, while Edric and his warriors drove straight into the village.

A line of houses concealed the initial clash from Roran, but he heard a chorus of frantic shouts, then a series of strange, metallic twangs, and then the screams of men and horses.

Worry knotted Roran's gut. *What was that noise? Could it be metal bows? Do they exist?* Regardless of the cause, he knew there should not have been so many horses crying out in agony. Roran's limbs went cold as he realized with utter certainty that the attack had somehow gone wrong and that the battle might already be lost.

He pulled hard on Snowfire's reins as they passed the last house, steering him toward the center of the village. Behind him, his men did the same. Two hundred yards ahead, Roran saw a triple line of soldiers positioned between two houses, so as to block their way. The soldiers seemed unafraid of the horses racing toward them.

Roran hesitated. His orders were clear: he and his men were to charge the western flank and cut their way through Galbatorix's troops until they rejoined Sand and Edric. However, Edric had not told Roran what he should do if riding straight up to the soldiers no longer seemed a good idea once he and his men were in position. And Roran knew that if he deviated from his orders, even if it was to prevent his men from being massacred, he would be guilty of insubordination and Edric could punish him accordingly.

Then the soldiers swept aside their voluminous cloaks and raised drawn crossbows to their shoulders.

In that instant, Roran decided that he would do whatever was necessary in order to ensure the Varden won the battle. He was not about to let the soldiers destroy his force with a single volley of arrows just because he wished to avoid the unpleasant consequences of defying his captain.

"Take cover!" shouted Roran, and wrenched Snowfire's head to the right, forcing the animal to swerve behind a house. A dozen quarrels buried themselves in the side of the building a second later. Turning around, Roran saw that all but one of his warriors had managed to duck behind nearby houses before the soldiers fired. The man who had been too slow lay bleeding in the dirt, a pair of quarrels projecting from his chest. The bolts had torn through his mail hauberk as if it were no thicker than a sheet of tissue. Frightened by the smell of blood, his horse kicked up its heels and fled the village, leaving a plume of dust rising in its wake.

Roran reached over and grasped the edge of a beam in the side of the house, holding Snowfire in place while he desperately tried to figure out how to proceed. The soldiers had him and his men pinned down; they could not step back out into the open without being shot so full of quarrels, they would resemble hedgehogs.

511

A group of Roran's warriors rode up to him from a house that his own building partially shielded from the soldiers' line of sight. "What should we do, Stronghammer?" they asked him. They did not seem bothered by the fact that he had disobeyed his orders; to the contrary, they looked at him with expressions of newfound trust.

Thinking as fast as he could, Roran cast his gaze around. By chance, his eyes alighted upon the bow and quiver strapped behind one of the men's saddles. Roran smiled. Only a few of the warriors fought as archers, but they all carried a bow and arrows so they could hunt for food and help feed the company when they were alone in the wilderness, without support from the rest of the Varden.

Roran pointed toward the house he was leaning against and said, "Take your bows and climb onto the roof, as many of you as will fit, but if you value your lives, stay out of sight until I say otherwise. When I tell you to, start shooting and keep shooting until you run out of arrows or until every last soldier is dead. Understood?"

"Yes, sir!"

"Get going, then. The rest of you, find buildings of your own where you can pick off the soldiers. Harald, spread the word to everyone else, and find ten of our best spearmen and ten of our best swordsmen and bring them here as fast as you can."

"Yes, sir!"

With a flurry of motion, the warriors hurried to obey. Those who were closest to Roran retrieved their bows and quivers from behind their saddles and then, standing upon the backs of their horses, pulled themselves onto the thatched roof of the house. Four minutes later, the majority of Roran's men were in place on the roofs of seven different houses—with about eight men per roof—and Harald had returned with the requested swordsmen and spearmen in tow.

To the warriors gathered around him, Roran said, "Right, now listen. When I give the order, the men up there will start shooting. As soon as the first flight of arrows strikes the soldiers, we're going to ride out and attempt to rescue Captain Edric. If we can't, we'll have to settle for giving the red-tunics a taste of good cold steel. The archers should provide enough confusion for us to close with the soldiers before they can use their crossbows. Am I understood?"

"Yes, sir!"

"Then fire!" Roran shouted.

With full-throated yells, the men stationed on the houses rose up above the ridges of the roofs and, as one, fired their bows at the soldiers below. The swarm of arrows whistled through the air like bloodthirsty shrikes diving toward their prey.

An instant later, when soldiers began to howl with agony at their wounds, Roran said, "Now *ride!*" and jabbed his heels into Snowfire.

Together, he and his men galloped around the side of the house, pulling their steeds into such a tight turn that they nearly fell over. Relying on his speed and the skill of the archers for protection, Roran skirted the soldiers, who were flailing in disarray, until he came upon the site of Edric's disastrous charge. There the ground was slick with blood, and the corpses of many good men and fine horses littered the space between the houses. Edric's remaining forces were engaged in hand-to-hand combat with the soldiers. To Roran's surprise, Edric was still alive, fighting back to back with five of his men.

"Stay with me!" Roran shouted to his companions as they raced into the battle.

Lashing out with his hooves, Snowfire knocked two soldiers to the ground, breaking their sword arms and staving in their rib cages. Pleased with the stallion, Roran laid about himself with his hammer, snarling with the fierce joy of battle as he felled soldier after soldier, none of whom could withstand the ferocity of his assault. "To me!" he shouted as he drew abreast of Edric and the other survivors. "To me!" In front of him, arrows continued to rain down upon the mass of soldiers, forcing them to cover themselves with their shields while at the same time trying to fend off the Varden's swords and spears.

Once he and his warriors had surrounded the Varden who were on foot, Roran shouted, "Back! Back! To the houses!" Step by step, the lot of them withdrew until they were out of reach of the soldiers' blades, and then they turned and ran toward the nearest house. The soldiers shot and killed three of the Varden along the way, but the rest arrived at the building unharmed.

Edric slumped against the side of the house, gasping for breath. When again he was able to speak, he gestured at Roran's men and said, "Your intervention is most timely and welcome, Stronghammer, but why do I see you here, and not riding out from among the soldiers, as I expected?"

Then Roran explained what he had done and pointed out the archers on the roofs.

A dark scowl appeared on Edric's brow as he listened to Roran's account. However, he did not chastise Roran for his disobedience but merely said, "Have those men come down at once. They have succeeded in breaking the soldiers' discipline. Now we must rely upon honest blade-work to dispose of them."

"There are too few of us left to attack the soldiers directly!" protested Roran. "They outnumber us better than three to one."

"Then we shall make up in valor what we lack in numbers!" Edric bellowed. "I was told you had courage, Stronghammer, but obviously rumor is mistaken and you are as timid as a frightened rabbit. Now do as you're told, and do not question me again!" The captain indicated one of Roran's warriors. "You there, lend me your steed." After the man dismounted, Edric pulled himself into the saddle and said, "Half of you on horse, follow me; I go to reinforce Sand. Everyone else, remain with Roran." Kicking his mount in the sides, Edric galloped away with the men who chose to follow him, racing from building to building as they worked their way around the soldiers clumped in the center of the village.

Roran shook with fury as he watched them depart. Never before had he allowed anyone to question his courage without answering his critic with words or blows. So long as the battle persisted, however, it would be inappropriate for him to confront Edric. *Very well*, Roran thought, *I shall demonstrate to Edric the courage he thinks I lack. But that is all he shall have from me. I will not send the archers to fight the soldiers face to face when they are safer and more effective where they are.*

Roran turned and inspected the men Edric had left to him. Among those they had rescued, Roran was delighted to see Carn, who was scratched and bloody but, on the whole, unharmed. They nodded to each other, and then Roran addressed the group: "You have heard what Edric said. I disagree. If we do as he wishes, all of us will end up piled in a cairn before sunset. We can still win this battle, but not by marching to our own deaths! What we lack in numbers, we can make up with cunning. You know how I came to join the Varden. You know I have fought and defeated the Empire before, and in just such a village! This I can do, I swear to you. But I cannot do it alone. Will you follow me? Think carefully. I will claim responsibility for ignoring Edric's orders, but he and Nasuada may still punish everyone who was involved."

"Then they would be fools," growled Carn. "Would they prefer that we died here? No, I think not. You may count on me, Roran."

As Carn made his declaration, Roran saw how the other men squared their shoulders and set their jaws and how their eyes burned with renewed determination, and he knew they had decided to cast their lot with him, if only because they would not want to be parted from the only magician in their company. Many was the warrior of the Varden who owed his life to a member of Du Vrangr Gata, and the men-at-arms Roran had met would sooner stab themselves in a foot than go into battle without a spellcaster close at hand.

"Aye," said Harald. "You may count on us as well, Stronghammer."

"Then follow me!" said Roran. Reaching down, he pulled Carn up onto Snowfire behind himself, then hurried with his group back around the village to where the bowmen on the roofs continued to fire arrows at the soldiers. As Roran and the men with him dashed from house to house, quarrels buzzed past them—sounding like giant, angry insects—and one even buried itself halfway through Harald's shield.

Once they were safely behind cover, Roran had the men who were still mounted give their bows and arrows to the men on foot, whom he then sent to climb the houses and join the other archers. As they scrambled to obey him, Roran beckoned to Carn, who had jumped off Snowfire the moment they ceased moving, and said, "I need a spell of you. Can you shield me and ten others from these bolts?"

Carn hesitated. "For how long?"

"A minute? An hour? Who knows?"

"Shielding that many people from more than a handful of bolts would soon exceed the bounds of my strength. . . . Although, if you don't care if I stop the bolts in their tracks, I could deflect them from you, which—"

"That would be fine."

"Who exactly do you want me to protect?"

Roran pointed at the men he had picked to join him, and Carn asked each of them their names. Standing with his shoulders hunched inward, Carn began to mutter in the ancient language, his face pale and strained. Three times he tried to cast the spell, and three times he failed. "I'm sorry," he said, and released an unsteady breath. "I can't seem to concentrate."

"Blast it, don't apologize," growled Roran. "Just do it!" Leaping down from Snowfire, he grasped Carn on either side of his head, holding him in place. "Look at me! Look into the center of my eyes. That's it. Keep staring at me. . . . Good. Now place the ward around us."

Carn's features cleared and his shoulders loosened, and then, in a confident voice, he recited the incantation. As he uttered the last word, he sagged slightly in Roran's grip before recovering. "It is done," he said.

Roran patted him on the shoulder, then clambered into

Snowfire's saddle again. Sweeping his gaze over the ten horsemen, he said, "Guard my sides and my back, but otherwise keep behind me so long as I am able to swing my hammer."

"Yes, sir!"

"Remember, the bolts cannot harm you now. Carn, you stay here. Don't move too much; conserve your strength. If you feel like you can't maintain the spell any longer, signal us before you end it. Agreed?"

Carn sat on the front step of the house and nodded. "Agreed."

Renewing his grip on his shield and hammer, Roran took a deep breath, attempting to calm himself. "Brace yourselves," he said, and clucked his tongue to Snowfire.

With the ten horsemen following, Roran rode out into the middle of the dirt street that ran between the houses and faced the soldiers once more. Five hundred or so of Galbatorix's troops remained in the center of the village, most of them crouching or kneeling behind their shields while they struggled to reload their crossbows. Occasionally, a soldier would stand and loose a bolt at one of the archers on the roofs before dropping back behind his shield as a flight of arrows sliced through the air where he had just been. Throughout the corpse-strewn clearing, patches of arrows studded the ground, like reeds sprouting from the bloody soil. Several hundred feet away, on the far side of the soldiers, Roran could see a knot of thrashing bodies, and he assumed that was where Sand, Edric, and whatever remained of their forces were fighting the soldiers. If the young woman and the boy were still in the clearing, he did not notice them.

A quarrel buzzed toward Roran. When the bolt was less than a yard from his chest, it abruptly changed direction and hurtled off at an angle, missing him and his men. Roran flinched, but the missile was already past. His throat constricted, and his heartbeat doubled.

Glancing around, Roran spotted a broken wagon leaning against a house off to his left. He pointed at it and said, "Pull that over here and lay it upside down. Block as much of the street as you can." To

517

the archers, he shouted, "Don't let the soldiers sneak around and attack us from the sides! When they come at us, thin out their ranks as much as you can. And as soon as you run out of arrows, come join us."

"Yes, sir!"

"Just be careful you don't shoot us by accident, or I swear I'll haunt your halls for the rest of time!"

"Yes, sir!"

More quarrels flew at Roran and the other horsemen in the street, but in every case, the bolts glanced off Carn's ward and veered into a wall or the ground or vanished into the sky.

Roran watched his men drag the wagon into the street. When they were nearly finished, he lifted his chin, filled his lungs, and then, projecting his voice toward the soldiers, he roared, "Ho there, you cowering carrion dogs! See how only eleven of us bar your way. Win past us, and you win your freedom. Try your hand if you have the guts. What? You hesitate? Where is your manhood, you deformed maggots, you bilious, swine-faced murderers? Your fathers were dribbling half-wits who should have been drowned at birth! Aye, and your mothers were poxy trollops and the consorts of Urgals!" Roran smiled with satisfaction as several of the soldiers howled with outrage and began to insult him in return. One of the soldiers, however, seemed to lose his will to continue fighting, for he sprang to his feet and ran northward, covering himself with his shield and darting from side to side in a desperate attempt to avoid the archers. Despite his efforts, the Varden shot him dead before he had gone more than a hundred feet. "Ha!" exclaimed Roran. "Cowards you are, every last one of you, you verminous river rats! If it will give you spine, then know this: Roran Stronghammer is my name, and Eragon Shadeslayer is my cousin! Kill me, and that foul king of yours will reward you with an earldom, or more. But you will have to kill me with a blade; your crossbows are of no use against me. Come now, you slugs; you leeches; you starving, white-bellied ticks! Come and best me if you can!"

518

With a flurry of battle-cries, a group of thirty soldiers dropped their crossbows, drew their flashing swords, and, with shields held high, ran toward Roran and his men.

From over his right shoulder, Roran heard Harald say, "Sir, there are many more of them than us."

"Aye," Roran said, keeping his eyes fixed on the approaching soldiers. Four of them stumbled and then lay motionless on the ground, pierced through by numerous shafts.

"If they all charge us at once, we won't stand a chance."

"Yes, but they won't. Look, they're confused and disorganized. Their commander must have fallen. As long as we maintain order, they cannot overwhelm us."

"But, Stronghammer, we cannot kill that many men ourselves!"

Roran glanced back at Harald. "Of course we can! We fight to protect our families and to reclaim our homes and our lands. They fight because Galbatorix forces them to. They have not the heart for this battle. So think of your families, think of your homes, and remember it is they you are defending. A man who fights for something greater than himself may kill a hundred enemies with ease!" As he spoke, Roran saw in his mind an image of Katrina clad in her blue wedding dress, and he smelled the scent of her skin, and he heard the muted tones of her voice from their discussions late at night.

Katrina.

Then the soldiers were upon them, and for a span Roran heard nothing but the thud of swords bouncing off his shield and the clang of his hammer as he struck the soldiers' helms and the cries of the soldiers as they crumpled underneath his blows. The soldiers threw themselves against him with desperate strength, but they were no match for him or his men. When he vanquished the last of the attacking soldiers, Roran burst out laughing, exhilarated. What a joy it was to crush those who would harm his wife and his unborn child!

He was pleased to see that none of his warriors had been seriously injured. He also noticed that during the fray, several of the archers had descended from the roofs to fight on horseback with them. Roran grinned at the newcomers and said, "Welcome to the battle!"

"A warm welcome indeed!" one of them replied.

Pointing with his gore-covered hammer toward the right side of the street, Roran said, "You, you, and you, pile the bodies over there. Make a funnel out of them and the wagon, so that only two or three soldiers can get to us at once."

"Yes, sir!" the warriors answered, swinging down from their horses.

A quarrel whizzed toward Roran. He ignored it and focused on the main body of soldiers, where a group, perhaps a hundred strong, was massing in preparation for a second onslaught. "Hurry!" he shouted to the men shifting the corpses. "They're almost upon us. Harald, go help."

Roran wet his lips, nervous, as he watched his men labor while the soldiers advanced. To his relief, the four Varden dragged the last body into place and clambered back onto their steeds moments before the wave of soldiers struck.

The houses on either side of the street, as well as the overturned wagon and the gruesome barricade of human remains, slowed and compressed the flow of soldiers, until they were nearly at a standstill when they reached Roran. The soldiers were packed so tightly, they were helpless to escape the arrows that streaked toward them from above.

The first two ranks of soldiers carried spears, with which they menaced Roran and the other Varden. Roran parried three separate thrusts, cursing the whole while as he realized that he could not reach past the spears with his hammer. Then a soldier stabbed Snowfire in the shoulder, and Roran leaned forward to keep from being thrown as the stallion squealed and reared.

As Snowfire landed on all fours, Roran slid out of the saddle, keeping the stallion between him and the hedge of spear-wielding soldiers. Snowfire bucked as another spear pierced his hide. Before the soldiers could wound him again, Roran pulled on Snowfire's reins and forced him to prance backward until there was enough room among the other horses for the stallion to turn around. "Yah!" he shouted, and slapped Snowfire on the rump, sending him galloping out of the village.

"Make way!" Roran bellowed, waving at the Varden. They cleared a path for him between their steeds, and he bounded to the forefront of the fight again, sticking his hammer through his belt as he did.

A soldier jabbed a spear at Roran's chest. He blocked it with his wrist, bruising himself on the hard wooden shaft, and then yanked the spear out of the soldier's hands. The man fell flat on his face. Twirling the weapon, Roran stabbed the man, then lunged forward and lanced two more soldiers. Roran took a wide stance, planting his feet firmly in the rich soil where once he would have sought to raise crops, and shook the spear at his foes, shouting, "Come, you misbegotten bastards! Kill me if you can! I am Roran Stronghammer, and I fear no man alive!"

The soldiers shuffled forward, three men stepping over the bodies of their former comrades to exchange blows with Roran. Dancing to the side, Roran drove his spear into the jaw of the rightmost soldier, shattering his teeth. A pennant of blood trailed the blade as Roran withdrew the weapon and, dropping to one knee, impaled the central soldier through an armpit.

An impact jarred Roran's left shoulder. His shield seemed to double in weight. Rising, he saw a spear buried in the oak planks of his shield and the remaining soldier of the trio rushing at him with a drawn sword. Roran lifted his spear above his head as if he were about to throw it and, when the soldier faltered, kicked him between the fork of his legs. He dispatched the man with a single blow. During the momentary lull in combat that followed, Roran disengaged his arm from the useless shield and cast it and the attached spear under the feet of his enemies, hoping to tangle their legs.

More soldiers shuffled forward, quailing before Roran's feral grin and stabbing spear. A mound of bodies grew before him. When it reached the height of his waist, Roran bounded to the top of the blood-soaked berm, and there he remained, despite the treacherous footing, for the height gave him an advantage. Since the soldiers were forced to climb up a ramp of corpses to reach him, he was able to kill many of them when they stumbled over an arm or a leg or stepped upon the soft neck of one of their predecessors or slipped on a slanting shield.

From his elevated position, Roran could see that the rest of the soldiers had chosen to join the assault, save for a score across the village who were still battling Sand's and Edric's warriors. He realized he would have no more rest until the battle had concluded.

Roran acquired dozens of wounds as the day wore on. Many of his injuries were minor—a cut on the inside of a forearm, a broken finger, a scratch across his ribs where a dagger had shorn through his mail—but others were not. From where he lay on the pile of bodies, a soldier stabbed Roran through his right calf muscle, hobbling him. Soon afterward, a heavyset man smelling of onions and cheese fell against Roran and, with his dying breath, shoved the bolt of a crossbow into Roran's left shoulder, which thereafter prevented Roran from lifting his arm overhead. Roran left the bolt embedded in his flesh, for he knew he might bleed to death if he pulled it out. Pain became Roran's ruling sensation; every movement caused him fresh agony, but to stand still was to die, and so he kept dealing deathblows, regardless of his wounds and regardless of his weariness.

Roran was sometimes aware of the Varden behind or beside him, such as when they threw a spear past him, or when the blade of a sword would dart around his shoulder to fell a soldier who was about to brain him, but for the most part Roran faced the soldiers alone, because of the pile of bodies he stood on and the restricted amount of space between the overturned wagon and the sides of the houses. Above, the archers who still had arrows maintained their lethal barrage, their gray-goose shafts penetrating bone and sinew alike.

Late in the battle, Roran thrust his spear at a soldier, and as the tip struck the man's armor, the haft cracked and split along its length. That he was still alive seemed to catch the soldier by surprise, for he hesitated before swinging his sword in retaliation. His imprudent delay allowed Roran to duck underneath the length of singing steel and seize another spear from the ground, with which he slew the soldier. To Roran's dismay and disgust, the second spear lasted less than a minute before it too shattered in his grip. Throwing the splintered remains at the soldiers, Roran took a shield from a corpse and drew his hammer from his belt. His hammer, at least, had never failed him.

Exhaustion proved to be Roran's greatest adversary as the last of the soldiers gradually approached, each man waiting his turn to duel him. Roran's limbs felt heavy and lifeless, his vision flickered, and he could not seem to get enough air, and yet he somehow always managed to summon the energy to defeat his next opponent. As his reflexes slowed, the soldiers dealt him numerous cuts and bruises that he could have easily avoided earlier.

When gaps appeared between the soldiers, and through them Roran could see open space, he knew his ordeal was nearly at an end. He did not offer the final twelve men mercy, nor did they ask it of him, even though they could not have hoped to battle their way past him as well as the Varden beyond. Nor did they attempt to flee. Instead, they rushed at him, snarling, cursing, desiring only to kill the man who had slain so many of their comrades before they too passed into the void.

In a way, Roran admired their courage.

Arrows sprouted from the chests of four of the men, downing them. A spear thrown from somewhere behind Roran took a fifth man under the collarbone, and he too toppled onto a bed of corpses. Two more spears claimed their victims, and then the men reached Roran. The lead soldier hewed at Roran with a spiked ax. Although Roran could feel the head of the crossbow bolt grating against his bone, he threw up his left arm and blocked the ax with his shield. Howling with pain and anger, as well as an overwhelming desire for the battle to end, Roran whipped his hammer around and slew the soldier with a blow to the head. Without pause, Roran hopped forward on his good leg and struck the next soldier twice in the chest before he could defend himself, cracking his ribs. The third man parried two of Roran's attacks, but then Roran deceived him with a feint and slew him as well. The final two soldiers converged on Roran from either side, swinging at his ankles as they climbed to the summit of the piled corpses. His strength flagging, Roran sparred with them for a long and wearisome while, both giving and receiving wounds, until at last he killed one man by caving in his helm and the other by breaking his neck with a well-placed blow.

Roran swayed and then collapsed.

He felt himself being lifted up and opened his eyes to see Harald holding a wineskin to his lips. "Drink this," Harald said. "You'll feel better."

His chest heaving, Roran consumed several draughts between gasps. The sun-warmed wine stung the inside of his battered mouth. He felt his legs steady and said, "It's all right; you can let go of me now."

Roran leaned against his hammer and surveyed the battleground. For the first time he appreciated how high the mound of bodies had grown; he and his companions stood at least twenty feet in the air, which was nearly level with the tops of the houses on either side. Roran saw that most of the soldiers had died of arrows, but even so, he knew that he had slain a vast number by himself.

"How . . . how many?" he asked Harald.

The blood-spattered warrior shook his head. "I lost count after thirty-two. Perhaps another can say. What you did, Stronghammer . . . Never have I seen such a feat before, not by a man of human abilities. The dragon Saphira chose well; the men of your family are fighters like no others. Your prowess is unmatched by any mortal, Stronghammer. However many you slew here today, I—"

"It was one hundred and ninety-three!" cried Carn, clambering toward them from below.

"Are you sure?" asked Roran, unbelieving.

Carn nodded as he reached them. "Aye! I watched, and I kept careful count. One hundred and ninety-three, it was—ninety-four if you count the man you stabbed through the gut before the archers finished him off."

The tally astounded Roran. He had not suspected the total was quite so large. A hoarse chuckle escaped him. "A pity there are no more of them. Another seven and I would have an even two hundred."

The other men laughed as well.

His thin face furrowed with concern, Carn reached for the bolt sticking out of Roran's left shoulder, saying, "Here, let me see to your wounds."

"No!" said Roran, and brushed him away. "There may be others who are more seriously injured than I am. Tend to them first."

"Roran, several of those cuts could prove fatal unless I stanch the bleeding. It won't take but a—"

"I'm fine," he growled. "Leave me alone."

"Roran, just look at yourself!"

He did and averted his gaze. "Be quick about it, then." Roran stared into the featureless sky, his mind empty of thought while Carn pulled the bolt out of his shoulder and muttered various spells. In every spot where the magic took effect, Roran felt his skin itch and crawl, followed by a blessed cessation of pain. When Carn had finished, Roran still hurt, but he did not hurt quite so badly, and his mind was clearer than before.

The healing left Carn gray-faced and shaking. He leaned against his knees until his tremors stopped. "I will go . . ." He paused for breath. ". . . go help the rest of the wounded now." He straightened and picked his way down the mound, lurching from side to side as if he were drunk.

Roran watched him go, concerned. Then it occurred to him to wonder about the fate of the rest of their expedition. He looked toward the far side of the village and saw nothing but scattered bodies, some clad in the red of the Empire, others in the brown wool favored by the Varden. "What of Edric and Sand?" he asked Harald.

"I'm sorry, Stronghammer, but I saw nothing beyond the reach of my sword."

Calling to the few men who still stood on the roofs of the houses, Roran asked, "What of Edric and Sand?"

"We do not know, Stronghammer!" they replied.

Steadying himself with his hammer, Roran slowly picked his way down the tumbled ramp of bodies and, with Harald and three other men by his side, crossed the clearing in the center of the village, executing every soldier they found still alive. When they arrived at the edge of the clearing, where the number of slain Varden surpassed the number of slain soldiers, Harald banged his sword on his shield and shouted, "Is anyone still alive?"

After a moment, a voice came back at them from among the houses: "Name yourself!"

"Harald and Roran Stronghammer and others of the Varden. If you serve the Empire, then surrender, for your comrades are dead and you cannot defeat us!"

From somewhere between the houses came a crash of falling metal, and then in ones and twos, warriors of the Varden emerged from hiding and limped toward the clearing, many of them supporting their wounded comrades. They appeared dazed, and some were stained with so much blood, Roran at first mistook them for captured soldiers. He counted four-and-twenty men. Among the final group of stragglers was Edric, helping along a man who had lost his right arm during the fighting.

Roran motioned, and two of his men hurried to relieve Edric of his burden. The captain straightened from under the weight. With slow steps, he walked over to Roran and looked him straight in the eye, his expression unreadable. Neither he nor Roran moved, and Roran was aware that the clearing had grown exceptionally quiet.

Edric was the first to speak. "How many of your men survived?"

"Most. Not all, but most."

Edric nodded. "And Carn?"

"He lives. . . . What of Sand?"

"A soldier shot him during his charge. He died but a few minutes ago." Edric looked past Roran, then toward the mound of bodies. "You defied my orders, Stronghammer."

"I did."

Edric held out an open hand toward him.

"Captain, no!" exclaimed Harald, stepping forward. "If it weren't for Roran, none of us would be standing here. And you should have seen what he did; he slew nearly two hundred by himself!"

Harald's pleas made no impression on Edric, who continued to hold out his hand. Roran remained impassive as well.

Turning to him then, Harald said, "Roran, you know the men are yours. Just say the word, and we will—"

Roran silenced him with a glare. "Don't be a fool."

Between thin lips, Edric said, "At least you are not completely devoid of sense. Harald, keep your teeth shut unless you want to lead the packhorses the whole way back."

Lifting his hammer, Roran handed it to Edric. Then he unbuckled his belt, upon which hung his sword and his dagger, and those too he surrendered to Edric. "I have no other weapons," he said.

Edric nodded, grim, and slung the sword belt over one shoulder. "Roran Stronghammer, I hereby relieve you of command. Have I your word of honor you will not attempt to flee?"

"You do."

"Then you will make yourself useful where you may, but in all else, you will comport yourself as a prisoner." Edric looked around and pointed at another warrior. "Fuller, you will assume Roran's position until we return to the main body of the Varden and Nasuada can decide what is to be done about this."

"Yes, sir," said Fuller.

* * *

For several hours, Roran bent his back alongside the other warriors as they collected their dead and buried them on the outskirts of the village. During the process, Roran learned that only nine of his eighty-one warriors had died in the battle, while between them, Edric and Sand had lost almost a hundred and fifty men, and Edric would have lost more, except that a handful of his warriors had remained with Roran after he rode to their rescue.

When they finished interring their casualties, the Varden retrieved their arrows, then built a pyre in the center of the village, stripped the soldiers of their gear, dragged them onto the pile of wood, and set it ablaze. The burning bodies filled the sky with a pillar of greasy black smoke that drifted upward for what seemed like miles. Through it, the sun appeared as a flat red disk.

The young woman and the boy the soldiers had captured were nowhere to be found. Since their bodies were not among the dead, Roran guessed the two had fled the village when the fighting broke out, which, he thought, was probably the best thing they could have done. He wished them luck, wherever they had gone.

To Roran's pleased surprise, Snowfire trotted back into the village minutes before the Varden were to depart. At first the stallion was skittish and standoffish, allowing no one to approach, but by talking to him in a low voice, Roran managed to calm the stallion enough to clean and bandage the wounds in the horse's shoulder. Since it would be unwise to ride Snowfire until he was fully healed, Roran tied him to the front of the packhorses, which the stallion took an immediate dislike to, flattening his ears, flicking his tail from side to side, and curling his lips to bare his teeth.

"Behave yourself," said Roran, stroking his neck. Snowfire rolled an eyeball at him and nickered, his ears relaxing slightly.

Then Roran pulled himself onto a gelding that had belonged to one of the dead Varden and took his place at the rear of the line of men assembled between the houses. Roran ignored the many glances they directed at him, although it heartened him when several of the warriors murmured, "Well done."

As he sat waiting for Edric to give the command to start forward, Roran thought of Nasuada and Katrina and Eragon, and a cloud of dread shadowed his thoughts as he wondered how they would react when they learned of his mutiny. Roran pushed away his worries a second later. *I did what was right and necessary,* he told himself. *I won't regret it, no matter what may come of it.*

"Move on out!" shouted Edric from the head of the procession.

Roran spurred his steed into a brisk walk, and as one, he and the other men rode west, away from the village, leaving the pile of soldiers to burn itself to extinction.

MESSAGE IN A MIRROR

The morning sun beat down on Saphira, suffusing her with a pleasant warmth.

She lay basking on a smooth shelf of stone several feet above Eragon's empty cloth-shell-tent. The night's activities, flying around scouting the Empire's locations—as she had every night since Nasuada sent Eragon to the big-hollow-mountain-Farthen Dûr—had left her drowsy. The flights were necessary to conceal Eragon's absence, but the routine wore on her, for while the dark held no terrors for her, she was not nocturnal by habit, and she disliked having to do anything with such regularity. Also, since it took the Varden so long to move from place to place, she spent most of her time soaring over much the same landscape every night. The only recent excitement was when she spotted stunted-thoughts-red-scales-Thorn low on the northeastern horizon the previous morning. He had not turned to confront her, however, but had continued on his way, heading deeper into the Empire. When Saphira had reported what she had seen, Nasuada, Arya, and the elves guarding Saphira had reacted like a flock of frightened jays, screaming and yammering at each other while darting every which way. They had even insisted that black-blue-wolf-hair-Blödhgarm fly with her in the guise of Eragon, which of course she had refused to allow. It was one thing to permit the elf to place a water-shadow-ghost of Eragon on her back every time she took off from or landed among the Varden, but she was not about to let anyone other than Eragon ride her unless a battle was imminent, and perhaps not even then.

Saphira yawned and stretched out her right foreleg, spreading the clawed fingers of her paw. Relaxing again, she wrapped her tail around her body and adjusted the position of her head on her paws, visions of deer and other prey drifting through her mind.

Not long afterward, she heard the patter of feet as someone ran through the camp, heading toward Nasuada's folded-wing-red-butterfly-chrysalis-tent. Saphira paid little attention to the sound; messengers were always hurrying to and fro.

Just as she was about to fall asleep, Saphira heard another runner dash past, then, after a brief interval, two more. Without opening her eyes, she extended the tip of her tongue and tasted the air. She detected no unusual odors. Deciding that the disturbance was not worth investigating, she drifted off into dreams of diving for fish in a cool green lake.

Angry shouting woke Saphira.

She did not stir as she listened to a large number of round-ear-two-legs arguing with each other. They were too far away for her to make out the words, but from the tone of their voices, she could tell they were angry enough to kill. Disputes sometimes broke out among the Varden, just as they did in any large herd, but never before had she heard so many two-legs argue for so long and with so much passion.

A dull throbbing formed at the base of Saphira's skull as the two-legs' shouting intensified. She tightened her claws against the stone beneath her, and with sharp cracks, thin wafers of the quartz-laden rock flaked off around the tips of her talons.

I shall count to thirty-three, she thought, *and if they have not stopped by then, they had better hope that whatever upset them was worth disrupting the rest of a daughter-of-the-wind!*

When Saphira reached the count of seven-and-twenty, the two-legs fell silent. *At last!* Shifting to a more comfortable position, she prepared to resume her much-needed slumber.

Metal clinked, plant-cloth-hides swished, skin-paw-coverings thudded against the ground, and the unmistakable scent of dark-skin-warrior-Nasuada wafted over Saphira. *What now?* she wondered, and briefly considered roaring at everyone until they fled in terror and left her alone.

Saphira opened a single eye and saw Nasuada and her six guards striding toward where she lay. At the lower end of the slab of stone, Nasuada ordered her guards to remain behind with Blödhgarm and the other elves—who were sparring with each other on a small expanse of grass—and then she climbed the slab by herself.

"Greetings, Saphira," Nasuada said. She wore a red dress, and the color seemed unnaturally strong against the green leaves of the apple trees behind her. Glints of light from Saphira's scales mottled her face.

Saphira blinked once, feeling no inclination to answer with words.

After glancing around, Nasuada stepped closer to Saphira's head and whispered, "Saphira, I must speak to you in private. You can reach into my mind, but I cannot reach into yours. Can you remain inside me, so I can think what I need to say and you will hear?"

Extending herself toward the woman's tense-hard-tired-consciousness, Saphira allowed her irritation at being kept from her sleep to wash over Nasuada, and then she said, *I can if I so choose, but I would never do so without your permission.*

Of course, Nasuada replied. *I understand.* At first Saphira received nothing but disjointed images and emotions from the woman: a gallows with an empty noose, blood on the ground, snarling faces, dread, weariness, and an undercurrent of grim determination. *Forgive me,* said Nasuada. *I have had a trying morning. If my thoughts wander overmuch, please bear with me.*

Saphira blinked again. *What is it that has stirred up the Varden so? A group of men roused me from my sleep with their ill-tempered wrangling, and before that, I heard an unusual number of messengers racing through the camp.*

Pressing her lips together, Nasuada turned away from Saphira and crossed her arms, cradling her healing forearms with cupped hands. The coloring of her mind became black as a midnight cloud, full of intimations of death and violence. After an uncharacteristically long pause, she said, *One of the Varden, a man by the name of Othmund, crept into the Urgals' camp last night and killed three of them while they were asleep around their fire. The Urgals failed to catch Othmund at the time, but this morning, he claimed credit for the deed and was boasting of it throughout the army.*

Why did he do this? Saphira asked. *Did the Urgals kill his family?*

Nasuada shook her head. *I almost wish they had, because then the Urgals would not be so upset; revenge, at least, they understand. No, that's the strange part of this affair; Othmund hates the Urgals for no other reason than they are Urgals. They have never wronged him, nor his kin, and yet he loathes Urgals with every fiber of his body. Or so I gather after having spoken with him.*

How will you deal with him?

Nasuada looked at Saphira again, a profound sadness in her eyes. *He will hang for his crimes. When I accepted the Urgals into the Varden, I decreed that anyone who attacked an Urgal would be punished as if he had attacked a fellow human. I cannot go back on my word now.*

Do you regret your promise?

No. The men needed to know I would not condone such acts. Otherwise, they might have turned against the Urgals the very day Nar Garzhvog and I made our pact. Now, however, I must show them I meant what I said. If I don't, there will be even more murders, and then the Urgals will take matters into their own hands, and once again, our two races shall be snapping at each other's throats. It is only right Othmund should die for killing the Urgals and for defying my order, but oh, Saphira, the Varden will not like this. I have sacrificed my own flesh to win their loyalty, but now they will hate me for hanging Othmund. . . . They will hate me for equating the lives of Urgals with the lives of humans. Lowering her arms, Nasuada tugged at the cuffs of her sleeves. *And I cannot say I like it any more than they will. For all my attempts to treat the Urgals openly and fairly and as equals, as my father would have, I cannot help but remember how they killed him. I cannot help but remember the sight of all those Urgals slaughtering the*

Varden during the Battle of Farthen Dûr. I cannot help but remember the many stories I heard when I was a child, stories of Urgals sweeping out of the mountains and murdering innocent people in their beds. Always Urgals were the monsters to be feared, and here I have joined our fate with theirs. I cannot help but remember all that, Saphira, and I find myself wondering if I have made the right decision.

You cannot help but be human, said Saphira, attempting to comfort Nasuada. *Yet you do not have to be bound by what those around you believe. You can grow beyond the limits of your race if you have the will. If the events of the past can teach us anything, it is that the kings and queens and other leaders who have brought the races closer together are the ones who have accomplished the greatest good in Alagaësia. It is strife and anger we must guard against, not closer relations with those who were once our foes. Remember your distrust of the Urgals, for they have well earned it, but also remember that once dwarves and dragons loved one another no more than humans and Urgals. And once dragons fought against the elves and would have driven their race extinct if we could have. Once those things were true, but no more, because people like you had the courage to set aside past hatreds and forge bonds of friendship where, previously, none existed.*

Nasuada pressed her forehead against the side of Saphira's jaw, then said, *You are very wise, Saphira.*

Amused, Saphira lifted her head off her paws and touched Nasuada on the brow with the tip of her snout. *I speak the truth as I see it, no more. If that is wisdom, then you are welcome to it; however, I believe you already possess all the wisdom you need. Executing Othmund may not please the Varden, but it will take more than this to break their devotion to you. Besides, I am sure you can find a way to mollify them.*

Aye, said Nasuada, wiping the corners of her eyes with her fingers. *I will have to, I think.* Then she smiled and her face was transformed. *But Othmund was not why I came to see you. Eragon just contacted me and asked for you to join him in Farthen Dûr. The dwarves—*

Arching her neck, Saphira roared toward the sky, sending the fire from her belly rippling out through her mouth in a flickering sheet of flame. Nasuada staggered back from her while everyone else within earshot froze and stared at Saphira. Rising to her feet, Saphira shook herself from head to tail, her weariness forgotten, and spread her wings in preparation for flight.

Nasuada's guards started toward her, but she waved them back. A patch of smoke swept over her, and she pressed the underside of a sleeve over her nose, coughing. *Your enthusiasm is commendable, Saphira, but—*

Is Eragon injured or hurt? Saphira asked. Alarm shot through her when Nasuada hesitated.

He's as healthy as ever, Nasuada replied. *However, there was an . . . incident . . . yesterday.*

What kind of incident?

He and his guards were attacked.

Saphira held herself motionless while Nasuada recalled for her everything Eragon had said during their conversation. Afterward, Saphira bared her teeth. *Dûrgrimst Az Sweldn rak Anhûin should be grateful I was not with Eragon; I would not have let them escape so easily for attempting to kill him.*

With a small smile, Nasuada said, *For that reason, it is probably better you were here.*

Perhaps, Saphira admitted, and then released a puff of hot smoke and lashed her tail from side to side. *It does not surprise me, though. Always this happens; whenever Eragon and I part, someone attacks him. It's gotten so it makes my scales itch to let him out of my sight for more than a few hours.*

He's more than capable of defending himself.

True, but our enemies are not without skill either. Impatient, Saphira shifted her stance, raising her wings even higher. *Nasuada, I am eager to be gone. Is there anything else I should know?*

No, said Nasuada. *Fly swift and fly true, Saphira, but do not tarry when you arrive in Farthen Dûr. As soon as you leave our camp, we shall have only a few days' grace before the Empire realizes I have not sent you and Eragon on a brief scouting trip. Galbatorix may or may not decide to* strike while you are away, but every hour you are absent will increase the possibility. Also, I would much prefer to have the two of you with us when we attack Feinster. We could take the city without you, but it will cost us many more lives. In short, the fate of the entire Varden depends upon your speed.

We shall be as swift as the storm-driven wind, Saphira assured her.

Then Nasuada bade her farewell and retreated from the stone slab, whereupon Blödhgarm and the other elves rushed to Saphira's side and strapped her uncomfortable-leather-patch-Eragon-seat-saddle onto her and filled the saddlebags with the food and equipment she would normally carry if embarking upon a trip with Eragon. She would not need the supplies—she could not even access them herself—but for the sake of appearances, she had to carry them. Once she was ready, Blödhgarm twisted his hand in front of his chest in the elves' gesture of respect and said in the ancient language, "Fare thee well, Saphira Brightscales. May you and Eragon return to us unharmed."

Fare thee well, Blödhgarm.

Saphira waited while the black-blue-wolf-hair-elf created a water-shadow-ghost of Eragon and the apparition walked out of Eragon's tent and climbed onto her back. She felt nothing as the insubstantial wraith stepped from her left foreleg to the upper part of her leg and then to her shoulder. When Blödhgarm nodded to her, indicating the not-Eragon was in place, she lifted her wings until they touched overhead, then leaped forward, off the end of the stone slab.

As Saphira fell toward the gray tents below, she drove her wings downward, propelling herself away from the break-bone-ground. She turned in the direction of Farthen Dûr and began climbing up to the layer of thin-cold-air high above, where she hoped to find a steady wind to aid her on her journey.

She circled over the wooded riverbank where the Varden had chosen to stop for the night and wriggled with a fierce joy. No longer did she have to wait while Eragon went off adventuring without her! No longer would she have to spend the entire night flying over the same patches of land again and again! And no longer would those who wished to hurt her partner-of-her-mind-and-heart be able to escape her wrath! Opening her jaws, Saphira roared her joy and confidence to the world, daring whatever gods there might be to challenge *her*, she who was the daughter of Iormûngr and Vervada, two of the greatest dragons of their age.

When she was more than a mile above the Varden and a strong southwestern wind was pressing against her, Saphira aligned herself with the torrent of air and allowed it to propel her forward, soaring over the sun-drenched land below.

Casting her thoughts out before her, she said, *I'm on my way, little one!*

✦ ✦ ✦

Four Strokes upon the Drum

Eragon leaned forward, every muscle in his body tense, as the white-haired dwarf woman Hadfala, chief of Dûrgrimst Ebardac, rose from the table where the clanmeet was gathered and uttered a short line in her native language.

Murmuring into Eragon's left ear, Hûndfast translated: "On behalf of mine clan, I vote for Grimstborith Orik as our new king."

Eragon released his pent-up breath. *One.* In order to become ruler of the dwarves, a clan chief had to win a majority of the votes from the other chiefs. If none achieved that feat, then according to Dwarvish law, the clan chief with the least votes would be eliminated from the competition and the meet could adjourn for up to three days before voting again. The process would continue as needed until a clan chief had achieved the necessary majority, at which point, the meet would swear fealty to him or her as their new monarch. Considering how pressed for time the Varden were, Eragon fervently hoped that the voting would not require more than one round, and if it did, that the dwarves would not insist upon taking a recess of more than a few hours. If that happened, he thought he might break the stone table in the center of the room out of frustration.

That Hadfala, the first clan chief to vote, had cast her lot with Orik boded well. Hadfala, as Eragon knew, had been backing Gannel of Dûrgrimst Quan before the attempt on Eragon's life. If Hadfala's allegiances had shifted, then it was also possible that the other member of Gannel's cohort—namely, Grimstborith Ûndin—might also give his vote to Orik.

Next, Gáldhiem of Dûrgrimst Feldûnost rose from the table, although he was so short, he was taller sitting than he was standing.

"On behalf of mine clan," he declared, "I vote for Grimstborith Nado as our new king."

Turning his head to one side, Orik looked back at Eragon and said to him in an undertone, "Well, that was as we expected."

Eragon nodded and glanced over at Nado. The round-faced dwarf was stroking the end of his yellow beard, appearing pleased with himself.

Then Manndrâth of Dûrgrimst Ledwonnû said, "On behalf of mine clan, I vote for Grimstborith Orik as our new king." Orik nodded toward him in thanks, and Manndrâth nodded in return, the tip of his long nose bobbing.

As Manndrâth sat, Eragon and everyone else looked at Gannel, and the room became so quiet, Eragon could not even hear the dwarves breathing. As chief of the religious clan, the Quan, and the high priest of Gûntera, king of the dwarf gods, Gannel carried enormous influence among his race; however he chose, so the crown was likely to go.

"On behalf of mine clan," Gannel said, "I vote for Grimstborith Nado as our new king."

A wave of soft exclamations broke out among the dwarves watching from the perimeter of the circular room, and Nado's pleased expression broadened. Clenching his interlaced hands, Eragon silently cursed.

"Don't give up hope yet, lad," Orik muttered. "We may yet pull through. It's happened before that the grimstborith of the Quan has lost the vote."

"How often does it happen, though?" whispered Eragon.

"Often enough."

"When did it *last* happen?"

Orik shifted and glanced away. "Eight hundred and twenty-four years ago, when Queen—"

He fell silent as Ûndin of Dûrgrimst Ragni Hefthyn proclaimed, "On behalf of mine clan, I vote for Grimstborith Nado as our new king."

Orik crossed his arms. Eragon could only see his face from the side, but it was obvious that Orik was scowling.

Biting the inside of his cheek, Eragon stared at the patterned floor, counting the votes that had been cast, as well as those that remained, trying to determine if Orik could still win the election. Even in the best of circumstances, it would be a close thing. Eragon tightened his grip, his fingernails digging into the back of his hands.

Thordris of Dûrgrimst Nagra stood and draped her long, thick braid over one arm. "On behalf of mine clan, I vote for Grimstborith Orik as our new king."

"That makes three to three," Eragon said in a low voice. Orik nodded.

It was Nado's turn to speak then. Smoothing his beard with the flat of a hand, the chief of Dûrgrimst Knurlcarathn smiled at the assembly, a predatory gleam in his eyes. "One behalf of mine clan, I vote for myself as our new king. If you will have me, I promise to rid our country of the outlanders who have polluted it, and I promise to devote our gold and warriors to protecting our own people, and not the necks of elves, humans, and *Urgals*. This I swear upon mine family's honor."

"Four to three," Eragon noted.

"Aye," said Orik. "I suppose it would have been too much to ask for Nado to vote for anyone but himself."

Setting aside his knife and wood, Freowin of Dûrgrimst Gedthrall heaved his bulk halfway out of his chair and, keeping his gaze angled downward, said in his whispering baritone, "On behalf of mine clan, I vote for Grimstborith Nado as our new king." Then he lowered himself back into his seat and resumed carving his raven, ignoring the stir of astonishment that swept through the room.

Nado's expression changed from pleased to smug.

"Barzûl," growled Orik, his scowl deepening. His chair creaked as he pressed his forearms down against the armrests, the tendons in his hands rigid with strain. "That false-faced traitor. He promised his vote to me!"

Eragon's stomach sank. "Why would he betray you?"

"He visits Sindri's temple twice a day. I should have known he would not go against Gannel's wishes. Bah! Gannel's been playing me this whole time. I—" At that moment, the attention of the clanmeet turned to Orik. Concealing his anger, Orik got to his feet and looked around the table at each of the other clan chiefs, and in his own language, he said, "On behalf of mine clan, I vote for myself as our new king. If you will have me, I promise to bring our people gold and glory and the freedom to live above the ground without fear of Galbatorix destroying our homes. This I swear upon mine family's honor."

"Five to four," Eragon said to Orik as he returned to his seat. "And not in our favor."

Orik grunted. "I can count, Eragon."

Eragon rested his elbows on his knees, his eyes darting from one dwarf to another. The desire to act gnawed at him. How, he knew not, but with so much at stake, he felt that he ought to find a way to ensure Orik would become king and, thus, that the dwarves would continue to aid the Varden in their struggle against the Empire. For all he tried, however, Eragon could think of nothing to do but sit and wait.

The next dwarf to rise was Havard of Dûrgrimst Fanghur. With his chin tucked against his breastbone, Havard pushed out his lips and tapped the table with the two fingers he still had on his right hand, appearing thoughtful. Eragon inched forward on his seat, his heart pounding. *Will he uphold his bargain with Orik?* Eragon wondered.

Havard tapped the table once more, then slapped the stone with the flat of his hand. Lifting his chin, he said, "On behalf of mine clan, I vote for Grimstborith Orik as our new king."

It gave Eragon immense satisfaction to watch as Nado's eyes widened, and then the dwarf gnashed his teeth together, a muscle in his cheek twitching. "Ha!" muttered Orik. "That put a burr in his beard."

The only two clan chiefs who had yet to vote were Hreidamar and Íorûnn. Hreidamar, the compact, muscular grimstborith of the Urzhad, appeared uneasy with the situation, while Íorûnn—she of Dûrgrimst Vrenshrrgn, the War Wolves—traced the crescent-shaped scar on her left cheekbone with the tip of a pointed finger-nail and smiled like a self-satisfied cat.

Eragon held his breath as he waited to hear what the two of them would say. *If Íorûnn votes for herself,* he thought, *and if Hreidamar is still loyal to her, then the election will have to proceed to a second round. There's no reason for her to do that, however, other than to delay events, and so far as I know, she would not profit from a delay. She cannot hope to become queen at this point; her name would be eliminated from con-sideration before the beginning of the second round, and I doubt she would be so foolish as to squander the power she has now merely so she can boast to her grandchildren that she was once a candidate for the throne. But if Hreidamar does part ways with her, then the vote will re-main tied and we will continue on to a second round regardless. . . . Argh! If only I could scry into the future! What if Orik loses? Should I seize control of the clanmeet then? I could seal the chamber so no one could enter or leave, and then . . . But no, that would be—*

Íorûnn interrupted Eragon's thoughts by nodding at Hreidamar and then directing her heavy-lidded gaze toward Eragon, which made him feel as if he were a prize ox she was examining. The rings of his mail hauberk clinking, Hreidamar stood upright and said, "On behalf of mine clan, I vote for Grimstborith Orik as our new king."

Eragon's throat constricted.

Her red lips curving with amusement, Íorûnn rose from her chair with a sinuous motion and in a low, husky voice said, "It seems it falls to me to decide the outcome of today's meet. I have listened most carefully to your arguments, Nado, and your arguments, Orik. While you have both made points I agree with upon a wide range of subjects, the most important issue we must decide is whether to commit ourselves to the Varden's campaign against the Empire. If theirs were merely a war between rival clans, it would not matter to me which side won, and I certainly would not consider sacrificing our warriors for the benefit of outlanders. However, this is not the case. Far from it. If Galbatorix emerges triumphant from this war, not even the Beor Mountains will protect us from his wrath. If our realm is to survive, we must see Galbatorix overthrown. Moreover, it strikes me that hiding in caves and tunnels while others decide the fate of Alagaësia is unbecoming for a race as old and as powerful as ours. When the chronicles of this age are written, shall they say we fought alongside the humans and the elves, as the heroes of old, or that we sat cowering in our halls like frightened peasants while a battle raged outside our doors? I, for one, know mine answer." Íorûnn tossed back her hair, then said, "On behalf of mine clan, I vote for Grimstborith Orik as our new king!"

The eldest of the five readers-of-law who stood against the circular wall stepped forward and struck the end of his polished staff against the stone floor and proclaimed, "All hail King Orik, the forty-third king of Tronjheim, Farthen Dûr, and every knurla above and below the Beor Mountains!"

"All hail King Orik!" the clanmeet roared, rising to their feet with a loud rustle of clothes and armor. His head swimming, Eragon did likewise, aware that he was now in the presence of royalty. He glanced at Nado, but the dwarf's face was a dead-eyed mask.

The white-bearded reader-of-law struck his staff against the floor again. "Let the scribes record at once the clanmeet's decision, and let the news be spread to every person throughout the realm. Heralds! Inform the mages with their scrying mirrors of what has transpired here today, and then seek out the wardens of the mountain and tell them, 'Four beats upon the drum. Four beats, and swing your mallets as you have never swung them before in all your lives, for we have a new king. Four beats of such strength, Farthen Dûr itself shall ring with the news.' Tell them this, I charge you. Go!"

After the heralds departed, Orik pushed himself out of his chair and stood looking at the dwarves around him. His expression, to

Eragon, seemed somewhat dazed, as if he had not actually expected to win the crown. "For this great responsibility," he said, "I thank you." He paused, then continued, "Mine only thought now is for the betterment of our nation, and I shall pursue that goal without faltering until the day I return to the stone."

Then the clan chiefs came forward, one by one, and they knelt before Orik and swore their fealty to him as his loyal subjects. When the time came for Nado to pledge himself, the dwarf displayed nothing of his sentiments but merely recited the phrases of the oath without inflection, the words dropping from his mouth like bars of lead. A palpable sense of relief rippled through the clanmeet once he had finished.

Upon the conclusion of the oath giving, Orik decreed that his coronation would take place the following morning, and then he and his attendants retired to an adjacent chamber. There Eragon looked at Orik, and Orik looked at Eragon, and neither made a sound until a broad smile appeared on Orik's face and he broke out laughing, his cheeks turning red. Laughing with him, Eragon grasped him by a forearm and embraced him. Orik's guards and advisers gathered around them, clapping Orik on the shoulder and congratulating him with hearty exclamations.

Eragon released Orik, saying, "I didn't think Íorûnn would side with us."

"Aye. I'm glad she did, but it complicates matters, it does." Orik grimaced. "I suppose I'll have to reward her for her assistance with a place within my council, at the very least."

"It may be for the best!" said Eragon, straining to make himself heard over the commotion. "If the Vrenshrrgn are equal to their name, we shall have great need of them before we reach the gates of Urû'baen."

Orik started to answer, but then a long, low note of portentous volume reverberated throughout the floor and the ceiling and the air of the room, causing Eragon's bones to vibrate with its force. "Listen!" cried Orik, and raised a hand. The group fell silent.

Four times in total the bass note sounded, shaking the room with each repetition, as if a giant were pounding against the side of Tronjheim. Afterward, Orik said, "I never thought to hear the Drums of Derva announce mine kingship."

"How large are the drums?" asked Eragon, awed.

"Close to fifty feet across, if memory serves."

It occurred to Eragon that although the dwarves were the shortest of the races, they built the biggest structures in Alagaësia, which seemed odd to him. *Perhaps*, he thought, *by making such enormous objects, they do not feel so small themselves.* He almost mentioned his theory to Orik but at the last moment decided that it might offend him, so he held his tongue.

Closing ranks around him, Orik's attendants began to consult with him in Dwarvish, often speaking over one another in a loud tangle of voices, and Eragon, who had been about to ask Orik another question, found himself relegated to a corner. He tried to wait patiently for a lull in the conversation, but after a few minutes, it became plain the dwarves were not about to stop plying Orik with questions and advice, for such, he assumed, was the nature of their discourse.

Therefore, Eragon said, "Orik Könungr," and he imbued the ancient language word for *king* with energy, that it would capture the attention of everyone present. The room fell silent, and Orik looked at Eragon and lifted an eyebrow. "Your Majesty, may I have your permission to withdraw? There is a certain . . . *matter* I would like to attend to, if it is not already too late."

Comprehension brightened Orik's brown eyes. "By all means, make haste! But you need not call me *majesty*, Eragon, nor *sire*, nor by any other title. We are friends and foster brothers, after all."

"We are, Your Majesty," Eragon replied, "but for the time being, I believe it is only proper I should observe the same courtesies as everyone else. You are the king of your race now, and my own king as well, seeing as how I am a member of Dûrgrimst Ingeitum, and that is not something I can ignore."

Orik studied him for a moment, as if from a great distance, and then nodded and said, "As you wish, Shadeslayer."

Eragon bowed and left the room. Accompanied by his four guards, he bounded through the tunnels and up the stairs that led to the ground floor of Tronjheim. Once they arrived at the southern branch of the four main hallways that divided the city-mountain, Eragon turned to Thrand, the captain of his guards, and said, "I mean to run the rest of the way. Since you won't be able to keep pace with me, I suggest you stop when you reach the south gate of Tronjheim and wait there for my return."

Thrand said, "Argetlam, please, you should not go alone. Cannot I convince you to slow yourself so we can accompany you? We may not be as fleet as the elves, but we can run from sunup to sundown, and in full armor too."

"I appreciate your concern," said Eragon, "but I would not tarry a minute longer, even if I knew there were assassins hiding behind every pillar. Farewell!"

And with that, he dashed down the broad hallway, dodging around the dwarves who blocked his way.

REUNION

It was nearly a mile from where Eragon started to the south gate of Tronjheim. He covered the distance in only a few minutes, his footsteps loud upon the stone floor. As he ran, he caught glimpses of the rich tapestries that hung above the arched entrances to the corridors on either side and of the grotesque statues of beasts and monsters that lurked between the pillars of blood-red jasper that lined the vaulted avenue. The four-story-high thoroughfare was so large, Eragon had little difficulty evading the dwarves who populated it, although at one point, a line of Knurlcarathn stepped in front of him, and he had no choice but to leap over the dwarves, who ducked, uttering startled exclamations. Eragon savored their looks of astonishment as he sailed over them.

With an easy, loping stride, Eragon ran underneath the massive timber gate that protected the southern entrance to the city-mountain, hearing the guards cry, "Hail, Argetlam!" as he flew past. Twenty yards beyond, for the gate was recessed into the base of Tronjheim, he sped between the pair of giant gold griffins that stared with sightless eyes toward the horizon and then emerged into the open.

The air was cool and moist and smelled like fresh-fallen rain. Though it was morning, gray twilight enveloped the flat disk of land that surrounded Tronjheim, land upon which no grass grew, only moss and lichen and the occasional patch of pungent toadstools. Above, Farthen Dûr rose over ten miles to a narrow opening, through which pale, indirect light entered the immense crater. Eragon had difficulty grasping the scale of the mountain when he gazed upward.

As he ran, he listened to the monotonous pattern of his breathing and to his light, quick footsteps. He was alone, save for a curious bat that swooped overhead, emitting shrill squeaks. The tranquil mood that permeated the hollow mountain comforted him, freed him of his usual worries.

He followed the cobblestone path that extended from Tronjheim's south gate all the way to the two black thirty-foot-high doors set into the southern base of Farthen Dûr. As he drew to a halt, a pair of dwarves emerged from hidden guardrooms and hurried to open the doors, revealing the seemingly endless tunnel beyond.

Eragon continued forward. Marble pillars studded with rubies and amethysts lined the first fifty feet of the tunnel. Past them the tunnel was bare and desolate, the smooth walls broken only by a single flameless lantern every twenty yards and at infrequent intervals by a closed gate or door. *I wonder where they lead,* Eragon thought. Then he imagined the miles of stone pressing down on him from overhead, and for a moment, the tunnel seemed unbearably oppressive.

He quickly pushed the image away.

Halfway through the tunnel, Eragon felt her.

"*Saphira!*" he shouted, with both his mind and his voice, her name echoing off the stone walls with the force of a dozen yells.

Eragon! An instant later, the faint thunder of a distant roar rolled toward him from the other end of the tunnel.

Redoubling his speed, Eragon opened his mind to Saphira, removing every barrier around who he was, so that they might join together without reservation. Like a flood of warm water, her consciousness rushed into him, even as his rushed into her. Eragon gasped and tripped and nearly fell. They enveloped each other within the folds of their thoughts, holding each other with an intimacy no physical embrace could replicate, allowing their identities to merge once again. Their greatest comfort was a simple one: they were no longer alone. To know that you were with one who cared for you, and who understood every fiber of your being, and who would not abandon you in even the most desperate of circumstances, *that* was the most precious relationship a person could have, and both Eragon and Saphira cherished it.

It was not long before Eragon sighted Saphira hurrying toward him as swiftly as she could without banging her head on the ceiling or scraping her wings against the walls. Her claws screeched on the stone floor as she slid to a stop in front of Eragon, fierce, sparkling, glorious.

Crying out with joy, Eragon leaped upward and, ignoring her sharp scales, wrapped his arms around her neck and hugged her as tightly as he could, his feet dangling several inches in the air. *Little one*, said Saphira, her tone warm. She lowered him to the floor, then snorted and said, *Little one, unless you wish to choke me, you should loosen your arms.*

Sorry. Grinning, he stepped back, then laughed and pressed his forehead against her snout and began to scratch behind both corners of her jaw.

Saphira's low humming filled the tunnel.

You're tired, he said.

I have never flown so far so fast. I stopped only once after I left the Varden, and I would not have stopped at all except I became too thirsty to continue.

Do you mean you haven't slept or eaten for three days?

She blinked at him, concealing her brilliant sapphire eyes for an instant.

You must be starving! Eragon exclaimed, worried. He looked her over for signs of injury. To his relief, he found none.

I am tired, she admitted, *but not hungry. Not yet. Once I have rested, then I will need to eat. Right now, I do not think I could stomach so much as a rabbit. . . . The earth is unsteady beneath me; I feel as if I am still flying.*

If they had not been apart for so long, Eragon might have reproached her for being reckless, but as it was, he was touched and grateful that she had pushed herself. *Thank you,* he said. *I would have hated to wait another day for us to be together again.*

549

As would have I. She closed her eyes and pressed her head against his hands as he continued to scratch behind her jaw. *Besides, I could hardly be late for the coronation, now could I? Who did the clanmeet—*

Before she could finish the question, Eragon sent her an image of Orik.

Ah, she sighed, her satisfaction flowing through him. *He will make a fine king.*

I hope so.

Is the star sapphire ready for me to mend?

If the dwarves have not already finished piecing it together, I'm sure they will have by tomorrow.

That is good. Cracking open an eyelid, she fixed him with her piercing gaze. *Nasuada told me of what Az Sweldn rak Anhûin attempted. Always you get into trouble when I am not with you.*

His smile widened. *And when you are?*

I eat the trouble before it eats you.

So you say. What about when the Urgals ambushed us by Gil'ead and took me captive?

A plume of smoke escaped from between Saphira's fangs. *That does not count. I was smaller then, and not as experienced. It would not happen now. And you are not as helpless as you once were.*

I've never been helpless, he protested. *I just have powerful enemies.*

For some reason, Saphira found his last statement enormously amusing; she started laughing deep within her chest, and soon Eragon was laughing as well. Neither of them was able to stop until Eragon was lying on his back, gasping for air, and Saphira was struggling to contain the darts of flame that kept shooting out of her nostrils. Then Saphira made a sound Eragon had never heard before, a strange jumping growl, and he noticed the oddest feeling through their connection.

Saphira made the sound again, then shook her head, as if trying to rid herself of a swarm of flies. *Oh dear,* she said. *I seem to have the hiccups.*

Eragon's mouth dropped open. He held that pose for a moment,

550

then he doubled over, laughing so hard, tears streamed down his face. Every time he was about to recover, Saphira would hiccup, bobbing her head forward like a stork, and he would go off into convulsions again. At last he plugged his ears with his fingers and stared at the ceiling and recited the true names of every metal and stone he could remember.

When he finished, he took a deep breath and stood.

Better? Saphira asked. Her shoulders shook as another hiccup racked her.

Eragon bit his tongue. *Better. . . . Come on, let's go to Tronjheim. You should have some water. That might help. And then you should sleep.*

Cannot you cure hiccups with a spell?

Maybe. Probably. But neither Brom nor Oromis taught me how. Saphira grunted her understanding, and a hiccup followed an instant later. Biting his tongue even harder, Eragon stared at the tips of his boots. *Shall we?*

Saphira extended her right foreleg in invitation. Eragon eagerly climbed up onto her back and settled into the saddle at the base of her neck.

Together, they continued through the tunnel toward Tronjheim, both of them happy, and both of them sharing in each other's happiness.

551

ASCENSION

The Drums of Derva sounded, summoning the dwarves of Tronjheim to witness the coronation of their new king.

"Normally," Orik had told Eragon the previous night, "when the clanmeet elects a king or queen, the knurla begins their rule at once, but we do not hold the coronation for at least three months, so that all who wish to attend the ceremony may have time to place their affairs in order and to travel to Farthen Dûr from even the most distant parts of our realm. It is not often we crown a monarch, so when we do, it is our custom to make much of the event, with weeks of feasting and song, and with games of wit and strength and contests of skill at forging, carving, and other forms of art. . . . However, these are hardly normal times."

Eragon stood next to Saphira just outside the central chamber of Tronjheim, listening to the pounding of the giant drums. On either side of the mile-long hall, hundreds of dwarves crowded the archways of each level, peering at Eragon and Saphira with dark gleaming eyes.

Saphira's barbed tongue rasped against her scales as she licked her chops, which she had been doing ever since she finished devouring five full-grown sheep earlier that morning. Then she lifted her left foreleg and rubbed her muzzle against it. The smell of burnt wool clung to her.

Stop fidgeting, said Eragon. *They're looking at us.*

A soft growl emanated from Saphira. *I can't help it. I have wool stuck between my teeth. Now I remember why I hate eating sheep. Horrible, fluffy things that give me hair balls and indigestion.*

I'll help you clean your teeth when we are finished here. Just hold still until then.

Hmph.

Did Blödhgarm pack any fireweed in the saddlebags? That would settle your stomach.

I don't know.

Mmm. Eragon thought for a moment. *If not, I'll ask Orik if the dwarves have any stored in Tronjheim. We ought to—*

He cut himself off as the final note from the drums faded into silence. The crowd shifted, and he heard the soft rustle of clothes and the occasional phrase of murmured Dwarvish.

A fanfare of dozens of trumpets rang forth, filling the city-mountain with its rousing call, and somewhere a choir of dwarves began to chant. The music made Eragon's scalp tingle and prickle and his blood flow faster, as if he were about to embark upon a hunt. Saphira whipped her tail from side to side, and he knew she felt the same.

Here we go, he thought.

As one, he and Saphira advanced into the central chamber of the city-mountain and took their place among the ring of clan chiefs, guild leaders, and other notables who girded the vast, towering room. In the center of the chamber rested the reconstructed star sapphire, encased within a framework of wooden scaffolding. An hour before the coronation, Skeg had sent a message to Eragon and Saphira, telling them that he and his team of artisans had just finished fitting together the last fragments of the gem and that Isidar Mithrim was ready for Saphira to make whole once more.

The black granite throne of the dwarves had been carried from its customary resting place underneath Tronjheim and placed upon a raised dais next to the star sapphire, facing the eastern branch of the four main hallways that divided Tronjheim, east because it was the direction of the rising sun and that symbolized the dawning of a new age. Thousands of dwarf warriors clad in burnished mail armor stood at attention in two large blocks before the throne, as well as in double rows along either side of the eastern hallway all the way to Tronjheim's eastern gate, a mile away. Many of the warriors carried spears mounted with pennants that bore curious designs. Hvedra, Orik's wife, stood at the forefront of the congregation; after the clanmeet had banished Grimstborith Vermûnd, Orik had sent for her in anticipation of becoming king. She had arrived in Tronjheim only that morning.

For half an hour, the trumpets played and the unseen choir sang as, step by deliberate step, Orik walked from the eastern gate to the center of Tronjheim. His beard was brushed and curled, and he wore buskins of the finest polished leather with silver spurs mounted upon the heels, gray wool leggings, a shirt of purple silk that shimmered in the lantern light, and, over his shirt, a mail hauberk, each link of which was wrought of pure white gold. A long ermine-trimmed cloak embroidered with the insignia of Dûrgrimst Ingeitum flowed over Orik's shoulders and onto the floor behind him. Volund, the war hammer that Korgan, first king of the dwarves, had forged, hung at Orik's waist from a wide, ruby-studded belt. Because of his lavish raiment and his magnificent armor, Orik seemed to glow from within; to look at him dazzled Eragon's eyes.

Twelve dwarf children followed Orik, six male and six female, or so Eragon assumed based upon the cut of their hair. The children were garbed in tunics of red and brown and gold, and they each carried in their cupped hands a polished orb six inches across, every orb a different species of stone.

As Orik entered the center of the city-mountain, the chamber dimmed and a pattern of dappled shadows appeared on everything within. Confused, Eragon glanced upward and was astonished to behold pink rose petals drifting downward from the top of Tronjheim. Like soft, thick snowflakes, the velvety petals settled upon the heads and shoulders of those in attendance, and also upon the floor, suffusing the air with their sweet fragrance.

The trumpets and the choir fell silent as Orik knelt on one knee before the black throne and bowed his head. Behind him, the twelve children stopped and stood motionless.

Eragon placed his hand on Saphira's warm side, sharing his concern and excitement with her. He had no idea what would happen next, for Orik had refused to describe the ceremony past that point.

Then Gannel, clan chief of Dûrgrimst Quan, stepped forward, breaking the ring of people around the chamber, and walked to stand on the right-hand side of the throne. The heavy-shouldered dwarf was appareled in sumptuous red robes, the borders of which gleamed with runes outlined with metal thread. In one hand, Gannel bore a tall staff with a clear, pointed crystal mounted on the top.

Lifting the staff over his head with both hands, Gannel brought it down upon the stone floor with a resounding crack. "Hwatum il skilfz gerdûmn!" he exclaimed. He continued to speak in the tongue of the dwarves for some minutes, and Eragon listened without comprehending, for his translator was not with him. But then the tenor of Gannel's voice shifted, and Eragon recognized his words as belonging to the ancient language, and he realized Gannel was weaving a spell, although it was a spell unlike any Eragon was familiar with. Instead of directing the incantation at an object or an element of the world around them, the priest said, in the language of mystery and power: "Gûntera, creator of the heavens and the earth and the boundless sea, hear now the cry of your faithful servant! We thank you for your magnanimity. Our race flourishes. This and every year, we have offered to you the finest rams of our flocks and also flagons of spiced mead and a portion of our harvests of fruits and vegetables and grain. Your temples are the richest in the land, and none may hope to compete with the glory that is yours. O mighty Gûntera, king of the gods, hear now mine plea and grant me this request: time is for us to name a mortal ruler of our earthly affairs. Will you deign to bestow your blessing upon Orik, Thrifk's son, and to crown him in the tradition of his predecessors?"

At first Eragon thought Gannel's request would go unanswered, for he felt no surge of magic from the dwarf when he finished speaking. However, Saphira nudged him then and said, *Look.*

Eragon followed her gaze and, thirty feet above, saw a disturbance among the tumbling petals: a gap, a void where the petals would not fall, as if an invisible object occupied the space. The disturbance spread, extending all the way to the floor, and the void outlined by the petals assumed the shape of a creature with arms and legs like a dwarf or a man or an elf or an Urgal, but of different proportions than any race Eragon had knowledge of; the head was nearly the width of the shoulders, the massive arms hung below the knees, and while the torso was bulky, the legs were short and crooked.

Thin, needle-sharp rays of watery light radiated outward from the shape, and there appeared the nebulous image of a gigantic, shaggy-haired male figure of the form the petals had traced. The god, if god he was, wore nothing but a knotted loincloth. His face was dark and heavy and seemed to contain equal amounts of cruelty and kindness, as if he might veer between the extremes of both without warning.

As he noticed those details, Eragon also became aware of the presence of a strange, far-reaching consciousness within the chamber, a consciousness of unreadable thoughts and unfathomable depths, a consciousness that flashed and growled and billowed in unexpected directions, like a summer thunderstorm. Eragon quickly sequestered his mind from the touch of the other. His skin prickled, and a cold shiver ran down him. He did not know what he had felt, but fear gripped him, and he looked at Saphira for comfort. She was staring at the figure, her blue cat eyes sparkling with unusual intensity.

With a single motion, the dwarves sank to their knees.

The god spoke then, and his voice sounded like the grinding of boulders and the sweep of the wind over barren mountain peaks and the slap of waves against a stony shore. He spoke in Dwarvish, and though Eragon knew not what was said, he shrank from the power of the god's speech. Three times the god questioned Orik, and three times Orik replied, his own voice faint in comparison. Apparently pleased with Orik's answers, the apparition extended his glowing arms and placed his forefingers on either side of Orik's bare head.

The air between the god's fingers rippled, and upon Orik's brow materialized the gem-encrusted helm of gold that Hrothgar had worn. The god slapped his belly and uttered a booming chuckle and then faded into oblivion. The rose petals resumed their fall uninterrupted.

"Ûn qroth Gûntera!" Gannel proclaimed. Loud and brassy, the trumpets blared.

Rising from his knee, Orik ascended the dais, turned to face the assembly, and then he sank into the hard black throne.

"Nal, Grimstnzborith Orik!" the dwarves shouted, and struck their shields with their axes and their spears and stamped the floor with their feet. "Nal, Grimstnzborith Orik! Nal, Grimstnzborith Orik!"

"All hail King Orik!" cried Eragon. Arching her neck, Saphira roared her tribute and released a jet of flame over the heads of the dwarves, incinerating a swath of rose petals. Eragon's eyes watered as a blast of heat washed over him.

Then Gannel knelt before Orik and spoke some more in Dwarvish. When he finished, Orik touched him upon the crown of his head, and then Gannel returned to his place at the edge of the chamber. Nado approached the throne and said many of the same things, and after him, so did Manndrâth and Hadfala and all the other clan chiefs, with the sole exception of Grimstborith Vermûnd, who had been banned from the coronation.

They must be pledging themselves to Orik's service, Eragon said to Saphira.

Did not they already give him their word?

Aye, but not in public. Eragon watched Thordris walk toward the throne before saying, *Saphira, what do you think we just saw? Could*

*that really have been Gûntera, or was it an illusion? His mind seemed
real enough, and I do not know how one might fake that, but . . .*

It may have been an illusion, she said. *The dwarves' gods have never
helped them upon the field of battle, nor in any other endeavor I am
aware of. Nor do I believe that a true god would come running at
Gannel's summons like a trained hound. I would not, and should not a
god be greater than a dragon? . . . But then, there are many inexplicable things in Alagaësia. It is possible we have seen a shade from a long-
forgotten age, a pale remnant of what once was that continues to haunt
the land, longing for the return of its power. Who can know for sure?*

Once the final clan chief had presented himself to Orik, the guild
leaders did the same, and then Orik gestured toward Eragon. With a
slow, measured pace, Eragon walked forward between the rows of
dwarf warriors until he reached the base of the throne, where he
knelt and, as a member of Dûrgrimst Ingeitum, acknowledged Orik
as his king and swore to serve and protect him. Then, acting as
Nasuada's emissary, Eragon congratulated Orik on behalf of Nasuada
and the Varden and promised him the Varden's friendship.

Others went to speak with Orik as Eragon withdrew, a seemingly
endless train of dwarves eager to demonstrate their loyalty to their
new king.

The procession continued for hours, and then the gift giving began. Each of the dwarves brought Orik an offering from their clan or
their guild: a goblet of gold filled to the brim with rubies and diamonds, a corselet of enchanted mail that no blade could pierce, a
tapestry twenty feet long woven of the soft wool the dwarves
combed from the beards of the Feldûnost goats, a tablet of agate inscribed with the names of every one of Orik's ancestors, a curved
dagger ground from the tooth of a dragon, and many other treasures.
In exchange, Orik presented the dwarves with rings as tokens of his
gratitude.

Eragon and Saphira were the last to go before Orik. Once again
kneeling at the base of the dais, Eragon drew from his tunic the gold
armband he had begged from the dwarves the previous night. He

held it up toward Orik, saying, "Here is my gift, King Orik. I did not make the armlet, but I have set on it spells to protect you. So long as you wear it, you need fear no poison. If an assassin tries to hit or stab you or throw any kind of object at you, the weapon will miss. The band will even shield you from most hostile magic. And it has other properties as well, which you may find of use if your life is in danger."

Inclining his head, Orik accepted the band from Eragon and said, "Your gift is most appreciated, Eragon Shadeslayer." In full view of everyone, Orik slid the band onto his left arm.

Saphira spoke next, projecting her thoughts to everyone who was watching: *My gift is this, Orik.* She walked past the throne, her claws clacking against the floor, and reared up and placed her forefeet upon the edge of the scaffolding around the star sapphire. The stout wood beams creaked under her weight, but held. Minutes passed and nothing happened, but Saphira remained where she was, gazing at the huge gemstone.

The dwarves watched her, never blinking, hardly breathing.

Are you sure you can do this? Eragon asked, reluctant to break her concentration.

I don't know. The few times I used magic before, I didn't pause to consider whether I was casting a spell or not. I just willed the world to change, and it did. It was not a deliberate process. . . . I suppose I will have to wait until the moment feels right for me to mend Isidar Mithrim.

Let me help. Let me work a spell through you.

No, little one. This is my task, not yours.

A single voice, low and clear, wafted across the chamber, singing a slow, wistful melody. One by one, the other members of the hidden dwarf choir joined in the song, filling Tronjheim with the plaintive beauty of their music. Eragon was going to ask for them to be silent, but Saphira said, *It's all right. Leave them alone.*

Although he did not understand what the choir sang, Eragon could tell from the tone of the music that it was a lamentation for things that had been and were no more, such as the star sapphire.

As the song built toward its conclusion, he found himself thinking of his lost life in Palancar Valley, and tears welled in his eyes.

To his surprise, he sensed a similar strain of pensive melancholy from Saphira. Neither sorrow nor regret was a normal part of her personality, so he wondered at it and would have questioned her, except that he also sensed a stirring of something deep within her, like the awakening of some ancient part of her being.

The song ended on a long, wavering note, and as it faded into oblivion, a surge of energy rushed through Saphira—so much energy, Eragon gasped at its magnitude—and she bent and touched the star sapphire with the tip of her snout. The branching cracks within the giant gemstone flared bright as bolts of lightning, and then the scaffolding shattered and fell to the floor, revealing Isidar Mithrim whole and sound again.

But not quite the same. The color of the jewel was a deeper, richer shade of red than before, and the innermost petals of the rose were shot through with streaks of dusky gold.

The dwarves stared in wonder at Isidar Mithrim. Then they leaped to their feet, cheering and applauding Saphira with such enthusiasm, it sounded like the pounding roar of a waterfall. She dipped her head toward the crowd and then walked back to Eragon, crushing rose petals under her feet. *Thank you,* she said to him.

For what?

For helping me. It was your emotions that showed me the way. Without them, I might have stayed there for weeks before I felt inspired to fix Isidar Mithrim.

Lifting his arms, Orik quieted the crowd, and then he said, "On behalf of our entire race, I thank you for your gift, Saphira. Today you have restored the pride of our realm, and we shall not forget your deed. Let it not be said that knurlan are an ungrateful lot; from now until the end of time, your name shall be recited at the winter festivals, along with the lists of Master Makers, and when Isidar Mithrim is returned to its setting at the peak of Tronjheim, your name will be engraved in the collar surrounding the Star Rose, along with that of Dûrok Ornthrond, who first gave shape to the jewel."

To both Eragon and Saphira, Orik said, "Once again you have demonstrated your friendship to mine people. It pleases me that, by your actions, you have vindicated my foster father's decision to adopt you into Dûrgrimst Ingeitum."

After the conclusion of the multitude of rituals that followed the coronation, and after Eragon had helped remove the wool caught between Saphira's teeth—a slippery, slimy, smelly task that left him needing a bath—the two of them attended the banquet held in Orik's honor. The feasting was loud and boisterous and lasted long into the night. Jugglers and acrobats entertained the guests, as well as a troupe of actors who performed a play called *Az Sartosvrenht rak Balmung, Grimstnzborith rak Kvisagûr*, which Hûndfast told Eragon meant *The Saga of King Balmung of Kvisagûr*.

When the celebrations had died down some and most of the dwarves were deep in their cups, Eragon leaned toward Orik, who sat at the head of the stone table, and said, "Your Majesty."

Orik waved a hand. "I won't have you calling me *Your Majesty* all the time, Eragon. It won't do. Unless the occasion demands it, use mine name as you always have. That's an order." He reached for his goblet but missed and nearly knocked the container over. He laughed.

Smiling, Eragon said, "Orik, I have to ask, Was that really Gûntera who crowned you?"

Orik's chin sank to his chest, and he fingered the stem of the goblet, his expression growing serious. "It was as close to Gûntera as we are ever likely to see on this earth. Does that answer your question, Eragon?"

"I . . . I think so. Does he always answer when called upon? Has he ever refused to crown one of your rulers?"

The gap between Orik's eyebrows narrowed. "Have you ever heard of the Heretic Kings and the Heretic Queens before?"

Eragon shook his head.

"They are knurlan who failed to secure Gûntera's blessing as our next ruler and yet who nevertheless insisted upon taking the throne." Orik's mouth twisted. "Without exception, their reigns were short and unhappy ones."

A band seemed to tighten around Eragon's chest. "So, even though the clanmeet elected you their leader, if Gûntera had failed to crown you, you would not be king now."

"That or I would be king of a nation at war with itself." Orik shrugged. "I was not overly worried about the possibility. With the Varden in the midst of invading the Empire, only a madman would risk tearing our country apart merely to deny me the throne, and while *Gûntera* is many things, he is not mad."

"But you did not know for certain," said Eragon.

Orik shook his head. "Not until he placed the helm upon mine head."

WORDS OF WISDOM

"**S**orry," said Eragon as he bumped the basin.

Nasuada frowned, her face shrinking and elongating as a row of ripples ran through the water in the basin. "What for?" she asked. "I should think congratulations are in order. You have accomplished everything I sent you to do and more."

"No, I—" Eragon stopped as he realized she could not see the disturbance in the water. The spell was designed so that Nasuada's mirror would provide her with an unobstructed view of him and Saphira, not the objects they were gazing at. "I struck the basin with my hand, that is all."

"Oh. In that case, let me formally congratulate you, Eragon. By ensuring Orik became king—"

"Even if it was by getting myself attacked?"

Nasuada smiled. "Yes, even if it was by getting yourself attacked, you have preserved our alliance with the dwarves, and that might mean the difference between victory and defeat. The question now becomes, How long until the rest of the dwarves' army will be able to join us?"

"Orik has already ordered the warriors to ready themselves for departure," said Eragon. "It will probably take the clans a few days to muster their forces, but once they do, they'll march immediately."

"It's a good thing too. We can use their assistance as soon as possible. Which reminds me, when can we expect you to return? Three days? Four days?"

Saphira shuffled her wings, her breath hot on the back of Eragon's neck. Eragon glanced at her, and then, choosing his words with care, he said, "That depends. Do you remember what we discussed before I left?"

Nasuada pursed her lips. "Of course I do, Eragon. I—" She looked off to the side of the image and listened as a man addressed her, his voice an unintelligible murmur to Eragon and Saphira. Returning her attention to them, Nasuada said, "Captain Edric's company has just returned. They appear to have suffered heavy casualties, but our watchmen say that Roran survived."

"Was he injured?" asked Eragon.

"I'll let you know once I find out. I would not worry too much, though. Roran has the luck of—" Once again, the voice of an unseen person distracted Nasuada, and she stepped out of view.

Eragon fidgeted while he waited.

"My apologies," said Nasuada, her visage reappearing in the basin. "We are closing in on Feinster, and we are having to fight off marauding groups of soldiers Lady Lorana sends from the city to harass us. . . . Eragon, Saphira, we need you for this battle. If the people of Feinster see only men, dwarves, and Urgals gathered outside their walls, they may believe they have a chance of holding the city, and they will fight all the harder because of it. They can't hold Feinster, of course, but they have yet to realize that. If they see a dragon and Rider leading the charges against them, however, they will lose the will to fight."

"But—"

Nasuada raised her hand, cutting him off. "There are other reasons for you to return as well. Because of my wounds from the Trial of the Long Knives, I cannot ride into battle with the Varden, as I have before. I need *you* to take my place, Eragon, in order to see that my commands are carried out as I intend and also to prop up the spirits of our warriors. What's more, rumors of your absence are already coursing through the camp, despite our best efforts to the contrary. If Murtagh and Thorn attack us directly as a result, or if Galbatorix sends them to reinforce Feinster . . . well, even with the elves by our sides, I doubt we could withstand them. I'm sorry,

Eragon, but I cannot allow you to return to Ellesméra right now. It's too dangerous."

Pressing his hands against the edge of the cold stone table upon which the basin rested, Eragon said, "Nasuada, please. If not now, then when?"

"Soon. You must be patient."

"Soon." Eragon drew a deep breath, tightening his grip on the table. "How soon exactly?"

Nasuada frowned at him. "You cannot expect me to know that. First we must take Feinster, and then we must secure the country-side, and then—"

"And then you intend to march on Belatona or Dras-Leona, and then to Urû'baen," said Eragon. Nasuada attempted to reply, but he did not allow her the opportunity. "And the closer you get to Galbatorix, the likelier it will be that Murtagh and Thorn will attack you, or even the king himself, and you will be ever more reluctant to let us go. . . . Nasuada, Saphira and I do not have the skill, the knowledge, nor the strength to kill Galbatorix. You know that! Galbatorix could end this war at any time if he was willing to leave his castle and confront the Varden directly. We *have* to talk with our teachers again. They can tell us where Galbatorix's power is coming from, and they might be able to show us a trick or two that will allow us to defeat him."

Nasuada gazed downward, studying her hands. "Thorn and Murtagh could destroy us while you were gone."

"And if we do not go, Galbatorix will destroy us when we reach Urû'baen. . . . Could you wait a few days before you attack Feinster?"

"We could, but every day we camp outside the city will cost us lives." Nasuada rubbed her temples with the heels of her palms. "You are asking a lot in exchange for an uncertain reward, Eragon."

"The reward may be uncertain," he said, "but our doom is inevitable unless we try."

"Is it? I am not so sure. Still . . ." For an uncomfortably long time, Nasuada was silent, gazing past the edge of the image. Then she nodded once, as if confirming something to herself, and said, "I can delay our arrival at Feinster for two or three days. There are several towns in the area we can seize first. Once we do reach the city, I can pass another two or three days having the Varden build siege engines and prepare fortifications. No one will think strangely of it. After that, though, I will have to set upon Feinster, if for no other reason but that we need their supplies. An army that sits still in enemy territory is an army that starves. At the most, I can give you six days, and perhaps only four."

As she spoke, Eragon made several quick calculations. "Four days won't be long enough," he said, "and six might not be either. It took Saphira three days to fly to Farthen Dûr, and that was without stopping to sleep and without having to carry my weight. If the maps I have seen are accurate, it's at least as far from here to Ellesméra, maybe farther, and about the same from Ellesméra to Feinster. And with me on her back, Saphira won't be able to cover the distance as quickly."

No, I won't, Saphira said to him.

Eragon continued: "Even under the best of circumstances, it would still take us a week to reach you at Feinster, and that would be without staying for more than a minute in Ellesméra."

An expression of profound exhaustion crossed Nasuada's face. "Must you fly all the way to Ellesméra? Wouldn't it be sufficient to scry with your mentors once you are past the wards along the edge of Du Weldenvarden? The time you would save could be crucial."

"I don't know. We can try."

Nasuada closed her eyes for a moment. In a hoarse voice, she said, "I may be able to delay our arrival at Feinster for four days. . . . Go to Ellesméra or don't; I leave the decision up to you. If you do, then stay however long is needed. You're right; unless you find a way to defeat Galbatorix, we have no hope of victory. Even so, keep you in mind the tremendous risk we are taking, the lives of the Varden I will be sacrificing in order to buy you this time, and how many more of the Varden will die if we lay siege to Feinster without you."

Somber, Eragon nodded. "I won't forget."

"I should hope not. Now go! Do not tarry any longer! Fly. Fly! Fly faster than a diving hawk, Saphira, and do not let anything slow you." Nasuada touched the tips of her fingers to her lips and then pressed them against the invisible surface of the mirror, where he knew she beheld the moving likeness of him and Saphira. "Luck on your journey, Eragon, Saphira. If we meet again, I fear it will be on the field of battle."

And then she hurried from their sight, and Eragon released his spell, and the water in the basin cleared.

✦　✦　✦

THE WHIPPING POST

Roran sat bolt upright and stared past Nasuada, his eyes fixed upon a wrinkle in the side of the crimson pavilion.

He could feel Nasuada studying him, but he refused to meet her gaze. During the long, dull silence that enveloped them, he contemplated a host of dire possibilities, and his temples throbbed with a feverish intensity. He wished he could leave the stifling pavilion and breathe the cool air outside.

At last Nasuada said, "What am I going to do with you, Roran?"

He straightened his spine even more. "Whatever you wish, my Lady."

"An admirable answer, Stronghammer, but in no way does it resolve my quandary." Nasuada sipped wine from a goblet. "Twice you defied a direct order from Captain Edric, and yet if you hadn't, neither he nor you nor the rest of your band might have survived to tell the tale. However, your success does not negate the reality of your disobedience. By your own account, you knowingly committed insubordination, and I *must* punish you if I am to maintain discipline among the Varden."

"Yes, my Lady."

Her brow darkened. "Blast it, Stronghammer. If you were anyone else but Eragon's cousin, and if your gambit had been even one whit less effective, I would have you strung up and hanged for your misconduct."

Roran swallowed as he imagined a noose tightening around his neck.

With the middle finger of her right hand, Nasuada tapped the arm of her high-backed chair with increasing speed until, stopping, she said, "Do you wish to continue fighting with the Varden, Roran?"

"Yes, my Lady," he replied without hesitation.

"What are you willing to endure in order to remain within my army?"

Roran did not allow himself to dwell upon the implications of her question. "Whatever I must, my Lady."

The tension in her face eased, and Nasuada nodded, appearing satisfied. "I hoped you would say that. Tradition and established precedent leave me only three choices. One, I can hang you, but I won't . . . for a multitude of reasons. Two, I can give you thirty lashes and then discharge you from the ranks of the Varden. Or three, I can give you fifty lashes and keep you under my command."

Fifty lashes isn't that many more than thirty, Roran thought, trying to bolster his courage. He wet his lips. "Would I be flogged where all could see?"

Nasuada's eyebrows rose a fraction of an inch. "Your pride has no part in this, Stronghammer. The punishment must be severe so that others are not tempted to follow in your footsteps, and it must be held in public so that the whole of the Varden can profit by it. If you are even half as intelligent as you seem, you knew when you defied Edric that your decision would have consequences and that those consequences would most likely be unpleasant. The choice you must now make is simple: will you stay with the Varden, or will you abandon your friends and family and go your own way?"

Roran lifted his chin, angry that she would question his word. "I shall not leave, Lady Nasuada. No matter how many lashes you assign me, they cannot be as painful as losing my home and my father was."

"No," said Nasuada softly. "They could not. . . . One of the magicians of Du Vrangr Gata will oversee the flogging and attend to you afterward, to ensure that the whip causes you no permanent damage. However, they shall not entirely heal your wounds, nor may you seek out a magician on your own to mend your back."

"I understand."

"Your flogging will be held as soon as Jörmundur can marshal the troops. Until then, you will remain under guard in a tent by the whipping post."

It relieved Roran that he would not have to wait any longer; he did not want to have to labor for days under the shadow of what lay before him. "My Lady," he said, and she dismissed him with a motion of her finger.

Turning on his heel, Roran marched out of the pavilion. Two guards took up positions on either side of him as he emerged. Without looking at or speaking to him, they led Roran through the camp until they arrived at a small, empty tent not far from the blackened whipping post, which stood upon a slight rise just beyond the edge of the camp.

The post was six and a half feet high and had a thick crossbeam near the top, to which prisoners' wrists were tied. Rows of scratches from the fingernails of scourged men covered the crossbeam.

Roran forced himself to look away and then ducked inside the tent. The only piece of furniture inside was a battered wooden stool. He sat and concentrated upon his breathing, determined to remain calm.

As the minutes passed, Roran began to hear the tromp of boots and the clink of mail as the Varden assembled around the whipping post. Roran imagined the thousands of men and women staring at him, including the villagers from Carvahall. His pulse quickened, and sweat sprang up upon his brow.

After about half an hour, the sorceress Trianna entered the tent and had him strip down to his trousers, which embarrassed Roran, although the woman seemed to take no notice. Trianna examined him all over, and even cast an additional spell of healing on his left shoulder, where the soldier had stabbed him with the bolt of a crossbow. Then she declared him fit to continue and gave him a shirt made of sackcloth to wear in place of his own.

Roran had just pulled the shirt over his head when Katrina

pushed her way into the tent. As he beheld her, an equal measure of joy and dread filled Roran.

Katrina glanced between him and Trianna, then curtsied to the sorceress. "May I please speak with my husband alone?"

"Of course. I shall wait outside."

Once Trianna had departed, Katrina rushed to Roran and threw her arms around him. He hugged her just as fiercely as she hugged him, for he had not seen her since he had returned to the Varden.

"Oh, how I've missed you," Katrina whispered in his right ear.

"And I you," he murmured.

They drew apart just far enough so that they could gaze into each other's eyes, and then Katrina scowled. "This is wrong! I went to Nasuada, and I begged her to pardon you, or at least to reduce the number of lashes, but she refused to grant my request."

Running his hands up and down Katrina's back, Roran said, "I wish that you hadn't."

"Why not?"

571

"Because I said that I would remain with the Varden, and I will not go back on my word."

"But this is wrong!" said Katrina, gripping him by his shoulders. "Carn told me what you did, Roran: you slew almost two hundred soldiers by yourself, and if not for your heroism, none of the men with you would have survived. Nasuada ought to be plying you with gifts and praise, not having you whipped like a common criminal!"

"It does not matter whether this is right or wrong," he told her. "It is necessary. If I were in Nasuada's position, I would have given the same order myself."

Katrina shuddered. "Fifty lashes, though. . . . Why does it have to be so many? Men have died from being whipped that many times."

"Only if they had weak hearts. Don't be so worried; it will take more than that to kill me."

A false smile flickered across Katrina's lips, and then a sob escaped her and she pressed her face against his chest. He cradled her in his arms, stroking her hair and reassuring her as best he could, even though he felt no better than she. After several minutes, Roran heard a horn being winded outside the tent, and he knew that their time together was drawing to a close. Extricating himself from Katrina's embrace, he said, "There is something I want you to do for me."

"What?" she asked, dabbing at her eyes.

"Go back to our tent and do not leave it until after my flogging."

Katrina appeared shocked by his request. "No! I shall not leave you . . . not now."

"Please," he said, "you should not have to see this."

"And you should not have to endure it," she retorted.

"Leave that. I know you wish to stay by my side, but I can bear this better if I know that you aren't here watching me. . . . I brought this upon myself, Katrina, and I do not want you to suffer because of it as well."

Her expression became strained. "The knowledge of your fate shall pain me regardless of where I am standing. However . . . I shall do as you ask, but only because it will help you through this ordeal. . . . You know that I would have the whip fall upon my own body instead of yours, if I could."

"And you know," he said, kissing her on both cheeks, "that I would refuse to let you take my place."

Tears welled up in her eyes again, and she pulled him closer, hugging him so tightly, he had difficulty breathing.

They were still wrapped in each other's arms when the entrance flap to the tent was swept back and Jörmundur entered, along with two of the Nighthawks. Katrina disengaged herself from Roran, curtsied to Jörmundur, and then, without a word, slipped out of the tent.

Jörmundur extended a hand toward Roran. "It's time."

Nodding, Roran rose and allowed Jörmundur and the guards to escort him to the whipping post outside. Row after row of the Varden boxed in the area around the post, every man, woman, dwarf, and Urgal standing with stiff spines and squared shoulders. After his initial glimpse of the assembled army, Roran gazed off toward the horizon and did his best to ignore the onlookers.

The two guards lifted Roran's arms above his head and secured his wrists to the crossbeam of the whipping post. While they did, Jörmundur walked around in front of the post and held up a leather-wrapped dowel. "Here, bite down on this," he said in a low voice. "It will keep you from hurting yourself." Grateful, Roran opened his mouth and allowed Jörmundur to fit the dowel between his teeth. The tanned leather tasted bitter, like green acorns.

Then a horn and a drumroll sounded, and Jörmundur read out the charges against Roran, and the guards cut off Roran's sackcloth shirt.

He shivered as the cold air washed across his bare torso.

An instant before it struck, Roran heard the whip whistling through the air.

It felt as if a rod of hot metal had been laid across his flesh. Roran arched his back and bit down on the dowel. An involuntary groan escaped him, although the dowel muffled the sound so he thought no one else heard.

"One," said the man wielding the whip.

The shock of the second blow caused Roran to groan again, but thereafter he remained silent, determined not to appear weak before the whole of the Varden.

The whipping was as painful as any of the numerous wounds Roran had suffered over the past few months, but after a dozen or so blows, he gave up trying to fight the pain and, surrendering to it, entered a bleary trance. His field of vision narrowed until the only thing he saw was the worn wood in front of him; at times, his sight flickered and went blank as he drifted into brief spates of unconsciousness.

After an interminable time, he heard the dim and faraway voice intone, "Thirty," and despair gripped him as he wondered, *How can I possibly withstand another twenty lashes?* Then he thought of Katrina and their unborn child, and the thought gave him strength.

✳ ✳ ✳

Roran woke to find himself lying on his stomach on the cot inside the tent he and Katrina shared. Katrina was kneeling next to him, stroking his hair and murmuring in his ear, while someone daubed a cold, sticky substance over the stripes on his back. He winced and stiffened as the anonymous person poked a particularly sensitive spot.

"That is *not* how I would treat a patient of mine," he heard Trianna say in a haughty tone.

"If you treat all of your patients as you were treating Roran," another woman replied, "I'm amazed that any survived your attentions." After a moment, Roran recognized the second voice as belonging to the strange, bright-eyed herbalist Angela.

"I beg your pardon!" said Trianna. "I will not stand here and be insulted by a lowly *fortuneteller* who struggles to cast even the most basic spell."

"Sit, then, if it pleases you, but whether you sit or stand, I will continue to insult you until you admit that his back muscle attaches *here* and not *there*." Roran felt a finger touch him in two different places, each a half inch apart.

"Oh!" said Trianna, and left the tent.

Katrina smiled at Roran, and for the first time, he noticed the tears streaking her face. "Roran, do you understand me?" she asked. "Are you awake?"

"I . . . I think so," he said, his voice raspy. His jaw ached from biting the dowel so hard for so long. He coughed, then grimaced as every one of the fifty stripes on his back throbbed in unison.

"There we go," said Angela. "All finished."

"It's amazing. I didn't expect you and Trianna to do so much," said Katrina.

"On Nasuada's orders."

"Nasuada? . . . Why would—"

"You'll have to ask her yourself. Tell him to stay off his back if he can help it. And he ought to be careful twisting from side to side, or he might tear open the scabs."

"Thank you," Roran mumbled.

Behind him, Angela laughed. "Think nothing of it, Roran. Or rather, think something of it, but do not consider it overly important. Besides, it amuses me to have tended injuries on both your back and Eragon's. Right, then, I'll be off. Watch out for ferrets!"

When the herbalist had gone, Roran closed his eyes again. Katrina's smooth fingers stroked his forehead. "You were very brave," she said.

"Was I?"

"Aye. Jörmundur and everyone else I spoke to said that you never cried out or begged for the flogging to stop."

"Good." He wanted to know how serious his wounds were, but he was reluctant to force her to describe the damage to his back.

Katrina seemed to sense his desire, however, for she said, "Angela believes that with a bit of luck, you won't scar too badly. In either case, once you're completely healed, Eragon or another magician can remove the scars from your back and it will be as if you were never whipped in the first place."

"Mmh."

"Would you like something to drink?" she asked. "I have a pot of yarrow tea steeping."

"Yes, please."

As Katrina rose, Roran heard another person enter the tent. He opened one eye and was surprised to see Nasuada standing next to the pole at the front of the tent.

"My Lady," Katrina said, her voice razor-sharp.

In spite of the lances of pain from his back, Roran pushed himself partially up and, with Katrina's help, swung himself into a sitting position. Leaning on Katrina, he started to stand, but Nasuada lifted a hand. "Please don't. I do not wish to cause you any more distress than I already have."

"Why have you come, Lady Nasuada?" asked Katrina. "Roran needs to rest and recover, not to spend his time talking when he does not have to."

Roran placed a hand on Katrina's left shoulder. "I can talk if I must," he said.

Moving farther into the tent, Nasuada lifted the hem of her green dress and sat on the small chest of belongings Katrina had brought with her from Carvahall. After arranging the folds of her skirt, she said, "I have another mission for you, Roran: a small raid similar to those you have already participated in."

"When will I leave?" he asked, puzzled that she would bother to inform him in person of such a simple assignment.

"Tomorrow."

Katrina's eyes widened. "Are you mad?" she exclaimed.

"Katrina . . . ," Roran murmured, attempting to placate her, but she shrugged off his hand and said, "The last trip you sent him on nearly killed him, and you've just had him whipped within an inch of his life! You can't order him back into combat so soon; he wouldn't last more than a minute against Galbatorix's soldiers!"

"I can, and I must!" said Nasuada with such authority, Katrina held her tongue and waited to hear Nasuada's explanation, although Roran could tell that her anger had not subsided. Gazing at him intensely, Nasuada said, "Roran, as you may or may not be aware, our alliance with the Urgals is upon the verge of collapse. One of our own murdered three of the Urgals while you were serving under Captain Edric, who, you may be pleased to know, is a captain no more. Anyway, I had the miserable wretch who killed the Urgals hanged, but ever since, our relations with Garzhvog's rams have become increasingly precarious."

"What does this have to do with Roran?" Katrina demanded.

Nasuada pressed her lips together, then said, "I need to convince the Varden to accept the presence of the Urgals without further bloodshed, and the best way I can do that is to *show* the Varden that our two races can work together in peaceful pursuit of a common goal. Toward that end, the group you shall be traveling with will contain equal numbers of both humans and Urgals."

"But that still doesn't—" Katrina started to say.

"And I am placing the whole lot of them under your command, Stronghammer."

"Me?" Roran rasped, astonished. "Why?"

With a wry smile, Nasuada said, "Because you will do whatever you have to in order to protect your friends and family. In this, you are like me, although my family is larger than yours, for I consider the whole of the Varden my kin. Also, because you are Eragon's cousin, I cannot afford to have you commit insubordination again, for then I will have no choice but to execute you or expel you from the Varden. Neither of which I wish to do.

"Therefore, I am giving you your own command so that there is no one above you to disobey, except me. If you ignore *my* orders, it had better be to kill Galbatorix; no other reason will save you from far worse than the lashes you earned today. And I am giving you *this* command, because you have proven that you are able to convince others to follow you, even in the face of the most daunting circumstances. You have as good a chance as any of maintaining control over a group of Urgals and humans. I would send Eragon if I could, but since he is not here, the responsibility falls to you. When the Varden hear that Eragon's own cousin, Roran Stronghammer—he who slew nigh on two hundred soldiers by himself—went on a mission with Urgals and that the mission was a success, then we may yet keep the Urgals as our allies for the duration of this war. *That* is why I had Angela and Trianna heal you more than is customary: not to spare you your punishment, but because I need you fit to command. Now, what say you, Stronghammer? Can I count on you?"

Roran looked at Katrina. He knew she desperately wished he would tell Nasuada that he was incapable of leading the raid. Dropping his gaze so he did not have to see her distress, Roran thought of the immense size of the army that opposed the Varden, and then, in a hoarse whisper, he said:

"You may count on me, Lady Nasuada."

577

AMONG THE CLOUDS

From Tronjheim, Saphira flew the five miles to Farthen Dûr's inner wall, then she and Eragon entered the tunnel that burrowed east, miles through Farthen Dûr's base. Eragon could have run the length of the tunnel in about ten minutes, but since the height of the ceiling prevented Saphira from flying or jumping, she would not have been able to keep up, so he limited himself to a brisk walk.

An hour later, they emerged in Odred Valley, which ran north to south. Nestled among the foothills at the head of the narrow, fern-filled valley was Fernoth-mérna, a fair-sized lake that was like a drop of dark ink between the towering mountains of the Beor range. From the northern end of Fernoth-mérna flowed the Ragni Darmn, which wound its way up the valley until it joined with the Az Ragni by the flanks of Moldûn the Proud, the northernmost mountain of the Beors.

They had departed Tronjheim well before dawn, and although the tunnel had slowed them, it was still early morning. The ragged strip of sky overhead was barred with rays of pale yellow where sunlight streamed between the peaks of the towering mountains. Within the valley below, ridges of heavy clouds clung to the sides of the mountains like vast gray snakes. Coils of white mist drifted up from the glassy surface of the lake.

Eragon and Saphira stopped at the edge of Fernoth-mérna to drink and to replenish their waterskins for the next leg of their journey. The water came from melted snow and ice high in the mountains. It was so cold, it made Eragon's teeth hurt. He screwed up his eyes and stamped the ground, groaning as a spike of cold-induced pain shot through his skull.

As the throbbing subsided, he gazed across the lake. Between the curtains of shifting mist, he spotted the ruins of a sprawling castle built upon a bare stone spur on one mountain. Thick ropes of ivy strangled the crumbling walls, but aside from that, the structure appeared lifeless. Eragon shivered. The abandoned building seemed gloomy, ominous, as if it were the decaying carcass of some foul beast.

Ready? Saphira asked.

Ready, he said, and climbed into the saddle.

From Fernoth-mérna, Saphira flew northward, following Odred Valley out of the Beor Mountains. The valley did not lead directly toward Ellesméra, which was farther west, yet they had no choice but to remain in the valley, as the passes between the mountains were over five miles high.

Saphira flew at as lofty an altitude as Eragon could endure because it was easier for her to traverse long distances in the rarefied upper atmosphere than in the thick, moist air near the ground. Eragon protected himself against the freezing temperatures by wearing several layers of clothes and by shielding himself from the wind with a spell that split the stream of freezing air so it flowed harmlessly to either side.

Riding Saphira was far from restful, but since she flapped in a slow and steady rhythm, Eragon did not have to concentrate upon maintaining his balance as he did when she turned or dove or engaged in other, more elaborate maneuvers. For the most part, he divided his time between talking with Saphira, thinking back upon the events of the past few weeks, and studying the ever-changing vista below them.

You used magic without the ancient language when the dwarves attacked you, said Saphira. *That was a dangerous thing to do.*

I know, but I didn't have time to think of the words. Besides, you never use the ancient language when you cast a spell.

That's different. I'm a dragon. We do not need the ancient language to state our intentions; we know what we want, and we do not change our minds as easily as elves or humans.

The orange sun was a handsbreadth above the horizon when Saphira sailed through the mouth of the valley and out over the flat, empty grasslands that abutted the Beor Mountains. Straightening in the saddle, Eragon gazed around them and shook his head, amazed by how much distance they had covered. *If only we could have flown to Ellesméra the first time,* he said. *We would have had so much more time to spend with Oromis and Glaedr.* Saphira indicated her agreement with a silent mental nod.

Saphira flew until the sun had set and the stars covered the sky and the mountains were a dark purple smudge behind them. She would have continued on until morning, but Eragon insisted they stop to rest. *You are still tired from your trip to Farthen Dûr. We can fly through the night tomorrow, and the day after as well, if necessary, but tonight you must sleep.*

Although Saphira did not like his proposal, she agreed to it and landed by a patch of willow trees growing alongside a stream. As he dismounted, Eragon discovered his legs were so stiff, he had difficulty remaining on his feet. He unsaddled Saphira, then spread his bedroll on the ground next to her and curled up with his back against her warm body. He had no need of a tent, for she sheltered him with a wing, like a mother hawk protecting her brood. The two of them soon sank into their respective dreams, which mingled in strange and wonderful ways, for their minds remained linked even then.

As soon as the first hint of light appeared in the east, Eragon and Saphira continued on their way, soaring high above the verdant plains.

A fierce headwind sprang up in midmorning, which slowed Saphira to half her normal speed. Try as she might, she could not rise above the wind. All day she fought against the rushing air. It was arduous work, and although Eragon gave her as much of his strength as he dared, by afternoon her exhaustion was profound. She swooped down and alighted on a knoll in the grasslands and sat there with her wings draped across the ground, panting and trembling.

We should stay here for the night, Eragon said.

No.

Saphira, you're in no condition to go on. Let's make camp until you recover. Who knows, the wind might die down by evening.

He heard the wet rasp of her tongue as she licked her chops and then the heave of her lungs as she resumed panting.

No, she said. *On these plains, it might blow for weeks or even months on end. We cannot wait for calm.*

But—

I will not give up merely because I hurt, Eragon. Too much is at stake. . . .

Then let me give you energy from Aren. There is more than enough in the ring to sustain you from here to Du Weldenvarden.

No, she repeated again. *Save Aren for when we have no other recourse. I can rest and recover in the forest. Aren, however, we may have need of at any moment; you should not deplete it merely to ease my discomfort.*

I hate to see you in such pain, though.

A faint growl escaped her. *My ancestors, the wild dragons, would not have shrunk from a puny breeze like this, and neither will I.*

And with that, she jumped back into the air, carrying him with her as she drove herself into the gale.

As the day was drawing to an end and the wind still howled around them, pushing against Saphira as if fate were determined to keep them from reaching Du Weldenvarden, Eragon thought of the dwarf woman Glûmra and of her faith in the dwarven gods, and for the first time in his life, he felt the desire to pray. Withdrawing from his mental contact with Saphira—who was so tired and preoccupied, she did not notice—Eragon whispered, "Gûntera, king of the gods, if you exist, and if you can hear me, and if you have the power, then, please, still this wind. I know I'm not a dwarf, but King Hrothgar adopted me into his clan, and I think that gives me the right to pray to you. Gûntera, please, we have to get to Du Weldenvarden as fast as possible, not only for the good of the Varden but also for the good of your people, the knurlan. Please, I beg of you, still this wind. Saphira cannot keep this up much longer." Then, feeling slightly foolish, Eragon extended himself toward Saphira's consciousness, wincing in sympathy as he felt the burning within her muscles.

Late that night, when all was cold and black, the wind abated and, thereafter, only occasionally buffeted them with a gust.

When morning came, Eragon looked down and saw the hard, dry land of the Hadarac Desert. *Blast it,* he said, for they had not come as far as he had hoped. *We won't make it to Ellesméra today, will we?*

Not unless the wind decides to blow in the opposite direction and carry us there upon its back. Saphira labored in silence for another few minutes, then added, *However, barring any other unpleasant surprises, we should arrive at Du Weldenvarden by evening.*

Eragon grunted.

They landed only twice that day. Once, while they were on the ground, Saphira devoured a brace of ducks that she caught and killed with a burst of fire, but other than that, she went without food. To save time, Eragon ate his own meals in the saddle.

As Saphira had predicted, Du Weldenvarden came into sight even as the sun neared setting. The forest appeared before them as an endless expanse of green. Deciduous trees—oaks and beeches and maples—dominated the outer parts of the forest, but farther in, Eragon knew, they gave way to the forbidding pine trees that formed the bulk of the woods.

Dusk had settled over the countryside by the time they arrived at the edge of Du Weldenvarden, and Saphira glided to a soft landing under the outstretched branches of a massive oak. She folded her wings and sat still for a while, too tired to continue. Her crimson tongue hung loose from her mouth. While she rested, Eragon listened to the rustle of leaves overhead and to the hoot of owls and the chirp of evening insects.

When she was sufficiently recovered, Saphira walked forward and passed between two giant, moss-covered oak trees and so crossed into Du Weldenvarden on foot. The elves had made it impossible for anyone or anything to enter the forest by means of magic, and since dragons did not rely upon their bodies alone to fly, Saphira could not enter while in the air, else her wings would fail her and she would fall from the sky.

That should be far enough, Saphira said, stopping in a small meadow several hundred feet from the perimeter of the forest.

Eragon unbuckled the straps from around his legs and slid down Saphira's side. He searched the meadow until he found a bare patch of earth. With his hands, he scooped out a shallow hole a foot and a half wide. He summoned forth water to fill the hole, then uttered a spell of scrying.

The water shimmered and acquired a soft yellow glow as Eragon beheld the interior of Oromis's hut. The silver-haired elf was sitting at his kitchen table, reading a tattered scroll. Oromis looked up at Eragon and nodded with unsurprised recognition.

"Master," Eragon said, and twisted his hand over his chest.

"Greetings, Eragon. I have been expecting you. Where are you?"

"Saphira and I just reached Du Weldenvarden. . . . Master, I know we promised to return to Ellesméra, but the Varden are only a few days away from the city of Feinster, and they are vulnerable without us. We don't have the time to fly all the way to Ellesméra. Could you answer our questions here, through the scrying pool?"

Oromis leaned back in his chair, his angled face grave and pensive. Then he said, "I will not instruct you at a distance, Eragon. I can guess at some of the things you wish to ask me, and they are subjects we must discuss in person."

"Master, please. If Murtagh and Thorn—"

"No, Eragon. I understand the reason for your urgency, but your studies are just as important as protecting the Varden, maybe even more so. We must do this properly, or not at all."

Eragon sighed and slumped forward. "Yes, Master."

Oromis nodded. "Glaedr and I will be waiting for you. Fly safe and fly fast. We have much to talk about."

"Yes, Master."

Feeling numb and worn-out, Eragon ended the spell. The water soaked back into the ground. He held his head in his hands, staring at the patch of moist dirt between his feet. Saphira's heavy breathing was loud beside him. *I guess we have to keep going,* he said. *I'm sorry.*

Her breathing paused for a moment as she licked her chops. *It's all right. I'm not about to collapse.*

He looked up at her. *Are you sure?*

Yes.

Eragon reluctantly hoisted himself upright and climbed onto her back. *As long as we're going to Ellesméra,* he said, tightening the straps around his legs, *we should visit the Menoa tree again. Maybe we can finally figure out what Solembum meant. I could certainly use a new sword.*

When Eragon had first met Solembum in Teirm, the werecat had told him, *When the time comes and you need a weapon, look under the roots of the Menoa tree. Then, when all seems lost and your power is insufficient, go to the Rock of Kuthian and speak your name to open the Vault of Souls.* Eragon still did not know where the Rock of Kuthian was, but during their first stay in Ellesméra, he and Saphira had had several chances to examine the Menoa tree. They had discovered no clue as to the exact whereabouts of the supposed weapon. Moss, dirt, bark, and the occasional ant were the only things they had seen among the roots of the Menoa tree, and none of them indicated where to excavate.

Solembum might not have meant a sword, Saphira pointed out. *Werecats love riddles nearly as much as dragons do. If it even exists, this weapon might be a scrap of parchment with a spell inscribed on it, or a* book, or a painting, or a sharp piece of rock, or any other dangerous thing.

Whatever it is, I hope we can find it. Who knows when we will have the chance to return to Ellesméra again?

Saphira raked aside a fallen tree that lay before her, then crouched and unfurled her velvety wings, her massive shoulder muscles bunching. Eragon yelped and grabbed the front of his saddle as she surged up and forward with unexpected force, rising above the tops of the trees in a single vertiginous bound.

Wheeling over the sea of shifting branches, Saphira oriented herself in a northwesterly direction and then set out toward the elves' capital, the beats of her wings slow and heavy.

✦ ✦ ✦

BUTTING HEADS

The raid on the supply train went almost exactly as Roran had planned: three days after leaving the main body of the Varden, he and his fellow horsemen rode down from the lip of a ravine and struck the meandering line of wagons broadside. Meanwhile, the Urgals sprang out from behind boulders scattered across the floor of the ravine and attacked the supply train from the front, stopping the procession in its tracks. The soldiers and wagoners put up a brave fight, but the ambush had caught them while sleepy and disorganized, and Roran's force soon overwhelmed them. None of the humans or Urgals died in the attack, and only three suffered wounds: two humans and one Urgal.

Roran killed several of the soldiers himself, but for the most part, he hung back and concentrated upon directing the assault, as was his responsibility now. He was still stiff and sore from the flogging he had endured, and he did not want to exert himself any more than necessary, for fear of cracking the mat of scabs that covered his back.

Until that point, Roran had had no difficulty maintaining discipline among the twenty humans and twenty Urgals. Although it was obvious that neither group liked nor trusted the other—an attitude he shared, for he regarded the Urgals with the same degree of suspicion and distaste as would any man who had been raised in proximity to the Spine—they had succeeded in working together during the past three days with nary a raised voice. That both groups had managed to cooperate so well had, he knew, little to do with his prowess as a commander. Nasuada and Nar Garzhvog had taken great care in picking the warriors who were to travel with him, selecting only those with a reputation for a quick blade, sound judgment, and, above all, a calm and even disposition.

However, in the aftermath of the attack on the supply train, as his men were busy dragging the bodies of the soldiers and the wagoners into a pile, and Roran was riding up and down the line of wagons overseeing the work, he heard an agonized howl from somewhere by the far end of the train. Thinking that perhaps another contingent of soldiers had chanced upon them, Roran shouted to Carn and several other men to join him and then touched his spurs to Snowfire's flanks and galloped toward the rear of the wagons.

Four Urgals had tied an enemy soldier to the trunk of a gnarled willow tree and were amusing themselves by poking and prodding him with their swords. Swearing, Roran jumped down from Snowfire and, with a single blow of his hammer, put the man out of his misery.

A swirling cloud of dust swept over the group as Carn and four other warriors galloped up to the willow tree. They reined in their steeds and spread out on either side of Roran, holding their weapons at the ready.

The largest Urgal, a ram named Yarbog, stepped forward. "Stronghammer, why did you stop our sport? He would have danced for us for many more minutes."

From between clenched teeth, Roran said, "So long as you are under my command, you will not torture captives without cause. Am I understood? Many of these soldiers have been forced to serve Galbatorix against their will. Many of them are our friends or family or neighbors, and while we must fight them, I will not have you treat them with unnecessary cruelty. If not for the whims of fate, any one of us humans might be standing in their place. They are not our enemy; Galbatorix is, as he is yours."

The Urgal's heavy brow beetled, nearly obscuring his deep-set yellow eyes. "But you will still kill them, yes? Why cannot we enjoy seeing them wriggle and dance first?"

Roran wondered if the Urgal's skull was too thick to crack with his hammer. Struggling to restrain his anger, he said, "Because it is wrong, if nothing else!" Pointing at the dead soldier, he said, "What if *he* had been one of your own race who had been enthralled by the Shade, Durza? Would you have tormented him as well?"

"Of course," said Yarbog. "They would want us to tickle them with our swords so that they would have an opportunity to prove their bravery before they died. Is it not the same with you hornless humans, or have you no stomach for pain?"

Roran was not sure how serious an insult it was among the Urgals to call another *hornless*, but even so, he had no doubt that questioning someone's courage was as offensive to Urgals as it was to humans, if not more so. "Any one of us could withstand more pain without crying out than you, Yarbog," he said, tightening his grip on his hammer and shield. "Now, unless you wish to experience agony the likes of which you cannot imagine, surrender your sword to me, then untie that poor wretch and carry him over to the rest of the bodies. After that, go see to the packhorses. They are yours to care for until we return to the Varden."

Without waiting for an acknowledgment from the Urgal, Roran turned and grasped Snowfire's reins and prepared to climb back onto the stallion.

"No," growled Yarbog.

Roran froze with one foot in a stirrup and silently swore to himself. He had hoped that just such a situation would not arise during the trip. Swinging around, he said, "No? Are you refusing to obey my orders?"

Drawing back his lips to expose his short fangs, Yarbog said, "No. I challenge you for leadership of this tribe, Stronghammer." And the Urgal threw back his massive head and bellowed so loudly that the rest of the humans and Urgals stopped what they were doing and ran toward the willow tree until all forty of them were clustered around Yarbog and Roran.

"Shall we attend to this creature for you?" Carn asked, his voice ringing out.

Wishing that there were not so many onlookers, Roran shook his head. "No, I shall deal with him myself." Despite his words, he was glad to have his men beside him, opposite the line of hulking, gray-skinned Urgals. The humans were smaller than the Urgals, but all except Roran were mounted on horses, which would give them a slight advantage if there were a fight between the two groups. If that came to pass, Carn's magic would be of little help, for the Urgals had a spellcaster of their own, a shaman named Dazhgra, and from what Roran had seen, Dazhgra was the more powerful magician, if not as skilled in the nuances of their arcane art.

To Yarbog, Roran said, "It is not the custom of the Varden to award leadership based upon trial by combat. If you wish to fight, I will fight, but you will gain nothing by it. If I lose, Carn will assume my command, and you will answer to him instead of me."

"Bah!" said Yarbog. "I do not challenge you for the right to lead your own race. I challenge you for the right to lead us, the fighting rams of the Bolvek tribe! You have not proven yourself, Strong-hammer, so you cannot claim the position of chieftain. If you lose, I will become chieftain here, and we shall not lift our chins to you, Carn, or any other creature too weak to earn our respect!"

Roran pondered his situation before accepting the inevitable. Even if it cost him his life, he had to try to maintain his authority over the Urgals, else the Varden would lose them as allies. Taking a breath, he said, "Among my race, it is customary for the person who has been challenged to choose the time and place for the fight, as well as the weapons both parties will use."

Chortling deep in his throat, Yarbog said, "The time is now, Stronghammer. The place is here. And among my race, we fight in a loincloth and without weapons."

"That is hardly fair, since I have no horns," Roran pointed out. "Will you agree to let me use my hammer to compensate for my lack?"

Yarbog thought about it, then said, "You may keep your helmet and shield, but no hammer. Weapons are not allowed when we fight to be chief."

"I see. . . . Well, if I can't have my hammer, I will forgo my helmet and shield as well. What are the rules of combat, and how shall we decide the winner?"

"There is only one rule, Stronghammer: if you flee, you forfeit the match and are banished from your tribe. You win by forcing your rival to submit, but since I will never submit, we will fight to the death."

Roran nodded. *That might be what he intends to do, but I won't kill him if I can help it.* "Let us begin," he cried, and banged his hammer against his shield.

At his direction, the men and Urgals cleared a space in the middle of the ravine and pegged out a square, twelve paces by twelve paces. Then Roran and Yarbog stripped, and two Urgals slathered bear grease over Yarbog's body while Carn and Loften, another human, did the same for Roran.

"Rub as much as you can into my back," Roran murmured. He wanted his scabs to be as soft as possible so as to minimize the number of places they would crack.

Leaning close to him, Carn said, "Why did you refuse the shield and helmet?"

"They would only slow me. I'll have to be as fast as a frightened hare if I'm to avoid being crushed by him." As Carn and Loften worked their way down his limbs, Roran studied his opponent, searching for any vulnerability that would help him defeat the Urgal.

Yarbog stood well over six feet tall. His back was broad, his chest deep, and his arms and legs covered with knotted muscles. His neck was as thick as a bull's, as it had to be in order to sustain the weight of his head and his curled horns. Three slanting scars marked the left side of his waist, where he had been clawed by an animal. Sparse black bristles grew over the whole of his hide.

At least he's not a Kull, thought Roran. He was confident of his own strength, but even so, he did not believe that he could overpower Yarbog with sheer force. Rare was the man who could hope to match the physical prowess of a healthy Urgal ram. Also, Roran knew that Yarbog's large black fingernails, his fangs, his horns, and his leathery hide would all provide Yarbog with considerable advantages in the unarmed combat they were about to engage in. *If I can, I will*, Roran decided, thinking of all the low tricks he could use against the Urgal, for fighting Yarbog would not be like wrestling with Eragon or Baldor or any other man from Carvahall; rather, Roran was sure that it would be like the ferocious and unrestrained brawling between two wild beasts.

Again and again, Roran's eyes returned to Yarbog's immense horns, for those, he knew, were the most dangerous of the Urgal's features. With them, Yarbog could butt and gore Roran with impunity, and they would also protect the sides of Yarbog's head from any blows Roran could deliver with his bare hands, although they limited the Urgal's peripheral vision. Then it occurred to Roran that just as the horns were Yarbog's greatest natural gift, so too they might be his undoing.

Roran rolled his shoulders and bounced on the balls of his feet, eager for the contest to be over.

When both Roran and Yarbog were completely covered with bear grease, their seconds retreated and they stepped into the confines of the square pegged out on the ground. Roran kept his knees partially flexed, ready to leap in any direction at the slightest hint of movement from Yarbog. The rocky soil was cold, hard, and rough beneath the soles of his bare feet.

A slight gust stirred the branches of the nearby willow tree. One of the oxen harnessed to the wagons pawed at a clump of grass, his tack creaking.

With a rippling bellow, Yarbog charged Roran, covering the distance between them with three thundering steps. Roran waited until Yarbog was nearly upon him, then jumped to the right. He underestimated Yarbog's speed, however. Lowering his head, the Urgal rammed his horns into Roran's left shoulder and tossed him sprawling across the square.

Sharp rocks poked into Roran's side as he landed. Lines of pain flashed across his back, tracing the paths of his half-healed wounds. He grunted and rolled upright, feeling several scabs break open, exposing his raw flesh to the stinging air. Dirt and small pebbles clung to the film of grease on his body. Keeping both feet on the ground, he shuffled toward Yarbog, never taking his eyes off the snarling Urgal.

Again Yarbog charged him, and again Roran attempted to jump out of the way. This time his maneuver succeeded, and he slipped past the Urgal with inches to spare. Whirling around, Yarbog ran at him for a third time, and once more, Roran managed to evade him.

Then Yarbog changed tactics. Advancing sideways, like a crab, he thrust out his large, hooked hands to catch Roran and pull him into his deadly embrace. Roran flinched and retreated. Whatever happened, he had to avoid falling into Yarbog's clutches; with his immense strength, the Urgal could soon dispatch him.

The men and Urgals gathered around the square were silent, their faces impassive as they watched Roran and Yarbog scuffle back and forth in the dirt.

For several minutes, Roran and Yarbog exchanged quick glancing blows. Roran avoided closing with the Urgal wherever possible, trying to wear him out from a distance, but as the fight dragged on and Yarbog seemed no more tired than when they had begun, Roran realized that time was not his friend. If he was going to win, he had to end the fight without further delay.

Hoping to provoke Yarbog into charging again—for his strategy depended upon just that—Roran withdrew to the far corner of the square and began to taunt him, saying, "Ha! You are as fat and slow as a milk cow! Can't you catch me, Yarbog, or are your legs made of lard? You should cut off your horns in shame for letting a human make a fool of you. What will your prospective mates think when they hear of this? Will you tell them—"

Yarbog drowned out Roran's words with a roar. The Urgal sprinted toward him, turning slightly, so as to crash into Roran with his full weight. Skipping out of the way, Roran reached out for the tip of Yarbog's right horn but missed his mark and fell stumbling into the middle of the square, skinning both knees. He cursed to himself as he regained his footing.

Checking his headlong rush just before momentum carried him beyond the boundaries of the square, Yarbog turned back, his small yellow eyes searching for Roran. "Yah!" shouted Roran. He stuck out his tongue and made every rude gesture he could think of. "You couldn't hit a tree even if it was in front of you!"

"Die, puny human!" Yarbog growled, and sprang at Roran, arms outstretched.

Two of Yarbog's nails carved bloody furrows across Roran's ribs as Roran darted to his left, but he still managed to grasp and hang on to one of the Urgal's horns. Roran grabbed the other horn as well before Yarbog could throw him off. Using the horns as handles, Roran wrenched Yarbog's head to one side and, straining every muscle, cast the Urgal to the ground. Roran's back flared in angry protest at the motion.

As soon as Yarbog's chest touched the dirt, Roran placed a knee on top of his right shoulder, pinning him in place. Yarbog snorted and bucked, trying to break Roran's grip, but Roran refused to let go. He braced his feet against a rock and twisted the Urgal's head as far around as it would go, pulling so hard he would have broken the neck of any human. The grease on his palms made it difficult to hold on to Yarbog's horns.

Yarbog relaxed for a moment, then pushed himself off the ground with his left arm, lifting Roran as well, and scrabbled with his legs in an effort to get them underneath his body. Roran grimaced and leaned against Yarbog's neck and shoulder. After a handful of seconds, Yarbog's left arm buckled and he fell flat on his stomach again.

Both Roran and Yarbog were panting as heavily as if they had run a race. Where they touched, the bristles on the Urgal's hide poked Roran like pieces of stiff wire. Dust coated their bodies. Thin streams of blood ran down from the scratches on Roran's side and from his aching back.

Yarbog resumed kicking and flailing once he had regained his breath, flopping around in the dirt like a hooked fish. It took all of Roran's strength, but he hung on, trying to ignore the stones that cut his feet and legs. Unable to free himself by those methods, Yarbog let his limbs go limp and then began to flex his neck again and again, in an attempt to exhaust Roran's arms.

They lay there, neither of them moving more than a few inches as they struggled against each other.

A fly buzzed over them and landed on Roran's ankle.

Oxen lowed.

After nearly ten minutes, sweat drenched Roran's face. He could not seem to get enough air into his lungs. His arms seared with agony. The stripes on his back felt as if they were about to tear asunder. His ribs throbbed where Yarbog had clawed him.

Roran knew he could not continue for much longer. *Blast it!* he thought. *Won't he ever give up?*

Just then, Yarbog's head quivered as a muscle in the Urgal's neck cramped. Yarbog grunted, the first sound he had made in over a minute, and in an undertone, he muttered, "Kill me, Stronghammer. I cannot best you."

Adjusting his grip on Yarbog's horns, Roran growled in an equally low tone, "No. If you want to die, find someone else to kill you. I have fought by your rules, now you will accept defeat according to mine. Tell everyone that you submit to me. Say you were wrong to challenge me. Do that, and I'll let you go. If not, I'll keep you here until you change your mind, no matter how long it takes."

Yarbog's head twitched under Roran's hands as the Urgal tried once more to free himself. He huffed, blowing a small cloud of dust into the air, then rumbled, "The shame would be too great, Stronghammer. Kill me."

"I don't belong to your race, and I won't abide by your customs," said Roran. "If you are so worried about your honor, tell those who are curious that you were defeated by the cousin of Eragon Shadeslayer. Surely there is no shame in that." When several minutes had passed and Yarbog still had not replied, Roran yanked on Yarbog's horns and growled, "Well?"

Raising his voice so that all of the men and Urgals could hear, Yarbog said, "Gar! Svarvok curse me; I submit! I should not have challenged you, Stronghammer. You are worthy to be chief, and I am not."

As one, the men cheered and shouted, banging the pommels of their swords on their shields. The Urgals shifted in place and said nothing.

Satisfied, Roran released Yarbog's horns and rolled away from the gray Urgal. Feeling almost as if he had endured another flogging, Roran slowly got to his feet and hobbled out of the square to where Carn was waiting.

Roran winced as Carn draped a blanket over his shoulders and the fabric rubbed against his abused skin. Grinning, Carn handed him a wineskin. "After he knocked you down, I thought for sure he would kill you. I should have learned by now to never count you out, eh, Roran? Ha! That was just about the finest fight I've ever seen. You must be the only man in history to have wrestled an Urgal."

"Maybe not," Roran said between sips of wine. "But I might be the only man who has survived the experience." He smiled as Carn laughed. Roran looked over at the Urgals, who were clustered around Yarbog, talking with him in low grunts while two of their brethren wiped the grease and grime from Yarbog's limbs. Although the Urgals appeared subdued, they did not seem angry or resentful, so far as he was able to judge, and he was confident that he would have no more trouble from them.

Despite the pain of his wounds, Roran felt pleased with the outcome of the match. *This won't be the last fight between our two races,* he thought, *but as long as we can return safely to the Varden, the Urgals won't break off our alliance, at least not on account of me.*

After taking one last sip, Roran stoppered the wineskin and handed it back to Carn, then shouted, "Right, now stop standing around yammering like sheep and finish drawing up a list of what's in those wagons! Loften, round up the soldiers' horses, if they haven't already wandered too far away! Dazhgra, see to the oxen. Make haste! Thorn and Murtagh could be flying here even now. Go on, snap to!

"And, Carn, where the blazes are my clothes?"

✦ ✦ ✦

GENEALOGY

On the fourth day after leaving Farthen Dûr, Eragon and Saphira arrived in Ellesméra.

The sun was clear and bright overhead when the first of the city's buildings—a narrow, twisting turret with glittering windows that stood between three tall pine trees and was grown out of their intermingled branches—came into view. Beyond the bark-sheathed turret, Eragon spotted the seemingly random collection of clearings that marked the location of the sprawling city.

As Saphira planed over the uneven surface of the forest, Eragon quested with his mind for the consciousness of Gilderien the Wise, who, as the wielder of the White Flame of Vándil, had protected Ellesméra from the elves' enemies for over two and a half millennia. Projecting his thoughts toward the city, Eragon said in the ancient language, *Gilderien-elda, may we pass?*

A deep, calm voice sounded in Eragon's mind. *You may pass, Eragon Shadeslayer and Saphira Brightscales. So long as you keep the peace, you are welcome to stay in Ellesméra.*

Thank you, Gilderien-elda, said Saphira.

Her claws brushed the crowns of the dark-needled trees, which rose over three hundred feet above the ground, as she glided across the pinewood city and headed toward the slope of inclined land on the other side of Ellesméra. Between the latticework of branches below, Eragon caught brief glimpses of the flowing shapes of buildings made of living wood, colorful beds of blooming flowers, rippling streams, the auburn glow of a flameless lantern, and, once or twice, the pale flash of an elf's upturned face.

Tilting her wings, Saphira soared up the slope of land until she reached the Crags of Tel'naeír, which dropped over a thousand feet to the rolling forest at the base of the bare white cliff and extended for a league in either direction. Then she turned right and flew north along the ridge of stone, flapping twice to maintain her speed and altitude.

A grass-covered clearing appeared at the edge of the cliff. Set against the backdrop of the surrounding trees was a modest, single-story house grown out of four different pines. A chuckling, gurgling stream wandered out of the mossy forest and passed underneath the roots of one of the pines before disappearing into Du Weldenvarden once again. And curled up next to the house, there lay the golden dragon Glaedr, massive, glittering, his ivory teeth as thick around as Eragon's chest, his claws like scythes, his folded wings soft as suede, his muscled tail nearly as long as all of Saphira, and the striations of his one visible eye sparkling like the rays within a star sapphire. The stump of his missing foreleg was concealed on the other side of his body. A small round table and two chairs had been placed in front of Glaedr. Oromis sat in the chair closest to him, the elf's silver hair gleaming like metal in the sunlight.

Eragon leaned forward in his saddle as Saphira reared upright, slowing herself. She descended with a jolt upon the sward of green grass and ran forward several steps, raking her wings backward before she came to a halt.

His fingers clumsy from exhaustion, Eragon loosened the slip-knots that bound the straps around his legs and then attempted to climb down Saphira's right front leg. As he lowered himself, his knees buckled and he fell. He raised his hands to protect his face and landed upon all fours, scraping his shin on a rock hidden within the grass. He grunted with pain and, feeling as stiff as an old man, started to push himself onto his feet.

A hand entered his field of vision.

Eragon looked up and saw Oromis standing over him, a faint smile upon his timeless face. In the ancient language, Oromis said,

"Welcome back to Ellesméra, Eragon-finiarel. And you as well, Saphira Brightscales, welcome. Welcome, both of you."

Eragon took his hand, and Oromis pulled him upright without apparent effort. At first Eragon was unable to find his tongue, for he had barely spoken aloud since they had left Farthen Dûr and because fatigue blurred his mind. He touched the first two fingers of his right hand to his lips and, also in the ancient language, said, "May good fortune rule over you, Oromis-elda," and then he twisted his hand over his sternum in the gesture of courtesy and respect the elves used.

"May the stars watch over you, Eragon," replied Oromis.

Then Eragon repeated the ceremony with Glaedr. As always, the touch of the dragon's sanguine consciousness awed and humbled Eragon.

Saphira did not greet either Oromis or Glaedr; she remained where she was, her neck drooping until her nose brushed the ground and her shoulders and haunches trembling as if with cold. Dry yellow foam encrusted the corners of her open mouth. Her barbed tongue hung limp from between her fangs.

By way of explanation, Eragon said, "We ran into a headwind the day after we left Farthen Dûr, and . . ." He fell silent as Glaedr lifted his giant head and swung it across the clearing until he was looking down upon Saphira, who made no attempt to acknowledge his presence. Then Glaedr breathed out upon her, fingers of flame burning within the pits of his nostrils. A sense of relief washed over Eragon as he felt energy pour into Saphira, stilling her tremors and strengthening her limbs.

The flames in Glaedr's nostrils vanished with a wisp of smoke. *I went hunting this morning,* he said, his mental voice resonating throughout Eragon's being. *You will find what is left of my kills by the tree with the white branch at the far end of the field. Eat what you want.*

Silent gratitude emanated from Saphira. Dragging her limp tail across the grass, she crawled over to the tree Glaedr had indicated and then settled down and began to tear at the carcass of a deer.

"Come," said Oromis, and gestured toward the table and chairs. On the table was a tray with bowls of fruit and nuts, half a round of cheese, a loaf of bread, a decanter of wine, and two crystal goblets. As Eragon sat, Oromis indicated the decanter and asked, "Would you care for a drink to wash the dust from your throat?"

"Yes, please," said Eragon.

With an elegant motion, Oromis unstoppered the decanter and filled both goblets. He handed one to Eragon and then settled back into his chair, arranging his white tunic with long, smooth fingers.

Eragon sipped the wine. It was mellow and tasted of cherries and plums. "Master, I—"

An upraised finger from Oromis stopped him. "Unless it is unbearably urgent, I would wait until Saphira joins us before we discuss what has brought you here. Are you agreed?"

After a moment's hesitation, Eragon nodded and concentrated upon eating, savoring the flavor of the fresh fruit. Oromis seemed content to sit beside him in silence, drinking his wine and gazing out over the edge of the Crags of Tel'naeír. Behind him, Glaedr watched over the proceedings like a living statue of gold.

The better part of an hour passed before Saphira rose from her meal, crawled over to the stream, and lapped the water for another ten minutes. Drops of water still clung to her jaws when she turned away from the stream and, with a sigh, sprawled next to Eragon, her eyes heavy-lidded. She yawned, her teeth flashing, then exchanged salutations with Oromis and Glaedr. *Talk as you want*, she said. *However, do not expect me to say much. I may fall asleep at any moment.*

If you do, we shall wait for you to wake before we continue, said Glaedr.

That is most . . . kind, replied Saphira, and her eyelids drifted even lower.

"More wine?" Oromis asked, and lifted the decanter an inch off the table. When Eragon shook his head, Oromis replaced the decanter, then pressed the tips of his fingers together, his round fingernails like polished opals. He said, "You do not need to tell me what has befallen you these past weeks, Eragon. Since Islanzadí left the forest, Arya has kept her informed of the news of the land, and every three days, Islanzadí sends a runner from our army back to Du Weldenvarden. Thus, I know of your duel with Murtagh and Thorn on the Burning Plains. I know of your trip to Helgrind and how you punished the butcher from your village. And I know you attended the dwarves' clanmeet in Farthen Dûr and the outcome thereof. Whatever you wish to say, then, you may say without fear of having to educate me about your recent doings."

Eragon rolled a plump blueberry in the palm of his hand. "Do you know of Elva and what happened when I tried to free her of my curse?"

"Yes, even that. You may not have succeeded in removing the whole of the spell from her, but you paid your debt to the child, and that is what a Dragon Rider is supposed to do: fulfill his obligations, no matter how small or difficult they be."

"She still feels the pain of those around her."

"But now it is by her own choice," said Oromis. "No longer does your magic force it upon her. . . . You did not come here to seek my opinion concerning Elva. What is it that weighs upon your heart, Eragon? Ask what you will, and I promise I shall answer all of your questions to the best of my knowledge."

"What," said Eragon, "if I don't know the right questions to ask?"

A twinkle appeared in Oromis's gray eyes. "Ah, you begin to think like an elf. You must trust us as your mentors to teach you and Saphira those things of which you are ignorant. And you must also trust us to decide when it is appropriate to broach those subjects, for there are many elements of your training that should not be spoken of out of turn."

Eragon placed the blueberry in the precise center of the tray, then in a quiet but firm voice said, "It seems as if there is much you have not spoken of."

For a moment, the only sounds were the rustle of branches and the burble of the stream and the chatter of distant squirrels.

If you have a quarrel with us, Eragon, said Glaedr, *then give voice to it and do not gnaw on your anger like a dry old bone.*

Saphira shifted her position, and Eragon imagined he heard a growl from her. He glanced at her, and then, fighting to control the emotions coursing through him, he asked, "When I was last here, did you know who my father was?"

Oromis nodded once. "We did."

"And did you know that Murtagh was my brother?"

Oromis nodded once more. "We did, but—"

"Then why didn't you tell me!" exclaimed Eragon, and jumped to his feet, knocking over his chair. He pounded a fist against his hip, strode several feet away, and stared at the shadows within the tangled forest. Whirling around, Eragon's anger swelled as he saw that Oromis appeared as calm as before. "Were you ever going to tell me? Did you keep the truth about my family a secret because you were afraid it would distract me from my training? Or was it that you were afraid I would become like my father?" A worse thought occurred to Eragon. "Or did you not even consider it important enough to mention? And what of Brom? Did he know? Did he choose Carvahall to hide in because of me, because I was the son of his enemy? You can't expect me to believe it was coincidence he and I happened to be living only a few miles apart and that Arya just *happened* to send Saphira's egg to me in the Spine."

"What Arya did was an accident," asserted Oromis. "She had no knowledge of you then."

Eragon gripped the pommel of his dwarf sword, every muscle in his body as hard as iron. "When Brom first saw Saphira, I remember he said something to himself about being unsure whether 'this' was a farce or a tragedy. At the time, I thought he was referring to the fact that a common farmer like myself had become the first new Rider in over a hundred years. But that's not what he meant, was it? He was wondering whether it was a farce or a tragedy that Morzan's youngest son should be the one to take up the Riders' mantle!

"Is that why you and Brom trained me, to be nothing more than a weapon against Galbatorix so that I may atone for the villainy of my father? Is that all I am to you, a balancing of the scales?" Before Oromis could respond, Eragon swore and said, "My whole life has been a lie! Since the moment I was born, no one but Saphira has wanted me: not my mother, not Garrow, not Aunt Marian, not even Brom. Brom showed interest in me only because of Morzan and Saphira. I have always been an inconvenience. Whatever you think of me, though, I am *not* my father, nor my brother, and I refuse to follow in their footsteps." Placing his hands on the edge of the table, Eragon leaned forward. "I'm not about to betray the elves or the dwarves or the Varden to Galbatorix, if that's what you are worried about. I will do what I must, but from now on, you have neither my loyalty nor my trust. I will not—"

The ground and the air shook as Glaedr growled, his upper lip pulling back to reveal the full length of his fangs. *You have more reason to trust us than anyone else, hatchling,* he said, his voice thundering in Eragon's mind. *If not for our efforts, you would be long dead.*

Then, to Eragon's surprise, Saphira said to Oromis and Glaedr, *Tell him,* and it alarmed him to feel the distress in her thoughts.

Saphira? he asked, puzzled. *Tell me what?*

She ignored him. *This arguing is without cause. Do not prolong Eragon's discomfort anymore.*

One of Oromis's slanted eyebrows rose. "You know?"

I know.

"You know what?" Eragon bellowed, on the verge of tearing his sword from its sheath and threatening all of them until they explained themselves.

With one slim finger, Oromis pointed toward the fallen chair. "Sit." When Eragon remained standing, too angry and full of resentment to obey, Oromis sighed. "I understand this is difficult for you, Eragon, but if you insist upon asking questions and then refuse to listen to the answers, frustration will be your only reward. Now, please sit, so we can talk about this in a civilized manner."

Glaring, Eragon righted the chair and dropped into it. "Why?" he asked. "Why didn't you tell me that my father was Morzan, the first of the Forsworn?"

"In the first place," said Oromis, "we shall be fortunate if you are anything like your father, which, indeed, I believe you are. And, as I was about to say before you interrupted me, Murtagh is not your brother, but rather your half brother."

The world seemed to tilt around Eragon; the sensation of vertigo was so intense, he had to grab the edge of the table to steady himself. "My half brother . . . But then, who . . . ?"

Oromis plucked a blackberry from a bowl, contemplated it for a moment, and then ate it. "Glaedr and I did not wish to keep this a secret from you, but we had no choice. We both promised, with the most binding of oaths, that we would never reveal to you the identity of your father or of your half brother, nor discuss your lineage, unless you had discovered the truth on your own or unless the identity of your relatives had placed you in danger. What transpired between you and Murtagh during the Battle of the Burning Plains satisfies enough of those requirements that we can now speak freely on this topic."

Trembling with barely restrained emotion, Eragon said, "Oromis-elda, if Murtagh is my half brother, then who is my father?"

Look into your heart, Eragon, said Glaedr. *You already know who he is, and you have known for a long time.*

Eragon shook his head. "I don't know! I don't know! Please . . ."

A gout of smoke and flame jetted from Glaedr's nostrils as he snorted. *Is it not obvious? Your father is Brom.*

Two Lovers Doomed

ragon gaped at the gold dragon.

"But how?" he exclaimed. Before either Glaedr or Oromis could respond, Eragon whirled toward Saphira and, with both his mind and his voice, he said, "You knew? You knew, and yet you let me believe Morzan was my father this whole time, even though it . . . even though I—I . . ." His chest heaving, Eragon stuttered and trailed off, unable to speak coherently. Unbidden, memories of Brom flooded through him, washing away his other thoughts. He reconsidered the meaning of Brom's every word and expression, and in that instant, a sense of rightness settled over Eragon. He still wanted explanations, but he did not need them in order to determine the veracity of Glaedr's claim, for in his bones, Eragon felt the truth of what Glaedr had said.

Eragon started as Oromis touched him on the shoulder. "Eragon, you need to calm yourself," said the elf in a soothing tone. "Remember the techniques I taught you for meditating. Control your breathing, and concentrate upon letting the tension drain out of your limbs into the ground beneath you. . . . Yes, like that. Now again, and breathe deeply."

Eragon's hands grew still and his heartbeat slowed as he followed Oromis's instructions. Once his thoughts had cleared, he looked at Saphira again and in a soft voice said, "You knew?"

Saphira lifted her head from the ground. *Oh, Eragon, I wanted to tell you. It pained me to see how Murtagh's words tormented you and yet to be unable to help you. I tried to help—I tried so many times—but like Oromis and Glaedr, I too swore in the ancient language to keep Brom's identity a secret from you, and I could not break my oath.*

"Wh-when did he tell you?" Eragon asked, so agitated that he continued speaking out loud.

The day after the Urgals attacked us outside of Teirm, while you were still unconscious.

"Was that also when he told you how to contact the Varden in Gil'ead?"

Yes. Before I knew what Brom wished to say, he had me swear to never speak of this with you unless you found out on your own. To my regret, I agreed.

"Is there anything else he told you?" demanded Eragon, his anger rising again. "Any other secrets I ought to know, like that Murtagh isn't my only sibling, or perhaps how to defeat Galbatorix?"

During the two days Brom and I spent hunting the Urgals, Brom recounted the details of his life to me so that if he died, and if ever you learned of your relation to him, his son could know what kind of a man he was and why he had acted as he did. Also, Brom gave me a gift for you.

A gift?

A memory of him speaking to you as your father and not as Brom the storyteller.

"Before Saphira shares this memory with you, however," said Oromis, and Eragon realized she had allowed the elf to hear her words, "it would be best, I think, if you knew how this came to pass. Will you listen to me for a while, Eragon?"

Eragon hesitated, unsure of what he wanted, then nodded.

Lifting his crystal goblet, Oromis drank of his wine, then returned the goblet to the table and said: "As you know, both Brom and Morzan were my apprentices. Brom, who was the younger by three years, held Morzan in such high esteem, he allowed Morzan to belittle him, order him about, and otherwise treat him most shamefully."

In a raspy voice, Eragon said, "It's hard to imagine Brom letting anyone order him about."

Oromis inclined his head in a quick, birdlike dip. "And yet, so it was. Brom loved Morzan as a brother, despite his behavior. It was only once Morzan betrayed the Riders to Galbatorix and the Forsworn killed Saphira, Brom's dragon, that Brom realized the true nature of Morzan's character. As strong as Brom's affection for Morzan had been, it was like a candle before an inferno compared with the hatred that replaced it. Brom swore to thwart Morzan however and wherever he could, to undo his accomplishments and reduce his ambitions to bitter regrets. I cautioned Brom against a path so full of hate and violence, but he was mad with grief from the death of Saphira, and he would not listen to me.

"In the decades that followed, Brom's hatred never weakened, nor did he falter in his efforts to depose Galbatorix, kill the Forsworn, and, above all else, to repay Morzan the hurts he had suffered. Brom was persistence embodied, his name a nightmare for the Forsworn and a beacon of hope for those who still had the spirit to resist the Empire." Oromis looked toward the white line of the horizon and took another draught of his wine. "I am rather proud of what he achieved on his own and without the aid of his dragon. It is always heartening for a teacher to see one of his students excel, however it might be. . . . But I digress. It so happened, then, that some twenty years ago, the Varden began to receive reports from their spies within the Empire about the activities of a mysterious woman known only as the Black Hand."

"My mother," said Eragon.

"Your mother and Murtagh's," said Oromis. "At first the Varden knew nothing about her, save that she was extremely dangerous and that she was loyal to the Empire. In time, and after a great deal of bloodshed, it became apparent that she served Morzan, and Morzan alone, and that he had come to depend upon her to carry out his will throughout the Empire. Upon learning of this, Brom set out to kill the Black Hand and so to strike at Morzan. Since the Varden could not predict where your mother might appear next, Brom traveled to Morzan's castle and spied upon it until he was able to devise a means of infiltrating the hold."

"Where was Morzan's castle?"

"*Is*, not *was*; the castle still stands. Galbatorix uses it for himself now. It is situated among the foothills of the Spine, near the northwestern shore of Leona Lake, hidden well away from the rest of the land."

Eragon said, "Jeod told me that Brom snuck into the castle by pretending to be one of the servants."

"He did, and it was no easy task. Morzan had impregnated his fortress with hundreds of spells designed to protect him from his enemies. He also forced everyone who served him to swear oaths of fealty, and often with their true names. However, after much experimentation, Brom managed to find a flaw in Morzan's wards that allowed him to procure a position as a gardener on his estate, and it was in that guise he first met your mother."

Glancing down at his hands, Eragon said, "And then he seduced her to hurt Morzan, I suppose."

"Not at all," replied Oromis. "That may have been his intention to begin with, but then something happened neither he nor your mother anticipated: they fell in love. Whatever affection your mother once had for Morzan had vanished by then, expunged by his cruel treatment of her and their newborn child, Murtagh. I do not know the exact sequence of events, but at some point Brom revealed his true identity to your mother. Instead of betraying him, she began to supply the Varden with information about Galbatorix, Morzan, and the rest of the Empire."

"But," said Eragon, "didn't Morzan have her swear oaths of fealty to him in the ancient language? How could she turn against him?"

A smile appeared on Oromis's thin lips. "She could because Morzan allowed her somewhat more freedom than his other servants so that she could use her own ingenuity and initiative while carrying out his orders. In his arrogance, Morzan believed that her love for him would ensure her loyalty better than any oath. Also, she was not the same woman who had bound herself to Morzan; becoming a mother and meeting Brom altered her character to such a degree that her true name changed, which released her from her previous commitments. If Morzan had been more careful—if, for example, he had cast a spell that would alert him if ever she failed to abide by her promises—he would have known the moment he lost control over her. But that was always a shortcoming of Morzan's; he would devise a cunning spell, but then it would fail because, in his impatience, he overlooked some crucial detail."

Eragon frowned. "Why didn't my mother leave Morzan once she had the chance?"

"After all she had done in Morzan's name, she felt it was her duty to help the Varden. But more importantly, she could not bring herself to abandon Murtagh to his father."

"Couldn't she have taken him with her?"

"If it had been within her power, I am sure she would have. Morzan realized that the child gave him a vast amount of control over your mother. He forced her to surrender Murtagh to a wet nurse and only allowed her to visit him at infrequent intervals. What Morzan did not know is that, during those intervals, she also visited Brom."

Oromis turned to watch a pair of swallows cavorting in the blue sky. In profile, his delicate, slanted features reminded Eragon of a hawk or a sleek cat. Still gazing at the swallows, Oromis said, "Not even your mother could anticipate where Morzan would send her next, nor when she could return to his castle. Therefore, Brom had to remain on Morzan's estate for extended lengths of time if he wished to see her. For nigh on three years, Brom served as one of Morzan's gardeners. Now and then, he would slip away to send a message to the Varden or to communicate with his spies throughout the Empire, but other than that, he did not leave the castle grounds."

"Three years! Wasn't he afraid that Morzan might see him and recognize him?"

Oromis lowered his gaze from the heavens, returning it to Eragon. "Brom was most adept at disguising himself, and it had been many years since he and Morzan had last stood face to face."

"Ah." Eragon twisted his goblet between his fingers, studying how the light refracted through the crystal. "Then what happened?"

"Then," said Oromis, "one of Brom's agents in Teirm made contact with a young scholar by the name of Jeod who wished to join the Varden and who claimed to have discovered evidence of a hitherto-secret tunnel that led into the elf-built portion of the castle in Urû'baen. Brom rightly felt that Jeod's discovery was too important to ignore, so he packed his bags, made his excuses to his fellow servants, and then departed for Teirm with all possible haste."

"What of my mother?"

"She had left a month before on another of Morzan's missions."

Struggling to weld a cohesive whole out of the fragmented accounts he had heard from various people, Eragon said, "So then . . . Brom met with Jeod, and once he was convinced the tunnel was real, he arranged for one of the Varden to attempt to steal the three dragon eggs Galbatorix was holding in Urû'baen."

Oromis's face darkened. "Unfortunately, for reasons that have never become entirely clear, the man they selected for the task, a certain Hefring of Furnost, succeeded in filching only one egg—Saphira's—from Galbatorix's treasury, and once he had possession of it, he fled from both the Varden and Galbatorix's servants. Because of his betrayal, Brom had to spend the next seven months chasing Hefring back and forth across the land in a desperate attempt to recapture Saphira."

"And during that time, my mother traveled in secret to Carvahall, where she gave birth to me five months later?"

Oromis nodded. "You were conceived just before your mother set forth upon her last mission. As a result, Brom knew nothing of her condition while he was pursuing Hefring and Saphira's egg. . . . When Brom and Morzan finally confronted each other in Gil'ead, Morzan asked Brom whether he had been responsible for the disappearance of his Black Hand. It is understandable that Morzan would suspect Brom's involvement, since Brom had arranged the deaths of several of the Forsworn. Brom, of course, immediately concluded that something terrible had befallen your mother. He later told me it was that belief which gave him the strength and fortitude he needed to kill Morzan and his dragon. Once they were dead, Brom took Saphira's egg from Morzan's corpse—for Morzan had already located Hefring and seized the egg from him—and then Brom left the city, pausing only long enough to hide Saphira where he knew the Varden would eventually find her."

"So that's why Jeod thought Brom died in Gil'ead," said Eragon.

Again Oromis nodded. "Stricken by fear, Brom dared not wait for his companions. Even if your mother was alive and well, Brom worried that Galbatorix would decide to make Selena his own Black Hand and that she would never again have the chance to escape her service to the Empire."

Eragon felt tears wet his eyes. *How Brom must have loved her, to leave everyone behind as soon as he knew she was in danger.*

"From Gil'ead, Brom rode straight to Morzan's estate, stopping only to sleep. For all his speed, however, he was still too slow. When he reached the castle, he discovered that your mother had returned a fortnight prior, sick and weary from her mysterious journey. Morzan's healers tried to save her, but in spite of their efforts, she had passed into the void just hours before Brom arrived at the castle."

"He never saw her again?" Eragon asked, his throat tightening.

"Never again." Oromis paused, and his expression softened. "Losing her was, I think, almost as difficult for Brom as losing his dragon, and it quenched much of the fire within his soul. He did not give up, though, nor did he go mad as he had for a time when the Forsworn slew Saphira's namesake. Instead, he decided to discover the reason for your mother's death and to punish those who were responsible if he could. He questioned Morzan's healers and forced them to describe your mother's ailments. From what they said, and also from gossip he heard among the servants on the estate, Brom guessed the truth about your mother's pregnancy. Possessed of that hope, he rode to the one place he knew to look: your mother's home in Carvahall. And there he found you in the care of your aunt and uncle.

"Brom did not stay in Carvahall, however. As soon as he assured himself that no one in Carvahall knew your mother had been the Black Hand and that you were in no imminent danger, Brom returned in secret to Farthen Dûr, where he revealed himself to Deynor, who was the leader of the Varden at that time. Deynor was astounded to see him, for until that moment, everyone had believed that Brom had perished in Gil'ead. Brom convinced Deynor to keep his presence a secret from all but a select few, and then—"

Eragon raised a finger. "But why? Why pretend to be dead?"

"Brom wanted to live long enough to help instruct the new Rider, and he knew the only way he could avoid being assassinated in retaliation for killing Morzan would be if Galbatorix believed he was already dead and buried. Also, Brom hoped to avoid attracting unwarranted attention to Carvahall. He intended to settle there in order to be close to you, as indeed he did, but he was determined that the Empire should not learn of your existence as a result.

"While in Farthen Dûr, Brom helped the Varden negotiate the agreement with Queen Islanzadí over how the elves and the humans would share custody of the egg and how the new Rider would be trained, if and when the egg should hatch. Then Brom accompanied Arya as she carried the egg from Farthen Dûr to Ellesméra. When he arrived, he told Glaedr and me what I have now told you, so that the truth about your parentage would not be forgotten if he should die. That was the last time I ever saw him. From here, Brom returned to Carvahall, where he introduced himself as a bard and storyteller. What happened thereafter, you know better than I."

Oromis fell silent, and for a time, no one spoke.

Staring at the ground, Eragon reviewed everything Oromis had told him and tried to sort out his feelings. At last he said, "And Brom really is my father, not Morzan? I mean, if my mother was Morzan's consort, then . . ." He trailed off, too embarrassed to continue.

612

"You are your father's son," Oromis said, "and your father is Brom. Of that there is no doubt."

"No doubt whatsoever?"

Oromis shook his head. "None."

A sense of giddiness gripped Eragon, and he realized he had been holding his breath. Exhaling, he said, "I think I understand why"—he paused to fill his lungs—"why Brom didn't say anything about this before I found Saphira's egg, but why didn't he tell me afterward? And why did he swear you and Saphira to such secrecy? . . . Didn't he want to claim me as his son? Was he ashamed of me?"

"I cannot pretend to know the reasons for everything Brom did, Eragon. However, of this much I am confident: Brom wanted nothing more than to name you his son and to raise you, but he dared not reveal that you were related, lest the Empire should find out and try to hurt him through you. His prudence was warranted too. Look how Galbatorix strove to capture your cousin so that he could use Roran to force you to surrender."

"Brom could have told my uncle," Eragon protested. "Garrow wouldn't have betrayed Brom to the Empire."

"Think, Eragon. If you had been living with Brom, and if word of Brom's survival had reached the ears of Galbatorix's spies, you both would have had to flee Carvahall for fear of your lives. By keeping the truth hidden from you, Brom hoped to protect you from those dangers."

"He didn't succeed. We had to flee Carvahall anyway."

"Yes," said Oromis. "Brom's mistake, as it were, although I judge it has yielded more good than ill, was that he could not bear to separate himself entirely from you. If he had had the strength to refrain from returning to Carvahall, you never would have found Saphira's egg, the Ra'zac would not have killed your uncle, and many things that were not, would have been; and many things that are, would not be. He could not cut you out of his heart, though."

Eragon clenched his jaw as a tremor coursed through him. "And after he learned Saphira had hatched for me?"

Oromis hesitated, and his calm expression became somewhat troubled. "I am not sure, Eragon. It may have been that Brom was still trying to protect you from his enemies, and he did not tell you for the same reason he did not bring you to the Varden straightaway: because it would have been more than you were ready for. Perhaps he was planning to tell you just before you went to the Varden. If I had to guess, though, I would guess that Brom held his tongue not because he was ashamed of you but because he had become accustomed to living with his secrets and was loath to part with them. And because—and this is no more than speculation—because he was uncertain how you might react to his revelation. By your own account, you were not that well acquainted with Brom before you left Carvahall with him. It is quite possible he was afraid that you might hate him if he told you he was your father."

"Hate him?" exclaimed Eragon. "I wouldn't have hated him. Although . . . I might not have believed him."

"And would you have trusted him after such a revelation?"

Eragon bit the inside of his cheek. *No, I wouldn't have.*

Continuing, Oromis said, "Brom did the best he could in what were incredibly trying circumstances. Before all else, it was his responsibility to keep the two of you alive and to teach and advise you, Eragon, so that you would not use your power for selfish means, as Galbatorix has done. In that, Brom acquitted himself with distinction. He may not have been the father you wished him to be, but he gave you as great an inheritance as any son has ever had."

"It was no more than he would have done for whoever became the new Rider."

"That does not diminish its value," Oromis pointed out. "But you are mistaken; Brom did more for you than he would have for anyone else. You need only think of how he sacrificed himself to save your life to know the truth of that."

With the nail of his right index finger, Eragon picked at the edge of the table, following a faint ridge formed by one of the rings in the wood. "And it really was an accident that Arya sent Saphira to me?"

"It was," Oromis confirmed. "But it was not entirely a coincidence. Instead of transporting the egg to the father, Arya made it appear before the son."

"How could that be if she had no knowledge of me?"

Oromis's thin shoulders rose and fell. "Despite thousands of years of study, we still cannot predict or explain all of the effects of magic."

Eragon continued to finger the small ridge in the edge of the table. *I have a father*, he thought. *I watched him die, and I had no idea who he was to me.* . . . "My parents," he said, "were they ever married?"

"I know why you ask, Eragon, and I do not know if my answer will satisfy you. Marriage is not an elvish custom, and the subtleties of it often escape me. No one joined Brom's and Selena's hands in marriage, but I know that they considered themselves to be husband and wife. If you are wise, you will not worry that others of your race may call you a bastard but rather be content to know that you are your parents' child and that they both gave their lives that you might live."

It surprised Eragon how calm he felt. His entire life he had speculated about the identity of his father. When Murtagh had claimed it was Morzan, the revelation had shocked Eragon as deeply as had the death of Garrow. Glaedr's counterclaim that Eragon's father was Brom had also shocked him, but the shock did not seem to have lasted, perhaps because, this time, the news was not as upsetting. Calm as he was, Eragon thought that it might be many years before he was certain of his feelings toward either of his parents. *My father was a Rider and my mother was Morzan's consort and Black Hand.*

"Could I tell Nasuada?" he asked.

Oromis spread his hands. "Tell whomever you wish; the secret is now yours to do with as you please. I doubt you would be in any more danger if the whole world knew you were Brom's heir."

"Murtagh," Eragon said. "He believes we are full brothers. He told me so in the ancient language."

"And I am sure Galbatorix does as well. It was the Twins who figured out that Murtagh's mother and your mother were one and the same person, and this they conveyed to the king. But they could not have informed him of Brom's involvement, for there was no one among the Varden who was privy to that information."

Eragon glanced up as a pair of swallows swooped by overhead, and he allowed himself a wry half smile.

"Why do you smile?" Oromis asked.

"I'm not sure you would understand."

The elf folded his hands in his lap. "I might not; that is true. But then, you cannot know for certain unless you try to explain."

It took Eragon a while to find the words he needed. "When I was younger, before . . . all of *this*"—he gestured at Saphira and Oromis and Glaedr and the world in general—"I used to amuse myself by imagining that, because of her great wit and beauty, my mother had been taken in among the courts of Galbatorix's nobles. I imagined that she had traveled from city to city and supped with the earls and ladies in their halls and that . . . well, she had fallen desperately in love with a rich and powerful man, but for some reason, she was forced to hide me from him, so she gave me to Garrow and Marian for safekeeping, and one day she would return and tell me who I was and that she had never wanted to leave me behind."

"That is not so different from what happened," said Oromis.

"No, it isn't, but . . . I imagined that my mother and my father were people of importance and I was someone of importance as well. Fate gave me what I wanted, but the truth of it is not as grand or as happy as I thought it would be. . . . I was smiling at my own ignorance, I suppose, and also at the unlikeliness of everything that has befallen me."

A light breeze swept across the clearing, feathering the grass at their feet and stirring the branches of the forest around them.

616

Eragon watched the fluttering of the grass for a few moments, then slowly asked, "Was my mother a good person?"

"I could not say, Eragon. The events of her life were complicated. It would be foolish and arrogant of me to presume to pass judgment on one I know so little of."

"But I need to know!" Eragon clasped his hands, pressing his fingers between the calluses on his knuckles. "When I asked Brom if he had known her, he said that she was proud and dignified and that she always helped the poor and those less fortunate than her. How could she, though? How could she be that person and also the Black Hand? Jeod told me stories about some of the things— horrible, terrible things—she did while she was in Morzan's service. . . . Was she evil, then? Did she not care if Galbatorix ruled or not? Why did she go with Morzan in the first place?"

Oromis paused. "Love can be a terrible curse, Eragon. It can make you overlook even the largest flaws in a person's behavior. I doubt that your mother was fully aware of Morzan's true nature when she left Carvahall with him, and once she had, he would not have allowed her to disobey his wishes. She became his slave in all but name, and it was only by changing her very identity that she was able to escape his control."

617

"But Jeod said that she enjoyed what she did as the Black Hand."

An expression of faint disdain altered Oromis's features. "Accounts of past atrocities are often exaggerated and distorted. That much you should keep in mind. No one but your mother knows exactly what she did, nor why, nor how she felt about it, and she is not still among the living to explain herself."

"Whom should I believe, though?" pleaded Eragon. "Brom or Jeod?"

"When you asked Brom about your mother, he told you what he thought were her most important qualities. My advice would be to trust in his knowledge of her. If that does not quell your doubts, remember that whatever crimes she may have committed while acting as the Hand of Morzan, ultimately your mother sided with the Varden and went to extraordinary lengths to protect you. Knowing that, you should not torment yourself further about the nature of her character."

Propelled by the breeze, a spider hanging from a gossamer strand of silk drifted past Eragon, rising and falling on the invisible eddies of air. When the spider had floated out of view, Eragon said, "The first time we visited Tronjheim, the fortuneteller Angela told me that it was Brom's wyrd to fail at everything he attempted, except for killing Morzan."

Oromis inclined his head. "One might think that. Another might conclude that Brom achieved many great and difficult things. It depends upon how you choose to view the world. The words of fortunetellers are rarely easy to decipher. It has been my experience that their predictions are never conducive to peace of mind. If you wish to be happy, Eragon, think not of what is to come nor of that which you have no control over but rather of the now and of that which you are able to change."

A thought occurred to Eragon then. "Blagden," he said, referring to the white raven who was Queen Islanzadí's companion. "He knows about Brom as well, doesn't he?"

One of Oromis's sharp eyebrows lifted. "Does he? I never spoke of it to him. He is a fickle creature and not to be relied upon."

"The day Saphira and I left for the Burning Plains, he recited a riddle to me. . . . I can't remember every line, but it was something about one of two being one, while one might be two. I think he might have been hinting that Murtagh and I only share a single parent."

"It is not impossible," said Oromis. "Blagden was here in Ellesméra when Brom told me about you. I would not be surprised if that sharp-beaked thief happened to be perched in a nearby tree during our conversation. Eavesdropping is an unfortunate habit of his. It might also be that his riddle was the result of one of his sporadic fits of foresight."

A moment later, Glaedr stirred, and Oromis turned and glanced back at the golden dragon. The elf rose from his chair with a graceful motion, saying, "Fruit, nuts, and bread are fine fare, but after your trip, you should have something more substantial to fill your belly. I have a soup that needs tending simmering in my hut, but please, do not bestir yourself. I will bring it to you when it is ready." His footsteps soft upon the grass, Oromis walked to his bark-covered house and disappeared inside. As the carved door closed, Glaedr huffed out his breath and closed his eyes, seeming to fall asleep.

And all was silent, save the rustle of the wind-tossed branches.

INHERITANCE

ragon remained sitting at the round table for several minutes, then he stood and walked to the edge of the Crags of Tel'naeír, where he gazed out over the rolling forest a thousand feet below. With the tip of his left boot, he pushed a pebble over the cliff and watched it bounce off the slanted face of the stone until it vanished into the depths of the canopy.

A branch cracked as Saphira approached from behind. She crouched by his side, her scales painting him with hundreds of shifting flecks of blue light, and stared in the same direction as he. *Are you angry with me?* she asked.

No, of course not. I understand that you could not break your oath in the ancient language. . . . I just wish that Brom could have told me this himself and that he hadn't felt it necessary to hide the truth from me.

She swung her head toward him. *And how do you feel, Eragon?*

You know as well as I.

A few minutes ago, I did, but not now. You have grown still, and looking into your mind is like peering into a lake so deep, I cannot see the bottom. What is in you, little one? Is it rage? Is it happiness? Or have you no emotions to give?

What is in me is acceptance, he said, and turned to face her. *I cannot change who my parents are; I reconciled myself with that after the Burning Plains. What is is, and no amount of gnashing teeth on my part will change that. I am . . . glad, I think, to consider Brom my father. But I'm not sure. . . . It's too much to grasp all at once.*

Perhaps what I have to give you will help. Would you like to see the memory Brom left for you, or would you prefer to wait?

No, no waiting, he said. *If we delay, you may never have the opportunity.*

Then close your eyes and let me show you what once was.

Eragon did as she directed, and from Saphira, there flowed a stream of sensations: sights, sounds, smells, and more, everything that she had been experiencing at the time of the memory.

Before him, Eragon beheld a glade in the forest somewhere among the foothills piled against the western side of the Spine. The grass was thick and lush, and veils of chartreuse lichen hung from the tall, drooping, moss-covered trees. Due to the rains that swept inland from the ocean, the woods were far greener and wetter than those of Palancar Valley. As seen through Saphira's eyes, the greens and reds were more subdued than they would have been to Eragon, while every hue of blue shone with additional intensity. The smell of moist soil and punky wood suffused the air.

And in the center of the glade lay a fallen tree, and upon the fallen tree sat Brom.

The hood of the old man's robe was pulled back to expose his bare head. Across his lap lay his sword. His twisted, rune-carved staff stood propped against the log. The ring Aren glittered on his right hand.

For a long while, Brom did not move, and then he squinted up at the sky, his hooked nose casting a long shadow across his face. His voice rasped, and Eragon swayed, feeling disjointed in time.

Brom said, "Ever the sun traces its path from horizon to horizon, and ever the moon follows, and ever the days roll past without care for the lives they grind away, one by one." Lowering his eyes, Brom gazed straight at Saphira and, through her, Eragon. "Try though they might, no being escapes death forever, not even the elves or the spirits. To all, there is an end. If you are watching me, Eragon, then my end has come and I am dead and you know that I am your father."

From the leather pouch by his side, Brom drew forth his pipe, filled it with cardus weed, then lit it with a soft muttering of "Brisingr." He puffed on the pipe several times to set the fire before he resumed talking. "If you do see this, Eragon, I hope that you are safe and happy and that Galbatorix is dead. However, I realize that's unlikely, if for no other reason than you are a Dragon Rider, and a Dragon Rider may never rest while there is injustice in the land."

A chuckle escaped Brom and he shook his head, his beard rippling like water. "Ah, I have not the time to say even half of what I would like; I would be twice my current age before I finished. In the pursuit of brevity, I shall assume that Saphira has already told you how your mother and I met, how Selena died, and how I came to be in Carvahall. I wish that you and I could have this talk face to face, Eragon, and perhaps we still shall and Saphira will have no need to share this memory with you, but I doubt it. The sorrows of my years press on me, Eragon, and I feel a cold creeping into my limbs the likes of which has never troubled me before. I think it is because I know it is now your turn to take up the standard. There is much I still hope to accomplish, but none of it is for myself, only for you, and you shall eclipse everything I have done. Of that, I am sure. Before my grave closes over me, though, I wanted to be able, at least this once, to call you my son. . . . My son. . . . Your whole life, Eragon, I have longed to reveal to you who I was. It has been a pleasure like no other for me to watch you growing up, but also a torture like no other because of the secret I held in my heart."

Brom laughed then, a harsh, barking sound. "Well, I didn't exactly manage to keep you safe from the Empire, now did I? If you are still wondering who was responsible for Garrow's death, you need look no further, for here he sits. It was my own foolishness. I should never have returned to Carvahall. And now look: Garrow dead, and you a Dragon Rider. I warn you, Eragon, beware of whom you fall in love with, for fate seems to have a morbid interest in our family."

Wrapping his lips around the stem of his pipe, Brom drew on the smoldering cardus weed several times, blowing the chalk-white smoke off to one side. The pungent smell was heavy in Saphira's nostrils. Brom said, "I have my share of regrets, but you are not one of them, Eragon. You may occasionally behave like a moon-addled fool, such as letting these blasted Urgals escape, but you are no more of an idiot than I was at your age." He nodded. "Less of an idiot, in fact. I am proud to have you as my son, Eragon, prouder than you will ever know. I never thought that you would become a Rider as I was, nor wished that future upon you, but seeing you with Saphira, ah, it makes me feel like crowing at the sun like a rooster."

Brom drew on the pipe again. "I realize you may be angry at me for keeping this from you. I can't say I would have been happy to discover the name of my own father this way. Whether you like it or not, though, we are family, you and I. Since I could not give you the care I owed you as your father, I will give you the one thing I can instead, and that is advice. Hate me if you wish, Eragon, but heed what I have to say, for I know whereof I speak."

With his free hand, Brom grasped the sheath of his sword, the veins prominent on the back of his hand. He fixed the pipe in one corner of his mouth. "Right. Now, my advice is twofold. Whatever you do, protect those you care for. Without them, life is more miserable than you can imagine. An obvious statement, I know, but no less true because of it. There, that is the first part of my advice. As for the rest . . . If you are so fortunate as to have already killed Galbatorix—or if *anyone* has succeeded in slitting that traitor's throat—then congratulations. If *not*, then you must realize that Galbatorix is your greatest and most dangerous enemy. Until he is dead, neither you nor Saphira will ever find peace. You may run to the farthest corners of the earth, but unless you join the Empire, one day you will have to confront Galbatorix. I am sorry, Eragon, but that is the truth of it. I have fought many magicians, and several of the Forsworn, and so far, I have always defeated my opponents." The lines on Brom's forehead deepened. "Well, all but once, but that was because I was not yet fully grown. Anyway, the reason I have always emerged triumphant is that I use my brain, unlike most.

623

I am not a strong spellcaster, nor are you, compared with Galbatorix, but when it comes to a wizards' duel, *intelligence* is even more important than strength. The way to defeat another magician is not by battering blindly against his mind. No! In order to ensure victory, you have to figure out how your enemy interprets information and reacts to the world. Then you will know his weaknesses, and there you strike. The trick isn't inventing a spell no one else has ever thought of before; the trick is finding a spell your enemy has overlooked and using it against him. The trick isn't plowing your way through the barriers in someone's mind; the trick is slipping underneath or around the barriers. No one is omniscient, Eragon. Remember that. Galbatorix may have immense power, but he cannot anticipate every possibility. Whatever you do, you must remain nimble in your thinking. Do not become so attached to any one belief that you cannot see past it to another possibility. Galbatorix is mad and therefore unpredictable, but he also has gaps in his reasoning that an ordinary person would not. If you can find those, Eragon, then perhaps you and Saphira can defeat him."

Brom lowered his pipe, his face grave. "I hope you do. My greatest desire, Eragon, is that you and Saphira will live long and fruitful lives, free from fear of Galbatorix and the Empire. I wish that I could protect you from all of the dangers that threaten you, but alas, that is not within my ability. All I can do is give you my advice and teach you what I can *now* while I am still here. . . . My son. Whatever happens to you, know that I love you, and so did your mother. May the stars watch over you, Eragon Bromsson."

As Brom's final words echoed in Eragon's mind, the memory faded away, leaving behind empty darkness. Eragon opened his eyes and was embarrassed to find tears running down his cheeks. He uttered a choked laugh and wiped his eyes on the edge of his tunic. *Brom really was afraid that I would hate him*, he said, and sniffed.

Are you going to be all right? Saphira asked.

Yes, said Eragon, and lifted his head. *I think I will, actually. I don't like some of the things Brom did, but I am proud to call him my father and*

*to carry his name. He was a great man. . . . It bothers me, though, that
I never had the opportunity to talk to either of my parents as my parents.*

*At least you were able to spend time with Brom. I am not so fortunate;
both my sire and my mother died long before I hatched. The closest I can
come to meeting them are a few hazy memories from Glaedr.*

Eragon put a hand on her neck, and they comforted each other
as best they could while they stood upon the edge of the Crags of
Tel'naeír and gazed out over the forest of the elves.

Not long afterward, Oromis emerged from his hut, carrying two
bowls of soup, and Eragon and Saphira turned away from the crags
and slowly walked back to the small table in front of Glaedr's immense bulk.

SOULS OF STONE

As Eragon pushed away his empty bowl, Oromis said, "Would you like to see a fairth of your mother, Eragon?"

Eragon froze for a moment, astonished. "Yes, please."

From within the folds of his white tunic, Oromis withdrew a shingle of thin gray slate, which he passed to Eragon.

The stone was cool and smooth between Eragon's fingers. On the other side of it, he knew he would find a perfect likeness of his mother, painted by means of a spell with pigments an elf had set within the slate many years ago. A flutter of uneasiness ran through Eragon. He had always wanted to see his mother, but now that the opportunity was before him, he was afraid that the reality might disappoint him.

With an effort, he turned the slate over and beheld an image—clear as a vision seen through a window—of a garden of red and white roses lit by the pale rays of dawn. A gravel path ran through the beds of roses. And in the middle of the path was a woman, kneeling, cupping a white rose between her hands and smelling the flower, her eyes closed and a faint smile upon her lips. She was very beautiful, Eragon thought. Her expression was soft and tender, yet she wore clothes of padded leather, with blackened bracers upon her forearms and greaves upon her shins and a sword and dagger hanging from her waist. In the shape of her face, Eragon could detect a hint of his own features, as well as a certain resemblance to Garrow, her brother.

The image fascinated Eragon. He pressed his hand against the surface of the fairth, wishing that he could reach into it and touch her on the arm.

Mother.

Oromis said, "Brom gave me the fairth for safekeeping before he left for Carvahall, and now I give it to you."

Without looking up, Eragon asked, "Would you keep it safe for me as well? It might get broken during our traveling and fighting."

The pause that followed caught Eragon's attention. He wrenched his gaze away from his mother to see that Oromis appeared melancholy and preoccupied. "No, Eragon, I cannot. You will have to make other arrangements for the preservation of the fairth."

Why? Eragon wanted to ask, but the sorrow in Oromis's eyes dissuaded him.

Then Oromis said, "Your time here is limited, and we still have many matters to discuss. Shall I guess which subject you would like to address next, or will you tell me?"

With great reluctance, Eragon placed the fairth on the table and rotated it so that the image was upside down. "The two times we have fought Murtagh and Thorn, Murtagh has been more powerful than any human ought to be. On the Burning Plains, he defeated Saphira and me because we did not realize how strong he was. If not for his change of heart, we would be prisoners in Urû'baen right now. You once mentioned that you know how Galbatorix has become so powerful. Will you tell us now, Master? For our own safety, we need to know."

"It is not my place to tell you this," said Oromis.

"Then whose is it?" demanded Eragon. "You can't—"

Behind Oromis, Glaedr opened one of his molten eyes, which was as large as a round shield, and said, *It is mine. . . . The source of Galbatorix's power lies in the hearts of dragons. From us, he steals his strength. Without our aid, Galbatorix would have fallen to the elves and the Varden long ago.*

Eragon frowned. "I don't understand. Why would you help Galbatorix? And how could you? There are only four dragons and an egg left in Alagaësia . . . aren't there?"

Many of the dragons whose bodies Galbatorix and the Forsworn slew are still alive today.

"Still alive . . . ?" Bewildered, Eragon glanced at Oromis, but the elf remained quiet, his face inscrutable. Even more disconcerting was that Saphira did not seem to share Eragon's confusion.

The gold dragon turned his head on his paws to better look at Eragon, his scales scraping against one another. *Unlike with most creatures,* he said, *a dragon's consciousness does not reside solely within our skulls. There is in our chests a hard, gemlike object, similar in composition to our scales, called the Eldunarí, which means "the heart of hearts." When a dragon hatches, their Eldunarí is clear and lusterless. Usually it remains so all through a dragon's life and dissolves along with the dragon's corpse when they die. However, if we wish, we can transfer our consciousness into the Eldunarí. Then it will acquire the same color as our scales and begin to glow like a coal. If a dragon has done this, the Eldunarí will outlast the decay of their flesh, and a dragon's essence may live on indefinitely. Also, a dragon can disgorge their Eldunarí while they are still alive. By this means, a dragon's body and a dragon's consciousness can exist separately and yet still be linked, which can be most useful in certain circumstances. But to do this exposes us to great danger, for whosoever holds our Eldunarí holds our very soul in their hands. With it, they could force us to do their bidding, no matter how vile.*

The implications of what Glaedr had said astounded Eragon. Shifting his gaze to Saphira, he asked, *Did you already know about this?*

The scales on her neck rippled as she made an odd, serpentine motion with her head. *I have always been aware of my heart of hearts. Always I have been able to feel it inside of me, but I never thought to mention it to you.*

How could you not when it's of such significance?

Would you think it worthy of mention that you have a stomach, Eragon? Or a heart or a liver or any other organ? My Eldunarí is an integral part of who I am. I never considered its existence worthy of note. . . . At least not until we last came to Ellesméra.

So you did know!

Only a little. Glaedr hinted that my heart of hearts was more impor-

tant than I had originally believed, and he warned me to protect it, lest I inadvertently deliver myself into the hands of our enemies. More than that he did not explain, but since then, I inferred much of what he just said.

Yet you still did not think this was worth mentioning? demanded Eragon.

I wanted to, she growled, *but as with Brom, I gave my word to Glaedr that I would speak of this to no one, not even to you.*

And you agreed?

I trust Glaedr, and I trust Oromis. Do you not?

Eragon scowled and turned back to the elf and the golden dragon. "Why didn't you tell us of this sooner?"

Unstoppering the decanter, Oromis refilled his goblet with wine and said, "In order to protect Saphira."

"Protect her? From what?"

From you, Glaedr said. Eragon was so surprised and outraged, he failed to regain his composure well enough to protest before Glaedr resumed speaking. *In the wild, a dragon would learn about his Eldunarí from one of his elders when he was old enough to understand the use of it. That way, a dragon would not transfer themself into their heart of hearts without knowing the full import of their actions. Among the Riders, a different custom arose. The first few years of partnership between a dragon and a Rider are crucial to establishing a healthy relationship between the two, and the Riders discovered that it was better to wait until newly joined Riders and dragons were well familiar with each other before informing them of the Eldunarí. Otherwise, in the reckless folly of youth, a dragon might decide to disgorge his heart of hearts merely to appease or impress his Rider. When we give up our Eldunarí, we are giving up a physical embodiment of our entire being. And we cannot return it to its original place within our bodies once it is gone. A dragon should not undertake the separation of their consciousness lightly, for it will change how they live the rest of their lives, even if they should endure for another thousand years.*

"Do you still have your heart of hearts within you?" Eragon asked.

The grass around the table bent under the blast of hot air that erupted from Glaedr's nostrils. *That is not a meet question to ask any dragon but Saphira. Do not presume to put it to me again, hatchling.*

Although Glaedr's rebuke made Eragon's cheeks sting, he still had the wherewithal to respond as he should, with a seated bow and the words "No, Master." Then he asked, "What . . . what happens if your Eldunarí breaks?"

If a dragon has already transferred their consciousness to their heart of hearts, then they will die a true death. With an audible click, Glaedr blinked, his inner and outer eyelids flashing across the rayed orb of his iris. *Before we formed our pact with the elves, we kept our hearts in Du Fells Nángoröth, the mountains in the center of the Hadarac Desert. Later, after the Riders established themselves on the island of Vroengard and therein built a repository for the Eldunarí, wild dragons and paired dragons both entrusted their hearts to the Riders for safekeeping.*

"So then," said Eragon, "Galbatorix captured the Eldunarí?"

Contrary to Eragon's expectations, it was Oromis who replied. "He did, but not all at once. It had been so long since anyone had truly threatened the Riders, many of our order had become careless about protecting the Eldunarí. At the time Galbatorix turned against us, it was not uncommon for a Rider's dragon to disgorge their Eldunarí merely for the sake of convenience."

"Convenience?"

Anyone who holds one of our hearts, said Glaedr, *may communicate with the dragon from which it came without regard for distance. The whole of Alagaësia might separate a Rider and dragon, and yet if the Rider had with him his dragon's Eldunarí, they could share thoughts as easily as you and Saphira do now.*

"In addition," said Oromis, "a magician who possesses an Eldunarí can draw upon the dragon's strength to bolster his spells, again without regard for where the dragon might be. When—"

A brilliantly colored hummingbird interrupted their conversation by darting across the table. Its wings a throbbing blur, the bird hovered over the bowls of fruit and lapped at the liquid oozing from a crushed blackberry, then flitted up and away, vanishing among the trunks of the forest.

Oromis resumed speaking: "When Galbatorix killed his first Rider, he also stole the heart of the Rider's dragon. During the years Galbatorix spent hiding in the wilderness thereafter, he broke the dragon's mind and bent it to his will, likely with the help of Durza. And when Galbatorix began his insurrection in earnest, with Morzan by his side, he was already stronger than most every other Rider. His strength was not merely magical but mental, for the force of the Eldunarí's consciousness augmented his own.

"Galbatorix did not just try to kill the Riders and dragons. He made it his goal to acquire as many of the Eldunarí as he could, either by seizing them from Riders or by torturing a Rider until his dragon disgorged its heart of hearts. By the time we realized what Galbatorix was doing, he was already too powerful to stop. It helped Galbatorix that many Riders traveled not only with the Eldunarí of their own dragon but also with Eldunarí of dragons whose bodies were no more, for such dragons often became bored with sitting in an alcove and yearned for adventure. And of course, once Galbatorix and the Forsworn sacked the city of Doru Araeba on the island of Vroengard, he gained possession of the entire hoard of Eldunarí stored therein.

"Galbatorix engineered his success by using the might and wisdom of the dragons against all of Alagaësia. At first he was unable to control more than a handful of the Eldunarí he had captured. It is no easy thing to force a dragon to submit to you, no matter how powerful you might be. As soon as Galbatorix crushed the Riders and had installed himself as king in Urû'baen, he dedicated himself to subduing the rest of the hearts, one by one.

"We believe the task preoccupied him for the main part of the next forty years, during which time he paid little attention to the affairs of Alagaësia—which is why the people of Surda were able to secede from the Empire. When he finished, Galbatorix emerged from seclusion and began to reassert his control over the Empire and the lands beyond. For some reason, after two and a half years of additional slaughter and sorrow, he withdrew to Urû'baen again, and there he has dwelt ever since, not so solitary as before, but obviously focused upon some project known only to him. His vices are many, but he has not abandoned himself to debauchery; that much the Varden's spies have determined. More than that, though, we have not been able to discover."

Lost deep in thought, Eragon stared off into the distance. For the first time, all of the stories he had heard about Galbatorix's unnatural power made sense. A faint feeling of optimism welled up within Eragon as he said to himself, *I'm not sure how, but if we could release the Eldunarí from Galbatorix's control, he would be no more powerful than any normal Dragon Rider.* Unlikely as the prospect seemed, it heartened Eragon to know that the king did have a vulnerability, no matter how slight.

As Eragon continued to muse upon the subject, another question occurred to him. "Why is it that I've never heard mention of the hearts of dragons in the stories of old? Surely if they are so important, the bards and scholars would speak of them."

Oromis laid a hand flat on the table then and said, "Of all the secrets in Alagaësia, that of the Eldunarí is one of the most closely guarded, even among my own people. Throughout history, dragons have striven to hide their hearts from the rest of the world. They revealed their existence to us only after the magical pact between our races was established, and then only to a select few."

"But why?"

Ah, said Glaedr, *often we despised the need for secrecy, but if ever the Eldunarí had become common knowledge, every low-minded scoundrel in the land would have attempted to steal one, and eventually some would have achieved their goal. It was an outcome we went to great lengths to prevent.*

"Is there no way for a dragon to defend themselves through their Eldunarí?" Eragon asked.

Glaedr's eye seemed to twinkle brighter than ever. *An apt question. A dragon who has disgorged their Eldunarí but who still enjoys the use of their flesh can, of course, defend their heart with their claws and their fangs and their tail and with the battering of their wings. A dragon whose body is dead, however, possesses none of those advantages. Their only weapon is the weapon of their mind and, perhaps, if the moment is right, the weapon of magic, which we cannot command at will. That is one reason why many dragons did not choose to prolong their existence beyond the demise of their flesh. To be unable to move of your own volition, to be unable to sense the world around you except through the minds of others, and to only be able to influence the course of events with your thoughts and with rare and unpredictable flashes of magic; it would be a difficult existence to embrace for most any creature, but especially dragons, who are the freest of all beings.*

"Why would they, then?" asked Eragon.

Sometimes it happened by accident. As their body was failing, a dragon might panic and flee into their Eldunarí. Or if a dragon had disgorged their heart before their body died, they would have no choice but to continue to endure. But mostly, the dragons who chose to live on in their Eldunarí were those who were old beyond measure, older than Oromis and I are now, old enough that the concerns of the flesh had ceased to matter to them and they had turned in on themselves and wished to spend the rest of eternity pondering questions younger beings could not comprehend. We revered and treasured the hearts of such dragons on account of their vast wisdom and intelligence. It was common for wild dragons and paired dragons alike, as well as Riders, to seek advice from them on matters of importance. That Galbatorix enslaved them is a crime of almost unimaginable cruelty and evil.

Now I have a question, said Saphira, the rich thrum of her thoughts running through Eragon's mind. *Once one of our kind becomes confined to their Eldunarí, must they continue to exist, or is it possible for them, if they could no longer endure their condition, to release their hold on the world and pass into the darkness beyond?*

"Not on their own," said Oromis. "Not unless the inspiration to use magic should sweep over the dragon and allow them to break their Eldunarí from within, which to my knowledge has happened but rarely. The only other option would be for the dragon to convince someone else to smash the Eldunarí for them. That lack of control is another reason why dragons were extremely wary of transferring themselves into their heart of hearts, lest they trap themselves in a prison from which there was no escape."

Eragon could feel Saphira's loathing at the thought of that prospect. She did not speak of it, however, but asked, *How many Eldunarí does Galbatorix hold in his thrall?*

"We do not know the exact number," said Oromis, "but we estimate that his hoard contains many hundreds."

A wriggle shimmered down Saphira's glittering length. *So then, our race is not on the verge of extinction after all?*

Oromis hesitated, and it was Glaedr who answered. *Little one*, he said, startling Eragon with the use of the epithet, *even if the ground were covered with Eldunarí, our race would still be doomed. A dragon preserved within an Eldunarí is still a dragon, but they possess neither the urges of the flesh nor the organs with which to fulfill them. They cannot reproduce.*

The base of Eragon's skull began to throb, and he became increasingly aware of his weariness from the past four days of traveling. His exhaustion made it difficult to keep hold of thoughts for more than a few moments; at the slightest distraction, they slipped out of his grasp.

The tip of Saphira's tail twitched. *I am not so ignorant as to believe that Eldunarí could beget offspring. However, it comforts me to know I am not as alone as I once thought. . . . Our race may be doomed, but at least there are more than four dragons alive in the world, whether they be cloaked in their flesh or not.*

"That is true," said Oromis, "but they are as much Galbatorix's captives as Murtagh and Thorn."

Freeing them gives me something to strive for, though, along with rescuing the last egg, said Saphira.

"It is something for us both to strive for," said Eragon. "We are their only hope." He rubbed his brow with his right thumb, then said, "There is still something I don't understand."

"Oh?" asked Oromis. "Wherein lies your confusion?"

"If Galbatorix draws his power from these hearts, how do they produce the energy he uses?" Eragon paused, searching for a better way to phrase his question. He gestured at the swallows flitting about in the sky. "Every living thing eats and drinks to sustain itself, even plants. Food provides the energy our bodies need to function properly. It also provides the energy we need to work magic, whether we rely upon our own strength to cast a spell or make use of the strength of others. How can that be, though, with these Eldunarí? They don't have bones and muscles and skin, do they? They don't eat, do they? So then, how do they survive? Where does their energy come from?"

Oromis smiled, his longish teeth glossy as enameled porcelain. "From magic."

"Magic?"

"If one defines magic as the manipulation of energy, which properly it is, then yes, magic. Where exactly the Eldunarí acquire their energy is a mystery to both us and the dragons; no one has ever identified the source. It may be they absorb sunlight, as do plants, or that they feed off the life forces of the creatures closest to them. Whatever the answer, it has been proven that when a dragon undergoes body death and their consciousness takes up sole residence in their heart of hearts, they bring with them however much spare strength was available within their body when it ceased to function. Thereafter, their store of energy increases at a steady pace for the next five to seven years, until they attain the full height of their power, which is immense indeed. The total amount of energy an Eldunarí can hold depends upon the size of the heart; the older a dragon, the larger their Eldunarí and the more energy it can absorb before becoming saturated."

Thinking back to when he and Saphira had battled Murtagh and Thorn, Eragon said, "Galbatorix must have given Murtagh several Eldunarí. That's the only explanation for his increase in strength."

Oromis nodded. "You are fortunate Galbatorix did not lend him any more hearts, else it would have been easy for Murtagh to overwhelm you, Arya, and all the other spellcasters with the Varden."

Eragon remembered how, both times he and Saphira had encountered Murtagh and Thorn, Murtagh's mind had felt as if it contained multiple beings. Eragon shared his recollection with Saphira and said, *Those must have been the Eldunarí I sensed. . . . I wonder where Murtagh put them? Thorn carried no saddlebags, and I didn't see any odd bulges in Murtagh's clothing.*

I don't know, said Saphira. *You do realize that Murtagh must have been referring to his Eldunarí when he said that instead of tearing out your own heart, it would be better to tear out his hearts. Hearts, not heart.*

You're right! Maybe he was trying to warn me. Inhaling, Eragon loosened the knot between his shoulder blades and leaned back in his chair. "Aside from Saphira's heart of hearts, and Glaedr's, are there any Eldunarí that Galbatorix hasn't captured?"

Faint lines appeared around the corners of Oromis's down-turned mouth. "None that we know of. After the fall of the Riders, Brom went searching for Eldunarí that Galbatorix might have overlooked, but without success. Nor, in all my years of scouring Alagaësia with my mind, have I detected so much as a whisper of a thought from an Eldunarí. Every Eldunarí was well accounted for when Galbatorix and Morzan initiated their attack on us, and none of them vanished without explanation. It is inconceivable that any great store of Eldunarí might be lying hidden somewhere, ready to help us if we could but locate them."

Although Eragon had expected no other answer, he still found it disappointing. "One last question. When either a Rider or a Rider's dragon dies, the surviving member of the pair would often waste away or commit suicide soon afterward. And those that didn't usually went mad from the loss. Am I right?"

You are, said Glaedr.

"What would happen, though, if the dragon transferred their consciousness to their heart and then their body died?"

Through the soles of his boots, Eragon felt a faint tremor shake the ground as Glaedr shifted his position. The gold dragon said, *If a dragon experienced body death and yet their Rider still lived, together they became known as Indlvarn. The transition would hardly be a pleasant one for the dragon, but many Riders and dragons successfully adapted to the change and continued to serve the Riders with distinction. If, however, it was a dragon's Rider who died, then the dragon would often smash their Eldunarí, or arrange for another to smash it for them if their body was no more, thus killing themselves and following their Rider into the void. But not all. Some dragons were able to overcome their loss—as were some Riders, such as Brom—and continue to serve our order for many years afterward, either through their flesh or through their heart of hearts.*

You have given us much to think about, Oromis-elda, said Saphira. Eragon nodded but stayed silent, for he was busy pondering all that had been said.

HANDS OF A WARRIOR

Eragon nibbled on a warm, sweet strawberry while he stared into the fathomless depths of the sky. When he finished eating the berry, he set the stem on the tray before him, pushing it into just the right spot with the tip of his forefinger, and then opened his mouth to speak.

Before he could, Oromis said, "What now, Eragon?"

"What now?"

"We have spoken at length on those subjects about which you were curious. What now do you and Saphira wish to accomplish? You cannot linger in Ellesméra, so I wonder what else you hope to achieve by your visit, or is it your intention to depart again tomorrow morning?"

"We had hoped," Eragon said, "that, when we returned, we would be able to continue our training as before. Obviously, we haven't time for that now, but there is something else I would like to do."

"And that would be?"

". . . Master, I have not told you everything that happened to me when Brom and I were in Teirm." And then Eragon recounted how curiosity had lured him into Angela's shop and how she had told him his fortune, and the advice Solembum had given him afterward.

Oromis drew a finger across his upper lip, his demeanor contemplative. "I have heard this fortuneteller mentioned with increasing frequency throughout this past year, both by you and in Arya's reports from the Varden. This Angela seems to be most adept at turning up whenever and wherever events of significance are about to take place."

That she is, confirmed Saphira.

Continuing, Oromis said, "Her behavior reminds me very much of a human spellcaster who once visited the halls of Ellesméra, although she did not go by the name of Angela. Is Angela a woman of short stature, with thick, curly brown hair, flashing eyes, and a wit that is as sharp as it is odd?"

"You have described her perfectly," said Eragon. "Is she the same person?"

Oromis made a small flicking motion with his left hand. "If she is, she is an extraordinary person. . . . As for her prophecies, I would not devote much thought to them. Either they will come true or they will not, and without knowing more, none of us can influence the outcome.

"What the werecat said, though, is worthy of far more consideration. Unfortunately, I cannot elucidate either of his statements. I have never heard of any such place as the Vault of Souls, and while the Rock of Kuthian strikes a familiar chord in my memory, I cannot recall where I have encountered the name. I will search my scrolls for it, but instinct tells me I will find no mention of it in elvish writings."

"What of the weapon underneath the Menoa tree?"

"I know of no such weapon, Eragon, and I am well acquainted with the lore of this forest. In all of Du Weldenvarden, there are perhaps only two elves whose learning exceeds my own where the forest is concerned. I will inquire of them, but I suspect it will be a futile endeavor." When Eragon expressed his disappointment, Oromis said, "I understand that you require a suitable replacement for Zar'roc, Eragon, and this I can help you with. Besides my own blade, Naegling, we elves have preserved two other swords of the Dragon Riders. They are Arvindr and Támerlein. Arvindr is currently held in the city of Nädindel, which you have not the time to visit. But Támerlein is here, in Ellesméra. It is a treasure of House Valtharos, and while the lord of their house, Lord Fiolr, would not part with it eagerly, I think he would give it to you if you asked him respectfully. I will arrange for you to meet with him tomorrow morning."

"And what if the sword does not fit me?" asked Eragon.

"Let us hope it does. However, I shall also send word to the smith Rhunön that she may expect you later in the day."

"But she swore she would never forge another sword."

Oromis sighed. "She did, but her advice would still be worth seeking out. If anyone can recommend the proper weapon for you, it would be she. Besides, even if you like the feel of Támerlein, I am sure Rhunön would want to examine the sword before you left with it. Over a hundred years have elapsed since Támerlein was last used in battle, and it might need some slight refurbishing."

"Could another elf forge me a blade?" asked Eragon.

"Nay," said Oromis. "Not if it were to match the craftsmanship of Zar'roc or whichever stolen sword Galbatorix has chosen to wield. Rhunön is one of the very oldest of our race, and it is she alone who has made the swords for our order."

"She is as old as the Riders?" said Eragon, amazed.

"Older even."

Eragon paused. "What shall we do between now and tomorrow, Master?"

Oromis looked over Eragon and Saphira, then said, "Go and visit the Menoa tree; I know you will not rest easy until you have. See there if you can find the weapon the werecat enticed you with. When you have satisfied your curiosity, retire to the quarters of your tree house, which Islanzadí's servants keep in readiness for you and Saphira. Tomorrow we shall do what we can."

"But, Master, we have so little time—"

"And the pair of you are far too tired for any more excitement today. Trust me, Eragon; you will do better for the rest. I think the hours between will help you to digest all we have spoken of. Even by the measure of kings, queens, and dragons, this conversation of ours has been no light exchange."

Despite Oromis's assurances, Eragon felt uneasy about spending the remainder of the day in leisure. His sense of urgency was so great, he wanted to continue working even when he knew he ought to be recuperating.

Eragon shifted in his chair, and by the motion he must have revealed something of his ambivalence, for Oromis smiled and said, "If it will help you relax, Eragon, I promise you this: before you and Saphira leave for the Varden, you may pick any use of magic, and in the brief while we have, I will teach you everything I can concerning it."

With his thumb, Eragon pushed his ring around his right index finger and considered Oromis's offer, trying to decide what, of all areas of magic, he would most like to learn. At last he said, "I would like to know how to summon spirits."

A shadow passed over Oromis's face. "I shall keep my word, Eragon, but sorcery is a dark and unseemly art. You should not seek to control other beings for your own gain. Even if you ignore the immorality of sorcery, it is an exceptionally dangerous and fiendishly complicated discipline. A magician requires at least three years of intensive study before he can hope to summon spirits and not have them possess him.

"Sorcery is not like other magics, Eragon; by it, you attempt to force incredibly powerful and hostile beings to obey your commands, beings who devote every moment of their captivity to finding a flaw in their bonds so that they can turn on you and subjugate you in revenge. Throughout history, never has there been a Shade who was also a Rider, and of all the horrors that have stalked this fair land, such an abomination could easily be the worst, worse even than Galbatorix. Please choose another subject, Eragon: one less perilous for you and for our cause."

"Then," said Eragon, "could you teach me my true name?"

"Your requests," said Oromis, "grow ever more difficult, Eragonfiniarel. I might be able to guess your true name if I so wished." The silver-haired elf studied Eragon with increased intensity, his eyes heavy upon him. "Yes, I believe I could. But I will not. A true name can be of great importance magically, but it is not a spell in and of itself, and so it is exempt from my promise. If your desire is to better understand yourself, Eragon, then seek to discover your true name on your own. If I gave you it, you might profit thereof, but you would do so without the wisdom you would otherwise acquire during the journey to find your true name. A person must earn enlightenment, Eragon. It is not handed down to you by others, regardless of how revered they be."

Eragon fiddled with his ring for another moment, then made a noise in his throat and shook his head. "I don't know. . . . My questions have run dry."

"That I very much doubt," said Oromis.

Eragon found it difficult to concentrate upon the matter at hand; his thoughts kept returning to the Eldunarí and to Brom. Again Eragon marveled at the strange series of events that had led Brom to settle in Carvahall and, eventually, to Eragon himself becoming a Dragon Rider. *If Arya hadn't* . . . Eragon stopped and smiled as a thought occurred to him. "Will you teach me how to move an object from place to place without delay, just as Arya did with Saphira's egg?"

Oromis nodded. "An excellent choice. The spell is costly, but it has many uses. I am sure it will prove most helpful to you in your dealings with Galbatorix and the Empire. Arya, for one, can attest to its effectiveness."

Lifting his goblet from the table, Oromis held it up to the sun, and the radiance from above rendered the wine transparent. He studied the liquid for a long while, then lowered the goblet and said, "Before you venture into the city, you should know that he whom you sent to live among us arrived here some time ago."

A moment passed before Eragon realized to whom Oromis was referring. "Sloan is in Ellesméra?" said Eragon, astonished.

"He lives alone in a small dwelling by a stream on the western edge of Ellesméra. Death was close upon him when he staggered out of the forest, but we tended the wounds of his flesh, and he is healthy now. The elves in the city bring him food and clothes and otherwise see to it he is well cared for. They escort him wherever he wishes to go, and sometimes they read to him, but for the most part, he prefers to sit alone, saying nothing to those who approach. Twice he has attempted to leave, but your spells prevented it."

I'm surprised he arrived here so quickly, Eragon said to Saphira.

The compulsion you placed upon him must have been stronger than you realized.

Aye. In a quiet voice, Eragon asked, "Have you seen fit to restore his vision?"

"We have not."

The weeping man is broken inside, Glaedr said. *He cannot see clearly enough for his eyes to be of any use.*

"Should I go and visit him?" asked Eragon, unsure of what Oromis and Glaedr expected.

"That is for you to decide," said Oromis. "Meeting you again might only upset him. However, you are responsible for his punishment, Eragon. It would be wrong for you to forget him."

"No, Master, I won't."

With a brisk motion of his head, Oromis set his goblet on the table and moved his chair closer to Eragon. "The day grows old, and I would keep you here no longer, lest I interfere with your rest, but there is one more thing I wish to attend to before you depart: your hands, may I examine them? I would like to see what they say about you now." And Oromis held out his own hands toward Eragon.

Extending his arms, Eragon placed his hands palm-downward on top of Oromis's, shivering at the touch of the elf's thin fingers against the inside of his wrists. The calluses on Eragon's knuckles cast long shadows across the backs of his hands as Oromis tilted them from side to side. Then, exerting a slight but firm pressure, Oromis turned Eragon's hands over and inspected his palms and the undersides of his fingers.

"What do you see?" asked Eragon.

Oromis twisted Eragon's hands around again and gestured at his calluses. "You now have the hands of a warrior, Eragon. Take care they do not become the hands of a man who revels in the carnage of war."

THE TREE OF LIFE

From the Crags of Tel'naeír, Saphira flew low over the swaying forest until she arrived at the clearing wherein stood the Menoa tree. Thicker than a hundred of the giant pines that encircled it, the Menoa tree rose toward the sky like a mighty pillar, its arching canopy thousands of feet across. The gnarled net of its roots radiated outward from the massive, moss-bound trunk, covering more than ten acres of forest floor before the roots delved deeper into the soft soil and vanished beneath those of lesser trees. Close to the Menoa tree, the air was moist and cool, and a faint but constant mist drifted down from the mesh of needles above, watering the broad ferns clustered about the base of its trunk. Red squirrels raced along the branches of the ancient tree, and the bright calls and chirrups of hundreds of birds burst forth from the bramble-like depths of its foliage. And throughout the clearing, the sense of a watchful presence pervaded, for the tree contained within it the remnants of the elf once known as Linnëa, whose consciousness now guided the growth of the tree and that of the forest beyond.

Eragon searched the uneven field of roots for any sign of a weapon, but as before, he found no object he would consider carrying into battle. He pried a loose slab of bark from the moss at his feet and held it up to Saphira. *What do you think?* he asked. *If I imbued it with enough spells, could I kill a soldier with this?*

You could kill a soldier with a blade of grass if you wanted to, she answered. *However, against Murtagh and Thorn, or the king and his black dragon, you might as well attack them with a strand of wet wool as that bark.*

You're right, he said, and tossed it away.

It seems to me, she said, *that you should not need to make a fool of yourself in order for Solembum's advice to prove true.*

No, but perhaps I should approach the problem differently if I am going to find this weapon. As you pointed out before, it could just as easily be a stone or a book as a blade of some sort. A staff carved from the branch of the Menoa tree would be a worthy weapon, I would think.

But hardly equal to a sword.

No. . . . And I would not dare lop off a branch without permission from the tree herself, and I have no idea how I could go about convincing her to grant my request.

Saphira arched her sinuous neck and gazed upward at the tree, then shook her head and shoulders to rid herself of the droplets that had accumulated on the sharp edges of her faceted scales. As the spray of cold water struck him, Eragon yelped and jumped backward, shielding his face with his arm. *If any creature tried to harm the Menoa tree,* she said, *I doubt they would live long enough to regret their mistake.*

For several more hours, the two of them prowled the clearing. Eragon continued to hope they would stumble across some nook or cranny among the knotted roots where they would find the exposed corner of a buried chest, which would contain a sword. *Since Murtagh has Zar'roc, which is his father's sword,* Eragon thought, *by all rights, I ought to have the sword Rhunön made for Brom.*

It would be the right color too, Saphira added. *His dragon, my namesake, was blue as well.*

At last, in desperation, Eragon reached out with his mind toward the Menoa tree and attempted to attract the attention of her slow-moving consciousness, to explain his search and ask for her help. But he might as well have been trying to communicate with the wind or the rain, for the tree took no more notice of him than he would of an ant flailing its feelers by his boots.

Disappointed, he and Saphira left the Menoa tree even as the rim of the sun kissed the horizon. From the clearing, Saphira flew to the center of Ellesméra, where she glided to a landing within the bedroom of the tree house the elves had given them to stay in. The

645

house was a cluster of several globular rooms that rested in the crown of a sturdy tree, several hundred feet above the ground.

A meal of fruit, vegetables, cooked beans, and bread was waiting for Eragon in the dining room. After eating a little, Eragon curled up next to Saphira on the blanket-lined basin set into the floor, ignoring the bed in preference for Saphira's company. He lay there, alert and aware of his surroundings, while Saphira sank into a deep sleep. From his place by her side, Eragon watched the stars rise and set above the moonlit forest and thought of Brom and the mystery of his mother. Late in the night, he slipped into the trancelike state of his waking dreams, and there he spoke with his parents. Eragon could not hear what they said, for his voice and theirs were muted and indistinct, but somehow he was aware of the love and pride his parents felt for him, and although he knew they were no more than phantoms of his restless mind, ever after he treasured the memory of their affection.

At dawn, a slim elf maid led Eragon and Saphira through the paths of Ellesméra to the compound of the family Valtharos. As they passed between the dark boles of the gloomy pines, it struck Eragon how very empty and quiet the city was compared with their last visit; he descried only three elves among the trees: tall, graceful figures who glided away on silent footsteps.

When the elves march to war, Saphira observed, *few remain behind.*

Aye.

Lord Fiolr was waiting for them inside an arched hall illuminated by several floating werelights. His face was long and stern and angled more sharply than those of most elves, so that his features reminded Eragon of a thin-bladed spear. He wore a robe of green and gold, the collar of which flared high behind his head, like the neck feathers of an exotic bird. In his left hand, he carried a wand of white wood carved with glyphs from the Liduen Kvaedhí. Mounted upon the end was a lustrous pearl.

Bending at the waist, Lord Fiolr bowed, as did Eragon. Then they exchanged the elves' traditional greetings, and Eragon thanked the lord for being so generous as to allow him to inspect the sword Támerlein.

And Lord Fiolr said, "Long has Támerlein been a prized possession of my family, and it is especially dear to my own heart. Know you the history of Támerlein, Shadeslayer?"

"No," said Eragon.

"My mate was the most wise and fair Naudra, and her brother, Arva, was a Dragon Rider at the time of the Fall. Naudra was visiting with him in Ilirea when Galbatorix and the Forsworn did sweep down upon the city like a storm from the north. Arva fought alongside the other Riders to defend Ilirea, but Kialandí of the Forsworn dealt him a mortal blow. As he lay dying on the battlements of Ilirea, Arva gave his sword, Támerlein, to Naudra that she might protect herself. With Támerlein, Naudra fought free of the Forsworn and returned here with another dragon and Rider, although she died soon afterward of her wounds."

With a single finger, Lord Fiolr stroked the wand, eliciting a soft glow from the pearl in response. "Támerlein is as precious to me as the air in my lungs; I would sooner part with life than part with it. Unfortunately, neither I nor my kin are worthy of wielding it. Támerlein was forged for a Rider, and Riders we are not. I am willing to lend you it, Shadeslayer, in order to aid you in your fight against Galbatorix. However, Támerlein will remain the property of House Valtharos, and you must promise to return the sword if ever I or my heirs ask for it."

Eragon gave his word, and then Lord Fiolr led him and Saphira to a long, polished table grown out of the living wood of the floor. At one end of the table was an ornate stand, and resting upon the stand was the sword Támerlein and its sheath.

The blade of Támerlein was colored a dark, rich green, as was its sheath. A large emerald adorned the pommel. The furniture of the sword had been wrought of blued steel. A line of glyphs adorned the crossguard. In Elvish, they said, *I am Támerlein, bringer of the final*

647

sleep. In length, the sword was equal to Zar'roc, but the blade was wider and the tip rounder and the build of the hilt was heavier. It was a beautiful, deadly weapon, but just by looking at it, Eragon could see that Rhunön had forged Támerlein for a person with a fighting style different from his own, a style that relied more on cutting and slashing than the faster, more elegant techniques Brom had taught him.

As soon as Eragon's fingers closed around Támerlein's hilt, he realized that the hilt was too large for his hand, and at that moment he knew that Támerlein was not the sword for him. It did not feel like an extension of his arm, as had Zar'roc. And yet, despite his realization, Eragon hesitated, for where else could he hope to find so fine a sword? Arvindr, the other blade Oromis had mentioned, lay in a city hundreds of miles distant.

Then Saphira said, *Do not take it. If you are to carry a sword into battle, if your life and mine are to depend upon it, then the sword must be perfect. Nothing else will suffice. Besides, I do not like the conditions Lord Fiolr has attached to his gift.*

And so Eragon replaced Támerlein on its stand and apologized to Lord Fiolr, explaining why he could not accept the sword. The narrow-faced elf did not appear overly disappointed; to the contrary, Eragon thought he saw a flash of satisfaction appear in Fiolr's fierce eyes.

From the halls of the family Valtharos, Eragon and Saphira made their own way through the dim caverns of the forest to the tunnel of dogwood trees that led to the open atrium in the center of Rhunön's house. As they emerged from the tunnel, Eragon heard the clink of a hammer on a chisel, and he saw Rhunön sitting at a bench by the open-walled forge in the middle of the atrium. The elf woman was busy carving a block of polished steel that lay before her. Whatever she was sculpting, Eragon could not guess, for the piece was still rough and indistinct.

"So, Shadeslayer, you are still alive," said Rhunön, without taking her eyes off her work. Her voice grated like pitted millstones. "Oromis told me that you lost Zar'roc to the son of Morzan."

Eragon winced and nodded, even though she was not looking at him. "Yes, Rhunön-elda. He took it from me on the Burning Plains."

"Hmph." Rhunön concentrated on her hammering, tapping the back of her chisel with inhuman speed, then she paused and said, "The sword has found its rightful owner, then. I do not like the use to which—what is his name? ah yes—*Murtagh* is putting Zar'roc, but every Rider deserves a proper sword, and I can think of no better sword for the son of Morzan than Morzan's own blade." The elf woman glanced up at Eragon from underneath her lined brow. "Understand me, Shadeslayer, I would prefer it if you had kept hold of Zar'roc, but it would please me even more if you had a sword that was made for you. Zar'roc may have served you well, but it was the wrong shape for your body. And do not even speak to me of Támerlein. You would have to be a fool to think you could wield it."

"As you can see," said Eragon, "I did not bring it with me from Lord Fiolr."

Rhunön nodded and resumed chiseling. "Well then, good."

"If Zar'roc is the right sword for Murtagh," said Eragon, "wouldn't Brom's sword be the right weapon for me?"

A frown pinched Rhunön's eyebrows together. "Undbitr? Why would you think of Brom's blade?"

"Because Brom was my father," said Eragon, and felt a thrill at being able to say that.

"Is that so now?" Laying down her hammer and chisel, Rhunön walked out from under the roof of her forge until she stood opposite Eragon. Her posture was slightly stooped from the centuries she had spent hunched over her work, and because of it, she appeared an inch or two shorter than he. "Mmh, yes, I can see the similarity. He was a rude one, he was, Brom; he said what he meant and wasted no words. I rather liked it. I cannot abide how my race has become. They are too polite, too refined, too precious. Ha! I remember when elves used to laugh and fight like normal creatures. Now they have become so withdrawn, some seem to have no more emotion than a marble statue!"

Saphira said, *Are you referring to how elves were before our races joined themselves to one another?*

Rhunön turned her scowl onto Saphira. "Brightscales. Welcome. Yes, I was speaking of a time before the bond between elves and dragons was sealed. The changes I have seen in our races since, you would hardly credit as possible, but so they are, and here I am, one of the few still alive who can remember what we were like before."

Then Rhunön whipped her gaze back to Eragon. "Undbitr is not the answer to your need. Brom lost his sword during the fall of the Riders. If it does not reside in Galbatorix's collection, then it may have been destroyed or it may be buried in the earth somewhere, underneath the crumbling bones of a long-forgotten battlefield. Even if it could be found, you could not retrieve it before you would have to face your enemies again."

"What, then, should I do, Rhunön-elda?" asked Eragon. And he told her of the falchion he had chosen when he was among the Varden and of the spells he had reinforced the falchion with and of how it had failed him in the tunnels underneath Farthen Dûr.

Rhunön snorted. "No, that would never work. Once a blade has been forged and quenched, you can protect it with an endless array of spells, but the metal itself remains as weak as ever. A Rider needs something more: a blade that can survive the most violent of impacts and one that is unaffected by most any magic. No, what you must do is sing spells over the hot metal while you are extracting it from the ore and also while you are forging it, so as to alter and improve the structure of the metal."

"How can I get such a sword, though?" Eragon asked. "Would you make me one, Rhunön-elda?"

The wire-thin lines on Rhunön's face deepened. She reached over and rubbed her left elbow, the thick muscles in her bare forearm writhing. "You know that I swore that I would never create another weapon so long as I live."

"I do."

"My oath binds me; I cannot break it, no matter how much I might wish to." Continuing to hold her elbow, Rhunön walked back to her bench and sat before her sculpture. "And why should I, Dragon Rider? Tell me that. Why should I loose another soul-reaver upon the world?"

Choosing his words with care, Eragon said, "Because if you did, you could help put an end to Galbatorix's reign. Would not it be fitting if I killed him with a blade you forged when it was with your swords he and the Forsworn slew so many dragons and Riders? You hate how they have used your weapons. How better to balance the scales, then, than by forging the instrument of Galbatorix's doom?"

Rhunön crossed her arms and looked up at the sky. "A sword . . . a new sword. After so long, to again ply my craft. . . ." Lowering her gaze, she jutted her chin out at Eragon and said, "It is possible, just possible, that there might be a way I could help you, but it is futile to speculate, for I cannot try."

Why not? asked Saphira.

"Because I have not the metal I need!" Rhunön growled. "You do not think that I forged the Riders' swords out of ordinary steel, do you? No! Long ago, while I was wandering through Du Weldenvarden, I happened upon fragments of a shooting star that had fallen to the earth. The pieces contained an ore unlike any I had handled before, and so I returned with it to my forge, and I refined it, and I discovered that the mix of steel that resulted was stronger, harder, and more flexible than any of earthly origin. I named the metal *brightsteel*, on account of its uncommon brilliance, and when Queen Tarmunora asked me to forge the first of the Riders' swords, it was brightsteel I used. Thereafter, whenever I had the opportunity, I would search the forest for more fragments of the star metal. I did not often find any, but when I did, I would save them for the Riders.

"Over the centuries, the fragments became ever more rare, until at last I began to think none were left. It took me four-and-twenty years to find the last deposit. From it, I forged seven swords, among them Undbitr and Zar'roc. Since the Riders fell, I have searched for brightsteel only once more, and that was last night, after Oromis spoke to me about you." Rhunön tilted her head, and her watery eyes bored into Eragon. "I wandered far and wide, and I cast many spells of finding and binding, but I came across not a single speck of brightsteel. If some could be procured, then we might begin to consider a sword for you, Shadeslayer. Otherwise, this discussion is no more than pointless blathering."

Eragon bowed to the elf woman and thanked her for her time, then he and Saphira left the atrium through the green leafy tunnel of dogwood.

As they walked side by side toward a glade from which Saphira could take off, Eragon said, *Brightsteel; that has to be what Solembum meant. There must be brightsteel underneath the Menoa tree.*

How would he know?

Perhaps the tree told him herself. Does it matter?

Brightsteel or not, she said, *how are we supposed to get at anything that the roots of the Menoa tree cover? We cannot chop through them. We do not even know where to chop.*

I have to think about it.

From the glade by Rhunön's house, Saphira and Eragon flew over Ellesméra back to the Crags of Tel'naeír, where Oromis and Glaedr were waiting. Once Saphira had landed and Eragon climbed down, she and Glaedr leaped off the cliff and spiraled high overhead, not really going anywhere, but rather enjoying the pleasure of each other's presence.

While the two dragons danced among the clouds, Oromis taught Eragon how a magician could transport an object from one place to another without having the object traverse the intervening distance. "Most forms of magic," said Oromis, "require ever more energy to sustain as the distance between you and your target increases. However, that is not the case in this particular instance. It would require the same amount of energy to send the rock in my hand to the other side of that stream as it would to send it all the way to the Southern Isles. For that reason, the spell is most useful when you need to transport an item with magic across a distance so vast, it would kill you to move it normally through space. Even so, it is a demanding spell, and you should only resort to it if all else has failed. To shift something as large as Saphira's egg, for example, would leave you too exhausted to move."

Then Oromis taught Eragon the wording of the spell and several variations on it. Once he had memorized the incantations to Oromis's satisfaction, the elf had him attempt to shift the small rock he was holding.

As soon as Eragon uttered the spell in its entirety, the rock vanished from the palm of Oromis's hand and, an instant later, reappeared in the middle of the clearing with a flash of blue light, a loud detonation, and a surge of burning hot air. Eragon flinched from the noise and then gripped the branch of a nearby tree to steady himself as his knees buckled and cold crept over his limbs. His scalp tingled as he gazed at the rock, which lay in a circle of charred and flattened grass, and he remembered the moment when he had first beheld Saphira's egg.

"Well done," said Oromis. "Now, can you tell me why the stone made that sound when it materialized in the grass?"

Eragon paid close attention to everything Oromis said, but throughout the lesson, he continued to ponder the question of the Menoa tree, even as he knew Saphira did as she soared high above. The longer he considered it, the more he despaired of ever finding a solution.

When Oromis had finished teaching him how to shift objects, the elf asked, "Since you have declined Lord Fiolr's offer of Támerlein, will you and Saphira stay in Ellesméra much longer?"

"I don't know, Master," replied Eragon. "There is something more

I wish to try with the Menoa tree, but if it does not succeed, then I suppose we will have no choice but to depart for the Varden empty-handed."

Oromis nodded. "Before you leave, return here with Saphira one last time."

"Yes, Master."

As Saphira winged her way toward the Menoa tree with Eragon on her back, she said, *It didn't work before. Why should it now?*

It will work because it must. Besides, do you have a better idea?

No, but I like it not. We do not know how she might react. Remember, before Linnëa sang herself into the tree, she killed the young man who betrayed her affections. She might resort to violence again.

She won't dare, not while you are there to protect me.

Mmh.

With a faint whisper of wind, Saphira alighted upon a knuckle-like root several hundred feet from the base of the Menoa tree. The squirrels in the enormous pine screamed warnings to their brethren as they noticed her arrival.

Sliding down onto the root, Eragon rubbed his palms on his thighs, then muttered, "Right, let's not waste time." With light footsteps, he ran up the root to the trunk of the tree, holding his arms out on either side to maintain his balance. Saphira followed at a slower pace, her claws splitting and cracking the bark she trod over.

Eragon squatted on a slippery patch of wood and hooked his fingers through a crevice in the trunk of the tree in order to keep himself from toppling over. He waited until Saphira was standing above him, and then he closed his eyes, breathed deeply of the cool, moist air, and pushed his thoughts out toward the tree.

The Menoa tree made no attempt to stop him from touching her mind, for her consciousness was so large and alien, and so intertwined with that of the other plant life of the forest, it did not need to defend itself. Anyone who attempted to seize control of the tree would also have to establish their mental dominance over a large swath of Du Weldenvarden, a feat which no single person could hope to achieve.

From the tree, Eragon felt a sense of warmth and light and of the earth pressing against her roots for hundreds of yards in every direction. He felt the stir of a breeze through the tree's tangled branches and the flow of sticky sap seeping over a small cut in its bark, and he received a host of similar impressions from the other plants the Menoa tree watched over. Compared with the awareness it had displayed during the Blood-oath Celebration, the tree almost seemed to be asleep; the only sentient thought Eragon could detect was so long and slow-moving, it was impossible to decipher.

Summoning all of his resources, Eragon flung a mental shout at the Menoa tree. *Please, listen to me, O great tree! I need your help! The entire land is at war, the elves have left the safety of Du Weldenvarden, and I do not have a sword to fight with! The werecat Solembum told me to look under the Menoa tree when I needed a weapon. Well, that time has come! Please, listen to me, O mother of the forest! Help me in my quest!* While he spoke, Eragon pressed against the tree's consciousness images of Thorn and Murtagh and the armies of the Empire. Adding several more memories to the mix, Saphira bolstered his efforts with the force of her own mind.

Eragon did not rely on words and images alone. From within himself and Saphira, he funneled a steady stream of energy into the tree: a gift of good faith that he hoped might also rouse the Menoa tree's curiosity.

Several minutes elapsed, and still the tree did not acknowledge them, but Eragon refused to abandon their attempt. The tree, he reasoned, moved at a slower pace than humans or elves; it was only to be expected that it would not immediately respond to their request.

We cannot spare much more of our strength, said Saphira, *not if we are to return to the Varden in a timely fashion.*

Eragon agreed and reluctantly stemmed the flow of energy.

While they continued to plead with the Menoa tree, the sun

reached its zenith and then began to descend. Clouds billowed and shrank and scuttled across the dome of the sky. Birds darted over the trees, angry squirrels chattered, butterflies meandered from spot to spot, and a line of red ants marched past Eragon's boot, carrying small white larvae in their pincers.

Then Saphira snarled, and every bird within hearing fled in fright. *Enough of this groveling!* she declared. *I am a dragon, and I will not be ignored, not even by a tree!*

"No, wait!" Eragon cried, sensing her intentions, but she ignored him.

Stepping back from the trunk of the Menoa tree, Saphira crouched, sank her claws deep into the root underneath her, and, with a mighty wrench, tore three huge strips of wood out of the root. *Come out and speak with us, elf-tree!* she roared. She drew back her head like a snake about to strike, and a pillar of flame erupted from between her jaws, bathing the trunk in a storm of blue and white fire.

Covering his face, Eragon leaped away to escape the heat.

"Saphira, stop!" he shouted, horrified.

I will stop when she answers us.

A thick cloud of water droplets fell to the ground. Looking up, Eragon saw the branches of the pine trembling and swaying with increasing agitation. The groan of wood rubbing against wood filled the air. At the same time, an ice-cold breeze struck Eragon's cheek, and he thought he felt a low rumble beneath his feet. Glancing around, he saw that the trees that ringed the clearing seemed taller and more angular than before, and they seemed to be leaning inward, their crooked branches reaching toward him like talons.

And Eragon was afraid.

Saphira . . . , he said, and sank into a half crouch, ready to either run or fight.

Closing her jaws and thus ending the stream of fire, Saphira looked away from the Menoa tree. As she beheld the ring of menacing trees, her scales rippled and the tips rose from her hide like the ruff on a riled cat. She growled at the forest, swinging her head from side to side, then unfolded her wings and began to retreat from the Menoa tree. *Quick, get on my back.*

Before Eragon could take a single step, a root as thick as his arm sprouted out of the ground and coiled itself around his left ankle, immobilizing him. Even thicker roots appeared on either side of Saphira and grasped her by the legs and tail, holding her in place. Saphira roared in fury and arched her neck to loose another deluge of fire.

The flames in her mouth flickered and went out as a voice sounded in her mind and Eragon's, a slow, whispering voice that reminded Eragon of rustling leaves, and the voice said: *Who dares to disturb my peace? Who dares to bite me and burn me? Name yourselves, so I will know who it is I have killed.*

Eragon grimaced in pain as the root tightened around his ankle. A little more pressure and it would break the bone. *I am Eragon Shadeslayer, and this is the dragon with whom I am bonded, Saphira Brightscales.*

Die well, Eragon Shadeslayer and Saphira Brightscales.

Wait! Eragon said. *I have not finished naming us.*

A long silence followed, then the voice said, *Continue.*

I am the last free Dragon Rider in Alagaësia, and Saphira is the last female dragon in all of existence. We are perhaps the only ones who can defeat Galbatorix, the traitor who has destroyed the Riders and conquered half of Alagaësia.

Why did you hurt me, dragon? the voice sighed.

Saphira bared her teeth as she answered: *Because you would not talk with us, elf-tree, and because Eragon has lost his sword and a werecat told him to look under the Menoa tree when he needed a weapon. We have looked and looked, but we cannot find it on our own.*

Then you die in vain, dragon, for there is no weapon under my roots.

Desperate to keep the tree talking, Eragon said, *We believe the werecat might have meant brightsteel, the star metal Rhunön uses to forge the blades of the Riders. Without it, she cannot replace my sword.*

657

The surface of the earth rippled as the network of roots that covered the clearing shifted slightly. The disturbance flushed hundreds of panicked rabbits, mice, voles, shrews, and other small creatures from their burrows and dens, and sent them scampering across the open ground toward the main body of the forest.

Out of the corner of his eye, Eragon saw dozens of elves running toward the clearing, their hair streaming behind them like silk pennants. Silent as apparitions, the elves stopped underneath the boughs of the encircling trees and stared at him and Saphira but made no move to approach or to assist them.

Eragon was about to call with his mind for Oromis and Glaedr when the voice returned. *The werecat knew whereof he spoke; there is a nodule of brightsteel ore buried at the very edge of my roots, but you shall not have it. You bit me and you burned me, and I do not forgive you.*

Alarm tempered Eragon's excitement at hearing of the ore's existence. *But Saphira is the last female dragon!* he exclaimed. *Surely you would not kill her!*

Dragons breathe fire, whispered the voice, and a shudder ran through the trees at the edge of the clearing. *Fires must be extinguished.*

Saphira growled again and said, *If we cannot stop the man who destroyed the Dragon Riders, he will come here and he will burn the forest around you, and then he will destroy you as well, elf-tree. If you help us, though, we may be able to stop him.*

A screech echoed among the trees as two branches scraped against each other. *If he tries to kill my seedlings, then he will die,* said the voice. *No one is as strong as the whole of the forest. No one can hope to defeat the forest, and I speak for the forest.*

Is not the energy we gave you enough to repair your wounds? asked Eragon. *Is not it compensation enough?*

The Menoa tree did not answer but rather probed at Eragon's mind, sweeping through his thoughts like a gust of wind. *What are you, Rider?* said the tree. *I know every creature that lives among this forest, but never have I encountered one like you.*

I am neither elf nor human, said Eragon. *I am something in between. The dragons changed me during the Blood-oath Celebration.*

Why did they change you, Rider?

So that I could better fight Galbatorix and his empire.

I remember I felt a warping in the world during the celebration, but I did not think it was important. . . . So little seems important now, save the sun and the rain.

Eragon said, *We will heal your root and trunk if that will satisfy you, but please, may we have the brightsteel?*

The other trees creaked and moaned like abandoned souls, and then, soft and fluttering, the voice came again. *Will you give me what I want in return, Dragon Rider?*

I will, Eragon said without hesitation. Whatever the price, he would gladly pay it for a Rider's sword.

The canopy of the Menoa tree grew still, and for several minutes, all was quiet in the clearing. Then the ground began to shake and the roots in front of Eragon began to twist and grind, shedding flakes of bark as they pulled aside to reveal a bare patch of dirt, out of which emerged what appeared to be a lump of corroded iron roughly two feet long and a foot and a half wide. As the ore came to rest on the surface of the rich black soil, Eragon felt a slight twinge in his lower belly. He winced and rubbed at the spot, but the momentary flare of discomfort had already vanished. Then the root around his ankle loosened and retreated into the ground, as did those that had been holding Saphira in place.

Here is your metal, whispered the Menoa tree. *Take it and go. . . .*

But— Eragon started to ask.

Go . . . , said the Menoa tree, its voice fading away. *Go. . . .* And the tree's consciousness withdrew from him and Saphira, receding deeper and deeper into itself until Eragon could barely sense its presence. Around them, looming pines relaxed and resumed their usual positions.

"But . . . ," Eragon said out loud, puzzled that the Menoa tree had not told him what she wanted.

Still perplexed, he went over to the ore, slid his fingers under the edge of the metal-laced stone, and hoisted the irregular mass into his arms, grunting at its weight. Hugging it against his chest, he turned away from the Menoa tree and started the long walk toward Rhunön's house.

Saphira sniffed the brightsteel as she joined him. *You were right,* she said. *I should not have attacked her.*

At least we got the brightsteel, said Eragon, *and the Menoa tree . . . well, I don't know what she got, but we have what we came for, and that's what matters.*

The elves gathered alongside the path Eragon had chosen to follow and gazed at Eragon and Saphira with an intensity that made Eragon quicken his pace and the skin on the nape of his neck prickle. Not once did the elves speak, only stared with their slanting eyes, stared as if they were watching a dangerous animal stalk through their homes.

A puff of smoke billowed from Saphira's nostrils. *If Galbatorix does not kill us first,* she said, *I think we shall live to regret this.*

MIND OVER METAL

"Where did you find that?" demanded Rhunön as Eragon staggered into the atrium of her house and dropped the lump of brightsteel ore onto the ground by her feet.

In as few words as possible, Eragon explained about Solembum and the Menoa tree.

Squatting next to the ore, Rhunön caressed the pitted surface, her fingers lingering over the metallic patches interspersed among the stone. "You were either very foolish or very brave to test the Menoa tree as you did. She is not one to trifle with."

Is there enough ore for a sword? Saphira asked.

"Several swords, if past experience is anything to judge by," said Rhunön, rising to her full height. The elf woman glanced at her forge in the center of the atrium, then clapped her hands together, her eyes lighting up with a combination of eagerness and determination. "Let us to it, then! You need a sword, Shadeslayer? Very well, I shall give you a sword the likes of which has never been seen before in Alagaësia."

"But what of your oath?" Eragon asked.

"Think not of it for the time being. When must the two of you return to the Varden?"

"We should have left the day we arrived," said Eragon.

Rhunön paused, her expression introspective. "Then I shall have to hurry that which I do not normally hurry and use magic to craft that which would otherwise require weeks of work by hand. You and Brightscales will help me." It was not a question, but Eragon nodded in agreement. "We shall not rest tonight, but I promise you, Shadeslayer, you shall have your sword by tomorrow morning." Bending at the knees, Rhunön lifted the ore from the ground without discernible effort and carried it to the bench with her carving in progress.

Eragon removed his tunic and shirt, so he would not ruin them during the work to come, and in their place Rhunön gave him a tight-fitting jerkin and a fabric apron treated so that it was impervious to fire. Rhunön wore the same. When Eragon asked her about gloves, she laughed and shook her head. "Only a clumsy smith uses gloves."

Then Rhunön led him to a low, grotto-like chamber set within the trunk of one of the trees out of which her house was grown. Inside the chamber were bags of charcoal and loose piles of whitish clay bricks. By means of a spell, Eragon and Rhunön lifted several hundred bricks and carried them outside, next to the open-walled forge, then did the same with the bags of charcoal, each of which was as large as a man.

Once the supplies were arranged to Rhunön's satisfaction, she and Eragon built a smelter for the ore. The smelter was a complex structure, and Rhunön refused to use much magic to construct it, so the project took them most of the afternoon. First they dug a rectangular pit five feet deep, which they filled with layers of sand, gravel, clay, charcoal, and ash, and in which they embedded a number of chambers and channels to wick away moisture that would otherwise dampen the heat of the smelting fire. When the contents of the pit were level with the ground, they assembled a trough of bricks on top of the layers below, using water and unfired clay as their mortar. Ducking inside her house, Rhunön returned with a pair of bellows, which they attached to holes at the base of the trough.

They broke then to drink and to eat a few bites of bread and cheese.

After the brief repast, Rhunön placed a handful of small branches in the trough, lit them on fire with a murmured word, and, when the flames were well set, laid medium-sized pieces of seasoned oak along the bottom. For nearly an hour, she tended the fire, cultivating it with the care of a gardener growing roses, until the wood had burned down to an even bed of coals. Then Rhunön nodded to Eragon and said, "Now."

Eragon lifted the lump of ore and gently lowered it into the trough. When the heat on his fingers became unbearable, he released the ore and jumped back as a fountain of sparks swirled upward like a swarm of fireflies. On top of the ore and the coals, he shoveled a thick blanket of charcoal as fuel for the fire.

Eragon brushed the charcoal dust from his palms, then grasped the handles of one set of bellows and began to pump it, as did Rhunön the bellows on the other side of the smelter. Between them, they supplied the fire with a steady stream of fresh air so that it burned ever hotter.

The scales on Saphira's chest, as well as on the underside of her head and neck, sparkled with dazzling flashes of light as the flames in the smelter danced. She crouched several yards away, her eyes fixed upon the molten heart of the fire. *I could help with this, you know,* she said. *It would take me but a minute to melt the ore.*

"Yes," said Rhunön, "but if we melt it too quickly, the metal will not combine with the charcoal and become hard and flexible enough for a sword. Save your fire, dragon. We shall need it later."

The heat from the smelter and the effort of pumping the bellows soon had Eragon covered in a sheen of sweat; his bare arms shone in the light from the fire.

Every now and then, he or Rhunön would abandon their bellows to shovel a new layer of charcoal over the fire.

The work was monotonous, and as a result, Eragon soon lost track of the time. The constant roar of the fire, the feel of the bellows' handle in his hands, the whoosh of rushing air, and Saphira's vigilant presence were the only things he was aware of.

It came as a surprise to him, then, when Rhunön said, "That should be sufficient. Leave the bellows."

Wiping his brow, Eragon helped as she shoveled the incandescent coals out of the smelter and into a barrel filled with water. The coals sizzled and emitted an acrid smell as they struck the liquid.

When they finally exposed the glowing pool of white-hot metal at the bottom of the trough—the slag and other impurities having run off during the process—Rhunön covered the metal with an inch of fine white ash, then leaned her shovel against the side of the smelter and went to sit on the bench by her forge. "What now?" Eragon asked as he joined her.

"Now we wait."

"For what?"

Rhunön gestured toward the sky, where the light from the setting sun painted a tattered array of clouds red and purple and gold. "It must be dark when we work the metal if we are to correctly judge its color. Also, the brightsteel needs time to cool so that it will be soft and easy to shape."

Reaching around behind her head, Rhunön undid the cord that held back her hair, then gathered up her hair again and retied the cord. "In the meantime, let us talk about your sword. How do you fight, with one hand or two?"

Eragon thought for a minute, then said, "It varies. If I have a choice, I prefer to wield a sword with one hand and carry a shield with my other. However, circumstances have not always been favorable to me, and I have often had to fight without a shield. Then I like being able to grip the hilt with both hands, so I can deliver a more powerful stroke. The pommel on Zar'roc was large enough to grasp with my left hand if I had to, but the ridges around the ruby were uncomfortable and they did not afford me a secure hold. It would be nice to have a slightly longer hilt."

"I take it you do not want a true two-handed sword?" said Rhunön.

Eragon shook his head. "No, it would be too big for fighting indoors."

"That depends upon the size of the hilt and the blade combined, but in general, you are correct. Would you be amenable to a hand-and-a-half sword instead?"

An image flashed in Eragon's mind of Murtagh's original sword, and he smiled. *Why not?* thought Eragon. "Yes, a hand-and-a-half sword would be perfect, I think."

"And how long would you like the blade?"

"No longer than Zar'roc's."

"Mmh. Do you want a straight blade or a curved blade?"

"Straight."

"Have you any preferences as to the guard?"

"Not especially."

Crossing her arms, Rhunön sat with her chin touching her breastbone, her eyes heavy-lidded. Her lips twitched. "What of the width of the blade? Remember, no matter how narrow it is, the sword shall not break."

"Perhaps it could be a little wider at the guard than Zar'roc was."

"Why?"

"I think it might look better."

A harsh, cracked laugh broke from Rhunön's throat. "But how would that improve the use of the sword?"

Embarrassed, Eragon shifted on the bench, at a loss for words.

"Never ask me to alter a weapon merely in order to improve its appearance," admonished Rhunön. "A weapon is a tool, and if it is beautiful, then it is beautiful because it is useful. A sword that could not fulfill its function would be ugly to my eyes no matter how fair its shape, not even if it were adorned with the finest jewels and the most intricate engraving." The elf woman pursed her lips, pushing them out as she thought. "So, a sword equally suited for the unrestrained bloodshed of a battlefield as it is for defending yourself in the narrow tunnels under Farthen Dûr. A sword for all occasions, of middling length, but for the hilt, which shall be longer than average."

"A sword for killing Galbatorix," said Eragon.

Rhunön nodded. "And as such, it must be well protected against magic. . . ." Her chin sank to her chest again. "Armor has improved a great deal in the past century, so the tip will need to be narrower than I used to make them, the better to pierce plate and mail and to slip into the gaps between the various pieces. Mmh." From a pouch by her side, Rhunön withdrew a knotted piece of twine, with which she took numerous measurements of Eragon's hands and arms. Afterward, she retrieved a wrought-iron poker from the forge and tossed it toward Eragon. He caught it with one hand and raised an eyebrow at the elf woman. She motioned toward him with a finger and said, "Go on now. Up on your feet and let me see how you move with a sword."

Walking out from under the roof of the open-walled forge, Eragon obliged her by demonstrating several of the forms Brom had taught him. After a minute, he heard the clink of metal on stone, then Rhunön coughed and said, "Oh, this is hopeless." She stepped in front of Eragon, holding another poker. Her brow furrowed with a fierce scowl as she raised the poker before her in a salute and shouted, "Have at you, Shadeslayer!"

Rhunön's heavy poker whistled through the air as she swung at him with a strong slashing blow. Dancing to the side, Eragon parried the attack. The poker jumped in his hand as the two rods of metal collided. For a brief while, he and Rhunön sparred. Although it was obvious she had not practiced her swordsmanship for some time, Eragon still found her a formidable opponent. At last they were forced to stop because the soft iron of the pokers had bent until the rods were as crooked as the branches of a yew tree.

Rhunön collected Eragon's poker, then carried the two mangled pieces of metal over to a pile of broken tools. When she returned, the elf woman lifted her chin and said, "Now I know exactly what shape your sword should have."

"But how will you make it?"

A twinkle of amusement appeared in Rhunön's eyes. "I won't. You shall make the sword instead of me, Shadeslayer."

Eragon gaped at her for a moment, then sputtered and said, "Me? But I was never apprenticed to a blacksmith or a bladesmith. I have not the skill to forge even a common brush knife."

The twinkle in Rhunön's eyes brightened. "Nevertheless, you shall be the one to make this sword."

"But how? Will you stand beside me and give me orders as I hammer the metal?"

"Hardly," said Rhunön. "No, I shall guide your actions from within your mind so that your hands may do what mine cannot. It is not a perfect solution, but I can think of no other means of evading my oath that will also allow me to ply my craft."

Eragon frowned. "If you move my hands for me, how is that any different from making the sword yourself?"

Rhunön's expression darkened and, in a brusque voice, she said, "Do you want this sword or not, Shadeslayer?"

"I do."

"Then refrain from pestering me with such questions. Making the sword through you is different because I think it is different. If I believed otherwise, then my oath would prevent me from participating in the process. So, unless you wish to return to the Varden empty-handed, you would be wise to remain silent on the subject."

"Yes, Rhunön-elda."

They went to the smelter then, and Rhunön had Saphira pry the still-warm mass of congealed brightsteel from the bottom of the brick trough. "Break it into fist-sized pieces," Rhunön directed, and withdrew to a safe distance.

Lifting her front leg, Saphira stamped upon the rippled beam of brightsteel with all her strength. The earth shook, and the brightsteel cracked in several places. Three more times Saphira stamped upon the metal before Rhunön was satisfied with the results.

The elf woman gathered up the sharp lumps of metal in her apron and carried them to a low table next to her forge. There she sorted the metal according to its hardness, which, or so she told Eragon, she was able to determine by the color and texture of the fractured metal. "Some is too hard and some is too soft," she said, "and while

I could remedy that if I wanted to, it would require another heating. So we will only use the pieces that are already suitable for a sword. On the edges of the sword will go a slightly harder steel"—she touched a cluster of pieces that had a brilliant, sparkling grain— "the better to take a keen edge. The middle of the sword shall be made of a slightly softer steel"—she touched a cluster of pieces that were grayer and not so bright—"the better to bend and to absorb the shock of a blow. Before the metal can be forged into shape, though, it must be worked to rid it of the remaining impurities."

How is that done? asked Saphira.

"That you shall see momentarily." Rhunön went to one of the poles that supported the roof of the forge, sat with her back against it, crossed her legs, and closed her eyes, her face still and composed. "Are you ready, Shadeslayer?" she asked.

"I am," said Eragon, despite the tension gathered in his belly.

The first thing Eragon noticed about Rhunön as their minds met was the low chords that echoed through the dark and tangled landscape of her thoughts. The music was slow and deliberate and cast in a strange and unsettling key that scraped on his nerves. What it implied about Rhunön's character, Eragon was not sure, but the eerie melody caused him to reconsider the wisdom of allowing her to control his flesh. But then he thought of Saphira sitting next to the forge, watching over him, and his trepidation receded, and he lowered the last of the defenses around his consciousness.

It felt to Eragon like a piece of raw wool sliding over his skin as Rhunön enveloped his mind with hers, insinuating herself into the most private areas of his being. He shivered at the contact and almost withdrew from it, but then Rhunön's rough voice sounded within his skull: *Relax, Shadeslayer, and all shall be well.*

Yes, Rhunön-elda.

Then Rhunön began to lift his arms, shift his legs, roll his head, and otherwise experiment with the abilities of his body. Strange as it was for Eragon to feel his head and limbs move without his direction, it was stranger still when his eyes began to flick from place to place, seemingly of their own accord. The sensation of helplessness kindled a burst of sudden panic within Eragon. When Rhunön walked him forward and his foot struck the corner of the forge and it seemed as if he were going to fall, Eragon immediately reasserted command over his faculties and grabbed the horn of Rhunön's anvil to steady himself.

Do not interfere, snapped Rhunön. *If your nerve fails you at the wrong moment during the forging, you could cause yourself irreparable harm.*

So could you if you're not careful, Eragon retorted.

Be patient, Shadeslayer. I shall have mastered this by the time it is dark.

While they waited for the last of the light to fade from the velvet sky, Rhunön prepared the forge and practiced wielding various tools. Her initial clumsiness with Eragon's body soon disappeared, although once she reached for a hammer and rammed the tips of his fingers into the top of a table. The pain made Eragon's eyes water. Rhunön apologized and said, *Your arms are longer than mine.* A few minutes later, when they were about to begin, she commented, *It is fortunate you have the speed and strength of an elf, Shadeslayer, else we would have no hope of finishing this tonight.*

Taking the pieces of hard and soft brightsteel she had decided to use, Rhunön placed them into the forge. At the elf's request, Saphira heated the steel, opening her jaws only a fraction of an inch so that the blue and white flames that poured from her mouth remained focused in a narrow stream and did not spill over into the rest of the workshop. The roaring pillar of fire illuminated the entire atrium with a fierce blue light and made Saphira's scales sparkle and flash with blinding brilliance.

Rhunön had Eragon remove the brightsteel from the torrent of flames with a pair of tongs once the metal began to glow cherry red. She laid it on her anvil and, with a series of quick blows from a sledgehammer, flattened the lumps of metal into plates that were no

669

more than a quarter of an inch thick. The surface of the red-hot steel glittered with incandescent motes. As she finished with each plate, Rhunön dropped it into a nearby trough of brine.

Having flattened all of the brightsteel, Rhunön pulled the plates out of the trough, the brine warm against Eragon's arm, and scoured each plate with a piece of sandstone to remove the black scales that had formed on the surface of the metal. The scouring exposed the crystalline structure of the metal, which Rhunön examined with great attentiveness. She further sorted the metal by relative hardness and purity according to the qualities the crystals displayed.

Eragon was privy to Rhunön's every thought and feeling, by reason of their closeness. The depth of her knowledge amazed him; she saw things within the metal he had not suspected existed, and the calculations she made concerning its treatment were beyond his understanding. He also sensed she was dissatisfied with how she had handled the sledgehammer while flattening the steel.

Rhunön's dissatisfaction continued to grow until she said, *Bah! Look at these dents in the metal! I cannot forge a blade like this. My control over your arms and hands is not fine enough to craft a sword worthy of note.*

Before Eragon could attempt to reason with her, Saphira said, *The tools do not the artist make, Rhunön-elda. Surely you can find a way to compensate for this inconvenience.*

Inconvenience? snorted Rhunön. *I have no more coordination than a fledgling. I am a stranger in a stranger's house.* Still grumbling, she subsided into mental deliberations that were incomprehensible to Eragon, then said, *Well, I may have a solution, but I warn you, I shall not continue if I am unable to maintain my usual level of craftsmanship.*

She did not explain the solution to either Eragon or Saphira but, one by one, placed the plates of steel on the anvil and cracked them into flakes no wider than rose petals. Gathering up half the flakes of the harder brightsteel, Rhunön stacked them into a brick, which she then coated with clay and birch bark to hold them together.

The brick went on a thick steel paddle with a seven-foot-long handle, similar to those used by bakers to insert and remove loaves of bread from a hot oven.

Rhunön laid the end of the paddle in the center of the forge and then backed Eragon as far away as she could and still have him hold on to the handle. Then she asked Saphira to resume breathing fire, and again the atrium glowed with a flickering blue radiance. The heat was so intense, Eragon felt as if his exposed skin were crisping, and he saw that the granite stones of which the forge was made had acquired a bright yellow glow.

The brightsteel could easily have taken over half an hour to reach the appropriate temperature in a charcoal fire, but it required only a few minutes in the withering inferno of Saphira's flames before it turned white. The moment it did, Rhunön ordered Saphira to cease breathing fire. Darkness engulfed the forge as Saphira closed her jaws.

Rushing Eragon forward, Rhunön had him transport the glowing brick of clay-covered steel to the anvil, where she seized a hammer and welded the disparate flakes of brightsteel into a cohesive whole. She continued to pound on the metal, elongating it out into a bar, then made a cut in the middle, folded the metal back on itself, and welded the two pieces together. The bell-like peals of ringing metal echoed off the ancient trees that surrounded the atrium.

Rhunön had Eragon return the brightsteel to the forge once its color had faded from white to yellow, and again Saphira bathed the metal with the fire from her belly. Six times Rhunön heated and folded the brightsteel, and each time the metal became smoother and more flexible, until it could bend without tearing.

As Eragon hammered the steel, his every action dictated by Rhunön, the elf woman began to sing, both with his tongue and her own. Together, their voices formed a not-unpleasant harmony that rose and fell with the beats of the hammer. A tingle crawled down Eragon's spine as he felt Rhunön channel a steady flow of energy

671

into the words they were mouthing, and he realized that the song contained spells of making, shaping, and binding. With their voices two, Rhunön sang of the metal that lay on the anvil, describing its properties—altering them in ways that exceeded Eragon's understanding—and imbuing the brightsteel with a complex web of enchantments designed to give it strength and resilience beyond that of any ordinary metal. Of Eragon's hammer arm Rhunön also sang, and under the gentle influence of her crooning, every blow she struck with his arm landed upon its intended target.

Rhunön quenched the bar of brightsteel after the sixth and final fold was complete. She repeated the entire process with the other half of the hard brightsteel, forging an identical bar to the first. Then she gathered up the fragments of the softer steel, which she folded and welded ten times before forming it into a short, heavy wedge.

Next, Rhunön had Saphira reheat the two bars of harder steel. Rhunön lay the shining rods side by side on her anvil, grasped both of them at either end with a pair of tongs, and then twisted the rods around each other seven times. Sparks shot into the air as she hammered upon the twists to weld them into a single piece of metal. The resulting mass of brightsteel Rhunön folded, welded, and pounded back out to length another six times. When she was pleased with the quality of the metal, Rhunön flattened the brightsteel into a thick rectangular sheet, cut the sheet in half lengthwise with a sharp chisel, and bent each of the two halves down their middle, so they were in the shape of long, shallow V's.

And all that, Eragon estimated, Rhunön was able to accomplish within the course of an hour and a half. He marveled at her speed, even though it was his own body that carried out the tasks. Never before had he seen a smith shape metal with such ease; what would have taken Horst hours took her only minutes. And yet no matter how demanding the forging was, Rhunön continued to sing, weaving a fabric of spells within the brightsteel and guiding Eragon's arm with infallible accuracy.

Amid the frenzy of noise, fire, sparks, and exertion, Eragon thought he glimpsed, as Rhunön raked his eyes across the forge, a trio of slender figures standing by the edge of the atrium. Saphira confirmed his suspicion a moment later when she said, *Eragon, we are not alone.*

Who are they? he asked. Saphira sent him an image of the short, wizened werecat Maud, in human form, standing between two pale elves who were no taller than she. One of the elves was male, the other female, and they were both extraordinarily beautiful, even by the standards of the elves. Their solemn teardrop faces seemed wise and innocent in equal measure, which made it impossible for Eragon to judge their age. Their skin displayed a faint, silvery sheen, as if the two elves were so filled with energy, it was seeping out of their very flesh.

Eragon queried Rhunön as to the identity of the elves when she paused to allow his body a brief rest. Rhunön glanced at them, affording him a slightly better view, then, without interrupting her song, she said with her thoughts, *They are Alanna and Dusan, the only elf children in Ellesméra. There was much rejoicing when they were conceived twelve years ago.*

They are like no other elves I have met, he said.

Our children are special, Shadeslayer. They are blessed with certain gifts—gifts of grace and gifts of power—which no grown elf can hope to match. As we age, our blossom withers somewhat, although the magic of our early years never completely abandons us.

Rhunön wasted no more time talking. She had Eragon place the wedge of brightsteel between the two V-shaped strips and hammer on them until the strips nearly enveloped the wedge and friction held the three pieces together. Then Rhunön welded the pieces into a whole, and while the metal was still hot, she began to draw it out and form a rough blank of the sword. The soft wedge became the spine of the blade, while the two harder strips became the sides, edges, and point. Once the blank was nearly as long as the finished sword, the work slowed as Rhunön returned to the tang and carefully hammered her way up the blade, establishing the final angles and proportions.

Rhunön had Saphira heat the blade in segments of no more than six or seven inches at a time, which Rhunön arranged by holding the blade over one of Saphira's nostrils, through which Saphira would release a single jet of fire. A host of writhing shadows fled toward the perimeter of the atrium every time the fire sprang into existence.

Eragon watched with amazement as his hands transformed the crude lump of metal into an elegant instrument of war. With every blow, the outline of the blade became clearer, as if the brightsteel *wanted* to be a sword and was eager to assume the shape Rhunön desired.

At last the forging came to a close, and there on the anvil lay a long black blade, which, although it was still rough and incomplete, already radiated a sense of deadly purpose.

Rhunön allowed Eragon's tired arms to rest while the blade cooled by air, then she had Eragon take the blade to another corner of her workshop, where she had arranged six different grinding wheels and, on a small bench, a wide assortment of files, scrapers, and abrasive stones. She fixed the blade between two blocks of wood and spent the next hour planing the sides of the sword with a drawknife, as well as refining the contours of the blade with files. As with the hammering, every stroke of the drawknife and every scrape of a file seemed to have twice the effect it normally would; it was as if the tools knew exactly how much steel to remove and would remove no more.

When she was done filing, Rhunön built a charcoal fire in her forge, and while she waited for the fire to mature, she mixed a slurry of dark, fine-grained clay, ash, powdered pumice, and crystallized juniper sap. She painted the blade with the concoction, slathering twice as much on the spine as she did along the edges and by the point. The thicker the solution of clay, the slower the underlying metal would cool when it was quenched and, as a result, the softer that area of the sword would become.

The clay lightened as Rhunön dried it with a quick incantation. At the direction of the elf woman, Eragon went to the forge. He lay the sword flat upon the bed of scintillating coals and, pumping the bellows with his free hand, slowly pulled it toward his hip. Once the tip of the blade came free of the fire, Rhunön turned it over and repeated the sequence. She continued to draw the blade through the coals until both edges had acquired an even orange tone and the spine of the sword was bright red in color. Then, with a single smooth motion, Rhunön lifted the sword from the coals, swept the glowing bar of steel through the air, and plunged it into the trough of water next to the forge.

An explosive cloud of steam erupted from the surface of the water, which hissed and sizzled and bubbled around the blade. After a minute, the roiling water subsided, and Rhunön withdrew the now pearl-gray sword. Returning it to the fire, she brought the whole sword to the same low heat, so as to reduce the brittleness of the edges, and then quenched it once more.

Eragon had expected Rhunön to relinquish her hold on his body after they had forged, hardened, and tempered the blade, but to his surprise, she remained in his mind and continued to control his limbs.

Rhunön had him douse the forge, then she walked Eragon back to the bench with the files and scrapers and abrasive stones. There she sat him, and making use of ever finer stones, she polished the blade. From her memories, Eragon learned that she would normally spend a week or more polishing a blade, but because of the song they sang, she, through him, was able to complete the task in a mere four hours, in addition to carving a narrow groove down the middle of each side of the blade. As the brightsteel grew smoother, the true beauty of the metal was revealed; within it, Eragon could see a shimmering, cable-like pattern, every line of which marked the transition between two layers of the velvety steel. And along each edge of the sword was a rippling, silvery white band as wide as his thumb, which made it appear as if the edges burned with tongues of frozen fire.

The muscles in Eragon's right arm gave way as Rhunön was covering the tang with decorative cross-hatching, and the file he was holding slipped off the tang and fell from his fingers. The extent of his exhaustion surprised him, for he had been concentrating upon the sword to the exclusion of all else.

Enough, said Rhunön, and she removed herself from Eragon's mind without further ado.

Shocked by her sudden absence, Eragon swayed on his seat and nearly lost his balance before he regained control over his rebellious limbs. "But we're not finished!" he protested, turning toward Rhunön. The night sounded unnaturally quiet to him without the strains of their extended duet.

Rhunön rose from where she had been sitting cross-legged against the pole and shook her head. "I have no more need of you, Shadeslayer. Go and dream until dawn."

"But—"

"You are tired, and even with my magic, you are liable to ruin the sword if you continue to work on it. Now that the blade is done, I can attend to the rest without interference from my oath, so go. You will find a bed on the second floor of my house. If you are hungry, there is food in the pantry."

Eragon hesitated, reluctant to leave, then nodded and shambled away from the bench, his feet dragging in the dirt. As he passed her, he ran a hand over Saphira's wing and bade her good night, too weary to say more. In return, she tousled his hair with a warm puff of air and said, *I shall watch and remember for you, little one.*

Eragon paused on the threshold of Rhunön's house and looked across the shadowy atrium to where Maud and the two elf children were still standing. He raised a hand in greeting, and Maud smiled at him, baring her sharp, pointed teeth. A tingle crawled down Eragon's neck as the elf children gazed at him; their large, slanted eyes were slightly luminous in the gloom. When they made no other motion, he ducked his head and hurried inside, eager to lie down upon a soft mattress.

A RIDER IN FULL

ake, little one, said Saphira. *The sun has risen and Rhunön is impatient.*

Eragon bolted upright, throwing off his blankets as easily as he cast off his waking dreams. His arms and shoulders were sore from his exertions of the previous day. He pulled on his boots, fumbling with the laces in his excitement, grabbed his grimy apron from the floor, and bounded down the elaborately carved stairs to the entryway of Rhunön's curved house.

Outside, the sky was bright with the first light of dawn, although shadow still enveloped the atrium. Eragon spotted Rhunön and Saphira by the open-walled forge and trotted over to them, combing his hair into place with his fingers.

Rhunön stood leaning against the edge of the bench. There were dark bags under her eyes, and the lines on her face were heavier than before.

The sword lay before her, concealed beneath a length of white cloth.

"I have done the impossible," she said, the words hoarse and broken. "I made a sword when I swore I would not. What is more, I made it in less than a day and with hands that were not my own. Yet the sword is not crude or shoddy. No! It is the finest sword I have ever forged. I would have preferred to use less magic during the process, but that is my only qualm, and it is a small one compared with the perfection of the results. Behold!"

Grasping the corner of the cloth, Rhunön pulled it aside, revealing the sword.

Eragon gasped.

He had thought that in the handful of hours since he had left her, Rhunön would only have had enough time to fabricate a plain hilt and crossguard for the sword, and maybe a simple wooden scabbard. Instead, the sword Eragon saw on the bench was as magnificent as Zar'roc, Naegling, and Támerlein and, in his opinion, more beautiful than any of them.

Covering the blade was a glossy scabbard of the same dark blue as the scales on Saphira's back. The color displayed a slight variegation, like the mottled light at the bottom of a clear forest pond. A piece of blued brightsteel carved in the shape of a leaf capped the end of the scabbard while a collar decorated with stylized vines encircled the mouth. The curved crossguard was also made of blued brightsteel, as were the four ribs that held in place the large sapphire that formed the pommel. The hand-and-a-half hilt was made of hard black wood.

Overcome by a sense of reverence, Eragon reached out toward the sword, then paused and glanced at Rhunön. "May I?" he asked.

She inclined her head. "You may. I give it to thee, Shadeslayer."

Eragon lifted the sword from the bench. The scabbard and the wood of the hilt were cool to the touch. For several minutes, he marveled at the details on the scabbard and the guard and the pommel. Then he tightened his grip around the hilt and unsheathed the blade.

Like the rest of the sword, the blade was blue, but of a slightly lighter shade; it was the blue of the scales in the hollow of Saphira's throat rather than the blue of those on her back. And as it was on Zar'roc, the color was iridescent; as Eragon moved the sword about, the color would shimmer and shift, displaying any of the many tones of blue present on Saphira herself. Through the wash of color, the cable-like patterns within the brightsteel and the pale bands along the edges were still visible.

With a single hand, Eragon swung the sword through the air, and he laughed at how light and fast it felt. The sword almost seemed alive. He grasped the sword with both his hands then and was delighted to find that they fit perfectly on the longer hilt. Lunging forward, he stabbed at an imaginary enemy and was confident they would have died from the attack.

"Here," said Rhunön, and pointed at a bundle of three iron rods planted upright in the ground outside the forge. "Try it on those."

Eragon allowed himself a moment to focus his thoughts, then took a single step toward the rods. With a yell, he slashed downward and cut through all three rods. The blade emitted a single pure note that slowly faded into silence. When Eragon examined the edge where it had struck the iron, he saw that the impact had not damaged it in the slightest.

"Are you well pleased, Dragon Rider?" Rhunön asked.

"More than pleased, Rhunön-elda," said Eragon, and bowed to her. "I do not know how I can thank you for such a gift."

"You may thank me by killing Galbatorix. If there is any sword destined to slay that mad king, it is this one."

"I shall try my hardest, Rhunön-elda."

The elf woman nodded, appearing satisfied. "Well, you finally have a sword of your own, which is as it ought to be. *Now* you are truly a Dragon Rider!"

"Yes," said Eragon, and held the sword up toward the sky, admiring it. "Now I am truly a Rider."

"Before you leave, one last thing remains for you to do," said Rhunön.

"Oh?"

She flicked a finger toward the sword. "You must name it so I can mark the blade and scabbard with the appropriate glyph."

Eragon walked over to Saphira and said, *What do you think?*

I am not the one who must carry the blade. Name it as you see fit.

Yes, but you must have some ideas!

She lowered her head toward him and sniffed at the sword, then said, *Blue-gem-tooth is what I would name it. Or Blue-claw-red.*

That would sound ridiculous to humans.

Then what of Reaver or Gutripper? Or maybe Battleclaw or Glitter-

thorn or *Limbhacker? You could name it Terror or Pain or Armbiter or Eversharp or Ripplescale: that on account of the lines in the steel. There is also Tongue of Death and Elfsteel and Starmetal and many others besides.*

Her sudden outpouring surprised Eragon. *You have a talent for this,* he said.

Inventing random names is easy. Inventing the right name, however, can try the patience of even an elf.

What of Kingkiller? he asked.

And what if we actually kill Galbatorix? What, then? Will you do nothing else of worth with your sword?

Mmh. Placing the sword alongside Saphira's left foreleg, Eragon said, *It's exactly the same color as you. . . . I could name it after you.*

A low growl sounded in Saphira's chest. *No.*

He fought back a smile. *Are you sure? Just imagine if we were in battle and—*

Her claws sank into the earth. *No. I am not a thing for you to wave about and make fun of.*

No, you're right. I'm sorry. . . . Well, what if I named it Hope in the ancient language? Zar'roc means "misery," so wouldn't it be fitting if I were to wield a sword that by its very name would counteract misery?

A noble sentiment, said Saphira. *But do you really want to give your enemies hope? Do you want to stab Galbatorix with hope?*

It's an amusing pun, he said, chuckling.

Once, maybe, but no more.

Stymied, Eragon grimaced and rubbed his chin, studying the play of light across the glittering blade. As he gazed into the depths of the steel, his eye chanced upon the flamelike pattern that marked the transition between the softer steel of the spine and that of the edges, and he recalled the word Brom had used to light his pipe during the memory Saphira had shared with him. Then Eragon thought of Yazuac, where he had first used magic, and also of his duel with Durza in Farthen Dûr, and in that instant he knew without doubt that he had found the right name for his sword.

Eragon consulted with Saphira, and when she agreed with his

choice, he lifted the weapon to shoulder level and said, "I am decided. Sword, I name thee Brisingr!"

And with a sound like rushing wind, the blade burst into fire, an envelope of sapphire-blue flames writhing about the razor-sharp steel.

Uttering a startled cry, Eragon dropped the sword and jumped back, afraid of being burned. The blade continued to blaze on the ground, the translucent flames charring a nearby clump of grass. It was then that Eragon realized it was he who was providing the energy to sustain the unnatural fire. He quickly ended the magic, and the fire vanished from the sword. Puzzled by how he could have cast a spell without intending to, he picked up the sword again and tapped the blade with the tip of a finger. It was no hotter than before.

A heavy scowl on her brow, Rhunön stalked forward, seized the sword from Eragon, and examined it from tip to pommel. "You are fortunate I have already protected it with wards against heat and damage, else you would have just scratched the guard and destroyed the temper of the blade. Do not drop the sword again, Shadeslayer—even if it should turn into a snake—or else I shall take it back and give you a worn-out hammer instead." Eragon apologized, and appearing somewhat mollified, Rhunön handed the sword back to him. "Did you set fire to it on purpose?" she asked.

"No," said Eragon, unable to explain what had happened.

"Say it again," ordered Rhunön.

"What?"

"The name, the name, say it again."

Holding the sword as far away from his body as he could, Eragon exclaimed, "Brisingr!"

A column of flickering flames engulfed the blade of the sword, the heat warming Eragon's face. This time Eragon noticed the slight drain on his strength from the spell. After a few moments, he extinguished the smokeless fire.

Once more Eragon exclaimed, "Brisingr!" And once more the blade shimmered with blue, wraithlike tongues of flame.

Now there is a fitting sword for a Rider and dragon! said Saphira in a delighted tone. *It breathes fire as easily as I do.*

"But I wasn't trying to cast a spell!" protested Eragon. "All I did was say *Brisingr* and—" He yelped and swore as the sword again caught fire, which he put out for the fourth time.

"May I?" asked Rhunön, extending a hand toward Eragon. He gave her the sword, and she too said, "Brisingr!" A shiver seemed to run down the blade, but other than that, it remained inanimate. Her expression contemplative, Rhunön returned the sword to Eragon and said, "I can think of two explanations for this marvel. One is that because you were involved with the forging, you imbued the blade with a portion of your personality and therefore it has become attuned to your wishes. My other explanation is that you have discovered the true name of your sword. Perhaps both those things are what has happened. In any event, you have chosen well, Shadeslayer. Brisingr! Yes, I like it. It is a good name for a sword."

A very good name, Saphira agreed.

Then Rhunön placed her hand over the middle of Brisingr's blade and murmured an inaudible spell. The Elvish glyph for *fire* appeared upon both sides of the blade. She did the same to the front of the scabbard.

Again Eragon bowed to the elf woman, and both he and Saphira expressed their gratitude to her. A smile appeared on Rhunön's aged face, and she touched each of them upon their brows with her callused thumb. "I am glad I was able to help the Riders this once more. Go, Shadeslayer. Go, Brightscales. Return to the Varden, and may your enemies flee with fear when they see the sword you now wield."

So Eragon and Saphira bade her farewell, and together they departed Rhunön's house, Eragon cradling Brisingr in his arms as he would a newborn child.

◆ ◆ ◆

683

GREAVES AND BRACERS

A single candle lit the inside of the gray wool tent, a poor substitute for the radiance of the sun.

Roran stood with his arms outstretched while Katrina laced up the sides of the padded jerkin she had fitted for him. When she finished, she tugged on the hem of the jerkin, smoothing out the wrinkles, and said, "There now. Is it too tight?"

He shook his head. "No."

She retrieved his greaves from the cot they shared and knelt before him in the flickering candlelight. Roran watched as she buckled the greaves onto his lower legs. She cupped the curve of his calf with her hand as she secured the second piece of armor, her flesh warm against his through the fabric of his trousers.

Standing, she turned to the cot again and picked up his bracers. Roran held out his arms toward her and stared into her eyes, even as she stared into his. With slow, deliberate motions, she fastened the bracers onto his forearms, then drew her hands from the inside of his elbow down to his wrists, where he clasped her hands with his own.

She smiled and pulled free of his gentle grip.

Next from the cot, she took his shirt of mail. She rose up onto the tips of her toes and lifted the hauberk over his head and held it there while he fit his arms into the sleeves. The mail tinkled like ice as she released it and it fell onto his shoulders, unfurling so that the lower edge hung level with his knees.

On his head, she set his leather arming cap, tying it firmly in place with a knot under his chin. She held his face between her hands for a moment, then kissed him once upon the lips and fetched his peaked helm, which she carefully slid over the arming cap.

Roran slipped his arm around her thickening waist as she started back toward the cot, stopping her. "Listen to me," he said. "I'll be fine." He tried to convey all his love for her through the tone of his voice and the strength of his gaze. "Don't just sit here all alone. Promise me that. Go to Elain; she could use your help. She's sick, and her child is overdue."

Katrina lifted her chin, her eyes gleaming with tears he knew she would not shed until after he had left. "Must you march in the front line?" she whispered.

"Someone must, and it might as well be me. Whom would you send in my stead?"

"Anyone . . . anyone at all." Katrina looked down and was silent for a span, then she removed a red kerchief from the bodice of her dress and said, "Here, carry this favor of mine, so that the whole world may know how proud I am of you." And she tied the kerchief to his sword belt.

Roran kissed her twice and released her, and she fetched his shield and spear from the cot. He kissed her a third time as he took them from her, then fit his arm through the strap on his shield.

"If something does happen to me—" he began to say.

Katrina placed a finger upon his lips. "Shh. Speak not of it, lest it should come true."

"Very well." He hugged her one last time. "Be safe."

"And you."

Although he hated to leave her, Roran raised his shield and strode out of the tent into the pale light of dawn. Men, dwarves, and Urgals streamed westward through the camp, heading toward the trampled field where the Varden were assembling.

Roran filled his lungs with the cool morning air and then followed, knowing that his band of warriors would be waiting for him. Once he arrived at the field, he sought out Jörmundur's division and, after reporting to Jörmundur, made his way to the front of the group, where he chose to stand next to Yarbog.

The Urgal glanced at him, then grunted, "A good day for a battle."

"A good day."

A horn sounded at the forefront of the Varden as soon as the sun broke over the horizon. Roran hefted his spear and began to run forward, like everyone else around him, howling at the top of his lungs as arrows rained down upon them and boulders whistled past overhead, flying in either direction. Ahead of him, a stone wall eighty feet tall loomed.

The siege of Feinster had begun.

✦ ✦ ✦

LEAVE-TAKING

From Rhunön's house, Saphira and Eragon flew back to their tree house. Eragon gathered up his belongings from the bedroom, saddled Saphira, and then returned to his usual place upon the crest of her shoulders.

Before we go to the Crags of Tel'naeír, he said, *there is one more thing I must do in Ellesméra.*

Must you? she asked.

I won't be content unless I do.

Saphira leaped out from the tree house. She glided westward until the number of buildings began to diminish, and then she angled downward for a soft landing upon a narrow, moss-covered path. After asking for, and getting, directions from an elf who was sitting in the branches of a nearby tree, Eragon and Saphira continued through the woods until they arrived at a small one-room house grown out of the bole of a fir tree that stood at an acute angle, as if a constant wind pressed against it.

To the left of the house was a soft bank of earth taller by several feet than Eragon. A rivulet of water tumbled over the edge of the bank and poured itself into a limpid pool before meandering off into the dim recesses of the forest. White orchids lined the pool. A bulbous root protruded out of the ground from among the slender flowers that grew along the near shore, and sitting cross-legged upon the root was Sloan.

Eragon held his breath, not wanting to alert the other man to his presence.

The butcher wore robes of brown and orange, after the fashion of the elves. A thin black strip of cloth was tied around his head, concealing the gaping holes where his eyes had been. In his lap, he held a length of seasoned wood, which he was whittling with a small, curved knife. His face was covered with far more lines than Eragon remembered, and upon his hands and arms were several new scars, livid against the surrounding skin.

Wait here, Eragon said to Saphira, and slipped off her back.

As Eragon approached him, Sloan paused in his carving and cocked his head. "Go away," he rasped.

Not knowing how to respond, Eragon stopped where he was and remained silent.

The muscles in his jaw rippling, Sloan removed another few curls from the wood he held, then tapped the tip of his knife against the root and said, "Blast you. Can you not leave me alone with my misery for a few hours? I don't want to listen to any bard or minstrel of yours, and no matter how many times you ask me, I won't change my mind. Now go on. Away with you."

Pity and anger welled up inside Eragon, and also a sense of displacement at seeing a man he had grown up around, and had so often feared and disliked, brought to such a state. "Are you comfortable?" Eragon asked in the ancient language, adopting a light, lilting tone.

Sloan uttered a growl of disgust. "You know I cannot understand your tongue and I do not wish to learn it. The words ring in my ears longer than they ought to. If you will not speak in the language of my race, then do not speak to me at all."

Despite Sloan's entreaty, Eragon did not repeat the question in their common language, nor did he depart.

With a curse, Sloan resumed his whittling. After every other stroke, he ran his right thumb over the surface of the wood, checking the progress of whatever he was carving. Several minutes passed, and then in a softer voice, Sloan said, "You were right; having something to do with my hands calms my thoughts. Sometimes . . . sometimes I can almost forget what I have lost, but the memories always return, and I feel as if I am choking on them. . . .

I am glad you sharpened the knife. A man's knives should always be sharp."

Eragon watched him for a minute more, then he turned away and walked back to where Saphira was waiting. As he pulled himself into the saddle, he said, *Sloan does not seem to have changed very much.*

And Saphira replied, *You cannot expect him to become someone else entirely in such a short time.*

No, but I had hoped he would learn something of wisdom here in Ellesméra and that maybe he would repent of his crimes.

If he does not wish to acknowledge his mistakes, Eragon, nothing can force him to. In any event, you have done all you can for him. Now he must find a way to reconcile himself with his lot. If he cannot, then let him seek the solace of the everlasting grave.

From a clearing close to Sloan's house, Saphira launched herself up and over the surrounding trees and headed north toward the Crags of Tel'naeír, flapping as hard and fast as she could. The morning sun sat full upon the horizon, and the rays of light that streamed out over the treetops created long, dark shadows that, as one, pointed to the west like purple pennants.

Saphira descended toward the clearing by Oromis's pinewood house, where Glaedr and Oromis stood waiting for them. Eragon was startled to see that Glaedr was wearing a saddle nestled between two of the towering spikes on his back and that Oromis was garbed in heavy traveling robes of blue and green, over which he wore a corselet of golden scale armor, as well as bracers upon his arms. A tall, diamond-shaped shield was slung across his back, an archaic helm rested in the crook of his left arm, and around his waist was belted his bronze-colored sword, Naegling.

With a gust of wind from her wings, Saphira alighted upon the sward of grass and clover. She flicked out her tongue, tasting the air as Eragon slid to the ground. *Are you going to fly with us to the Varden?* she asked. The tip of her tail twitched with excitement.

"We shall fly with you as far as the edge of Du Weldenvarden, but there our paths must part," said Oromis.

Disappointed, Eragon asked, "Will you return to Ellesméra then?"

Oromis shook his head. "No, Eragon. Then we shall continue onward to the city of Gil'ead."

Saphira hissed with surprise, a sentiment Eragon shared. "Why to Gil'ead?" he asked, bewildered.

Because Islanzadí and her army have marched there from Ceunon, and they are about to lay siege to the city, said Glaedr. The strange, gleaming structures of his mind brushed against Eragon's consciousness.

But do not you and Oromis wish to keep your existence hidden from the Empire? Saphira asked.

Oromis closed his eyes for a moment, his expression withdrawn and enigmatic. "The time for hiding has passed, Saphira. Glaedr and I have taught the two of you everything we could in the brief while you were able to study under us. It was a paltry education compared with that you would have received of old, but given how events press on us, we are fortunate to have been able to teach you as much as we did. Glaedr and I are satisfied that you now know everything that might help you to defeat Galbatorix.

"Therefore, since it seems unlikely that either of you will have a chance to return here for further instruction before the conclusion of this war, and since it seems even more unlikely that there shall ever be another dragon and Rider for us to instruct while Galbatorix still bestrides the warm earth, we have decided that we no longer have any reason to remain sequestered in Du Weldenvarden. It is more important that we help Islanzadí and the Varden overthrow Galbatorix than we tarry here in idle comfort while we wait for another Rider and dragon to seek us out.

"When Galbatorix learns that we are still alive, it shall undermine his confidence, for he shall not know if other dragons and Riders have survived his attempt to exterminate them. Also, knowledge of our existence shall bolster the spirits of the dwarves and the Varden and counteract any adverse effects Murtagh and

Thorn's appearance on the Burning Plains may have had upon the resolution of their warriors. And it may well increase the number of recruits Nasuada receives from the Empire."

Eragon glanced at Naegling and said, "Surely, though, Master, you do not intend to venture into battle yourselves."

"And why should we not?" inquired Oromis, tilting his head to one side.

Since he did not want to offend Oromis or Glaedr, Eragon was uncertain how to respond. At last he said, "Forgive me, Master, but how can you fight when you cannot cast spells that require more than a small amount of energy? And what of the spasms you sometimes suffer? If one were to strike in the middle of a battle, it could prove fatal."

Oromis replied, "As you ought to know well by now, mere strength rarely decides the victor when two magicians duel. Even so, I have all the strength I need here, in the jewel of my sword." And he reached across his body and placed the palm of his right hand on the yellow diamond that formed the pommel of Naegling. "For over a hundred years, Glaedr and I have stored every iota of our excess strength in this diamond, and others have added their strength to the pool as well; twice a week, several elves from Ellesméra visit me here and transfer as much of their life force into the gem as they can without killing themselves. The amount of energy contained within this stone is formidable, Eragon; with it, I could shift an entire mountain. It is a small matter, then, to defend Glaedr and myself from swords and spears and arrows, or even from a boulder cast by a siege engine. As for my seizures, I have attached certain wards to the stone in Naegling that will protect me from harm if I become incapacitated upon the battlefield. So you see, Eragon, Glaedr and I are far from helpless."

Chastened, Eragon dipped his head and murmured, "Yes, Master."

Oromis's expression softened somewhat. "I appreciate your concern, Eragon, and you are right to be concerned, for war is a perilous endeavor and even the most accomplished warrior may find death waiting for him amid the heated frenzy of battle. However, our cause is a worthy one. If Glaedr and I go to our deaths, then we go willingly, for by our sacrifice, we may help to free Alagaësia from the shadow of Galbatorix's tyranny."

"But if you die," said Eragon, feeling very small, "and yet we still succeed in killing Galbatorix and freeing the last dragon egg, who will train that dragon and his Rider?"

Oromis surprised Eragon by reaching out and clasping him by the shoulder. "If that should come to pass," said the elf, his face grave, "then it shall be your responsibility, Eragon, and yours, Saphira, to instruct the new dragon and Rider in the ways of our order. Ah, do not look so apprehensive, Eragon. You would not be alone in the task. No doubt Islanzadí and Nasuada would ensure that the wisest scholars of both our races would be there to help you."

A strange sense of unease troubled Eragon. He had often longed to be treated as more of an adult, but nevertheless, he did not feel ready to take Oromis's place. It seemed wrong to even contemplate the notion. For the first time, Eragon understood that he would eventually become part of the older generation, and that when he did, he would have no mentor to rely upon for guidance. His throat tightened.

Releasing Eragon's shoulder, Oromis gestured at Brisingr, which lay in Eragon's arms, and said, "The entire forest shuddered when you woke the Menoa tree, Saphira, and half the elves in Ellesméra contacted Glaedr and me with frantic pleas for us to rush to her aid. Moreover, we had to intervene on your behalf with Gilderien the Wise, so as to prevent him from punishing you for employing such violent methods."

I shall not apologize, said Saphira. *We had not the time to wait for gentle persuasion to work.*

Oromis nodded. "I understand, and I am not criticizing you, Saphira. I only wanted you to be aware of the consequences of your actions." At his request, Eragon handed his newly forged sword to

Oromis and held his helm for him while the elf examined the sword. "Rhunön has outdone herself," Oromis declared. "Few weapons, swords or otherwise, are the equal of this. You are fortunate to wield such an impressive blade, Eragon." One of Oromis's sharp eyebrows rose a fraction of an inch as he read the glyph on the blade. "Brisingr . . . a most apt name for the sword of a Dragon Rider."

"Aye," said Eragon. "But for some reason, every time I utter its name, the blade bursts into . . . ," he hesitated, and instead of saying *fire*—which, of course, was *brisingr* in the ancient language—he said, "flames."

Oromis's eyebrow climbed even higher. "Indeed? Did Rhunön have an explanation for this unique phenomenon?" As he spoke, Oromis returned Brisingr to Eragon in exchange for his helm.

"Yes, Master," said Eragon. And he recounted Rhunön's two theories.

When he had finished, Oromis murmured, "I wonder . . . ," and his gaze drifted past Eragon toward the horizon. Then Oromis gave a brief shake of his head and again focused his gray eyes upon Eragon and Saphira. His face became even more solemn than before. "I am afraid I have let my pride speak for me. Glaedr and I may not be helpless, but neither, as you pointed out, Eragon, are we entirely whole. Glaedr has his wound, and I have my own . . . impairments. It is not for nothing I am called the Cripple Who Is Whole.

"Our disabilities would not be a problem if our only enemies were mortal men. Even in our current state, we could easily slay a hundred ordinary humans—a hundred or a thousand, it would matter little which. However, our enemy is the most dangerous foe we or this land has ever faced. As much as I dislike acknowledging it, Glaedr and I are at a disadvantage, and it is quite possible that we shall not survive the battles yet to come. We have lived long and full lives, and the sorrows of centuries press upon us, but the two of you are young and fresh and full of hope, and I believe your

693

prospects of defeating Galbatorix are greater than those of anyone else."

Oromis glanced at Glaedr, and the elf's face became troubled. "Therefore, in order to help ensure your survival, and as a precaution against our possible demise, Glaedr has, with my blessing, decided to . . ."

I have decided, said Glaedr, *to give you my heart of hearts, Saphira Brightscales, Eragon Shadeslayer.*

Saphira's astonishment was no less than Eragon's. Together, they stared at the majestic gold dragon who towered high above them. Saphira said, *Master, you honor us beyond words, but . . . are you sure that you wish to entrust your heart to us?*

I am sure, said Glaedr, and lowered his massive head until it was only slightly above Eragon. *For many reasons, I am sure. If you hold my heart, you shall be able to communicate with Oromis and me—no matter how far apart we may be—and I shall be able to aid you with my strength whenever you are in difficulty. And if Oromis and I should fall in battle, our knowledge and experience, and also my strength, shall still be at your disposal. Long have I pondered this choice, and I am confident it is the right one.*

"But if Oromis were to die," said Eragon in a soft voice, "would you really want to live on without him, and as an Eldunarí?"

Glaedr turned his head and focused one of his immense eyes upon Eragon. *I do not wish to be parted from Oromis, but whatever happens, I shall continue to do what I can to topple Galbatorix from his throne. That is our only goal, and not even death shall deter us from pursuing it. The idea of losing Saphira horrifies you, Eragon, and rightly so. However, Oromis and I have had centuries to reconcile ourselves with the fact that such a parting is inevitable. No matter how careful we are, if we live long enough, eventually one of us will die. It is not a happy thought, but it is the truth. Such is the way of the world.*

Shifting his stance, Oromis said, "I cannot pretend that I regard this with favor, but the purpose of life is not to do what we want but what needs to be done. This is what fate demands of us."

So now I ask you, said Glaedr, *Saphira Brightscales and Eragon Shadeslayer, will you accept my gift and all that it entails?*

I will, said Saphira.

I will, replied Eragon after a brief hesitation.

Then Glaedr drew back his head. The muscles of his abdomen rippled and clenched several times, and his throat began to convulse, as if something were stuck in it. Widening his stance, the gold dragon extended his neck straight out in front of him, every cord and sinew of his body standing in high relief underneath the armor of his sparkling scales. Glaedr's throat continued to flex and relax with increasing speed until at last he lowered his head so that it was level with Eragon and opened his jaws, hot, pungent air pouring from his massive maw. Eragon squinted and tried not to gag. As he gazed into the depths of Glaedr's mouth, Eragon saw the dragon's throat contract one last time, and then a hint of gold light appeared between the folds of dripping, blood-red tissue. A second later, a round object about a foot in diameter slid down Glaedr's crimson tongue and out of his mouth so fast, Eragon nearly missed catching it.

As his hands closed around the slippery, saliva-covered Eldunarí, Eragon gasped and staggered backward, for he suddenly felt Glaedr's every thought and emotion, and all of the sensations of his body. The amount of information was overwhelming, as was the closeness of their contact. Eragon had expected as much, but it still shocked him to realize he was holding Glaedr's entire being between his hands.

Glaedr flinched, shaking his head as if he had been stung, and quickly shielded his mind from Eragon, although Eragon could still sense the flicker of his shifting thoughts, as well as the general color of his emotions.

The Eldunarí itself was like a giant gold jewel. Its surface was warm and covered with hundreds of sharp facets, which varied somewhat in size and sometimes projected at odd, slanting angles. The center of the Eldunarí glowed with a dull radiance, similar to

695

that of a shuttered lantern, and the diffuse light throbbed with a slow, steady beat. Upon first inspection, the light appeared uniform, but the longer Eragon gazed at it, the more details he saw within it: small eddies and currents that coiled and twisted in seemingly random directions, darker motes that barely moved at all, and flurries of bright flashes no larger than the head of a pin that would flare for a moment, then fade back into the underlying field of light. It was alive.

"Here," said Oromis, and handed Eragon a sturdy cloth sack.

To Eragon's relief, his connection with Glaedr vanished as soon as he placed the Eldunarí in the bag and his hands were no longer touching the gemlike stone. Still somewhat shaken, Eragon clasped the cloth-covered Eldunarí against his chest, awed by the knowledge that his arms were wrapped around Glaedr's essence and afraid of what might happen to it if he allowed the heart of hearts out of his grasp.

"Thank you, Master," Eragon managed to say, bowing his head toward Glaedr.

We shall guard your heart with our lives, Saphira added.

"No!" exclaimed Oromis, his voice fierce. "Not with your lives! That is the very thing we wish to avoid. Do not allow any misfortune to befall Glaedr's heart because of carelessness on your part, but neither should you sacrifice yourself to protect him or me or anyone else. You have to stay alive at all costs, else our hopes shall be dashed and all will be darkness."

"Yes, Master," Eragon and Saphira said at the same time, he with his tongue and she with her thoughts.

Said Glaedr, *Because you swore fealty to Nasuada, and you owe her your loyalty and obedience, you may tell her of my heart if you must, but only if you must. For the sake of dragons everywhere, what few of us remain, the truth about the Eldunarí cannot become common knowledge.*

May we tell Arya? asked Saphira.

"And what about Blödhgarm and the other elves Islanzadí sent to protect me?" asked Eragon. "I allowed them into my mind when

Saphira and I last fought Murtagh. They will notice your presence, Glaedr, if you help us in the midst of a battle."

You may inform Blödhgarm and his spellcasters of the Eldunarí, said Glaedr, *but only after they have sworn oaths of secrecy to you.*

Oromis placed his helm on his head. "Arya is Islanzadí's daughter, and so I suppose it is proper she should know. However, as with Nasuada, do not tell her unless it becomes absolutely necessary. A secret shared is no secret at all. If you can be so disciplined, do not even think of it, nor of the very fact of the Eldunarí, so that no one may steal the information from your minds."

"Yes, Master."

"Now let us be gone from here," said Oromis, and drew a pair of thick gauntlets over his hands. "I have heard from Islanzadí that Nasuada has laid siege to the city of Feinster, and the Varden have great need of you."

We have spent too long in Ellesméra, said Saphira.

Perhaps, said Glaedr, *but it was time well spent.*

Taking a short running start, Oromis bounded up Glaedr's single foreleg and onto his high, jagged back, where Oromis settled into his saddle and began to tighten the straps around his legs. "As we fly," said the elf, calling down to Eragon, "we can review the lists of true names you learned during your last visit."

Eragon went to Saphira and carefully climbed onto her back, wrapped one of his blankets around Glaedr's heart, and packed the bundle in his saddlebags. Then he secured his legs in the same manner as had Oromis. Behind him, he could feel a constant thrum of energy radiating from the Eldunarí.

Glaedr walked to the edge of the Crags of Tel'naeír and unfurled his voluminous wings. The earth shook as the gold dragon leaped toward the cloud-streaked sky, and the air boomed and shuddered as Glaedr drove his wings downward, pulling away from the ocean of trees below. Eragon gripped the spike in front of him as Saphira followed, flinging herself out into open space and falling several hundred feet in a steep dive before she ascended to Glaedr's side.

Glaedr assumed the lead as the two dragons oriented themselves toward the southwest. Each of them flapping at a different tempo, Saphira and Glaedr sped over the rolling forest.

Saphira arched her neck and uttered a ringing roar. Ahead, Glaedr responded likewise. Their fierce cries echoed across the vast dome of the sky, frightening the birds and beasts below.

FLIGHT

From Ellesméra, Saphira and Glaedr flew without stopping over the ancient forest of the elves, soaring high above the tall, dark pine trees. Sometimes the forest would break, and Eragon would see a lake or a contorted river winding across the land. Often there was a herd of small roe deer gathered along the edge of the water, and the animals would stop and lift their heads to watch the dragons soar past. For the most part, however, Eragon paid little attention to the scenery because he was busy reciting within his mind every word of the ancient language Oromis had taught him, and if he forgot any or made a mistake in pronunciation, Oromis would have him repeat the word until he had memorized it.

They arrived at the edge of Du Weldenvarden by late afternoon of the first day. There, above the shadowed boundary between the trees and the fields of grass beyond, Glaedr and Saphira circled one another, and Glaedr said, *Keep safe your heart, Saphira, and mine as well.*

I will, Master, Saphira replied.

And Oromis shouted from Glaedr's back, "Fair winds to you both, Eragon, Saphira! When next we meet, let it be before the gates of Urû'baen."

"Fair winds to you as well!" Eragon called in return.

Then Glaedr turned and followed the line of the forest westward—which would lead him to the northernmost tip of Isenstar Lake, and the lake thence to Gil'ead—while Saphira continued in the same southwesterly direction as before.

Saphira flew all through that night, landing only to drink and so Eragon could stretch his legs and relieve himself. Unlike during their flight to Ellesméra, they encountered no headwinds; the air remained clear and smooth, as if even nature were eager for them to return to the Varden. When the sun rose on their second day, it found them already deep within the Hadarac Desert and heading straight south, so as to skirt the eastern border of the Empire. And by the time darkness had again engulfed the land and sky and held them in its cold embrace, Saphira and Eragon were beyond the confines of the sandy wastes and were again soaring over the verdant fields of the Empire, their course such that they would pass between Urû'baen and Lake Tüdosten on their way to the city of Feinster.

After flying for two days and two nights without sleep, Saphira was unable to continue. Swooping down to a small thicket of white birch trees by a pond, she curled up in their shade and napped for a few hours while Eragon kept watch and practiced his swordsmanship with Brisingr.

Ever since they had parted with Oromis and Glaedr, a sense of constant anxiety had troubled Eragon as he pondered what awaited him and Saphira at Feinster. He knew that they were better protected than most from death and injury, but when he thought back to the Burning Plains, and to the Battle of Farthen Dûr, and when he remembered the sight of blood spurting from severed limbs and the screams of wounded men and the white-hot lash of a sword slicing through his own flesh, then Eragon's gut would roil and his muscles would shake with suppressed energy, and he did not know whether he wished to fight every soldier in the land or flee in the opposite direction and hide in a deep, dark hole.

His dread only worsened when he and Saphira resumed their journey and spotted lines of armed men marching over the fields below. Here and there, pillars of pale smoke rose from sacked villages. The sight of so much wanton destruction sickened him. Averting his gaze, he squeezed the neck spike in front of him and squinted until the only thing visible through the bars of his blurry eyelashes was the white calluses on his knuckles.

Little one, said Saphira, her thoughts slow and tired. *We have done this before. Do not allow it to disturb you so.*

Regretting that he had distracted her from flying, he said, *I'm sorry. . . . I'll be fine when we get there. I just want it to be over.*

I know.

Eragon sniffed and wiped his cold nose on the cuff of his tunic. *Sometimes I wish I enjoyed fighting as much as you do. Then this would be so much easier.*

If you did, she said, *the entire world would cower before our feet, including Galbatorix. No, it is good you do not share my love of blood. We balance each other out, Eragon. . . . Apart we are incomplete, but together we are whole. Now clear your mind of these poisonous thoughts and tell me a riddle that will keep me awake.*

Very well, he said after a moment. *I am colored red and blue and yellow and every other hue of the rainbow. I am long and short, thick and thin, and I often rest coiled up. I can eat a hundred sheep in a row and still be hungry. What am I?*

A dragon, of course, she said without hesitation.

No, a woolen rug.

Bah!

Their third day of traveling crept past with agonizing slowness. The only sounds were those of Saphira's wings flapping, the steady rasp of her panting, and the dull roar of air rushing past Eragon's ears. His legs and lower back ached from sitting in the saddle for so long, but his discomfort was slight compared with Saphira's; her flight muscles burned with an almost unbearable amount of pain. Still, she persevered and did not complain, and she refused his offer to alleviate her suffering with a spell, saying, *You will need the strength when we arrive.*

Hours after dusk, Saphira wobbled and dropped several feet in a single, sickening lurch. Eragon straightened, alarmed, and looked around for any clues as to what had caused the disturbance but saw only blackness below and the glittering stars above.

I think we just reached the Jiet River, said Saphira. *The air here is cool and moist, as it would be over water.*

Then Feinster shouldn't be much farther ahead. Are you sure you can find the city in the dark? We could be a hundred miles north or south of it!

No, we could not. My sense of direction may not be infallible, but it is certainly better than yours or that of any other earthbound creature. If the elf maps we have seen were accurate, then we cannot be off by more than fifty miles north or south of Feinster, and at this height, we can easily see the city over that distance. We may even be able to smell the smoke from their chimneys.

And so it was. Later that night, when dawn was only a few hours away, a dull red glow appeared upon the western horizon. Seeing it, Eragon twisted around and removed his armor from the saddlebags, then donned his mail hauberk, his arming cap, his helm, his bracers, and his greaves. He wished he had his shield, but he had left it with the Varden before running to Mount Thardûr with Nar Garzhvog.

Then Eragon rummaged with one hand through the contents of his bags until he found the silver flask of faelnirv Oromis had given him. The metal container was cool to the touch. Eragon drank a small sip of the enchanted liqueur, which seared the inside of his mouth and which tasted of elderberries and mead and mulled cider. Heat suffused his face. Within seconds, his weariness began to recede as the restorative properties of the faelnirv took effect.

Eragon shook the flask. To his concern, it felt as if a third of the precious liqueur was already gone, even though he had only consumed a single mouthful once before. *I have to be more careful with it in the future*, he thought.

As he and Saphira drew closer, the glow on the horizon resolved into thousands of individual points of light, from small handheld lanterns to cookfires to bonfires to huge patches of burning pitch that poured a foul black smoke into the night sky. By the ruddy light of the fires, Eragon saw a sea of flashing spearpoints and gleaming helmets surging against the base of the large, well-fortified city, the walls of which teemed with tiny figures busy firing arrows at the army below, pouring cauldrons of boiling oil between the merlons of the parapet, cutting ropes thrown over the walls, and pushing away the rickety wooden ladders the besiegers kept leaning against the ramparts. Faint calls and cries floated upward from the ground, as well as the boom of a battering ram crashing against the city's iron gates.

The last of Eragon's weariness vanished as he studied the battle-field and noted the placement of the men and the buildings and the various pieces of war machinery. Extending outward from the walls of Feinster were hundreds of ramshackle hovels crammed one against another, with hardly enough room for a horse to pass be-tween: the dwellings of those too poor to afford a house within the main part of the city. Most of the hovels appeared deserted, and a wide swath had been demolished so that the Varden could approach the city walls in force. A score or more of the mean huts were burn-ing, and even as he watched, the fires spread, leaping from one thatched roof to another. East of the hovels, curved black lines scored the earth where trenches had been excavated to protect the Varden's camp. On the other side of the city were docks and wharves similar to those Eragon remembered from Teirm, and then the dark and restless ocean that seemed to extend to infinity.

A thrill of feral excitement ran through Eragon, and he felt Saphira shiver underneath him at the same time. He gripped the hilt of Brisingr. *They don't seem to have noticed us yet. Shall we an-nounce our arrival?*

Saphira answered him by loosing a roar that made his teeth rattle and by painting the sky in front of them with a thick sheet of blue fire.

Below, the Varden at the foot of the city and the defenders upon the ramparts paused, and for a moment, silence enveloped the bat-tlefield. Then the Varden began to cheer and bang their spears and swords against their shields while great groans of despair wafted from the people of the city.

Ah! exclaimed Eragon, blinking. *I wish you hadn't done that. Now I can't see anything.*

Sorry.

Still blinking, he said, *The first thing we should do is find a horse that just died, or some other animal, so that I can replenish your strength with theirs.*

You don't have—

Saphira stopped talking as another mind touched theirs. After a half second of panic, Eragon recognized the consciousness as that of Trianna. *Eragon, Saphira!* cried the sorceress. *You're just in time! Arya and another elf scaled the walls, but they were trapped by a large group of soldiers. They won't survive another minute unless someone helps them! Hurry!*

BRISINGR!

Saphira tucked her wings close to her body and tipped into a steep dive, hurtling toward the dark buildings of the city. Eragon ducked his head against the blast of wind that tore at his face. The world spun around them as Saphira rolled to her right so that the archers on the ground would have difficulty shooting her.

Eragon's limbs grew heavy as Saphira pulled out of the dive. Then she leveled out and the weight pressing down on him vanished. Like strange, shrieking hawks, arrows whistled past them, some missing their mark, while Eragon's wards deflected the rest.

Swooping low over the outer city walls, Saphira roared again and lashed out with her claws and tail, knocking groups of screaming men off the parapet and toward the hard ground eighty feet below.

A tall, square tower armed with four ballistae stood at the far end of the southern wall. The huge crossbows fired twelve-foot-long javelins toward the Varden massed before the city gates. Inside the curtain wall, Eragon and Saphira spotted a hundred or so soldiers gathered around a pair of warriors, who stood with their backs pressed against the base of the tower, desperately trying to fend off a thicket of thrusting blades.

Even in the gloom and from high above, Eragon recognized one of the warriors as Arya.

Saphira leaped down from the parapet and landed in the midst of the soldiers, crushing several men beneath her feet. The rest scattered, screaming with fear and surprise. Saphira roared, frustrated that her prey was escaping, and whipped her tail across the dirt, flattening a dozen more soldiers. A man tried to run past her. Fast as a striking snake, she caught him between her jaws and shook her head, snapping his spine. She disposed of another four in a similar manner.

By then the remaining men had vanished among the buildings.

Eragon quickly pulled loose his leg straps, then jumped to the ground. The additional weight of his armor drove him to one knee as he landed. He grunted and pushed himself up onto his feet.

"Eragon!" cried Arya, running up to him. She was panting and drenched with sweat. Her only armor was a padded jerkin and a light helm painted black so it would not cast unwanted reflections.

"Welcome, Bjartskular. Welcome, Shadeslayer," purred Blödhgarm from by her side, his short fangs orange and glistening in the torchlight, his yellow eyes glowing. The ruff of fur on the elf's back and neck stood on end, which made him appear even fiercer than usual. Both he and Arya were stained with blood, although Eragon could not tell if the blood was theirs.

"Are you hurt?" he asked.

Arya shook her head, and Blödhgarm said, "A few scratches, but nothing serious."

What are you doing here without reinforcements? asked Saphira.

"The gates," said Arya, gasping. "For three days, we've tried to break them, but they're impervious to magic, and the battering ram has barely dented the wood. So I convinced Nasuada to . . ."

When Arya paused to regain her breath, Blödhgarm picked up the thread of her narrative. "Arya convinced Nasuada to stage tonight's attack so that we could sneak into Feinster without being noticed and open the gates from within. Unfortunately, we encountered a trio of spellcasters. They engaged us with their minds and prevented us from using magic while they summoned soldiers to overwhelm us with sheer numbers."

While Blödhgarm spoke, Eragon placed a hand on the chest of one of the dead soldiers and transferred what energy remained in the man's flesh into his own body, and thence to Saphira. "Where are the spellcasters now?" he asked, proceeding to another corpse.

Blödhgarm's fur-covered shoulders rose and fell. "They seem to have taken fright at your appearance, Shur'tugal."

As well they should, growled Saphira.

Eragon drained the energy from three more soldiers, and from the last, he also took the man's round wooden shield. "Well then," he said, standing, "let us go open the gates for the Varden, shall we?"

"Yes, and without delay," said Arya. She started forward, then cast a sideways glance at Eragon. "You have a new sword." It was not a question.

He nodded. "Rhunön helped me to forge it."

"And what is the name of your weapon, Shadeslayer?" asked Blödhgarm.

Eragon was about to answer when four soldiers ran out from the mouth of a dark alleyway, spears lowered. In a single, smooth motion, he drew Brisingr from its sheath and slashed through the haft of the lead man's spear and, continuing with the blow, decapitated the soldier. Brisingr seemed to shimmer with savage delight. Arya lunged forward and stabbed two of the other men before they could react while Blödhgarm leaped sideways and tackled the last soldier, killing him with his own dagger.

"Hurry!" cried Arya, and started to run toward the city gates.

Eragon and Blödhgarm raced after her while Saphira followed close behind, her claws loud against the paving stones of the street. Archers fired arrows at them from the parapet above, and three different times, soldiers rushed out from the main bulk of the city and flung themselves against them. Without slowing, Eragon, Arya, and Blödhgarm cut down the attackers, or else Saphira blasted them with a withering torrent of fire.

The steady boom of the battering ram became ever louder as they approached the forty-foot-tall gates of the city. Eragon saw two men and a woman, who were garbed in dark robes, standing before the ironbound doors, chanting in the ancient language and swaying from side to side with upheld arms. The three spellcasters fell silent when they noticed Eragon and his companions and, with their robes flapping, ran up the main street of Feinster, which led to the keep at the far side of the city.

Eragon longed to pursue them. However, it was more important to let the Varden into the city, where they would no longer be at the mercy of the men on the walls. *I wonder what mischief they have planned*, he thought, worried as he watched the spellcasters depart.

Before Eragon, Arya, Blödhgarm, and Saphira arrived at the gates, fifty soldiers in gleaming armor streamed out of the guard towers and positioned themselves in front of the huge wooden doors.

One of the soldiers pounded the hilt of his sword against his shield and shouted, "Never shall you pass, foul demons! This is our home, and we shall not allow Urgals and elves and other inhuman monsters to enter! Begone, for you shall find nothing but blood and sorrow in Feinster!"

Arya pointed at the guard towers and murmured to Eragon, "The gears for opening the gates are hidden within there."

"Go," he said. "You and Blödhgarm sneak around the men and slip into the towers. Saphira and I will keep them occupied in the meantime."

Arya nodded, then she and Blödhgarm disappeared into the pools of inky shadows that surrounded the houses behind Eragon and Saphira.

Through his bond with her, Eragon sensed that Saphira was gathering herself to pounce upon the group of soldiers. He put a hand on one of her forelegs. *Wait*, he said. *Let me try something first.*

If it doesn't work, then may I tear them to shreds? she asked, licking her fangs.

Yes, then you may do what you wish with them.

Eragon slowly walked toward the soldiers, holding his sword and shield out to either side. An arrow shot toward him from above, only to stop dead in the air three feet from his chest and drop straight to the ground. Eragon looked over the soldiers' frightened faces, then raised his voice and said, "My name is Eragon Shade-slayer! Perhaps you have heard of me, and perhaps not. In either case, know this: I am a Dragon Rider, and I have sworn to help the Varden remove Galbatorix from his throne. Tell me, have any of you sworn fealty in the ancient language to Galbatorix or the Empire? . . . Well, have you?"

The same man who had spoken before, who appeared to be the captain of the soldiers, said, "We would not swear fealty to the king even if he held a sword to our necks! Our loyalty belongs to Lady Lorana. She and her family have ruled us for four generations, and they've done a fine job of it too!" The other soldiers muttered in agreement.

"Then join us!" cried Eragon. "Lay down your weapons, and I promise no harm shall come to you or your families. You cannot hope to hold Feinster against the combined might of the Varden, Surda, the dwarves, and the elves."

"So you say," shouted one of the soldiers. "But what if Murtagh and that red dragon of his should come here again?"

Eragon hesitated, then said in a confident tone, "He is no match for me and the elves who fight with the Varden. We have already driven him off once before." To the left of the soldiers, Eragon saw Arya and Blödhgarm sidle out from behind one of the stone staircases that led to the top of the walls and, with silent footsteps, creep toward the leftmost guard tower.

The captain of the soldiers said, "We may not have pledged ourselves to the king, but Lady Lorana has. What will you do to her, then? Kill her? Imprison her? No, we will not betray our trust and allow you to pass, nor the monsters clawing at our walls. You and the Varden hold nothing but the promise of death for those who have been forced to serve the Empire!

"Why couldn't you have left well enough alone, eh, Dragon Rider? Why couldn't you have kept your head down so the rest of us could live in peace? But no, the lure of fame and glory and riches was too great. You had to bring wrack and ruin to our homes so that you could satisfy your ambitions. Well, I curse you, Dragon Rider! I curse you with all my heart! May you leave Alagaësia and never return!"

A chill crept over Eragon, for the man's curse echoed that which the last Ra'zac had cast upon him in Helgrind, and he remembered how Angela had foretold that very future for him. With an effort, he put aside such thoughts and said, "I do not wish to kill you, but I will if I must. Lay down your weapons!"

Arya silently opened the door at the bottom of the leftmost guard tower and slipped inside. Stealthy as a hunting wildcat, Blödhgarm crept behind the soldiers toward the other tower. If any of the men had turned around, they would have seen him.

The captain of the soldiers spat on the ground by Eragon's feet. "You don't even look human yourself! You're a traitor to your race, you are!" And with that, the man raised his shield and hefted his sword and slowly walked toward Eragon. "Shadeslayer," growled the soldier. "Ha! I'd as soon believe my brother's twelve-year-old son had killed a Shade as a youth like you."

Eragon waited until the captain was only a few feet away. Then he took a single step forward and stabbed Brisingr through the center of the man's embossed shield, through his arm underneath, and then through the man's chest and out his back. The man convulsed once and was still. As Eragon pulled his blade free of the corpse, there was a discordant clamor from within the guard towers as gears and chains began to turn and the massive beams that held closed the city gates began to withdraw.

"Lay down your weapons or die!" Eragon shouted.

Bellowing in unison, twenty soldiers ran at him, brandishing their swords. The others either dispersed and fled toward the heart of the city or else took Eragon's advice and placed their swords and spears and their shields on the gray paving stones and knelt by the side of the street with their hands on their knees.

A fine mist of blood formed around Eragon as he cut his way through the soldiers, dancing from one to the next faster than they could react. Saphira knocked two of the soldiers over, then set another two on fire with a short burst of flame from her nostrils, cooking them in their armor. Eragon slid to a stop several feet beyond the rearmost soldier and held his position, his sword arm outstretched from the blow he had just dealt, and waited until he heard the man topple to the ground, first one half, and then the other.

Arya and Blödhgarm emerged from the guard towers just as the gates groaned and swung outward, revealing the blunt and splintered end of the Varden's massive battering ram. Above, the archers on the parapet cried out in dismay and retreated toward more defensible positions. Dozens of hands appeared around the edges of the gates and pulled them farther apart, and Eragon saw a mass of grim-faced Varden, men and dwarves alike, crowded in the archway beyond.

"Shadeslayer!" they shouted, and also "Argetlam!" and "Welcome back! The hunting is good today!"

"These are my prisoners!" Eragon said, and pointed with Brisingr at the soldiers kneeling by the side of the street. "Bind them and see that they are treated well. I gave my word that no harm would come to them."

Six warriors hurried to follow his order.

The Varden rushed forward, streaming into the city, their jangling armor and pounding boots creating a continuous, rolling thunder. Eragon was pleased to see Roran and Horst and several other men from Carvahall in the fourth rank of the warriors. He hailed them, and Roran raised his hammer in greeting and ran toward him.

Eragon grasped Roran's right forearm and pulled him into a rough hug. Drawing back, he noticed that Roran seemed older and hollow-eyed compared with before.

"About time you got here," Roran grunted. "We've been dying by the hundreds trying to take the walls."

"Saphira and I came as fast as we could. How's Katrina?"

"She's fine."

"Once this is over, you'll have to tell me everything that's happened to you since I left."

Roran pressed his lips together and nodded. Then he pointed at Brisingr and said, "Where did you get the sword?"

"From the elves."

"What's it called?"

"Bris—" Eragon started to say, but then the eleven other elves whom Islanzadí had assigned to protect him and Saphira sprinted out of the column of men and surrounded the two of them. Arya and Blödhgarm rejoined them as well, Arya wiping clean the slim blade of her sword.

Before Eragon could resume speaking, Jörmundur rode through the gates and hailed him, shouting, "Shadeslayer! Well met indeed!"

Eragon greeted him in return and asked, "What should we do now?"

"Whatever you see fit," Jörmundur replied, reining in his brown charger. "We have to fight our way up to the keep. It doesn't look as if Saphira would fit between most of the houses, so fly around and harry their forces where you can. If you could break open the keep or capture Lady Lorana, it would be a great help."

"Where's Nasuada?"

Jörmundur gestured over his shoulder. "At the rear of the army, coordinating our forces with King Orrin." Jörmundur glanced out over the influx of warriors, then looked back at Eragon and Roran. "Stronghammer, your place is with your men, not gossiping with your cousin." Then the lean, wiry commander spurred his horse forward and rode up the gloomy street, shouting orders to the Varden.

As Roran and Arya started to follow, Eragon grabbed Roran by the shoulder and tapped Arya's blade with his own. "Wait," he said.

"What!" both Arya and Roran demanded in exasperated tones.

Yes, what? Saphira asked. *We should not be sitting and talking when there is sport to be had.*

"My father," Eragon exclaimed. "It's not Morzan, it's Brom!"

Roran blinked. "Brom?"

"Yes, Brom!"

Even Arya appeared surprised. "Are you sure, Eragon? How do you know?"

"Of course I'm sure! I'll explain later, but I couldn't wait to tell you the truth."

Roran shook his head. "Brom. . . . I never would have guessed, but I suppose it makes sense. You must be glad to be rid of Morzan's name."

"More than glad," Eragon said, grinning.

Roran clapped him on the back, then said, "Watch yourself, eh?" and trotted after Horst and the other villagers.

Arya moved away in the same direction, but before she went more than a few steps, Eragon called her name and said, "The Cripple Who Is Whole has left Du Weldenvarden and joined Islanzadí at Gil'ead." Arya's green eyes widened and her lips parted, as if she were about to ask a question. Before she could, the column of inrushing warriors swept her deeper into the city.

Blödhgarm sidled closer to Eragon. "Shadeslayer, why did the Mourning Sage leave the forest?"

"He and his companion felt that the time had come to strike against the Empire and to reveal their presence to Galbatorix."

The elf's fur rippled. "That is indeed momentous news."

Eragon climbed back onto Saphira. To Blödhgarm and his other guards, he said, "Work your way up to the keep. We'll meet you there."

Without waiting for the elf to answer, Saphira jumped onto the stairs leading to the top of the city walls. The stone steps cracked under her weight as she climbed up to the wide parapet, from which she took flight over the burning hovels outside Feinster, flapping quickly to gain altitude.

Arya will have to give us permission before we can tell anyone else about Oromis and Glaedr, said Eragon, remembering the oath of secrecy he, Orik, and Saphira had sworn to Queen Islanzadí during their first visit to Ellesméra.

I am sure she will once she hears our account, said Saphira.

Aye.

Eragon and Saphira flew from place to place within Feinster, landing wherever they spotted a large clump of men or wherever members of the Varden appeared beleaguered. Unless someone immediately attacked, Eragon attempted to convince each group of enemies to surrender. He failed as often as he succeeded, but he felt better for having tried, for many of the men who thronged the streets were ordinary citizens of Feinster, and not trained soldiers. To each, Eragon said, "The Empire is our foe, not you. Do not take up arms against us and you shall have no cause to fear us." The few times Eragon saw a woman or child running through the dark city, he ordered them to hide in the nearest house, and without exception, they obeyed.

Eragon examined the minds of every person around him and Saphira, searching for magicians who might mean them harm, but he found no other spellcaster besides the three they had already seen, and the three were careful to keep their thoughts hidden from him. It concerned him that they did not seem to have rejoined the fight in any noticeable way.

Maybe they intend to abandon the city, he said to Saphira.

Would Galbatorix let them leave in the middle of a battle?

I doubt he wants to lose any of his spellcasters.

Maybe, but we should still tread with care. Who knows what they are planning?

Eragon shrugged. *For now, the best thing we can do is help the Varden secure Feinster as quickly as possible.*

She agreed and angled toward a skirmish in a nearby square.

Fighting in a city was different from fighting in the open, as Eragon and Saphira were accustomed to. The narrow streets and close-set buildings hampered Saphira's movements and made it difficult to react when soldiers attacked, even though Eragon could sense the men approaching long before they arrived. Their encounters with the soldiers devolved into dark and desperate struggles, broken only by the occasional burst of fire or magic. More than once, Saphira wrecked the front of a house with a careless sweep of her tail. She and Eragon always managed to escape permanent injury—through a combination of luck, skill, and Eragon's wards—but the attacks made them even more cautious and tense than they normally were in battle.

The fifth such confrontation left Eragon so enraged that when the soldiers began to withdraw, as they always did in the end, he gave chase, determined to kill every last one. They surprised him by swerving off the street and crashing through the barred door of a millinery shop.

Eragon followed, leaping over the cracked wreckage of the door. The inside of the shop was pitch-black and smelled like chicken feathers and stale perfume. He could have lit the shop with magic, but since he knew the soldiers were at a greater disadvantage than he was, he refrained. Eragon felt their minds nearby, and he could hear their ragged breathing, but he was uncertain of what lay between him and them. He inched deeper into the inky shop, feeling his way with his feet. He held his shield in front of him and Brisingr over his head, ready to strike.

Faint as a line of thread falling to the floor, Eragon heard an object flying through the air.

He jerked backward and staggered as a mace or a hammer struck his shield, breaking it into pieces. Shouts erupted. A man knocked over a chair or a table and something shattered against a wall. Eragon lashed out and felt Brisingr sink into flesh and bury itself in bone. A weight dragged on the end of his sword. Eragon yanked it free, and the man he had struck collapsed across his feet.

Eragon dared a glance back at Saphira, who was waiting for him in the narrow street outside. Only then did Eragon see that there was a lantern mounted on an iron post beside the street and that the light it cast rendered him visible to the soldiers. He quickly moved from the open doorway and threw away the remnants of his shield.

Another crash echoed through the shop, and there was a confusion of footsteps as the soldiers rushed out the back and up a flight of stairs. Eragon scrambled after them. The second story was the living quarters of the family who owned the store below. Several people screamed and a baby began to wail as Eragon bounded through a maze of small rooms, but he ignored them, intent as he was on his prey. At last he cornered the soldiers in a cramped sitting room illuminated by a single flickering candle.

Eragon slew the four soldiers with four strokes of his sword, wincing as their blood splattered him. He scavenged a new shield from one, then paused and studied the corpses. It seemed rude to leave them lying in the middle of the sitting room, so he threw them out a nearby window.

On his way back to the stairs, a figure stepped around a corner and stabbed a dagger toward Eragon's ribs. The tip of the dagger stopped a fraction of an inch from Eragon's side, halted by his wards. Startled, Eragon swept Brisingr upward and was about to strike his attacker's head from his shoulders when he realized that the holder of the dagger was a thin boy of no more than thirteen.

Eragon froze. *That could be me*, he thought. *I would have done the same if I were in his shoes.* Looking past the boy, he saw a man and a woman standing in their nightgowns and knit caps, clutching each other and staring at him with horror.

A tremor ran through Eragon. He lowered Brisingr and, with his free hand, removed the dagger from the boy's now-soft grip. "If I were you," Eragon said, and the loudness of his voice shocked him, "I would not go outside until the battle is over." He hesitated, then added, "I'm sorry."

Feeling ashamed, he hurried from the shop and rejoined Saphira. They continued along the street.

Not far from the millinery shop, Eragon and Saphira came across several of King Orrin's men carrying gold candlesticks, silver plates and utensils, jewelry, and an assortment of furnishings out of a well-appointed mansion the men had broken into.

Eragon dashed a pile of rugs from the arms of one man. "Put these things back!" he shouted to the entire group. "We're here to *help* these people, not steal from them! They are our brothers and sisters, our mothers and fathers. I'll let you off this once, but spread the word that if you or anyone else goes looting, I'll have you strung up and whipped as the thieves you are!" Saphira growled, emphasizing his point. Under their watchful gaze, the chastened warriors returned the spoils to the marble-clad mansion.

Now, Eragon said to Saphira, *maybe we can—*

"Shadeslayer! Shadeslayer!" shouted a man, running toward them from deeper within the city. His arms and armor identified him as one of the Varden.

Eragon tightened his grip on Brisingr. "What?"

"We need your help, Shadeslayer. And yours too, Saphira!"

They followed the warrior through Feinster until they arrived at a large stone building. Several dozen Varden sat hunched behind a low wall in front of the building. They appeared relieved to see Eragon and Saphira.

"Stay back!" said one of the Varden, gesturing. "There's a whole group of soldiers inside, and they have bows aimed at us."

Eragon and Saphira halted just out of sight of the building. The warrior who had brought them said, "We can't get at them. The doors and windows are blocked, and they shoot at us if we try to chop our way in."

Eragon looked at Saphira. *Shall I, or shall you?*

I'll attend to it, she said, and jumped into the air with a rush of spreading wings.

The building shook, windows shattering, as Saphira landed on the roof. Eragon and the other warriors watched with awe as she fit the tips of her claws into the mortared grooves between the stones and, snarling from the effort, tore the building apart until she exposed the terrified soldiers, whom she killed like a terrier kills rats.

When Saphira returned to Eragon's side, the Varden edged away from her, clearly frightened by her display of ferocity. She ignored them and began licking her paws, cleaning the gore from her scales.

Have I ever told you how glad I am we're not enemies? Eragon asked.

No, but it's very sweet of you.

Throughout the city, the soldiers fought with a tenacity that impressed Eragon; they gave ground only when forced and made every attempt to slow the Varden's advance. Because of their determined resistance, the Varden did not arrive at the western side of the city, where the keep stood, until the first faint light of dawn began to spread across the sky.

The keep was an imposing structure. It was tall and square and adorned with numerous towers of differing height. The roof was made of slate, so attackers could not set it on fire. In front of the keep was a large courtyard—in which were several low outbuildings and a row of four catapults—and encircling the lot was a thick curtain wall interspersed with smaller towers of its own. Hundreds of soldiers manned the battlements and hundreds more teemed within the courtyard. The only way to enter the courtyard on the ground was through a wide, arched passageway in the curtain wall, which was closed off by both an iron portcullis and a set of thick oaken doors.

718

Several thousand of the Varden stood pressed against the curtain wall, striving to break through the portcullis with the battering ram they had brought from the main gate of the city or else to surmount the walls with grappling hooks and ladders, which the defenders kept pushing away. Flocks of whining arrows arched back and forth over the wall. Neither side seemed to have the advantage.

The gate! said Eragon, pointing.

Saphira swept down from on high and cleared the parapet above the portcullis with a jet of billowing fire, smoke venting from her nostrils. She dropped onto the top of the wall, jarring Eragon, and said, Go. *I'll see to the catapults before they start lobbing rocks at the Varden.*

Be careful. He lowered himself to the parapet from her back.

It is they *who must be careful!* she replied. She snarled at the pikemen gathering around the catapults. Half of them turned and fled inside.

The wall was too high for Eragon to comfortably jump to the street below, so Saphira draped her tail over the side and wedged it between two merlons. Eragon sheathed Brisingr, then climbed down, using the spikes on her tail like rungs on a ladder. When he reached the tip, he released his hold and fell the remaining twenty feet. He rolled to lessen the impact as he landed amid the press of Varden.

"Greetings, Shadeslayer," said Blödhgarm, emerging from the crowd, along with the eleven other elves.

"Greetings." Eragon drew Brisingr again. "Why haven't you already opened the gate for the Varden?"

"The gate is protected by many spells, Shadeslayer. It would require much strength to break and shatter. My companions and I are here to protect you and Saphira, and we cannot fulfill our duty if we exhaust ourselves on other tasks."

Biting back a curse, Eragon said, "Would you rather Saphira and I exhaust ourselves, Blödhgarm? Will that make us safer?"

The elf stared at Eragon for a moment, his yellow eyes inscrutable, then he bowed his head slightly. "We shall open the gate at once, Shadeslayer."

"No, don't," growled Eragon. "Wait here."

Eragon pushed his way to the front of the Varden and strode toward the lowered portcullis. "Give me room!" he shouted, gesturing at the warriors. The Varden backed away from him, forming an open area twenty feet across. A javelin shot from a ballista glanced off his wards and flew spinning down a side street. Saphira roared from inside the courtyard, and there came the sounds of timbers breaking and of taut rope snapping in twain.

Grasping his sword with both hands, Eragon lifted it overhead and shouted, "Brisingr!" The blade burst into blue fire, and the warriors behind him uttered exclamations of amazement. Eragon stepped forward then and smote one of the crossbars of the portcullis. A blinding flash lit the wall and surrounding buildings as the sword sliced through the thick piece of metal. At the same time,

Eragon noticed a sudden increase in his fatigue as Brisingr severed the wards protecting the portcullis. He smiled. As he had hoped, the spells of countermagic with which Rhunön had imbued Brisingr were more than sufficient to defeat the enchantments.

Moving at a quick but steady pace, Eragon cut as large a hole as he could in the portcullis, then stood aside as the loose piece of grating fell flat onto the stones of the street with a discordant clang. He stepped past the grating and walked forward to the oaken doors recessed farther within the curtain wall. He aligned Brisingr with the hairline crack between the two doors, put his weight behind the sword, and pushed the blade through the narrow gap and out the other side. Then he increased the flow of energy to the fire blazing around the blade until it was hot enough to burn its way through the dense wood as easily as a knife cuts through fresh bread. Copious amounts of smoke billowed from around the blade, making his throat sting and his eyes smart.

Eragon worked the sword upward, burning through the immense wooden beam that barred the doors shut from the inside. As soon as he felt the resistance against Brisingr's blade lessen, he withdrew the sword and extinguished the flame. He wore thick gloves, so he did not shrink from grasping the glowing edges of one door and pulling it open with a mighty heave. The other door also swung outward, seemingly of its own accord, although a moment later, Eragon saw that it was Saphira who had pushed it open; she sat to the right of the entryway, peering at him with sparkling sapphire eyes. Behind her, the four catapults lay in ruins.

Eragon went to stand with Saphira as the Varden poured into the courtyard, filling the air with their clamorous battle-cries. Exhausted by his efforts, Eragon placed a hand over the belt of Beloth the Wise and bolstered his flagging strength with some of the energy he had stored within the twelve diamonds hidden inside the belt. He offered the rest of it to Saphira, who was equally tired, but she declined, saying, *Keep it for yourself. You haven't that much left. Besides, what I really need is a meal and a full night's sleep.*

Eragon leaned against her and allowed his eyelids to drift halfway closed. *Soon*, he said. *Soon this will all be over.*

I hope so, she replied.

Among the warriors who streamed past was Angela, garbed in her strange, flanged armor of green and black and carrying her hûthvír, the double-bladed staff weapon of the dwarf priests. The herbalist paused next to Eragon and, with an impish expression, said, "An impressive display, but don't you think you're overdoing it a bit?"

"What do you mean?" asked Eragon, frowning.

She lifted an eyebrow. "Come now, was it really necessary to set your sword on fire?"

Eragon's expression cleared as he understood her objection. He laughed. "Not for the portcullis, no, but I enjoyed it. Besides, I can't help it. I named the sword *Fire* in the ancient language, and every time I say the word, the blade flares up like a branch of dry wood in a bonfire."

"You named your sword Fire?" Angela exclaimed with a note of incredulity. "Fire? What kind of a boring name is that? You might as well name your sword Blazing Blade and be done with it. Fire indeed. Humph. Wouldn't you rather have a sword called Sheepbiter or Chrysanthemum Cleaver or something else with imagination?"

"I already have one Sheepbiter here," said Eragon, and laid a hand on Saphira. "Why would I need another?"

Angela broke out into a wide smile. "So you're not entirely devoid of wit after all! There just might be hope for you." And she danced off toward the keep, twirling her double-bladed staff by her side and muttering, "Fire? Bah!"

A soft growl emanated from Saphira, and she said, *Be careful whom you call Sheepbiter, Eragon, or you might get bitten yourself.*

Yes, Saphira.

SHADOW OF DOOM

y then, Blödhgarm and his fellow elves had joined Eragon and Saphira in the courtyard, but Eragon ignored them and looked for Arya. When he spotted her, running alongside Jörmundur on his charger, Eragon hailed her and brandished his shield to attract her attention.

Arya heeded his call and loped over, her stride as graceful as a gazelle's. She had acquired a shield, a full-sized helm, and a mail hauberk since they had parted, and the metal of her armor gleamed in the gray half-light that pervaded the city. As she drew to a stop, Eragon said, "Saphira and I are going to enter the keep from above and try to capture Lady Lorana. Do you want to come with us?"

Arya agreed with a terse nod.

Springing from the ground onto one of Saphira's front legs, Eragon climbed into her saddle. Arya followed his example an instant later and sat close behind him, the links of her hauberk pressing against his back.

Saphira unfurled her velvety wings and took flight, leaving Blödhgarm and the other elves gazing up at her with looks of frustration.

"You should not abandon your guards so lightly," Arya murmured in Eragon's left ear. She wrapped her sword arm around his waist and held him tightly as Saphira wheeled above the courtyard.

Before Eragon could respond, he felt the touch of Glaedr's vast mind. For a moment, the city below vanished, and he saw and felt only what Glaedr saw and felt.

Little-stinging-hornet-arrows bounced off his belly as he rose above the scattered wood-caves of the two-legs-round-ears. The air was smooth and firm beneath his wings, perfect for the flying he would need to do. On his back, the saddle rubbed against his scales as Oromis altered his position.

Glaedr flicked his tongue out and tasted the enticing aroma of burnt-wood-cooked-meat-spilled-blood. He had been to this place many times before. In his youth, it had been known by a different name than Gil'ead, and then the only inhabitants had been the somber-laughing-quick-tongued-elves and the friends of elves. His previous visits had always been pleasant, but it pained him to remember the two nest-mates who had died here, slain by the twisted-mind-Forsworn.

The lazy-one-eye-sun hovered just above the horizon. To the north, the big-water-Isenstar was a rippling sheet of polished silver. Below, the herd of pointed-ears commanded by Islanzadí was arrayed around the broken-anthill-city. Their armor glittered like crushed ice. A pall of blue smoke lay over the whole area, thick as cold morning mist.

And from the south, the small-angry-rip-claw-Thorn winged his way toward Gil'ead, bellowing his challenge for all to hear. Morzan-son-Murtagh sat upon his back, and in Murtagh's right hand, Zar'roc shone as bright as a nail.

Sorrow filled Glaedr as he beheld the two miserable hatchlings. He wished he and Oromis did not have to kill them. Once more, he thought, dragon must fight dragon and Rider must fight Rider, and all because of that egg-breaker-Galbatorix. His mood grim, Glaedr quickened his flapping and spread his claws in preparation for tearing at his oncoming foes.

Eragon's head whipped on his neck as Saphira lurched to one side and dropped a score of feet before she regained her equilibrium. *Did you see that as well?* she asked.

I did. Worried, Eragon glanced back at the saddlebags, where Glaedr's heart of hearts was hidden, and wondered if he and Saphira should try to help Oromis and Glaedr but then reassured himself with the knowledge that there were numerous spellcasters among the elves. His teachers would not want for assistance.

"What is wrong?" asked Arya, her voice loud in Eragon's ear.

Oromis and Glaedr are about to fight Thorn and Murtagh, said Saphira.

Eragon felt Arya stiffen against him. "How do you know?" she asked.

"I'll explain later. I just hope they don't get hurt."

"As do I," said Arya.

Saphira flew high above the keep, then floated downward on silent wings and alighted upon the spire of the tallest tower. As Eragon and Arya clambered onto the steep roof, Saphira said, *I will meet you in the chamber below. The window here is too small for me.* And she took off, the gusts from her wings buffeting them.

Eragon and Arya lowered themselves over the edge of the roof and dropped to a narrow stone ledge eight feet below. Ignoring the vertigo-inducing fall that awaited him if he slipped, Eragon inched along the ledge to a cross-shaped window, where he pulled himself into a large square room lined with sheaves of quarrels and racks of heavy crossbows. If anyone had been in the room when Saphira landed, they had already fled.

Arya climbed through the window after him. She inspected the room, then gestured at the stairs in the far corner and padded toward them, her leather boots silent on the stone floor.

As Eragon followed her, he sensed a strange confluence of energies below them and also the minds of five people whose thoughts were closed to him. Wary of a mental attack, Eragon withdrew into himself and concentrated upon reciting a scrap of elvish poetry. He touched Arya on the shoulder and whispered, "Do you feel that?"

She nodded. "We should have brought Blödhgarm with us."

Together, they descended the stairs, making every effort to be quiet. The next room in the tower was much larger than the last; the ceiling was over thirty feet high, and from it hung a lantern with faceted panes of glass. A yellow flame burned inside. Hundreds of oil paintings covered the walls: portraits of bearded men in ornate robes and expressionless women sitting amid children with sharp, flat teeth; gloomy, windswept seascapes depicting the drowning of sailors; and scenes of battle, where humans slaughtered bands of grotesque Urgals. A row of tall wooden shutters set within the northern wall opened onto a balcony with a stone balustrade. Opposite the window, near the far wall, was a collection of small round tables littered with scrolls, three padded chairs, and two oversized brass urns filled with bouquets of dried flowers. A stout, gray-haired woman garbed in a lavender dress sat in one of the chairs. She bore a strong resemblance to several of the men in the paintings. A silver diadem adorned with jade and topaz rested upon her head.

In the center of the room stood the three magicians Eragon had glimpsed before in the city. The two men and a woman were facing each other, the hoods of their robes thrown back and their arms extended out to each side, so that the tips of their fingers touched. They swayed in unison, murmuring an unfamiliar spell in the ancient language. A fourth person sat in the middle of the triangle they formed: a man garbed in an identical fashion, but who said nothing, and who grimaced as if in pain.

Eragon threw himself at the mind of one of the male spellcasters, but the man was so focused on his task, Eragon failed to gain entry to his consciousness and thus was unable to subordinate him to his will. The man did not even seem to notice the attack. Arya must have attempted the same thing, for she frowned and whispered, "They were trained well."

"Do you know what they are doing?" he murmured.

She shook her head.

Then the woman in the lavender dress looked up and saw Eragon and Arya crouched upon the stone stairs. To Eragon's surprise, the woman did not call for help but rather placed a finger upon her lips, then beckoned.

Eragon exchanged a perplexed glance with Arya. "It could be a trap," he whispered.

"It most likely is," she said.

"What should we do?"

"Is Saphira almost here?"

"Yes."

"Then let us go and greet our host."

Matching their steps, they padded down the remaining stairs and snuck across the room, never taking their eyes off the engrossed magicians. "Are you Lady Lorana?" asked Arya in a soft voice as they halted before the seated woman.

The woman inclined her head. "That I am, fair elf." She turned her gaze upon Eragon then and said, "And are you the Dragon Rider of whom we have heard so much about recently? Are you Eragon Shadeslayer?"

"I am," said Eragon.

A relieved expression appeared upon the woman's distinguished face. "Ah, I had hoped you would come. You must stop them, Shadeslayer." And she gestured at the magicians.

"Why don't you order them to surrender?" whispered Eragon.

"I cannot," said Lorana. "They answer only to the king and his new Rider. I have sworn myself to Galbatorix—I had no choice in the matter—so I cannot raise a hand against him or his servants; otherwise, I would have arranged their destruction myself."

"Why?" asked Arya. "What is it you fear so much?"

The skin around Lorana's eyes tightened. "They know they cannot hope to drive off the Varden as they are, and Galbatorix has not sent reinforcements to our aid. So they are attempting, I do not know how, to create a Shade in the hope that the monster will turn against the Varden and spread sorrow and confusion throughout your ranks."

Horror enveloped Eragon. He could not imagine having to fight another Durza. "But a Shade might just as easily turn against them and everyone else in Feinster as it would against the Varden."

Lorana nodded. "They do not care. They only wish to cause as much pain and destruction as they can before they die. They are insane, Shadeslayer. Please, you must stop them, for the sake of my people!"

As she finished speaking, Saphira landed upon the balcony outside the room, cracking the balustrade with her tail. She knocked aside the shutters with a single blow of her paw, breaking their frames like so much tinder, and then pushed her head and shoulders into the chamber and growled.

The magicians continued to chant, seemingly oblivious to her presence.

"Oh my," said Lady Lorana, gripping the arms of her chair.

"Right," said Eragon. He hefted Brisingr and started toward the magicians, as did Saphira from the opposite direction.

The world reeled around Eragon, and again he found himself peering through Glaedr's eyes.

Red. Black. Flashes of throbbing yellow. Pain . . . Bone-bending pain in his belly and in the shoulder of his left wing. Pain as he had not felt for over a hundred years. Then relief as partner-of-his-life-Oromis healed his injuries.

Glaedr regained his balance and looked for Thorn. The little-red-shrike-dragon was stronger and faster than Glaedr had anticipated, due to Galbatorix's meddling.

Thorn slammed into Glaedr's left side, his weak side, where he had lost his foreleg. They spun around each other, plummeting toward the hard-flat-wing-crushing-ground. Glaedr snapped and tore and raked with his hind feet, trying to batter the smaller dragon into submission.

You will not best me, youngling, he vowed to himself. I was old before you were born.

White-dagger-claws scratched Glaedr along his ribs and underside. He flexed his tail and struck snarling-long-fang-Thorn across one leg, stabbing him in the thigh with a spike on his tail. The fighting had long since exhausted both of their invisible-spell-shields, leaving them vulnerable to every sort of wound.

When the twirling ground was only a few thousand feet away, Glaedr inhaled and drew back his head. He tightened his neck, clenched his belly, and drew forth the dense-liquid-of-fire from deep within his gut. The liquid ignited as it combined with the air in his throat. He opened his jaws to their full extent and sprayed the red dragon with fire, engulfing him in a blistering cocoon. The torrent of hungry-grasping-writhing-flames tickled the inside of Glaedr's cheeks.

He closed off his throat, terminating the flow of fire as he and the squirming-squealing-slash-claw-dragon pulled away from each other. From on his back, Glaedr heard Oromis say, "Their strength is fading; I can see it in their bearing. Another few minutes and Murtagh's concentration shall fail and I will be able to assume control over his thoughts. That or we shall slay them with sword and fang."

Glaedr growled in agreement, frustrated that he and Oromis dared not communicate with their minds, as they usually did. Rising on warm-wind-from-tilled-earth, he turned toward Thorn, whose limbs dripped with crimson blood, and roared and prepared to grapple with him once more.

Eragon stared at the ceiling, disoriented. He was lying on his back within the keep tower. Kneeling next to him was Arya, concern etched upon her face. She grasped him by an arm and helped him upright, steadying him as he wobbled. Across the room, Eragon saw Saphira shake her head, and he felt her own confusion.

The three magicians still stood with their arms outstretched, swaying and chanting in the ancient language. The words of their spell rang with unusual force and lingered in the air long after they should have faded to silence. The man who sat at their feet gripped his knees, his entire body shuddering as he thrashed his head from side to side.

"What happened?" asked Arya in a strained undertone. She pulled Eragon closer and lowered her voice even further. "How can you know what Glaedr is thinking from so far away, and when his mind is closed even to Oromis? Forgive me for touching your thoughts without your permission, Eragon, but I was worried about your welfare. What sort of a bond do you and Saphira share with Glaedr?"

"Later," he said, and squared his shoulders.

"Did Oromis give you an amulet or some other trinket that allows you to contact Glaedr?"

"It would take too long to explain. Later, I promise."

Arya hesitated, then nodded and said, "I shall hold you to that."

Together, Eragon, Saphira, and Arya advanced toward the magicians and struck at a separate one each. A metallic peal filled the room as Brisingr glanced aside before it reached its intended target, wrenching Eragon's shoulder. Likewise, Arya's sword rebounded off a ward, as did Saphira's right front paw. Her claws screeched against the stone floor.

"Concentrate on this one!" Eragon shouted, and pointed at the tallest spellcaster, a pale man with a snarled beard. "Hurry, before they manage to summon any spirits!" Eragon or Arya could have attempted to circumvent or deplete the spellcasters' wards with spells of their own, but using magic against another magician was always a perilous proposition unless the magician's mind was under your control. Neither Eragon nor Arya wanted to risk being killed by a ward they were as yet ignorant of.

Attacking in turns, Eragon, Saphira, and Arya cut, stabbed, and battered at the bearded spellcaster for nearly a minute. None of their blows touched the man. Then, at last, after only the slightest hint of resistance, Eragon felt something give way beneath Brisingr, and the sword continued on its way and lopped off the spellcaster's head. The air in front of Eragon shimmered. At the same instant, he felt a sudden drain on his strength as his wards defended him from an unknown spell. The assault ceased after a few seconds, leaving him dizzy and light-headed. His stomach rumbled. He grimaced and fortified himself with energy from the belt of Beloth the Wise.

The only response the other two magicians evinced at the death of their companion was to increase the speed of their invocation.

Yellow foam encrusted the corners of their mouths, and spittle flew from their lips, and the whites of their eyes showed, but still they made no attempt to flee or to attack.

Continuing on to the next spellcaster—a corpulent man with rings on his thumbs—Eragon, Saphira, and Arya repeated the process they had used on the first magician: alternating blows until they succeeded in wearing down his wards. It was Saphira who slew the man, knocking him through the air with a swipe of her claws. He hit the side of the staircase and cracked open his skull on the corner of a step. This time there was no magical retaliation.

As Eragon moved toward the female spellcaster, a cluster of multicolored lights hurtled into the room through the broken shutters and converged upon the man seated on the floor. The glowing spirits flashed with angry virulence as they whirled around the man, forming an impenetrable wall. He threw up his arms as if to shield himself and screamed. The air hummed and crackled with the energy that radiated from the flickering orbs. A sour, ironlike taste coated Eragon's tongue, and his skin prickled. The hair on the female spellcaster's head was standing on end. Across from her, Saphira hissed and arched her back, every muscle in her body rigid.

A bolt of fear shot through Eragon. *No!* he thought, feeling sick. *Not now. Not after all we've gone through.* He was stronger than he had been when he faced Durza in Tronjheim, but if anything, he was even more aware of just how dangerous a Shade could be. Only three warriors had ever survived the killing of a Shade: Laetrí the Elf, Irnstad the Rider, and himself—and he had no confidence he could duplicate the feat. *Blödhgarm, where are you?* Eragon shouted with his mind. *We need your help!*

And then everything around Eragon winked out of existence, and in its place he beheld:

Whiteness. Blank whiteness. The cold-soft-sky-water was soothing against Glaedr's limbs after the stifling heat of combat. He lapped at the air, welcoming the thin coat of moisture that accumulated on his dry-sticky-tongue.

He flapped once more and the sky-water parted before him, revealing the glaring-scorchback-sun and the hazy-green-brown-earth. Where is he? Glaedr wondered. He swung his head, looking for Thorn. The little-red-shrike-dragon had fled high above Gil'ead, higher than any bird normally flew, where the air was thin and one's breath water-smoked.

"Glaedr, behind us!" Oromis shouted.

Glaedr twisted, but he was too slow. The red dragon crashed into his right shoulder, knocking him tumbling. Snarling, Glaedr wrapped his single remaining foreleg around the nipping-scratching-ferocious-hatchling and strove to crush the life out of Thorn's squirming body. The red dragon bellowed and climbed halfway out of Glaedr's embrace, digging his claws into Glaedr's chest. Glaedr arched his neck and sank his teeth into Thorn's left hind leg and, with it, held him in place, although the red dragon writhed and kicked like a pinned wildcat. Hot-salty-blood filled Glaedr's mouth.

As they plummeted downward, Glaedr heard the sound of swords striking shields as Oromis and Murtagh exchanged a flurry of blows. Thorn convulsed, and Glaedr glimpsed Morzan-son-Murtagh. Glaedr thought the human appeared frightened, but he was not entirely sure. Even after so long bonded with Oromis, he still had difficulty deciphering the expressions of two-legs-no-horns, what with their soft, flat faces and their lack of tails.

The clanging of metal ceased, and Murtagh shouted, "Curse you for not showing yourself sooner! Curse you! You could have helped us! You could have—" Murtagh seemed to choke on his tongue for a moment.

Glaedr grunted as an unseen force brought their fall to an abrupt halt, nearly shaking him loose from Thorn's leg, and then lifted the four of them up through the sky, higher and higher, until the broken-anthill-city was only a faint blotch below and even Glaedr had difficulty breathing in the rarefied air.

What is the youngling doing? Glaedr wondered, concerned. Is he trying to kill himself?

Then Murtagh resumed speaking, and when he did, his voice was richer and deeper than before, and it echoed as if he were standing in an empty hall. Glaedr felt the scales on his shoulders crawl as he recognized the voice of their ancient foe.

"So you survived, Oromis, Glaedr," said Galbatorix. His words were round and smooth, like those of a practiced orator, and their tone was deceptively friendly. "Long have I thought that the elves might be hiding a dragon or a Rider from my sight. It is gratifying to have my suspicions confirmed."

"Begone, foul oath-breaker!" cried Oromis. "You shall not have any satisfaction from us!"

Galbatorix chuckled. "Such a harsh greeting. For shame, Oromis-elda. Have the elves forgotten their fabled courtesy over the past century?"

"You deserve no more courtesy than a rabid wolf."

"Tut-tut, Oromis. Remember what you said to me when I stood before you and the other Elders: 'Anger is a poison. You must purge it from your mind or else it will corrupt your better nature.' You should heed your own advice."

"You cannot confuse me with your snake's tongue, Galbatorix. You are an abomination, and we shall see to it that you are eliminated, even if it costs us our lives."

"But why should it, Oromis? Why should you pit yourself against me? It saddens me that you have allowed your hate to distort your wisdom, for you were wise once, Oromis, perhaps the wisest member of our entire order. You were the first to recognize the madness eating away at my soul, and it was you who convinced the other Elders to deny my request for another dragon egg. That was very wise of you, Oromis. Futile, but wise. And somehow you managed to escape from Kialandí and Formora, even after they had broken you, and then you hid until all but one of your enemies had died. That too was wise of you, elf."

A brief pause marked Galbatorix's speech. "There is no need to continue fighting me. I freely admit that I committed terrible crimes in my youth, but those days are long past, and when I reflect upon the blood I have shed, it torments my conscience. Still, what would you have of me? I cannot undo my deeds. Now, my greatest concern is ensuring the peace and prosperity of the empire over which I find myself lord and master. Cannot you see that I have lost my thirst for vengeance? The rage that drove me for so many years has burned itself to ashes. Ask yourself this, Oromis: who is responsible for the war that has swept across Alagaësia? Not I. The Varden were the ones who provoked this conflict. I would have been content to rule my people and leave the elves and the dwarves and the Surdans to their own devices. But the Varden could not leave well enough alone. It was they who chose to steal Saphira's egg, and they who cover the earth with mountains of corpses. Not I. You were wise once before, Oromis, and you can become wise once again. Give up your hatred and join me in Ilirea. With you by my side, we can bring an end to this conflict and usher in an era of peace that will endure for a thousand years or more."

Glaedr was not persuaded. He tightened his crushing-piercing-jaws, causing Thorn to yowl. The pain-noise seemed incredibly loud after Galbatorix's speech.

In clear, ringing tones, Oromis said, "No. You cannot make us forget your atrocities with a balm of honeyed lies. Release us! You have not the means to hold us here much longer, and I refuse to exchange pointless banter with a traitor like yourself."

"Bah! You are a senile old fool," said Galbatorix, and his voice acquired a harsh, angry cast. "You should have accepted my offer; you would have been first and foremost among my slaves. I will make you regret your mindless devotion to your so-called justice. And you are wrong. I can keep you thus as long as I want, for I have become as powerful as a god, and there are none who can stop me!"

"You shall not prevail," said Oromis. "Even gods do not endure forever."

At that Galbatorix uttered a foul oath. "Your philosophy does not constrain me, elf! I am the greatest of magicians, and soon I will be even greater still. Death will not take me. You, however, shall die. But first you will suffer. You will both suffer beyond imagining, and then I will kill you, Oromis, and I shall take your heart of hearts, Glaedr, and you will serve me until the end of time."

"Never!" exclaimed Oromis.

And Glaedr again heard the clash of swords on armor.

Glaedr had excluded Oromis from his mind for the duration of the fight, but their bond ran deeper than conscious thought, so he felt it when Oromis stiffened, incapacitated by the searing pain of his bone-blight-nerve-rot. Alarmed, Glaedr released Thorn's leg and tried to kick the red dragon away. Thorn howled at the impact but remained where he was. Galbatorix's spell held the two of them in place—neither able to move more than a few feet in any direction.

There was another metallic clang from above, and then Glaedr saw Naegling fall past him. The golden sword flashed and gleamed as it tumbled toward the ground. For the first time, the cold claw of fear gripped Glaedr. Most of Oromis's word-will-energy was stored within the sword, and his wards were bound to the blade. Without it, he would be defenseless.

Glaedr threw himself against the limits of Galbatorix's spell, struggling with all his might to break free. In spite of his efforts, however, he could not escape. And just as Oromis began to recover, Glaedr felt Zar'roc slash Oromis from shoulder to hip.

Glaedr howled.

He howled as Oromis had howled when Glaedr lost his leg.

An inexorable force gathered inside of Glaedr's belly. Without pausing to consider whether it was possible, he pushed Thorn and Murtagh away with a blast of magic, sending them flying like windblown leaves, and then tucked his wings against his sides and dove toward Gil'ead. If he could get there fast enough, then Islanzadí and her spellcasters would be able to save Oromis.

The city was too far away, though. Oromis's consciousness was faltering . . . fading . . . slipping away. . . .

Glaedr poured his own strength into Oromis's ruined frame, trying to sustain him until they reached the ground. But for all the energy he gave to Oromis, he could not stop the bleeding, the terrible bleeding.

Glaedr . . . release me, Oromis murmured with his mind.

A moment later, in an even fainter voice, he whispered, Do not mourn me.

And then the partner of Glaedr's life passed into the void.

Gone.

Gone!

GONE!

Blackness. Emptiness.

He was alone.

A crimson haze descended over the world, throbbing in unison with his pulse. He flared his wings and looped back the way he had come, searching for Thorn and his Rider. He would not let them escape; he would catch them and tear at them and burn them until he had eradicated them from the world.

Glaedr saw the red-shrike-dragon diving toward him, and he roared his grief and redoubled his speed. The red dragon swerved at the last moment, in an attempt to flank him, but he was not fast enough to evade Glaedr, who lunged and snapped and bit off the last three feet of the red dragon's tail. A fountain of blood sprayed from the stump. Yelping in agony, the red dragon wriggled away and darted behind Glaedr. Glaedr started to twist around to face him, but the smaller dragon was too quick, too nimble. Glaedr felt a sharp pain at the base of his skull, and then his vision flickered and failed.

Where was he?

He was alone.

He was alone and in the dark.

He was alone and in the dark, and he could not move or see.

He could feel the minds of other creatures close by, but they were not the minds of Thorn and Murtagh but of Arya, Eragon, and Saphira.

And then Glaedr realized where he was, and the true horror of the situation broke upon him, and he howled into the darkness. He howled and he howled, and he abandoned himself to his agony, not caring what the future might bring, for Oromis was dead, and he was alone.

Alone!

With a start, Eragon returned to himself.

He was curled into a ball. Tears streaked his face. Gasping, he pushed himself up off the floor and looked for Saphira and Arya.

It took him a moment to comprehend what he saw.

The female spellcaster Eragon had been about to attack lay before him, slain by a single sword thrust. The spirits she and her companions had summoned were nowhere to be seen. Lady Lorana was still ensconced in her chair. Saphira was in the process of struggling to her feet on the opposite side of the room. And the man who had been sitting on the floor amid the three other spellcasters was standing next to him, holding Arya in the air by her throat.

The color had vanished from the man's skin, leaving him bone white. His hair, which had been brown, was now bright crimson, and when he looked at Eragon and smiled, Eragon saw that his eyes had become maroon. In every aspect of appearance and bearing, the man resembled Durza.

"Our name is Varaug," said the Shade. "Fear us." Arya kicked at him, but her blows seemed to have no effect.

The burning pressure of the Shade's consciousness pressed against Eragon's mind, trying to break down his defenses. The force of the attack immobilized Eragon; he could barely repel the burrowing tendrils of the Shade's mind, much less walk or swing a sword. For whatever reason, Varaug was even stronger than Durza, and Eragon was not sure how long he could withstand the Shade's might. He saw that Saphira was also under attack; she sat stiff and motionless by the balcony, a snarl carved on her face.

The veins in Arya's forehead bulged, and her face turned red and purple. Her mouth was open, but she was not breathing. With the palm of her right hand, she struck the Shade's locked elbow and broke the joint with a loud crack. Varaug's arm sagged, and for a moment, Arya's toes brushed the floor, but then the bones in the Shade's arm popped back into place, and he lifted her even higher.

"You shall die," growled Varaug. "You shall all die for imprisoning us in this cold, hard clay."

Knowing that Arya's and Saphira's lives were in peril stripped Eragon of every emotion, save that of implacable determination. His thoughts as sharp and clear as a shard of glass, he drove himself at the Shade's seething consciousness. Varaug was too powerful, and the spirits that resided within him too disparate, for Eragon to overwhelm and control, so Eragon sought to isolate the Shade. He surrounded Varaug's mind with his own: every time Varaug attempted to reach out toward Saphira or Arya, Eragon blocked the mental ray, and every time the Shade attempted to shift his body, Eragon counteracted the urge with a command of his own.

They battled at the speed of thought, fighting back and forth along the perimeter of the Shade's mind, which was a landscape so jumbled and incoherent, Eragon feared it would drive him mad if he gazed at it for long. Eragon pushed himself to the utmost as he dueled with Varaug, striving to anticipate the Shade's every move, but he knew that their contest could only end with his own defeat. As fast as he was, Eragon could not outthink the numerous intelligences contained within the Shade.

Eragon's concentration eventually wavered, and Varaug seized upon the opportunity to force himself further into Eragon's mind, trapping him . . . transfixing him . . . suppressing his thoughts until Eragon could do no more than stare at the Shade with dumb rage. An excruciating tingling filled Eragon's limbs as the spirits raced through his body, coursing down every one of his nerves.

"Your ring is full of light!" exclaimed Varaug, his eyes widening with pleasure. "Beautiful light! It will feed us for a long time!"

Then he growled with anger as Arya grabbed his wrist and broke it in three places. She twisted free of Varaug's grip before he could heal himself and dropped to the ground, gasping for air. Varaug kicked at her, but she rolled out of the way. She reached for her fallen sword.

Eragon trembled as he struggled to cast off the Shade's oppressive presence.

Arya's hand closed around the hilt of her sword. A wordless bellow escaped the Shade. He pounced on her, and they rolled across the floor, wrestling for control of the weapon. Arya shouted and struck Varaug in the side of his head with the pommel of the sword.

The Shade went limp for an instant, and Arya scrambled backward, pushing herself upright.

In a flash, Eragon freed himself from Varaug. Without consideration for his own safety, he resumed his attack on the Shade's consciousness, his only thought to restrain the Shade for a few moments.

Varaug rose onto one knee, then faltered as Eragon redoubled his efforts.

"Get him!" Eragon shouted.

Arya lunged forward, her dark hair flying. . . .

And she stabbed the Shade through his heart.

Eragon winced and extricated himself from Varaug's mind even as the Shade recoiled from Arya, pulling himself off her blade. The Shade opened his mouth and uttered a piercing, dithering wail that shattered the panes of glass in the lantern above. He reached out toward Arya and tottered in her direction, then stopped as his skin faded and became transparent, revealing the dozens of glittering spirits trapped within the confines of his flesh. The spirits throbbed, growing in size, and Varaug's skin split along the bellies of his muscles. With a final burst of light, the spirits tore Varaug apart and fled the tower room, passing through the walls as if the stone were insubstantial.

Eragon's pulse gradually slowed. Then, feeling very old and very tired, he walked over to Arya, who stood leaning against a chair, cupping the front of her neck with a hand. She coughed, spitting up blood. Since she seemed incapable of talking, Eragon placed his hand over hers and said, "Waíse heill." As the energy to mend her injuries flowed out of him, Eragon's legs weakened, and he had to brace himself against the chair.

"Better?" he asked as the spell finished its work.

"Better," Arya whispered, and favored him with a weak smile. She motioned toward where Varaug had been. "We killed him. . . . We killed him, and yet we did not die." She sounded surprised. "So few have ever killed a Shade and lived."

"That is because they fought alone, not together, like us."

"No, not like us."

"I had you to help me in Farthen Dûr, and you had me to help you here."

"Yes."

"Now I shall have to call *you* Shadeslayer."

"We are both—"

Saphira startled them by loosing a long, mournful keen. Still keening, she raked her claws across the floor, chipping and scratching the stones. Her tail whipped from side to side, smashing the furniture and the grim paintings on the walls. *Gone!* she said. *Gone! Gone forever!*

"Saphira, what's wrong?" exclaimed Arya. When Saphira did not answer, Arya repeated the question to Eragon.

Hating the words he spoke, Eragon said, "Oromis and Glaedr are dead. Galbatorix killed them."

Arya staggered as if she had been hit. "Ah," she said. She gripped the back of the chair so hard, her knuckles turned white. Tears filled her slanted eyes, then spilled over onto her cheeks and coursed down her face. "Eragon." She reached out and grasped his shoulder, and almost by accident, he found himself holding her in his arms. Eragon felt his own eyes grow wet. He clenched his jaw in an effort to maintain his composure; if he started crying, he knew he would not be able to stop.

He and Arya remained locked together for a long while, consoling each other, then Arya withdrew and said, "How did it happen?"

"Oromis had one of his seizures, and while he was paralyzed, Galbatorix used Murtagh to—" Eragon's voice broke, and he shook his head. "I'll tell you about it along with Nasuada. She should know about this, and I don't want to have to describe it more than once."

Arya nodded. "Then let us go and see her."

SUNRISE

As Eragon and Arya escorted Lady Lorana down from the room in the tower, they encountered Blödhgarm and the eleven other elves running up the staircase four steps at a time.

"Shadeslayer! Arya!" exclaimed a female elf with long black hair. "Are you hurt? We heard Saphira's lament, and we thought one of you might have died."

Eragon glanced at Arya. His oath of secrecy to Queen Islanzadí would not allow him to discuss Oromis or Glaedr while in the presence of anyone not from Du Weldenvarden—such as Lady Lorana—without permission from the queen, Arya, or whoever might succeed Islanzadí to the knotted throne in Ellesméra.

She nodded and said, "I release you from your vow, Eragon, both of you. Speak of them to whomever you choose."

"No, we are not hurt," Eragon said. "However, Oromis and Glaedr have just died, slain in battle over Gil'ead."

As one, the elves cried out in shock and then began to ply Eragon with dozens of questions. Arya raised a hand and said, "Restrain yourselves. Now is not the time or place to satisfy your curiosity. There are still soldiers about, and we do not know who might be listening. Keep your sorrow hidden within your hearts until we are safe and secure." She paused and looked at Eragon, then said, "I will explain the full circumstances of their deaths to you once I know them myself."

"Nen ono weohnata, Arya Dröttningu," they murmured.

"Did you hear my call?" Eragon asked Blödhgarm.

"I did," the fur-covered elf said. "We came as fast as we could, but there were many soldiers between there and here."

Eragon twisted his hand over his chest in the elves' traditional gesture of respect. "I apologize for leaving you behind, Blödhgarm-elda. The heat of battle made me foolish and overconfident, and we nearly died because of my mistake."

"You need not apologize, Shadeslayer. We too made a mistake today, one which I promise we shall not repeat. From now on, we will fight alongside you and the Varden without reserve."

Together, they all trooped down the stairs to the courtyard outside. The Varden had killed or captured most of the soldiers within the keep, and the few men who were still fighting surrendered once they saw that Lady Lorana was in the custody of the Varden. Since the stairwell was too small for her, Saphira had descended by wing to the courtyard and was waiting for them when they arrived.

Eragon stood with Saphira, Arya, and Lady Lorana while one of the Varden fetched Jörmundur. When Jörmundur joined them, they informed him of what had happened within the tower—which amazed him greatly—and then gave over Lady Lorana to his custody.

Jörmundur bowed to her. "You may rest assured, Lady, we shall treat you with the respect and dignity due your station. We may be your enemies, but we are still civilized men."

"Thank you," she replied. "I am relieved to hear it. However, my main concern now is for the safety of my subjects. If I might, I would like to speak with your leader, Nasuada, about her plans for them."

"I believe she wishes to speak with you as well."

As they parted, Lady Lorana said, "I am most grateful to you, elf, and to you as well, Dragon Rider, for killing that monster before he could wreak sorrow and destruction upon Feinster. Fate has placed us on opposite sides of this conflict, but that does not mean I cannot admire your bravery and prowess. We may never meet again, so fare thee well, both of you."

Eragon bowed and said, "Fare thee well, Lady Lorana."

"May the stars watch over you," said Arya.

Blödhgarm and the elves under his command accompanied

Eragon, Saphira, and Arya as they searched Feinster for Nasuada. They found her riding her stallion through the gray streets, inspecting the damage to the city.

Nasuada greeted Eragon and Saphira with evident relief. "I'm glad you have finally returned. We've needed you here these past few days. I see you have a new sword, Eragon, a Dragon Rider's sword. Did the elves give it to you?"

"In an indirect way, yes." Eragon eyed the various people standing nearby and lowered his voice. "Nasuada, we must talk with you alone. It's important."

"Very well." Nasuada studied the buildings that lined the street, then pointed at a house that appeared abandoned. "Let us talk in there."

Two of Nasuada's guards, the Nighthawks, ran forward and entered the house. They reappeared a few minutes later and bowed to Nasuada, saying, "It's empty, my Lady."

"Good. Thank you." She dismounted her steed, handed the reins to one of the men in her retinue, and strode inside. Eragon and Arya followed.

The three of them wandered through the shabby building until they found a room, the kitchen, with a window large enough to accommodate Saphira's head. Eragon pushed opened the shutters, and Saphira laid her head on the wooden counter. Her breath filled the kitchen with the smell of charred meat.

"We may speak without fear," Arya announced after casting spells that would prevent anyone from eavesdropping on their conversation.

Nasuada rubbed her arms and shivered. "What is this all about, Eragon?" she asked.

Eragon swallowed, wishing that he did not have to dwell upon Oromis and Glaedr's fate. Then he said, "Nasuada . . . Saphira and I were not alone. . . . There was another dragon and another Rider fighting against Galbatorix."

"I knew it," breathed Nasuada, her eyes shining. "It was the only explanation that made sense. They were your teachers in Ellesméra, weren't they?"

They were, said Saphira, *but no more.*

"No more?"

Eragon pressed his lips together and shook his head, tears blurring his vision. "Just this morning they died at Gil'ead. Galbatorix used Thorn and Murtagh to kill them; I heard him speak to them with Murtagh's tongue."

The excitement drained from Nasuada's face, replaced by a dull, empty expression. She sank into the nearest chair and stared at the cinders in the cold fireplace. The kitchen was silent. At last she stirred and said, "Are you sure they are dead?"

"Yes."

Nasuada wiped her eyes on the hem of her sleeve. "Tell me about them, Eragon. Would you, please?"

So for the next half hour, Eragon spoke of Oromis and Glaedr. He explained how they had survived the fall of the Riders and why they had chosen to keep themselves hidden thereafter. He explained about their respective disabilities, and he spent some time describing their personalities and what it had been like to study under them. Eragon's sense of loss deepened as he remembered the long days he had spent with Oromis on the Crags of Tel'naeír and the many things the elf had done for him and Saphira. As he came to their encounter with Thorn and Murtagh at Gil'ead, Saphira lifted her head off the counter and began to keen again, her mournful wail soft and persistent.

Afterward, Nasuada sighed and said, "I wish I could have met Oromis and Glaedr, but alas, it was not to be. . . . There is one thing I still do not understand, Eragon. You said you *heard* Galbatorix speaking to them. How could you?"

"Yes, I would like to know that as well," said Arya.

Eragon looked for something to drink, but there was no water or wine in the kitchen. He coughed, then launched into an account of their recent trip to Ellesméra. Saphira occasionally made a comment, but for the most part, she left it to him to tell the story. Starting with the truth about his parentage, Eragon proceeded in quick succession through the events of their stay, from their discovery of the brightsteel under the Menoa tree to the forging of Brisingr to his visit with Sloan. Last of all, he told Arya and Nasuada about the dragons' heart of hearts.

"Well," said Nasuada. She stood and walked the length of the kitchen and then back again. "You the son of Brom, and Galbatorix leeching off the souls of dragons whose bodies have died. It's almost too much to comprehend. . . ." She rubbed her arms again. "At least we now know the true source of Galbatorix's power."

Arya stood motionless, breathless, her expression stunned. "The dragons are still alive," she whispered. She clasped her hands together in a prayer-like fashion and held them against her chest. "They are still alive after all these years. Oh, if only we could tell the rest of my race. How they would rejoice! And how terrible their wrath would be when they heard of the enslavement of the Eldunarí! We would run straight to Urû'baen, and we would not rest until we had freed the hearts of Galbatorix's control, no matter how many of us died in the process."

But we cannot tell them, said Saphira.

"No," said Arya, and lowered her gaze. "We cannot. But I wish we could."

Nasuada looked at her. "Please do not take offense, but I wish that your mother, Queen Islanzadí, had seen fit to share this information with us. We could have made use of it long ago."

"I agree," said Arya, frowning. "On the Burning Plains, Murtagh was able to defeat the two of you"—she indicated Eragon and Saphira—"because you did not know that Galbatorix might have given him some of the Eldunarí and thus you failed to act with appropriate caution. If not for Murtagh's conscience, you would both be trapped in Galbatorix's service even now. Oromis and Glaedr, and my mother too, had sound reasons for keeping the Eldunarí a secret, but their reticence was nearly our undoing. I will discuss this with my mother when next we speak."

Nasuada paced between the counter and the fireplace. "You have given me much to think about, Eragon. . . ." She tapped the floor with the tip of her boot. "For the first time in the history of the Varden, we know of a way to kill Galbatorix that might actually succeed. If we can separate him from these heart of hearts, he will lose the better part of his strength, and then you and our other spell-casters will be able to overpower him."

"Yes, but how can we separate him from his hearts?" Eragon asked.

Nasuada shrugged. "I could not say, but I am sure it must be possible. From now on, you will work on devising a method. Nothing else is as important."

Eragon felt Arya studying him with unusual concentration. Unsettled, he made a questioning face at her.

"I always wondered," said Arya, "why Saphira's egg appeared to you, and not somewhere in an empty field. It seemed too great a co-incidence to have occurred purely by chance, but I could not think of any plausible explanation. Now I understand. I should have guessed that you were Brom's son. I did not know Brom well, but I did know him, and you share a certain resemblance."

745

"I do?"

"You should be proud to call Brom your father," said Nasuada. "By all accounts, he was a remarkable man. If not for him, the Varden wouldn't exist. It seems fitting that you are the one to carry on his work."

Then Arya said, "Eragon, may we see Glaedr's Eldunarí?"

Eragon hesitated, then went outside and retrieved the pouch from Saphira's saddlebags. Careful not to touch the Eldunarí, he loosened the drawstring at the top and allowed the pouch to slide down around the golden, gemlike stone. In contrast to when he had last seen it, the glow within the heart of hearts was dim and feeble, as if Glaedr were barely conscious.

Nasuada leaned forward and stared into the swirling center of the Eldunarí, her eyes gleaming with reflected light. "And Glaedr is really inside of here?"

He is, said Saphira.

"Can I speak with him?"

"You could try, but I doubt he would respond. He just lost his Rider. It will take him a long time to recover from the shock, if ever. Please leave him be, Nasuada. If he wished to speak with you, he would have done so already."

"Of course. It was not my intention to disturb him in his time of grief. I shall wait to meet him until such time as he has regained his composure."

Arya moved closer to Eragon and placed her hands on either side of the Eldunarí, her fingers less than an inch away from its surface. She gazed at the stone with an expression of reverence, seemingly lost within its depths, then whispered something in the ancient language. Glaedr's consciousness flared slightly, as if in response.

Arya lowered her hands. "Eragon, Saphira, you have been given the most solemn responsibility: the safekeeping of another life. Whatever happens, you must protect Glaedr. With Oromis gone, we shall need his strength and wisdom more than ever before."

Do not worry, Arya, we won't allow any misfortune to befall him, Saphira promised.

Eragon covered the Eldunarí with the pouch again and fumbled with the drawstring, exhaustion rendering him clumsy. The Varden had won an important victory and the elves had taken Gil'ead, but the knowledge brought him little joy. He looked at Nasuada and asked, "What now?"

Nasuada lifted her chin. "Now," she said, "we will march north to Belatona, and when we have captured it, we will proceed onward to Dras-Leona and seize it as well, and then to Urû'baen, where we will cast down Galbatorix or die trying. That is what we shall do now, Eragon."

After they left Nasuada, Eragon and Saphira agreed to leave Feinster for the Varden's camp so that they could both rest undisturbed by the cacophony of noises within the city. With Blödhgarm and the rest of Eragon's guards ranged around them, they walked toward the main gates of Feinster, Eragon still carrying Glaedr's heart of hearts in his arms. Neither of them spoke.

Eragon stared at the ground between his feet. He paid little attention to the men who ran or marched past; his part in the battle was finished, and all he wanted to do was lie down and forget the sorrows of the day. The last sensations he had felt from Glaedr still reverberated through his mind: *He was alone. He was alone and in the dark. . . . Alone!* Eragon's breath caught as a wave of nausea swept over him. *So that is what it's like to lose your Rider or your dragon. No wonder Galbatorix went insane.*

We are the last, Saphira said.

Eragon frowned, not understanding.

The last free dragon and Rider, she explained. *We are the only ones left. We are . . .*

Alone.

Yes.

Eragon stumbled as his foot struck a loose stone he had overlooked. Miserable, he closed his eyes for a moment. *We can't do this by ourselves,* he thought. *We can't! We're not ready.* Saphira agreed, and her grief and anxiety, combined with his, nearly incapacitated him.

When they arrived at the city gates, Eragon paused, reluctant to push his way through the large crowd gathered in front of the opening, trying to flee Feinster. He glanced around for another route. As his eyes passed over the outer walls, a sudden desire gripped him to see the city in the light of day.

Veering away from Saphira, he ran up a staircase that led to the top of the walls. Saphira uttered a short growl of annoyance and followed, half opening her wings as she jumped from the street to the parapet in a single bound.

They stood together on the battlements for the better part of an hour and watched as the sun rose. One by one, rays of pale gold light streaked across the verdant fields from the east, illuminating the countless motes of dust that drifted through the air. Where the rays struck a column of smoke, the smoke glowed orange and red and billowed with renewed urgency. The fires among the hovels outside the city walls had mostly died out, although since Eragon and Saphira had arrived, the fighting had set a score of houses within Feinster ablaze, and the pillars of flame that leaped up from the disintegrating houses lent the cityscape an eerie beauty. Behind Feinster, the shimmering sea stretched out to the far, flat horizon, where the sails of a ship plowing its way northward were just visible.

As the sun warmed Eragon through his armor, his melancholy gradually dissipated like the wreaths of mist that adorned the rivers below. He took a deep breath and exhaled, relaxing his muscles.

No, he said, *we are not alone. I have you, and you have me. And there is Arya and Nasuada and Orik, and many others besides who will help us along our way.*

And Glaedr too, said Saphira.

Aye.

Eragon gazed down at the Eldunarí that lay covered within his arms and felt a rush of sympathy and protectiveness toward the dragon who was trapped inside the heart of hearts. He hugged the stone closer to his chest and laid a hand upon Saphira, grateful for their companionship.

We can do this, he thought. *Galbatorix isn't invulnerable. He has a weakness, and we can use that weakness against him. . . . We can do this.*

We can, and we must, said Saphira.

For the sake of our friends and our family—

—and for the rest of Alagaësia—

—we must do this.

Eragon lifted Glaedr's Eldunarí over his head, presenting it to the sun and the new day, and he smiled, eager for the battles yet to come, so that he and Saphira might finally confront Galbatorix and kill the dark king.

HERE ENDS THE THIRD BOOK

OF THE INHERITANCE CYCLE.

THE STORY WILL CONTINUE AND CONCLUDE

IN BOOK FOUR.

ON THE ORIGIN OF NAMES:

To the casual observer, the various names an intrepid traveler will encounter throughout Alagaësia might seem but a random collection of labels with no inherent integrity, culture, or history. However, as with any land that different cultures—and in this case, different species—have repeatedly colonized, Alagaësia acquired names from a wide array of unique sources, among them the languages of the dwarves, elves, humans, and even Urgals. Thus, we can have Palancar Valley (a human name), the Anora River and Ristvak'baen (elven names), and Utgard Mountain (a dwarf name) all within a few square miles of each other.

While this is of great historical interest, practically it often leads to confusion as to the correct pronunciation. Unfortunately, there are no set rules for the neophyte. You must learn each name upon its own terms, unless you can immediately place its language of origin. The matter grows even more confusing when you realize that in many places the resident population altered the spelling and pronunciation of foreign words to conform to their own language. The Anora River is a prime example. Originally *anora* was spelled *äenora*, which means *broad* in the ancient language. In their writings, the humans simplified the word to *anora*, and this, combined with a vowel shift wherein *äe* (ay-eh) was said as the easier *a* (uh), created the name as it appears in Eragon's time.

To spare readers as much difficulty as possible, I have compiled the following list, with the understanding that these are only rough guidelines to the actual pronunciation. The enthusiast is encouraged to study the source languages in order to master their true intricacies.

Pronunciation:

Ajihad—AH-zhi-hod

Alagaësia—al-uh-GAY-zee-uh

Arya—AR-ee-uh

Blödhgarm—BLAWD-garm

Brisingr—BRISS-ing-gur

Carvahall—CAR-vuh-hall

Dras-Leona—DRAHS-lee-OH-nuh

Du Weldenvarden—doo WELL-den-VAR-den

Ellesméra—el-uhs-MEER-uh

Eragon—EHR-uh-gahn

Farthen Dûr—FAR-then DURE (*dure* rhymes with *lure*)

Galbatorix—gal-buh-TOR-icks

Gil'ead—GILL-ee-id

Glaedr—GLAY-dur

Hrothgar—HROTH-gar

Islanzadí—iss-lan-ZAH-dee

Jeod—JODE (rhymes with *load*)

Murtagh—MUR-tag (*mur* rhymes with *purr*)

Nasuada—nah-soo-AH-dah

Nolfavrell—NOLL-fah-vrel (*noll* rhymes with *toll*)

Oromis—OR-uh-miss

Ra'zac—RAA-zack

Saphira—suh-FEAR-uh

Shruikan—SHREW-kin

Sílthrim—SEAL-thrim (*síl* is a hard sound to transcribe; it's made by flicking the tip of the tongue off the roof of the mouth)

Skgahgrezh—skuh-GAH-grezh

Teirm—TEERM

Trianna—TREE-ah-nuh

Tronjheim—TRONJ-heem

Urû'baen—OO-roo-bane

Vrael—VRAIL

Yazuac—YAA-zoo-ack

Zar'roc—ZAR-rock

754

THE ANCIENT LANGUAGE:

Adurna rïsa.—Water, rise.

Agaetí Blödhren—Blood-oath Celebration (held once a century to honor the original pact between elves and dragons)

älfa-kona—elf woman

Äthalvard—an organization of elves dedicated to the preservation of their songs and poems

Atra du evarínya ono varda, Däthedr-vodhr.—May the stars watch over you, honored Däthedr.

Atra esterní ono thelduin, Eragon Shur'tugal.—May good fortune rule over you, Eragon Dragon Rider.

Atra guliä un ilian tauthr ono un atra ono waíse sköliro fra rauthr.—May luck and happiness follow you and may you be shielded from misfortune.

audr—up

Bjartskular—Brightscales

Blödhgarm—Bloodwolf

brisingr—fire

Brisingr, iet tauthr.—Fire, follow me.

Brisingr raudhr!—Red fire!

deyja—die

draumr kópa—dream stare

dröttningu—princess

Du deloi lunaea.—Smooth the earth/dirt.

Du Namar Aurboda—The Banishing of the Names

Du Vrangr Gata—The Wandering Path

edur—a tor or prominence

Eka eddyr aí Shur'tugal . . . Shur'tugal . . . Argetlam.—I am a
    Dragon Rider . . . Dragon Rider . . . Silver Hand.

Eka elrun ono.—I thank you.

elda—a gender-neutral honorific suffix of great praise, attached
    with a hyphen

Eldhrimner O Loivissa nuanen, dautr abr deloi/Eldhrimner nen
    ono weohnataí medh solus un thringa/Eldhrimner un fortha onr
    fëon vara/Wiol allr sjon.—Grow, O beautiful Loivissa, daughter
    of the earth/Grow as you would with sun and rain/Grow and put
    forth your flower of spring/For all to see.

Eldunarí—the heart of hearts

Erisdar—the flameless lanterns both the elves and the dwarves use
    (named after the elf who invented them)

faelnirv—elven liqueur

fairth—a picture taken by magical means on a shingle of slate

fell—mountain

finiarel—an honorific suffix for a young man of great promise,
    attached with a hyphen

flauga—fly

fram—forward

Fricai onr eka eddyr.—I am your friend.

gánga—go

Garjzla, letta!—Light, stop!

gedwëy ignasia—shining palm

Helgrind—The Gates of Death

Indlvarn—a certain type of pairing between a Rider and dragon

jierda—break; hit

könungr—king

Kuldr, rïsa lam iet un malthinae unin böllr.—Gold, rise to my hand
and bind into an orb.

kveykva—lightning

lámarae—a fabric made by cross-weaving wool and nettle threads
(similar in construction to linsey-woolsey, but of higher
quality)

letta—stop

Liduen Kvaedhí—Poetic Script

loivissa—a blue, deep-throated lily that grows in the Empire

maela—quiet

naina—make bright

nalgask—a mixture of beeswax and hazelnut oil used to moisten
the skin

Nen ono weohnata, Arya Dröttningu.—As you will, Princess Arya.

seithr—witch

Shur'tugal—Dragon Rider

slytha—sleep

Stenr rïsa!—Stone, rise!

svit-kona—a formal honorific for an elf woman of great wisdom

talos—a cactus found near Helgrind

thaefathan—thicken

Thorta du ilumëo!—Speak the truth!

vakna—awaken

vodhr—a male honorific suffix of middling praise, attached with a
hyphen

Waíse heill!—Be healed!

yawë—a bond of trust

The Dwarf Language:

Ascûdgamln—fists of steel

Az Knurldrâthn—The Trees of Stone

Az Ragni—The River

Az *Sartosvrenht rak Balmung, Grimstnzborith rak Kvisagûr*—The Saga
of King Balmung of Kvisagûr

Az Sindriznarrvel—The Gem of Sindri

barzûl—curse someone with ill fate

delva—a term of endearment among the dwarves; also a form of
gold nodule indigenous to the Beor Mountains that the dwarves
greatly prize

dûr—our

dûrgrimst—clan (literally, "our hall," or "our home")

dûrgrimstvren—clan war

eta—no

Eta! Narho ûdim etal os isû vond! Narho ûdim etal os formvn
mendûnost brakn, az Varden, hrestvog dûr grimstnzhadn! Az
Jurgenvren qathrid né dômar oen etal— No! I will not let that
happen! I will not let these beardless fools, the Varden, destroy
our country. The Dragon War left us weak and not—

Fanghur—dragon-like creatures that are smaller and less
intelligent than their cousins (native to the Beor Mountains)

Farthen Dûr—Our Father

Feldûnost—frostbeard (a species of goat native to the Beor Mountains)

Gáldhiem—Bright/shining head

Ghastgar—spear-throwing contest akin to jousting and fought on
the backs of Feldûnost

grimstborith—clan chief (literally, "hall chief"; plural is *grimstborithn*)

grimstcarvlorss—arranger of the house

grimstnzborith—ruler of the dwarves, whether king or queen
(literally, "halls' chief")

hûthvír—double-bladed staff weapon used by Dûrgrimst Quan

Hwatum il skilfz gerdûmn!—Listen to mine words!

757

Ingeitum—fire workers; smiths

Isidar Mithrim—Star Rose (the star sapphire)

knurla—dwarf (literally, "one of stone"; plural is *knurlan*)

knurlaf—woman/she/her

knurlag—man/he/him

knurlagn—men

Knurlcarathn—stoneworkers; masons

Knurlnien—Stone Heart

Ledwonnû—Kílf's necklace; also used as a general term for *necklace*

menknurlan—unstone ones/those who are not, or are without, stone (the worst insult in Dwarvish; cannot be directly translated into English)

mérna—lake/pool

Nagra—giant boar, native to the Beor Mountains

Nal, Grimstnzborith Orik!—Hail, King Orik!

ornthrond—eagle eye

Ragni Darmn—River of Small Red Fish

Ragni Hefthyn—River Guard

Shrrg—giant wolf, native to the Beor Mountains

Skilfz Delva—Mine Delva (see *delva* for translation)

thriknzdal—the temper line on the blade of a differentially tempered weapon

Tronjheim—Helm of Giants

Ûn qroth Gûntera!—Thus spoke Gûntera!

Urzhad—giant cave bear, native to the Beor Mountains

Vargrimst—clanless/banished

Vrenshrrgn—War Wolves

werg—the dwarves' equivalent of *ugh* (used humorously in the place name Werghadn; *Werghadn* translates as either "the land of ugh" or, more liberally, "the ugly land")

THE NOMAD LANGUAGE:

no—an honorific suffix attached with a hyphen to the main name
of someone you respect

THE URGAL LANGUAGE:

Herndall—Urgal dams who rule their tribes
namna—woven strips containing Urgal family narratives that are
placed by the entrances to their huts
nar—a title of great respect
Urgralgra—Urgals' name for themselves (literally, "those with
horns")

ACKNOWLEDGMENTS

Kvetha Fricaya. Greetings, Friends.

Brisingr was a fun, intense, and sometimes difficult book to write. When I started, I felt as if the story were a vast, three-dimensional puzzle that I had to solve without hints or instructions. I found the experience to be immensely satisfying, despite the challenges it occasionally posed.

Because of its complexity, *Brisingr* ended up much larger than I anticipated—so much larger, in fact, that I had to expand the series from three books to four. Thus, the Inheritance trilogy became the Inheritance cycle. I'm pleased with the change too. Having another volume in the series has allowed me to explore and develop the characters' personalities and relationships at a more natural pace.

As with *Eragon* and *Eldest*, I never would have been able to complete this book without the support of a whole host of talented people, to whom I am ever grateful. They are:

At home: Mom, for her food, tea, advice, sympathy, endless patience, and optimism; Dad, for his unique perspective, razor-sharp observations on story and prose, helping me to name the book, and for coming up with the idea of having Eragon's sword burst into flame every time he says its name (very cool); and my one and only sister, Angela, for once again consenting to reprise her character and for numerous pieces of information on names, plants, and all things wool.

At Writers House: Simon Lipskar, my agent, for his friendship, his hard work, and for giving me a much-needed kick in the pants early on in *Brisingr* (without which I might have taken another two years to finish the book); and his assistant Josh Getzler for all he does on behalf of Simon and the Inheritance cycle.

At Knopf: my editor, Michelle Frey, who did an awesome job of helping me to clean up and tighten the manuscript (the first draft was *much* longer); associate editor Michele Burke, who also labored over the editing and who helped pull together the synopsis of *Eragon* and *Eldest*; head of communications and marketing Judith Haut, who from the beginning spread word of the series throughout the land; publicity director Christine Labov; art director Isabel Warren-Lynch and her team for again putting together such a classy-looking book; John Jude Palencar for a majestic cover painting (I don't know how he can top it with the fourth book!); executive copy editor Artie Bennett for checking every word, real or invented, in *Brisingr* with such consummate care; Chip Gibson, head of the children's division at Random House; Knopf publishing director Nancy Hinkel for her unwavering support; Joan DeMayo, director of sales and her team (huzzah and many thanks!); head of marketing John Adamo, whose team designed such impressive materials; Linda Leonard, new media, for all her efforts with online marketing; Linda Palladino, Milton Wackerow, and Carol Naughton, production; Pam White, Jocelyn Lange, and the rest of the subsidiary rights team, who have done a truly extraordinary job of selling the Inheritance cycle in countries and languages throughout the world; Janet Renard, copyediting; and everyone else at Knopf who has supported me.

At Listening Library: Gerard Doyle, who brings the world of Alagaësia to life with his voice; Taro Meyer for getting the pronunciation of my languages just right; Orli Moscowitz for pulling all the threads together; and Amanda D'Acierno, publisher of Listening Library.

Thank you all.

The Craft of the Japanese Sword by Leon and Hiroko Kapp and Yoshindo Yoshihara provided me with much of the information I needed to accurately describe the smelting and forging process in the chapter "Mind over Metal." I highly recommend the book to anyone who is interested in learning more about (specifically Japanese) swordmaking. Did you know that Japanese smiths used to start their fires by hammering on the end of a bar of iron until it was red-hot, then touching it to a cedar shingle that was coated with sulfur?

Also, for those who understood the reference to a "lonely god" when Eragon and Arya are sitting around the campfire, my only excuse is that the Doctor can travel everywhere, even alternate realities.

Hey, I'm a fan too!

Finally, and most importantly, thank you. Thank you for reading *Brisingr*. And thank you for sticking with the Inheritance cycle through all these years. Without your support, I never would have been able to write this series, and I can't imagine anything else I would rather be doing.

Once again Eragon and Saphira's adventures are over, and once again we have arrived at the end of this wandering path . . . but only for the time being. Many more miles still lie before us. Book Four will be published just as soon as I can finish it, and I can promise you, it's going to be the most exciting installment in the series. I can't wait for you to read it!

Sé onr sverdar sitja hvass!

Christopher Paolini
September 20, 2008